By Anne Tyler

IF MORNING EVER COMES
THE TIN CAN TREE
A SLIPPING-DOWN LIFE
THE CLOCK WINDER
CELESTIAL NAVIGATION
SEARCHING FOR CALEB
EARTHLY POSSESSIONS
MORGAN'S PASSING
DINNER AT THE HOMESICK RESTAURANT
THE ACCIDENTAL TOURIST
BREATHING LESSONS

IF MORNING EVER COMES
THE TIN CAN TREE
A SLIPPING-DOWN LIFE

IF MORNING EVER COMES
THE TIN CAN TREE
A SLIPPING-DOWN LIFE

◆

ANNE TYLER

QUALITY PAPERBACK BOOKS NEW YORK

A somewhat abridged form of this novel appeared in the January 1970 issue of *Redbook* magazine.

This edition was specially created in 1990 for Quality Paperback Books by arrangement with Alfred A. Knopf, Inc.

Printed in the United States of America

IF MORNING EVER COMES

1

WHEN BEN JOE HAWKES left home he gave his sister Susannah one used guitar, six shelves of *National Geographic,* a battered microscope, and a foot-high hourglass. All of these things he began to miss as soon as he hit New York. He considered writing home and asking for them—Susannah probably hadn't even listened when he gave them to her—but he figured she might laugh at him. His family was the kind that thought only children during their first summer at Scout camp should miss anything. So he kept quiet about what he missed and just dropped Susannah a postcard, with a picture on it of the UN building by night, asking if she had learned to play the guitar yet. And six weeks later he got a card back, but not the picture kind, postmarked Sandhill, N.C., and badly rained-on. He turned the card over and learned, from Susannah's jet-black, jerky script, that she had just changed to a job with the Sandhill School Library and was getting rich and could have her hair done every week now. She signed it "So long—S," and then there was a P.S. saying she was going to start learning to play the guitar tomorrow. Ben Joe read this over two or three times, although what she had said was perfectly clear: she had only just now remembered that the guitar existed. Probably she had got up in the midst of doing something else to drag it from his closet and twang the slack strings, but having discovered that she wasn't born knowing how to play and might have to work at it awhile she had dropped it again and drifted on to something else that came to mind. Ben Joe thought about starting up a whole *string* of cards—asking on the next one, for instance, whether that hourglass was still keeping time okay—until she got snappy with him and packed everything up and sent it to New York. But Susannah was flighty, like almost all his sisters, and rarely finished anything she started reading even if it was as short as a postcard; he didn't think she would notice that he might be missing something. So he stopped the postcards and just wrote his regular letters after that, addressed to the family as a whole, asking about the health of his mother and all his sisters and saying he thought of them often.

By then it was November. He had left home late in August, just after his twenty-fifth birthday, to start law school at Columbia, and although he was doing well, even with three years of empty space behind him since college, he didn't like Columbia. On campus the wind up from the river cut clean through him no matter what he wore, and his classmates were all quick and sleek and left him nothing to say to them. They looked like the men who modeled Italian wool jackets in men's magazines;

he plodded along beside them, thin and shivering, and tried to think about warm things. Nor did he like law; it was all memory work. The only reason he had chosen it was that it was at least practical, whereas the other ideas he had had were not, and practicality was a good thing when you headed up a family of six women. So all through September, October, and most of November he sat through Columbia's law classes and jiggled one foot across his knee and peeled his fingernails off.

On this particular Thursday the wind was so cold that Ben Joe became personally angry at it. He stepped out of the law building, pulling his collar up over his ears, and the wind suddenly hit him full in the face and left him gasping. That decided him; he changed direction and headed toward the apartment. Lately he had taken to spending the really cold days in bed with a murder mystery, and he was beginning to think he should have done that this morning.

On Broadway he stayed close to the buildings, hoping that there would be less wind there. He passed the brass nameplate on one of the concrete walls and for an instant saw his face reflected there, made yellow by the brass, with his mouth open and his jaw clenched and his teeth gnashed against the cold. If it had been any other day he would have smiled, and maybe stopped to peer into the brass until the passers-by wondered what he was doing, but not today. Today he only hunched his gray topcoat around him more securely and kept going.

His apartment was five blocks from the campus, in a tiny dark old building with unbelievably high, sculptured ceilings. Opening the front door of it took all the strength he had. And all the way up the three flights of stairs he could smell what every family had eaten for the last day and a half—mainly bacon and burnt beans, he gathered. Ordinarily the smells made him feel a little sick, but today they seemed warm and comforting. He climbed more quickly, making each wooden step creak beneath his feet. By the time he was at his own door and digging through his pockets for the keys he was whistling under his breath, even though his face was stiff with cold.

"That you?" his roommate called from the kitchen.

"It's me."

He took the key out of the door and slammed the door shut behind him. Inside it was almost as cold as it was in the street; all it needed was the wind. The living room was taller than it was wide, and very dark, with high-backed stuffed furniture and long, narrow windows that rattled when a gust of wind blew. The mantel and the coffee tables were bare and dusty. There were none of the flower pots and photographs and china do-dads that he was used to from the houseful of women in which he had been raised, but a huge clutter of other objects lay around—newspapers, tossed-off jackets, textbooks, playing cards. In the middle of the dark wooden floor was a square scatter rug colored like a chessboard, and ridiculously tiny plastic chess pieces sat upon it in a middle-of-the-game confusion.

Ben Joe stripped his topcoat and his suit jacket off and threw them onto an easy chair. He untied his tie and stuffed it into the pocket of the jacket. From the daybed he picked up a crazy quilt from home and began swaddling himself in it, covering even his head and huddling himself tightly inside it.

"For Pete's sake," his roommate said from the kitchen doorway.

"Well, I'm cold."

He backed up to the daybed and sat down. The bed was a wide one; he worked himself back until he was leaning against the wall and his legs were folded Indian fashion in front of him, and then he frowned.

"Forgot to take off my shoes," he said.

He patiently undid the quilt and untied his shoes. They fell to the floor with two dull thuds. With his cold feet pressed beneath the warmth of his legs, he reached again for the quilt and began pulling it around him.

"Hey, Jeremy," he said, "grab this corner, will you?"

His roommate left the doorway and came over, carrying a cup of coffee in one hand. "I've never seen the like," he said. "You wait till it's really winter. Which one?"

"The one in my left hand. There. Thanks."

He leaned back against the wall again and Jeremy drifted over to the window, slurping up his coffee as he went. He was younger than Ben Joe—twenty-one at the most, and an undergraduate—but Ben Joe liked him better than most of the other people he had met here. Maybe because he didn't have that sleek look either. He was from Maine, and wore sneakers and dungarees and dirty red Brewster jackets to class. His hair was so black it was startling; it gave him a wild look even when he smiled.

"I thought you had *two* classes on Thursdays," Jeremy said.

"I did. But I only went to the one. I got cold."

"Oh, pooh." He sat down on the edge of the window sill and swung one sneaker back and forth. "In Maine," he said, "we'd be swimming in this weather."

"In Sandhill we'd be sending for federal aid."

"Oh, now, don't you give me that."

He stood up and began tugging at the window. It screeched open; a gust of wind blew the newspaper's society section into Ben Joe's lap.

"Will you shut that *window!*" Ben Joe said.

"In a minute, in a minute. I'm trying to see what the thermometer says. Thirty-four. Thirty-four! Not even freezing."

"It's the wind," Ben Joe said.

The window slid shut again, leaving the apartment suddenly silent.

"Want to walk with me to the drugstore, Ben Joe?"

"Not me."

"I got to get a toothbrush."

"Nope."

Jeremy sighed and headed for the bedroom, twirling his empty coffee cup by the handle.

"Last night," he said as he walked, "I figured out the prettiest-sounding word in the English language. I did. And now I can't remember it."

"Hmm," Ben Joe said. He reached behind him to flick on the wall switch and smoothed out the newspaper in his lap. It was last Sunday's, but he hadn't got desperate enough to read the society section till now. It crackled dully on his knees, looking gray and smudgy under the flat light from the ceiling.

"I mean," Jeremy said from the bedroom, "usually you can think of a word that's *one* of the prettiest-sounding. But no, sir, this was *the* word. *Really* the word. I meant to tell this comp professor about it, that I see in the cafeteria. And then I woke up this morning and it was gone. It had an *s* in it, I think. An *s*."

"*That* should narrow it down," Ben Joe said. He grinned and tipped his head back so that it was resting against the wall.

"You want a date tonight, Ben Joe?"

"Who with?"

"This real cute freshman, has red hair and brown eyes, which is my favorite combination, and comes from, um—"

"Too young."

He opened the society section and folded it back, letting his arms emerge partway from the blanket.

"Thank you anyway," he called as an afterthought.

"Oh, that's okay." Jeremy was standing in the doorway now, with one end of a pillow in his teeth. "I've decided to clean the bedroom," he said. The words came out muffled but still intelligible. "I haven't changed my sheets in three weeks." He shook out a pillowcase, held it below the pillow, and opened his mouth to let the pillow drop into the case. Then he tossed the pillow toward his bed and vanished from sight again.

Ben Joe started reading the society section, holding it upside-down in front of him. He had started learning to read when he was three, but his parents wanted him to wait until school age; they made him stand facing them when they read him bedtime stories, so that the book was turned the wrong way around. It wasn't until too late that they realized he was reading upside-down. Usually he read the right way now unless he was bored, and then upside-down words came to his mind more clearly. He held the newspaper at arm's length and frowned, studying an upside-down description of a golden anniversary where the couple had had another wedding performed all over again.

"What's this mess of lima beans doing on the floor of the closet?" Jeremy called.

"Oh, leave them. I'll take care of them."

"I know, but what are they *doing* there?"

"I forget. Hey, Jeremy, if you were having your golden anniversary would you have another wedding performed all over again?"

"Hell, no. I wouldn't have the first one."

On the next page there were ads to run through, detailed little line drawings of silver patterns and china patterns and ring sets. He yawned and then set to picking out a ring set, ending up with a large, oddly shaped diamond and a wedding band that was fine except for a line of dots at each edge that bothered him. Then he chose a silver pattern and a very expensive china pattern, platinum-rimmed, but he was already beginning to be tired of the game and abruptly he turned the paper right-side up, picked out a bride for himself that he considered most likely to meet all his requirements, and, with that finished, pushed the society news to the floor and stood up.

"Where's last Sunday's crossword?" he called.

"I already did it."

"You did it the week before, too."

"Well, I waited till *Wednesday*, for God's sake."

Ben Joe went into the bedroom. Jeremy was sitting on the floor with one of the bureau drawers beside him; he was slowly going through a stack of postcards and throwing some out but keeping most of them. The rest of the room was in chaos; Ben Joe's bed was unmade, Jeremy's was made but covered with the things he had decided to throw out, and there was a heap of dirty sheets on the floor between the two beds.

"Worse than it was before," Ben Joe said.

"I know. That's the trouble with cleaning up."

Ben Joe leaned his elbows on the dresser and looked into the mirror with his chin in his hands. The mirror was wavy and speckled, but he could at least recognize himself: his thin, flat-planed face, which almost never needed shaving and took on a sort of yellow look in the wintertime; his level gray eyes, so narrow that they looked as if he were constantly suspecting people; and his hair, dark yellow and hanging in shocks over his forehead. It was getting shaggy at the back and sides; he looked like an orphan. And walked like one, letting his shoulders hitch forward and burying his hands deeply in his pockets so that his arms could remain stiff and his elbows could dig into his sides. One of his sisters had once told him, meaning it kindly, that he was homely, all right, but *trustworthy*-looking; if people could do what they liked to strangers on the street, they would stop him and reach up to pat the top of his head. He sighed and straightened up and began moving around the room, kicking dust balls with his stockinged feet.

"I thought you were going out for a toothbrush," he said to Jeremy.

"I am. Soon as I finish this drawer. A red one."

"A red what?"

"*Tooth*brush." Jeremy threw a stack of postcards in the direction of the wastebasket. "I always buy a red toothbrush for the wintertime."

"Oh." Ben Joe sat down on the edge of his bed and frowned at the sheets on the floor. After a minute he said, "You ever seen one of those toothbrushes with a bird on the end? The kind that gives a soft little whistle when you blow on it?"

"Sure. That's for kids, to make them want to brush their teeth."

"Well, I know it." He lay back crosswise on the bed and stared at the ceiling. "My sister had one of those once," he said. "My older sister, Joanne. She's away now. But she had a little pink toothbrush with a bird on the end, and it wasn't when she was a little girl, either. It was when she was in high school and had taken to wearing red dresses and gold hoop earrings and flinging that black hair of hers around. One night I was writing this philosophy paper. I came out of my room for a drink of water and I felt like hell—my mind all confused and tired but still popping off like a machine gun. And out of the bathroom just then came Joanne, not in red but in a little quilty white bathrobe, and sort of dreamily blowing the bird on her toothbrush. She didn't see me. But it was so damned *comforting*. I went to bed and slept like a rock, no more machine guns in my head."

He lay quiet for a minute, following the sculptured molding around the ceiling with his eyes.

"What was I saying?"

"About toothbrushes."

"Oh. Well, that was all."

He turned and rose up on one elbow to see what Jeremy was doing. Jeremy was reading all the postcards he had saved.

"Hey, Ben Joe," he said.

"Hmm."

"You want to hear something funny?"

"What."

"It's from this buddy of mine that goes to college out west, with a picture of this gorge, real deep down with a river at the bottom. Says, 'This gorge is habit-forming. Threw a bowling ball down it to hear how it sounded and it sounded so good I moved on to bigger and better things and last night me and some buddies threw a piano down it.' A *piano*. What do you guess it looked like when it hit? Ben Joe?"

Ben Joe looked up.

"Ah, you're not listening," said Jeremy. He put the postcard back in the drawer and moved on to the next one.

Ben Joe sat up, running his fingers through his hair. "What time is it?" he asked.

"I don't know. Eleven or so."

He reached over and pulled open the top drawer of his own bureau. At the right was a stack of letters; he pulled the top one out, looked at it to make sure it had been signed by his sister Jenny (she was the official family letter writer), and then lay back down, holding the letter over his head, right-side up, to read it:

Dear Ben Joe:

We received yours of the 12th. Yes, of course we are well. I don't know why you keep asking us, since you know as well as we do that the last time any of us was in the hospital was five years ago when Susannah had all four wisdom teeth pulled at once. Mama says to tell you you worry too much. We are getting along beautifully & hope you are too.

Financially things are going smoothly. Next month both of the twins are getting raises at the bank, but Lisa is getting $6 more a month than Jane, which make family relationships kind of tense. Tessie is taking drawing lessons after school now for $2 a lesson, which I think we can afford, & the only extra expense this month has been the eaves pipe falling down from the roof outside Tessie's & my window due to Tessie's standing on it. Tessie didn't, tho. Fall, I mean. I'll never know why.

I wish you would write a letter to the family suggesting that we go back to a policy of my doing the grocery shopping. Specially since it was me you left in charge of the money. Gram has been doing it lately & the results are disaster. She gets anything she feels like, minced clams & pickled artichoke hearts & pig's feet & when I ask where are the meat & potatoes she says it's time we had a little change around here. She's ruining us.

Enclosed is next month's check for your expenses, etc. I hope you will remember to send a receipt this time as it makes my bookkeeping neater.

Sincerely,
Jennifer.

Enc.

Ben Joe folded the letter and sat up again. "I wish someone besides Jenny would do the letter writing in my family," he said.

"Why?"

"I don't know." He began walking around the room

with his hands in his pockets. "You never know what's going *on*, exactly. Just about the dratted eavespipes and stuff."

"The what?" Jeremy sat back and stared, and when Ben Joe didn't answer, he said, "Oh, now, are you getting started on your family again? What you worried about?"

Ben Joe stopped in front of the window and looked out. There was a venetian blind between him and the outdoors; the buildings across from him were divided into dozens of horizontal strips.

"Someone's lost a red balloon," he said. "They must've lost it out a window, it's flying so high."

"Maybe it's a gas balloon."

"Maybe. What bothers me is, sometimes I think my family doesn't know *when* to get upset—the most amazing things happen and they forget to even tell me. I try to keep quiet, but all the time I'm thinking, 'I wonder what's going on back there. I wonder if maybe I shouldn't just chuck everything and go on back and see for myself, set my mind at rest if nothing . . .' "

He was sitting on Jeremy's bed now, and reaching for the phone.

"You going to call home?" Jeremy asked.

"I reckon."

"You want me to get out?"

"Nah, that's all right— Operator, I want Sandhill, North Carolina, two four oh—"

"You got a Southern accent," she said. She was snappy and cross, with a New York twang to her voice. "I can't tell if you said 'four' or 'five'; you don't—"

"I haven't got one, either. I said 'two, four, oh—' "

"Yes you do. You said 'Ah.' 'Ah haven't got—' "

"I did not. My mother's a Northerner, even."

"Number, please."

"Two four oh, six seven five four. If I had an accent I'd say 'foh.' No 'r.' But I said the 'r.' "

"And *your* number, please."

"Academy four, six five five nine."

"Station to station?"

"Yes'm."

The telephone had a familiar plastic smell; the receiver was warm and already a little damp in his hand. He hated using the telephone. The thought of speaking to someone, and listening to him, without seeing him was as panicky as not being able to breathe. How could he tell anything about a person if he couldn't see him? Sometimes he thought something must be wrong with his ears; what he heard told him almost nothing. And usually he read too much harshness into a voice. He could hang up a telephone receiver and feel hurt and bewildered for days and then find out, weeks later when he asked what he had done to annoy them, that they were just talking above the noise from a TV set. So now, to make it easier for himself, he tried to picture exactly what was going on at the other end. He pictured the house in Sandhill at eleven o'clock on a Thursday morning, with the autumn sun shining palely through the long bay windows in the living room. His sisters would all be at work, he guessed, except for Tessie, who was still in grade school. Or was it her lunch hour? No, too early. That left only his mother, and maybe even she would be gone; she worked part time at a book store.

The phone rang twice. He waited, tensed against the pillows.

"Hello?" his mother said. He could tell her from his sisters, although their voices were almost the same, by that way she had of seeming to expect the worst when she answered the telephone.

"Hi," he said.

"I beg your pardon?"

"It's me. Ben Joe."

"Ben Joe! What's wrong?"

"Nothing's wrong. I called to see how you were."

"Didn't you get our last letter?"

"Well, yes. I guess I did. The one about the eaves-pipe falling down?"

"I think that was it. Did you get it?"

"*Yes*, I got it."

"Oh. I thought maybe you were worried because you hadn't heard from us."

"No, I heard."

"Well, that's nice."

Ben Joe waited, frowning into the receiver, twining the coils of the telephone cord around his index finger. He tried desperately to picture what she looked like right now, but all he came up with was her hair, dust-colored with the curls at the side of her face pressed flat by the receiver. That was no help. Give him anything—eyes, mouth, just a stretch of cheek, even—and he could tell something, but not *hair*, for goodness' sake. He tried again.

"Well," he said, "how *is* everyone?"

"Oh, fine."

"That's good. I'm glad to hear it."

"It's too bad you called while the girls were away. Joanne's the only one here now. They'd have liked to talk to you."

"Susannah, you mean."

"What?"

"You mean, *Susannah's* the only one here."

"No, Susannah's switched to a full-time job now. I thought Jenny told you. She's working at the school library. I don't know why that should be tiring, but apparently it is. She comes home all cross and snappy, and last night she had a date with the Lowry boy and ended up shoving his face into a cone of buttered popcorn at the Royal Crown theater. I forget what movie they were showing."

"Never mind," said Ben Joe. "What I'm asking is, *who* is it that's the only one home but you?"

"Joanne. I told you."

"Joanne?"

"Well, yes."

"Mom," Ben Joe said, "*Joanne's* been gone for seven *years*."

"Oh. I thought Jenny wrote you about that."

"Wrote me about *what?*" He was up off the bed now; Jeremy looked over at him curiously.

"I think maybe you *didn't* get our last letter," his mother said. "Come to think of it, it was the *next*-to-the-last letter about the eaves pipe falling down. The last one should get there today or so. Have you gotten today's mail yet?"

"No."

"Why, what time is it?"

"Mom," Ben Joe said, "is Joanne home or isn't she?"

"*Yes,* she's home."

"Well, then, why? And when did she get there? Why didn't you—"

"She left," his mother said vaguely.

"Just now? Didn't she know I was on the phone?"

"No, I mean she left Kansas."

"Obviously she left."

"She took the baby and ran away from her husband."

"*What?*"

Ben Joe sat down again on the edge of Jeremy's bed. Jeremy took a sidelong glance at him and then got up and left the room.

"Ben Joe, is there a bad connection on your end? Can't you hear me?"

"I can hear you."

"Well, don't be so dramatic, then. What's done is done, and it's nonc of our affair."

Ben Joe closed his eyes, briefly; he wondered how many times in his life he had heard his mother say that.

"Are you there, Ben Joe?"

"Yes'm. How is she?"

"Oh, fine. And the baby's a darling. Very well behaved."

"Has she changed much? Joanne, I mean. What's she like now?"

"Oh, the same as ever."

"Can I talk to her?"

"She's asleep. She stayed up last night to watch the late show."

Ben Joe took a breath, hesitated, and then said, "I'm coming home, Mom."

"Ben Joe—"

"It won't hurt to cut a few classes. I want to just see how everything is."

"Everything's *fine.*"

"I know, but I want to set my mind at rest. I've been worrying."

"You're always worrying."

"I'll see you tomorrow, Mom."

"Ben *Joe—*"

Ben Joe hung up, neatly and quietly. There was that giddy feeling in his head that always came from talking for any period of time with his mother, or even sometimes with his sisters; he felt confused and uncertain, as if he and his family were a set of square dancers coming to clap the palms of their hands to each others', only their hands missed by inches and encountered nothing. It was only after he had gone over the conversation in his mind, arranging it in a logical order and trying to convince himself that everything was really all right, that he felt better. He stepped to the door and said, "Jeremy?"

"Yeah, Ben Joe." Jeremy came in, looking quickly at Ben Joe's face. "Trouble?"

"I'm going home for a few days. If the university calls, you tell them I'll be back, will you?"

"Sure."

"I'll take that night train. Be there by morning." He pulled his suitcase out from under the bed and then sat down, staring at it blankly.

"You see what I mean," he said. He spread his arms helplessly, looking up at Jeremy, who was leaning against the wall with his hands in the pockets of his dungarees and his face worried. "You get these cheerful little financial statements, and meanwhile what's going on? Joanne's run away from her husband and come home, after seven years of only phone calls and letters from her—"

"Joanne," Jeremy said. "She the one with the red dress and bangles?"

"Yep. Her. On the way out to get your toothbrush, will you pick up today's mail? I bet they tell about it in a P.S., that's what."

"You going to try and make her go back to her husband?"

"No, just going to see her."

"Well, I'll go get the mail," said Jeremy.

"Okay."

Ben Joe crossed back to his bureau. The drawer was still open; he pulled out a large leather jewelry box and flipped the lid up. Inside were all the odds and ends that he never knew what to do with. He searched through two-cent postage stamps and Canadian nickels and old scraps of addresses and worn-out snapshots and eventually he came across the torn-off flap of an envelope with train times scrawled across it. He picked out the night train to North Carolina. Then, whispering the time to himself as he walked, he went to his closet to choose the clothes he would wear home.

2

His car on the train was only half full; rushing through the darkness it made a hollow, rattling sound. It was cramped and peeling inside, with dirty plush seats and a painted tin roof. At the front hung a huge black-and-white photograph of some people on a beach in Florida, to show that this was the southbound train. Maybe once the photograph had been shiny and exciting, so that passengers gazing at it had counted the hours until they could see the real thing. But now the plastic sheet over it had grown scratched and dull, and the people in it—dozens of tiny people in homely old bathing suits, caught forever in the act of skipping hand in hand toward gray waves or sitting close together under gray-and-white umbrellas—seemed as sad and silent as the flat, still palm trees above them. For a while Ben Joe gave himself up to just staring at it, until the strange feeling it gave him was gone and it was only a photograph again. Then he turned away and looked at the people who shared this car with him.

Mostly they were upright, energetic Negro housewives, sitting like wide shade trees over their clusters of children. Around their feet were diaper bags and paper sacks and picnic baskets; above their heads, in the baggage racks, was an abundance of feathered hats and woolen scarves and sturdy, dark-colored coats. Like Ben Joe, who had a sheepskin-lined jacket folded across his lap, they had come prepared for the time when the hot, stuffy car would suddenly turn too cold for sleeping. They clucked to their children constantly and passed them hot lemonade and pieces of Kleenex, dug up from the bottoms of grocery sacks whenever they heard someone sniff, whether it was their own child or not.

"Here your pacifier, Bertie."

"You let Sadie at the window now; you been at it a sufficient time."

A thin blond man in a pea jacket passed through, carrying a box of toys with "80 cts" printed on it in purple nail polish. He came even with the children just across the aisle from Ben Joe and from the box he pulled out a toy—a rubber donkey with a cord and squeeze-bulb attached to it. The children reached for it, their hands like four little black spiders.

"Want it?" the man asked.

The children looked at their mother. She was a comfortable, smiling woman sitting in the seat ahead of them with a friend. When she heard the man's voice she turned and looked at the children and smiled more broadly, and then frowned and gently shook her head.

"Watch," the man said.

He pressed the bulb and the donkey bucked, tossed his

head, kicked up his heels. Then the little rubber knees buckled in the wrong places and the donkey was lying down in the man's hand, limp and ridiculous-looking.

"Only eighty cents," the man said.

The children watched, round-eyed. With one hand the little girl began stroking the back of her mother's head, patting the curls of her hair with soft, tiny pats.

"How much you say?" the mother asked. She turned only halfway, so that she seemed to be asking the woman beside her.

"Eighty cents, ma'am. Eighty little pieces of copper."

"No sir," the mother said. She turned to the children and said, "No sir. You wait, chirren, we'll get us something in Efram. In Efram, we'll see."

"Eighty cents," the man said.

"No sir." She reached out to straighten the collar of the smaller child, the girl, and then gave her a soft pat on the shoulder and smiled at her.

"How about you?" the man said to Ben Joe.

"No."

"No kiddies at home?"

"No."

"Ah, well."

The man moved on. At the back of the car it began to be noisier; that was where the men sat. Some of them were apparently the women's husbands, and others—the younger, more carelessly dressed ones, slouching in their seats and tipping hip flasks—belonged to no one. They offered swigs to the married men now and their conversation became gayer and louder. Up front, the women clicked their tongues at each other.

"Lemuel Barnes, I coming back there after you if you don't hush!" one called.

"You watch it now, you men, you watch it!"

That was the woman ahead of Ben Joe, a young, plump woman with a baby whose head rested on its mother's shoulder like a little brown mushroom button. She was sitting alone, but she had been talking steadily ever since she boarded the train, calling to her husband at the rear and soothing her baby and carrying on conversations with the other women passengers. Now she stood up and faced the rear, with the baby still over her shoulder, and shouted in a piercing voice:

"You all going to wake the baby, Brandon, you hear? Going to wake up Clara Sue. You want me come back and check on you?"

She started into the aisle, obviously not meaning to go through with it, and stopped when Brandon shouted back, "Aw, Matilda, this Jackie boy the one. *He* stirring all the trouble up."

The other women chuckled.

"That Jackie, he become a pest afore we even got out of the station."

"Brought him *two* bottles. Say no one bottle'd do him."

"Need a wife to keep him still, that boy."

"*Hoo,* Lord."

Matilda smiled down at them and sat down slowly. "Going to make that Brandon come up *here* he don't behave," she said loudly to the window. "I *mean* it, now."

Ben Joe tried smiling at the children across the aisle,

stretching his mouth farther than it wanted to go, but the children stared soberly back at him with little worried frowns. Ahead of them, their mother opened a paper sack and handed back two pieces of fried chicken. The children accepted them automatically, their eyes still fixed on Ben Joe.

"When I get home," their mother said to the woman beside her, "I going to have me a mess of collard greens."

"You got you a good idea there," Matilda called.

The woman turned back and nodded gravely. "They don't feed you right in New York," she said. "Don't know how a person keep himself alive, in New York."

"Ain't *that* the truth."

They were quiet a minute, picturing home. For a minute Ben Joe pictured it with them, knowing almost for a certainty exactly what their homes were like. Who could be that definite about where *he* came from? A hundred years ago, maybe, you could look at a Carolina white man and know what he would have for supper that night, in what kind of house and with what sort of family sitting around him. But not any more—not in his case, at least. He felt suddenly pale and plain, going back to a big pale frame house that no one could tell was his. He looked at his reflection in the black windowpane and frowned, seeing only the flat planes of his cheeks and the worried hollows of his eyes.

"The way they does their chicken in New York," called Matilda, "they puts it in the oven stark nekkid and let it lay awhile. I *seen* it done that way. With a cut-up *frying* chicken I seen it."

"That's so, I know. That's so."

"Ticket, please."

Ben Joe looked up at the conductor, standing stolidly beside him and smiling down over a huge stomach. He handed him his ticket, already a little frayed, and the conductor tore off one section of it.

"Won't have to change," he said. He gave the rest of the ticket back and swayed on to the next passenger.

Someone sat down beside him, so suddenly that Ben Joe was almost frightened for a minute by the jounce in the springs. He turned from the window and found himself no more than three inches from the pointy nose of a curly-haired boy, who was leaning so closely toward him in order to see his face that he was practically lying on his side against Ben Joe.

"*Pardon* me," the boy said. He sat up straight again, folded his coat in his lap, and stared ahead of him at Matilda's baby.

Ben Joe settled back more firmly on his side of the seat and examined the boy's face. He would judge him to be about fifteen, but a New York fifteen; he was very self-assured and his face, except for that one moment of inquisitiveness, was tightly closed and smooth. When he became aware of Ben Joe's stare, he turned toward him again and said, explaining himself, "Just wanted to see what you looked like. See you didn't talk a lot or weren't drunk or nothing."

"I don't talk and I'm not drunk," Ben Joe snapped.

"Okay, okay. But I was sitting with this old man, see, and he was talking all the time. Made me nervous. *All* these guys make me nervous."

"That's *your* problem," Ben Joe said.

"The old man's dying."

Ben Joe looked around, alarmed. "Which one?" he asked.

"White fellow, sitting way back. Can't see him from here."

"Why didn't you tell me before? What—"

"Re*lax*. He's only dying slowly, of old age."

"But—"

"He's *okay*, see."

Ben Joe sat back and stared out the window. The rushing sound of the train and the deep blackness outside made everything seem dreamy and unreal. It was hard to believe that the train was going anywhere at all; it was only standing still and swaying slightly, against a moving screen of darkness and the occasional pinpoints of lights. He told himself that he was finally going home, after all that worrying about his family and wanting desperately to see them again. He told himself what was even more real than that: that when he got there he would immediately feel sad and confused again, the way he always did. But no, Joanne was back. Joanne could change things; just by smiling that smile of hers she could make everything seem safe and in its right place. He closed his eyes, picturing home. He pictured his house as another kind of train, lighted also, floating through darkness. But with the sound of his own train in his ears he couldn't hear their voices; he stood outside his family's windows and watched their movements without hearing a single sound.

His mother would be moving rapidly around the house, pursing her lips tight and flouncing her hair because Ben Joe *couldn't* come home, she wouldn't have it, and then going off to put clean sheets on his bed. His grandmother would be standing on a counter in the kitchen to see what Ben Joe might like from her special private stock of food on the top shelf. And in the ruffly, perfumey closed circles of their worlds, his sisters would hear Ben Joe was returning and then forget again until his return was an actuality and they could get briefly excited over it. Joanne would laugh. She would look at her feet, propped bare on their father's leather hassock, and laugh easily for no reason at all.

(Only would she? It was seven years now since he'd seen Joanne; why couldn't he ever realize the happening of a thing? Surely she'd be different now—calmer and more even-tempered. Or did she wear a low-necked, swinging red dress when she took the baby for a stroll? And toss her hair and flash that teasing smile when she ironed her husband's shirt for him?)

"Plate of okra!" Matilda shouted. "That's what *my* mind fixed on!"

"Be right good. I declare if it wouldn't be."

Ben Joe reached into his shirt pocket. From behind a crumpled pack of cigarettes and an old lighter of his mother's he pulled out this morning's letter, already dingy at the creases. He held it up under the tiny bulb that was supposed to be a reading lamp and read, once more:

Dear Ben Joe:

We received yours of the 21st & are glad to hear you are well. It is too bad that the Asian flu shots gave you Asian flu. Also we are sorry to hear that you are cold.

The big news of course is that Joanne is home. She left her husband altho it's not clear why and of course the first thing Mama asked was was he unfaithful, they all are, & Joanne just laughed at her. The baby is as cute as she can be & is going to be spoiled rotten.

Tessie is going to have to have braces, which will be quite an expense. Gram is going to knit you a sweater for the cold but has forgotten the measurement from the tip of your shoulder to your wrist & would like you to tell her. Also what is your favorite color & if it's still purple forget it, because whenever she knits you a purple sweater she gets to seeing polka dots in front of her eyes before she goes to bed at night.

Ben Joe, you did not write telling Gram not to shop any more. Last night we had crabmeat and black olives in our Monday-night casserole. She also thinks I am not handling the money right & so yesterday she went over the bank books and decided the bank had credited us with $112 too much so she quick withdrew it and put it in another bank before they could find out. I had to go & change banks back again this noon.

Let us hear from you & don't worry.

Sincerely,
Jennifer.

Ben Joe put the letter back in his shirt pocket. He pulled the lever under the arm of his chair and pushed against the back of the seat to make it slant more. There was no point in staying awake worrying about things.

Someone sat down in the curly-haired boy's lap. The boy awoke with a start and said, "Hey! What you—" and began fighting, flailing his arms out and heaving his body and hitting mainly Ben Joe. Whoever sat in the boy's lap was big and solid and quiet, in a heavy tweed overcoat, calmly tipping a bottle to his mouth.

"*Brandon!*" Matilda shrieked. She stood up and, with one hand still holding the baby to her shoulder, reached out and grabbed a handful of Brandon's hair and shook him by it, hard. "You no-count you, Brandon—"

"I'm just *set*ting, Matilda," said Brandon.

"You setting on some*body*, Brandon."

Brandon turned around and looked beneath him.

"Oh, hey," he said.

"You are *sitting* on me," said the boy. He was breathing hard, and looked as if he might start crying.

"I surely am sorry, sir. I didn't see you atall, sir, I come to say hey to this yellow-haired gentleman—"

"Get yourself *offen* him, Brandon."

Brandon rose, confused, and bent over Ben Joe's rumpled seatmate. "I surely do hope I didn't hurt you none," he said. "I surely am sorry. I surely am."

"For*get* it," the boy said. He straightened his jacket and then settled down further in his seat and closed his eyes, determinedly.

"Aren't you *ashamed* of yourself, Brandon."

"Yes'm."

"He ain't *never* like this," she said to Ben Joe. "It's that Jackie egg him on. Brandon has always been a real pillar to me, a real— Come up here and set, Brandon."

"Yes'm, just a minute. I want to speak some with this *yellow*-haired—"

He sat down heavily on the arm of Ben Joe's seat, but taking care not to touch the boy, and leaned across to look at Ben Joe.

"Believe you Ben Joe Hawkes," he said. He switched the bottle to his left hand and shook Ben Joe's hand several times, up and down. His breath smelled of gin, but other than his first mistake he didn't act like a drunken man. His face was sharp and alert, and although he seemed very young there were the beginnings of lines at each corner of his mouth, downward-pulling lines that made him look as if he were in pain. "I'm Brandon Hayes. This here my wife, Matilda. Matilda, this Dr. Hawkes's boy. Dr. *Phillip* Hawkes—him."

"That so?" Matilda said. She turned to Ben Joe, still uncertain, and when Ben Joe nodded, she look relieved. "Looks like you know a *little*, Brandon, I will say. I remember about him having a boy, though I ain't met you ever." She switched the baby to her other shoulder and sat down again, sideways, so that she could see them over the back of the seat. "Your daddy fixed Brandon here's leg," she said. "Was broke in two places, back when he a boy and me just a girl in the same Sunday school class with him. I remember."

"It's true," Brandon said. He settled down more comfortably on the arm of the chair. "Way I saw you, you were in the office with him, wanting him to come home for supper. You mustn't of been but twelve or so but I remembered. I good at faces, yes sir. Been eight years since I even *seen* Sandhill, but there's many I remember though they mightn't remember me. How your daddy now?"

"Well . . ." Ben Joe said, startled. "He, uh, he's dead. Died some six years back."

Brandon looked down at his knees and shook his head, silently. His wife made a sad little cooing sound.

"I do say," Brandon said finally. "Well, I do say. I

surely am sorry to hear it. We been gone so long, they don't write the news like they should . . . I surely am sorry."

"How he go?" Matilda asked.

"Heart attack."

"Law, law." She shook her head too, echoing Brandon. "Well, I know it was a dignified passing. Wan't it?'

Ben Joe, taken off guard, didn't answer.

"Oh, I sure it was *very* dignified, Matilda," Brandon said soothingly.

In the cramped space between the wall and the curly-haired boy, Ben Joe carefully crossed his foot over his knee and twisted one shoelace, staring down at it.

"*Well*, now," said Matilda, suddenly becoming very brisk. "How about your mama?"

"Oh, she's fine."

"And there more of you, ain't there? A passle of sisters? I recollect that. How they?"

"Oh, they're fine, too. The oldest one's got a baby of her own now."

"Well, glory. She marry a Sandhill boy?"

"No. She left Sandhill a little before Dad died, and got a job, and then a few years back she called to say she was married to this boy from Georgia. Haven't seen her since, or the boy, either. They live in Kansas. But she's at home now."

"Well, I know you be glad to see her. I bet your mamma went to Kansas when the baby come, hey?"

"No."

"That daddy of yours a fine man," Brandon said. "Fine man."

"Well," said Matilda, "your mama had enough to do with chirren of her own, I reckon. Maybe just couldn't *make* it all the way to Kansas."

"That's a nice-looking baby *you* got," said Ben Joe.

"Well, thank you. Name's Clara Sue. I *knew* it'd be a girl. I got fatter and fatter in the behind all the time I carrying her."

"Now, Matilda, he don't want to hear about that."

"Well, I just mentioning. You want to sleep, Mr. Ben Joe, and I know Brandon he wild to get back to that gin."

"It was good seeing you," Ben Joe said. He and Brandon stood up and shook hands, and then Brandon left and Matilda turned around to face forward again.

When he was settled back in his seat, Ben Joe leaned his head against the windowpane and closed his eyes, trying to ignore the vibration of the pane against his skin. He wished he knew what state they were passing through. The last of New Jersey, maybe. He felt unsure of his age; in New York he was small and free and too young, and in Sandhill he was old and tied down and enormous, but what age was he here?

With his eyes closed, the division between sleeping and waking became blurred and airy. He saw the sunlit front porch of his house in Sandhill floating up toward him through the darkness behind his eyelids. His father came out of the house, humming a tune beneath his breath, and began crossing the yard to the front gate.

"You come pick me up when it's suppertime, Ben Joe," he said, speaking to the empty air. "I'll be in my office."

The sun shone on his lined face, and on the top of his white hair. From somewhere far off, Ben Joe shouted, "But I'm not there! I'm over here!"

His father made a shoulder-patting motion in space. "We'll walk home together," he said.

Ben Joe began running, trying to be beside his father before he reached the gate, but he was too late. When he got there his father was gone, and his mother had come out on the porch holding a glass of lemonade that flashed piercingly in the sun.

"You've been dreaming about your father," she said.

But Ben Joe said, "No. No, I didn't. I never did."

He awoke, and found that the sill of the train window had pressed a wide deep line into his cheekbone.

3

It was still very early in the morning when Ben Joe reached Sandhill. The wooden station house seemed deserted and the parking lot behind it was white and empty, with the pale sunlight glinting on the flecks of mica in the gravel. Beyond that was a thin row of trees and then, after that, Main Street, running parallel to the railroad tracks and lined with the little stores that made up the downtown section of Sandhill. From where Ben Joe was standing, beside the tracks, all he could see of Sandhill was smoking chimneys and white steeples. The town looked small and clean and perfect, as if it were one of those miniature plastic towns sitting beside a child's electric railroad.

The only other passengers to get off at Sandhill were Brandon's family and a tiny old snuff-chewing white man whom Ben Joe had not seen before. They all stood by the tracks in a group, motionless, soaking in the early morning sunshine and listening to the train fading away behind them. When the air was completely silent again Brandon said, "Sure do feel different from New York."

"Sure do," the old man said.

They turned to look at him.

"Softer, I guess," he said. "I don't know."

They nodded and turned away again. Ben Joe felt as if they might almost be a family, the five of them, standing so close together and so watchful. The sleepiness and the sudden silence seemed to have left an odd gentleness, in himself and in the others, that made him reluctant to leave the station.

"Can't see much of a change from *here*," Brandon said. "See they ain't fixed the clock on the Sand-Bottom Baptists' steeple tower yet."

He was holding the baby now, and in his other hand was a large striped cardboard suitcase, Beside him his wife clutched a diaper bag to her stomach. In the sunlight they both looked much younger; Brandon was bundled into a woolly-collared maroon windbreaker that a little boy might wear, and his wife had a thin brown topper on, girlishly awkward and too short-sleeved, and a simple blue dress that had faded a little. Beside them stood the little old man, also faded but still very clean and polished-looking, as if some brisk daughter-in-law had scrubbed him like an apple with a clean white cloth before she packed him on the train. He had a funny way of breathing—short and fast, with a tiny kitten's mew at the end of each intake. Ben Joe wondered if he were the one that the curly-haired boy had said was dying.

"Anyone know where Setdown Street is?" the old man was asking.

"I do," said Ben Joe.

"I want to find it. Be mighty obliged."

"I'll show you."

A dusty black Chevrolet pulled into the parking lot. It seemed stuffed with laughing brown faces, piled three deep, and even before it had come to a complete stop, the doors had popped open and a whole wealth of brightly dressed Negroes had begun pouring out. Brandon gave a joyous hoot of laughter that was almost a shout and said, "*Hey*, man, hey, Matilda, look who *here*!" and the baby woke up and blinked her round berry eyes at Ben Joe.

"You waking Clara Sue," Matilda said.

"It's *all* of them done come, man, all of them!"

"Mr. Ben Joe," said Matilda, turning halfway to him while she seemed still to be looking toward the Chevrolet, "won't your family planning on meeting you? Because we'n take you in the Chevy, you know. That Brandon's brother driving."

"Well, I reckon my family's not even up yet," Ben Joe said. "But the walk'll do me good. Thanks anyway."

"You, sir?" she said to the old man.

"Oh, I'll be going with him. Iffen it's not too far." He looked up at Ben Joe, questioning him, and Ben Joe shook his head.

"Well, good to see you," Matilda said. She turned to catch up with Brandon and her baby. Across the chilly air the voices of their relatives rang cheerfully; they were grinning and standing awkwardly in a cluster now beside their open-doored car, as if they wanted to give Brandon and Matilda time to get used to them again before they descended on them all at once. And Brandon and Matilda seemed in no hurry. They walked slowly and with careful dignity, proud to have such a large turnout for them. Over Brandon's shoulder the baby waved both fists helplessly.

"Might as well start," said the old man.

"I guess."

"Sure it's not far?"

"Sure."

The old man picked up a large, very new suitcase and Ben Joe led the way, with his own lightweight suitcase swinging easily in his hand. "Ought to be just far enough to get you hungry for breakfast," he called back over his shoulder.

"Good to hear that. Been traveling too long for *my* preference."

They cut through the station, through the large, hot waiting room with its rows and rows of naked, dark wooden benches. Ben Joe could never figure out why Sandhill had provided space for so many passengers. The waiting room was divided in two by a slender post, with half the room reserved for white people and the other half for Negroes. Since times had changed, the wooden letters saying "White" and "Colored" had been removed, but the letters had left cleaner places on the wall that spelled out the same words still. A fat, red-haired lady sat in the ticket both between the two halves of the waiting room; she frowned at the old man and Ben Joe and tapped a pencil against her teeth.

As soon as they were outside, going up the short gravel driveway that cut through the trees onto Main Street, the old man became talkative.

"You shouldn't of mentioned breakfast, boy," he said. "Lord, I'm hungry. Wonder what they'll feed me."

"Who?" Ben Joe asked.

"Oh, them. And you know them colored folks off the same train as us? Know what they're doing now? Setting down to the table with their relations, partaking of buckwheat cakes and hot buttered syrup and them little link sausages. Makes me hungry just thinking of it."

His breath was squeaking more now; the nostrils of his small, bent nose widened and fluttered as he drew in bigger and bigger amounts of air.

"My son got me this suitcase special, just for the trip. It was real expensive. I said, 'Sam,' I said, '*you* don't need to spend all that money on me, son,' but Sam he said, 'It's the least I can do.' 'It's the least I can do,' he tells me. He wanted to come take the trip with me, but I could see he was busy and all. I wouldn't allow it. Law, I am eighty-four years old now and *capable*, it's what I keep telling him. Capable. Though I will admit the train was something bumpy, and I feared that it would jounce all my insides out of place. I got this fear, someday my intestines will get tied in a bow by accident, like shoelaces. You ever thought of that?"

"Not that I can remember," Ben Joe said. He was getting worried now; the old man's voice had become a mere wheezing sound, and he was so out of breath that Ben Joe's own throat grew tight and breathless in sympathy.

"Well, I have. Often I have. I don't know if you ever knew my son Sam. He's a businessman, like on Wall Street, except that he happens to be in Connecticut instead. Got a real nice family, too. Course I think he could of made a better choice in wives, but then Sally's right pretty and I reckon I can see his point in picking her. Just a mite bossy, in all. And then her family's Jehovah's Witnesses. Now, I got no quarrel to pick with *any* religion, excepting maybe a few, but I heard somewheres that Jehovah's Witnesses they turn off all the lights and get under the chairs and tables and look for God. They do. Ain't found Him yet, neither. Course Sally she's reformed now, but *still* and all, still and all . . ."

On Main Street he became suddenly silent. He walked along almost on tiptoe, looking around him with a white, astonished face. Sometimes he would whisper, "Oh, my, look at that!" and purse his mouth and widen his eyes at some ordinary little store front. Ben Joe couldn't understand him. What was so odd about Sandhill? Main Street was wide and white and almost bare of cars; a few shopkeepers whistled cheerfully as they swept in front of their stores, and a pretty girl Ben Joe had never seen before passed by, smiling. Except for the new hotel, there wasn't a single building over three stories high in the whole town. Above the squat little shops the owners' families lived, and their flowered curtains hung cozily behind narrow dark windows.

At the third block they turned left and started uphill on a small, well-shaded street. Main Street was the only commercial district in the town; as soon as they turned off it they were among large family houses with enormous old pecan trees towering over them. The old man had stopped exclaiming now, but he was still tiptoeing and wide-eyed. Although his baggy coat seemed paper thin and the morning was very cool, the surface of his face was shiny with perspiration. With a small grunt he switched his suitcase to his other hand and it banged against the side of his knee.

"I'll trade you suitcases for a while," Ben Joe said.

"No no. No no. You know, when I was a boy we'd of been plumb through town by now."

"Sir?"

"Town's *grown* some, I said."

"Oh. You mean you've been here before?"

"Born here, I was. But I ain't seen it since I was eighteen years old and that's a fact. Went off to help my uncle make bed linens in Connecticut. Though at the time I never wanted to. I wanted to go to Africa."

"*Africa?*"

"Africa." He stopped and set down his suitcase in order to wipe his forehead with a carefully folded handkerchief from his breast pocket. "Wadn't but two streets that was paved then," he said. "Main and Dower. Dower's *my* name. It was named after my daddy, who moved out west soon after I went north on account of the humidity here being bad for my mother's ankle bones. But there wadn't no street called Setdown then. Got no idea where *that* is."

"Well, it's not far," Ben Joe said. "You got relatives living there?"

"Nope. Nope."

"Where you going?"

"Home for the aged."

"Oh."

Ben Joe stood in silence for a minute, not knowing what to say next. Finally he cleared his throat and said, "Well, that's where it is, all right."

"Course it is. Going to die there."

"Well. Well, um, I trust that'll be a long time from now."

"Don't trust too hard," the old man said. He seemed irritated by Ben Joe's embarrassment; he picked up his suitcase with a jerk and they continued on up the hill. As they walked, Ben Joe kept looking over at him sideways.

"Don't you corner your eyes like that," Mr. Dower said. "Not at me you don't."

"Well, I was just thinking."

"Don't have to corner your eyes just to be thinking, do you?"

"I've been away some time myself," Ben Joe said. "Some time for *me*, anyway. Going on four months. It seemed longer, though, and I sort of left planning not to return."

"Then what you *here* for?" Mr. Dower snapped.

"Well, I don't know," Ben Joe said. "I just can't seem to *get* anywhere. Nowhere permanent."

"*I* can. Can and did. Went away permanent and now I've come back to die permanent."

"How can you have gone away permanent if you've come back?" Ben Joe asked.

"Because what I left ain't here to come back to, that's

why. Therefore my going away can be counted as permanent."

"That's what they all say," said Ben Joe. "But they're fooling themselves."

"Well." Mr. Dower stopped again to wipe his forehead. "How much farther, boy?"

"Not far. Right at the end of this block."

"Long blocks you've got. Long blocks. This here," the old man said, pointing to an old stone house, "is where Jonah Barnlott lived, that married my sister. Like to broke my family's heart doing it, too. He was a no-count boy, that Jonah. Became a doctor, finally, down in Georgia, but never had any patients to speak of. Was inflicted with athlete's foot, he was, and decided shoes were what gave it to him, so he loafed about his office playing patience in a white uniform and pure-T bare feet, which scared all his patients away. My sister left him, finally, and got remarried to a lawyer. Lawyers're better. Not so concerned with bodily matters. So now it's Saul Bowen lives in that house. I reckon you know *him*."

"No, sir."

"Not know Saul Bowen? Fat old guy who goes around town all day eating pudding from a dish?"

"No, sir."

"Well, no," Mr. Dower said after a minute. "I guess not. I guess not."

They were silent for the rest of the block. The old man's shoes made a shuffling, scratchy noise on the sidewalk and the mewing of his breath was loud and unsteady, so that Ben Joe became frightened.

"Sir," he said at the corner, "it's just one block down from here, on the left. But I'd be happy to walk you the rest of the way."

"I can make it. I can make it."

"Well, it's a big yellow house with a sign in front. You sure you're all right?"

"I am *dying*," said the old man. "But otherwise I'm fine and I'd appreciate to walk by myself for a spell."

"Well. Good-by, Mr. Dower."

"Bye, boy."

The old man started down Setdown Street, his suitcase banging his knees at every step. For a minute Ben Joe watched after him, but the shabby little figure was pushing doggedly on with no help from him and there was nothing more he could do. Finally he turned and started walking again, on toward his own home.

The houses in this area were big and comfortable, although most of them were poorly cared-for. On some of the lawns the trees were so old and thick that there was a little whitening of frost on the grass beneath their limbs, even now that most of their leaves were gone. Ben Joe began shivering. He walked more quickly, past the wide, deserted porches and down the echoing sidewalk. Then he was on the corner, and across the street was his own house.

A long, low wire gate stood in front of it, although the fence that went with it had been torn down years ago when the last of the children had left the toddler stage. The lawn behind it had been allowed to grow wild and weedy, half as high as a wheat field and dotted here and there with little wiry shrubs and seedy, late-fall flowers.

And the sidewalk from the gate to the front porch was cracked and broken; little clumps of grass grew in it. Towering above such an unkempt expanse of grass, the house took on a half-deserted look in spite of the lace curtains that hung primly in all the windows. It was an enormous white frame house, in need of a little touch-up with a paint brush, and it could easily be the ugliest house in town. Round stained-glass windows popped up in unexpected places; the front bay window was too tall and narrow, and the little turret, with its ridiculously curlicued weather vane, looked as if it must be stuffed with bats and cobwebs. People said—although Ben Joe never believed them—that the first time his mother had seen the house she had laughed so hard that she got hiccups and a neighbor had had to bring her a glass of peppermint water. And all the while that Ben Joe was growing up, little boys used to ask him jealously if his room was in the turret. He always said yes, although the truth was that nobody lived there; it was just a huge hollow space above the stairwell. The only thing that saved the house from looking haunted was the front porch, big and square and friendly. A shiny green metal glider sat there, and in the summertime the whole porch railing was littered with bathing suits and Coke bottles and the lounging figures of whatever boys his sisters were dating at the time. In front of the door, Ben Joe could just make out a rolled-up newspaper. That brought him to life again; he crossed the yard cheerfully, stopped on the porch to pick up the paper, and opened the front door.

Inside, there was the mossy brown smell that he had been raised with, that seemed to be part and parcel of the house and was a wonderful smell if you were glad to be home and an unbearable smell if you were not. And mingled with it were the more temporary, tangible smells—bacon, coffee, hot radiators, newly ironed dresses, bath powder. He was standing in the narrow hallway and looking into the living room, which was stuffed with durable old ugly furniture that had stood the growing up of seven children. On the walls hung staid oil paintings of ships at sea and summer landscapes. The coffee tables were littered with things that had been there as long as Ben Joe could remember—little china figurines, enameled flower pots, conch shells. Periodically his mother tried to move them, but Gram always put them back again. On the floor was an interrupted Monopoly game, a pair of fluffy slippers, a beer can, and a pink baby sweater that reminded him of Tessie. It must belong to Joanne's baby now. He set down the suitcase and the newspaper and crossed into the living room to pick the sweater up between two fingers. It seemed to him that every girl in the family had worn that. But had it really been that tiny?

In the kitchen a voice said, "I'll tell you what. I'll tell you what, Jane. Every time I even pick *up* a glass of frozen orange juice, it makes me think of vitamin pills. Does it you?"

Someone answered. It could have been any one of them; they all had that low, clear voice of their mother's. And then the first voice again: "I'd rather squeeze oranges in my bare hands than drink my orange juice frozen."

Ben Joe smiled and headed through the hallway toward the voices, with the sweater still in one hand. At the open doorway to the kitchen he stopped and looked in at the five girls sitting around the table. "Anybody home?" he asked.

They all turned at the same moment to look at him, and then their chairs were scraped back and five cheeks were pressed briefly to his and questions hurled around his head.

"What you doing here, Ben Joe?"

"What you think Mama's going to say?"

"How'd you get *in*, is what I want to know."

"Sure, a burglar could've walked in. We'd never even heard him."

"Would anyone be a burglar before breakfast? And what's to steal?"

"Where's your luggage, Ben Joe?"

He stood smiling, unable to get a word in edgewise. They were circled around him, looking soft and happy in their pastel bathrobes, and if they had been still a minute he would have said he was glad to see them, even if it *would* embarrass them, but they didn't give him a chance. Lisa reached for the baby sweater in his hand and held it up above her head for the others to see and laugh at.

"Why, Ben Joe, you bring us a sweater? Isn't that nice, except I don't reckon it'll *fit* us too well."

"He's been away so long, forgotten how big we'd have grown."

"Aren't you exhausted?"

"I am at that," said Ben Joe. "Feels like my head's come unscrewed at the neck."

"I'll get you some coffee," Jenny said. She was the next-to-youngest—it was only last spring that she'd graduated from high school—but, of all of them, she was the most down-to-earth. She went to the cupboard and took down the huge earthenware mug that Ben Joe always used. "Mama didn't know if you meant it about coming home," she said, "and says she hopes you *didn't*, but she changed your bed, anyway."

"I'm going to it, too, soon as I've had my breakfast. Hello there, Tessie. You're so little still I damn near overlooked you. Maybe it's you this sweater's for."

"Not me it's not," said Tessie. "It's too little for Carol, even."

"Who's Carol?"

"Carol's our *niece*."

"Oh. Where's Joanne?"

"In bed. So's Carol."

"I forgot about her being named Carol," Ben Joe said. "One more girl to remember. Hoo boy." He took off his jacket and turned to hang it on the back of his chair. "Ma gone to work already?"

"Yup. This man's bringing a truckload of books real early."

The mug was set before him, full of steaming coffee. Tessie passed him a plate of cinnamon buns and said, "You notice anything different about me?"

"Well . . ." Ben Joe said. He frowned at her, and she frowned steadily back. Of all the Hawkes children, she and Ben Joe were the only blond ones. The others had dark hair, which they wore short and curly, and their eyes were so black it was hard to tell where they were looking. They were almost round-eyed, too, whereas Ben Joe and Tessie had their father's too-narrow eyes. And there was something tricky about their coloring. At one moment they could seem very pale and at the next their skin would be almost olive-toned. But all of the girls, even Tessie, had little pointed faces and small, careful features, a little too sharp; all of them wore quick, watchful expressions and their oval-nailed hands were thin and restless. People said they were the prettiest girls in town, and the ficklest. Thinking of that, Ben Joe smiled at them, and Tessie tugged at his arm impatiently and said, "Not them, *me*."

"You." He turned back to her. "You've gone and gotten married on us."

"Oh, Ben *Joe*." Her giggle was like Joanne's, light and chuckly. "I'm only ten years *old*," she said. "Don't you see *anything* different?"

"Nope."

"I've had my ears pierced!"

"Aha," said Ben Joe. He took her face in his hands and turned it first one way and then the other, examining the tiny gold rings in her ears. "What for?"

"Oh, just because. Joanne and Susannah and the twins have pierced ears. Why not me?"

"Did it hurt?"

"Yup."

"Did you cry?"

"Nope. Well, tears came out, but I went on smiling."

"Good girl," Ben Joe said. "Better run along and get ready for school, now. You'll be late."

"You'll all be late," Susannah said.

The others got up and left; the pinks and blues of their bathrobes clustered together for a minute at the doorway and then vanished into the hall. Ben Joe could hear their soft slippers padding up the stairs, and somewhere a door slammed. "What about you?" he asked.

"I've got another half-hour."

"Is Gram up?"

"Yes. She's up in her room, making a gun belt for Tessie out of an old leather skirt."

He watched Susannah silently for a while, following her quick little movements around the kitchen. She hadn't changed any; she got the coffee grounds half emptied and fled to the orange-juicer and then to sponge the top of the stove off before she remembered the coffee grounds again.

"Have you talked to Joanne?" he asked.

"Oh, sure."

"What'd she say?"

"What about?"

"About leaving Gary."

"Oh." She tossed the insides of the coffee pot into the sink and went dashing across the kitchen after a cream pitcher. "I don't know," she said. "It never came up."

"Oh, for heaven's sake."

"Well, it's none of *my* business."

"She's your sister, isn't she?"

"That still doesn't make it my business."

"What does, then?" Ben Joe asked.

"*Nothing.*" She lifted up one soapy hand and pushed a piece of hair off her forehead with the back of her wrist.

"You're the one that's so worried. Why don't *you* talk to her, if you think you know where she'd be happier."

"It's not that I much want her to go *back* to him," Ben Joe said slowly. "Gary's an awful name. Whatever he's like. It reminds me of a G.I. with a crew cut, and 'Mom' tattooed on his chest, and lots of pin-up pictures on his wall."

"Oh, you," Susannah said. "That's beside the point. Go up and get some sleep, Ben Joe. The house'll be bedlam when Carol wakes up."

"Okay. Have a good day at work."

"Thank you."

He stood watching her for a minute, but Susannah had already forgotten him. She was on her hands and knees under the table now, crawling after one of her slippers, and it was as if Ben Joe had never been there.

4

WHEN HE AWOKE, his mother was in the doorway watching him. He was not sure whether she had spoken his name or not; in his sleep he seemed to have heard her voice. But maybe all that had awakened him was the feel of her eyes—wide eyes, as dark as her daughters', but with small lines now at the corners. She was the kind of woman who did not become very wrinkled as she aged but instead acquired only a few lines around her mouth and eyes, and those so deep that they were actual crevices even when her face was calm. She was smiling a little, so that the mouth lines curved and deepened even more, and she stood with one hand on her hip and the other on the doorknob and watched Ben Joe.

"Ben Joe Hawkes," she said finally, "what on *earth* are you doing home?"

Ben Joe sat up in the familiar wooden bed and pushed his hair back from his forehead. "I already told you," he said. "I told you the reason on the phone."

"That was no reason." She shook her head. "Of all the things to do . . . What's going to happen to your school work?"

"I don't have to be there every minute."

"If you make good grades you do. If you're going to be any kind of decent lawyer."

Ben Joe shrugged and pulled his pillow up behind him so that he could sit against it. The sheets smelled crisp and newly ironed; his mother had smoothed them tight on the bed herself and turned the covers down for him, and he could hold that thought securely in his mind even when she scolded him for returning. You had to be a sort of detective with his mother; you had to search out the fresh-made bed, the flowers on the bureau, and the dinner table laid matter-of-factly with your favorite supper, and then you forgot her crisp manners. He wondered, watching her, whether his sisters knew that. Or did they even need to know? Maybe it was only Ben Joe, still watching his mother with those detective eyes even though he was a grown man now and should have stopped bothering.

"Have you had breakfast?" his mother was asking.

"Yes'm. Had it with the girls before they went to work."

"Well, I'm home for lunch now. You want a bite to eat?"

"I guess."

She came further into the room and opened his closet door. From the front rack she took a bathrobe and tossed it to him, not watching where it landed, and then crossed to pull the shade up. He saw that she was still wearing those wide walking skirts with the mid-calf hem that had been popular some fifteen years ago. On her, with her bony height and her swinging walk, they still looked up to date. Her hair was a light, dusty color, once as blond as his and Tessie's. It was short and a little too frizzy around the sharp angles of her face, but she still didn't seem like an old woman. He gave up watching her and, pulling the bathrobe around him, stepped barefoot to the floor.

"You're thinner," she said. She had stopped fiddling with the window shade and was taking stock of him now, with her hands deep in the pockets of her skirt. "You've been cooking for yourself, I'll bet."

"Yes'm. What time is it?"

"About twelve."

"Is Joanne up?"

"Oh, yes. She and Carol are in the den, I think."

"Is she okay?"

"Of *course* she's okay. And it's her own business, Ben Joe—nothing we have any right to touch. I don't want to hear about your meddling in it. Hurry up and get dressed, will you? Lunch is nearly ready."

She swung out of the door and vanished, humming something beneath her breath as she went downstairs. Behind her, Ben Joe sighed and tied his bathrobe around him. It would be a good time to shave; none of the older girls came home for lunch.

When he came downstairs he could smell lunch already—all the varied smells of odds and ends left over in the refrigerator and reheated now in tiny saucepans. Although he was rested now, his stomach still felt shaky from the trip and he made a face as the smell of lunch hit him on the stairs. Gram must be doing the cooking today; she was an old Southerner and floated all her vegetables in grease.

He pushed open the kitchen door and found his grandmother standing by the stove just lifting the lid off a steaming saucepan. She was his father's mother, and close to eighty now, but there was a steely, glinting endurance to her. Joanne used to say her grandmother reminded her of piano wires. She was small and bony; she wore men's black gym shoes that tied around her bare ankles, and her dress, as usual, was a disgrace—a sort of blue denim coat that was fastened with one string at the back of the neck and hung open the rest of the way down the back to expose a black lace slip. (Her underwear was her one luxury; she had seven different colors in her bureau drawer.) As she stirred the leftovers she sang, just as she always did, in a deafening roar that came effortlessly from the bottom of her tiny rib cage:

> "I ain't gonna knock on your window no more,
> Ain't gonna bang on your door . . ."

"Hello, Gram," Ben Joe said in her ear.

She spun around, just missing him with the saucepan lid. "Ben *Joe!*" she said. "I hear you came in this morning and didn't even say hey to me. That true?"

"You were up in the attic making a gun belt," he said.

He hugged her and she hugged him back, so hard that he could feel her hard, bony chest and the point of her chin just below his shoulder.

"We're having leftovers," she said. "I know what view you hold of leftovers, but you just wait till tonight. You just *see* what manner of things we're preparing."

She replaced the saucepan lid and undid her hair. It was her habit to take three bobby pins from her head, at least twenty times a day, and let her straight white hair fall almost to her shoulders. Then, with the bobby pins clamped tightly in her mouth, she deftly wound her hair around one finger, squashed it on top of her head in a bun, and nailed it there again with the three bobby pins. All this took less than a minute. While she was doing it she kept right on talking, shifting the bobby pins to one corner of her mouth so that they wouldn't interrupt her speech.

"Turkey we're having," she said, "and giblet dressing, and yams— Ben Joe, you got to talk to Jenny about her grocery rut. She's got into a rut about grocery shopping. Buys the same old thing every time. No imagination. Now, Jenny, she is a right good cook and I want to see her get married, real soon. I don't hold with a girl staying and looking after her family and being a little old secretary all her life when she is as home-minded as Jenny is. Got to get a family of her own. But what man'll marry a girl feeds him hamburgers every night? Course she does all *manner* of clever things to dress them up a little, but still and all it's hamburger and the cheap kind of hamburger at that. Ever since you left and put her in charge of the money matters she's been *parsimonious,* is what, taking it too serious. Call people to eat, will you? Your ma's upstairs and the others're in the den."

"Yes'm."

He left the kitchen and headed for the den, which was through the living room and at the other end of the house. It had once been his father's study, and although the medical books on the shelves had long since been disposed of, there was still the extra telephone on the desk, installed when the girls had first become old enough to tie up the lines on the regular phone. Since their father's death the room was used as a TV room, and now the set was blaring so loudly that Ben Joe could hear it way before he crossed the living room. And once he was inside the den the sound hurt his ears. The shades were down and at first it was too dark to see anything but the silhouettes of the people watching and beyond them the screen, bluish and snow-flecked. A fat man was shouting, "Whaddaya say, kiddies? Huh? Whaddaya say?" and behind his voice was a loud, angry humming from the set itself. Ben Joe blinked and looked around.

All he could see of Joanne was the white line that edged her profile from the light of the TV screen on her face. She had her eyes lowered to something in her lap—a piece of cloth. And she was sewing on it, pushing the needle through and then stretching her arm as far out as it would reach in order to pull the thread tight. Joanne was the type of person who used just one enormous length of thread instead of several short practical lengths. On the cane chair in front of her sat Tessie, also just a silvery profile but with a snatch of yellow over her forehead where the light hit her blond hair. And farthest in front, so that her back was toward Ben Joe, sat a small child in a child's rocking chair. Of her Ben Joe could see nothing, except that she was so small (she would have been two only last June) her feet stuck out in front of her on the chair, and she was rocking violently. He could make out her small hands gripping the chair arms tightly; she flung her head first forward and then back, to make the chair rock. From here he could almost swear her hair was red, although that was improbable. He took another step into the room and said, "Has she got *red* hair?"

Joanne started and looked at him.

"Hi, Joanne," he said.

"Ben Joe, come here! No, wait. Come out into the living room. It's dark as night in here."

She rose and pulled him out into the light and kissed him on both cheeks, hard, and hugged him around the waist. The little dress she was sewing was still in one hand, but the needle had slipped off its thread and was lying on the rug at her feet. It was funny how the tiniest thing Joanne did was exactly like her, even now, even after all these years. Any of the other girls would have stuck her needle into the cloth for safekeeping before she went to kiss her brother. "God, you're thin," she said. She was laughing, and her hair was mussed from hugging him. "I can't believe it's really you. Have you gone back to being a vegetarian?"

"No. Mom says it's eating my own cooking that does it."

"Mm-hm. You're older, too. But that's all right. I don't reckon you're *ever* going to get any lines in your face."

"That's from having no character," he said absently.

He was trying to decide what was different about her; something was making him feel a little shy, as if she were a stranger. Probably the way she dressed was partly responsible for it. In place of the blazing red dress of the old days was a soft yellow sacklike thing that hung loosely from her shoulders. She was still thin, though, with a face just slightly rounder than her sisters'. Almost immediately he decided what the change in her was; she was pretty much the same, with that same warm chuckly laugh, but she had a different way of showing it. A subtler one, he thought. Yet the bangles were still on her arms, and the twinkling, chin-ducking smile still on her face. He smiled back.

"I see you're not old yet," he said.

"Almost I am. Did you have a good trip?"

"I guess so. I came to call you to lunch, by the way. Gram's dishing up."

"I'll get the children."

She pattered back into the den, barefoot, and came out again with Carol in her arms and Tessie trailing behind her, blinking in the sunlight. The TV had been forgotten; accordion music seesawed out noisily from the empty room.

"You met Carol yet?" Joanne asked.

Ben Joe looked at Carol, checking her hair first because he was curious to see whether it was red or not. It was. It was cut, cup-like, around a small, round face that was still so young it could tell Ben Joe nothing. "Can you talk yet?" he asked her.

She smiled, not telling.

"Only when she's in the mood," Joanne said. "She's

got to say a word exactly right or she refuses to say it at all. A perfectionist. I don't know where she gets it."

"What about her red hair?"

"What?"

"Where's she get *that*?"

Joanne frowned. "Where you get any kind of hair," she said finally. "Genes."

"Oh."

"I sure am glad to see you, Ben Joe," she said as they crossed the living room. "I am. You don't know how glad."

Embarrassed, Ben Joe smiled down at her and said nothing. At the stairway he stopped and yelled up, "Mom!" and then continued on into the kitchen, not looking at Joanne or waiting for his mother's answer. But just before they reached the doorway he said, "Well, I'm happy to see *you*."

That's good," she said cheerfully.

In the kitchen Gram was bustling around, ladling food onto the plates on the table. Joanne pulled the old high chair up and sat Carol in it. "Don't you go wiggling around," she told her. She gave her a little pat on the knee. It made Ben Joe feel strange, watching Joanne with Carol. He never had really thought about the fact that she was a mother now with a child of her own.

"Where's your mama?" Gram asked.

"Coming."

"Well, her meal's getting cold. Sit down, Joanne. Sit down, Ben Joe. Tessie, you got to hurry now. What happened to your napkin?"

"It's on the screen porch."

"Well, it's not supposed to be. No, don't go get it. More important to get your meal down you hot—stave off germs that way. Ben Joe, honey, aren't you tired to pieces?"

"Not any more I'm not."

"Well, you have a big helping of these here beans. Carol just threw her bib on the floor, Joanne."

She put another scoop of beans on Ben Joe's plate, shaking the spoon vigorously. Seeing her hands, so much older than the rest of her, reminded Ben Joe of the old man from the train. He said, "Gram, did you ever know a man named Dower?"

"Dower." She sat down at her own place, smoothing the front of her apron across her lap. "Lord yes, I did. There was a whole heap of Dowers here at one time, though most have died out or moved on. There was the good Dowers and there was the bad Dowers. The good ones were very great friends of the family once. I near about lived at their house when I was a teeny-iney girl. They're all dead now, I reckon. But the bad ones are living here yet. Wouldn't you know. No relation to the good ones, of course. Living off the county and letting chickens in the kitchen. That kind just hangs on and *hangs* on. I don't know why. They're so spindly-legged and pasty-faced, but they keep on long after stronger men's in their graves."

She stopped to take a breath. Ben Joe's mother came into the kitchen and pulled up a chair for herself. Carol threw her bib on the floor again and said, "Carrot."

"We're going to have to tie a double knot in your bib from now on," Ben Joe's mother told her. She took a raw carrot from the plate on the table and handed it to her. "Gram, what are those little things in the dish over there?"

"Smoked oysters. And that child shouldn't have a carrot."

"Smoked *oysters*?"

"That's what I said. Won't have this grocery rut of Jenny's one day longer. My mind's made up. Ellen, take that carrot away from her."

"Why? She's got teeth."

"But it's a big *thick* carrot."

"Well, we can't mollycoddle her. The rest of the girls had carrots at her age."

"Not while I was around," Gram said. "She'll choke on it."

Joanne looked up anxiously and Gram nodded to her.

"On the little pieces of it. She'll choke. I've seen it happen."

"Oh, don't be silly," said Ellen Hawkes.

Joanne reached over and took the carrot away, replacing it with a soda cracker immediately so that Carol didn't have time to start crying. Ben Joe's mother turned back to her meal, resigned. Neither she nor Gram paid much attention to these quibbling arguments of theirs; they were used to them. Gram said Ellen Hawkes was coldhearted and Ellen Hawkes said Gram was soft-cored. The rest of the family was as used to the feud as they were. They went on eating now, cheerfully, and Carol began gnawing at her cracker.

"The reason I asked about the Dowers," Ben Joe said,

"is that I met an old man from the train by that name. He said he was born right here in Sandhill."

"That's funny. Good Dower or bad Dower?"

"Well, Gram, I doubt if he'd have said."

"If he was a bad Dower he would have. He would have said he was a good Dower."

Joanne laughed.

"He said there was a street named for his father," Ben Joe said. "I remember that much. He said that when he was here, Main and Dower were the only real streets in town."

Gram looked up, interested now. "That's so," she said. "It's true, that's so."

Carol spilled her milk. It trickled off the high-chair tray and into her lap, and when she felt the coldness of it she squealed.

"I'll get a rag," said Tessie.

She started for the sink, but her mother reached around and grabbed her back by the the sash. "You sit right there, young lady. You have to be at school in fifteen minutes."

"It won't take long, Mama."

But Joanne was already up, reaching for paper towels and then lifting Carol out of her high chair to sponge her off. "There, there," she was saying, although Carol was only squealing for the joy of hearing her own voice now and had started pulling out all the bobby pins from Joanne's hair.

"He went off to help his uncle make bed sheets in Connecticut!" Ben Joe shouted above the uproar.

His mother stopped chewing and stared at him.

"Mr. Dower, I'm talking about. And then his family moved away because his mother's ankle bones started hurting—"

"Ben Joe," his mother said, "if all of you children would cast your minds back to when you were small and I told you *never,* on *any* account, to speak to those strange-looking people you seem to keep meeting up with—"

"How old was he when he began in bed sheets?" Gram asked.

"Eighteen, he told me."

"My Lord in heaven!" She laid her fork on the table and stared at him. "Why, that couldn't be anyone but *Jamie* Dower. Jamie Dower, I'll be. My Lord in heaven."

"Was he a good Dower?"

"Good as they come. Shoot, yes. He was six years older'n me, but you'd never believe the crush I had on him. That was the *reason* I practically lived at the Dowers'—following him around all the time. I thought he was Adam, back then."

"*Adam?*" Tessie said. "How was he dressed?"

Her mother pushed her plate closer to her. "Eat your beans, Tessie. Stop that dawdling."

"Where was he going to?" Gram asked.

"Well, um—the home for the aged, is what he told me."

"The home for the aged." She shook her head. "My, my, who'd have believed it? He was a real handsome boy, you know—kind of tall for back then, though nothing to compare with some of those basketball players you see around nowadays. Real fond of stylish clothes, too.

What would we have thought, I wonder, had someone told us back then where Jamie Dower would end up?"

"Tessie," said Ellen Hawkes, "I give you to the count of five to drink that milk up. What's that on your front? Beans?"

"Nothing," said Tessie. She finished the last of her milk and wiped the white mustache off her upper lip with the back of her hand.

"That's a funny-looking nothing."

"Well, anyway, I gotta go. Good-by, Mama. Good-by, everybody."

She vanished out the kitchen door, grabbing her jacket as she went. Her mother stared after her and shook her head. "You practically have to *drag* her to school," she said. "Sometimes I think the brains just sort of dribbled away toward the end in this family."

"She's plenty bright," said Gram.

"Well, maybe. But not like Joanne and Ben Joe were —not like them."

"Rubbish," said Gram. She began reaching for the plates and scraping them while she sat at her place. "Too much emphasis on brains in this family. What good's it do? Joanne quit after one year of college and the others, excepting Ben Joe, never went. And Ben Joe—look at him. He just kept trying to figure out what that all-fired mind of his was given him for, and first he thought it was for science and then for art and then for philosophy and now what's he got? Just a mish-mash, is all. Just nothing. Won't read a thing now but murder mysteries."

"Neither *one* of you knows what you're talking about," Ben Joe said cheerfully. He had been through all this before; he listened with only half an ear, tipping back in his chair and watching his grandmother scrape plates. "And pooh, what do the girls want to go to college for? I say they're smart choosing not to—"

"Well, sure you do," his mother said. "Sure you do, when all you've got to judge it by is *Sandhill* College. Might as well not have gone at all, as far as I'm concerned—"

"No fault of his," Gram said.

"Well, it's no fault of *mine*."

"If my son'd had his say," Gram said, "Ben Joe'd have gone to Harvard, that's where."

"Your son could've had his say. If he'd come back he could've had his say and welcome *to* it, but what'd he do instead?" She was sitting up straight now, with one hand clasping her fork so tightly that the knuckles were white.

"Who made him like that?" Gram shouted. "Who made his house so cold he chose to go live in another's, tell me that!"

Ben Joe cleared his throat. "Actually," he said, "if I'd made better grades I'd have gotten a scholarship to Harvard. I don't see how it's anyone's fault but my—"

"And who didn't give a hoot when he left?" Gram shouted triumphantly above Ben Joe. "Answer me *that*, now, answer me—"

"That will *do*, Gram," said Ellen Hawkes.

She unclasped her hand from the fork and rose, suddenly calm. "I'll be home by six," she said to Joanne and Ben Joe. They nodded, silently; she pushed her chair in and left. Joanne was staring at the tablecloth as if it were impossible to drag her eyes away from it.

"Cracker," Carol said.

Ben Joe handed her one. She seized it and immediately began crumbling it over her tray.

"I *am* sorry," Gram said after a minute. "There was no call to act like that. I didn't mean to bring it up."

Joanne nodded, still staring at the tablecloth. "I thought you'd have settled that," she said.

"Oh, no. No, just let it slip from being uppermost in my mind, is all. You missed the worst of it. Things went on like before even after you up and left home over it, though you'd think some people might try and change a little. Ah, well, least said soonest . . ."

She sighed and rose to take the stack of dishes to the sink. "Ben Joe, honey," she called over her shoulder, "you reckon Jamie Dower might like a visitor?"

"I don't know why not, Gram."

"You and me'll go, then, sometime this week. I'll start thinking about it."

Joanne rose to help Gram, with her face still pale and too sober. For a while Ben Joe watched them, following their quick, sure movements around the kitchen, but then Carol began blowing cracker crumbs at him and he turned back to her and lifted her out of the high chair.

"Does she get a nap?" he asked Joanne.

"Well, yes. But I'm reading this book that says the same person has got to put her to bed all the time. You better wait and let me do it."

"All right." He headed for the living room, with Carol snuggled in the crook of his arm. "Wouldn't want to make you maladjusted," he told her. She smiled and sucked on a corner of her cracker.

In the living room he sat down in the rocking chair. He pried the soggy mass of cracker from Carol's hand and put it in the ash tray, and then he began absent-mindedly rocking. Carol's head dropped heavily against his chest; her red hair was tickling a point just under his chin. He could feel the small dead weight of her, but he remained unconvinced of her realness and for a long time he just rocked silently, frowning above her head at the faded wallpaper.

5

By evening Ben Joe was beginning to feel the weight of home settling back on him, making him feel heavy and old and tired. He had eaten too much for supper; his stomach ached and he didn't want to admit it to anyone, or to show it by lying down, for fear that his mother and his grandmother would be hurt after all that special cooking. So he wandered aimlessly through the house, searching out something to do or think about. In the den Tessie and Jenny watched television, scowling intently at the screen and not looking up when he came to stand in the doorway. The twins, dressed in different colors now that they were older but still looking exactly the same in every other way, were popping popcorn with their dates in the kitchen, and Susannah and Gram were playing honeymoon bridge. None of them took any notice of him. He went upstairs, hoping to find someone up there who would talk to him, but his mother was using the sewing machine, her mouth full of pins and her eyes narrowed at the sleeve of a dress for Tessie. Joanne was giving Carol a bath. He could hear them even with the door half shut—Carol squealing and splashing, Joanne calming her with low, soothing noises and then occasionally laughing along with her.

"Can I come in?" Ben Joe called.

"Carol, you mind if a man comes to watch your bath?"

Carol made a louder splash, probably with the flat of her hand, and giggled.

"Well, she didn't say no," said Joanne.

Ben Joe pushed the door open and stepped inside. The room was warm and steamy, and cluttered with towels and cast-off clothes. Beside the bathtub knelt Joanne, wearing a terry-cloth bathrobe, with her hair hanging wet and stringy down her neck and her face shiny from her own bath. She had rolled the sleeves of the robe up to her elbows so that she could bathe Carol, who sat in a heap of rubber toys that blocked out almost all sight of bathwater and laughed at Ben Joe.

"Can't be a true Hawkes," said Ben Joe. "No bubble bath."

"Oh, that'll start soon enough."

Ben Joe leaned back against the sink with one foot on a tiny old step stool that read: "For doing some job that's bigger than me." He tested his full weight on the edge of the sink, decided not to risk it, and stood up again.

"I meant to tell you," Joanne said. "Don't feel bad."

"What?"

"Don't you feel bad about what Gram said. About your mind being a mish-mash. It's been in the back of my mind all day to tell you, she didn't meant it. She just said it for the sake of argument."

"I don't feel bad."

"Okay."

She started soaping Carol's hair, expertly, turning the pinkish-red hair dark auburn with her quick, firm fingers. For the first time he noticed that she wasn't wearing a wedding ring. What had she done with it? He pictured her throwing it in Gary's face, but it sounded improbable. Even in her ficklest days, Joanne had never done things that way. No, it would be more like her not even to tell Gary she was going. Or maybe it had been *Gary* who had left *her*; who knew?

"Where's your wedding ring?" he asked.

"In my jewelry box."

"What on earth for?"

"Well, I don't know. I thought maybe I should wear it so I wouldn't look like an unwed mother, but when I got here Mama said there was no point. She never wears *hers,* she said. It would just keep reminding her."

She took Carol by the chin and the back of the neck and ducked her back into the water swiftly. Before Carol could utter more than one sharp squeak she was upright again, with her hair rinsed and streaming.

"Mom's advice is the *last* I would take," Ben Joe said.

"Now, don't go being mean."

"I'm not. She wants you to say, 'Oh, who cares about *him?*' and then your whole problem is solved. You saw what that did for her."

"Mom's not as coldhearted as Gram keeps telling you, Ben Joe. You know that."

"Oh, I know."

"Besides, this isn't the same kind of thing."

"What kind of thing *is* it?" Ben Joe asked.

Joanne picked out a rubber duck and pushed it toward Carol, who ignored it. Carol was raising and lowering one round knee, watching it emerge sleek and gleaming and then lowering it again when the water had drained off to mere drops on her skin. Joanne watched too, thoughtfully, and Ben Joe watched Joanne.

"I always did like first dates," she said after a minute. "I was good at those. I knew what to wear—not so dressy it made them shy and not so sloppy they thought I didn't give a hoot—and how to act and what to say, and by the time I was ready to come in I'd have them all the way in love with me or know the reason why. But the dates after that are different. Once they loved me, what was I supposed to do *then*? Once I've accomplished that, where else is there to go? So I ended up confining myself to first dates. I got so good at them that I could first-date *anyone*—I mean even the people that were on *seventh* dates with me, or even people that weren't dates at all. I could first-date my own *family*, even—just figure out what would make them love me at a certain moment and then do it, easy as that."

She leaned forward suddenly, resting her elbows on the rim of the bathtub and staring into the water at Carol's gleeful face.

"Then I got married," she said.

Ben Joe waited, not pushing her. Joanne stood up and reached for a towel and then just stayed there, holding the towel forgotten in her hands.

"The trouble is," she said, "you have to stop clinking your bracelets and dancing like a maniac after a while. You have to *rest* now and then. Which may have been okay with Gary, but not with me. I didn't know what to do once I had sat down to rest, and so I started being just terrible. Following him around telling him what a awful wife I was. Waking him up in the middle of the night to accuse him of not believing I loved him. He was all sleepy and didn't know *what* was coming off. He'd say sure he believed me and go back to sleep leaving me to lie awake counting the dust specks that floated around in the dark, and making all kinds of plans to get my hair done and have him take me dancing." She frowned at the towel. "Got so I couldn't bear my own self," she said. "I left."

She wrapped the towel around Carol and lifted her out onto the bath mat.

"What'd you come back *here* for?" Ben Joe asked.

She dried Carol silently for a minute. Then she said, "Well, I want Carol to be with some kind of people that know her if I am going to get a job. That's why."

She had finished scrubbing Carol with the towel and now she pulled a white flannel nightgown over the baby's head, saying, "Where's Carol? Oh, I can't find Carol. *Where's* Carol?" until Carol's face poked through the neck of the nightgown, small and round and grinning.

"Besides," Joanne said, tying the ribbon under Carol's chin, "it's not the same place I'm coming back to, really. Not even if I wanted it to be."

"Oh, for God's sake," said Ben Joe.

"What's wrong?"

"You and Mama. You and the girls. And Mr. Dower, even. Of course it's the same place. What would it have gone and changed into? Always pulling up the same silly argument to fool yourselves with—"

"Now, now," said Joanne soothingly. She picked Carol up. "It's *not* the same place really, is it?"

He gave up, helplessly, and followed her out of the bathroom. There was no argument he could give that would convince her; she was too blindly cheerful, giving Carol little pecks on the cheek and talking to her happily as she crossed the hallway. At her mother's door she stopped and looked in. "Gone downstairs," she said. "Come on, Ben Joe. I want to ask you something."

"What?" he asked suspiciously.

"Come *on.*"

He followed her to her own room. It was cluttered with Joanne's odds and ends, and the old white crib had been moved down from the attic to a spot beside Joanne's bed. Other than that, it was almost the same as when she had left it. Huge stuffed animals, won by long-ago boy-friends at state fairs, littered the window seat; perfume bottles and hair ribbons and bobby pins lay scattered on the bureau. She laid Carol carefully in the crib and said, "Where were you when Dad died?"

"Where— Oh, no," Ben Joe said. "No, don't you start that."

"Why not?" She straightened up from kissing Carol good night and turned to face him. "That's not fair, Ben Joe. Nobody'll tell me *anything* about it. I even wrote a letter asking them to tell me. Nobody ever answered."

"Well, you were away," Ben Joe said.

"That doesn't change anything." She spread a blanket over Carol and began tying it down at the corners. "It happened just after Jenny began writing all the family's letters," she said. "Only Jenny didn't write this particular one, I remember. She went through a stage when she wouldn't write or speak the fact that Dad was dead. Susannah told me that. So the twins had to take over the letter writing. Jane and Lisa, they handled everything, although neither one of them will touch a pen ordinarily and you can tell it from their letters. But it was just as well, I guess—their writing the letters, I mean—because I suppose Jenny would just have sent a list of the funeral costs. Or would she, that far back? When did Jenny learn to be so practical? Anyway, there was this note from Lisa saying, 'Dad just passed away last night but felt no pain' —as if anyone could *know* what he felt—and that's all I ever heard. What happened, Ben Joe?"

"What difference does it make?" he asked.

"It makes a lot of difference. Who *won* makes a lot of difference."

"What?"

"Who won. Mama or that other woman."

"Well, that's the—"

"I know." She turned the lamp around so that it wouldn't shine in Carol's eyes and sat down on the foot of the bed. "It's an awful thing to wonder. And none of my business, anyway. But it's important to know, for all kinds of reasons."

He began searching through his crumpled cigarette pack for the last cigarette, not looking at her.

"Here, take mine," she said.

"Not menthol."

"They won't kill you."

She threw the pack at him; it fell on the floor in front of him and he picked it up and leaned back against the bureau.

"Two weeks before he died," Joanne said, "he was at home. I know he was. Jenny put it just beautifully, in this letter she wrote me. She said, 'You'll be happy to know Daddy has got back from his trip'—'trip'; that's an interesting choice of words—'and he's living at home now.' Now, where was he when he died? Still at home?"

"At Lili Belle's," Ben Joe said.

"At— Oh." She shook her head. "Lately I've stopped thinking about her by her name," she said. "What with Gram calling her 'Another's House' all the time."

"Well, he didn't *mean* to go and die there," said Ben Joe. "He'd just been drinking a little, is all. Went out to get ice cubes and then forgot which home he was supposed to be going back to. Mom explained that to Lili Belle."

"*Mom* explained it to *Lili* Belle?"

"Well, yes. It was her that Lili Belle called soon as he died. He got to Lili Belle's with a pain in his chest and died a little after. So Lili Belle called Mom, and Mom came to explain how it was our house he'd really intended going back to and not hers; just a mistake. And Lili Belle hadn't really won after all."

"Looks like to me she had."

"But it was by *mistake* he went there."

"Oh, pshaw," Joanne said. She turned to see how Carol was and then faced Ben Joe again. "What about their little boy, his and Lili Belle's? That was named after Daddy? That's more'n *you* were named for. I don't see that *your* name is Phillip. Do you think he would have walked off and left a baby named Phillip for good?"

"That's beside the point. You know, Joanne, sometimes I wonder whose side you're on."

She smiled and ground out her cigarette and stood up. "Don't you lose sleep on it," she said. "Come on, we're keeping Carol awake. I'm going to do my nails and I reckon you have people you'll want to visit."

"I don't know who."

But he straightened up anyway and followed Joanne out of the room. In the hall she gave him a little pat on the arm and then turned toward the bathroom, and he started for the stairs. He stopped at the hall landing, which looked down over the long stairway, and put one hand on the railing.

"You know where the emery boards are?" Joanne called from the bathroom.

He didn't answer; he leaned both elbows on the railing and stared downward, thinking.

"Oh, never mind. I found them."

He was remembering one night six years ago; this spot always reminded him of it. He had been studying in his room and at about ten o'clock he had decided to go downstairs for a beer. With his mind still foggy with facts and dates, he had wandered out into the hallway, had put one hand on the railing and was about to take the first step down, when the noise began. He could hear that noise still, although he always did his best to forget it.

First he thought it sounded like an angry bull wheezing and bellowing in a circle around the house. But it was too reedy and penetrating to be that; he thought then that it must be an auto horn. Kerry Jamison had an auto horn like that. Only Kerry Jamison was a well-bred boy and didn't honk for Ben Joe when he came visiting him. And he certainly didn't drive on the Hawkes's carefully tended lawn.

All over the house the girls had come swarming out of the various rooms, asking what the racket was. Tessie, who was scarcely more than a baby then and should have been asleep for hours, inched her bedroom door open and peeked out to ask Ben Joe if she could come downstairs with the others, because there was a trumpet blowing outside that wouldn't hush for her. She spoke in a whisper; their mother was reading in bed in the room next to Tessie's and would surely say no if she heard what Tessie was asking. But what neither Ben Joe nor Tessie realized at the time was that their mother was answering the telephone in her room, listening to Lili Belle Mosely tell her her husband was dead. Right then shc wouldn't have cared if Tessie never went to bed again, but Tessie couldn't know that and she went on in her whispery voice: "Can I, Ben Joe? Say yes. Can I?"

"No," said Ben Joe. "I'll go down and shut it up, whatever it is. Get back in bed, Tessie."

"But it's so *scary*, Ben—"

Their mother's door opened. Tessie popped back into her room just as Ellen Hawkes flew out of hers; they were like the two figures in a weather house. Ellen had on a pair of blue cotton pajamas and her hair was rumpled and she was struggling into a khaki raincoat of her husband's as she ran.

"Your father's dead," she said, and rushed down the stairs.

Ben Joe put both hands on the railing and leaned down. His mother had passed the little landing at the curve of the stairs and now she was directly below him, still running down; he could see the top of her head, and the curls lifting a little as she came down hard on each step. "Your father's dead," she repeated to the girls downstairs. Above her voice came the eerie sound from outside, wheezing and bellowing its way around to the front of the house.

Ben Joe let go of the railing and tore down the stairs after his mother. His shirt was open, and the tails of it flew out behind him as he ran. He had no shoes on. On one of the steps his stockinged foot slipped and he almost fell, but he caught himself and kept on going. The girls were waiting for him at the bottom, with stunned white faces. Tessie had come out to stand on the landing where Ben Joe had stood a minute ago and now she looked down at the others and began to cry without knowing why. She had poked her head through the bars because she was not yet tall enough to see over the railing. Her mother, holding on to the newel post at the bottom of the stairs while she struggled into a pair of Susannah's loafers, looked up at Tessie briefly and said, "She'll have got her head caught in those bars again. Better get her out, somebody."

Tessie's head was a tiny yellow circle on the second floor, outlined against the dark cupola that rose above the stairwell. The house seemed enormous, suddenly. The whole world seemed enormous.

"Where are you going?" Ben Joe asked his mother.

"To your father's friend's house," she said, without expression. "I'll be back. Gram's asleep now. Don't wake her. And try and figure some way of getting Tessie's head free without sawing the bars down again, will you?"

Ben Joe nodded. None of it made sense. Everything was harried and nightmarish and yet the same small practical things were going on at the same time. His mother patted his shoulder and then, abruptly, she was off, out the front door and into the darkness of the moonless, early-autumn night. As she crossed the front porch the eerie, wailing sound from outside became louder; as she descended the steps down to the front walk a soldier came into view playing a bagpipe. He was small and serious, with his eyes fixed only on his instrument, and he walked in a straight line across their front lawn and then around to the other side of the house. He and Ellen crossed paths with only inches between them; neither one of them paused or looked toward the other one.

Jenny, standing with the rest of them on the front porch, said, "It's a *bagpipe*."

From out in back of the house came the sound of their mother's car starting, rising above the piercing sound of the bagpipes. A minute later the yellow, dust-filled beams of two headlights backed past them out into the street and then swung sharply around and disappeared.

Susannah stopped staring after the car and turned to Jenny, frowning, trying to sort her thoughts and figure what should be done.

"It's no bagpipe *I* ever heard," she said finally. "Bagpipes make tunes. This is only making one note."

"Maybe he can't play," Jenny said. She was only twelve then, a thin, nervous little girl, and she was shivering and seemed to be trying desperately to get a grasp on herself. "I'm sure that's it," she said. "He'll practice this note for a while and then go to the next, and then go—"

"Not in *our* yard he won't," Susannah said. "Run around the back and stop him, Ben Joe."

But there was no need to; the soldier had come around the front again. Apparently he liked having an audience. He emerged from the side of the house at a scurrying little run, with his short legs pumping as fast as they could go, and then as soon as he came into the light from the front porch he slowed to a leisurely stroll in order to parade before them for as long as possible. His chest heaved up and down from the running he had done, and the horrible wailing sound was jerky and breathless now.

"Um . . ." Ben Joe said. He stepped down from the porch and the little soldier stopped. "You think you could do that somewhere else?"

The soldier grinned. He had a small, bony face, with the skin stretched tight and shining across it when he smiled. "No sir," he said. "No sir. Man said no."

"What?"

"Your daddy. 'No,' he says. No."

"I don't—"

"Saw me hitchhiking, your dad did. Told me could I play that thing, I allowed yes I could but not *this* way, with all but one reed gone so there wasn't but one sound.

He said anyway, anyway, he said, to play it round his house for a joke and not give up till he come back. When he comes he'll give me a bottle. A free bottle."

He grinned again and put the mouthpiece to his lips, but Ben Joe reached out and took a gentle hold on his arm. "He won't be back," he said. He turned toward Susannah. "Get a bottle of bourbon, Susannah. Bourbon all right with you, friend?"

"Oh yes, oh yes—"

Jenny suddenly came to life. She raced down the front steps and yanked Ben Joe's hand from the soldier's arm. "Leave him be," she said. "You leave him. Let him play." Her face was white and pinched-looking; Ben Joe thought if she shook any harder she would fall down.

"He's getting tired of playing," he told her.

"You leave him."

Susannah came out of the house again, slamming the screen door behind her. "Here," she said.

"Why, thank you, Ma'am. I am much—"

"You play, you," said Jenny to the soldier.

Susannah reached over Jenny's head with the bottle; the soldier held out his hand and Jenny made a grab for the bottle but missed.

"Wait," she said.

"Wouldn't change a thing, making him keep playing," Ben Joe told her gently. "If he played till you had grandchildren, it wouldn't bring back—"

"You wait, you *wait*!"

She was rigid now, not shaking any more but with her hands folded into tense fists and her face wet with tears. When Ben Joe put one hand on her shoulder she spun toward him, not actually fighting him but letting her arm stay rigid, so that her fist swung hard into his stomach and knocked all the wind from him. The soldier clicked his tongue, his eyes round. Ben Joe started coughing and bent over, but he kept hold of Jenny, pinning her arms down at her sides and holding her tight while he and Susannah guided her toward the stairs.

"I told you and *told* you!" she was screaming. "Now you've sent him away and he'll *never* come back—"

The soldier, mistaking her meaning, smiled cheerfully and waved his bottle at her. "*Sure* I'll be back," he called comfortingly. "*Don't* you worry ma'am!"

He set off toward the street, whistling. On the porch, Jane and Lisa took Jenny from Ben Joe while he leaned over the railing and coughed himself hoarse, trying to get his wind again. Susannah whacked him steadily on the back.

"You'll be all right," she said over and over. "You'll be all right. You'll be all right."

She did her best, but she couldn't say it the way Joanne did. And right then he wished for Joanne more than anyone in the world. He thought probably they all did. If she came walking up the steps right now she would fold every single person up close to her and cry, and pat them softly; and they could start crying too and telling her all the secret fears swamping their minds at this minute and then they would realize everything that had happened. If they could only *realize* something, things could start getting better again.

But Joanne didn't come up the steps, and when his coughing fit was through, Ben Joe straightened up and followed Susannah into the house again. Up on the second floor, Tessie was crying.

"You get the twins to give Jenny one of Dad's sleeping pills," Ben Joe told Susannah. "I'll try and get Tessie out of the railings."

Now, six years later, he thought he could still name the two posts where Tessie's head had been caught. All seven children, from Joanne to Tessie, had been stuck in this railing at least once in their lives. But he thought he knew which posts Tessie had been between *that* night, because it was still so clear in his mind. He had soothed Tessie, who had been through this before and was not very frightened, and while he was trying to pull her out he thought about the same thing he always thought when he did this: he must put some screening here, to stop all these ridiculous goings-on. Even if Gram *did* say it would ruin the looks of the railing. Under his hands was the feel of Tessie's head—the thin, soft hair, the tight little bones of her skull. He had turned her face gently, holding her small ears flat against her head, and worked her out from between the bars and scooped her up to carry her back to bed. It was then, standing there with the weight of her against his shoulder, that the first sorrow hit him—just one deep bruise inside that made him catch his breath. He could remember it still. That, and the little flannel nightgown Tessie wore, and the soft sounds of Jenny crying in the room she shared with Tessie . . .

It was so clear still that he could have told Joanne, and by telling her proved that Lili Belle hadn't won. For if his father had *meant* to go to Lili Belle's, he wouldn't have played that bagpipe joke on them. He loved every one of his children; he wouldn't have left them with any unkind tricks. But even though he had thought about telling her, Ben Joe had stopped himself. It was one of those things that wasn't mentioned in this house. Not even he and his other sisters mentioned it.

What else didn't they mention? He looked down the stairs and frowned, wondering what went on behind their cool, bright smiles. What did they think about before they went to sleep at night? He leaned further down, listening. The twins were chattering away in the kitchen; in the living room, someone laughed and Tessie gave a small squeal. He began to feel a sort of admiration for them. It was like watching a man who has been to Africa drink tea in the parlor and make small talk, with all those things known and done behind him that he is not even thinking about. Behind him, Joanne padded back to her bedroom with a pack of emery boards in her hand, but Ben Joe didn't look around. He remained in his own thoughts, with his hand resting absently on the stair railing.

6

When finally he came downstairs he made another tour of the house, just to see if anyone was free to talk to him yet. He started with his mother, who had joined the others in the living room and was taking tiny stitches in a white collar.

"Finish Tessie's dress?" he asked.

"Obviously not, since that's what I'm stitching on."

He stood in the middle of the room, chewing on his thumbnail while he tried to think of another opening.

"Well, how's the book store going?" he asked finally.

"It's all right. What's the matter, Ben Joe, haven't you any plans for tonight?"

"Not offhand."

"You certainly are restless."

He took this as an invitation to sit down and did so at once on the leather hassock beside her. On the couch opposite him Susannah and Gram collected the cards that lay between them and Susannah began shuffling them. The cards made a quick, snapping noise under her fingers.

"Carol sure doesn't look like a Hawkes, does she?" he said.

His mother held the dress up at arm's length and frowned at it. "No, I don't suppose she does," she said finally. She lowered the dress into her lap again and then, feeling that something more seemed to be expected of her, said, "It's really too young to tell yet."

"I wouldn't say that," Gram said. "Has the Hawkes nose, I'll say *that*. Small and pointy. And Joanne's little pointy chin."

There was another silence. Susannah began dealing, slapping down a loud card for Gram and a soft one for herself in a steady rhythm. Ben Joe stood up again and moved aimlessly over to the game.

"I thought we might go see Jamie Dower tonight, Gram," he said. "Car's free."

"Oh, well, I don't think so, Ben Joe. Not tonight."

"Why not?"

"Well . . ." She frowned at the cards in her hand. "I'd rather wait awhile," she said. "He wouldn't have settled his self properly yet."

"What's to settle?"

"Can't be much of a host when you're still feeling like a guest yourself, can you? Give him a couple more days."

"A couple more *days*?" said Ben Joe's mother. "How long are you planning on staying here, Ben Joe?"

"I don't know."

"Well, it seems to me you should be gone by then. Columbia's not going to wait on you forever."

"Oh, well," Ben Joe said. He was wandering back and forth with his hands in his pockets, occasionally kicking gently at a leg of the coffee table as he passed it. "Susannah?" he said.

"Hmm."

"Where's the guitar and the hourglass and all?"

"I'm not sure."

"What you mean, you're not sure?"

She brushed a piece of hair off her forehead with the back of her wrist and then switched a card in her hand from the left end of the fan to the right.

"I asked you if you wanted them," Ben Joe said. "I asked if you would take care of them. 'Yes, Ben Joe. Oh yes, Ben Joe.' " He made his voice into a silly squeak, imitating her. Of all his sisters, Susannah was the only one he was ever rude to—maybe because she was always so cool and brisk that he figured she wouldn't change toward him no matter *what* he did. "I can just see it," he said now. "Bet the whole shebang has just mildewed away to nothing, right?"

"In the *winter*?" Gram said.

"I bid two spades," said Susannah. "Ben Joe, I am sure everything's right where you left it. Except the guitar. The rest of the things I just hadn't assimilated yet."

"Well, where's the guitar, now that you've assimilated that? In the bathtub? Out in the garden holding up a tomato plant?"

"In the *winter*?" Gram said again. "A tomato plant in the winter?"

Ellen Hawkes laughed. When they turned to look at

her she stopped and looked down at her sewing again, still smiling.

"I declare," said Gram, "you got no sense of *season,* Ben Joe."

"Where's the guitar?"

"Under the couch in the den."

"Aha, I wasn't far wrong. Right where it belongs."

"Ben Joe," said his mother, "there's no reason to get so excited about a few possessions you've already given away. What's the matter with you tonight?"

"But they're my *favorite* possessions. That I missed all the time I was gone."

"Then you shouldn't have given them away. You're too old to be missing things, anyway. Why don't you stop that pacing and read something?"

He picked the newspaper up from the coffee table and began to read it listlessly as he stood there.

"And *not* upside-*down*!" his mother said.

"Ah, hell."

He threw down the paper and turned toward the den.

"You need someone to take you out walking with a leash around your neck," said Susannah. "Are you going to bid or not, Gram?"

"Pass."

Ben Joe stuck his head inside the doorway of the TV room. "Tessie," he said.

"Sssh."

"Tess, I want to ask you something."

"I'm watching television."

"It's only a cigarette commercial."

"Leave her in peace," said Jenny. "And don't hold that door open, Ben Joe. The noise'll bother the others."

"Don't either one of you want to go to the movies?"

Tessie shook her head, not taking her eyes from the screen. "It's only what it just about always is," she said. "*Phantom of the Opera.*"

"Why don't you come in and watch TV?" Jenny asked.

"I don't feel like it. I feel all yellow inside."

"Well, close the door, then."

He closed the door and came back into the living room.

"What happened to all those boys you used to go around with?" his mother asked.

"They went *north*, all of them. A long time ago."

"Do you know any girls any more?"

"Them too," he said.

"What?"

"They went north too."

"Oh."

"Gram," said Susannah, "if you keep holding your hand that way I'm going to have to shut my *eyes* not to see what cards you have."

"What about Shelley Domer?" his mother asked.

"Oh, Mom. She was my *first* girl. Her family went off to Savannah seven years ago."

"Gram, wasn't that Shelley Domer we saw the other day?"

"It was," said Gram. "You have another diamond, Susannah. I know you do."

"I don't either. Want to see my hand?"

"What's she doing *here*?" Ben Joe asked.

"I don't know," said his mother. "Their family kept

their house here, I think. Kept planning to come back someday."

"You mean she's living in her old home?"

"She wouldn't have been sweeping the front porch of it if she *wasn't*, would she?"

"I'd go see her if you've nothing better to do," Gram said. "Be something to keep you occupied. And you saw right much of her once upon a time."

"Oh, she was all right."

"That all you can find to say about her? *Spades* are trumps, Susannah. Keep your mind on your game. Only thing *I* ever had against Shelley Domer was her family, to be frank."

"What was wrong with her family, for heaven's sake?"

"Well, I'm not saying they didn't have money. Or weren't nice. But money and niceness neither one isn't all there is. Mrs. Domer still went grocery shopping in shuffly old slippers with pansies sewn on them, and that Shelley, well, she was a sweet child and it was no fault of hers, but many's the time I seen her in a flowered calico skirt and a plaid blouse *together*, like a tenant farmer's girl would wear, and in wintertime overalls under her dress, which is a *sure* sign, a sure sign. As if having those glass-blue, empty-looking eyes like the bad Dowers have wasn't enough—"

"Well, for one who wears black *gym* shoes to the grocery store—" Ellen Hawkes began.

"I can afford to. My family is different, and don't have to worry about being taken for the wrong kind."

Ben Joe's mother bit a thread off the white collar. "Well, I don't see what slippers have to do with it," she said. "Shelley Domer can't help her ancestry, that's for sure. No, all I ever had against her was the way she hung on Ben Joe all the time. None of *my* girls has ever been a boy chaser, I'll say that for them. They've been raised to have pride, and—"

"Pride nothing," Gram snapped. "Nicest thing *about* that girl was her being so sweet on Ben Joe. She used to wait for him every day after school, I remember. Even in wintertime. Till he'd come ambling out at whatever hour he chose to say hey to her."

"That's what I'm—"

"Oh, forget it," said Ben Joe. "I'll go and see her now while you two are arguing." He went to the hall closet and pulled his jacket from a hanger. "Anyone want anything from outside?"

"No, thank you. Have a nice evening."

"Okay."

Outside it was beginning to get cold. There was a little chill around his neck where his collar was open, but he just walked more quickly to make up for it. With his hands in his pockets and his lips pursed in a silent whistle he headed east, down past rows of medium-sized, medium-aged houses that jangled faintly with the TV or radio noises locked inside them. Occasionally he caught glimpses of families moving around behind lace curtains, but no one was out on the sidewalk. A dog rushed past, trailing a leash; nobody attempted to follow him. And at one house an old woman in a man's overcoat rocked on a cold porch glider.

"Hey," she said.

"Hey," said Ben Joe.

"No moon out tonight."

"No."

He turned up Evers and walked more slowly. None of the walk took any thinking. When he was in high school it had become second nature, like going downstairs in the morning for breakfast and then realizing, once he was down there, that the actual descent had been an utter blank in his memory. The first few times he had come here actually shaking, with his hair slicked down and his face thin from the tension of keeping his teeth from chattering. He would have gone to the bathroom six or seven times in the half-hour before, just from nervousness. But gradually it became just an ordinary thing, this walk. Even when there was no definite date planned he would go, just to sit in the living room with Shelley and talk to her. She wasn't very quick-witted and she didn't entertain him with fast talk and bubbles of laughter the way his sisters entertained their dates, but she did listen. No matter what he talked about she would listen, smiling happily at him all the time, and when he was done she would just hug him or tell him how much she liked the way the barber had cut his hair this week, but he knew she had heard what he had to say, anyway. He smiled into the darkness, thinking about that, and cut through a vacant lot to Holland Street and the Domer house.

The lights were turned on inside. The place was the same as always—big and worn and comfortable, with years of dead leaves piled around it. He would have thought Mr. Domer had raked those up by now; Mr. Domer was a small and tidy man. When Ben Joe crossed the front lawn the leaves roared around his ankles. He climbed the long steps to the front door. Years ago, in the summertime, they would stop at this top step when they came in from a date. They would look up to the open window upstairs and there would be the little triangular-faced, white-nightgowned blur of Shelley's sister Phoebe peering down at them. She must have been about seven, that first year. She had thought, from seeing the cartoons in the *Saturday Evening Post*, that all boys kissed their dates on the girls' doorsteps, and every night she had lain in wait in her bedroom, watching hopefully. How old would she be now? Sixteen or seventeen, he supposed. And gone from that window. There was only the closed glass pane now, and the still white organdy curtains behind it.

He knocked twice. A figure came toward him and peered out the window glass in the door, still only a silhouette behind a mesh curtain. Then she opened the door and let him step in. She seemed stunned for a minute; her mouth was slightly open.

"Ben Joe!" she said. "Is that you?"

"Sure it is. Have I gone and changed all that much?"

"No. No, only it's been such a long . . . Well, hey, anyway."

"Hey."

Shelley stood awkwardly in front of him, beginning to look happy and a little scared. She never had known what to do about greeting people. If she had been one of the girls he had dated after her, she would have come tripping up and shrieked, "For goodness *sake*!" and kissed him loudly on the mouth even if she didn't remember his name. But not Shelley. Shelley stood straight before him, with her hands pleating little bunches of her skirt at the sides, and smiled at him.

"Mom said she saw you sweeping the front porch," he said. "I'm home for a little vacation. I thought I'd stop by and see how you were getting on."

"Oh, well, I'm fine. Just seems funny to see you, I think . . ."

She moved over almost soundlessly to shut the door behind him, and he turned to watch her. There were little changes in her; he could see that even under the dim light in the hallway. Her hair, which used to hang almost to her shoulders in such straight blond ribbons that it had made him think of corn syrup, was bunched scratchily behind her head now and held there by a few pins, much like Gram's bun. Her face was prettier and more clearly defined, but she still gave the impression of a waifish kind of thinness that made her seem more like fifteen than twenty-five. Partly it was because she was pale and without make-up, and her eyes were such a light blue; partly it was because she was wearing old clothes that must have been her mother's and were far too big for her. The skirt was a dingy pink, accordion-pleated and very long; the sweater was an old bulky maroon one that somehow made her shoulder blades stick out more in back than her breasts did in front. But she still moved the same way—almost frightenedly and without a sound, and always in slow motion. Now she slowly opened her hands at her sides, as if she were consciously telling herself to relax, and looked down at her clothes.

"Now, Ben Joe," she said, "I have to go put another

dress on. I didn't know I was about to have company. You wait in the living room, hear? I'll be right—"

"But I'm just going to stay a minute," Ben Joe said. "I only came to say hello."

"Well, you just wait."

She turned and darted up the curving stairs, and Ben Joe had to go into the living room alone. He chose a seat at the end of the sofa, nearest the unlit fireplace. The room seemed to him like the huge front room of a long-unused summer house; all the things that were not particularly liked and yet still too good to discard had been left here by the Domers when they moved South. Wicker armchairs and threadbare sofas sat on an absolutely bare wooden floor, and the few decorative items scattered around were worthless—a china spaniel with three puppies chained to her collar by tiny gold chains; a huge framed photograph of a long-ago baseball team; a rosebudded cracked china slipper with earth in it but no plant. Ben Joe shivered. This had been a cheerful room once, back when he was in high school.

He heard Shelley's shoes on the stairs and a minute later she was in the living room, crossing in front of him with a company smile and a white skirt and sweater that fit better than the old ones. She had combed her hair, although he was sorry to see that it was still in a bun, and there was a little lipstick on her mouth.

"I'm going to get you some coffee," she said.

"No, I don't want any."

"It's already made, Ben Joe. You wait here and I'll—"

"No, *please*. I don't want any."

"Well, all right."

She sat down on the edge of a wicker armchair with her hands on her knees.

"Where's Phoebe?" Ben Joe asked.

"Phoebe."

"Phoebe your *sister.*"

"Oh," she said. All the breath seemed to have left her; she gasped a little and said, "Phoebe and Mama and Daddy, all of them, they're dead, you mustn't have heard, it only happened a while—"

"Oh, no, I never—"

"They had a wreck."

"I'm sorry," Ben Joe said. He thought of the small white blur in the upstairs window, still almost realer than Shelley herself. He watched Shelley's fingers twisting a pearl button on her sweater. "Nobody told me," he said helplessly.

"I only been back a while now. Not many people know about it."

"Was . . . How old was Phoebe?"

"Seventeen."

"Oh." He fell silent again, and tugged gently at one of the little cotton balls on the sofa upholstery.

"How are *your* sisters?" Shelley asked suddenly.

"They're fine." Almost immediately he felt guilty for that; he thought a minute and then offered: "Joanne's left her husband, though."

"Left him?"

"Yes."

"Well, I declare."

"She's back home now."

"Well."

"Her and her baby."

"I'm going to get you some coffee," Shelley said.

"No, wait. I've got to be—"

"It's *hot* already." She stood up and almost ran to the kitchen, still managing to make it slow motion. Behind her, Ben Joe shifted in his seat uneasily and crossed his legs.

"You're hungry too, I bet," she said when she entered the room again.

"No, I'm all right."

"You look right thin to me, Ben Joe. I got this marble cake from the Piggly-Wiggly. Course it's not real homemade, but anway—"

"Shelley, I really don't want it."

"Well, all right, Ben Joe."

She was carrying a chipped tin tray with two cups of coffee on it and a sugar bowl and cream pitcher that didn't match. When she set it on the coffee table everything clinked like the too-loud clinking of tea sets in movies.

"You take yourself lots of sugar," she said. "I declare, you *are* thin." She hovered over him, shadowlike, while he took up his coffee cup. He could smell her perfume now—a light, pink-smelling perfume—and when she bent over the table to hand him the sugar bowl, he could even smell perfume in her hair. Then she moved back to her seat, and he relaxed against the sofa cushions.

"Seems like I have got to get used to you all over again, it's been so long," Shelley said. "Are you feeling talky?"

He had forgotten that. She always asked him that question, to give him a chance before she plunged into her own slow, circuitous small talk. This time he remained silent, choosing to have her carry on the conversation, and smiled at her above his coffee cup because he liked her suddenly for remembering. Shelley waited another minute, sitting back easily in her chair. Once the first awkward moments were over, Shelley could be as relaxed as anyone.

"I don't know if I did right or not," she said finally, "coming back here like this. But my family's passing came so sudden. Left me strap-hanging in empty space, like. And I chose to come to Sandhill. I don't know why, except I was helping to run this nursery school for working mothers' children down in Georgia and so *sick* of it, you've got no idea, and saw no way out. I think I got something against Georgia. I really do. Seems like if there is one thing makes me ill, it's those torn-up circus posters on old barns. You know? And Seven-up signs. Well, Georgia's plumb full of those, though one time this girl I worked with told me she thought it was real snotty of me to say a thing like that. That's what our trouble was down there—the trash thought we were snotty and the snotty thought we were trash. Now, my daddy had to work himself up the hard way, but you know how fine he was, and anyway his mama's folks were Montagues, which should have *some* bearing. And there's nothing wrong with Mama's side of the family, either. But anyway I was lonely there. Didn't seem like there was any group we could really say we belonged to. Back in Sandhill it was better. I always have remembered Sandhill. And I still carry your picture."

She smiled happily at Ben Joe.

"That real goofy-looking one," she said, "that we had taken of you in the Snap-Yourself Photo Booth. Mama used to tease me about keeping it—said I might as well throw it out now. Though she always did like you. When you wrote me that letter, after we'd moved, about you starting to date Gloria Herman I thought Mama would cry. She said Gloria was real fast and loud, though it was my opinion that you knew better than Mama who was good for you. And at least you were right honest, telling me. I said that to Mama, too. And then a month later Susan Harpton wrote to tell how Gloria had moved on to someone new and you'd started dating Pat Locker. It got so I couldn't keep up with you any more. But I wasn't mad. Things like that happen when people get separated from each other."

"Well, it was a long time ago," Ben Joe said.

"It was. I know. Well, don't you worry, Ben Joe, I'm dating a real nice boy now. You'd like him. His name is John Horner and he's starting up a construction firm in Sandhill. You know him?"

"Horner." Ben Joe frowned. "Not offhand," he said.

"Well. You'd like him, though. Course we aren't too serious yet—I only been in town a month or so. But he is the *kindest* man. I don't know if I could marry him, yet."

"Has he asked you?"

"No. But I reckon he will one of these days."

The idea of Shelley's marrying someone else surprised him. He looked at her as a stranger suddenly, evaluating her. She smiled back at him.

"Course," she said, "I was surprised he even wanted to

date me. But I figured if maybe he could just endure through the first few dates, till I got easy with him and not so silly and tongue-tied any more, it'd be all right. And he did. He endured."

"Well, I'm glad to hear it."

She nodded, finished with that piece of news, and then frowned into space a minute as if she were fishing in her mind for the next piece.

"Oh, I know," she said finally. "I know. Ben Joe, I was so sorry to hear about your daddy. I wrote you about it and you never answered. But I hope it was a peaceful passing. He was a sweet man, your daddy."

"Thank you," said Ben Joe.

"Susan Harpton told me about it. And about your going to work at the bank after classes and Joanne getting married and all. She said the whole town missed your daddy."

"I did too," said Ben Joe. "Took to riding trains."

"What?"

"Trains. Riding trains. I rode trains all the time. One time I spent a whole month's salary that way. Mom about had a conniption fit—I was almost the family's only support back then."

"Oh," Shelley said. She frowned; she was on uncertain ground now. "Well, anyway, I just wanted to tell you I missed him. And if he lived a little different from most people, I don't think anybody held it against him. Not your daddy. Remember how when he got to drinking he always wanted someone to sing to him? 'Life Is Like a Mountain Railroad,' that's what he liked. Many's the time I've sung it to him."

"And 'Nobody Knows the Trouble I've Seen,'" said Ben Joe.

"That's right." She smiled into her coffee cup and then looked up again, with the next subject decided upon. "I hear you're in law school up north," she said. "Mrs. Murphy told me that. She's the one that's been keeping an eye on the house all these years. She's nice, though I found when I came back that she'd looked through the photograph albums and all Mama's love letters. When your mama and grandma passed by the porch as I was sweeping I called out 'hey' to them, meaning to ask about you, but I had trouble making myself heard, as your grandma was doing some of that singing of hers and your mama was trying real hard to hush her. When your grandma saw me she recognized me right off, though. She shouted out to tell me you weren't married yet, which I already knew, and a minute later your mama remembered me too. Your mama is a little slow in recognizing folks, but I don't hold with what Mrs. Murphy says, that she's on *purpose* slow. This town has always been of the opinion she is coldhearted, but I think it's because your daddy was their fair-haired boy, and they didn't want him hurt. Not that I think she *meant* to hurt him. I reckon she is just a little prideful and thinks pride's the same as dignity so she doesn't try and change herself. Mrs. Murphy said many's the time she herself went to your mama to tell her all she had to do was let herself get to crying and then, as soon as the tears got started good, go to . . . um, where your father lived at and tell him she wanted him back, but your mama always just tossed her hair and said who cared and offered Mrs. Murphy a slice of angel-food cake.

It was the doctor's business and no one else's, she would say, though if it wasn't the doctor's *wife's* business too, then what did they get married for?

"Well, anyway, I never did get to ask how you were doing up north, since your mama and grandma were in a hurry. But I know it can be a lonely place. I went up there once to work for the Presbyterian church and stayed for a month, rooming with a girl I'd met who turned out to be a bit touched in the head. Went around in a chiffon gown with a candle in her hand at four a.m. and talked about craning her swanlike neck in the rain. I went home again. I always have been a homebody. I don't know what I'll do without my family. Even Phoebe, and her so mischievous. The last night that Phoebe was . . . was living, the last night I ever saw her, she was in the kitchen with her boy-friend and when—"

"Phoebe had a *boy*-friend?" Ben Joe asked.

"Well, yes, and when I walked in, they were robbing this loose-change bank of my mama's, shaped like an Indian with a slot in the top of his head where she puts the money in, for odds and ends-like that she wants to buy—they were robbing this bank so they could go to the movies. The boy-friend had just got out his pocketknife to put through the slot and Phoebe was holding out her hand and saying, 'scalpel,' and that's the last I ever saw of her. I'm awful glad to meet up with you again, Ben Joe. All these years I been missing you."

"I'm glad to see *you*," said Ben Joe. He smiled at her in silence for a minute and then looked at his watch and stood up. "I've got to go. I was on the train all last night. Need to catch up on my sleep."

"Oh, don't you hurry."

"I've got to."

He picked up his jacket from the couch and put it on as he followed Shelley to the door. Outside it was raining; the sight surprised them both and they stood there looking at it.

"Don't come out with me," Ben Joe said.

"I won't melt."

"No, stay inside."

"I want to see you safely to the street," Shelley said.

Her face was serious, and she looked worried about him. Without knowing why, Ben Joe said, "Um, this Jack Horner—"

"John Horner."

"*John* Horner. Do you think he'd mind if I came back again?"

"I don't know. I don't— You come see me anyway, Ben Joe. You come anyway."

She was smiling now, looking up at him with the porch light shining clear through those sky-blue eyes of hers. Her face was so close he could bend down and kiss her. He had never kissed her on her doorstep before, despite all Phoebe's hopes; he had kissed her in his mother's old Buick, parked somewhere in the darkness, with that pink smell of her perfume circling him and her arms thin and warm around his neck. Her face hovered under his, still close; she looked up at him. But as he was about to bend toward her he thought that maybe this might commit him again; maybe everything would begin all over again, and time would get even more jumbled up in his head than it was already. So he drew back from the pale oblong of her face and said, "Is Sunday evening all right? About nine?"

"Yes."

"Well."

He stood looking at her for a minute longer, and then straightened his shoulders.

"I'll see you then," he said.

"Good night, Ben Joe."

"Good night."

He turned and started down the long steps, being careful not to slip on the soggy layers of leaves beneath his feet. The rain was no more than an unsteady dripping sound now, with an occasional cool drop landing on his face. Once on the street again, he shoved his hands deep into his trouser pockets and walked very slowly, frowning, sorting his thoughts out. But his thoughts wouldn't sort; he felt as if he was never again going to know the reason for anything he did. The puddles on the sidewalk began soaking into his shoes, and he started running toward home.

7

The next day was Saturday. Ben Joe awoke with a hollow, bored feeling; he dawdled over his breakfast until it was cold and then went back to his room to read a detective novel upside-down on an unmade bed. Halfway through the morning one of the girls knocked on his door and said, "Ben Joe?"

"Mm-hmm."

"It's me. Lisa. Can I come in?"

"I guess so."

She stuck her head in the door and smiled. She was much calmer than her twin; it was the way Ben Joe had first learned to tell them apart. She was wearing a neat blue suit and high heels. "We're going downtown," she said. "Want to come?"

"You have to dress up *that* much just to go downtown?"

"Never can tell who you'll meet." She grinned, and

crossed to his bed to hand him a postcard. "Mail," she said. "Who's Jeremy?"

"My roommate. Do you have to read all my mail?"

He looked at the picture on it—the Guggenheim Museum, in an unreal shade of yellowish-white—and then turned the card over and began reading the large, rounded handwriting:

Dear Ben J.,

Hope you are thawing out down there. I borrowed your dinner jacket. That frizzly-haired girl keeps calling wanting to know when you'll be back, and I said Monday or so, right? Pack one of those sisters of yours in a suitcase and bring her along.

Jeremy.

"Which one are you going to pack up?" Lisa asked.

"What?"

"Which sister?"

"Oh. I don't know. Why—you feel like leaving home?"

"I surely do," Lisa said. She sat down with a little bounce on the foot of the bed and looked at her shoes. "I've used up all the boys in this town, that's what."

"What about those two you and Jane were with last night?"

"I'm getting tired of them. I keep thinking maybe I could start new someplace else, in another town."

"Well, I know the feeling," said Ben Joe. He turned the card over again and looked at it, frowning. "I wonder if I've missed any quizzes. Jeremy's right—I've got to get started back there pretty quick."

"Well, do you want to come to town or don't you?"

"No. I guess not."

Lisa stood up and left, and Ben Joe looked after her thoughtfully. "Don't you worry," he said when she reached the door. "New boys're always showing up."

"I know. Yell if you change your mind about coming downtown, Ben Joe."

"Okay."

He stared at the closed door for a few minutes and then got up and padded over to his bureau in his stocking feet. The top drawer looked like Jeremy's had in New York—stuffed with postcards and envelopes and canceled checks. He threw the postcard on top of the heap and then idly leafed through what was underneath. At the bottom was a stack of Shelley's letters from Savannah, neatly rubber-handed together. And a few postcards from the times his father had gone to medical conventions. They were dry and formal; his father had trouble saying things in writing. He stacked everything carelessly together again and was about to close the drawer when he saw something pink lying in the right-hand corner. It was a unique shade of pink—a deep rose that was almost magenta and never should have been used in writing paper—and it was one that had stuck in his mind for some six years now. Even when he saw something nearly that color in a dress or a magazine ad, even now, it made him wince. He pulled the envelope up and made himself examine it. Large, slanted pencil writing ran in a straight line across it, addressed to his father at his office on Main Street. Only his father had never seen it; Ben Joe had taken it from the box when he had gone to bring his father home for supper one day. He had seen the "L.B.M." on the upper left-hand corner and quietly stuffed it in his pocket. Now he stood staring at it without opening it, letting it lie flat in the palm of his hand. When he had stared at it so long that he could see it with his eyes shut, he suddenly slapped it into his shirt pocket, grabbed up his sneakers from the floor in front of the bureau, and slammed out of his room.

"Lisa!" he called.

His grandmother was on the landing, polishing the stair rail and singing only slightly more softly than usual, because she was intent upon her polishing:

"When I was *si-ingle*, .
I wandered at my *e-ease*.
Now that I am *ma-arried,*
Got a flat-heeled man to please . . ."

"Gram," Ben Joe said, "has Lisa gone downtown yet?"

She refolded her cloth and smiled at it, still singing, because she was at the loudest part and no one could stop her at a loud part:

"And it's oh, *Lo-o-ord,*
I wish I was but one lone girl again . . ."

"Oh, hell," Ben Joe said. He galloped on down the stairs, two at a time, with his sneakers still in his hands. "*Lisa!*"

"What you want, Ben Joe?"

He stepped over Carol, who was sticking toothpicks upright into the nap in the hall rug. Lisa was in the living room arguing with Jenny and Joanne over the grocery list.

"If she wants all those outlandish things," Jenny was saying, "she can darn well go get them herself, that's what *I* think."

Joanne took the list from her and ran her finger down it. "Well," she said finally, "I don't reckon it would *hurt* us any to start drinking burgundy with our meals—"

"But *I'm* the one Ben Joe left in charge of the money. What's the matter with Gram lately? Ben Joe, I want you to look at this."

Ben Joe sat down on the couch and began putting his sneakers on. "I've decided to hitch a ride downtown with you," he said.

"*Look,* will you, Ben Joe? Now Gram's making *me* go out and buy all her silly notions. Burgundy my foot. And her upstairs singing loud on purpose, been singing all morning without taking breath so that no one can interrupt and ask her what she wants with burgundy and oyster crackers and kippered herrings—"

"Oh, she's just tired of the same old things," Ben Joe said. "You going right away? Because if not, I'll just walk instead of—"

"No, we're coming. Come on, Joanne."

Jenny led the way, looking sensible and businesslike in her open trenchcoat. At the front door she took the car keys off a hook on the wall and stuck them in her pocket. "Where's Tessie?" she asked Lisa.

"In the car. Says you and she are going shoe shopping and she's in a hurry to get started."

"Okay. Close the door behind you, Ben Joe."

They crossed through the weedy grass to the driveway beside the house where the car was parked. Inside, on the front seat, Tessie bounced up and down in a short-sleeved plaid dress.

"Where's your jacket?" Jenny asked as she opened the door.

"In the house."

"Well, better go get it."

"Aw, Jenny—"

"Jenny, for Pete's sake," Ben Joe said. "I'm in a hurry."

"Well, I can't help that. Run on and get it, Tessie."

Tessie slammed out of the car, and Jenny turned the motor on to let it warm up. She seemed resigned to all these hindrances; she sat patiently waiting, while Ben Joe, squeezed between Joanne and Lisa, drummed his fingers on his knees and squirmed about irritably. When Tessie came out of the house, dragging her feet slowly as she worked her way into an old corduroy jacket, Ben Joe leaned forward and shouted, "Come *on*, Tessie!"

"What's the matter with *you*?" Jenny asked. She leaned across to open the door for Tessie. "What you suddenly in such an all-fired hurry for?"

"I've got a lot to get done."

"Ten minutes ago you were going to stay home all day," said Lisa.

"Well, not any more."

"Where you going?"

"Just around." He leaned back with his hands between his knees and stared out the window as the car slipped down the driveway into the street. "Got a couple of things I want to attend to," he said. "And Jeremy's postcard reminded me I don't have all year to do them in."

"Better go see your old music teacher," Lisa said. "And Miss Potter, the one that taught you third grade. She asks about you every time she sees me."

"Okay."

"She wants to know if you're a famous poet yet. Says you wrote your first poem in her class."

"*I* don't remember that."

"Well, she does. Says it went, 'My fish, my cat, my little world,' and she's keeping it still for when you get famous."

"My land," Ben Joe said. "Jenny, how far downtown are you going?"

"Just to the A & P."

"And the shoe store," Tessie reminded her.

"And the shoe store. Why you want to know?"

"Not past that?" asked Ben Joe.

"Well, no. What *is* past that?"

"Where is it you're going, anyway?" Joanne asked him.

He scowled at her and remained silent, and Joanne turned back to the window. They were still among lawns and houses; Jenny drove so slowly that a man walking at a brisk pace could keep up with her. At one point Joanne said, "Was that the Edmonds' house?"

Ben Joe leaned forward to see where she was pointing. Between two houses was a charred space with only a set of cement steps and a yellow brick fireplace left intact.

"It was," he said. "Burned down the year you left."

"Nobody told me about it."

"You used to date their son, I think." He had come upon them kissing in the den one night; Bobby was hugging her and kissing the hollow in her neck, and Ben Joe had left the room again without a sound.

"I'd forgotten that," Joanne said.

Sometimes he thought his sisters had been born senile.

When they reached the A & P on Main Street, Jenny parked the car. "We'll be in here awhile and then to Barton's for Tessie's shoes," she said. "If you're back in the car by then I'll drive you home. Otherwise you can just walk back whenever you're ready. Hurry, Ben Joe, you're holding Lisa up."

Ben Joe was sitting forward but not getting out. Lisa nudged him impatiently. "*Come* on, Ben Joe. I thought you were the one in such a rush."

"Okay, okay."

He climbed slowly out of the car and then just stood on the sidewalk beside Joanne with his hands in his pockets.

"Well," he said.

Joanne looked at him curiously. Jenny and Tessie were already heading toward the A & P, and Lisa was staring at a sweater in the window next door.

"Maybe I'll go wherever you're going," said Joanne.

"No."

"Well, where is it you're going?"

"Um. To call on Miss Potter, for one thing. You go on and do your shopping. Maybe I'll meet you in Stacy's for a cup of coffee later."

"All right."

She stood there still looking at him with that little half-smile. He wished she weren't so nosy. The others didn't know the meaning of privacy, they were continually bursting into his room unannounced or reading his postcards, but at least they didn't go ferreting around to see what he was thinking about, the way Joanne did. Sometimes he thought she had even *succeeded* in her ferreting—like today, when she remained absolutely motionless and smiled her knowing smile. He scowled back at her.

"So long," he said.

"So long."

When she still stood there, he whirled around abruptly and headed for the drugstore at a businesslike pace. Once inside, he peered out the glass door and saw that her back was to him now; she was calmly waiting for a car to pass before she crossed the street.

The drugstore smelled like his house did when all the girls were getting ready to go out on dates at once. It was spicy and perfumey, with several different kinds of scents that were mingled together and made him want to sneeze. He headed toward the back, where the toilet articles were kept. From the rack on top of the counter he chose a pack of razor blades, taking a long time to compare prices and brand names, and then he turned to the magazine counter and picked out a crossword-puzzle book that was made of dull comic-booklike paper which would depress him before he finished the first puzzle. These he paid for at the cash register; he counted out the exact change to pay a white-haired man he had not seen before.

"Don't bother about a bag," he said.

He dropped the razor blades into his shirt pocket, next to the pink envelope and his cigarettes. The crossword-puzzle book he rolled up carelessly and stuck into his back trouser pocket. Then he looked out toward the street again. This time there was not a sister of his in sight. He smiled good-by to the man at the cash register and headed outside.

Beyond the A & P, which was the last real store on Main Street, the millworkers' houses again. At first they were the big old houses that had been built by well-to-do families but had turned gray and peeling with "Room for Rent" signs on them. Their side yards, once grassy and shaded with oak trees, were now cement squares where Esso stations sat. And beyond these were smaller, grayer houses, most of them duplexes. Dirty-faced children played on the porches in skimpy sweaters; the yards were heaped with old tires and rusty scrap metal. Behind the houses, barely visible above the tar-paper roofs, were the tall smoking chimneys of the textile factory where all these people worked. They made blue denim, day in and day out. It was toward these chimneys that Ben Joe headed. He crossed a vacant lot, knee-high with weeds and brambles, and stumbled over a rusted-out potbellied stove that lay smack in the middle of the field. Then he was on the gravel road that ran down to the muddy little river where the factory was. Opposite the factory was Lili Belle Mosely's house.

He had been here before, many times. The first time was when his father was still alive, living at Lili Belle's as if it were his home and having his patients call him there in the night if they needed him. He had first rented a room there; people said that one night he had finished mending a millworker's arm and was setting out for home when it suddenly hit him that he couldn't bear to go home again, so he had stopped here and rented a room. His wife, hearing about it, clamped her mouth shut and said that was *his* lookout, nothing she could do about it. She said the same when she heard that he had taken to sharing a room with the landlady's daughter; and the same when she heard about little Phillip's being born. But Ben Joe, who never could resign himself to the fact that it was his father's lookout alone, had come to see his father at Lili Belle's one night with his heart pounding and his eyes wide with embarrassment. They had fed him supper—green beans cooked with fat back, hash-brown potatoes in a puddle of Mazola, pork chops coated with grease that turned white when he let the chops cool on his plate. Everyone laughed a lot, and his father ate more than Ben Joe had seen him eat in years. And Ben Joe had not been able to say a word to his father about coming home. He hadn't tried.

As he stood now, facing the long, squat house with its dingy front porch, he could almost see how he must have looked coming out of it. His head down, his face puzzled, his feet dragging. Not just once, but many times, because he had gone back again and again. First he had gone to see his father. Then his father died and left a request that Lili Belle and her son get a little money each month, which Ben Joe's mother could have contested but didn't; she said it wasn't worth her bother. So Ben Joe took Lili Belle her money in person once each month. And once each month his mother said, "Ben Joe, have you mailed off all our bills for this month?" and Ben Joe said, "Yes'm," not ever letting on he had taken it in person.

Every month he had taken it, up until he had left for New York and turned the money matters over to Jenny. Now Jenny mailed the money, as she was supposed to, in a business envelope. She wouldn't have that feeling Ben Joe always had, looking at his mother with pure guilt on his face and wondering why he kept on lying to her and visiting a woman whose name was never mentioned in the house. He couldn't have given a reason. When he was a senior in high school, his father came home for an hour one day (after he'd been gone a year) to say that all his life he had been saving the money for Ben Joe to go to Harvard and now there was enough. Ellen Hawkes said that unless he came home she wouldn't take a penny, and he said, well, he didn't see that it would really matter to her if he never came home again. Ellen Hawkes didn't answer that. So Ben Joe went to Sandhill College. But even so, even knowing that Lili Belle was the reason he had to go there, he still came to sit in Lili Belle's house and talk to her about the weather and he still threw little Phillip up in the air and caught him again, laughing.

He crossed the scrubby little yard and climbed up to the porch. The wooden floor boards made a hollow sound under his shoes. At the door he knocked and waited, and then knocked again. One corner of the chintz curtain rose slowly. The door swung open.

"Lili Belle?" he said.

"It's *me*, boy."

It was her old mother standing in the shadows behind the door. Ben Joe had seldom seen her before. She was fat and puffing but very dignified, and she had kept out of sight for sheer shame ever since the day her daughter's baby had been born. Now she closed the door sharply behind him and said, "What you want, anyway?"

"I want to see Lili Belle."

"Hmm." She crossed her fat arms under the shelf-like bosom of her black crepe dress. "Lilian Belle is very tired, Benjamin," she said. "Got troubles of her own. What you wanting to see her for?"

"Mrs. Mosely, I won't stay long. I just wanted to see her a minute. It's important."

"Well, I'll tell her. But I don't know, I don't know."

"Thank you, ma'am."

He followed her across the small, mousy-smelling hallway into the almost totally dark sitting room. Against the shaded window he could make out the outline of an unlit lamp, double-globed and beaded. Mrs. Mosely stood like a mountain barring the rest of the view; she called into the room, "Back."

Lili Belle was in the shadows, sitting on a cane chair. She stirred a little and said, "You say something, Mama?"

"Back again to pester us."

"Who?"

"Him." She jerked a thumb behind her. "Ben Joe."

"Oh, my goodness. Benjy, honey, come *in*!" She stood up and ran to the windows to raise the shades. In her right hand was a bowl of soup, which she shifted awkwardly to her left hand when she tried to maneuver the shade. The room was suddenly light again. With the light a feeling of relief came to Ben Joe; this wasn't going to be as hard as he thought. He always forgot how easy Lili Belle made him feel the minute he saw her.

"It's okay, Mama," she was saying now. "You can go on now. Come on in, Benjy honey. I do apologize for sitting in the dark like this, but my eyes is strained."

"It's okay," Ben Joe said.

He looked at her closely, noticing how tired she looked. It was hard to tell how old she was. Nine years ago, when his father had first met her, she had been about twenty. Now she could be any age. Her face seemed never to have resolved itself but stayed as vague and unformed as when she had been a girl. Her hair was straggly and colorless, and she was never anything but homely, but she had an enormous, bony frame that made people look a second time when they passed her on the street. There was not an ounce of fat on her. When she walked, her bones seemed to swing loosely, and she never hit hard upon the earth or seemed, for all her boniness, to have any sharp corners to her. Yet he could see the strain lines beginning around her eyes and mouth, and the way the skin of her face had grown white and dry.

"You sit yourself," she was saying now. "Wait a minute . . ." She looked around among the straight-backed chairs, searching for the most comfortable. When she found it she pushed the bowl of soup into Ben Joe's hands and ran to pull it up. "If we'd of known," she said, "I'd of cleaned up house a little. How come they've not told us you were back?"

"Well, I only got here yesterday."

"Sit, now. Oh my, let me take that soup bowl off your hands. What you think of New York?"

"I like it all right." He sat down on the chair and stretched his feet out in front of him. On the table under the window, among the doilies and flower pots and bronzed baby shoes, sat a photograph of his father. It was taken when he still had his mustache, long before he had ever met Lili Belle, but he looked much the same as he had when he died—rumpled hair, black then with only the first touches of white, and crinkling gray eyes and a broad, easy smile. Except for Gram's bedroom, where Ben Joe's mother never set foot, this was probably the only place in the world that still had a picture of Phillip Hawkes. Ben Joe reached out and turned it a little in his direction, looking at it thoughtfully.

"You have to excuse Mama's being so rude," Lili Belle was saying. "She has gotten like that more and more. The other day this lodger of ours, he stopped to talk to me on account of wanting to know where the clean towels were kept, and Mama clunked him in the chest with the griddle-cake-flipper. Didn't hurt him none, but I had a whole heap of explaining to do."

"Was she right about your having some kind of trouble?" Ben Joe asked.

"I'd say she was. That's why I was sitting in the dark like a spook. Little Phillip is in the hospital with pneumonia and I was resting my eyes from sitting up with him so much. I don't know where he got it. Folks tell me I take *too* good care of him, so it can't of been that he got too cold. Though he is right much of a puddle-wader, that could've done it. I told him and told him. When it was serious and I had reason to be worried I was just *possessed* by the thought of those puddles. I had it in mind, in this dream I had one night, to take me a vacuum cleaner and go vacuum all the puddles up. But the worrying part is over now. Doctor says another ten days or two weeks and he'll be out."

"How long's he been in?" Ben Joe asked.

"Two weeks."

"How're you managing the bills?"

"I plan to make it up gradual. I been working at the mill part time since little Phil started school, but not a full day, because I like to be home when he needs me. Oh, Mama would take care of him—says she's ashamed he was ever born, but I notice she's right fond of him. But I'd rather it be me. I'll work full time till the bill's paid off and then go back half-days again."

"We've got some money in the savings account," Ben Joe said.

"No, honey, I don't want it."

"But we never even touch it. It's the money Dad saved up and Mama won't use it no matter what—says it's only for emergencies. You're right, you shouldn't work when little Phillip's at home."

"I wouldn't take it, Benjy. It bothers me to take what we *do* take offen you all. Your sister Jenny's been bringing it real regular."

"Been what?"

"*You* know—the once-a-month money. She's not missed a time."

"But I thought— Doesn't she mail it?"

"Why, no." Lili Belle stopped playing with the folds of her skirt and looked up at him. "Neither *one* of you's ever *mailed* it," she said. "What she said the first time she came was, she would bring it the same as you'd always done."

"For Pete's sake." Ben Joe sat forward in his chair with his elbows on his knees. "I wonder how she knew."

"Oh, girls're smarter than you think." She laughed, and then became quiet again and looked at her hands. "She's a real nice little girl," she said. "First time she came I was just merely polite, you know, figuring that what's your mama's is your mama's and I didn't want to seem to be trying to make friends of your mama's own daughter. But she was so friendly—came in and taught little Phil how to play this game about scissors cutting rock and rock covering paper, or something. Real good with children, she is."

"She is," Ben Joe said. He sat quietly for a minute, and then he cleared his throat and said, "Lili Belle?"

"Hmm?"

"I've got something I want to talk to you about."

"Well, I'm listening."

"I thought I should get it said, in case I don't come back to Sandhill for a good while again. I figured . . ."

He was silent.

"I'm right here listening," she said. Her face was gentle and interested; Ben Joe wondered if it would become angry by the time he was through talking. Did Lili Belle ever get angry?

"I've got this letter," he said miserably.

"This . . . ?"

"Letter. Letter." He touched his pocket, where the rim of the pink envelope showed. "This, um—"

"*Oh*, yes."

"Ma'am?"

"Letter."

"Yes. And I wanted, wanted to show it to you because—"

"Well, I seen it before, Benjy honey.

"I know you have. That's what I'm trying to—"

"No, I mean I seen it on *you* before." She laughed gently, startling him. "Sure. First time you came after your daddy died, I seen it. Little piece of pink in your pocket, just like now. You'd not been to see me for two whole months, and then you came by but never said nothing about the letter. I figured you had found it in your daddy's office and read it, all about how I was asking him to come back to me and little Phillip. I was afraid you'd come to taunt me with it."

"Why to *taunt* you?"

"Account of the spelling, of course."

"The what?"

"The spelling. I never spelled too good."

"Oh," he said. He could think of nothing else to say; he was too surprised. For a moment he sat staring at her blankly and then he had to smile back at her.

"When you never did mention it," she was saying, "I figured you had just brought it along that one time to show me you had it safe. To show me you had took it from his office after he died so that no one else could see it. That why you brought it, Ben Joe?"

"No, ma'am," he said.

"No?"

"No, I took that letter *before* he ever died. What I came to tell you is, I took it before he even *saw* it."

He was afraid to look up at her. When he finally did, when she had been silent so long that he *had* to look, he saw that she didn't seem shocked or angry but was just absorbing the news still, shaking her head a little and trying to fit all this in with what she already knew.

"Lili Belle, I am awfully sorry," he said. "It's bothered me for so long I couldn't see any way to get rid of it now but to tell you, and say how sorry I am."

"Well, that's all right, Ben Joe." She licked her lips nervously, still frowning off into space. "That's all right—it didn't make no difference, did it? Everything would've happened the same, I reckon, letter or no letter."

"But I—"

"You didn't do nothing *wrong,* Benjy. Why, it seems to me your family is kind of queer-like sometimes. Meaning no offense. It's not *natural* to come see me and all, not even to speak to me on the street, but you do, and I reckon it's even a little relief, maybe, having you do something on your mother's side like most would do."

"Well—" Ben Joe stopped, not certain what to say. "What bothered me," he said, "is that maybe Dad would have gone back to you soon as he got your letter. And then, who knows, not had that heart attack a week later. Old Gram, she's blamed herself forever for forgetting to refill the ice-cube trays. Says that's why he died—going downtown to get ice. Though Mom says he could have stepped next door if he'd been sober enough to think of it. But sometimes when Gram gets on those ice-cube trays I'm almost tempted to show her the pink envelope, to prove it's not she that's to blame."

"Well, it surely ain't *you,*" Lili Belle said. She bent

forward to rub her eyes, tiredly, and then leaned her head back again and smiled at him. "I don't guess my letter would of made any change in him one way or the other. If your mother'd said one *word* he'd have stayed with her, always would have. He was just wanting her to ask him. But she didn't. He waited two weeks, and I guess he would have waited that long if I'd sent *fourteen* letters, even. Then he came back to me, not even planning to but just drunk and tired, and I took him in."

"But you can't say for sure," Ben Joe said.

"What?"

"You can't say for sure your letter wouldn't have made him come back earlier, you can't say—"

"Benjy honey, don't you worry. Can't say *nothing* for sure, if it comes to that. Don't you worry."

Both of them were silent for a minute, Lili Belle rocking steadily in her chair and filling the silence with slow creaks. Then she sat up straight again and said, "*Well*, how long you going to be here?"

"I don't know yet. Not too much longer, I guess."

"I heard your older sister's in town."

"That's right."

"Well, it'll work out. Her husband'll come and get her, you just watch. She's a right pretty girl—I seen her downtown before—and *he'll* come claim her. You just wait."

"Well, maybe so."

"Uh, you know my brother? Freeman? Well, Freeman he—"

"I thought his name was Donald."

"No, he changed it. That's what I was about to tell you. He said he was sick of this town and sick of blue denim and wanted to be free, so he changed his name to Freeman and went to work in a diner in New York. He likes it right much, I hear. Sent us this picture postcard saying, 'This here New York is a right swinging town.' That's what he said, 'a right swinging town.' You being in New York reminded me of it."

Her head was against the back of her chair again, lolling wearily. There was no telling how many nights she had sat up with little Phillip.

"You're tired," Ben Joe said. "I'll be going, Lili Belle. Here's the letter."

He pulled out the pink envelope and put it in one of her hands. She took it listlessly, stopping her rocking to frown down at it.

"Oh, land," she said. "Land."

She didn't go on speaking, though Ben Joe waited. She dropped the letter in her lap and went on rocking.

"I'll find my own way out," he said finally. "And I'm going to take care of that hospital bill, Lili Belle. Soon as I get it from the bank."

"No, Benjy, I don't—"

She was up on her feet now, wanting to protest, but he pulled on his jacket and left hurriedly. "You tell little Phil hey!" he called back.

"Well—"

He ran down the porch steps and into the yard. The sky above the river had grown churned and dark, and a cold wind was rising. As he walked he stuck his hands deep into his trouser pockets and hunched up his shoulders against the cold.

8

When he had finished what he had to do at the bank, Ben Joe headed toward Stacy's. It was a small, grim-looking café, but he and his friends had almost lived there once, back when they were in high school. They could meet up with almost anyone they wanted to see there if they waited long enough. Now, looking at the dirty gray front of the building while he waited for the traffic light to change, Ben Joe wondered why they had ever liked it. The picture window was dark and smudged, cluttered with neon beer signs and hand-lettered pizza posters. In front of it two weird-looking high school boys slouched, watching the people who passed by. When Ben Joe crossed the street and came closer to them, he stopped looking in their direction and stared steadfastly at Stacy's doorknob in order to avoid those amused eyes of theirs. But once inside it was no better; clustered in the dimness, lit briefly by the twirling rainbow from the jukebox, were more slouching boys and more leather jackets. Occasionally he caught a glimpse of a girl or two, with her hair piled in a fantastic frizzed mountain on her head and her skirt well above her knees. It was only after he had blinked a couple of times and strained his eyes into the farthest corners that he found Joanne.

She was sitting at a booth with her red coat thrown back behind her and a cup of coffee sitting on the table in front of her. But the coffee was going unnoticed; Joanne stared out at the empty dance floor with her mouth partly open and her eyes thoughtful.

"Hi," Ben Joe said.

She started a little and looked up at him. "Oh, hi," she said. She turned toward the cash register and called, "Stacy!"

Stacy was a fat blond woman who hated everyone under forty. No one knew why it was to her place that all the high school kids came. She bumbled toward them down the aisle, muttering something under her breath and slapping her round feet hard upon the floor at every step.

"*What*," she said.

"Ben Joe's here now."

"Hmm!" She stared at him blankly, with her eyes narrowed. "What you want?"

"Coffee. With double cream."

"With *what*?"

"Double cream."

"Double cream, hey. Double cream. My soul, double cream." She stamped off again, still muttering.

"Seven years gone by and she hasn't changed a mite," Joanne said. "How long's it been since you've come here, Ben Joe?"

"Oh, I don't know. Couple of years. Why?"

"I just wondered. Seems to me it used to be more lively."

"Mmm."

"Doesn't it to you? Seem that way?"

"I guess."

"On one of these tables there's a monument carved," she said. "It says, 'Memorial to Joanne, for her spirit.' Buddy Holler did that the day I walked out of chemistry class because it was boring."

Ben Joe smiled across the table at her. He wasn't listening to what she said; he was just glad to be having that cheerful voice of hers babble on. Before he had been walking too thin a line, losing sight of the division between Lili Belle's world and his mother's. Now there was Joanne to help. She was talking in an everyday voice about matter-of-fact things, and she was from home and reminding him that that was where he was from, too.

"Joanne," he said, "how well would you say you know Jenny?"

"Jenny our sister, you mean?"

"Yes."

She frowned. "Oh, I don't know. How old was she when I left—only eleven. Just barely getting a good start in life."

"You don't figure you know her very well?"

"No, not very well."

"Well, how about— What does she say in her letters to you?"

"Oh, *you* know." She grinned suddenly. "Just facts and figures—gotten much worse since you turned the money over to her."

"Does she say how she spends the money?"

"Sure."

"No, I mean does she tell you what bills she mails and what bills she takes in person? I mean . . ."

His coffee was set before him. He looked above the steam of it to Joanne's puzzled face.

"I'm not following," she said. "What do—"

"Well, does she say how the money is partitioned *up*, for instance? A certain amount to groceries, a certain amount for savings, and so on. Has she ever told you that?"

"Not even *Jenny* gets *that* specific," said Joanne. "What's the matter, Ben Joe?"

"Nothing. No, I just . . ."

He picked up his coffee and began drinking it, not meeting Joanne's eyes. She was giving him that amused little knowing smile again; he'd never find out how much she knew. Either she didn't know a thing or she was determined not to tell what she *did* know, and he'd never be able to find out which it was.

"I don't understand a soul in this world," he said.

"What makes you think you should? Especially girls. Think what a— Oh, hey, speaking of girls. Is that Shelley Domer?"

Ben Joe turned. Shelley was just coming in the door, dressed all in blue and carrying a coat over her arm. Behind her came a man Ben Joe didn't know.

"Who's he?" Joanne asked.

"I don't know."

"Sure looks familiar."

"Well, it might be Jack Horner. Shelley said the other night—"

"*John* Horner," Joanne said. "I remember all about him. Used to live just outside Sandhill, went to Murphy High School."

She put her chin in her hand and examined John Horner. So did Ben Joe, although he tried to look as if he were watching something else. He was surprised to see that Horner was a nice enough looking man, with a broad face and a mop of brown hair. For some reason, Ben Joe had pictured him as thin and sinister; he couldn't say why. Shelley was smiling up at him with that small, formal smile she always put on when she felt awkward, and when she saw Ben Joe she looked pleased and her smile broadened. Immediately she came over to their table, letting Horner follow if he wanted to.

"Hey, Ben Joe," she said. "Hey, Joanne. It's good to see you again."

"It's good to see *you*. Why don't you sit down?"

"Well, all right."

Shelley looked back and forth, first at the seat beside Joanne and then at the seat beside Ben Joe, and finally she chose the one beside Ben Joe and slid shyly into it. Opposite her, John Horner sat down by Joanne and began talking to her immediately, not waiting for an introduction to Ben Joe.

"You look kind of glum," Shelley said to Ben Joe.

"I do?"

"What you been doing that makes you look so glum?"

"Well, I don't know. What've *you* been doing?"

"Looking for a job. I didn't find one, though."

"Where'd you look?"

"Sesame Printery." She smiled, unexplainably, at her

fingernails. "I worked there one summer proofreading, remember? And they're so low on work that Mr. Crown —that's the boss—he's just thinking *up* things to keep the typesetters busy. This morning they turned out five hundred labels reading 'Strawberry Jam,' one hundred labels reading 'Pickled Pigs' Feet,' though Mrs. Crown hates them and won't pickle any no matter *what* inducement Mr. Crown offers, and seven school-book covers saying 'All cats look gray in the dark,' because that's little Sonny Crown's favorite quotation. This afternoon they'll print the Crowns' stationery. So I don't reckon they need any help."

Across the table, Horner was laughing at something Joanne had said. Shelley looked over at them and said, "I'd introduce you to John if he wasn't talking just now. But anyway, that's the John Horner I was telling you about. You like him?"

"Well, what I see of him I do," Ben Joe said.

"He and I are going roller-skating this afternoon. I just know I'll break my neck."

"Has he asked you yet?"

"Asked me what?"

"About marrying him."

"No, not yet."

"What you going to say?"

"Oh . . ."

"Come on, now," he said. He was teasing her, but she turned suddenly serious and began pleating the paper napkin beside his saucer. "Haven't decided yet?" he asked her more gently.

She shook her head.

"You couldn't *drag* me in this place again," Joanne was saying to John. "It's all taken over by hoods, looks like. Used to be a real happy place, everybody dancing together—"

"Remember Barney Pocket?" John asked. "Remember how he used to make up dances all by himself? Lord, he was a funny guy. Put himself through college, later, calculating how soon people would die and then borrowing money from them. It worked, too."

"He walked to Newfoundland one summer," Joanne said. "On a dare."

Ben Joe cleared his throat. "Joanne," he said, "I think Gram expects us home for lunch."

"Okay, Ben Joe."

Shelley and John stood up to let them out. While Ben Joe was struggling into his jacket, Shelley edged closer and said, "You coming tomorrow?"

"Sure," Ben Joe said. "I'll be by at—"

"Hush!" She frowned toward where John was standing talking with Joanne and then turned back to Ben Joe. "Will you *hush?*"

The urge to tease came over him again. He grinned down at her and said, "Don't tell me he doesn't *know* I'm coming! Why, Shelley Domer, that amounts to outright two-timing. I swear if you're not—"

"I *mean* it, now!" Her face was white and miserable; Ben Joe immediately felt sorry. "He *is* a steady boyfriend, after all," she said. "I don't want to—"

"Okay, okay."

He reached around to help her with her coat, and then raised one hand in Horner's direction.

"See you," he said.

"So long."

When they were outside, Joanne stopped to button up her coat. "It's getting kind of chilly," she said. "Shelley hasn't changed much, has she?"

"I don't know."

"I mean, she's still sort of quiet and drifty. You always did alternate between two extremes, come to think of it—first a dreamy, drifty girl and then a shrieky, dancing one."

"Well."

"That all you got to say?"

He watched the traffic light patiently, not hearing her.

"What you got on your mind, Ben Joe?"

"I don't know. Joanne?"

"What?"

"Would you say about ten dollars a day is enough to pay for a stay in a hospital?"

"That depends on the circumstances."

"Well, I don't know the circumstances, really. It's just this friend of mine. I'm worried about how much money he'd need."

"Light's changed."

She pulled him impatiently into the street, but once they had crossed she walked more slowly, studying the question.

"It sounds like a fair guess," she said. "Yes, I'd say so."

"Well, I don't know," said Ben Joe. "I keep thinking it should be more, somehow."

"That's *your* problem," said Joanne.

9

OVERNIGHT the weather turned much colder. The wind howled and rattled at the bones of the house, and dry leaves scraped along the sidewalk. In the evening, when Ben Joe began dressing for his date with Shelley, his whole family pounced on him out of sheer boredom and wanted to know where he was going.

"Just out," he said.

He was in the living room, buttoning up the shirt Jenny had just ironed.

"I thought you might take me to see Jamie Dower tonight," Gram said.

"In *this* weather?"

"Well . . . it's Sunday. Good visiting time."

"I'll take you tomorrow," he said. "I don't know why we can't get synchronized on this Jamie Dower thing. If I'm ready to go you've got an iron-bound excuse *not* to, and now that I'm busy you're almost out in the car honking for me. Where's Susannah? I bet you anything she took my cuff links."

"She's in the attic," said Tessie. "Hunting squirrels."

"Oh."

"She took the only gun of mine that really shoots and she's been up there since suppertime. Got a whole soup can full of B-B's beside her."

"Funny way for a grown woman to spend her time. You notice if she's wearing my cuff links?"

"The squirrels have been nesting there," his mother said. "*Someone* has to get rid of them. Besides, your shirt has button cuffs."

"Oh. Well, then, it's the wrong shirt. I asked for the one with the French cuffs on it."

Jenny, sitting on the rug with a book, looked up and made a face at him. "Serve you right if I'd made you iron it yourself," she said.

"That one looks just as nice, Ben Joe."

"Okay, okay. How can she hunt squirrels in the dark?"

"She's got the extension lamp," Tessie said. "She's really mad at them."

"She'll never shoot one."

"Ben Joe, your shirt tail is out."

"I know it."

He jammed it into his trousers and went to the hall mirror to put his tie on. In the wavy glass he saw his face, sullen and heavy with the boredom of a long day at home. Behind him a part of his family was reflected, looking just as bored as he did. His mother sat in the rocking chair, absently glancing through a newspaper; her neck was made funny and crooked by a flaw in the mirror. Beside her sat Tessie, doing nothing at all but looking admiringly at her new shoes and occasionally wetting one finger and bending down to wipe at an imaginary scuff. The shoes were not reflected, but he had been asked to give an opinion of them so many times in the last day and a half that he thought he would be seeing them in his sleep forever—clumsy, too-white oxfords that were still new enough to look enormous on her feet. Also in the mirror were Jenny's legs, but not the rest of her. He thought even her legs looked bored.

He finished knotting his tie, made a ferocious face in the mirror to see if his teeth needed brushing, and went back into the living room for his jacket.

"I'm going," he said.

"Are you going to be anywhere near the drugstore?"

"Or the newsstand?"

"Nope," he said. "Not going anywhere near anything."

"Well, it's hard to believe when you're dressed up so handsome," Gram said. "Come kiss me good night."

He bent down and kissed her cheekbone, and then kissed the tops of Tessie's and his mother's head for good measure.

"I won't be late," he said.

"All right, Ben Joe."

At the doorway he turned to look at them again. He was in one of those faraway moods when everything he saw seemed to be inside a shining goldfish bowl, and he suddenly saw how closed-off his family looked. They went peacefully on with what they were doing; Ben Joe, having vanished, might as well not exist. When he stepped outside he gave the door an enormous slam, just to make himself exist a minute longer.

The wind bit at his face and his bare hands. It was very dark, without a moon, but he could see the white clouds swimming rapidly past the house tops. And before he had even reached the front gate, the cold had begun to seep in all over. He didn't care. He was glad to get out in the fresh air after the long, stuffy day, and he was glad to be going to Shelley's, although he couldn't say why. There were times when even Shelley's shyness and her slowness seemed to be exactly what he needed. And he would like the way she greeted him at the door, with her face so formal.

He hurried on, making his arms hang loosely instead of huddling them close to his body, because the cold air still felt good. A twig from one of the trees along the sidewalk stung across his face. He ducked and then turned in, whistling now, to climb the long steps to Shelley's house.

She answered almost as soon as he knocked. He saw the outline of her behind the mesh curtain, running in order to let him in quickly. The minute the door was open she tugged at his arm with both hands and said, "Get in, Ben Joe, aren't you *frozen?*"

He nodded, smiling at her, and stepped inside so that she could shut the door behind him.

"Come on in," she said, "come in. I declare, I think you're just frozen stiff and silent. Take off your coat, now. That's right."

She took the coat from him and smiled into his eyes. It had been a long time since he had seen her looking so pretty. Her hair was down, the way she had worn it when she was in high school, and it was well brushed and shining. There was something besides lipstick on her face—rouge, he thought—that made her look excited and bright-eyed, and she was watching him with that half-scared expression.

"I sure am glad to see *you*," he said suddenly.

"Well, thank the Lord you've said something. I thought maybe you were going to be speechless all evening."

She took a hanger from the closet for his coat, and Ben Joe went into the living room. A fire had been lit in the fireplace, a tall fire that roared out and glinted on the bare wood floor. The thought of having to go out again, away from all this warmth, was depressing. But as soon as Shelley came into the living room he turned and said, "Do you want to go somewhere?"

"Oh, I don't care. What do you want to do?"

"Well, anything you want to."

"No, you say."

He spread his hands helplessly. "*You* say," he said.

"I really don't have a preference in this world, Ben Joe."

"You must have."

"Oh . . ." She put her hands together and stared into the fire. "I hate to be the one to say," she said finally.

The fire light kept moving and flickering on her face. And her hair just brushed the top of her collar. Something about her—the expectant way she stood, the dress-up navy dress with its spotless white collar—reminded him of a night he thought he had forgotten, back when his sisters were still very young. Joanne had thrown a barbecue party, with what seemed like millions of couples, and had suggested offhandedly than anyone in the family could have some barbecue with them if they wanted to. At the time Jenny was no more than eleven, but she was just beginning to notice boys and had started reading beauty magazines. The night of the barbecue the whole house reeked of some heavy-scented bath oil and no one knew why; but then down the stairs came Jenny, wearing a white puff-sleeved dress, with her hair perfectly combed and a thick envelope of perfume encircling her wherever she moved. She had come down and sat quietly on the lawn with the older couples, who were in sloppy Bermudas and T shirts, and she hadn't spoken unless spoken to, but all evening she watched the party with that same happy, frightened look. He had wanted to cry for her, without knowing why—or at least hug her. He wanted to hug Shelley now, but she had awakened from her staring into the fire and was watching him.

"What're you thinking about?" she asked.

"I don't know."

"Well, I tell you. One thing I do know about New York is that when they have dates they like as not never set *foot* in a movie house or a skating rink. The girls just serve them cocktails in their apartments. So I have bought some bourbon, in case that's what you're used to doing. Is that all right?"

"It's a wonderful idea," Ben Joe said.

She ran out to the kitchen immediately; for some reason she didn't seem to be in slow motion tonight. Ben Joe sat down on the couch and relaxed happily against the cushions. The fire was slowly drawing the cold out of him, leaving him warm and comfortable. He could hear glasses tinkling in the kitchen.

"I've put you some ice and a little water," Shelley said when she came in again.

"That's perfect."

She had brought the bottle in on a tray, and next to it stood their two glasses, her own very pale. When Ben Joe picked his glass up, she watched his face carefully to see if he liked it, and smiled when he nodded to her.

"Just right," he said.

"I'm glad."

She picked up her own glass and, after turning over in her mind the problem of where to sit, chose a spot next to Ben Joe on the couch, settling there so delicately that her drink hardly wavered in its glass.

"Is it you that's going to talk?" she asked.

"Well, I don't know."

"I think it is."

"Why?"

"Oh . . ." She took a sip of her drink and began turning her glass around, smiling into it. "When you come in slow and smiling, likely something is on your mind. Also if you're too much the other way. And then me, I'm not in a real talky mood myself. So I figured it would be you to talk."

"Maybe so." He slid down, so that his feet were under the coffee table and his weight was upon the small of his back, and scratched the top of his head. "I'm thinking about it," he explained when she laughed.

"Well, tell me what you did with your day."

"My day. Lord. Nothing to speak of. It was Sunday. We all got the Sunday blues. Got them so bad that Susannah's up in the attic hunting squirrels with a B-B gun now. Nobody went out. Me, I slept and then I read the funny papers twice through, and then I finished a murder mystery and peeled potatoes for Gram. It's been a God-awful day, considering."

He sat up straighter and took a swallow of his drink.

"You know," he said, "except for an occasional Sunday, they don't make days like they used to. I mean, they don't make them *whole* any more. You noticed?"

He looked over at Shelley, but she only shook her head, puzzled.

"Oh, well, what I mean is, the days seem to come in pieces now. They used to be in blocks—all one solid color to them. Sometimes whole *weeks* would be in blocks. Someone could say, 'What's this week been like?' and right off the bat you could say, 'Oh, lousy. My father won't let me have the car because he caught me scratching off in front of Stacy's café the other day.' Or it would be a great week, for another reason just that clear-cut. It's not that way any more."

"Well . . ." Shelley said. She was trying, but in the end she gave up and said, "I reckon I never did notice that, Ben Joe."

"No, I guess not."

"You tell me about the pieces, then."

"All right."

He settled back again and thought a minute. "What I'm mainly wondering," he said, "is whether Mom ever looks at the bank records. I've never actually seen her do it. She's real funny that way. Sometimes I think Jenny is the one who manages the family now, as if Mom weren't there. Jenny tells her what's going on but only to keep her informed, not to ask her for any decisions. So maybe she doesn't know anything about the bank books."

"What difference does it make if she does?" Shelley asked.

"Well, I took some money out when I shouldn't have. I don't know what she'd do if she knew. I'm worried about it."

He drained the last of his drink and then balanced the glass on his knee. It made a cold, dark ring in the fabric of his trousers. "I don't know why it's always so hard deciding which side I'm on," he said.

"Let me pour you another drink, Ben Joe."

"Also, I found out Joanne's asking for a divorce," Ben Joe said. He watched Shelley's hands as she poured his bourbon; they were long, thin hands that seemed uncertain about what they were touching. "She says she just *left* Gary, not even telling him about it. The lawyer's getting in touch with him now. Sometimes I'm hoping Gary'll say no, she can't have the divorce, and Joanne will leave Sandhill and go back and be happy in Kansas again. But most times I'm hoping she'll get divorced and stay with us. That Gary, I don't know whether I like him or not. Well, hell, I've never even *seen* him. Except in this blurred snapshot Joanne sent us of him holding Carol when she was just newborn. There was all kinds of excitement when Carol was born. The girls went around calling each other 'Aunt'—even Tessie—and Mom was 'Grandma' for I don't know how long. Then they forgot about it. But Gary sent out these birth announcements that say there's a new product on the market, giving the name of the manufacturers—that's the parents—and all."

"I think that's *nice*," Shelley said.

"Well. It just seems funny in our particular family, is all. Like that sentimental kind of letter he wrote us after Joanne called to say they were married. It began, 'Dear Mom,' in this unreadable handwriting, and Mom looked at the greeting and then at the closing to see what stranger was calling her Mom and she said, 'Who's Gary?' It wasn't till she'd read the letter that she figured it out. No, that's a nice idea but it doesn't fit, somehow, and I kind of hope he'll give Joanne the divorce." He sat up straight again and stared into the fire. "Why can't they all just let *me* take care of them? My sisters are so separate. I'd be happy to take care of them."

"I know," Shelley said comfortingly.

He smiled at her. She was sitting very straight and still, almost touching him, and listening completely to what he said. Anyone else he knew would be getting restless by now.

"*You* talk," he said.

"I got nothing to say, Ben Joe."

"Neither do I, seems like." He bent to untie his shoelaces and slip the shoes off. Then he swung his legs up and settled his feet on the coffee table. "Tomorrow we're going to see Jamie Dower," he said. "He's eighty-four. How do you reckon it would feel to be eighty-four? Do you think you'd *realize* you were that old? I don't realize I'm twenty-five. I keep thinking I'm about eighteen or so. I don't even know if Gram realizes how old *she* is. Somehow I think not, or she wouldn't still be making a fuss about bygone things. Still keeping up the old war with Mom. She never did like her much. Grandpa, now, he thought Mom was wonderful. Said she had backbone. First time she came to visit here before she and Dad got married, she came down to breakfast saying she was thirsty and Grandpa poured her a glass of water. Only it turned out not to be water but moonshine, that clear kind that comes out of a Mason jar. Mom was right surprised but she drank it anyway, without coughing, and Grandpa said, 'Honey, *you're* no Yankee,' and loved her like a daughter ever since. But Gram, she said all it proved was that she was no lady. Oh, hell, I'm getting off the subject. Whatever the subject was."

"It's all right," Shelley said. "Don't you worry, Ben Joe."

"Me? I'm not worried."

"Well. Anyway, it's all right."

She looked sad, and Ben Joe didn't know why. He didn't know what to do about it. He put one arm along the back of the couch behind her, not actually touching her but just protecting her, and looked at her face to see what was bothering her. There were lots of things he *might* do; he might say something funny and make her laugh, for instance. But for some reason he didn't. He pulled his hand in tighter, around the curve of her shoulder, and then leaned forward and kissed her cheek.

"Nothing's worrying me," he said.

She turned her face full toward him, and he put his other arm around her and kissed her mouth that was as familiar as if he had been kissing her only last night instead of almost seven years ago. Even the taste of her lipstick was the same—like strawberries. And she had the same way of hugging him; the minute she hugged him she stopped seeming scared and became soft and warm, first kissing him and then gently laying her cheek against his as if he were a child to be comforted. For a minute he relaxed against her, but then he began to feel a crick in his neck. He sat up straight again and cleared his throat.

"Um . . ." he said. He leaned forward a little, with his elbows on his knees. "I forgot about Horner," he said.

"What?"

"Horner. I forgot about him."

"Oh."

He lit a cigarette and puffed on it a few times before he looked at her again. "Have you got an ash tray?" he asked her.

"I'll get you one." She stood up and crossed to the desk. She was the kind of person who rumpled easily; her hair was fluffed now and her lipstick was a little blurred. When she came back with the ash tray she said, "We're not *engaged*, after all. I just go out with him some."

"Well, still."

"Of course, I *like* him and all . . ."

"Oh, sure. Sure, he looked like a nice person."

"He is. He's real nice, he really is."

"Where did you meet up with him?" he asked.

"At my aunt's house. She used to know his family."

"That's right. Joanne said he was from around Sandhill. I don't know where *she* met up with him."

"At a basketball game," said Shelley, "when Joanne was still in high school."

"How you know that?"

"Oh, John's told me *all* about his past." She settled back against the cushions, smiling a little now.

"His *past?* Does that include just meeting a girl at a basketball game? He must have been pretty thorough."

"Oh, no, he dated her a while. But he felt—" She stopped, and looked into her half-empty glass.

"He felt what?"

"Oh, now I've forgotten what I was going to say."

"Come on, Shelley."

She kept on staring at her drink, pressing the corners of her mouth down. Finally she said, "Well, I suppose he just met her at . . . at one of those ages when girls are in a sort of, um, wild stage. I mean, rebellious. That's what I mean. *Rebellious* stage."

Ben Joe sat up straighter.

"Now, Ben Joe, I'm sure he didn't mean to—"

"Who does he think he—"

"Ben Joe, I *know* he didn't mean to carry tales. He wouldn't do that."

"Oh, never mind." He sat back again. "She *was* kind of a *flirt* in high school," he said. "The way she dressed and all. I suppose if you just met her a couple of times you'd think she really *was* wild."

"But—" Shelley looked down in her drink again. "Well, yes, Ben Joe, I'm sure that's what he meant. You want another drink?"

"No."

"There's lots more."

"No. People who just look at them on the surface, *they've* got no right to say what my sisters are like."

"I know that."

"Okay."

She was still watching him, trying to tell if he was feeling better. He looked back at her blankly.

"Ben Joe," she said finally, "have you got a girl in New York?"

"Why?"

"Because I want to know."

"Not one steady girl. No."

She nodded, satisfied. "Anyway," she said, "I'm sorry I told you what I just did. I wouldn't have you worried for anything."

"I'm *not worried!*"

"All right."

She put her hands on his shoulders and he settled down next to her again, fitting his head beneath her chin. Against his back he could feel her hands patting him softly, so lightly he could hardly feel it.

"The trouble is," he said into her collarbone, "I'm reversible."

The words were muffled. She pulled back a little and looked down at him and said, "What?"

"I don't guess you're hardly *alive* if you're as reversible as I am. But the *ir*reversible people, they get someplace. Good or bad. Murder is irreversible, for that matter. Even if it's bad, you can tell you're getting somewhere definite. But me, I am reversible."

"You silly," Shelley said. "You talk like you're some kind of raincoat, Ben Joe. Don't get upset, now."

He was pulled in next to her again, and soothed with the same small pats. Gradually he closed his eyes and let the full weight of his head rest against her chest.

He heard Shelley's voice beginning above him, faraway and soft, saying, "You were the first person I ever wanted to ask me out. There'd been two other boys asked me out before, but I didn't like them and I've forgotten now where we ever went or what we did. One was that fat little Junior Gerby, who was shorter than me, and the other was Kenny Burke, who was so greasy and hoody back in those days. Though later on he changed. His mama says he's right nice now. She was always afraid he'd end up in Alcatraz. But when I started thinking about you asking me out, now that you weren't just a little boy to play roll-a-bat with any more, I'd pray every night for you to ask me. I'd say, 'Please, God, you let Ben Joe Hawkes ask me out and I will never ask for anything more as long as I live.' Though I knew at the time it was next to impossible. There were three other girls after you and all of them prettier than me, though you never noticed and were always playing baseball and fiddling with your microscope. I took to shoplifting lipsticks, even if I *did* have plenty allowance, and trying on all manner of different shades in front of the mirror. Then I figured God was mad at me for it and I buried all my lipsticks in the backyard, where they are to this day."

He moved his head a little, and she let him settle down again and then began stroking his hair with her hand.

Above him the voice went on; he barely listened to the words but just concentrated on the sound, slow and murmuring above him.

"And then they announced how the Future Homemakers were going to have a supper at the Parnells' Restaurant out by the college and we could ask dates, and I asked you, although I was shaking so hard I had to lean against the wall while I was talking to you. When you said yes I got all happy, but then when it came time to go I was terrified and wished I'd never asked you. I was afraid I'd vomit at the dinner table. And I didn't know what to order. I could order spaghetti and get a big, long, endless strand of it and have to keep sucking it up from the plate just indefinitely. Or pizza, and misjudge how soon it had cooled, the way I always did, and take a hot bite and have to spit it out. Or chicken, and have it slide from under my knife and fork right across the table into somebody else's plate, like it had done once before."

"What did you order?" Ben Joe asked sleepily.

"A roast-beef sandwich. Only the meat was tough, and when I took a bite the whole slab of beef came out of the sandwich and hung from my teeth."

She was quiet a minute. Ben Joe stirred again, sitting up straighter so that his face was level with Shelley's.

"I love you, Ben Joe," she said.

This time when he kissed her her mouth was softer, with that first stickiness of her lipstick gone, and he didn't care whether there was a crick in his neck or not now. He wanted to say he loved her back, but he couldn't because her mouth was in the way, and then when she drew back to nestle down next to his shoulder, he felt too warm and comfortable to say anything at all. He just sat still, letting her nuzzle a little place for her face between his neck and his shoulder. It was only when he knew that they were about to fall asleep that he spoke again, and then in the softest whisper, as if her family was still alive and gently watchful in other parts of the house.

"Shelley."

"What?"

"I better go home."

"It's early still."

"I know, but anyway."

"Well, all right."

They both stood up, Shelley patting her hair down as she rose. The minute Ben Joe was up he was awake again and felt almost sorry that he had mentioned going home. But he took the coat when she handed it to him and kissed the top of her head and said, "When can I come back?"

"Tuesday. You going to?"

"Yes."

She pulled the door open and a blast of cold air came in, taking both their breaths away.

"You hurry, now," she said. "You're going to freeze, Ben Joe!"

"Good night," he said.

"Night."

Then the door closed behind him, and all he could hear was the shrieking of the wind.

10

OUTSIDE it was sheer blackness, rolling in around him with the wind. He walked down Shelley's steps slowly, pausing when he reached the street to button up the collar of his coat. But walking was too quiet; he wanted to run. And if no one had been within earshot he would have started singing, too, or laughing at nothing, because he felt happy and easy. But it was the hour just before bedtime, when everyone had something to do outdoors —walk the dog, or set out the milk bottles, or simply take a breath of fresh air in the yard before they shut themselves up in their houses for the night. So he ran silently; he doubled up his fists and tore down the sidewalk with the leaves rattling behind him and people occasionally pausing on their porches to turn and watch him run.

Someone came down a front walk and set a cat down outside the gate. It was a small cat of some nameless color, with its sling-eyes glowing, and when its owner turned to go inside, the cat hunched sullenly on the sidewalk as if it resented being put out for the night. It stared unblinkingly at Ben Joe. Ben Joe stooped down to pat it.

"There, there, cat," he said. His hand reached out for the cat almost blindly, aiming only for a blurred patch of darkness against the lighter background of the sidewalk. When he felt the cat's head under his hand he stroked it gently. "I'll take care of you," he said.

The cat was used to people; it began purring instantly and pressing its little head against Ben Joe's hand. Ben Joe picked it up and began walking again, hugging the cat next to his chest to keep it warm. He was afraid to run, for fear the cat would become frightened, but he was tired, anyway, and contented himself with walking fast.

Some of the houses were already dark; most of them still had soft yellow lights in the windows. He could see people moving around upstairs, pulling down shades or simply walking about their rooms in bathrobes. In one house a woman stood brushing her hair, and Ben Joe stopped to watch the dreamlike rhythm of it. Then the little cat stirred restlessly, and Ben Joe went on. The sky above the lights of the houses was a deep blue-black, but when he stepped out into the street and kept his eyes away from the lights it was pale and glowing, and stretched almost white behind the black skeletons of trees. He was almost running again, and the cat began mewing softly and squirming in his arms.

"Now, don't you worry, cat," Ben Joe said. "No call to worry."

He laughed, for no reason he could name. Laughing

made his teeth cold. He closed his mouth and his teeth felt cold and dry against the inside of his lips.

"That you, Ben Joe?" someone called.

He turned; a dark figure was standing on the sidewalk.

"It's me," he said. "Who's that?"

"Jenny."

"Oh. What *you* doing out?"

"Nothing." She stepped off the sidewalk and walked over to him. "I went to bed early and just got myself all wound up in the bed sheets," she said. "Thought I'd have a walk and hot milk and then try going to bed all over again. What's that you got?"

"A cat. There's something I meant to talk to you about."

"Where'd you get him?" She bent forward to see the cat, and then touched it. All he could see of her was a pale face and the dark hollows where her eyes were. "Doesn't like being carried," she said.

"I'm keeping it warm. I wanted to ask you—"

"It doesn't *want* to be kept warm."

"It does too. Jenny, there's a sort of money matter I'd like to—"

"You better put it *down*, Ben Joe."

"He *likes* me, I tell you."

"Got his own little overcoat sewn right on him, doesn't he? What's he want to be kept warm for? No, when they squirm like that, Ben Joe . . ."

He gave in, knowing she was right, and bent to let the cat hop down and run away.

"It's much happier now," she said.

"*Jenny!*"

"Well, I'm listening."

He smiled suddenly, without knowing why. "Oh, never mind," he said. "Oh, what the hell, what the hell . . ."

"Well, good night, Ben Joe."

"Night."

He was off again, tearing along the cracked pavement and leaving Jenny far behind. He swung three times around the tree on his corner, the way he had always done for good luck when he was small. Then he clattered through the wire gate and up the walk to the porch. The bark from the tree had left his palm gritty: he rubbed his hand against the side of his coat as he climbed the steps. At the front door, dark now with only the softest yellow light glimmering through the round stained-glass window, he bumped smack into a girl and boy.

"Excuse me, excuse me," he said, and found himself smiling again. "I didn't see you. Funny house this is—they just never think of leaving the light on for you. They forget all about you, the minute you—"

He opened the screen door with a flourish, almost bumping into the couple, and with his hand on the knob of the inside door he turned back again.

"Excuse me," he said.

John Horner and Joanne were looking at him, their faces serious and lit very dimly by the pale-yellow light. Joanne's hand was clasped in John's, against John's chest, but it was forgotten now as they both stared at him.

"*Quite* all right," said John Horner.

The heat inside the house burned Ben Joe's cold face. As soon as he had slammed the door behind him he ripped off his overcoat and threw it on a chair in the hallway and began undoing his collar as he climbed the stairs.

"That you, Ben Joe?" his mother called.

"Yup."

"Come on into the living room and say hello, why don't you?"

"I can't," Ben Joe said.

He stopped on the stairs, hearing his mother's footsteps in the hallway, and turned to look down at her.

"Why can't you?" she said.

"I just can't. I just can't. I can't be bothered with that right now."

"You can't be—"

He climbed the rest of the stairs at a steady, slow pace. His tie trailed by one hand. It wasn't until he was in the upstairs hallway that he let the actual picture of the couple on the porch come back to him, and then all he did was stop and stare tiredly at the wallpaper. After a minute he turned and started doggedly down the hall toward his room.

11

"BEN JOE," Gram said, "a promise is a promise. If you didn't want to see Jamie Dower you shouldn't have told me he was here."

Ben Joe pushed a rubbery piece of scrambled egg around his plate.

"You hear me, Ben Joe?"

"Yes'm."

"Well, you going to take me there or aren't you?"

"All I'm doing is being honest about it," he said. "I just honestly dont *feel* like going to the home, Gram. Never have liked going. That time I went to see Mrs. Gray with you I couldn't get it out of my mind again."

His grandmother poured him a second cup of coffee and then slammed the pot back on the stove. "Liking's got nothing to do with it," she said. "What's the matter with it, anyway? No, I don't enjoy thinking of my friends in an old folks' home, but this I *will* say: homes are a lot more cheerful nowadays. They don't *depress* the tar out of you."

"I don't care if they depress me. I just get confused in homes. I walk out of there all confused and I never can tell what time it is."

"What difference is the time of day? What difference does it make?"

"Well, the time of *day* doesn't make *any* difference, Gram. That's not what I'm talking about."

"You." She flounced into the chair opposite him and began pulling out her three bobby pins. "Now, it's got to be this morning that we go, Ben Joe, because I got to take Tessie to her drawing lesson this afternoon. Your mother's too busy. *Busy.*" She jabbed one of the bobby pins back in.

"What you need me along for? To go to the home, I mean. What good'll I do? You tell me a good reason, I'll be glad to come."

"I just want someone with me. Besides."

"What."

"Besides, I want you to remember how I tagged around after Jamie Dower when I was little. Then you'll see how it might seem a little forward for me to be going there alone today."

"I don't see why," Ben Joe said. "You're seventy-eight years old now, Gram."

"That's not too old to do things ladylike."

"All right, I'll go." He knew it was no use arguing; he shrugged resignedly and speared another piece of egg.

"You promise?"

"I promise. Give me a minute to finish my breakfast."

"Well, do you think I look all right?"

He looked at her carefully for the first time that morning. She was wearing a huge black turtle-neck sweater, knitted in haste, and a wrap-around denim skirt, and on her feet were the usual black gym shoes. But there were a few small changes that he hadn't noticed: her face looked feverish with its dabs of rouge and the careful line of orange lipstick that ordinarily she never wore; and next to the worn little wedding band on her finger was a huge diamond engagement ring that was used only for church-going.

"You look fine," he said.

"I bet he won't recognize me."

"I bet he won't."

"Last time he saw me I was a little roly-poly fat girl with lollypop juice down my front. I bet he won't know what name to call me by, even."

"No, I bet he won't."

"Come *on*, Ben Joe."

He gulped down the last of his coffee and stood up. "Where are the keys?" he asked.

"On the wall, where they belong. Put your dishes in the sink, now. Jenny was raising the roosters about how you don't do your share of picking up around here."

"Oh, pick up, pick up." He stacked the dishes helter-skelter in the sink and then knelt to tie his shoe. "*Joanne* never picks up. I had to scrape pablum off the damn *toaster* this morning."

"That was Jane that fed Carol. Joanne's still in bed."

"No wonder," he said.

"No wonder what?"

"No wonder she's still in bed. Get your coat, Gram."

"I've got it right here." She picked up one of his father's old lab coats from the back of a chair and began putting it on. It came down almost to the top of her gym shoes, but she looked at it proudly and stuck her hands in the pockets.

"You going to be warm enough in that?" he asked.

"Course I am."

"Well, it's your lookout."

He followed her across the living room, which was still cluttered with all the things the family had been doing the night before. His heel crushed something; it was the flatiron from the Monopoly set. He scraped it off his shoe and kept going.

Outside it was bright and still. The wind was gone but it was still cold, and in shady places there was something that was either very heavy frost or light patches of snow. He turned on the windshield wipers in the car to get rid of the thin covering of frost.

"Now, I want you to be very polite to Jamie," his grandmother said.

"Am I ever *not* polite?"

"Sometimes. Sometimes. Or at least, absent-minded. So you watch it, Ben Joe. Jamie Dower is older even than I am. I used to think maybe someday he'd save my life."

"How would he do that?"

"Oh you know. Pull me out of the water or something. I'm just saying that to show how *much* older he is. Old enough to be kind of looked up to and admired, so's the only way he'd really notice me would be for me to die or something."

"All right," Ben Joe said. "I'll be polite."

She settled back, satisfied. But when they had pulled out into the street and were drawing closer to the home, the anxious expression came back to her face and she crossed her legs and began picking at the white rubber circle at the ankle of her gym shoes, a sure sign she was worrying.

"Maybe I should've brought him something," she said.

"I thought you were going to."

"No. No, ordinarily I would, would have brought something to pretty up his room or tempt his appetite. But Jamie never liked that kind of thing. When I was little I would walk to his house every day and bring him my dessert from lunchtime, but he never wanted it."

"Well, that was nearly seventy years ago. You want to stop at a florist's?"

"No thank you, Ben Joe."

She settled back again, still frowning. When they drew up in front of the home, which looked like just a larger sort of yellow brick family house, she remained in her seat and looked at it through the window pane without changing her expression or giving any sign that she was about to go in.

"Would you rather not go?" Ben Joe asked gently. "I could bring you back another time, if you want."

"No, no. I was just thinking, oughtn't to ever put brownish curtains in a yellow house. It's ugly." She swung her door open and got out, grunting a little as her feet hit the ground. "Don't know what they could have been thinking of," she said.

"We'll get inside where we don't have to look at it."

But she kept standing there, looking up at the home.

"You're going to stay right by me, aren't you, Benjy?" she asked.

"Course I am."

"They say," she said, beginning to walk slowly across the yard, "they say when people get old they take to reading the obituary column to see if their names're in it. Well, I'm not to that yet, but one thing I have noticed: I do hate going to the home for the aged, for fear I can't get out again. They might mistake me, you know. When I said I wasn't a patient, they might think I was just planning to escape."

Ben Joe took her by the elbow and began walking with her. "I'll watch out for you," he said. "Besides, they must have a sort of roll book here. And your name's not on it. They couldn't keep you here."

"Oh, don't be so *reasonable*, Ben Joe." She made an exasperated face and pinched the arm that she was hanging onto. "You're just like your mother. So reasonable. Just like her."

"I am not."

"Well, no, but you surely are an annoyance."

"If you're not more polite I'm going to leave you here," Ben Joe said. "And sneak up and put your name on the roll book just to make sure you stay." He gave her a small pat on the back.

The front door of the home was huge and heavy. Ben Joe pulled it open and they stepped inside, into suffocating heat and the smell of furniture polish. The flowered brown rug they stood on was deep and made everything seem too quiet; it stretched for what seemed like miles across a huge sort of social room. There were easy chairs arranged next to the walls, and in them sat a few old people talking or playing checkers or staring into space. In the center of the room hung a great tarnished chandelier that Ben Joe could almost have reached on tiptoe. He stared past it at the old people, but his grandmother looked fixedly at the chandelier, never letting her eyes move from it.

"Can I help you?" a nurse said. She had come up soundlessly on her thick-soled shoes, and now she faced them with her arms folded across the cardboard white of her uniform and her face strangely young and cheerful.

"We've come to visit a Mr. Dower," Ben Joe said.

"Algernon Hector James Dower the Third," said his grandmother, still looking intently at the chandelier.

"You members of his family?"

"Raised together."

"Well, he's not feeling too good. He's a bed patient. If you'll only stay a few minutes . . ."

"We'll be quiet," said Ben Joe.

"Follow me, then."

She led them through the social room, toward an elevator around the corner. As they passed the other patients there was a whispering and a stirring, and everyone stared at them. "Mr. Dower," the nurse told them. They nodded and kept staring. The nurse turned back to Ben Joe and his grandmother and gave them a sudden, reassuring smile; when she smiled, her nose wrinkled like a child's and the spattering of freckles stood out in a little brown band across her face.

"If you'll just step in here," she said.

The elevator smelled dark and soapy. It was so small that it made Ben Joe nervous, and he could see that his grandmother was beginning to get that lost look on her face and was twisting her engagement ring. He smiled at her, and she cleared her throat and smiled back.

"Here we are," the nurse said cheerfully.

The door slid open. Gram bounded out like a young goat, with a suprising little kick of her heels, and looked back at the nurse.

"My, I wish *our* people were as spry as *you* are!" the nurse said.

Gram smiled.

"Are those—those are very, um, sensible shoes you're wearing," the nurse went on pleasantly. "They must be—"

"I get them at Pearson's Sport Shop," Gram said.

"Ah, I see. Down this corridor, please."

The corridor was very long and silent. It was hard to imagine that such an average-looking house could hold it all. The walls were covered with a heavy brown paper that had columns of palm leaves up and down it, and the doors were of some dark wood. At the next to the last door, which was slightly open, the nurse stopped and tapped lightly with her fingernails.

"Mr. Dower?" she called.

She peeked in, all smiles, and said, "We have company, Mr. Dower."

Then she looked backed at Ben Joe and Gram and said, "You can come in. Don't stay long, now. I'll be out here when you want to go down again."

They tiptoed in, Gram ahead of Ben Joe. Jamie Dower

was lying in a spotless white iron bed, with his white hair fluffed out around his polished little face. His eyes were as alert as when Ben Joe had first seen him, but his breathing was worse; even when he was lying flat now, there was that squeaky kittenish sound that had been there when he'd climbed the hill.

"Oh, young man," he said, recognizing Ben Joe.

"Hello, Mr. Dower."

"Who is—"

Gram stepped forward. She had her hands folded primly in front of her and she looked very small and uncertain. For a long time she looked at Jamie Dower, taking in every change she must have seen in him. Then she dropped her hands and became brisk and lively, the way she always did at a sickbed. "I look familiar?" she asked him. She flounced over to sit on the edge of the chair beside his bed and smiled brightly at him. "I look like anyone you know, Jamie Dower?"

"A doctor—"

"Oh, no, no." She twisted out of the white lab coat impatiently and flung it behind her. "Now?" she asked.

"Well, ma'am . . ."

"*I'm* Bethany Jane *Chrisawn*!" she caroled out loudly. The nurse came swiftly to the doorway and put one finger to her lips, but Gram was watching only Jamie Dower. "*Now* you remember?"

"Bethany . . ." He raised himself up on one elbow and stared at Gram puzzledly. For a minute Ben Joe held his breath; then the old man's face slowly cleared and he said, "Bethany! Bethy Jay *Chrisawn*, that's who!"

Ben Joe breathed again, and Gram nodded smugly.

"Bethy *Jay*!" the old man roared.

"Mr. Dower, *please*," the nurse said.

"Well, I'll be," said Jamie Dower. He lay back down and shook his head as he stared at her. "Bethy," he said, "you surely have changed some."

Gram turned around and beamed at Ben Joe. "I told you," she said. "Didn't I? Before we even left the house I said to Ben Joe, I said, 'I bet he won't recognize me.' This is Ben Joe Hawkes, Jamie. My grandson. He's the one told me you were here."

"I'm going," the nurse called across to Ben Joe, barely mouthing the words. She trilled the fingers of one hand at him, gave him a warning look, and vanished.

"Never thought you'd still be alive," Jamie said.

"Why, I'll be! I'm younger'n *you* are."

"Well, I know that. I know."

He tried to sit up higher, and Gram reached behind him to pull the pillows up.

"You're looking good, Jamie," she said.

"That's funny. View of the fact that I'm dying."

"Oh, now, *you're* not dying."

"Don't argue, Bethy Jay. Your word against the doctor's and I'll take the doctor's any day. Yes sir, I'm dying and I come to die where I was born at, like any good man should. Not that I'd *recognize* the damn place."

"Language, Jamie. You're right, town has changed some."

"Sure has. This your grandson, hey? You got married?"

"Well, of *course* I got married. What'd you think?" She sat up straighter and glared at him. "I married Lemuel Hawkes, that's who."

"Lemuel *Hawkes?*"

"Why, sure."

"That kind of chubby guy whose voice wasn't changed?"

"Well, by the time I *married* him it was changed," Gram said. "Good *heavens*, Jamie."

"When I knew, when I knew—" He laughed, and the laugh ended in a wheezy little cough. "When I knew him he was sending away for all kinds of creams and secret remedies, that's what. He had this kind of black syrup made by the Indians, you're supposed to put it on your throat and lie out in the moonlight with it, and it was guaranteed to give a manly vibrance to your voice. A 'manly vibrance,' that's the exact words. Only his mother found him lying under the clothesline and all she could see was something dark and wet all over his neck, oh, God—" He choked and choked again and still laughed, with his little wheezing breaths pulling him almost to a sitting position.

"When *I* knew him," Gram said firmly, "he sang bass in the Baptist choir. Had his own business, and—"

"Did he have a little sort of pot above his belt? With his navel sitting on it like a button on a mountain? Oh, God—" and he was off again, laughing delicately this time so as not to choke.

"*And*," Gram said, "I married him and had four girls and a boy and all of them healthy. Lemuel he died after the children were grown on account of having influenza, but the children are all alive to this day excepting Phillip, who passed on due to a combination of circumstances. And he left behind him seven children, Joanne Ben Joe

Susannah Lisa Jane Jenny and Tessie and a wife and a granddaughter Carol who is just as—"

"Let me say mine," the old man said. He struggled up higher against the pillows and folded his hands across the sheet. "While making bed linens in New Jersey I married my secretary though of good family and not just an every*day* secretary, mind you, and to my grief she died having Samuel our son—"

"You're not married any more?"

"Don't interrupt me. You always were one to interrupt me. I raised him honest and respectful and first he kept books—"

"A *bookie?*"

"A book*keeper*, for our company and gradually rose to an even higher position than I ever had. He has now got a wife and six healthy children Donald Sandra Mara Alex Abigail and uh, uh, Suzanne and one of them—"

"*I* got a grandchild named Susannah," Gram said.

"*One* of them, I say—"

"How's she spell it?"

"*One* of them went to *Europe!*" the old man shouted joyfully.

"Is that so!"

"Summer before last, she went."

"*My* Susannah is spelled kind of like 'Savannah,' Georgia," said Gram. "Only it's *Sus*annah."

"Well, mine's not. It was Sandra that went to Europe. She got to see the Pope."

"The Pope!" Gram's mouth fell open. "Why, Jamie Dower, you haven't gone and become a—"

"Oh, no. Oh, no. But she went with this touring group,

her and her aunt, and the itinerary said they could have an audience with the Pope. The family came to me and asked what I thought of it; they ask me about everything important. And I said, 'Sandra, honey,' I said, 'I'll tell you what do. You go visit the Pope and then right after that, the very same day, you go see a *Protestant* minister too. And encourage him in his work and all.' Only it turned out the touring group had to move on before she could track down a Protestant. She was heart*broken* about not keeping her promise."

"Did she sell the clothes the Pope blessed her in?" Gram asked.

"Oh, yes. Excepting her shoes. I think it's good to keep *some*thing he blessed her in, just in case, you know."

"Ma'am," the nurse said, "remember what I said about keeping it short, now. If you could be thinking about drawing your visit to a close . . ."

She was standing in the doorway with her hands pressed neatly together in front of her, and when they looked up she smiled. Ben Joe, leaning silently upon the window sill, nodded at her. When she was gone he turned back to look out at the view, but Gram and Jamie kept on staring blankly at the place where she had been. Their faces seemed crushed and pale. Finally Gram forced her bright smile again and began anxiously working her dry little hands together.

"Um, Jamie," she said. "Do you remember the time your cousin Otis bought a wild horse?"

"Horse?"

"I was thinking about it while watching a Western

the other night. He bought this wild horse that couldn't *no*body tame and rode off on it practically upside-down, the horse was bucking so bad, but he was waving his scarf and shouting all the same, with your mother and your aunt on the porch watching after him and crying and wringing their hands. And after dark he came back safe and sound and singing, with the horse so polite, and dismounted into the sunken garden and broke his leg in two places. Oh, law, I reckon I never *will* forget—"

"You know," said Jamie, "I just can't recall it."

"Well, it came to me out of the blue, sort of."

He nodded, and for a minute there were only the kitten squeaks of his breathing.

"Then I reckon you remember Grandfather Dower getting religion," he said finally.

"Not offhand I don't."

"Sure you do. Along came this revivalist by the name of Hezekiah Jacob Lee, preaching how nothing material is real and things of the spirit is all that counts. He only stayed for some three days of preaching, but Grandfather Dower, he latched right on. Gave up his swaggering ways and his collecting of old American saloon songs and went around acting unfit to live with. And one day, after Hezekiah Jacob Lee had been gone about a month, Great-Aunt Kazi got stung by a bee on the wrist knob and naturally she went to Grandfather, him being a doctor, and he stamped his foot and shouted, 'Don't bother *me* with your material matters; put mud on it, woman!' when suddenly he frowned and his eyes kind of opened and he said to her, 'Why,' he says, '*why* do you reckon Hezekiah Jacob Lee went off and left me holding the bag this way?' And what a party there was *that* night, with alcohol floating on the garden path—"

"I declare," Gram said, "it rings a bell, sort of. I just vaguely do remember."

They were quiet again, thinking. Jamie Dower drew the edge of his sheet between his small, brittle fingers.

"About all that's left now is Arabella," said Gram.

"Arabella."

"Your cousin, the fat one. Auntie Adams's little girl."

"Oh, her."

"I don't see her much," Gram said. "She was always kind of a prissy girl."

"She was. She was at that. She went to study in Virginia, I remember, before I'd even left home. We heard from her regular but stopped reading her letters."

"It was on account of her mother, I believe," Gram said. "She was the same way. Told Arabella to watch out for germs in public places. Every letter Arabella sent us after that sounded like something from a health inspector. All these long detail-ly descriptions of every— You remember that? Auntie Adams finally wrote back and said she would take Arabella's word for it, but I don't recall that Arabella paid her any mind."

"How about her brother Willie?" Jamie asked.

"Oh, he was prissy too. That whole *section* of the family was prissy."

"No, I mean, what is he doing now?"

"Oh. Well, he's dead. He died about a year ago."

"I didn't know that."

"And of course Auntie Adams is dead. She died."

"I remember someone telling me."

"All that's left now," said Gram, "is Arabella."

They both stared at a place in Jamie's blanket. Behind them the door cracked open softly and the nurse poked her head in and said, "About time to be saying our good-bys now."

"Do you remember," Jamie said suddenly, "do you remember that funny old L-shaped bench that sat on your front porch?"

"What color was it?"

"Green. Dark green. Forest green, I think they call it. Us kids used to sit all together on it in the summer afternoons and eat fresh peaches out of a baskety box. Remember?"

"Well, no."

"I do. I do. You-all were having Hulda Ballew as your maid then, and is was she that set the peaches out for us to dice up small with sharp kitchen knives and eat in little bitty bites, the boys to poke a bite on the tip of a knife to some girl they liked and she to bite it off, dainty like, on summer afternoons. You got to remember that."

"Well, I don't," Gram said. "I remember Hulda Ballew, but no green bench comes to mind."

"You got to remember."

"Ma'am," the nurse said.

Something in her voice made Gram know it was time to give up. Her shoulders sagged and she fell silent, but she kept staring at the blanket.

"Say bye to our guests, Mr. Dower."

"I'm coming," said Gram. "We'll come back, Jamie Dower. If you want us."

"That'll be right nice, Beth. Funny thing," he said,

looking at her suddenly. "You were such a *fat* little girl."

Gram patted his hand on the sheet and then stood up and left the room, so suddenly that she took all of them by surprise.

"Well, good-by," said Ben Joe.

"Good-by, young man."

"You take a nice little nap now," the nurse said. She pulled the venetian blinds shut and then tiptoed out of the room behind Ben Joe, closing the door behind her. "He's not well at all," she whispered as they walked down the hall. "I don't know how he lasted this long, or managed to get here all by himself."

"Hush," Ben Joe said. They were approaching Gram, who stood waiting by the elevator. The nurse nodded without surprise and clamped her mouth shut.

When they were out in the car again Ben Joe said, "Put on your coat, Gram, you'll catch cold."

"All right, Ben Joe."

"You want me to turn the heat on?"

"Oh, no."

He started the motor but let it idle while he watched her, trying to think whether there was something to say or whether there was even any need for anything to be said. Her face, with its clown's coating of rouge, told him nothing. When he kept on watching her, she folded her arms across her chest and turned away, so that she was looking out of the window toward the home. Ben Joe let the car roll out into the street again.

"That house," Gram said, looking back at the home, "wasn't even *here* when Jamie Dower was born."

"I know."

"It wasn't even here when we were growing up, did you know *that?* They hadn't laid the first brick yet. They hadn't even dug the foundation yet. There were only trees here, trees and brambly bushes with those little seedy blackberries on them that aren't fit for pies, even—"

"I know. I know."

She grew silent. He didn't know what her face looked like now. And he didn't try to find out, either. He just looked straight ahead at the road they drove on, and kept quiet.

12

On the wall behind the silverware drawer in the kitchen was a combination blackboard and bulletin board, frayed at the edges now from so many years of use. Ben Joe stood leaning against the refrigerator with a tomato in his hand and studied the board very carefully, narrowing his eyes. First the blackboard part. Jenny's great swooping handwriting took up half the board:

Eggs
Lavoris
Contact lense fluid

Who in this family wore contact lenses? He frowned and shook his head; he felt like a stranger. Under Jenny's list his grandmother had written, in straight little angry letters:

Chewing gum

And then came Tessie's writing, round and grade-schoolish, filling up the rest of the board right down to the bottom:

What shall we do about it? I will think of somthing. What I want to know is, how do you think?

He switched the tomato to his left hand and picked up the piece of chalk that hung by a string from the board. With his mouth clamped tight from concentrating, he bent forward, inserted an "e" in "somthing," and then stepped back to look at it. After a minute he underlined the "e" twice and then dropped the chalk and reread the whole message. Something about it still confused him.

His eyes moved over to the bulletin-board part. In the old days it had been crowded with the children's drawings, ranging from kindergarten-level pictures of houses with smoking chimneys up to the tiny complicated landscapes Ben Joe had done in upper grade school. Now only one of them was left—a drawing done by Jenny, when she was six, of a circle superimposed on a furry cylinder, which she had said was the Lone Ranger and Silver seen from above. Other than that, there were only two yellowed scraps of paper. The first was one of the few reminders of his father that had been allowed to remain; it was a note written by Susannah, back when her writing was as uncertain as Tessie's, saying:

Mama, the last five times that Gram has gone to a church supper and you've gone to a Legal Women Voters' supper both at the same time Daddy has fed us as follows: (1) popcorn (2) grilled cheese sandwiches (3) fudge (4) popcorn (5) ice cream, please talk to him.

Ben Joe frowned again, considered changing the comma to a semicolon, but eventually let it go for some reason and turned to the next piece of paper. This was his own, in crooked, preschool capitals, and he could not remember when or for what reason he had written it. It said:

Song By
Benjamin Josiah Hawkes

What shall we do with the trunk-ed sailor
Is a matter worth disgusting.
Everybody's pinto is agoing to heaven
Heaven, in the morning.

It had a tune, his mother had told him, something like the scissors-mender's chant, all on one note, except that the last word in each line was several notes lower. They said he used to sing it at the beach, but he had no memory of it now.

He looked down at his tomato. There was a bite in it, although he hadn't noticed he had taken one. He considered storming into the den and accusing Tessie of spit-backing, which was a habit she had developed after biting into chocolates that turned out to be caramel-filled; but on second thought he decided he might have taken a bite after all. There was no telling. He had been confused and absent-minded all day; he attributed it to the visit at the home for the aged, but just knowing the reason didn't help him any. All he could think of that might help was to isolate himself in the kitchen for a while after supper and stare at the bulletin board, where years arranged themselves one on top of the other in layers before his eyes. Sometimes that helped. Sometimes it didn't, too. He sighed, took another bite from his tomato, and began rereading the blackboard.

Eggs
Lavoris . . .

"What are *you* doing here?" Jenny asked.

"Why?"

"I thought you were just going out to get a snack. You missed the last half of the program."

"Oh. Okay."

He moved aside to let her get into the refrigerator.

"Ben Joe . . ."

"*What*," he said. Every time she interrupted him he had to go back to the very top of the blackboard and begin reading all over again.

"Never mind," she said.

"Well, go *on*, now that you've interrupted me."

"I just wanted to know where the ice water is. I'm getting some for Gram. What's the matter with you tonight?"

"I don't know. I went with Gram to the old folks' home." He jammed his hands into his pockets and with the toe of his sneaker he began tracing patterns in the linoleum. There was no sense in going back to reading the blackboard until Jenny was out of the room again.

She had found the ice water. She poured it into an orange-juice glass and put the jar back in the refrigerator.

"Hey, I wonder . . ." she said suddenly.

But Ben Joe, off on another track now, interrupted her. "Who in this family wears contact lenses?" he asked.

"Contact— Oh, you're talking about the list. Susannah does."

"How come I didn't know?"

"You weren't here," Jenny said.

"Oh."

"She got them with her first pay check from the library, after she switched jobs."

"I never heard about it."

"You weren't *here*, I said." She picked up the glass of water and started out again. At the door she stopped. "What I was just wondering," she said, "was it this morning you went to the home? With Gram?"

"Yes."

"Well, why don't you come out into the living room? Gram just heard an old friend of hers died. She says she only saw him this morning, so that must be who it is. That Mr. Dower."

"He's dead?"

"That's what she said."

"But he can't be. We only saw him this morning."

"Doesn't stop him from being dead, does it? Why do people always—"

"Ah, no," said Ben Joe. He shook his head gently and turned his back to the bulletin board. (What good would it do him now?) There was no reason for him to feel so sad, but he did, anyway, and he just kept staring at a corner of the kitchen cabinet while Jenny watched him curiously.

"Why don't you come talk to Gram?" she asked him.

"Well . . ."

"Come on."

She backed against the door to open it and let Ben Joe pass through ahead of her. "All I ever know to do is get people water," she said, "I know when *I'm* sad *I* don't want water, and I don't guess others do, either, but it's all I know to do."

"Well, I'm sure she'd like it," Ben Joe said.

"Maybe so."

In the living room he found his grandmother upright on the couch, sitting very stiffly with her hands in her lap and her eyes dry. Around her was clustered most of the family, some sitting next to her and some on chairs around the room.

"Only this morning," she was saying. "Only this morning." She caught sight of Ben Joe and called out, "Wasn't it, Ben Joe? Wasn't it only this morning?"

"Yes," said Ben Joe.

"There. Ben Joe can tell you." She turned to nod at the others and then, realizing that Ben Joe hadn't yet heard the whole story, she looked his way again. "I called the home," she said. "I wanted to tell him about something I'd forgotten. This evening I was just hunting under the bed for Carol's hair brush and suddenly it came to me, so clear: Jamie's mustache cup."

"His what?" Ben Joe asked.

"Mustache cup. Mustache cup. You know, Jamie Dower was the only man I ever knew who really did use a mustache cup. That was something wonderful, when I was twelve. He got it just the last year he was home, on account of this lovely mustache he was growing. He was kind of a dandy, Jamie Dower. *Always* was. But it was a beautiful mustache, I have to say. Ben *Joe* knows. You tell them, Ben Joe."

"Well . . ." Ben Joe said. The picture of Jamie's face was before him, small and white and clean-shaven.

"Ben Joe knows," Gram said to the rest of them. She smiled down at her hands. "I know it's a small thing, but I suddenly thought of that mustache cup, white with pink rosebuds, it was, and I just had to tell him about it.

So I called the home, and after a right long spell of hemming and hawing they told me. They said he had passed on just an hour ago. I didn't let on how it hit me. I just said I hoped he'd had a peaceful passing, and hung up." Her mouth shook for a minute, and the first tear slid down the dry paper of her cheek. "But it was only this *morning* . . ." she said.

A glass of water was poked suddenly under her chin. Gram drew back and blinked at it through her tears. Her eyes traveled slowly from the glass itself to the poker-stiff arm that held it and above that to Jenny's face, sober and embarrassed.

"Why, thank you," she said. She took the glass, looked at it a minute, and then smiled at Jenny and drank until the glass was empty. "There is nothing like clear water," she told Jenny formally.

Ben Joe looked around at the rest of the family. His mother was in the easy chair, looking worried; Tessie was on the arm of the chair, and the twins and Susannah were sitting around their grandmother on the couch. All of them were unusually quiet. When the silence had gone unbroken for at least a full minute, his mother cleared her throat and said, "We'll have to send a nice wreath of flowers, Gram."

"He wouldn't like it," Gram said. "Used to get angry when I brought him my dessert."

"Your— Well, anyway. It'd be a nice gesture to send a small wreath, just to show—"

"I will *not* send him *flowers!*" Gram said.

Ellen Hawkes was quiet a moment, figuring this out. Finally she said, "Well, some people prefer the money to go to a worthy cause instead. Maybe to the missionary league of his church, if he has one—"

"I tell you, no, Ellen. He never could accept a gift graciously. My mother said accepting gifts graciously is the true test of a gentleman, but I don't go along with that. Jamie Dower was a gentleman all the way through. He just didn't like gifts, is all."

"But that was some seventy *years* ago, Gram—"

"No point discussing it," said Ben Joe. "We don't send flowers."

Gram began crying again. The girls fluttered and crowded in around her and Jenny backed toward the door, in case she had to get more ice water. Ellen Hawkes clicked her tongue.

"What's going on?" Joanne said.

She was standing in the doorway dressed to go out and carrying a coat over her arm. Everyone looked up except Gram, who had just been handed Ben Joe's handkerchief and was now blowing her nose in it.

"Gram's lost an old friend," Susannah said.

"Oh, no." She came quickly over to the couch and knelt down in front of her grandmother. "Who was it?"

"Jamie Dower," said Gram, "and I can't send him flowers."

"Well, of course you can. What's the matter with this family? Mom, since when have we got so poor we can't send—"

"My God," her mother said. She stood up and left the room, not sharply but with a slow kind of weariness.

"It's not the money," Ben Joe said. "It's that Jamie never could accept a gift graciously."

"Oh, I see." She nodded and began gently stroking Gram's shoulder.

"If you see," her mother said from the doorway, "will you please explain it to *me?*"

"Well, it makes sense."

"Not to me it doesn't. Does it to you, Ben Joe?"

"Well, yes," said Ben Joe.

His mother vanished into the hallway.

"What *doesn't* make sense," Ben Joe said, "is why it makes you unhappy not sending him flowers. If you know he'd be happier not getting them."

"Because I *want* to send them, that's why," his grandmother said. "I always did want to give him flowers."

She began crying into her handkerchief, and the other girls moved over so that Joanne could sit beside her and hug her. "I know, I know," she said soothingly. "Now, I tell you what do, Gram. You just buy some flowers and give them to someone you like. Prettiest flowers you can find. And then you tell yourself you wouldn't have done it if Jamie Dower hadn't died. That way you solve the whole thing, right?"

"Well, maybe," Gram said.

The doorbell rang. Joanne gave Gram a brisk pat on the shoulder and stood up. "Don't bother," she told Ben Joe. "I'll get it. It's my date."

"What?"

But she didn't answer; she was already out of the room. Gram refolded the handkerchief to a dry place and then suddenly, in the middle of the process, stopped and looked up at Ben Joe. "What'd she say?" she asked.

"She said it was her date."

"Did she mean her appointment? Or did she mean her date?"

"Her date, is what she said."

All of them fell silent, listening. A young man laughed in the front hallway. Ben Joe could read in Gram's face the slow transition from grief to indignation.

"Why, *she* can't do that!" she said. "Joanne?"

The two voices ran on, ignoring her.

"*Joanne!*" Gram said.

Joanne reappeared, still carrying her coat over her arm.

"Who's that you got with you?" Gram asked.

"John Horner, Gram. Come on in, John."

John Horner appeared next to her, soundlessly. He still had his broad, open smile and he didn't seem to think it strange to be greeted by a whole silent, staring family grouped around a weeping old woman. He nodded to all of them in general and lifted a hand toward Ben Joe, whom he recognized.

"This is my grandmother," said Joanne. "And Ben Joe, and Susannah, and Jane, Lisa, Jenny, and Tessie. This is John Horner."

"How do you do?" John Horner said. He was addressing mainly Gram, as the oldest member of the family, but Gram just sat up straighter and stared narrowly at him.

"I wish I'd of married Jamie Dower," she said.

"Ma'am?"

"Gram has just heard that a friend passed away," Joanne began. Her voice was the old high-school Joanne's, soft and bubbling. She stood very close to John Horner while she talked to him. Under cover of Joanne's voice Gram went on muttering to the others.

"If I'd of married Jamie," she said, "I would of had a different family. On account of different genes mingling. They wouldn't all have gone and done queer things, or acted so—"

"Hush, Gram," Susannah said.

"Ben Joe?" Joanne called.

"What."

"John was asking you something."

"Excuse me?"

"I was just asking," said John, "aren't you the one that's at Columbia?"

"That's right."

"I was there for a while. Took a business course. Mrs. Hawkes, ma'am, I'm sorry to hear about your friend's passing."

Gram frowned. "Well," she said ungraciously. She thought a minute and then added, "Troubles always descend lots at a time, seems like."

"They do," said John. He came further into the room to sit on the arm of the rocker, and Joanne moved over to stand beside him. "My old man had a saying. My old man used to say, 'It never rains but it—' "

"Who is your daddy?" Gram asked suddenly.

"Jacob Hart Horner, ma'am."

"Jacob Hart Horner. That so."

"Yes'm."

"Oh. I know him."

"Do you really?" He smiled politely.

"*Yes,* I know him."

"Ah."

Gram nodded a while, considering.

"What you think he'd say if he saw you here?" she asked.

The silence before her question had been long enough so that John was just beginning to consider the conversation over. He froze now, in the act of turning toward Joanne, and looked back at Gram blankly.

"Ma'am?" he said. "What's that?"

"If he saw you here. If Jacob Hart Horner saw you here. What you think he'd say?"

"If he saw me *here?*"

"*Yes*, here."

"I don't—"

"Saw you taking Joanne out. Joanne Hawkes *Bentley* out. What you think he'd say?"

"Well, nothing, I don't guess."

"Nothing." She nodded again, with her eyes fixed veiled and thoughtful upon the floor. "No, I don't guess he would," she said finally. "*I* remember Jacob Hart Horner. Remember him well. Came here in his teens, he did, and took up with my boy Phillip. He was supposed to be working, but he didn't do much of *that*. Lived off little Sylvester Grant and my boy Phillip. I never *will* forget, one time he called his folks long distance from this very house and me sitting in the same room listening to him. I reckon they wanted to know had he got a steady job and he said yes, he was working in the chicken cannery. There was a chicken cannery then, down by the river near the blue-denim factory, but I never saw *him* near it. And I reckon they wanted to know what he did there, because he started talking about carrying grain —said that was his job. Now, I don't know what his folks were like and I don't *want* to know, but let me just ask you this: what kind of intelligence do you suppose they had, to believe a body could get a job carrying grain in a factory that deals with dead chickens?"

"Well, now, I don't know," John Horner said. He was laughing, and didn't seem to be insulted.

"There's bad blood there," Gram said. She looked at him a while, at the friendly face with the dark eyes made slits by laughter, and then she blew her nose and looked down into her lap. "I am getting old," she said.

The room grew silent. John looked over at Joanne soberly, and she clutched her coat more tightly to her and started toward the door.

"Gram," she said, "I hope you feel better."

"Well. New things come up. A minute ago Jamie Dower slipped from my mind altogether for a second."

"Sure. It's always that way. You'll—"

"What I was meaning to bring up a minute ago," Gram began, "what I wanted to say . . ."

She stopped and looked over at Ben Joe.

"Um," he said. He took his hands out of his pockets and walked over to where John was standing beside Joanne.

"What's the matter?" Joanne asked.

"Well, I was just wondering." He looked at her face, with its blank brown eyes, and then changed his mind and directed the question toward John. "What I think Gram was trying to say," he said, ". . . well, hell with it, what *I'm* trying to say is, it doesn't look to me like a good idea for you to be going out, Joanne." But he was still facing John; it was to John's more open eyes that he said it.

"Why *not,*" John said, turning it into a challenge instead of a question.

"Well, it's a small town. That's one reason."

"Small town, what's *that* got to do with it? Listen, boy, you and your family got to stop hanging on to your sister this way. Got to start—"

"But she's still *married,* damn it!"

His mother, coming in on the tail end of the sentence, stopped in the doorway and looked at Ben Joe.

"What?" she said.

Ben Joe turned to her. "Mom, I'm asking you, now. Do you think Joanne ought to go out on a date?"

His mother frowned. "Well," she said finally, "I don't know. If it's just an old friend of hers, I don't see the harm in her getting out of the house for a while. It's up to Joanne, after all. None of *our* business."

"But he's *not* just an old *friend*!"

"What is he, then?"

There was a silence. Everyone looked at him.

"Frankly," John said finally, "I don't see how—"

"No, listen. Please *listen*!"

"We're listening, Ben Joe," said his mother.

"No, you're not. You never are. Look, I was just worrying if people would *talk.*"

"What would they talk about?"

He sat down, realized immediately the disadvantage at which this put him when everyone else was standing, and stood up again.

"Joanne," he said, "don't you see my point?"

"No," Joanne said.

"John? *You* do."

"I'm sorry, I don't," said John.

"*You* talk, don't you?" Ben Joe said. He took a step closer to him. "Don't you?"

John blinked his eyes at him.

"Look," Ben Joe said. He was facing all of them now, with his arms straight by his sides and his fists clenched. "All I'm trying to do is stop one more of those amazing damned things that go on in this family and everyone takes for granted, pretends things are still all right and the world's still right-side up. The most amazing things go on in this family, the most *amazing* things, that no one *else* would *allow*, and this family just keeps on—"

"Just what sort of amazing things are you talking about?" his mother asked. She was looking at him straight on and sternly, with her eyes just slits. "This family's just like any other family, Ben Joe. There's nothing going on here that—"

"Oh, *no?*"

"No."

He slitted his eyes back at her.

"Just to give you a for-instance," he said, "I don't know if you all can dredge far enough back in your memories or not, but I can recall a time when Dad and the sheriff were out all one night in their pajamas—"

"That is *enough*," his mother said.

"—pajamas, chasing down to Dillon, South Carolina, because Joanne had run off with a total stranger that came here selling clear plastic raincoats one autumn afternoon, run off to get married as soon as he asked her, which as near as we could figure it was three seconds after she had opened the front door to his ringing, and Dad was frantically chasing down every highway to Dillon and finally found them at seven-thirty in the morning waiting to fill out a marriage license. And he brought her back and everyone just said, 'Well, let her sleep.' "

"It's true!" Gram said. "It's true. I remember it all!"

"What else could we have done?" his mother asked the clock.

"Which was fine, except didn't they wonder even what *led* to it, or *why*, or try to do something to help her? No, and at supper they all told jokes and passed the biscuits and there was Joanne with a new trick, a piece of plastic that looked just exactly like vomit—she'd bought it at the magic store—and she was retching and then throwing the plastic on the floor, and she squealed, 'Ooh, wouldn't my vomit go good on the living room *rug*!' and you all laughed and ran with her to the living room and life went on, and on, while—"

Joanne stepped up, and for a minute he thought she was going to hit him, but instead she pushed her coat in his face, choking him with the force of it, leaving him in a forest-green darkness that smelled of wool and spice perfume. He could feel the bones of her hands pressing through the wool to his face, and above the uproar John Horner was shouting, "Stop it, *stop* it!" but the coat was still being pushed against his face.

"Anybody home?" someone called.

There was a long, deep silence.

The coat fell away from Ben Joe's face and hung, crumpled, around his shoulders. He blinked his eyes several times. Everyone in the room was looking toward the door, with their faces blank, staring at the tallest man Ben Joe had ever seen. He was bony and freckled with a long, friendly face, and though his overcoat hung on him badly, there was something very easy and graceful about the way he was standing.

"I would have called," he said cheerfully, "but then if I had, you probably would be gone when I got here. And I would have waited for you to answer the door, but a man can't wait forever. Can he?" he asked, and grinned at Ben Joe.

People were coming out of their surprise now, opening their mouths to speak, but the stranger had moved rapidly into the center of the room with his hands still in his pockets and he said, "I knew the house. Know it anywhere. Though that glider has *got* to be new. I didn't know that. You people are—" he looked around at them, still cheerfully— "Gram, Ben Joe, Mom, uh . . . Jenny? and a man I don't know with, of course, Joanne—"

"You go away," Joanne said softly.

"But I only just got here."

"I'm telling you, Gary . . ."

But before the name was out of her mouth, Ben Joe knew. He suddenly recognized the hair, flaming red and pushed carelessly back from his forehead exactly like Carol's, and the familiar-looking eyes that had stared out of the dim snapshot. He stood gaping at the three of them—Joanne and Gary and John—in a brightly tensed, three-cornered group in the center of the room.

“I’m leaving,” he said.

“Ben Joe!” his mother called.

“I don’t care, I don’t care, I’m *leaving*!”

And he shoved the coat back in Joanne’s face. It fell to the floor, but she let it stay there and didn’t look his way. Jenny was in his path; he pushed her aside without even knowing it and flew through the hallway and out the door. Then he was outside. He was in the dark wind, with the cold already slapping at his face.

13

Shelley's face was small and white; her hair was a mass of sausage-shaped curlers, shrouded under a heavy black net. She stood behind her screen door and looked out to where Ben Joe stood on the porch, under the yellow outside light, and to Ben Joe it seemed as if she was suddenly considering every detail of him, weighing him in the back of her faraway mind. With one hand she reached up vaguely to touch her curlers, obeying that part of her that wondered always, no matter what, whether she was fit to be seen. But it was only the most absent-minded gesture. Her eyes were still fixed on him, and she frowned a little and bent forward to see him more clearly.

"It's me," Ben Joe said.

"I know."

She kept watching him. The two of them seemed to be standing between the two ticks of a clock, in a dead silence of time where there was no need to hurry about anything; as long as she stayed silent and watchful they were frozen stock-still between that clock's ticking. Then she gave up, not finished with whatever it was she was trying to do but just giving up in the middle of it, and, clutching her quilted bathrobe more tightly about her, opened the door for him.

"I've been walking for hours," he said.

She nodded. Nothing seemed to surprise her. When he stepped inside she held up both hands, in a gesture like a doll's in a toy-shop window, to take the light sweater he was wearing, and he shucked it off and handed it to her.

"I know you weren't expecting company," he told her as she turned to hang up his sweater. "You can go on and do whatever you were doing before. I won't mind."

She didn't answer. The hangers in the closet tinkled flatly as she rummaged among them, and when she lifted one from the rod another fell with it, making a blurred explosive sound as it landed on a floor full of old rubbers and high-heeled galoshes. She ignored it; her eyes concentrated upon what suddenly seemed, to Ben Joe, the impossibly complicated task of getting his sweater upon the hanger. What was wrong with Shelley? Her fingers fumbled tightly at the collar of the sweater, taking hours to make it lie straight around the hook of the hanger. If it had been any other night, Ben Joe would have gone on in, would have left her in the hallway and headed for the living-room sofa. But tonight he felt uneasy. He wanted to tread as delicately as possible so that she would turn out to be glad he came. So he stood clenching his cold aching hands together and waiting hopefully for

Shelley to finish this interminable business of getting his sweater up, and he never even looked toward the living room.

"I reckon you'll want some bourbon," she said.

"No."

"It'll do you good, if you're cold."

She headed toward the kitchen, making only the softest whispering noise across the floor in her bare feet. After a minute Ben Joe followed her. If she took so long to hang a sweater up, how long would she spend making a drink? And he really didn't want one; he felt awkward and foolish stumbling in here like this, and he didn't want to make it worse by accepting anything.

"I'm sorry I came without warning," he said.

"It's all right."

"I should have called first."

"It's all *right,* Ben Joe."

She stood on tiptoe to reach a liquor bottle from the cupboard, and Ben Joe leaned against the kitchen sink. He was surprised at how messy everything was; ordinarily Shelley was almost old-maidishly tidy. He could remember her spreading peanut butter on a piece of bread and then washing the knife and putting it and the peanut butter away even before she finished making the sandwich. And she had some sort of phobia about seeing that all the cannisters were neatly aligned along the counter and all the measuring spoons hung in order on the wall according to their sizes. But tonight the place was in chaos. Dishes and leftovers littered the counter; a recently washed sweater was balled up in the dish drainer and a shower cap was flung over the towel rack. He looked around at Shelley, trying to figure out what sort of mood she must be in. In her pale flowered bathrobe, a little too small for her, she looked wire-thin and brittle. But the shyness was gone, so much forgotten that she seemed not at all embarrassed at being caught in her bathrobe. In place of the shyness was a sort of heavy sullenness that he hadn't often seen in her before, that made her face look fuller and the lower lines of her cheeks sag. Her eyebrows had lost the high, uncertain arch they usually had and sat straight over blank eyes, and she was poking out her mouth in a way that made it seem like a pouting child's mouth. When she poured the drink she did it heavily, with finality.

"Have you got something on your mind?" Ben Joe asked.

She stopped, looked at the bottle, and then reached for another glass and poured a drink for herself.

"If you do," he said, "I wish you'd tell me. I hate this ferreting things out of people. I ask what's wrong and they say nothing, and then I say *please* to tell me and they say no, really, it's nothing, and I say well, I can just *feel* something's wrong. And by then we both hate each other. I keep thinking of everything bad I've done in the last ten years, things you wouldn't even begin to know, but somehow I start thinking maybe you've found out—"

"Oh, Ben Joe," Shelley said tiredly.

She handed him his drink and then picked up her own and headed for the living room. Behind her Ben Joe walked slowly, dragging his feet and watching the back of Shelley's head. The curlers bobbed up and down cheerfully, but her shoulders were slumped and careless.

When they entered the living room, Shelley chose a seat in the wicker chair by the fireplace and Ben Joe had to sit alone on the couch opposite her. He felt exposed and defenseless, with all that bare expanse of couch at either side of him.

"I would do anything to help," he said. "But I don't know what's wrong."

Shelley raised her eyebrows slightly, as if what he was saying was a curious little toy he had handed her and she wanted to act polite about it. He had forgotten that she could be this way. He had seen her angry only a few times in his life—once or twice when he had dated other girls, and then one memorable time when she had taken three months to knit him a sweater in high school and then found he had grown two inches while she was busy knitting. Each time that she had been angry, the change in her had surprised him all over again. She became suddenly cool and haughty, and she left him feeling bewildered. Tonight no matter how hard he looked at her, no matter how patiently he waited for her to speak, she was unchangingly cool and blank-faced, sitting aloof in her solitary wicker chair. He sighed and took a long drink of the straight warm bourbon. He thought about the bourbon winding slowly to his stomach; with his head cocked, he seemed to be listening to it, noting carefully which part of him it was burning now. Shelley was turned into a carefully shut-out inanimate object on the other side of the room. A tune began in his head, hummed nonchalantly by that sexless, anonymous voice that lived inside him and always spoke words as he read them and thoughts as he thought them.

"So I guess I won't be coming tomorrow night," he said absently. Shelley's fingernail, tapping rhythmically against her glass, was suddenly stilled. "I've got to go back to New York."

The fingernail resumed its tapping. Ben Joe watched a specific place on the coffee table, a corner where the dust had gathered between the table top and the raised rim of it in a tiny triangle. He suddenly thought, without meaning to or wanting to, that tomorrow night when he was rattling northward on the rickety little train, this table corner would be exactly the same, would exist solid and untouched no matter where he was. Shelley would wash and neatly stack her dishes, and Gram would roar songs at the top of her lungs while she polished the silver, and everything—the solid little coffee table, the narrow polished windows, the hundreds of curtained front doors, all this still, unchanging world of women—would stay the same while he rushed on through darkness across the garishly lit industrial plains of New Jersey and into the early-morning stillness of New York. He leaned forward, resting his chin on his hand, and stared at the floor.

"Every place I go," he said, "I miss another place."

Shelley was silent.

"I don't know why," he said, just as if she'd asked. "When I am away from Sandhill, sometimes the picture of it comes drifting toward me—just the picture of it, like some sunny little island I have got to get back to. And there's my family. Most of the time I seem to see them sort of like a bunch of picnickers in a nineteenth-century painting, sitting around in the grass with their picnic baskets and their pretty dresses and parasols, and floating past on that island. I think, I've got to get back. I think, they need me there and I have got to get back to them. But when I go back, they laugh at me and rumple my hair and ask why I'm such a worrier. And I can't tell them why. There's nothing I can tell them. Pretty soon I leave again, on account of seeing myself so weak and speechless and worried. I get to thinking about something I just miss like hell in *another* town, like this tree on a street in Atlanta that has a real electric socket in it, right in the trunk, or the trolley cars in Philadelphia making that faraway lonesome sound as they pass down an empty street in the rain, through old torn-down slum buildings with nothing but a wall-papered sheet of brick and a set of stone steps left standing . . ."

Shelley was staring at him now, with her forehead wrinkled, trying to understand and not succeeding. When he saw that he wasn't making sense he stopped, and spread his hands helplessly.

"Oh, well," he said.

"No, I'm listening."

"Well." He paused, trying to arrange his words better, but finally he gave up. "Nothing," he said. "So you go to Atlanta, and you *see* the damn electric socket, and you *go* to Philadelphia and you *see* the damn trolley cars. So what? They only turn out to be an electric socket and a trolley car, in the long run. Nothing to keep you occupied longer than five minutes, either one of them. Then, in the middle of being loose and strong and on my own, wherever I am, along through my mind floats this island of a town with my family on it, still smiling on the lawn beside their picnic baskets . . ."

Shelley nodded several times slowly, as if she understood. He couldn't tell if she really did or not. He thought probably she didn't, but what mattered more than that right now was whether she was still in that black mood of hers and whether she would tell him why. He looked across at her steadily; her face returned to its original blankness and she stared back at him.

"So you're going back to New York," she said.

"I guess."

She was silent again. He began twirling the bourbon around in his glass, watching it slosh up and leave its oily trail along the sides.

"So you just come," she said, "and then you leave."

"Well, that's what I've just been explaining to—"

"You're not fair, Ben Joe Hawkes."

He looked up; Shelley's eyes were narrowed at him and she was angry. As soon as he looked at her she reached one hand up to her curlers again and then began pulling them down, with hasty, fumbling fingers, ripping them out and tossing them into her lap, where her other hand was clenched so hard that the knuckles were white. In spite of all his worries, in spite of being concerned at her anger and sad at the way this whole night had been, a part of Ben Joe wondered detachedly why she was taking her curlers out and why she was choosing this moment to do it. He watched, fascinated. Her hair without the curlers remained still in little sausage shapes around her head, and since she had no comb handy, she began raking her fingers through the curls in order to loosen them. But all the while her face seemed unaware of what was going on, as if this business with her hair was just a nervous habit.

"You come and then you leave," she repeated, "just like that. You're not fair. The trouble with you, Ben Joe Hawkes, is you don't *think*. You're a kind enough person when you think about it, but that's not often, and most of the time you—"

"Don't think about what?" he asked.

"Your coming and your going."

"Shelley, for God's sake."

"And then on *top* of all that, there's your sister."

He stopped in the middle of putting his drink on the table and looked up. There was something nightmarish about this. It was like one of those dreams in which he was playing the leading role in a play on opening night and had no idea what the play was.

"My sister," he said.

"*Yes*, your sister."

"Which one?"

"Benjamin Hawkes, don't you joke with me."

"Well, but what *sister*?"

"What sister my foot. How can you—"

"I have six," Ben Joe said patiently. He took another breath to go on and then suddenly, realizing what she meant, let his breath out again and sank back. Once more John Horner and Joanne stood looking at him on the porch steps, stood defensively close together in the Hawkes's living room, and Ben Joe shook his head at his own stupidity. There was something about Joanne; the minute she met a man, that man seemed to belong to her. Even John Horner, whom Shelley had so definitely identified as her own, was associated in Ben Joe's mind only with Joanne now that he had seen the two of them together. He had seen them first, after all, the night that Shelley had seemed to forget about John Horner completely. It was too confusing; he shook his head and said, "Lord, I'm stupid."

"Why?" Shelley asked curiously. She seemed to have expected more of a fight, and now she was temporarily taken aback.

"Joanne, you meant."

"Well, of course." She put both hands together in her lap and stared down at them. "Mrs. Murphy told me," she said. "Well, if it hadn't of been her, it'd been someone else. This town knows everything. I know she's your sister, Ben Joe, but I tell you she's just wild. With a husband and a baby, even, she's wild. She's wild and no-count and after anyone who'll pay a little attention to her. Anyone can tell you that. Doesn't take a detective to figure it out. It's just you that won't listen. You don't hear facts too good if it's your own precious sister they concern."

"I hear them," Ben Joe said. He sat there, not looking at her, twisting his hands aimlessly between his knees.

"Oh, I didn't mean to go mud-slinging . . ." Shelley said suddenly. For the first time that evening Ben Joe saw the beginnings of tears in her eyes. She looked up shinily, with her mouth blurred and shaky, and stared hard at a point just above his head to keep from blinking the tears onto her cheeks. Shelley was the kind of girl who cried often, and from years of experience he had learned that with her the best thing was to be cheerful and brisk and to pay as little attention to the tears as possible. The little anonymous voice in his head picked up the tune again and went cheerfully da-da-deeing along. He kept his eyes upon an empty knickknack shelf in the corner behind Shelley's chair.

"Anyway," he said finally. He kept his voice pleasant and reasonable. "At least we've got to why you're angry with me."

"Why?" Shelley asked, and bit her lip hard and went on staring above him.

"Well, you were with me and therefore John went out with Joanne. It was black magic. Once in college I was in love with a coquette. She had a cute little pony tail that bobbed on the back of her head every time she took a step, and I thought she was wonderful. I would go for whole weeks without even looking at other girls, not even looking at one that I just saw on the campus somewhere, because I thought that then she wouldn't look at another boy. Sometimes it amazes me how superstitious I am. In the end, of course, she ran away and got married to this tuba player from Ditch 29, Arkansas—"

"You are just as lighthearted as a bird," Shelley said. "I declare, every time a body gets sad, it's a fact that someone'll come along all cheerful and tell them *their* problems, which aren't a bit more related—"

"I'm sorry," Ben Joe said. "I thought it was related. I'm sorry."

He began twisting his hands between his knees again, still not looking at her. When it seemed safe to start speaking again, when he was fairly sure that he hadn't sent her off into a real crying fit, he said, "All I meant was, that's why I'm to blame. Because it was me you were with. If you're superstitious too, of course. But I surely didn't mean to send John Horner off to my sister. God knows I—"

One of Shelley's tears must have escaped. She was too far away and the room was too dim for him to tell for sure, but he saw her hand flicker up to her cheek and then back to her lap again.

"Oh, well," he said, "you're probably not superstitious at all. It's probably nothing to do with that. But I'm trying to think what I've done and I can't come *up* with anything—"

"Oh, you silly," Shelley said. She hunched forward and began crying in earnest now, without trying to hide it any more, burying her face in her brittle white hands.

"Well," Ben Joe said for no reason. He searched hurriedly through his pockets, but there wasn't a handkerchief. On the mantel he spied a purse, a black leather clutch purse with a clasp, that always reminded him of old ladies. He rose and went to it just at the moment when the tune started up in his head again, but this time not even the little voice could drown out the whispery choking sounds behind him. He rushed through the contents of the purse—glasses, keys, coin purse, lipstick, arranged neatly inside—and found beneath them an unused Kleenex. Shaking the folds out of it as he went, he crossed over to Shelley and stuck the Kleenex in her hand.

"The way you talk," she said in a thick voice as she took the Kleenex, "you haven't done a thing in the world and are just asking what you did wrong to humor me, like. Well, I'll tell you what you've done." She blew her nose lightly. Ben Joe, standing over her, felt as if she might be Tessie or Carol. He wanted to say, "Come on now, blow hard. You'll never breathe again if you blow *that* way," but he resisted the urge and only waited silently for her to continue. "You just come to me when you want comforting," she said, "without ever thinking, without giving it any thought. My own mama told me that, although she thought the world of you. Like when things got bad at home you would drop over to get comforted and then leave, bam, no thought to it, and when it came time for the Pom-Pom prom you asked Dare Georges, who I *will* say was as *flighty* as the day is long, her and that little majorette suit she wore everywhere but church—"

"Oh, Shelley," Ben Joe said wearily, "try and stick to the subject, will you?"

She blew her nose and nodded at the floor. When Shelley cried she became almost ugly, with that translucent skin of hers suddenly mottled and blurred. As if she were thinking of this now, she passed one hand across her face and then through her uncombed hair, and she sat up straighter.

"It's worse this time," she said. "Worse than the times before, I mean. Because this time I had a steady boyfriend, who was getting serious, and then along you came and superstition *nothing,* it's plain fact I had to tell John Sunday night was out because of you. Well, I know it's my fault going out with you. And I know I shouldn't be crying if I turned him down for you, but he's *someone,* isn't he? Someone that'll stay, and think about me sometimes, and let me have a kitchen with pots and pans?"

She had worked herself up to a good crying session again. Her voice was shaky and her chin wobbled. Sometimes Ben Joe thought girls must actually enjoy crying, the way they kept dwelling on what made them sad. He reached down for her drink, which stood almost untouched beside her chair, and bent over her with it.

"Take a good drink," he said.

"No."

"Come on."

He held it to her mouth and she took a swallow and tried to smile. Her face was puffy, with her eyes sleepy little slits, like a child's, and her mouth smooth and swollen. He thought there must be something about tonight that made it right for crying. First Gram, and then Shelley, and in a way even he felt like crying now.

"One more drink," he said.

She drank obediently.

"You want a cigarette?"

She pressed her lips together stubbornly and shook her head. "No, thank you," she said. "They give me halitosis."

"Oh. Okay."

He took one for himself and lit it. It was the first he had had all day and it tasted bad, but he kept puffing hard and not looking at her.

"Well, it's really me to blame," Shelley said, as if they were in the middle of an unfinished conversation. "It's me. For years, now, I haven't let anyone sweep under my feet."

"Under your—"

"So that I wouldn't be an old maid. I worry too much

about having someone to settle down with, but I can't help it. Back home, when my family was alive, I would come in from work every day at the same time and climb the front steps of where we all lived thinking, 'It's five-ten just like it was yesterday and the day before, and just like then I am climbing these steps with no one but the family to greet me and the family to spend my evening with playing parcheesi and no man to care if I *ever* get home.' And I'd come in and head up the stairs toward my room and Mama would call from the parlor, she'd say, 'That you, Shelley?' and I'd say, 'It's me.' I'd climb the rest of the stairs and go toward my room and then out of Phoebe's room Phoebe would call, 'That you, Shelley?' and I'd say, 'It's me—' "

"Shelley, I don't think we're really getting anywhere with this," Ben Joe said.

"I'm explaining something, Ben Joe. I'm explaining. I'd go to my room and change to my house clothes, and I'd hang up my work dress neatly and I'd take my stockings to the bathroom and wash them out and hang them over the shower rail. Then I'd go back to my room and rearrange my underwear drawer, which I'd rearranged the week before, or I'd mend something or work a double crostic. At suppertime there'd be two questions for me. Daddy always said, 'You have a good day, Shelley?' and I said, 'Yes, Daddy,' and Mama'd say, 'You going to be doing anything special tonight?' and I'd say, 'I don't guess so, Mama.' Which was true and which went on and on, so sometimes I think I could have just sent a tape recording home from work with my same old answers on it and done as well—"

"Well, what are you telling me for?"

"I'm explaining why I'm mad at you."

"You're still mad?" he asked.

"Course I am."

"Oh, look now. Look, *don't* be mad at me."

"You come, you go," she said doggedly.

"I don't either."

"You don't?"

"Well, I won't," he said. He had a desperate, sinking feeling; there swam into his mind again the picture of himself on the train and Shelley behind in Sandhill calmly washing dishes as if he'd never been there.

"I don't believe you'll *ever* change, Ben Joe," she said.

"Shelley, *I* won't come and go. I won't go on not thinking. Look, you come with me. You come to New York."

"Oh, now, wouldn't *that* give people—"

"No, I mean it. We could . . . hell, get married. You hear? Come on, Shelley."

She stopped looking at her hands and stared at him. "I beg your pardon?" she said.

"We could . . ." The words in his mouth sounded absurd, like another line from the unknown play in his nightmare. He hesitated, and then went on. "Get married," he said.

"Why, Ben Joe, *that* wasn't what I was after. I wasn't asking—"

"No, I mean it, Shelley. I mean it. Don't be mad any more. You come with me on the train tomorrow and we'll be married in New York when we get there. You want to? Just pack a bag, and Jeremy will be our best man . . ."

She was beginning to believe him. She was sitting up

in the chair with her mouth a little open and her face half excited and half doubtful still, trying to search underneath his words to see how much he meant them.

"Sure," he said. "Oh, hell, who wants to go away and leave you with the dishes—"

"The what?"

"And come back like, I don't know, Jamie Dower maybe, with no one to recognize him but a girl, and even she went on and married someone else—"

"Ben Joe," Shelley said, "I'm not following you too well, but if you mean what you say—"

"Of course I do," Ben Joe said. And he did; he was becoming excited now, watching her face eagerly to see that she was convinced and not angry any more. "Do you want to, Shelley? I'll meet you at the station for the early-evening train tomorrow. Do you want to?"

"Well, I reckon so," Shelley said slowly. "I just don't know . . ." For the first time that evening she really smiled, even with her eyes, and she rose and crossed over to where he stood. "You won't be sorry?"

"No, I won't be sorry."

"All right," she said.

"Will *you*? Be sorry, I mean. Will you?"

"Oh, no. Didn't I always tell you that, even back in high school?"

"I guess so," he said.

"Seems like you are always loving the people that fly away from you, Ben Joe, and flying away from the people that love you. But if you've decided, this once, to do something the other way, I'll be happy to agree. I'll meet you at the station, then."

She reached up and kissed him and he smiled down at her, relieved.

"What time is it?" he asked.

"About one."

"Lord. Shelley, if it's all right with you, I want to sleep on your couch. I can't face going home right yet, and I'll be out of here before morning."

She looked a little doubtful, but then after a minute she nodded. "Won't do any harm, I guess," she said. "But it's bumpy."

"That's all right."

"Phoebe used to sleep there sometimes. She was a little bit sway-backed, and she said there was a poking-up spring on that couch that would support the curve in her back."

She gave his cheek a pat and then turned and went quickly over to the hall closet. From the top shelf she took a crazy quilt, permanently dingy from years of use.

"This ought to keep you warm," she said as she walked back to the couch. "You just hold this end, now, and I'll wrap you up in it. That's warmer than just having it over the top of you. Here."

He kicked off his shoes and then took the end of the quilt she handed him. Shelley walked around him in a circle, winding the blanket about him like a cocoon. When she was done she stood looking him over and then nodded to herself.

"You'll be fine in that," she said. "The lamp's above your head, and if you need anything you just call. Good night, Ben Joe."

"Good night."

He stood there by the couch, wrapped tightly in his quilt, until she had smiled for the last time and climbed the stairs to her room. When her bare feet padded gently across the floor above his head he laboriously unwound himself again and tucked the quilt around the foot of the couch. Then he took one of the throw cushions and placed it at the head for a pillow. He did these things with the special businesslike air that he always adopted when he didn't want to be bothered with thinking; if he let himself think tonight he would never get to sleep at all. So he sat on the couch and worked his feet down under the quilt methodically, concentrating solely upon the mechanical business of getting settled. And once he was in bed he made his mind into nothing but a blank, faceless blackboard, bare of everything that might remind him of the restless puzzling at the back of his mind.

14

IT WAS NOT YET MORNING when Ben Joe passed through the gate in front of his house again. The night was at the stage when the air seemed to be made up of millions of teeming dust specks, and although he could see everything, the outlines were fuzzy and the objects were flat and dim, like a barely tinted photograph. Ahead of him his house loomed, blank-faced. If he were passing by in a car at this hour, he would look at the house for a second and envy the people inside it, picturing them gently asleep in silent darkness. Even now he envied them, in a way. His eyes were gritty from a bad night and he thought of his sisters in their clean white beds beneath neatly curtained windows, most probably sound asleep and dreamless. But because he was no mere stranger passing by, he paused at the gate, and stared harder at the house than any stranger would have. It was such a locked-looking house, and so importantly secretive. In the daylight, especially in summer daylight, the house passed off those secrets carelessly and took on an open, joyous look; the screen door banged innumerable times and the girls in pastel dresses passed out lemonade to the young men lounging on the porch railing, and bumblebees buzzed among the overgrown hollyhocks beside the steps. But now, with those voices stilled and the porch deserted and all the windows black and closed against the winter darkness, who knew how many secrets lay inside? Who knew, from that self-important, tightly shut front door, what had gone on tonight and what new decisions his sleeping sisters had arrived at? He hesitated with his hand upon the gate and found himself swinging between loving that house and hating it, between rushing into the sleepy darkness of it and turning away and shrugging off its claim on him forever. Then the gate squeaked a little, and he pushed harder against it and walked on up the sidewalk to the front steps.

His feet on the cement made a gritty, too-clear sound; except for a few aimless chirpings in the trees around the house it was the only sound he heard. When he began climbing the steps his footsteps seemed dogged and heavy, and he thought again of how unreasonably tired he was. He had awakened often during the night, always with a sense of having forgotten something or left something undone, and even his sleep had been restless and strewn with brightly colored fragments of dreams. Now his head swam with just the effort of climbing the porch steps. Instead of going directly into the house, he turned toward the porch glider and let himself sink slowly down on it, to rest a minute and look out across the yard.

The cold of the metal glider soaked sharply through his trousers. He shivered and hugged his arms across his chest, and after a while his body became used to the cold and relaxed once more. The glider whined back and forth, making a lonesome, sleepy sound that sank into him as clearly as the sound of his footsteps had. If he were asleep now, safe inside his house in a warm, deep bed, and it were someone else upon this glider, those slow, gentle creaks would lull him into a deeper and deeper sleep. He would turn a little on his pillow and pull the blankets up closer around his ears, and the sound of the glider penetrating into his dreams would gradually build pictures in his mind of warm summer evenings and soft radio music drifting across green lawns . . .

He stood up sharply, feeling his eyes begin to mist over with sleep. If he were found asleep here in the morning, wouldn't they laugh then? Neighbors on their way to work would stop and look over the gate at him and smile. One sister would find him and would call the others delightedly, and they would all come out and laugh to see funny old Ben Joe torturing himself on a cold tin glider. Ben Joe the worrier. He would wake up to come in and have a sheepish breakfast among their little jokes, or he could sit huffishly out here and be even funnier. No, he didn't want to take a chance on falling asleep in the glider.

He sighed and crossed the wooden floor toward the front door. The backs of his legs were cold and stiff, like metal themselves, and there was a sore place in his side where Phoebe's favorite couch spring had poked him. As he was turning the key in the door he decided the only thing to do was go to his own bed. Tomorrow—or today—was going to be hectic enough and he might as well get rested up for it. The lock clicked open and he went through the complicated process of getting inside the house, ordinarily an automatic one but now, in his dreamlike state, as sharp in his mind as a slow-motion movie: press down the thumb latch, pull back hard on the door until it clicked, then abruptly press downward and inward upon the door until it gave and swung open, creaking a little and brushing across the hall carpet with a soft *sssh.* He stepped inside, pushing the front door shut behind him. There was a close, dusty smell in the hallway that rushed to meet him instantly, and for a minute he paused to adjust to the sudden darkness and warmth. He could see almost nothing. A pale flash on the wall identified the mirror; that was all. There was a deeper silence here than outdoors, but also there was the feeling that people were in the area. He no longer felt that he was by himself, even though there was no definite sound to prove it.

He headed blindly across the hall toward the stairs. As he passed the living room he looked through the wide archway of it and saw that the room was lighter, lit gray-white by the long bay windows. On the couch was a long, dark shape that stirred slightly as Ben Joe watched, and to satisfy his own curiosity, he changed direction and headed toward the couch. At his feet there was a sharp *ping;* a saucepan full of what looked like popcorn had been in his path. But the figure on the couch didn't move again, and after holding his breath for a minute, Ben Joe went on. He stopped at the head of the couch and stooped over, squinting his eyes in the attempt to see through the dusty dimness. It looked like Gary. His expression was hard to see, but Ben Joe could make out his pale face emerging from the depths of two feather pillows. His mouth was open but he was not snoring, only breathing gently and regularly in little even sighs. And his hair, drained of all its flaming color by the night, stuck out in sharp spikes against his pillows. Ben Joe watched him for a minute, considering the blandness of people asleep. Not even dreams or fits of restlessness seemed to bother Gary; he was peaceful and relaxed. Ben Joe shook his head and then, after putting away the thought of waking Gary up and asking him what had happened that evening, he turned back toward the hallway again.

Halfway up the stairs a sudden picture crossed his mind. He saw millions of houses, viewed from an airplane, and every couch in every tiny house was occupied by someone from yet another house. Everyone was shuffled around helter-skelter—Ben Joe on Shelley's couch, Gary on Ben Joe's couch, and God knew who on Gary's couch. The picture came to him sharply and without his willing it, and before it faded, it had nearly made him smile.

The upstairs hall was almost black; no windows opened onto it. He felt his way past the circle of tall white doors, all of them closed and with only the murmuring sounds of sleep behind them. Then he was in his own room, where his bed was a welcoming white blur with the covers turned neatly down and waiting for him. From the bedside stand he picked up his alarm clock and tilted it toward the light from the window, frowning as he tried to see where the hands stood. Five-thirty. That gave him at least another hour, and maybe more if only the girls would rise quietly for a change. The shade on his window was raised and a square of pale white shone through it onto the rug; he pulled the shade down to the sill so that the sun wouldn't waken him. Then he undressed, doing it slowly and methodically and hanging his clothes neatly in the closet so that he could go to sleep with the feeling that everything had been attended to in an orderly fashion. His socks he put in the small laundry hamper behind the door, making sure to lower the lid again without a sound. All his sisters slept lightly—downright night birds they were, and prone to wandering around at all hours—and right now there wasn't a one of them he wanted to see. He tiptoed to his bed and lay down, still in his underwear, and reached for his blankets gingerly so as not to creak the springs. The top sheet against his skin was cold and smooth and he felt immediately protected, and more ready for sleep than he had been under the rough, mothball-smelling quilt at Shelley's. He pulled the sheet up under his chin and closed his eyes, feeling them burn beneath the lids.

Wanting to be quiet kept him from changing his position. Gradually he grew stiff and tense, and his face muscles wouldn't loosen up, but he was afraid to move around. Why hadn't he got into bed on his stomach? He *knew* he couldn't sleep on his back. Carefully he turned on his side, trying to make his body light on the mattress and tightening his jaw with the effort. Now he was facing the center of the room, away from the wall. He could see all the dim objects he had grown up with and a white rim of pillow case besides (his right eye was half hidden in the pillow), and he couldn't *not* see them because his eyes wouldn't close. They kept springing open again. They looked around the room continually and searched out the smallest thing to stare at, while the rest of his body ached with tiredness and a headache began just above the back of his neck.

His room seemed to be made up of layers, the more recent layers never completely obliterating the earlier ones. Of the first layer only the peeling decals on the closet door remained—rabbits and ducks in polka-dotted clothes, left over from that time when he had been a small child. Then the layer from his early boyhood: a small red shoe bag, still in use, with a different symbol of the Wild West on each pocket, a dusty collection of horse books on the bottom shelf of the bookcase. And after that his later boyhood, most in evidence: a striped masculine wallpaper pattern, brown curtains, a microscope, the *National Geographics.* He tried closing his eyes again and thought about how each layer had become less distinct progressively; the top layer was flat and impersonal, consisting only of a grownup's clothes in the closet and a grownup's alarm clock on the stand, while the bottom layers were bright and vivid and always made him remember things, in striking detail, that had happened years and years before. He turned to the other side, grimacing at a creak in the springs, and faced the one picture on the wall: a black-and-white photograph of himself and Joanne on tricycles, in look-alike playsuits, with a younger, out-of-date mother between them in a mannish shoulder-padded suit and black lipstick. There had been another picture, with the cleaner square on the wall left to prove it, of his father in slacks on the mowed lawn with his hand on a teenaged Ben Joe's shoulder; but during the bad years Ben Joe had burned it, not knowing what else he was supposed to do.

He pushed his eyes shut; they popped open again. He turned on his back and looked at the ceiling and switched the room upside-down, picturing the furniture hanging from the ceiling and the light fixture sticking straight up from a bare and peeling plaster floor. To go out of the room, he must reach up an unusual height to the white china doorknob, and when the door was opened he must step over a two-foot threshold of striped wallpaper onto the chandeliered floor of the hallway . . .

The door opened. The crack of black at one side of it widened and widened until a girl's face appeared in it, a small oval that could have been any of them except that a sort of space helmet of lace above it identified the face as Jenny's. She didn't speak out but crept very stealthily toward his bed without so much as creaking the floor. To Ben Joe, lying there watching her from under heavy, aching eyelids, she seemed very funny all of a sudden—cautious and bent forward like a nearsighted old woman.

"Ben Joe?" she whispered.

He didn't answer.

"Ben *Joe.*"

Her whisper was piercing; she must have seen the slits

of his half-open eyes. Ben Joe stirred slowly and then muttered something, making his voice purposely sleepy-sounding.

"Come on," she said patiently. "*You're* not asleep."

She came to the foot of his bed, hugging her bathrobe around her, and sat down with a bounce that he was sure would wake the whole household. He sighed and drew his knees up.

"I'm *almost* asleep," he said.

"You're not."

She settled herself down more securely, tucking her feet up under her to keep them warm. Her face was lively and wide awake.

"How come you're up?" he asked.

"I don't know. Well, for one thing, I was wondering where you were."

"I'm all right," he said.

"Well, I was just wondering."

He lowered his knees and swung his feet to the other side of the bed so she would be more comfortable, and smiled at her, but all he could think of to say was "I'm all right" again.

"I know." She rested her chin in one hand and looked at him seriously. "Where'd you go?"

"Just out."

"Oh."

He paused a minute, and then finally gave in and said, "What happened to Gary?"

"He's sleeping on the couch."

"I know, but what happened to him? To him and Joanne?"

"Nothing, I guess." She began stirring around restlessly and after a minute she rose and pulled the window shade up. "Joanne said she was committed to a date and was darn well going to keep her commitments," she said. She was leaning her elbows on the window sill now; her whisper came back cool and sharp, resounding off the pane. "And even though that Horner guy said he thought it'd be better to take a rain check, she said no and went out real quick, leaving Gary kind of empty-handed-looking and Gram crying into the sofa cushions and wishing she'd married Jamie Dower—"

"What happened when she got back?" Ben Joe broke in.

"Joanne? I don't know. I don't think her date came inside with her when he brought her home again—"

"Thank God for small gifts," he said.

"Well, but she and Gary didn't talk too much. She just went on to bed after a few minutes. I reckon she's counting on getting it settled in the morning. While she was on her date, Gary stayed home and taught us how to make a French omelet. You take—"

"Jenny, I'm getting awful sleepy."

Jenny went on looking out the window, her face cheerful and her mouth pursed silently to whistle. "You should see Lisa," she said after a minute. "She's out walking under the clothesline. Can't get to sleep, I guess."

"Oh, Lord."

"Well, it's no wonder she had to go all the way outside, considering she shares a room with Jane. Can't make a sound in there. Step on a dust ball in your bare feet and Jane's wide awake wanting to know what that crunching sound was."

"Well, tell Lisa to come in," Ben Joe said. "Makes me nervous."

"You'd be more nervous if she did come in."

"No, I wouldn't."

"Oh, she'll come soon of her own accord, anyway. Don't worry about it."

"Well, all right," said Ben Joe. But he frowned and picked at the tufts on his bed spread. He never could have the feeling that the whole family was under one roof and taken care of; one always had to be out wandering around somewhere beyond his jurisdiction.

"You try and get some sleep, now," Jenny was saying. She straightened up and left the window, heading toward the door and tying the sash of her bathrobe as she walked. When she reached the hallway she turned back and said, "Night."

"Night."

"See you in the morning."

"If morning *comes*," Ben Joe said.

She smiled suddenly and closed the door on him with a gentle click. Ben Joe turned over on his side, facing the wall. He closed his eyes and found that this time they stayed closed, although the muscles of his face were still drawn tight. Against his cheek the pillow was cool and slightly rough. Every time he breathed, the pillow brushed his skin with a soft, crisp sound and it made itself into a rhythm, plunging him farther and farther down until he found himself in the black, teetering world of half-sleep.

His father was sitting at the sunlit breakfast table. His mustache was gone and his face was as lined and leathery as it had been the day he died, although Ben Joe himself was only a small boy sitting at the table beside him. Why wasn't he dreaming the ages correctly? Either his father should be a mustached, smooth-faced young man or Ben Joe should be at least old enough for high school. He pulled his mind up from the deep water of his dream and opened his eyes. He must get all this arranged right. No, he thought suddenly, he had to stop the dream altogether. He thought about flat, green things—leaves, chalk boards, lawns seen from a distance—to make his mind blank again. The face of his father stayed in one corner, twinkling and deeply lined.

He closed his eyes and gave in, sinking back into the stream of the dream. His father, frozen in one position at the breakfast table, became animated again, like a movie that has been stopped and then started at the same place. He was telling a story, one that they all knew by heart. Only he told it in that anonymous voice inside Ben Joe's head instead of his own deep booming one; Ben Joe's mind, searching frantically, was unable to recapture even the vaguest semblance of his father's voice. But the story came to him perfectly, word for word:

"When I was young, and liked to go places, my Uncle Jed said he'd take me to the Farmers' Market in Raleigh. *You* remember Uncle Jed. He was the one could walk barefoot on broken glass without feeling it and went on farming even after the family got their money. Well, sir, this was back in the days when the farmers went to market the night before and all slept on the ground in blankets so as to be up at five. And that's how I saw my first silly-minded boy.

"Not that I haven't seen plenty since.

"Big as an ox, he was, and kind of round-eyed, and hung his head like he knew he was silly and was damned ashamed of it, too. And well he might be. For soon's we all got to bed this boy began saying, 'What time's it, Pa?'

"And his pa would say, growly-like, "Bout ten o'clock, Quality.'

"Quality Jones, that's what his name was.

"Name like that would make anybody silly-minded.

"And then Quality would say, 'What time's it *now*, Pa?'

"And his pa'd say, 'Little after ten, Quality.'

"Well, sir, this went on for maybe two hours. Farmers are patient men. They got to be. Got to see those seeds come up week by week, fraction by fraction, and sweat it out for some days not knowing yet is it weeds or vegetables making all that greeny look. So they kept quiet—just sort of muttered around a little. And when Quality started snoring, there was this little relaxing kind of sigh, like a breeze through a cornfield, all over the Farmers' Market.

"What good's a clock to a man in bed? What good?

"But that wasn't the half of it. For soon's Quality started snoring, his pa raised up on one elbow and looked over at him and he says, 'Quality, son?'

" 'Huh, Pa?' says Quality, all sleepy-like.

" 'You all right?' his pa asks.

"And Quality says, 'Yes, Pa.'

"That's the way it was all night. A fellow didn't have

time to get his eyes shut properly before it'd be, 'You want to pee, son?', 'You want a drink of water, Quality?' Lord, I never will forget.

"After about two hours of this, my Uncle Jed he stood up and grabbed his army blanket and he shouted, to the whole market place he shouted, 'Folks,' he says, 'if morning ever comes, I hope you get to meet this Quality!'

"And everyone laughed, but Uncle Jed paid them no mind. He grabbed my blanket right up from under me and said, 'Come on, boy, we're going home,' and that sure enough is where we went.

"I never went back to that market place. Folks say it is still going, only modern now, but every time I think about it, it seems like the only way I can see it is at nighttime still, with Quality still on his crazy quilt, and all those men still waiting, waiting still, for morning to be coming. Yes, sir. Yes, sir."

His father smiled, and leaned back to look around at his family. In his sleep Ben Joe smiled too. (He was proud of himself; he'd dreamed it all correctly from beginning to end.) And there was the contented murmuring of the family settling back in their chairs in the sunlight. It was their favorite story. It belonged to them; their father always told it after a night like this one, when he said the women in this family thought night was only a darker kind of daytime, just as good as any time for wandering and for talking. Ben Joe leaned back in his chair exactly the way his father did, and looked around and smiled at his family smiling.

His mother said, "The *least* you could do is try to keep it a secret from the *children*."

(How had that got in? That was from another time; that was from years later.)

A man said, "Feel the calluses on my hand."

Ben Joe sat on an unfamiliar porch beside his mother. His mother was very angry. He looked down at the old man, way below him on the ground, reaching his hand to Ben Joe.

"Feel the *calluses,*" the old man said. "I've worked and worked."

"Don't do it," his mother said.

He looked at his mother and then at the old man. He bent down toward the man's upturned, lined face and then he touched the man's hand, and quick as a wink the hand gripped his, vice-like, and hauled him off the porch and down to blackness.

"*Mother*!" he screamed.

But his mother's hand, reaching for him, gripped him harder, yanked him until his shoulder snapped. He was torn from the blackness back toward the porch but too far, and too hard, and now he was in greenness and falling even faster.

"Wake up," a voice said.

He awoke and he was on the glider, only it was the wrong color. In front of him stood his mother, looking out thoughtfully across the lawn with her arms folded. When he opened his eyes the eyelids creaked and groaned and scraped like the heavy tops of old attic trunks, and at the sound his mother turned and glanced down at him.

"You've been dreaming about your father," she said.

"I haven't," said Ben Joe.

"Ben Joe, *please*. Wake *up*."

He opened his eyes for the second time; this time he knew without a doubt that he was really awake. At the foot of his bed stood his mother, with a faded corduroy bathrobe tossed hastily around her. She was bent over a little the way Jenny had been earlier, and she was watching him with kind, worried eyes.

"What?" he said.

"You had a bad dream, I guess," she said. "You screamed 'Mother!' I thought—Where's your pillow?"

"Oh . . . on the floor," said Ben Joe. He watched dazedly as she reached down to pick it up for him.

"Is something wrong?" she asked. She had stepped closer now, and he could see the deep lines around her mouth and the anxious twisting motion of her hands upon the cord of her bathrobe.

"I'm all right," he said. "You go back to bed now. I'll be fine."

"If you'd like for me to sit with you awhile—"

"No, no. You go back to bed. Please.

She stayed another minute, looking down at him anxiously, but he made his face smooth and cheerful and eventually she sighed and straightened up again.

"Well, all right," she said. "But if there's anything I can get you, now—"

"Good night, Mom."

"Good night."

He thought she would never leave. Finally she turned and went absently to the door, and after looking back at him one more time she was gone. He tried to unstiffen his muscles. His legs were rigid and cold, and he couldn't relax them for more than a second before they stiffened again. But gradually, as the dream faded piece by piece and image by image from his memory, his body relaxed again. All that was left was a faintly sad feeling because he was afraid he had been rude to his mother. In this house there was only one recognized cure for nightmares; you rushed to the dreamer's room and offered him Postum and pleasant conversation. Only with Ben Joe that always seemed to make it worse. Probably that was what his mother was telling the others now. He could hear her voice in the hall, murmuring along against a background of other voices, low and questioning. When was night going to end?

He lay back tensely, and with great determination he began naming all the places he had ever been. Even one-night stays in hotels. He pictured every single place (though the hotels tended to merge into a single dreary prototype) in his mind's eye, exactly as it would look at this very hour. His New York apartment, with Jeremy curled up like a bear in the pale light from the dirty window. The camp cabin he had slept in when he was ten, with half-finished lanyards dangling from all the nails on the wall. The boat he had stayed on one summer in Maine with his uncle, where the sunlight came to pick up the colors in the Hudson Bay blankets at something like five o'clock in the morning. Only no, it was winter now. He'd forgotten. Maine would be icy and gray with only the bleak Nova Scotia lobster boats moored in the tiny harbor. Maybe not even they would be there; he'd never seen it in the winter.

He reached back, turned his pillow over to the other

side, and let his head fall back into the coolness of it. At the back of his mind the little voice began prodding him, pushing him into the next subject. Shelley. He frowned at the ceiling, turning the idea of Shelley every possible way and trying to think how all this had come about. He pictured himself walking to the train station and meeting Shelley, taking her to New York and surprising the daylights out of Jeremy and the few other friends he had. Writing home and announcing he was married. It sounded to him like one of those wild little what-if thoughts that was always wandering through his head—nothing logical or concrete but only a little tale to pass the time. But when he forced himself to believe it, when he went over all the plain facts of it like actually buying Shelley's ticket, he began to believe it. He sat up straighter now, tenser than ever. He caught himself in the act of sitting up and tried to lie back down, but his eyes were doing their springing-open act again; it was no use.

The clock said 6:45. He stood up and stumbled toward the closet, not caring now *how* much racket he made. From the hangers he pulled down a white shirt and an old pair of slacks and piled himself into them hurriedly. He didn't want to stay in this room another minute.

Again the door opened. He heard the creak.

"What now?" he said, with his back to the door. He threaded his belt through the loops.

"Ben Joe?" Tessie said.

"Yes."

She padded over in her bare feet to stand beside him.

In her too-long bathrobe and rumpled hair, she looked no older than Carol, and so cross and sleepy that Ben Joe felt sorry for her.

"Ben Joe," she said, "is it time to get up yet?"

"I think we could say so."

"I'm so *glad*," she said.

She turned around and walked out again. Out in the hallway Gram started singing, just a little more softly than usual, as she came down the stairs from her attic room:

> "If you don't love me, love whom you please.
> Throw your arms round me, give my heart ease . . ."

The shower in the bathroom was turned on. One of the twins opened the door of their bedroom and shouted out, "Susannah, does milk chocolate remind you of Chicago?"

"Of what?" Susannah said. It sounded as if she were in her closet.

" 'Chicago,' I said."

"I've never *been* to Chicago."

"I've been thinking about it all night," said the twin. "Milk chocolate reminds me of Chicago."

"You've never been to Chicago either."

"Well."

Someone downstairs started playing the piano. Ben Joe got down on his hands and knees beside his bed and began fishing under it for his shoes with an unstrung tennis racket.

15

"GARY," Ben Joe said. "Hey, Gary. Wake up, will you?"

He hated to wake people up. His grandmother had told him after breakfast that it wasn't good for people to sleep late and especially not in the middle of the living room, and that it was his job to see that Gary got up, but Ben Joe had put it off all morning. Now it was almost eleven; he had spent the last half-hour whistling very loudly in other parts of the house and kicking the furniture in the hallway, but Gary was still peacefully asleep with his mouth open.

"You're worse than Joanne," Ben Joe said to the freckled face. "*Gary?*"

Gary opened his eyes, opaquely blue, and stared up at Ben Joe. "Hmm?" he said.

Ben Joe was instantly embarrassed, caught peering at the privacy of a man's face asleep.

"Uh, would you like some breakfast?"

"That wouldn't be half bad," Gary said. It was amazing how quickly he came alive. He sat straight up and swung his incredibly long, pajamaed legs off the couch and scratched his head.

"What time is it?" he asked.

"About eleven."

"Oh, Lord."

He reached for the faded blue bathrobe at the foot of the couch and stood up to put it on. "It's a disgrace," he said, grinning happily. "I should've been up hours ago. What goes *on* in this house at night? All night long it sounded like mice above my head, just scurrying around as busy as you please. They went to bed so early and I thought it was a peace-loving family. And then I find out they didn't go to bed at all, seems like, just adjourned upstairs to carry on where they'd left off before, slamming doors and visiting back and forth. Me, I've always thought sleep was a wonderful invention. Not that being awake isn't nice too, of course. But when I get up in the morning I think, boy, only fourteen more hours and I can be back to sleep again. I like to see the covers turned down and waiting and the pillows puffed up so I can hop right in. And I never dream, because it distracts my mind from pure sleeping, so to speak . . ."

He was dipping his arms into his robe and tying it and then folding up the bed clothes as he talked, stopping every now and then to gesture widely with one arm. There was something fascinating about that constant flow of speech. He was the way he had been the night before—big and graceful and always in the center of the room, chattering happily away in a steady stream that left his listeners virtually speechless. Even Ben Joe, who had been an incurable talker as a small boy and had once lost a family bet that he could keep totally silent for fifteen minutes straight, could find no place to break in.

"Not that I'm complaining," Gary was saying. I just think it's worth commenting on, is all. For years now I've been wondering at Joanne, wondering where she got her habits. You'll have to admit they're kind of odd. She's the only mother I know of that used to keep waking the *baby* all the time, instead of the baby waking her. And making milk shakes in the Waring blender at two a.m. Now, where, I'd think, as I'd wake up and hear her whistling and the blender going and the dishes clattering, *where* did she learn to live like that? Well, I'm mighty glad to meet your family, Ben Joe. It's good to see you."

He stuck out one long, bony hand and Ben Joe, taken off guard, stared at it a minute and then shook it.

"Uh, how about that breakfast?" he asked.

"Sure thing."

"I'll get it."

Ben Joe fled. He was glad to get out to the kitchen; Gary was much better than he had pictured him, but at the same time he felt inadequate around him. He couldn't welcome him or say he was glad to see him or make one small response to all that puppy-dog friendliness because Gary was too busy talking to hear. Where had Joanne ever met him? He dropped an egg in the frying pan and stared out the window, trying to remember, but it seemed to him that Joanne had never said. She had simply announced that she was married. Well,

Joanne never *was* one to tell much of her personal life. Her letters were full of things like how much wool cost in Kansas nowadays and what movies they had seen and how crabby Carol's pediatrician was. Everyone in the family wrote like that when they were away; it was probably because of Jenny's being the official letter writer. What *else* could you answer to a letter of Jenny's except the price of wool in Kansas? Still, he wondered where Joanne had met Gary. He cracked the second egg into the frying pan and went to the refrigerator for orange juice.

Gary appeared the instant his breakfast was ready, rubbing his hands together. He was dressed in a plaid shirt that clashed with his hair and a pair of corduroy slacks and he looked exuberant.

"Boy oh boy," he said, "I just love a big breakfast. They tell you what we had before bed last night? Pizza. A great big pizza with all *kinds* of stuff on— You seen Joanne?"

"She went out," Ben Joe said. "Downtown, I think." He cleared his throat. "I was just wondering where you and Joanne ever met up with each other."

"Oh, she was dating a buddy of mine. This was when I was in the Marines, back east. She was one of those gals that flits around a lot. Danced with practically everyone at this dance and I was one of them. Keeping her *with* me, now, that was harder than just dancing one dance with her. And she didn't like it that in civilian life I'm a salesman. Said salesmen always smiled even when they didn't want to, so how could she trust me. That's what she kept harping on, how could she trust me. And, besides, she thought I had no manners. You ever seen Joanne's feet?"

"What?"

"Her feet. You ever seen them?"

"Well, of course," Ben Joe said. "She's always barefoot."

Gary nodded and shoveled half a fried egg in his mouth. "That's why," he said with his mouth full. "Why they look like they do, I mean. The rest of her is kind of slim, but her feet are wide and smooth and brown like a gypsy's maybe, or a peasant's. You see her barefoot and *you'll* know what I mean. I always liked her feet. First time she ever met my mother she had little bare sandals on and her hair piled high and I was so proud of her I said, 'Mama, this is Joanne Hawkes. See her peasant feet?'

"And after we were alone again, you should have seen the row. She kept saying, 'I've never been so embarrassed in my life before; see my peasant feet, see my peasant feet?' and kicked me in the shin with one of them peasant feet so hard I can still feel it if I think on it awhile. That's why she said I was bad-mannered. That and this door-opening business. I believe in opening a car door for a girl when she gets *in*, mind you. But when she gets *out*, well, she just sits and sits all useless in the car while you get out and plod all the way around to the other side . . ."

He held his hand out toward the cream pitcher and Ben Joe, mesmerized, placed it in his hand while he kept staring at Gary's face.

"So," Gary said, "I went off on a fishing boat named

the *Sagacity* one weekend with a fellow from Norfolk. Figured there wasn't any use staying around right then. Joanne said she didn't trust me far as she could throw a tractor and then went and accepted five dates for that weekend. *Five,* mind you. There was this about Joanne back then: seems she liked drawing people to her. Once she got them, she sort of forgot what she was planning to do with them, like. But if you drew *away,* she'd be out to draw you to her again. So when she heard I had left she got them to radio the *Sagacity* to come in again. Saturday, it was. They kept calling the *Sagacity* but the catch was this: it was a borrowed boat and me and my buddy, who was the captain, thought its name was the *Saga City.* We didn't connect them, you see. Makes a difference. So the man told Joanne there wasn't an answer and he didn't know what could be the trouble, and she started crying and all, and by the time the mess was straightened out we were on dry land again and Joanne had her arms around my neck and said she'd marry me. That was quite some day," he said.

Ben Joe nodded, with his mouth open. Gary laid his fork down and rocked back easily on the kitchen chair.

"So we got married and all, and of course Carol came along. You get to see that first picture we took of her?"

"It's somewhere around the house right now," Ben Joe said.

"Well, I'm glad. It's a real good picture, I think. I was hoping you all thought so too. I always wondered why your mama didn't come when Carol was born, or one of your sisters maybe. Almost a custom, you might say. But no one came."

"Well, anyway, we were glad to hear about it," Ben Joe said.

"That so?" Gary looked happy.

"Um . . ." said Ben Joe. He bent forward to lean his elbows on the table. There was a long string of questions he wanted to ask, like why was Joanne here now and why was Gary himself here, but he would hate to see that happy face of Gary's get a closed, offended look. In the tiny silence he heard the front door open and a pair of high heels walk in, with little, soft baby steps beside them. He looked up at Gary to see if he had heard too, but Gary was musing along on some path of his own. The high heels climbed the stairs, and Ben Joe in his mind followed their journey to Joanne's bedroom.

"I'd like to have a lot more children," Gary said unexpectedly. "Dozens. I like kids. Joanne takes too good care of just the one. She needs a whole group of them. She's always saying how Carol's got to be secure-feeling, got to have no wonders about being loved or not. But this way she just makes Carol nervous—follows her around reading psychology books. Wants to know what her nightmares are about. I say let her alone—kids grow up all right. But that's just *like* Joanne. She got in this Little Theater play once back in Kansas and had a whole bunch of lines to learn and got all worried about it. So did she just take a deep breath and start learning them? No sir. The night before the play opened I asked her did she know her lines and she said no not yet but she *had* got almost all the way through this book called *How to Develop a Super-Power Memory*. If that isn't just like her . . ."

He smiled into his plate and then clasped both hands behind his neck and stared at the ceiling.

"She was like that about *me* once," he said. "Followed me around reading books about marriage. But when Carol came along she got sidetracked, sort of. It happens. So if she was too busy with Carol I'd just go bowling with the boys or watch TV maybe. And Joanne'd start feeling bad—say it was her fault and she was making the house cold for me. First time she said that was in a heat wave. You couldn't hardly see for the little squiggly lines of heat in the air. '*Cold?*' I says. '*Cold?* Honey, you make this house cold and I'll love you forever for it," but Joanne, she didn't think it was funny. Carol was crawling across the table in rubber pants and Joanne picked her up and spanked her for no reason and then started crying and saying history was repeating itself. Huh. You believe in history repeating itself, Ben Joe?"

"Well, not exactly," Ben Joe said.

"No, I mean it, now. Do you?"

"No," said Ben Joe. "I can't believe history's going anywhere at all, much less repeating itself."

Gary lit a slightly bent Chesterfield that he had pulled from his shirt pocket. He was enjoying himself now—as wrapped up in his story as if he were watching it unfold right there on the kitchen ceiling, he never even looked at Ben Joe.

"Course she meant *you*-all's history," he said, "which is so confusing I never *have* got it straight and don't intend to. Hardly worth it at this late date. But whatever it was, it's got no bearing on us and Joanne's house wasn't a cold one, no. But Joanne, she gets *i*-deas. And up and left one day. Well, I don't know why. But here I am, come to get her. I always say," he said, looking suddenly at Ben Joe, "no sense acting like you don't miss a person if you do. Never get 'em back pretending you wouldn't have them if they crawled."

"I hope you do," Ben Joe said suddenly. "Get her back, I mean."

"Thank you, sir. Thank you. It's a right nice house you have here. You born in this house?"

"Yes."

"I figured so. I always have wanted to come visit you all. Joanne, she sometimes talks about this place when she's rested and just sort of letting her mind drift. Tells about all the things that go on here just in one day. It's right fascinating to listen to. Tells about your daddy, and how his one aim in life was to go to Nashville, Tennessee, and watch real country-music singers, the way some people want to go to Paris, only he never did get there—"

"I'd forgotten that," Ben Joe said.

"Oh, Joanne didn't. She was full of things. I know about the time when your mamma and daddy were just married, and he bet her that she'd drop out first on a fifteen-mile hike to, to . . ."

"Burniston," said Ben Joe.

"Burniston, that's it. Only neither one of them dropped out, they both made it, but what really got your daddy peeved was that the whole town of Sandhill followed behind them for curiosity's sake, and none of *them* dropped out, either . . . O, ho . . ." He threw his head back, with his mouth wide and smiling for pure joy, so that Ben Joe had to smile back at him. "And how you are the only boy in Sandhill that they made a special town law for, forbidding you to whistle in the residential sections because it was so awful-sounding. And Susannah's cracker sandwiches, made with two pieces of bread and then a cracker in between—"

"Joanne told you all *that?*"

"She did."

Ben Joe was quiet for a minute. For the first time he actually pictured Joanne married, telling a person what she had noticed in a lifetime and giving someone bits of her mind that none of them had even known she had. What bits, he wondered, would he give Shelley (if there were any to give)? And how did one go about it? Would he just lie back and say what came into his mind the minute it came, removing that filter that was always there and that strained the useless thoughts and the secret thoughts from being made known? But how could *that* be any gift to her? He frowned, and marked the tablecloth over and over with his thumbnail.

"I'll do the dishes," Gary said.

There were some things Ben Joe didn't want to tell; he didn't care if she *was* his wife. He wouldn't want to tell all about his family, for instance, the way Joanne had done. Or about the little aimless curled-in-on-themselves things he was always wondering, like if you were an ant, how big would the rust on a frying pan look and could you actually see the molecules going around; and why was it that a sunlit train going through a tunnel did not retain the sunlight for a minute, the way the world did just at twilight, so that it was a little trainful of sunshine speeding through the dark like a lit-up aquarium—useless things that a child might think and that Ben Joe had never seemed to grow out of. What would Shelley say to him if she knew all that?

"Did you hear me?" Gary said. "I said, I'll do the dishes."

Ben Joe pulled his thoughts together. "No," he said, "Gram gets mad if we do them. She says that the only thinking time she has is when she's doing the dishes."

"You sure?"

"Sure."

"Well, then . . ."

For the first time that Ben Joe knew of, someone managed to interrupt Gary. It was Gram, bellowing from somewhere near the front of the house:

> "*Soft* as the *voices* of *a-angels* . . ."

"What on earth," Gary said.

He scraped his chair back and stood up to head for the sound, with Ben Joe trailing aimlessly after him. They found Gram in the den, standing in the middle of the floor with her head thrown back and her arms spread like a scarecrow's, roaring at the top of her lungs:

> "*Whisp*ering ho-o-ope
> Da da *da* da da . . ."

In front of her, Carol sat in her rocking chair and rocked like mad. Her little feet stuck out in front of her; her head was ducked so that she could throw her weight forward.

"You're not *listening,*" Gram told her. She dropped her arms and beamed at Gary and Ben Joe. "I'm teaching her 'Whispering Hope.' "

"What for?" asked Ben Joe.

"What *for? Every* little girl should know something like that. So she can stand up in a lacy little pinafore like the one she's got on now—that's what reminded me of it—and perform before refreshments are served on Sunday afternoons when callers come. All your *sisters* know how to do it. Joanne used to recite Longfellow's 'My Lost Youth' and then Susannah would sing 'Whispering—' "

"*I* don't remember that," Ben Joe said.

"Well, we never actually did it in front of guests. Your mother wouldn't allow it. But we had our own private tea parties, sort of."

"Well, I'm leaving," Ben Joe said.

But behind him, as he left, Gary was saying, "That's a *great* idea. Do you know 'My Heart Belongs to Daddy'? I'd like—"

Ben Joe climbed the stairs two at a time and crossed the hall to Joanne's door.

"Joanne?" he called.

"Who is it? That you, Ben Joe?"

"Yes. Can I come in?"

"Sure, I guess so."

He opened the door. Joanne was at the door of her closet, looking at herself in the full-length mirror that hung there. She had on one of the gypsy-red dresses that she used to wear in high school and that had been left behind in her closet because it had faded at the seams. Faded or not, it was still a brighter shade of red than

Ben Joe had been used to seeing lately. He blinked his eyes, and Joanne laughed and turned around to face him.

"I found it hanging here," she said. "I'd forgotten I had it. Do you remember when I used to wear this?"

"Of course I do," Ben Joe said. "You wore it up till the time you left home."

"I'd forgotten all about it."

She spun once more in front of the mirror and then stopped smiling and sat down abruptly on the bed with her shoulders sagging.

"Did you want something?" she asked.

"Well . . . no."

"Is Gary up?"

"Yes."

He took his hands out of his pockets and crossed to sit in the platform rocker opposite her.

"How do you like him?" she asked.

"Oh, fine."

There seemed to be no words that would fill in the silence. He got up again and wandered aimlessly around the room. At the bureau he stopped and began looking through a silver catch-all tray under the mirror, full of odds and ends like rolled-up postage stamps and paper clips and pieces of lint.

"Hey," he said, "here's my nail clippers."

"Take them."

"I can prove they're mine. See this little license tag on the chain? I got it from a cereal company when I was about twelve. It has the year on it and the—"

"*Take* it, for *goodness'* sakes."

She lit a Salem and threw the match in the direction

of the window. With the nail clippers in his pocket Ben Joe wandered back to his seat, still with nothing to say.

"I've been looking all over for them," he said finally. "Also there's a dent in the file part, where Jenny bit it when she was only—"

"Ben *Joe!*"

"What?"

"Nothing," she said after a minute.

"Well, what'd you say 'Ben Joe' for?"

"No reason."

"It seems kind of funny," he said, "just to scream 'Ben Joe!' at the top of your lungs as a way of making small talk. Why, I could think of a better topic than *that* if I—"

"Are you *trying* to irritate me?"

"Well, maybe so." He examined his fingernails. "Yes," he said after a minute, "I liked him fine. I did. Gary, I mean."

"You did?"

"Yes."

He looked up, saw that she was waiting for him to go on, and went back to frowning at his fingernails. "Came all the way here for you," he said finally. "That's something."

Joanne blew out an enormous cloud of smoke and nodded. She seemed still to be waiting for him to say more, but there was nothing else he could think of to say. When she saw that he was through speaking, she went over and sat down at her dressing table, still not speaking. She put her cigarette in the groove of a glass ash try and began unpinning her knot of hair.

"If I could just get *organized,*" she said. "I never have believed in going backwards instead of forwards."

Ben Joe looked up at her. He knew suddenly, without her telling him, what she had decided she was going to do about Gary. He could tell by her face, half happy and half embarrassed at having to announce that she was as reversible as anyone. He could almost read what she was thinking, and how she was trying to figure out the best way to say it gracefully.

Her hair fell to her neck in a little puff. She put the bobby pins in a china coaster, and picked up a comb and began pulling it through her hair. The red dress made her different, Ben Joe thought. It turned her into exactly the same old Joanne, right down to the swinging hair that she tossed with a little teasing movement of her neck. And this could be any day seven years ago: Ben Joe in the chair watching her get ready to go out, funny old fussy Ben Joe telling her she really should start coming in earlier; and Joanne thin and quick and vaguely dissatisfied in front of her oval mirror. Any minute one of the children would come in (they were still called "the children" back then, not "the girls") to watch, too. Going out was something exciting and mysterious then, something only Ben Joe and Joanne and Susannah were allowed to do; and the others always liked coming to watch the preparations. He felt suddenly sad, thinking about them—as if instead of merely growing up and still being right here they had died, and he was only now realizing it. He pictured all the children in a circle on the floor, newly bathed and ready for bed (it would have to be evening, then), all looking in the mirror to see the miraculous things Joanne did to her face. Joanne would be talking rapidly, teasing the children behind her and giving that saucy smile as she stared at her mascara in the glass—"Oh, it's only old Kim Laurence I'm going out with. I think I'll just stay home and let the baby go instead. You hear that, Tessie?" She would turn around and make a little face at Tessie, only three years old and already half asleep in the lap of a twin. "And won't Kim Laurence be surprised when his date comes rolling toward him in a baby carriage?" Or: "I'll tell you who I'm seeing tonight—it's Quality Jones. Quality Jones, and he's taking me to a New York night club and he's such a *fascinating* conversationalist. All he says is, 'What time is it, Joanne?' and I say, 'If morning ever comes, Quality, I'll be happy to tell you.'"

The image of the real Joanne, seven years older, glimmered in the mirror. Ben Joe bent his head and laid his index fingers across his eyelids, just lightly enough to cool them, but the muscles of his throat stayed hot and aching with all those tears held back, pressing forward for no reason he could name.

"Headache?" the face in the mirror asked.

Ben Joe nodded silently.

"I'll get you an aspirin." She stood up and started for the door. When she was directly in front of him she stopped there—looking down at him, he guessed—but she didn't say anything and after a minute she went on out.

She was gone long enough for him to be sitting up

straight and whistling a little tune under his breath before she entered again.

Soft as the voices of *a-an*gels . . .

he whistled. Downstairs Gram's voice, coming loudly and only a little indistinctly through three closed doors, tramped along with him.

"Here," Joanne said. She handed him an aspirin and a glass of water.

"Thank you," he said cheerfully.

He swallowed the pill with one gulp of water and set the glass down on the floor beside his chair. There was a frown on his face now; he sat with his hands clasped tightly together and tried to think of a way to help Joanne say what she wanted to.

"Um, if by any chance you changed your mind about leaving Kansas . . ." he said.

He paused, waiting without realizing it for Joanne to interrupt, but she didn't.

"If just by chance you did," he said finally, "I don't know that I would call it going backwards instead of forwards. Sometimes it's not the same place when a person goes back to it, or not the same . . ."

That little inner mind of his, always scrutinizing him as if it were a separate individual from him, winced. Ben Joe nodded and tipped his hat to it; the separate mind returned his bow and withdrew.

"Not the same person," he finished.

"Oh," Joanne said. She was looking down at her hands, acting as if this were a brand-new idea that would have to be given time to soak in.

"I don't know," she said finally. Her voice was relieved, and lighthearted. "That is something to think about, I guess . . ."

Ben Joe stood up. "Thank you for the aspirin," he said.

"That's all right. Bye."

"Good-by."

He bowed again, this time for real, and left, clicking the door gently shut behind him.

16

Ben Joe came downstairs as slowly and quietly as possible; his feet instinctively veered away from the centers of the steps, where the slightest pressure always brought forth a creaking noise. In his left hand was his suitcase, held high and away from his body so that it wouldn't bang against anything. His right hand was on the polished stair railing. His whole face seemed to be concentrated on the sleek wood of it and the thin film of wax that clung a little to his skin. He lifted his hand and rubbed his thumb and fingers together, frowning down, and then abruptly dropped his hand to his side and descended to the next step. As yet he had not made a single sound. He could go all the way downstairs and out the front door without anyone's ever knowing it if he wanted to. But he wasn't sure he wanted to. If he left without saying good-by, could he really feel he had left for good? He switched the suitcase to his other hand and began descending more rapidly, still frowning at how silly he would feel to announce so suddenly that he was leaving. In the back of his mind he knew he would never leave the house without telling anyone; yet his feet still moved cautiously and he still held the suitcase carefully away from the railing.

Once in the downstairs hall, he moved quickly across the half-lit area between the stairs and the front door. There was a square of warm yellow light on the rug, cast through the wide archway of the living room, and the murmuring voices of his sisters were as clear as if they were out in the hall also, but nobody noticed when he crossed the yellow square. At the front door he stopped, setting his suitcase by his feet, and stood there a minute and then turned back and entered the yellow square again.

"Mom?" he said at the living-room doorway.

"Mmm." She didn't look up. She was sitting on the couch, sipping her after-supper Tom Collins and leafing through a *Ladies' Home Journal.* Beside her Gram was reading Carol a chapter out of *Winnie-the-Pooh,* although Carol wasn't listening, and on the other side of the room Jenny and Tessie and the twins were arguing over a game of gin rummy. The other two were out somewhere—Susannah with the school phys-ed instructor and Joanne with Gary, showing him her home town before they went back to Kansas in the morning. But those who were still at home looked so calm and cheerful, sitting in their lamp-lit room, that Ben Joe almost wished he could stay with them and forget the suitcase at the front door.

"Hey, Mom," he said.

"What is it?" She looked up, holding one finger in the magazine to mark her place. "Oh, Ben Joe. Why don't you come on in?"

" 'Many happy returns of Eeyore's birthday,' " Gram was saying in her bright, reading-aloud voice. Carol sniffed and bent down to touch the bunny ears on one of her slippers, and Gram glared at her. "I said, 'Many happy returns of—' "

"I'm going back to school," Ben Joe said.

" 'Eeyore's birthday,' " Gram went on, no longer looking at the book but just finishing the sentence automatically. "Where you say you're going, Ben Joe?"

"To school," he said.

"You mean, *tonight* you're going?"

"Yes'm."

His mother folded the page over and then closed the magazine. "Well, I don't see—" she began.

"I just suddenly remembered this test I've got, Mom. I really have to go. I'm going to catch that early train . . ."

His sisters turned around from their card game and looked at him.

"Where's your suitcase?" Jane asked.

"Out in the hall. I just stopped in to say good-by."

"Well, I should hope *so,*" said his mother. "Why didn't you tell us earlier? Now I don't know what to do about those shirts of yours that are still in the laundry—"

"Don't worry about it. You can send them to me later." He felt awkward, just as he knew he would, standing empty-handed in the doorway with everyone staring at him. His grandmother was the first one to stand up. She came toward him briskly, her arms outstretched to hug him good-by, and he smiled at her and went to meet her halfway.

"If you'd only told us, I could've made some cookies," she said.

"No, I don't need—"

"Or at least some sandwiches. You want me to whip you up some sandwiches, Ben Joe?"

"I haven't got time," he said.

The rest of the family was clustered around him now; Carol had her arms about one of his knees as if he were a tree she was about to climb. Behind his sisters stood his mother, with her face no longer surprised but back to its practical, thoughtful expression.

"I suppose it's about time," she said. "Looked as if you'd *forgotten* school."

"We'll drive you to the station," said Lisa.

"No, thank you, I've got plenty of time."

"But you just said you *didn't* have—"

"No, really. I feel like walking. Come kiss me good-by, everyone."

There was a succession of soft, cool cheeks laid against his. His grandmother held Carol up and she kissed him loudly on the chin, leaving a little wet place that he wiped off absent-mindedly with the cuff of his sleeve.

"Look, Mom," he said, when his mother stepped forward to hug him, "you tell Joanne good-by for me, okay? And Susannah. Tell Joanne I'm sorry to leave without—"

"Of course I will," she said automatically. "Try to get some sleep on the train, Ben Joe."

Gram kissed him again, with her usual angry vigor, and said, "Don't buy a thing on the train if you can help it, Benjy. You never know how much they're going to upcharge. Me, now, I have some idea, because I used to be a good friend of Simon McCarroll that sold cigarettes and Baby Ruths on the train from here to Raleigh some twenty years back. He used to say to me, 'Bethy Jay,' he says, 'you'll never know how they upcharge on these here trains,' and I'd answer back, I'd say—" She stopped, staring off into space. It was her habit, when saying good-by's, to lead the conversation in another direction and ignore the fact that anyone was leaving. Taking advantage of her pause, Ben Joe's mother patted him on the shoulder and became brisk and cheerful, just as she always did at such times.

"I know you'll have a good trip, Ben Joe," she said.

"You got enough money?" Jenny asked.

"I think so. Jenny, you tell Susannah to take good care of my guitar, will you?"

"I will. Bye, Ben Joe."

"Good-by."

His sisters smiled and began turning back to their gin-rummy game. His mother led the way to the front door.

"You'll tell her too, won't you?" he said to her. "Tell her it's a good guitar, and a good hourglass and all. Don't let her go forgetting—"

"Oh, Ben Joe." She laughed and pulled the door open for him. "Everything'll take care of itself."

"Maybe."

"Everything works out on its own, with no effects from what anyone does . . ."

He bent to pick up his suitcase and smiled at her. "Good-by, Mom," he said.

"Good-by, Ben Joe. I want you to do well on that test."

He started out across the porch, and the door closed behind him.

When he was across the street from his house he turned and looked back at it. It sat silently in the twilight, with the bay windows lit yellow by the lamps inside and the irregular little stained-glass and rose windows glowing here and there against the vague white clapboards. When he was far away from home, and picturing what it looked like, this wasn't the way he saw it at all. He saw it as it had been when he was small—a giant of a place, with children playing on the sunlit lawn and yellow flowers growing in two straight lines along the walk. Now, as he looked at the house, he tried to make the real picture stay in his memory. If he remembered it only as it looked right now, would he miss it as much? He couldn't tell. He stood there for maybe five minutes, but he couldn't make the house register on his mind at all. It might be any other house on the block; it might be anyone's.

He turned again and set off for the station. The night was growing rapidly darker, and his eyes seemed wide and cool in his head from straining to see. Occasionally he met people going alone or in two's on after-supper errands, and because it was not really pitch-dark yet, almost all of them spoke cheerfully or at least nodded to Ben Joe whether they knew him or not. Ben Joe smiled back at them. To the older women, walking their dogs or talking to friends on front walks, he gave a deep nod that was almost a bow, just as his father had done before him. Two children playing hopscotch on white-chalked lines that they could barely see stepped aside to let him pass. He walked between the lines gingerly so as not to mess them up, and didn't speak until the smaller one, the boy, said hello.

"Hello," said Ben Joe.

"Hello," the little boy said again.

"Hello," Ben Joe called back.

"Hello—"

"You *hush* now," his sister whispered.

"Oh," the little boy said sadly. Ben Joe turned right on Main Street, smiling.

People were gathering sparsely around the glittering little movie house, and he could see dressed-up couples eating opposite each other in the small restaurant he passed. Just before he crossed to head down the gravel road to the station, a huge, red-faced old man in earmuffs stopped beside him and said, "You Dr. Hawkes's son?"

"Yes," Ben Joe said.

"Going away?"

"Yes."

"Funny thing," the man said, shaking his head. "I outlived my doctor. I outlived my doctor, whaddaya know."

It was what he always said. Ben Joe smiled, and when the light changed, he crossed the street.

The gravel road was just a path of grayish-white under his feet, but he could see well enough to walk without difficulty. Even so, he went very slowly. He stared ahead, to where the station house, with its orange windows, sat beside the railroad tracks. The tracks were mere silver ribbons now, gleaming under tall, curved lamps. All around there was nothing but darkness, marked occasionally by the dark, shining back of some parked car. Ben Joe shivered. He suddenly plunked his suitcase at his feet and after a minute sat on it, folding his arms, staring at the station house and still shivering so hard that he had to clamp his teeth together. He didn't know what he wanted; he didn't know whether he wanted Shelley to meet him there or never to show up at all. If she was there, what would he say? Would he be glad to see her? If she wasn't there, he would climb on the train and leave and then it would be *he* who was the injured party; something would at last be clearly settled and he could turn his back on it forever. He looked at the blank orange windows, still far away, as if they could by some sign let him know if she was there and tell him what to do about it. No sign appeared. A new idea came: he could wait a while, till after his train had left, and then surreptitiously catch a local to Raleigh and take the later train from there. But what good would that do? The picture arose in his mind of chains of future wakeful nights spent wondering whether he should have gone into the station or not. He rose, picked up his suitcase again, and continued on down the hill.

It was warm and bright inside, and the waiting room smelled of cigar smoke and pulp magazines. Nearest Ben Joe was a group of businessmen, all very noisy and active, who mulled around in a tight little circle calling out nicknames and switching their brief cases to their left hands as they leaned forward to greet someone.

"Excuse me," Ben Joe said.

They remained cheerfully in his path, too solid and fat to be sidled past. He changed directions, veering to the right of them and continuing down the next aisle. A small Negro man and his family stood there; the man, dressed stiffly and correctly for the trip north, was counting a small pile of wrinkled dollar bills. His wife and children strained forward, watching anxiously; the man wet his lips and fumbled through the bills.

"Excuse me," Ben Joe said.

The husband moved aside, still counting. With his suitcase held high and tight to his body so as not to bump anyone, Ben Joe edged past them and came into the center of the waiting room. He looked around quickly, for the first time since he had entered the station. His eyes skimmed over two sailors and a group of soldiers and an old woman with a lumber jacket on; then he saw Shelley.

She was sitting in the far corner, next to the door that led out to the tracks. At her feet were two suitcases and a red net grocery bag. Ben Joe let out his breath, not realizing until then that he had been holding it, but he didn't go over to her right away. He just stood there, holding onto the handle of his suitcase with both hands in front of him as if he were a child with a book satchel. He suddenly *felt* like a child, like a tiny, long-ago Ben Joe poised outside a crowded living room, knowing that sooner or later he must take that one step to the inside of the room and meet the people there, but hanging back anyway. He shifted the suitcase to one side. At that moment Shelley looked up at him, away from the tips of her new high-heeled shoes and toward the center of the waiting room, where she found, purely by accident, the silent, watchful face of Ben Joe. Ben Joe forced himself to life again. He crossed the floor, his face heavy and self-conscious under Shelley's grave stare.

"Hello," he said when he reached her.

"Hello."

Her dress was one he had not seen before—a waistless, pleated beige thing—and she had a round feathered hat and gloves the same color. So much beige, with her dark blond hair and her pale face, made her look all of one piece, like a tan statue carved from a single rock. Her face seemed tighter and more strained than usual, and her eyes were squinched up from the bright lights.

"Ben Joe?" she asked.

He sat down quickly in the seat opposite her and said, "What?"

For a minute she was silent, concentrating on lining up the pointed toes of her shoes exactly even with each other. In the space of her silence Ben Joe heard the whispery sound of the train, rushing now across the bridge at Dublin Cat River and drawing nearer every second. Men outside ran back and forth calling orders; a boy pushed a baggage cart through the door and drenched them for a second in the cold, sharp air from outside. Ben Joe hunched forward and said, "What is it, Shelley? What've you got to tell me?"

"I came by taxi," she said after a moment.

"What?"

"I said, taxi. I came by taxi."

"Oh. Taxi."

He stood up, with his hands in his pockets. Outside

the whistle blew, louder and closer this time. The two sailors had risen by now and were moving toward the door.

"I got my ticket," Shelley said. "And I've got, wait a minute . . ." She dug through the beige pocketbook beside her and came up with a navy-blue checkbook. "Travelers' checks," she said. "I don't want my money stolen. We didn't talk about it, but, Ben Joe, I want you to know I am going to get a job and all, so money won't be any—"

The train was roaring in now. It had a steamy, streamlined sound and it clattered to a stop so noisily that Shelley's words were lost. All Ben Joe could hear was the steaming and the shouts and above all that the garbled, rasping voice of the loud-speaker. Shelley was looking up at him with her eyes glass-clear and waiting, and he knew by her face she must have asked a question.

"What'd you say?" he asked when the train had stopped.

"I said, I wondered, do you still want me to come?"

She started lining up the toes of her shoes again. All he could see of her face were her pale lashes, lying in two semicircles against her cheeks, and the tip of her nose. When the shoes were as exactly even as they could get she looked up again, and it seemed to him suddenly that he could see himself through her eyes for a minute—Ben Joe Hawkes, pacing in front of her with his hands in his pockets, setting out in pure thoughtlessness toward his own narrow world while she looked hopefully up at him.

"Course I still want you," he said finally.

She smiled and at once began bustling around, checking in her purse for her ticket, leaping up to push all her baggage out into the middle of the floor and then stand frowning at it.

"We'll *never* get it all in," she said. "I tried to take just necessities and save the rest to be shipped, but—"

"Come on." He grabbed her two suitcases and left her to carry the grocery bag, which seemed to be filled with hair curlers and Kleenex, and his own, lighter suitcase. When she had picked them up, he held the door open for her, and they followed the straggling soldiers out into the cold night air, across the platform and up the clanging steps to the railroad car.

"Passengers to New York and Boston take the car to the right!" the conductor sang out cheerfully. He put one hand under Shelley's elbow to boost her up the steps. "Watch it there, lady, watch it—"

A thin white cloud of steam came out of Ben Joe's mouth every time he breathed. Ahead of them the soldiers paused, looking over the seats in the car, and Ben Joe was left half inside and half out, with his arms rigidly close to his body to keep himself warm. He looked at the back of Shelley's head. A few wisps of blond hair were straggling out from under her felt hat, and he couldn't stop staring at them. They looked so real; he could see each tiny hair. In that moment he almost threw down the suitcases and turned around to run, but then the soldiers found their seats and they could go on down the aisle.

The car was full of smoke and much too hot. They maneuvered their baggage past dusty seats where all they could see of the passengers were the tops of their heads, and then toward the end the car became more empty. Shelley ducked into the first vacant seat, but Ben Joe touched her shoulder.

"Keep going," he said. "There're two seats facing each other at the back."

She nodded, and got up again and continued down the aisle ahead of him. It seemed strangely silent here after the noise outside. All he could hear were the rustlings of newspapers and their own footsteps, and his voice sounded too loud in his ears.

At the last seat they stopped. Ben Joe put their luggage up on the rack, and then he took Shelley's coat and folded it carefully and put it on top of the luggage.

"Sit down," he told her.

She sat, obediently, and moved over to the window. When Ben Joe had put his own coat away he sat down opposite her, rubbing the backs of his hands against his knees to get them warm again.

"Are you comfortable?" he asked.

Shelley nodded. Her face had lost that strained look, and she seemed serene and unworried now. With one gloved finger she wiped the steam from the window and began staring out, watching the scattered people who stood in the lamplight outside.

"Mrs. Fogarty is seeing someone off," she said after a minute. "*You* remember Mrs. Fogarty; she's got that husband in the nursing home in Parten and every year she gives him a birthday party, with nothing but wild rice and birthday cake to eat because that's the only two things he likes. She mustn't of seen us. If she had she wouldn't still be here; she'd be running off to tell—"

She stopped and turned back to him, placing the palms of her hands together. "What did your family say?" she asked.

"I didn't tell them."

"Well, when *will* you tell them?"

"I don't know."

She frowned. "Won't it bother you, having to tell them we did this so sneaky-like?"

"They won't care," he said.

"Well. I still can't believe we're really going through this, somehow."

Ben Joe stopped rubbing his hands. "You mean more than usual you can't?" he asked.

"What?"

"You mean it's harder to believe than it usually is?"

"I don't follow your meaning," she said. "It's not usual for me to get married."

"Well, I know, but . . ." He gave up and settled back in his seat again, but Shelley was still watching him puzzledly. "What I meant," he said, "is it harder for you to believe a thing now than it was a week ago?"

"Well, no."

He nodded, not entirely satisfied. What if marrying Shelley meant that she would end up just like him, unable to realize a thing's happening or a moment's passing? What if it were like a contagious disease, so that soon she would be wandering around in a daze and incapable of putting her finger on any given thing and saying, that is that? He looked over at her, frightened now. Shelley smiled at him. Her lipstick was soft and worn away, with only the outlines of her lips a bright pink still, and her lashes were white at the tips. He smiled back, and relaxed against the cushions.

"When we get there," he said, "we'll look for an apartment to settle down in."

She smiled happily. "I tell you one thing," she said. "I always have read a lot of homemaking magazines and I have picked up all kinds of advice from them. You take a piece of driftwood, for instance, and you spray it with gold-colored—"

The train started up. It gave a little jerk and then hummed slowly out of the station and into the dark, and the tiny lights of the town began flickering past the black window.

"I bought me a white dress," Shelley was saying. "I know it's silly but I wanted to. Do you think it's silly?"

"No. No, I think it's fine."

"Even if we just go to a J.P., I wanted to wear white. And it won't *bother* me about going to a J.P. . . ."

The Petersoll barbecue house, flashing its neon-lit, curly-tailed pig, swam across the windowpane. In its place came the drive-in movie screen, where Ava Gardner loomed so close to the camera that only her purple, smiling mouth and half-closed eyes fitted on the screen. Then she vanished too. Across from Ben Joe, in her corner between the wall and the back of her seat, Shelley yawned and closed her eyes.

"Trains always make me sleepy," she said.

Ben Joe put his feet up on the seat beside her and

leaned back, watching her face. Her skin seemed paper-thin and too white. Every now and then her blue-veined eyelids fluttered a little, not quite opening, and the corner of her mouth twitched. He watched her intently, even though his own eyes were growing heavy with the sleepy ryhthm of the train. What was she thinking, back behind the darkness of her eyelids?

Behind his own eyelids the future rolled out like a long, deep rug, as real as the past or the present ever was. He knew for a certainty the exact look of amazement on Jeremy's face, the exact look of anxiety that would be in Shelley's eyes when they reached New York. And the flustered wedding that would embarrass him to pieces, and the careful little apartment where Shelley would always be waiting for him, like his own little piece of Sandhill transplanted, and asking what was wrong if he acted different from the husbands in the homemaking magazines but loving him anyway, in spite of all that. And then years on top of years, with Shelley growing older and smaller, looking the way her mother had, knowing by then all his habits and all his smallest secrets and at night, when his nightmares came, waking him and crooning to him until he drifted back to sleep, away from the thin, warm arms. And they might even have a baby, a boy with round blue eyes and small, struggling feet that she would cover in the night, crooning to him too. Ben Joe would watch, as he watched tonight, keeping guard and making up for all the hurried unthinking things that he had ever done. He shifted in his seat then, frowning; what future was ever a certainty? Who knew how many other people, myriads of people that he had met and loved before, might lie beneath the surface of the single smooth-faced person he loved now?

"Ticket, please," the conductor said.

Ben Joe handed him his ticket and then reached forward and gently took Shelley's ticket from her purse. The conductor tore one section off each, swaying above Ben Joe.

"Won't have to change," he said.

Ben Joe took his suit jacket off and folded it up on the seat beside him. He put his feet back on the opposite seat and slouched down as low as he could get, with his hands across his stomach, so that he could rest without going all the way to sleep. But his eyes kept wanting to sleep; he opened them wide and shook his mind awake. Shelley turned to face the aisle, and he fastened his eyes determinedly upon her, still keeping guard. His eyes drooped shut, and his head swayed back against the seat.

In that instant before sleep, with his mind loose and spinning, he saw Shelley and his son like two white dancing figures at the far end of his mind. They were suspended a minute, still and obedient, before his watching eyes and then they danced off again and he let them go; he knew he had to let them. One part of them was faraway and closed to him, as unreachable as his own sisters, as blank-faced as the white house he was born in. Even his wife and son were that way. Even Ben Joe Hawkes.

His head tipped sideways as he slept, with the yellow of his hair fluffed against the dusty plush. The conductor walked through, whistling, and the train went rattling along its tracks.

THE TIN CAN TREE

1

After the funeral James came straight home, to look after his brother. He left Mr. and Mrs. Pike standing on that windy hillside while their little boy wandered in circles nearby, and the only one who saw James go was Joan. She looked over at him, but she didn't say anything. When he was a few steps away he heard her say, "We have to go home now, Aunt Lou. We have to go down." But Mrs. Pike was silent, and all James heard for an answer was the roaring of the wind.

Going down the hill he took big steps—he was a tall man, and the steepness of the hill made him walk faster than he wanted to. It was too hot to walk fast. The sun was white and glaring and soaked deep in through the mat of his black hair, and his face felt slick when he wiped it with the back of his hand. Partway down the hill he stopped and took off his suit jacket. While he was rolling up his shirt sleeves he looked back at the grave to see if the others were coming, but their backs were still turned toward him. From here it seemed as if that wind hardly touched them; they stood like stones, wearing black, with their heads down and their figures making straight black marks against the sky. The only thing moving was little Simon Pike, as he picked his way down through the dry brambles toward James. Simon looked strange, dressed up. He had always worn Levi's and crumpled leather boots, but today someone had made him put his suit on. That would be Joan. Mrs. Pike had looked at nothing but the ground for two days now, and couldn't notice what Simon wore. Joan would have polished those white dress-shoes that Simon was getting all grass-stained, and taken out the last inch of cuff on his sleeves so that they could cover his wrists. There was a thin faint line above each of his cuffs where the old hem had been; James could see it clearly when Simon came up even with him. He stood staring at the cuffs for a long time, and then he shifted his eyes to Simon's face and saw Simon frowning up at him, his eyebrows squinched into one straight line across his forehead and his mouth held tight against the wind.

"I'm coming too," he told James. His voice had a low, froggy sound; he was barely ten, but in a year or two his voice would begin to change.

James nodded and finished rolling up his shirt sleeves. There was a band of dampness beneath his collar. He loosened his tie and unbuttoned the top button of his shirt, and then he began walking again with Simon beside him. Now he went more slowly, bracing himself against the steepness of the hill. Each time he took one step Simon took two, but when he looked over at Simon to see if he was growing tired, Simon ignored him and walked faster. He wasn't sweating at all. He looked cold. James wiped his face on his shirt sleeve and followed him down between the rocks.

"Getting near lunchtime," he said finally.

Simon didn't answer.

"Want to eat with Ansel and me?"

"Well."

"Don't worry about your mother. I'll tell her where you are."

Simon said something to his shoes, but James couldn't hear.

"What's that?" he asked.

"I wouldn't bother."

"We'll tell your cousin Joan then," said James. "Soon as she gets back."

The wind was so hot it burned his face; it made lulling sounds around his ears so that he couldn't hear his own footsteps. He pushed his hair off his forehead but it fell into his eyes again, hanging in a tangled web just at the top of his range of vision. Beside him, Simon was letting his hair do what it wanted. He had greased it down with something (it needed cutting, but Joan had been too busy with her aunt to see about that) and now it ruffled up in thick strings and stood out wildly in every direction. When James turned to look at him he nearly smiled. With his face sideways to the wind the roaring sound was quieter, so he kept looking in Simon's direction until Simon grew uneasy.

"What you staring at?" he asked.

"Nothing," said James. "Some wind we got." He

looked straight ahead again, and the roaring sound came back to hammer at his ears.

The ground they were treading was wild and weedy, with rocks sticking up here and there so white they might have been painted. There was no path to follow. Below them was the whole town of Larksville—the main street hidden by trees, but the outlying houses and the tobacco fields laid bare to the sun. At the foot of the hill was the white gravel road where Simon and James both lived. They lived in a three-family house that looked like only a long tin roof from here. No houses stood near it. James's brother Ansel said whoever built their house must have been counting on Larksville's becoming a city someday, but Larksville was getting smaller every year. When anyone went away to college it was taken for granted they'd never be back again, not for any longer than it took to eat a Christmas dinner in the house they'd started out in. Yet the long crowded house sat there, half a mile from town as a bird flies and a mile by car, and its three chimneys were jumbled tightly together with the smoke intermingling in wintertime.

The sight of that green part of town was cool and inviting; it made James think of cold beers in the tavern opposite the post office. He looked down at Simon, but Simon was hunched into the jacket of his suit and he still seemed cold.

"Do you like sardines?" James asked him.

"Not much."

"Or cold cuts?"

"No."

They stepped through a tangle of briars, with the thorns making little ripping sounds against their clothes. "I could eat a pizza," Simon said.

"You better talk to Ansel, then. He makes pizzas."

Simon tripped and caught himself. He looked down at the small rock that had tripped him and then began kicking it ahead of him down the hill, swerving out of his course to recover it every time the rock rolled sideways. Gray streaks began to show on his shoes, but James didn't try to stop him.

When they reached the gravel road they turned right and began heading in the direction of the house. Simon's rock rolled into a ditch; he left it lying there. It looked as if they might get all the way home this way—not talking much, and not saying anything when they *did* talk, just as if this were an ordinary walk on an ordinary day. That suited James. He had been thinking too much, these last two days—turning things over and over, figuring out how if just some single incident had happened, or hadn't happened, things might have been different. Now he ached all over, and thinking made him sick. He was just beginning to feel easier, ambling along in silence beside Simon, when Simon turned and began walking backwards ahead of James, fixing his frowning brown eyes on a point far down the road. He opened his mouth and closed it, and then he opened it again and said, "James."

"What."

"How far down in the ground before it starts getting cold?"

"Pretty soon," said James.

"*How* soon."

"Pretty soon."

"I'm just thinking," Simon said.

To keep him from thinking any more, James said, "But then it gets hot again, down towards the center of the earth. That's beyond digging distance."

"Six feet under is stone, stone cold," said Simon.

"Well, yes."

"Good old Janie Rose, boy."

"Now, wait," James said. "Now, Janie Rose don't feel if it's cold or it's not, Simon. Get that all straight in your mind."

"I know that."

"Get it straight *now*, before you go bothering your mother about it."

"I know all about that," said Simon. He spun around and began walking forward again, still ahead of James. Strands of his hair rose up and floated behind him, like the tail plumes of some strange bird. "You don't get what I mean," he called back.

"Maybe not."

"Now, you know Janie Rose."

"Yes," said James, and without his wanting it the picture of Janie Rose came to him, sharp and clear—Janie Rose looking exactly the way he thought her name sounded, six years old and blond and fat, with round pink cheeks and round thick glasses. He hadn't been planning to think about it. He said, "*Yes,* I know," and then waited for whatever would follow, keeping part of his mind far away.

"She just hated cold," said Simon. "Playing 'Rather' in the evenings after supper—which would you rather be, blind or deaf; which would you rather die of, heat or cold—she chose heat any day. She had a twenty-pound comforter on her bed, middle of summer."

"I already said to you—" James began.

"Well, I *know*," said Simon, and he started walking faster then and whistling. He whistled off-key, and the tune was carried away by the wind.

When they reached their house, which stood slightly swaybacked by the road with its one painted side facing forward, James stopped to look in his mailbox. There was only a fertilizer ad, which he stuck in his hip pocket to throw away later. "See what your mail is, why don't you," he told Simon.

Simon was walking in small neat circles around the three mailboxes. He stuck out a hand toward the box with "R. J. Pike" painted on it and flipped the door open, and then made another circle and came to a stop in front of the box to peer inside. "Fertilizer ad," he said. He pulled it out and dropped it on the roadside. "Letter for Mama." He pulled that out too, and dropped it on top of the first. "She'll never read it."

James picked the letter up and followed Simon along the dirt path to the house. Halfway through the yard the path split into three smaller ones, each leading to a separate door on the long front porch. Simon took the one on the far left, heading toward James's door, and James took the far right to deliver the Pikes' letter. The Pikes' part of the porch had a washing machine and an outgrown potty-chair and a collection of plants littering it;

he had to watch his step. When he bent to slide the letter under the door he heard a scratching sound and a little yelp, and he stood up and called to Simon, "Your dog wants out, all right?"

"All right."

He opened the door and a very old, fat Chihuahua slid through, dancing nervously on stiff legs as if her feet hurt her. "Okay, Nellie," he said, and bent to pat her once and then stepped over her and continued down the porch. On his way he passed the Potter sisters' window and waved to Miss Faye, smiling and shaking his head to show her he couldn't come in. She was sitting behind closed glass, full face to the window and as close to it as she could get, and when James shook his head the corners of her mouth turned down and she slumped back in her chair. Neither she nor Miss Lucy could climb that hill to the funeral, and they were counting on James to tell them about it.

Simon was standing at James's door, his hands in his pockets. "Why didn't you go on in?" James asked him, and Simon just shook his head.

"I reckoned I'd wait," he said.

"Ansel'd let you in."

"Well, anyway," said Simon, and stood back to let James open the door for him.

The inside of the house was cool and dim. It had unvarnished wooden floorboards, with no rugs, and when Simon walked in he clicked his heels sharply against the wood the way he did when he was wearing his boots. Walking that way, swinging his thin legs in heavy, too-big strides, made him look younger, like a small child entering a dark room. And he didn't look to his left, although he knew James's brother would be on the couch where he always was.

"Ansel?" James said.

"Here I am."

James closed the screen door behind him and looked toward the couch. Ansel was sitting there, with his back very straight and his feet on the floor. Usually he spent the day on his back (he had anemia, the kind that never got much better or much worse so long as he was careful), but today he had made a special effort to be up. He was wearing his Sunday black suit, and he had slicked his pale hair so tightly down with water that it was the same shape as the narrow bones of his head. Probably he had thought that was the least he could do for Janie Rose. When James came in Ansel didn't look in his direction; he was watching Simon. He waited until Simon finally turned around and faced him, and then he stood up and stooped toward him in what looked like a bow. "I hope this day wasn't too hard on you," he said formally, and then sat down and waited while Simon stood frowning at him.

"We got back before the others," James said. "I promised Simon lunch."

"Oh. Well, I doubt that he— Here, you want to sit down?"

He patted the couch where he sat, which meant that he was extending special privileges. Ordinarily he didn't like people sitting there. After a minute Simon shrugged and clicked his heels over to the couch, and Ansel moved aside to give him room.

"I haven't really talked to you since the, uh— It's been quite a few days. But I wanted to say—"

"I been busy," said Simon.

"Well, sure you have," Ansel said. "I know that." He was sitting forward now, placing the tips of his fingers together, gazing absently at the floor with those clear blue eyes of his. It made James nervous (Ansel had been known to get too serious at times like this) but before he could change the atmosphere any, Ansel had begun speaking again. "Uh, I wanted to tell you," he said, "I been meaning to say to you—sheesh! James, will you close the door?"

James gave the inner door a push and it clicked shut.

"Too much wind," Ansel said. "Well. I been meaning to, um, give you my condolences, Simon. And tell you how sorry I am not to go to the funeral. James said I shouldn't, but you don't know how I—"

"You didn't miss much," said Simon.

"What? Well, I just wish I could've come and paid my respects, so to speak. That's what I told James. But James said—"

Simon sat tight, his hands pressed between his knees and his eyes straight ahead. When James started into the kitchen Simon half stood, with that squinchy little frown on his face again, so James stopped and leaned back against the wall. He wasn't sure why; always before this it was Ansel that Simon followed, leaving James to Janie Rose. But now Simon sank back in his seat again, looking easier, and begun kicking one foot lazily in the direction of the coffee table. Ansel rambled on, his speech growing more certain.

"I had never been so shocked by *any* news," he said. "I was saying that to James. I said, 'Why, she and Simon were over here not but a while ago,' I said. 'Why, think how Simon must *feel.*' "

"I feel all right," Simon said.

"I mean—"

"I feel all right."

Ansel rubbed the bridge of his nose and looked over at James, and James straightened up from his position against the wall. "Mainly he feels hungry," he told Ansel. "I promised him lunch."

"Why, sure," said Ansel. "If he wants it. But I doubt he does. You hungry, Simon?"

"I'm starved," Simon said.

"You going to eat?"

"I *reckon* I am."

"I see," said Ansel.

Simon stood up and came over to James. When he got to James's side he just stood there and waited, with his eyes straight ahead and his back to Ansel. "We going to get that pizza?" he asked.

"Anything you want."

"Pizza?" Ansel said, and Simon turned then and looked up at James.

"That's what I promised him," James said.

"Why, Simon—"

"Hush," said James. "Now, Simon, we got three kinds of pizza mix out there. Sausage, and cheese, and something else. I forget. You go choose and then we'll cook it up. All right?"

"All right," Simon said. He turned and looked back at Ansel, and then he went on into the kitchen. When he was gone, James came over and sat down beside Ansel.

"Listen," he said.

Away from outsiders now, Ansel slumped back in his seat and let his shoulders sag. There were tired dark marks underneath his eyes; he hadn't slept well. "You're on my couch," he said automatically. "Do I have to tell you, James? Sitting like that makes the springs go wrong."

"Simon's folks are still on the hill," said James. "We've got to keep him here; I promised Joan he wouldn't sit in that house alone."

"Ah, sitting alone," Ansel said. He sighed. "That's no good."

"No. Will you help keep him busy?"

"The couch, James."

James stood up, and Ansel swung his feet around and slid down until he was lying prone. "I don't see how he can eat," he said.

"He's hungry."

"I *wonder* about this world."

"People handle things their own ways," James said. "Don't go talking to him about dying, Ansel."

"Well."

"Will you?"

"Well."

There was a crash of cans out in the kitchen. A cupboard door slammed, and Simon called, "Hey, James. I've decided."

"Which one?"

"The sausage. There was only just the two of them." He came into the living room, carrying the box of pizza mix, and Ansel raised his head to look over at him and then grunted and lay back and stared at the ceiling. For a minute Simon hesitated. Then he walked over to him and said, "*You're* the pizza-maker."

"Who said?" Ansel asked.

"Well, back there on the hill James said—"

"All right." Ansel sat up slowly, running his fingers through his hair. "It's always something," he said.

"Well, maybe—"

"No, no. I don't mind."

And then Ansel smiled, using his widest smile that dipped in the middle and turned up at the corners like a child's drawing of a happy man. When he did that his long thin face turned suddenly wide at the cheekbones, and his chin became shiny. "We'll make my specialty," he said. "It's called an icebox pizza. On refrigerator-defrosting days that's the way we clean the icebox; we load it all on a pizza crust and serve it up for lunch. You want to see how I make it?"

He was standing now, smoothing down his Sunday jacket and straightening his slumped shoulders. When he reached for the pizza mix Simon walked forward and gave it to him, not hanging back now but looking more at ease. Ansel said, "This is something every man should know. Even if he's married. He can cook it when his wife is sick and serve her lunch in bed. Do you want an apron?"

"No," said Simon.

"Don't blame you. Don't blame you at all. Well—" and he was heading for the kitchen now, reading the directions as he walked. His walk was slow, but not enough to cause James any worry. James could judge the way Ansel felt just by glancing at him, most of the time. He had to; Ansel would never tell himself. When he felt his best he was likely to call for meals on a tray, and when he was really sick he might decide to wall-paper the bedroom. He was a backward kind of person. James had a habit of looking at him as someone a whole generation removed from him, although in reality he was twenty-six, only two years younger than James himself. He was thinking that way now, watching with narrow, almost paternal eyes as Ansel made his way into the kitchen.

"Naturally there are no really *rules*," Ansel was saying, "since you never know what might be in the ice-box." And Simon's voice came floating back: "Fruit, even? Lettuce?" "*Well*, now . . ." Ansel said.

James smiled and went over to the easy chair to sit down, stretching his legs out in front of him. It felt good to be home again. The house was a dingy place, with yellow peeling walls and sunken furniture. And it was so rickety that whenever James had some photography job that required a long time-exposure he had to run around warning everyone. "Just *sit* a minute," he would say, and he would pull up chairs for everybody in the house and then go dashing off to take his picture before people started shaking the floors again. But at least it was a comfortable house, not far from town, and Ansel had that big front window in the living room where he could watch the road. He would sit on the couch with his elbows on the sill, and everything he saw passing—just an old truck, or a boy riding a mule—meant something to him. He had been watching that long, and he knew people that well.

Thinking of Ansel and his window made James look toward it, to see what was going on, but all he saw from where he sat was the greenish-yellow haze of summer air, framed by mesh curtains. He rose and went over to look out, with his hands upon the sill, and peered down the gravel road toward the hill he had just come from. No one was in sight. Maybe it would be hours before they returned; Joan might still be standing there, trying to make her aunt and uncle stop staring at that grass. But even so, James went on watching for several minutes. He could still feel the wind, gentler down here but strong enough to push the curtains in.

For a long time now, wind would make him think of today. He had climbed that hill behind all the others, and seen how the wind whipped the women's black skirts and ruffled little crooked parts down the backs of their hairdos. And when the first cluster of relatives had taken their leave at the end, stopping first to touch Mrs. Pike's folded arms or murmur something to Mr. Pike, the words they said were blown away and neither of the parents answered. Though they might not have answered anyway, even without the wind. The day that Janie Rose died, when James had spent thirty-six hours in the hospital waiting room and finally heard the news with only that tenth of his mind that was still awake, he had gone to Mrs. Pike and said, "Mrs. Pike, if there's anything I or Ansel can do for you, no matter what it is, we will want to do it." And Mrs. Pike had looked past him at the information desk and said, "Just falling off a *tractor* don't make a person die," and then had turned and left. So James had let them be, and went home and told Ansel to keep to himself a while and not go bothering the Pikes. "Not even to give our sympathy?" asked Ansel, and James said no, not even that. He hadn't liked the thought of Ansel's going to the funeral, either. Ansel said he had half a mind to go anyway—he could always rest on the way, he said—but James could picture that: Ansel toiling up the hill, clasping his chest from the effort and gasping out lines of funeral poetry, calling out for the whole procession to stop the minute he needed a rest. So James had gone alone, and quietly, and had promised to report to Ansel the minute it was over. The only one there that he had spoken to was Joan; the only two sounds he carried away with him were Joan's low voice and the roaring of the wind. He thought he would never like the sound of wind again.

Out in the kitchen now, Janie Rose's brother was talking on and on in his froggy little voice. "I never saw *peanut* butter on a pizza," he was saying. "You sure you know what you're doing, Ansel?"

"Just wait'll you taste it," Ansel said.

James left the window and went out to the kitchen. "How's it going?" he asked.

"It's coming along," Ansel said. He was swathed in a

big checked dishtowel, wrapped right over his suit jacket and safety-pinned at the back, and on the counter stood the almost finished pizza that Simon was decorating. The kitchen was rippling with heat. James took his shirt off and laid it on the counter, so that he was in just his undershirt, and he opened the back door.

"Aren't you hot?" he asked Simon.

But Simon said, "No," and went on laying wiener slices down. On the floor at his feet were little sprinklings of flour and Parmesan, and the front of his suit was practically another pizza in itself, but the important thing was keeping him busy. It was too bad the pizza-making couldn't go on for another hour or so, just for that reason; they would have to find something else for him to do.

Ansel said, "Now the olives, Simon."

"I don't think I like olives."

"Sure you do. Olives are good for the brain. Will you look at your shirt?"

Simon looked down at his shirt and then shrugged.

"It'll wash," he said.

"Your mama'll have a fit."

"Ah, she won't care."

"I bet she will."

"She won't care."

"*Any* mother would care about *that,*" said Ansel. "Makes quite a picture."

"Pictures," James said suddenly. He straightened up. "Hey, Simon. You seen my last photographs?"

"No," said Simon. "You get another customer?"

"Not in the last few days, no. But I took a bunch on

my own a while ago. When you're done I'll show you."

"Okay," said Simon.

"Olives," Ansel reminded him.

James went over to the back window and looked out. There was the Pikes' Nellie, burrowing her way through a tangle of wild daisies and bachelor's buttons. He had been planning to pick Joan a bunch of those daisies, before all this happened. They were her favorite flowers. Now he couldn't; the house would be stuffed with hothouse funeral flowers. And anyway, he couldn't just walk in there with a bunch of daisies in his hand and risk disturbing the Pikes. The daisies would have grown old there, waving in the sunshine on their long green stems, before he could go back to doing things like that again.

The pizza was in the oven. Ansel slammed the door on it and wiped his hands and said, "*There,* now."

"How much longer?" Simon asked.

"Oh, I don't know. Fifteen-twenty minutes. We'll go out where it's cool and wait on it. You coming, James?"

James followed them out to the living room. It seemed very dark and cool here now. Ansel settled down on his couch with a long contented groan, and Simon went over to Ansel's window and stood watching the road.

"Anybody seen those people?" he asked James.

"What people?"

"My mama and them. Anybody seen them?"

"No, not yet."

"Well, anyway," said Simon, "I reckon I'll just run on over and have a look, see if maybe they haven't—"

"I think we'd have seen them if they'd come," said James. "Or heard them, one."

"*Still* and all, I guess I'll just—"

"You two," Ansel said. "Do you have to stand over me like that?" He was lying full length now, with his head propped against one of thc sofa arms. "Kind of overwhelming," he said, and James moved Simon gently away by one shoulder.

"I almost forgot," he said. "You want to see my pictures?"

"Oh, well I—"

"They're good ones."

"Well."

James went down the little hallway to his darkroom. There was a damp and musky smell there, and only the dimmest light. He headed for the filing cabinet in the corner, where he kept his pictures, and opened the bottom drawer. The latest ones were at the front, laid away carefully (taking pictures for fun wasn't something he could afford very often), and when he pulled them out he handled them gently, examining the first two alone for a minute before he returned to the living room.

"Here you go," he said to Simon. "Your hands clean?"

"Yes."

His hands were covered with tomato sauce, but he held the pictures by the rims so James didn't say anything. The first picture didn't impress Simon. He studied it only a minute and then sniffed. "One of those," he said. James grinned and handed him the next one. Neither Simon nor Janie Rose had ever liked anything but straight, posed portraits—preferably of someone they could recognize, which always made them giggle. But when James wasn't taking wedding pictures, or photographs for the Larksville newspaper, he turned away from portraits altogether. He had the idea of photographing everyone he knew in the way his mind pictured them when they weren't around. And the way people stuck in his memory was odd—they were doing something without looking at him, usually, wheeling a wheelbarrow up a hill or hunting under the dining-room table for a spool of thread. Old girlfriends of his used to object to being photographed in their most faded blue jeans, the way he remembered them from some picnic. But almost always he won out in the end; the pictures of people in his mind and in his filing cabinet were nearly identical. Joan he imagined in a dust storm, the way he had first seen her (she had come down the road with two suitcases and a drawstring handbag, spitting dust out of her mouth and turning her face sideways to the wind as she walked.) For a long time now he had waited for another dust storm, and last week one had come. That was in those first two pictures, the ones that Simon had barely glanced at. Even when James said, "That's your cousin Joan, if you don't know," thinking to make Simon look twice, Simon only raised his eyebrows. It was the third picture he liked. In that one Ansel was lying on his couch, looking up at the sky through the window and absently playing with the cord of the shade. "Ansel!" Simon said, and Ansel turned his head and looked at him.

"What now?" he asked.

"I just seen your picture here."

"*Oh*, yes," Ansel said.

"Of you on your couch and all."

"Oh, yes. Here, let me look." He raised himself up on one elbow, reaching out toward the picture, and Simon brought it over to him. "That's me, all right," said Ansel. He studied it for a while, smiling. "It's not bad," he said.

"I think it's a right good picture."

"Yep. Not bad at all." He handed the picture back and lay down again, staring up at the ceiling and still smiling. "They're wonderful things, pictures," he said.

"Well, some of them."

"Very *remaining* things, you know?"

"I don't like them other kind, though," Simon said. "Dust clouds and all. I can't see what *they're* for."

"They're for me," said James. "Here, I got another one of Ansel."

"James," Ansel said, "do your legs ever get to feeling kind of numb? Kind of achey-numb?"

"Prop them up."

"Propping *up* won't do it."

"It's what you get for not having your shots," James said.

"Oh, well. Right behind the knee, it is." He propped his legs against the back of the couch and slid farther down, so that his feet were the highest part of him. "This couch is too short," he said. "Here, Simon. Hand me the next one."

The next picture had Ansel sitting up, looking self-conscious. When Ansel saw it he smiled his dippy little smile again and brought the picture closer to examine it. "This is one I posed myself," he said. "Had James take it like I wanted. James, I believe it's my *shoes* aggravating that feeling."

James set the rest of the pictures beside Simon and reached over to untie Ansel's shoes. "If you'd get the right *size*," he said.

"No, it's to do with my illness. I can tell."

"It's on Wednesdays you get your shots," said James. "This is Saturday. That's five times you missed."

"Lot you care. Listen—" He twisted around, so that he was facing Simon. "What was I talking about? The picture. That's right. I was about to say, in my estimation this picture is the best of the lot. The one of me sitting up." He tilted the picture toward the light. "Heroic, like," he said. "Profile to the window and all."

"The other one's better," said Simon.

"What other one?"

"The first one. You lying down."

"That's because you're used to me lying down," Ansel said. He sighed and tossed the picture onto the coffee table. "Everyone's used to it. When I stand up they hardly recognize me. Faces change, standing up. Become more bottom-heavy. Pass me the next one."

"I think the pizza must be done," said James. "Hey, Ansel?"

"Well, take it out. This one of Mr. Abbott—I'd be insulted if I was him. Troweling up the garden plot with his back to the camera and his rear end sticking out."

James got up and went to the kitchen. The pizza-smell filled the whole room, and when he opened the oven he thought it looked done. From a hook on the wall he took a pot-holder and then hauled the pizza out and set it on the counter, burning one finger on the way. "Ansel!" he called. He came to the living room doorway. Ansel was just bending over a picture, rocking slightly back and forth and frowning at it, and Simon was sorting through the rest of them. "Ansel," James repeated.

"This one here," said Ansel, "ought not to've been included."

"Which one?" Simon asked.

"I'm ashamed of James. You ought not to see it."

"Well, I just *saw* it," said Simon. "What's the matter with it?"

"Nothing's the matter. I'll just set it aside."

He pulled himself up and lay the picture face down on the back of the couch, looking over his shoulder to make sure Simon hadn't seen. "Shamed of James," he said.

"Well, for heaven's sake," James said from the doorway. "What's all that about, Ansel?"

"It ought never to've been included, that picture."

James crossed the living room and picked up the picture. It was a perfectly ordinary one—he'd done it as a favor for Miss Faye, who wanted her screened back porch photographed now that her nephew had spent half the summer building it. She had led James way behind the house, deep into the wild grass that grew there among scattered piles of rusted stoves and old car parts, and she directed him to photograph the whole long house so that her people in Georgia could get an idea how the porch was proportioned. "I think this is too *far*, ma'am," James told her, but she insisted and this was what had come of it—a wild, weedy-looking picture, with the house rising above a wave of grass like a huge seagoing barge. Miss Faye's porch was only a little bump sticking out along with a lot of other bumps—Janie Rose Pike's tacked-on back bedroom, the woodshed under James and Ansel's bathroom window, and the rusted old fuel barrel on its stilt legs beside the middle chimney. He hadn't shown the picture to Miss Faye yet, for fear of disappointing her. But it wasn't all *that* bad; he couldn't see what was upsetting Ansel.

"I don't get it," he said.

"Well, never you mind. Just give it back."

"What you trying to pull, Ansel?"

"Will you give it back?"

James handed it across, but before Ansel's fingers had quite touched it Simon reached out and took it away. He swung away from the couch, avoiding Ansel's long arm, and wandered out into the middle of the room with his eyes fixed frowningly on the picture. Ansel groaned.

"You see what you done," he told James.

"Ansel, I don't know why—"

"Then *listen*," Ansel said. He leaned forward, talking in a whisper now. "James, someone *departed* is in that picture—"

"Where?" Simon asked.

"Oh, Lord."

"Well, I don't see."

"Me neither," said James. "What're you up to, Ansel?"

Ansel stood up, supporting himself with both hands on the arm of the couch. When he walked over to Simon he walked like a man wading, sliding his stocking feet across the floor. He poked his finger at one corner of the picture, said "There," and then waded back again. "I'm going to lie down," he said to no one in particular.

"Ah, yes," said James. "I see."

"I don't," Simon said.

"Right here she is."

He pointed. His forefinger was just touching the Model A Ford that stood behind the house, resting on cinder-blocks that were hidden by the tall waving grass. All that could really be seen of the Ford was its glassless windows and its sunken roof—it had been submerged in that sea of grass a long time—and in the front window on the driver's side, no bigger than a little white button, was Janie Rose's moon-round face. She was too far away to have any expression, or even to have her spectacles show, but they could see the high tilt of her head as she eyed James and the two white dots of her hands on the steering wheel. She was pretending to be some haughty lady driving past. Yet when James drew back from the picture he lost her again immediately; she could have been one of the little patches of Queen Anne's lace that dotted the field. "I don't see how you found her," he told Ansel.

"No trouble."

Simon stared at the picture a while and then tilted it, moving Janie Rose out of his focus. "She just blurs right in again," he said. "She comes and goes. Like those pictures in little kids' magazines, where you try and find the pig in the tree."

"The *what?*" Ansel said. He raised his head and looked at Simon, open-mouthed.

"But it's her, sure enough," said James. "Isn't that something? I never saw her. Not even when I was enlarging it, and I looked it over right closely then."

"It's funny," Simon said.

"You hungry, Simon?"

"I guess." But he went on staring at the picture. He seemed not so much to be looking at Janie Rose as turning the whole thing over in his mind now, holding the picture absently in front of him. With his free hand he was pulling at a cowlick over his forehead.

"When our mother died," Ansel said suddenly, "I was beside myself."

Simon looked over at him.

"I couldn't think about her. I couldn't think her name. Yet people are different these days. I see that."

"Oh, well," Simon said. He returned to his picture. "James, is there such a thing as X-ray cameras? Could you take a picture of our house, like, and have the people show up from inside?"

"I don't know," said James. "I doubt it."

A fly buzzed in, humming its way in zigzags through the room, and Ansel followed it with his eyes. When the fly had disappeared into the kitchen he lay back again, gazing upwards. "I'm doing all my dying in one room now," he told the ceiling.

"Oh, stop that," James said.

"It's true. I'm getting contained in smaller and smaller spaces. First it was the whole of North Carolina; then this town; then this room. Soon no place. We *all* got to go."

"Look," James said. "I know of one stone-cold pizza in the kitchen. What do I do with it? Throw it out?"

"Well," said Ansel. He sat up and peered over at Simon. "Why do you keep looking at that picture?"

Simon put the picture down. He looked from Ansel to James, and then he stood up and stuck his hands in his pockets. "When I come to think of it," he said, "I don't want no pizza."

"Well, you don't have to eat it," said James.

"I think I'll just pass it up."

"All right."

"It's hard to say what's happening to people," Ansel said. "They don't seem to realize, no more. Don't think of *themselves* being dead someday; don't mourn no more. It's hard to say what they *do* do, when you stop and consider."

"Don't die of anemia no more, either," said James.

"What do you know about it?"

Simon was tilting gently back and forth, from his toes to his heels and his heels to his toes, with his shoulders hunched high and his eyes on a spot outside Ansel's window. He didn't seem to be listening.

"Nobody's perfect," Ansel said. "Janie wasn't exactly a pink-pinafore type, I admit it. Rattling through her prayers in purple pajamas: Deliver us from measles. But she's under the earth like you'll be someday, have you thought of that? *You* in that clay, and your survivors calling you a pig in a tree?"

"Ansel, there's not a thing in this world you do right," James said.

But Ansel waved him aside and sat forward, on the edge of his couch. "What will you do about *me?*" he asked. "How *about* that, now? When I am—"

Simon was crying. He was still rocking back and forth, still keeping his hands jammed tightly in his pockets, but there were wet paths running through the flour on his cheeks and his eyes were frowning and angry. "Well—" he said, and his voice came out croaky. He took a breath and cleared his throat. "Well, I reckon I'll be getting on home," he said.

"Oh, now," said Ansel.

But James said, "All right. It's all right."

He crossed over to open the door and Simon went out, stumbling a little. James followed him. He stood on the porch and watched Simon all the way down to his end of the house, hoping Simon might look back once, but he never did. He walked stiffly and blindly, with his sharp little shoulder-bones sticking out through the back of his jacket. When he reached his own door he hesitated, with his hand on the knob and his back still toward James. Then he said, "Well," again, and pulled the door open and went on in. The screen door slammed shut and rattled once and was still. James could hear Simon's footsteps clomping on across the hollow floor of the parlor.

The aluminum porch chair was still beneath the window, where Ansel had been sitting in it to watch the funeral go by. After a minute James went over and sat down on it. He let his arms rest along the arms of the chair and the metal burned him, making two lines of sunbaked heat down thc inside of his forearms. Behind him was the soft sound of the mesh curtains moving, and the sleeves of Ansel's rough black suit sliding across the splintery windowsill. "Hot out," Ansel said.

James squinted toward the road.

"I wish it was the season for tangerines."

There were no people passing now, only the yellow fields across the way rippling in the wind and one gray hound plodding slowly through the yard. In the house behind James were the soft, humming sounds of other people, murmuring indistinct words to one another and moving gently around. James closed his eyes.

"Hey, James."

He didn't answer.

"*James.*"

"What."

"James, I told you he wouldn't eat."

The wind began again, and James rose from his chair to go inside. He didn't want to sit here any more. Here it was too still; here there was only that wind, rushing over and around the house in its solitary position among the weeds.

2

Joan Pike was twenty-six years old, and had lived in bedrooms all her life. She lived the way a guest would—keeping her property strictly within the walls of her room, hanging her towel and washcloth on a bar behind her door. No one asked her to. Her aunt had even said to her, once, that she wished Joan would act more at home here. "You could at *least* hang your coat in the downstairs closet," she said. "Could you do that much?" And Joan had nodded, and from then on hung her coat with the others. But her towel stayed in her own room, because nobody had mentioned that to her. And she read and sewed sitting on her bed, unless she was expressly invited downstairs.

If they had asked her, point-blank, the way they must have wanted to—if they had asked, "Why do you have to be invited?" she wouldn't have known the answer. It was what she was used to; that was all. When she was born, her parents were already middle-aged. They weren't sure what they were supposed to do with her; they treated her politely, like a visitor who had dropped in unexpectedly. If she sat with them after supper they tried to make some sort of conversation, or gazed at her uneasily over the tops of their magazines until she retreated to her room. So now, a hundred miles from home and on her own, it felt only natural to be living in another bedroom, although she hadn't planned it that way. She had come here planning just to stay with the Pikes a week or two, until she found a place of her own, and then the children made her change her mind. When Janie Rose's hamster ran away, and Janie Rose stayed an hour in the bathroom shouting that it wasn't important, brushing her teeth over and over with scalding hot water that she didn't even notice and crying into the sink, Joan was the only one who could make her come away. After that the Pikes asked if she would like to live with them, and she said yes without appearing to think twice. This bedroom wasn't like the first one, after all. Here there was always something going on, and a full family around the supper table. When she went walking with Simon and Janie Rose, she pretended to herself that they were hers. She played senseless games with them, toasting marshmallows over candles and poking spiders in their webs to try and make them spin their names. For four years she had lived that way. Nine months of each year she worked as a secretary for the school principal, giving some of her salary to the Pikes and sending some home to her parents, and in the summers she worked part-time in the tobacco fields. In the evenings she sat with James, every evening talking of the same things and never moving forwards or backwards with him, and she spent a little time with the Pikes. But she still lived in her bedroom; she still waited for an invitation, and when any of the Pikes wanted to see her they had to go knock on her door.

Today no one knocked. Her aunt and uncle had gone straight to their room after the funeral and were there now—the sound of Mr. Pike's murmuring voice could just be heard—and Simon was alone in his room and seemed to be planning to stay there. That left Joan with a piece of time she knew would be her own, with no one interrupting, and at first she thought it was what she needed. She could sit down and get things sorted in her mind, and maybe catch some sleep later on. There was still that heavy feeling behind her eyes from the long aching wait in the hospital. But when she tried sorting her thoughts she found it was more than she could do just now, and then when she tried sleeping her eyes wouldn't shut. She lay on top of her bedspread, with her shoes off but her dress still on in case her aunt should call her, and her eyes kept wandering around the bland, motel-like cleanness of her room. It seemed every muscle she owned was tensed up and waiting to be called on. If she were alone in the house she would have gone down and scrubbed the kitchen floor, maybe, or at least had a long hot bath. But who knew whether her aunt would approve of that on a day like today?

When she finally thought of what she could do, she sat up quickly and frowned at herself for not thinking of it sooner. It was the one thing her aunt had asked of her all day: she had been sitting at the breakfast table, digging wells in her oatmeal and staring out into the back yard, and suddenly she had caught sight of Janie Rose's draggled blue crinoline flapping on the clothesline. "Take everything away, Joan," she said.

"What?"

"Take Janie's things away. Put them somewhere."

"All right," said Joan, but she was hunting raisins for Simon's oatmeal and hadn't really been thinking about it. Now she wasn't sure how much time she would have; Simon might come in at any moment. She wanted to do the job alone, keeping it from the rest of the family, because different things could bother different people. With her it had been Janie Rose's pocket collection—modeling clay and an Italian stamp and a handful of peas hidden away during supper, sitting on the edge of the tub where they had been dumped before a bath five nights ago. She didn't think any more could bother her now.

She opened her door and looked out into the hallway. No one was there. Behind the Pikes' door the mumbling voice still rambled on, faltering in places and then starting up again, louder than before. When Joan came out into the hall in her stocking feet, a floorboard creaked beneath her and the murmuring stopped altogether, but then her uncle picked up the thread and continued. Joan reached the steps and descended them on tiptoe, and when she got to the bottom she closed the door behind her and let out her breath.

Janie Rose's room opened off the kitchen hall. It had had to be built on for her especially, because the Pikes had never planned for more than one child and the room that was now Joan's had been taken up by a paying lodger at the time. Janie didn't like her room. She liked Simon's, with the porthole window in the closet and the cowboy wallpaper. When Simon wasn't around she did all her playing there, so that her own room looked almost unlived in. On her hastily made-up bed sat an eyeless teddy bear, tossed against the pillow the way Janie Rose must have seen it in her mother's copies of *House and Garden*. And her toys were neatly lined on the bookshelves, but wisps of clothes stuck out of dresser drawers and her closet was one heap of things she had kicked her way out of at night and thrown on the floor.

It was the closet Joan began with. She pulled back the flaps of a cardboard box from the hall and then began to fold the dresses up and lay them away. There weren't many. Janie Rose hated dresses, although her mother had dreams of outfitting her in organdy and dotted swiss. The dresses Janie chose for herself were red plaid, with the sashes starting to come off at the seams because she had a tendency to tie them too tightly. Then there were stacks of overalls, most of them home-sewn and inherited from Simon, and at the very bottom where the few things her mother had bought when Janie Rose wasn't along—pink and white things, with "Little Miss Chubby" labels sewn into the necklines. While she was folding those Joan had a sudden clear picture of Janie Rose on Sunday mornings, struggling into them. She dressed backwards. She refused to pull dresses over her head, for fear of becoming invisible. Instead she pulled them up over her feet, tugging and grunting and complaining all the way, and sometimes ripping the seams of dresses that weren't meant to be put on that way. She had a trick that she did with her petticoat, so that it wouldn't slide up with her dress—she bent over and tucked it between her knees, and while she was doing all this struggling with the dress she would be standing there knock-kneed and pigeon-toed, locking the petticoat in place and usually crying. She cried a lot, but quietly.

When Joan had finished with the closet, the cardboard box was only two-thirds full. The closet was bare, and the floor had just a few hangers and bubble gum wrappers scattered over it. It looked worse that way. She reached over and slammed the closet door shut, and then she dragged the box over to the dresser and began on that.

Upstairs, a door slammed. She straightened up and listened, hoping it was only the wind, but there were Simon's footsteps down the stairs. For a minute she was afraid he was coming to find her, but then she heard the soft puffing sound that the leather chair made when someone sat in it, and she relaxed. He must not want to be with people right now. She pushed her hair off her face and opened the next dresser drawer.

Janie Rose had more sachet bags than Joan thought existed. They cluttered every drawer, one smell mixed with another—lemon verbena and lavender and rose petals. And tossed in here and there were her mother's old perfume bottles with the tops off, adding their own heavy scent, so that Joan became confused and couldn't tell one smell from another any more. She wondered why Janie Rose, wearing all this fragant underwear, had still smelled only of Ivory soap and Crayolas. Especially when she wore so *much* underwear. On Janie Rose's bad days, when she thought things were going against her or she was frightened, she would pile on layer upon layer of undershirts and panties. Her jeans could hardly be squeezed on top of it all, and if she wore overalls the straps would be strained to the breaking point over drawersful of undershirts. Sometimes her mother made her take them off again and sometimes she didn't ("She's just hopeless," she would say, and give up), but usually, if the day turned better, Janie peeled off a few layers of her own accord. On the evenings of her bad days, when Simon came in for supper, he had a habit of reaching across the table and pinching her overall strap to see how many other straps lay beneath it. It was his way of asking how she was doing. If Janie was feeling all right by then she would just giggle at him, and he would laugh. But other days she jumped when he touched her and hunched up her shoulders, and then Simon would say nothing and fix all his attention on supper.

Out in the parlor now Joan heard the squeaking of leather as Simon rose, and the sound of his shoes across the scatter rug. She stopped in the act of closing the box and waited, silently; his footsteps came closer, and then he appeared in the doorway. "Hey, Joan," he said. There was something white on his face.

"Hey."

He looked at the cardboard boxes without changing expression, and then he went over to the bed and sat down, picking up the teddy bear in one hand. "Hey, Ernest," he said. He laid Ernest face down across his lap, circling the bear's neck with one hand, and leaned forward to watch Joan.

"I'm packing things away," she told him.

"Well, I see you are."

She folded the flaps of the box down, one corner over another so as to lock them, and then stood up and pushed the box toward the closet. "Some of your things're on the shelves there," she told Simon while she was opening the closet door. The box grated across the hangers on the floor. "You better take out what's yours, before I pack it away."

"None of it is," said Simon, without looking at the shelves.

"Some is. That xylophone."

"I don't play that any more. Don't you know I've stopped playing with that kind of thing?"

"All right," Joan said.

"I gave it for keeps."

"All right."

"Unliving things last much longer than living."

"That's true," Joan said. She chose an armload of things from the shelves—dolls, still shining and unused, a pack of candy Chesterfields, and an unbreakable yellow plastic record ordered off a cereal box. She dumped them helter-skelter into a second box and returned for another armload. "James give you a good lunch?" she asked.

"No."

"What was wrong with it?"

"Nothing," said Simon. "There just wasn't any. Because I didn't eat it."

"Oh."

"If I *had* of eaten it, it would have been a pizza."

"I see."

She dumped another armload in the box. It was half full now, and junky-looking, with the arms of dolls and the wheels of cars tangled together.

"I better make you a sandwich," she said finally.

"Naw."

"You want an apple?"

"Naw."

He crossed over to where she was standing and laid the bear gently on top of the other things. "James has got this photograph," he said, and went back to sit on the bed. "That Ansel, boy."

"What about him?"

"I just hate him. I hate him."

When it looked as if he weren't going to say any more, Joan began removing the last few things from the shelf. Every now and then she looked Simon's way, but he sat very quiet with his back against the wall and his face expressionless. Finally she said, "Well, Ansel has his days. You know that." But Simon remained silent.

The room was bare now; all that remained were the things on the clothesline. She pushed the second box into the closet and then said, "I'm going out back a minute. After that I'll fix you a sandwich." Simon stood up to follow her. "I'm only going for a minute," she said, but Simon came with her anyway, and they went down the hall and through the kitchen and out the back screen door.

It was hot and windy outside, with the acres of grass behind the house rumpling and tangling together. The few things on the line—Simon's bathing suit and Janie Rose's crinoline and Sunday blouse—were being whipped about by the wind so that they made little cracking sounds. While Joan unpinned Janie's things, Simon wandered nearby snapping the heads off the weeds.

"Simon," she called to him, "what kind of sandwich you want?"

"I ain't hungry."

"I'll just make you a little one. And go call your mama and daddy; they have to eat too."

"I wish *you* would."

"Come on, Simon."

He shrugged and started toward the house, still walking aimlessly and kicking at things. "All right," he said. "But I'll tell them it's your fault I came."

"They won't mind you coming."

"You think not?"

He banged the screen door behind him. After he was gone Joan stood in the yard awhile, clutching Janie's things against her stomach, feeling the dampness soak into her stocking feet. She wished she could just walk off. If it weren't for Simon, she would; she would go find some place to sit alone and think things out. But her feet were growing cold, and there were sandwiches to make; she shook her hair off her forehead and started back toward the house. The closer to the house she came the quieter the wind sounded, and when she stepped back into the kitchen there was a sudden silence in her ears that felt odd.

She put the things from the clothesline into the closet, and then she returned to the kitchen and leaned against the refrigerator while she planned a meal. The room was so cluttered it made thinking difficult. Small objects lay here and there, gathering dust because no one had ever found a place for them. The kitchen windows were curtainless, and littered with lost buttons and ripening tomatoes. And the wall behind the stove was covered with twenty or thirty drawings, scotch-taped so closely together they might have been wallpaper. Most of them were Simon's—soldiers and knights and masked men with guns. His mother thought he might be an artist someday. Scattered among them were Janie Rose's drawings, all of the same lollipop-shaped tree with hundreds of tiny round apples on it. She said it was the tree out back, but that was only a tiny scrubby tree with no leaves; it had never borne fruit and wouldn't have borne apples even if it had, since it was some other kind of tree. Once her mother said, "Janie, honey, why don't you draw something *else?*" and Janie had run out crying and wouldn't come down from the attic. But the next day she had said she would draw something different. She came into the kitchen where they were all sitting, carrying a box of broken crayons and a huge sheet of that yellow pulpy paper she always used. "What else *is* there to draw?" she asked, and her mother said, "Well, a house, for instance. Other children draw houses." Then they all hung over her, and she drew a straight up-and-down line and a window, and then a green circle above it with lots of red apples on it. Everybody sat back and looked at her; she had drawn an apple tree with a window in it. "*Oh*, my," she said apologetically, and then she smiled and began filling in the circle with green crayon. After that she never tried houses again. She labored away at apple trees, and signed them, "Miss J.R. Pike" in the corner, in large purple letters. Simon never signed his, but that was because his mother said she would recognize his style anywhere in the world.

When Simon came downstairs again he had changed into his boots; he was trying to make the floor shake when he walked. "Daddy's coming and Mama ain't," he said. "She ain't hungry."

"Did you ask if she wants coffee?"

"She didn't give me a chance. She said go on and let her rest."

"Well, run up again and ask her."

"*No*, sir," Simon said. He sat down firmly in one of the chairs.

"Just run up, Simon—"

"I won't do it," he said.

Joan thought a minute, and then she said, "Well, all right." She reached out to smooth his hair down and for a minute he let her, but just barely, and then shrugged her hand away.

"Daddy wants just a Co-Cola," he told her.

"He's got to have more than that."

"No. He said— Hey, Joan."

"What."

"I got an idea."

"All right."

"Why not you and me go *out* and eat. You like that?"

"We can't," Joan said.

"We could go to that place with the chicken."

"We have to stay home, Simon."

"I would pay for it."

"No," Joan said, and she touched one upright piece of his hair again. "Are you the one that doesn't like using other people's forks? That makes twice in two days you've had that idea."

"Well, anyway," said Simon. But he must have been expecting her to say no; he sat back quietly and began drumming his fingers on the table. Above them was the sound of Mr. Pike's footsteps, crossing the hall and beginning to descend the stairs, and Joan remembered why she was in the kitchen and went back to the refrigerator. She opened the door and stared inside, at shelves packed tightly with other people's casseroles. At the kitchen doorway her uncle said, "I only want a Coke, Joan," and came to stand beside her, bending down to peer at the lower shelves.

"You have to eat something solid," Joan told him.

"I can't." He straightened up and rubbed his forehead. He was a lean man, all bones and tough brown skin. Ordinarily he did construction work, but for the month of July he had been laid off and was spending his time the way Joan did, helping Mr. Terry get his tobacco in. Years of working outdoors had made his face look stained with walnut juice, and his eyes were squinted from force of habit even when he wasn't in the sun. They were narrow brown slits in his face, the same shade as

Simon's, and they were directed now at Joan while he waited for her to speak.

"There's a chicken salad here from Mrs. Betts," said Joan.

"No, thank you."

"The kind you like, with pimento."

"No."

"Now, eat a *little* something," she said. "I could be perking coffee for you to take Aunt Lou, if you'd sit down a minute."

"Oh, well," he said.

He sat down awkwardly, across from Simon, giving his Sunday pants a jerk at each knee to save the crease. "How you been getting along?" he asked Simon.

"Okay."

"Not giving Joan any trouble."

"No, sir."

"He's been just fine," said Joan. She set the salad out and laid three plates on the table. Her uncle studied his own plate seriously, hunching his shoulders over it and working his hands together.

"I'm glad to hear it," he said finally. When Joan looked over at him he said, "About Simon, I mean. James and Ansel feed you okay, boy?"

"No, sir."

"Well. Joan, Dr. Kitt left a prescription for your aunt but I don't see how I can go into town and leave her. I wonder, would you mind too much if—"

"I'll see to it after we eat," Joan said.

"All right."

He accepted his chicken salad wordlessly, keeping his

eyes on Joan's hands as she dished his share out. When she had passed on to the next plate, he said, "Thank you," and the words came out hoarse so that he had to clear his throat. "Thank you," he said again. Even then his voice was muffled-sounding. In the last three days he had been talking steadily, always mumbling something into Mrs. Pike's ear to keep her going. It was probably the most he had talked in a lifetime. Ordinarily he sat quiet and listened, with something like awe, while his wife rattled on; he seemed perpetually surprised and a little proud that she should have so much to say.

When Joan had sat down herself, after filling the others' plates and passing out forks, she said, "Eat, now." She looked at the other two, but neither of them picked up his fork. "*Come* on," she said, and then Simon sighed and tucked his paper napkin into his collar with a rustling sound.

"This feels like Sunday-night supper," he said.

"It does."

"Not like afternoon. Why're we eating in the afternoon? What the *day* feels like, is Wednesday."

"Wednesday?"

"Feels like Wednesday."

"Why does it feel like—?"

"She blames it on herself," said Mr. Pike.

"What?"

"It breaks my heart. She keeps saying how she was hemming Miss Brook's basic black at the time—I never *have* liked that Miss Brook—and Janie Rose comes up and says, 'Mama,' she says, 'I'm going off to—' and Lou just never did hear where. Miss Brook was going on about her bunions. 'Lou,' I told her, I said, 'Lou, *I* don't think that would have—' but Lou says that's how it come to happen. She *never* let Janie Rose play with those Marsh girls. Never would have let her go, if she had known. But she was—"

"Never let her ride no tractors, either," said Simon. "Shakes a girl's insides all up."

"Hush," Joan told him. "Both of you. There's not even a dent made in that chicken salad."

Her uncle picked his fork up and then leaned across the table toward her. "She *blames* herself," he said.

"I know."

"She keeps—"

"*Eat,* Uncle Roy."

He began eating. His fork made steady little clinking sounds on the plate, and he chewed rapidly with the crunchy sound of celery filling the silence. When he was done, Joan put another spoonful of salad on his plate and he kept on without pause, never looking up, making his way doggedly through the heap of food. Simon stopped eating and stared at him, until Joan gave his wrist a tap with her finger. Then he started eating again, but he kept his eyes on his father. When Mr. Pike reached for the bowl and dished himself another helping, still crunching on his last mouthful, chewing without breathing, like a thirsty man drinking water, Simon looked over at Joan with his eyes round above a forkful of food and she frowned at him and cleared her throat.

"Um, Mrs. Hammond phoned today," she said. "She's a very *cheering* person, Uncle Roy; maybe Aunt Lou could talk to her later on. I told her to call back in a day or—"

"Remember Janie Rose?" Simon asked.

His father stopped chewing. "Remember *what?*" he said.

"Remember how she did on the telephone? Never answering 'Hello,' but saying, 'I am listening to WKKJ, the all-day swinging station,' in case WKKJ was ever to call and give her the jackpot for answering that way. Only you know, WKKJ never *did* call—"

"Simon, I *mean* it," Joan said.

"Lou is breaking my heart," said Mr. Pike.

"Wouldn't you feel funny, if you was to call someone that answered like that? 'I am listening to—' "

"It wasn't her *fault,*" Mr. Pike said. "Janie never *asked* for no special attention, like. She just kind of—"

"God in heaven," Joan said.

The doorbell rang. It made a sharp, burring noise, and Joan stood up so quickly to answer it that her chair fell over backwards behind her. She let it stay. She escaped from the kitchen and crossed the parlor floor, smoothing her skirt down in front of her, making herself walk slowly. Behind the screen, standing close together with their faces side by side and peering in, were the Potter sisters from next door. They stepped backwards simultaneously so that Joan could swing the door open, and then Miss Faye entered first with Miss Lucy close behind her.

"We only stopped by for a minute," said Miss Faye. "We wanted to bring your supper."

"Well, come on in," Joan said. "Really, do. Come out to the kitchen, why don't you."

"Oh, I don't think—"

"No, I mean it." She took Miss Faye by one plump wrist, almost pulling her. "You don't know how glad I am to see you," she said.

"Well, if you really think—"

They walked on tiptoe, bearing their covered dishes before them like sacred offerings. When they reached the kitchen door, Mr. Pike stood up to greet them and his chair fell backwards too, so that the room with its overturned furniture looked stricken. "Why, Miss, um, Miss Lucy," he said. "And Miss Faye. I declare. Come in and have a—" and he bent down and pulled the chairs up by their backs, both at the same time. "Sit down, why don't you," he said.

Joan drew up the chair from beside the stove, and Miss Lucy sat down in it with a sigh while Miss Faye went to sit beside Simon. "We only mean to stay a minute," said Miss Lucy. She plopped the bowl she was carrying down on the table in front of her and then sat back, sliding her purse strap to a more comfortable position on her wrist. The Potter sisters always carried handbags and wore hats and gloves, even if they were only going next door. They were small, round women, in their early sixties probably, and for as long as Joan had known them they had had only one aim in life: they wanted to have swarms of neighborhood children clamoring at their door for cookies, gathering in their yard at the first smell of cinnamon buns. And although no one came ("Children nowadays prefer to buy Nutty Buddies," Miss Faye said), they still went on baking, eating the cookies themselves, growing fat together and comparing notes on their identical heart conditions. It was those heart conditions that Miss Faye was discussing right now. She was saying, "Now, you and Lou know, Roy, how much we wish we could have climbed that hill today. If there was *any* way, the merest *logging* trail, we would've got there. But as it was, it would just have meant more tragedy. You know that."

And Mr. Pike was saying, "Well, I know, I know," and nodding gently without seeming to be listening. There was chicken salad on his chin, which meant that both the Potters kept staring tactfully down at their gloves instead of looking at him. Joan passed him a paper napkin, but he ignored it; he sat forward on his chair and said, "It surely was nice of you to come. Nice to bring us supper."

"It's the *least* we could do," said Miss Lucy. She looked around her, toward the kitchen door, and then lowered her voice. "Tell me," she whispered. "How is she now? How's Lou?"

"It just breaks my heart," said Mr. Pike.

"Oh, my."

"Not a thing I can do, seems like. She just sits. If she would stop all this *blaming* herself—"

"They all do that," said Miss Faye.

"She said Janie was the one she never paid no mind to."

"Will you listen to that."

"Never gave her a fair share."

"If it's not one reason it's another," Miss Lucy said. "I've seen that happen plenty of times."

"Maybe if you talked to her," said Mr. Pike. He pushed his plate away and straightened up. "You think you could just run up there a minute?"

"Well, not *run*, no, but—"

"I didn't mean that," he said. "No, you can take the stairs as slow as you want to. But if you two would talk to her a minute, so long as you don't mind—"

"Why, we don't mind a bit," said Miss Faye. "We'd be proud." She reached up to set her flowered hat straighter, as if she might like to put an extra hat on top of the first one for such a special visit. And Miss Lucy pulled gloves to perfect smoothness, and then folded her hands tightly over her purse.

"I just don't like to trouble you," Mr. Pike said.

"You stop that, Roy Pike."

They rose simultaneously, with their backs very straight. But even making the trip across the kitchen they walked slowly, preparing themselves for the stairs. "Be careful," Joan told them. "Just see they don't get out of breath, Uncle Roy."

"I will."

But Simon was frowning as he watched them leave. "Hey, Joan," he said.

"Hmmm?"

"When they go up to bed at night, it takes them half an hour. They take two steps and then rest and talk; they bring their knitting along."

"Well, that's kind of silly," said Joan.

"Could they crumple up and die on our stairs?"

"No, they could not," she said. "It would take more than that."

"How do you know?"

"I heard Dr. Kitt tell them so. They just shouldn't get too out of breath, is all, or run in any marathons. He said—"

"I got an idea," Simon said.

"What?"

"Listen." He stood up from his place at the table and came around to face her, with his hands hitched through his belt loops. "How about us going to a movie," he said. "That Tarzan movie."

"We're not supposed to."

"Well, I got to get out," he said.

She looked down at him, considering. His face had a thin, stretched look; patches of flour still clung to it like some sort of sad clown makeup and his hair stuck up in wiry tangles. "Well, I do have to get Aunt Lou's prescription," she said. "Would you comb your hair first?"

"Sure."

"All right, we'll go."

"Right now?"

"If you want to."

He nodded, but with his face still wearing that strained look, and turned to go upstairs and then turned back again. "I'll wash downstairs," he said.

"There's no soap here."

"I don't care."

He turned on the water in the kitchen sink and splashed his face, and then he reached spluttering for the dishtowel. "My allowance money's all the way upstairs," he said. "I'll pay you back tomorrow, if you'll lend me the money."

"All right."

She went into the living room, with Simon following, and handed him a comb from her pocketbook. While he was combing his hair she went upstairs for her shoes. Mrs. Pike's door was open now. She was lying on her bed, with her head propped up on two pillows and the sisters beside her talking steadily, and when Joan walked past, her aunt followed her with her soft blue eyes but only vaguely, as if she weren't seeing her, so Joan didn't stop in to say anything. She put on her shoes and picked up a scarf and went downstairs, where Simon was waiting with his hand on the newel post and his face strained upward.

"What're they doing?" he asked her.

"I don't know."

"Are they crying?"

"I don't think so."

"Well. I *would*'ve gone upstairs," he said. "You know."

"I know."

"Did you think I wouldn't?"

"No." She sighed suddenly, looking back toward the stairs. "*I* don't know how to comfort people," she said.

"Well."

They went out the front door, across the porch, and down the wooden steps. It was beginning to get cool outside. Joan could hear tree frogs piping far away, and the wind had died down enough so that the sound of cars on the east highway reached her ears. She clasped her hands behind her back and followed Simon, cutting across the road and through the field toward town.

"Remember I've got heels on," she called.

"I remember."

"Remember that makes it hard walking."

He slowed down and waited for her, walking backwards. Behind him and all around him the field stretched wide and golden, with bits of tall yellow flowers stirring and glimmering like spangles in the sunlight. And when Joan came up even with him, so that he turned and walked forward again by her side, she could look down and see how his hair, bleached lighter on top, took on a varnished look out here and the little line of fuzz down the back of his neck had turned shiny and golden like the field he was walking in. "Right about here . . ." he said, but the wind started up just then and blew his words away.

"What?" she asked.

"Right about here is where I lost that ball. Will you keep a lookout for it?"

"I will."

"Do you reckon I'll ever find it?"

"No."

"I don't either," Simon said.

But they walked slowly anyway, keeping their eyes on the ground, kicking at clumps of wild wheat to see what might turn up.

3

"*Hold* STILL," JAMES SAID.

He bent over and peered through the camera. No one was holding still. Line upon line of Hammonds, from every corner of the state, littered the Larksville Hammonds' front lawn, sitting, kneeling, and standing, letting arms and legs and bits of dresses trail outside the frame of his camera. Whole babies were being omitted; they had crawled to other patches of grass. Yet the grown-ups stood there with their dusty blue, look-alike eyes smiling happily, certain that they and their children were being saved intact for future generations. James straightened up and shook his head.

"Nope," he said. "You've moved every which-away again. Close in tighter, now."

He waited patiently, with his hands on his hips. For five years he had been going through this. Every year there was a picture of the Hammond family reunion to be put in the Larksville paper, and another two or three for the Hammonds themselves to choose for their albums. By now he was resigned to it; he had even started enjoying himself. He smiled, watching all those hordes of Hammonds close in obligingly with sideways steps while their eyes stayed fixed on the camera. Moving like that made them look like chains of paper dolls, bright and shimmering in the heat. Eyelet dresses and seersucker suits blurred together; their whiteness was blinding. James shaded his eyes with one hand, and then he said, "Okay," and bent down over his camera again. But someone else was moving. It was Great-Aunt Hattie in the front row; she had started coughing. She was sitting in a cane-bottom chair, with children and animals tangled at her feet and the grown-ups forming a protective wall behind her. When she began her coughing fit, they closed in still tighter in a semicircle and the oldest nephew leaned down with his head next to hers. The coughs grew farther apart. After a minute the nephew raised his head and said, "She's sorry, she says." The others murmured behind him, saying it didn't matter. Swallowed down the wrong throat," said the nephew.

Someone called out, "Give her brown bread." And someone else said, "No, rock candy will do it." But the aunt spread her old hands out in front of her, palms down and fingers stretched apart, signifying she was better now and wanted to hear no more about it. "Back in your places," James said, and the twenty or thirty Hammonds closest to him drifted back to their original positions and made their faces stern again. Mothers looked anxiously down the rows, gripping their neighbors' arms and peering around them to make sure their children were at their best, and fathers hooked their thumbs into their belts and glared into the lens. "Hold it," James said. When he snapped the picture there was a little stirring through the group, and everyone relaxed. "That's the second," he called to the hostess. "You want another?"

"One more, James."

While he was fiddling with the camera people began talking again, still standing in their set places, and some lit cigarettes. He peered through the view-finder at them. If this were any other picture he would snap it now, catching them at their ease, but family pictures were different. He liked the way they stood so straight in jumbled, self-conscious rows, and molded themselves to make a block of tensed-up faces. "I'm ready," he warned them, and they did it again—closed their mouths and narrowed their eyes and set their shoulders. He snapped the picture that way. Then he said, "That's all," and watched the children as they shook themselves and scattered off to play.

The hostess walked up to him, trailing white lace, sinking into the ground at every step in her high-heeled pumps. "There's one more I want, James," she said, and then stopped and let her eyes wander after her youngest child. "Joey, you *know* not to ride that dog," she called.

"Yes, ma'am."

"I want you to photograph Great-Aunt Hattie alone," she told James. "She's getting old. Can you do that?"

"If she's willing," said James.

"She's not."

"Then maybe we should—"

"Now, don't you worry," said Mrs. Hammond. "I'll talk her around. They're serving up the ice cream over there. You go and get you some, and when you're through I'll have Aunt Hattie ready. Hear?"

"Well, okay," James said. But Mrs. Hammond hadn't stayed to hear his answer.

He folded his equipment up and put it on the porch, out of the way of the children. Then he went across the yard to the driveway, where the others were standing in line for ice cream. They looked different now, quick-moving and flexible, with the paper-doll stiffness gone. In a way James was sorry. Some of the best pictures he had were these poker-straight rows of families, Hammonds and Ballews and Burnetts; he kept copies of them filed away in his darkroom, and sometimes on long lonesome days he pulled them out and looked at them a while, with a sort of faraway sadness coming up in him if he looked too long. He might have seen any one of those families only that morning in the hardware store, but when he looked at their faces in pictures they seemed lost and long ago. ("I just wish once you'd take a *giggly* picture," Ansel said. "You make me so sorrowful.") Thinking about that made James smile, and the girl in front of him turned around and looked up at him.

"I'm thinking," he told her.

"That's what it looked like," she said. Her name was Maisie Hammond, and she lived across town from here and sometimes came visiting Ansel. She thought Ansel was wonderful. James was just considering this when she said, "How's that brother of yours?" and he smiled at her.

"Just fine," he said. "He's home reading magazines."

"Well, say hello to him." She moved up a space in line, still facing in James's direction and walking backwards. Standing out in the sunlight like this she was pretty, with her towhead shining and her white skin nearly transparent, but Ansel had always said she was homely and only out to catch a good husband (it was rumored James and Ansel came from an old family). Whenever she came visiting, Ansel turned his face to the wall and played sicker than he was. That was how he planned to scare her off, but Maisie only stayed longer then and fussed around his couch. She liked taking care of people. She would fetch pillows and ice-water, and Ansel would wave them away. When she was gone, James would say, "Ansel, what you want to treat her like that for?" But by that time Ansel had fooled even himself, and only tossed his head on the pillow and worried about how faint he felt. To make it up to Maisie now (although she wasn't aware there *was* anything to be made up), James stepped closer to her in the line and said, "Maisie, it's been a good two weeks since you've been by."

"Two *days*," said Maisie. "Day before yesterday I was there."

"I never heard about it."

"You were off somewhere. Taking care of some arrangements for the Pikes."

The man ahead of her left with his Dixie cup of ice

cream, and Maisie turned forward again and took two cups from the stack on the table. "Here," she said. She passed him a fudge ripple, with a little paper spoon lying across the top of it. "The children got to the strawberry before us."

"That's all right," said James. "I don't like strawberry."

He followed her back across the lawn, preferring to stick with her rather than interrupt the little individual reunions that were going on among the others. When she settled on the porch steps, fluffing her skirt out around her, he said, "You mind if I sit with you?" She shook her head, intent on opening her ice cream. "I'm going to take a picture of your great-aunt," he said.

"Oh, her."

"Do you like sitting out in the sun like this?"

"Yes," she said. But she looked hot; she was too thin and bird-boned, and being the slightest bit uncomfortable made her seem about to topple over. James was used to Joan, who was unbreakable and built of solid flesh.

When he had pried the lid off his own ice cream, and dipped into it with his paper spoon, he said, "It's sort of melty-looking." Maisie didn't answer. She was staring off across the yard. "Better eat yours before it turns to milk," he told her.

But Maisie said, "Ansel was laying down, when I went to see him."

"He does that," said James.

"I mean laying still. Not doing anything."

"Well, it was nice of you to come," he said.

She shrugged impatiently, as if he hadn't understood her. "You were out doing something," she told him. She seemed to be starting all over again now, telling the story a second time. "You weren't around."

"I was helping Mr. Pike with some arrangements," said James.

"That's what Ansel said."

"I'm sorry I wasn't around."

"Well. When I came in I said, 'Hey, Ansel,' and Ansel didn't even hear me. He was just laying there. I said, 'Hey!' and he jumped a foot, near about. He was a million miles away."

James was making soup out of his ice cream. He had it down to a sort of pulpy mess now, the way he liked it, and then he looked up and saw Maisie wrinkling her nose at it. He stopped stirring and took his first bite. "Ansel's a great one for daydreaming," he said with his mouth full.

"He wasn't daydreaming."

"Oh."

"He was crying, near about."

"*Ansel?*"

"Well, almost," said Maisie. She sat forward, with the ice cream still untasted in her hand. "I said, 'Ansel, *what's* the matter?' But he never did say. His eyes were all blurry."

"You got to remember Janie Rose," James said. "It was only three days ago."

"Well, I thought of that. But then I thought, no, Janie wasn't all that much to him. She was right bothersome, as a matter of fact. We had her over for supper just a month ago, her and her family; we gave them chicken. Mama forgot about Janie being vegetarian. Janie said, 'This chicken's *dead,*' and her daddy said, 'Well, I *hope* so,' and everybody laughed, but Mama's feelings were a little hurt. Though she went to the funeral and all, just like anyone else. I said, 'Ansel, is that what's bothering you? Janie Rose Pike being taken?' But the way he was acting, I don't think that was the real reason."

"His feet hurt him sometimes," said James.

"This is *serious*, James."

"I'm being serious."

"Anyway," Maisie sighed, and she took the first mouthful of her ice cream. It bothered him, the way she ate it; she chewed, slowly and carefully, even though the ice cream was nothing but liquid now. When she had swallowed, she said, "All he would talk about was dying. He said he could see how it would all turn out; they would mourn him like they mourn Janie Rose, not sad he died but sorry they hadn't liked him more. He'd rather they be sad he died, he said."

"Oh, now," said James. "He's been on that for days. It'll pass."

"Will you listen? I can't hardly sleep nights, for thinking about it. I keep wondering if he's all right."

"Of course he's all right," James said.

But Maisie was still hunching over, frowning into space. Her ice cream was forgotten. A child ran by, chased by another child, grabbing Maisie's knee for support as he pivoted past her, and Maisie only brushed his hand away absentmindedly. "Those times he goes away," she said finally, "those times he starts to get better and then goes off drinking for a night and can't be found till morning. He'll die of it."

"He won't die," said James. "He could lead a life like any other man, if he wasn't so scared of needles."

"He *might* die," Maisie said. "What if one of those nights of his, he don't come back?"

But James was getting tired of this. "Look," he said firmly. He swallowed the last of his ice cream and said, "Ansel only goes so far, you notice. Only enough to worry people. You ever thought of that?"

"What? Well, if that isn't the *coldest* thing. How do you know how far he'll go?"

"I just do," James said. "I been through this."

"Can you say for *sure* how far he'll go?"

"I been through it *hundreds* of times."

"I believe you don't even give it a thought," said Maisie. "That's what Ansel said. He said, 'What does *James* care—' "

"Well, we've got to be clearheaded about this," James said.

"You're clearheaded, all right." She jabbed her spoon into her ice cream and left it there, standing straight up in the middle of the cup. " 'What does James care,' he said, and then just lay there with his eyes all blurry—"

"I do everything I can think of," said James.

"Oh, foot."

"I try everything I know."

"Then tell me this, if you do so much all-fired good. Can you say that never, never once in all your life, have you thought about Ansel's going off and letting you be someday?"

"Well, for—"

"Never thought how nice it would be to live on your own for a change, just one little old TV dinner to pop into the—"

"I try *every*thing I *know!*" James shouted, and then noticed how loud his voice was and lowered it. "I mean—"

But Maisie just folded in the rim of her Dixie cup with all her concentration, as if her mind was made up. Then she rose and said, "Well, I'll be seeing you." Her skirt was rumpled in back, but she didn't bother smoothing it down. When she walked away James stood up, from force of habit, and waited until she was halfway across the yard before he sat down again. Inside he felt slow and heavy; he was chewing on his lower lip, the way he did when he didn't know what to say. All the way across the yard he watched her, and turned his empty ice cream cup around and around in his hands.

In front of him some children were playing statues. An out-of-town boy was flinging the others by one arm and then crying, "Hold!" so that they had to freeze there, and when he came to Janice Hammond, who was the littlest, he swung her around so hard that she spun halfway across the lawn and landed against Mrs. Hammond, who was heading over toward James. "Hold!" the boy said. Mrs. Hammond looked down at Janice, who was clutching her around the middle. She said, "*Oh*, Janice," tiredly, and was about to pull away, but the other children stopped her. "No, Janice has got to stay that way," said the out-of-town boy, and Mrs. Hammond seemed too tired to argue. She stood still, rising above Janice's circled arms like the figure of someone passively drowning, and called out, "James, we're ready with Aunt Hattie."

"Where is she?" he asked.

"Over there. Standing up. We wanted her to sit but she says no, she'll do it standing. Die with her boots on. She doesn't like cameras." She came to life suddenly and disentangled herself from Janice, ignoring the other children's protests. "She's fading," she said. James looked over at Janice, surprised, and Mrs. Hammond caught his look and shook her head. "Aunt Hattie, I mean," she said. "Just fading away."

"I'm sorry to hear that," said James. He gathered up his equipment and came after her. "She looked all right to me."

"Well, she fades out and then in again."

They circled a little group of women, all standing in identical positions with folded arms while they watched the children playing statues. "I don't like doing this if she don't want me to," James called. "Some people just have an allergy to cameras."

But Mrs. Hammond smiled brightly at him over her shoulder and kept walking. Out here on the grass the sun was still hot, and the back of Mrs. Hammond's powdered neck glistened faintly. She had the same brittle little bones as her niece Maisie, only covered now with a solid layer of flesh. James looked away from her and shifted his equipment to the other shoulder. "Right here would be a good place," he said. He hadn't really looked around; he just wanted to stop and not do anything any more. The heaviness inside was weighing him down. He set the camera on its tripod and then leaned on it, with his chin propped on his hand, and Mrs. Hammond said, "You all right?"

"I'm fine," James said.

"You look kind of tired."

He straightened up and tucked his shirt in. There was Great-Aunt Hattie, only a few yards away now, being led gingerly by Mrs. Hammond. Aunt Hattie looked neither to the right nor to the left; she seemed to be pretending Mrs. Hammond wasn't there. The closer they got to the camera, the farther away her eyes grew.

"Right here would be a good place," said Mrs. Hammond. "Don't you think so, James? In front of the roses?"

"Fine," James said. He had started adjusting his camera and wasn't really looking now. But when he raised his eyes again he saw that the old woman had been placed directly in front of a circular flower bed; she seemed to be rising from the middle of it, like an intricately sculptured garden decoration. James smiled. "I've changed my mind," he said. "I don't think she should have those flowers behind her."

"They're so pretty, though," Mrs. Hammond said sadly.

"Well. But I think she should have just grass behind her. You mind moving over, Miss Hattie?"

"I have just one thing to say," Miss Hattie said suddenly.

"Ma'am?"

"Don't push me. You can tell me where to go, but don't push me around."

"Oh, I won't," said James.

"The *last* time I had my picture taken—"

"I think he wants you to move over," Mrs. Hammond said. "Could you step this way, dear?"

The aunt stepped stiffly, jerking her chin up. "I was saying, Connie," she said, "the *last* man that took my picture was in need of an anatomy lesson. I told him so. He came right up to me and pushed my face sideways but my shoulders full-front, and my knees sideways but my feet full-front, so I swear, I felt like something on an Egyptian wall. You should have seen the photograph. Well, I don't have to tell you how it looked. I said—"

"If I were you I'd let my beads show," said Mrs. Hammond. "They're such nice ones."

"Well, just for that I won't," snapped Aunt Hattie. She raised her hands, heavy with old rings, and fumbled at the neck of her crepe dress until she had closed it high around her throat, hiding the beads from sight. "Now *no* one can see them," she said, and Connie Hammond sighed and turned to James with her hands spread hopelessly.

"I try and I try," she told him, and he looked up from fiddling with his camera and smiled.

"Why don't you go on and see to the others," he said, "and I'll call you when I'm through. I bet you haven't even had your ice cream yet."

"No. No, I've been so busy. Well, I might for just a minute, maybe—" She trailed off across the yard, looking relieved, and the last part of her to fade away was her voice, which still flowed on and on.

"She's putting on weight, don't you think?" Aunt Hattie asked.

James had the camera ready now, but he was waiting because he wanted the picture to be just right. He bent down and cleared away a dandelion from one of the tripod legs, and then over his shoulder he called, "You comfortable like that? Don't want to sit down?"

"No. I'll stand."

Connie Hammond wouldn't like that, but James was glad. To him Aunt Hattie looked just right this way—standing against a background of bare grass, holding her shoulders high to hide the beads and jutting her chin out at him. She had terrified high school students for forty years that way, back when she taught Latin I. People still told tales about her. She had declined her nouns in a deafening roar and slammed her yardstick against her desk on the ending of every verb. While students could lead other teachers off their subjects just by asking how they'd met their husbands, Miss Hattie had only strayed from Latin once a year, at Christmastime, when she read aloud from a condensed version of *Ben Hur*. James could picture that. He wished he had her in a classroom right now, to photograph her the way she stood in his mind. But all he had was this wide lawn, and he would have to make do with that. He stood there, pressing a dandelion between his fingers and squinting across at her. "That's right," he told her. "That's what I want."

She shifted her feet a little. "How many prints you plan to make of this?" she asked.

"Ma'am?"

"How many copies."

"Oh. As many as you want."

"Well, I want *none*," she said. "I'd like to request that you make the one picture asked of you and have that be that."

"Oh, now."

"Connie can have one, if she wants it so much. But that's because I don't like her. Nothing she could *do* would make me like her; I just constitutionally don't. Danny can't have one."

"Danny who?" he asked. "Raise your chin a little, please."

"Danny Hammond. Is there anyone in this world whose last name isn't Hammond?" She raised her chin but went on talking; James leaned his elbow on his camera and waited. "Danny I put up with," she said. "How long will they hide him away from me?"

"Danny *Hammond?* Why, I saw him only last—"

"*You* saw him. You saw him. But do you think *I* do? They rush him away the moment I come around; he looks back over his shoulder all bewildered. He's only seven."

"Could you turn more toward me?" asked James.

"They think he insulted me last Valentine's Day."

"Oh, I don't think Danny would—"

"Made me a present. None of these easy-breaking things from the gift shop. Made me a ceramic saltshaker in school, and it was the exact shape of my head, with even the wrinkles painted in."

"That's nice," said James.

"Do you know where the salt came out?"

"Well, no."

"My nose. Ho, out my nose. Two little holes punched

for nostrils, and out came the salt. Can you picture Connie's face?"

James laughed. "I sure can," he said.

"Well, of course she hadn't *seen* the thing, prior to my unwrapping it. She thought it was a bobby-pin holder or something. She said, 'Danny *Hammond!*' and made a grab for it, but I was too quick for her. I meant to *keep* it; it's not often I get such a personal present. But Connie rushed him off like I would eat him and there I sat, all alone with my saltshaker. No one to thank."

"Maybe you could—"

"I still use it, though."

"Ma'am?"

"The saltshaker. I use it daily."

"Well, I would too," said James.

"Then you see why he shouldn't have my picture."

That stumped him; he had to consider a minute. (If Miss Hattie Hammond was fading out, should he not just let it pass and agree with her?) But Miss Hattie seemed the same to him as ever, as sharp as a rock against the green of the lawn. "I don't see what you mean," he said.

"Ah well."

"I don't understand what pictures have got to do with it."

"Not much," she said. "But they're photographing me because I'm old, you know. They think I'm dying. (I'm not.) They think they'll have something to remember me by. But pictures are merely one way, Mr. Green. Should a person that I *like* have a picture of me?"

"I wouldn't let it worry me," said James. "I find no

one ever looks at pictures anyway, once they get hold of them."

"*I* don't want Danny remembering just a picture. Remembering something flat and of one tone. What is ever all one way?"

"Well," James said. He frowned down at his fingers, sticky now with dandelion mild. "Well, *plenty* of—"

"Photographs," said Miss Hattie, "are the only thing. Don't interrupt. Everything else is a mingling of things. Photographers don't agree, of course. Why else would they take pictures? Press everything flat on little squares of paper—well, that's all right. But not for people that you'd like to stay *interested* in you. Not for Danny Hammond."

"Now, wait a minute," said James, but Miss Hattie held up her hand.

"I already know," she said. "*I* know photographers."

James grinned and bent over his camera again. "As far as things that're all one way," he called, "I can name—"

"No. Not a thing, not a person, Mr. Green. Take your picture."

He gave up. Through the frame of his view-finder he saw her standing just the way he wanted her, old-fashioned-looking and symmetrical, with her hands across her stomach and her mouth tight. Her face was like a turtle's face, long and droopy. It had the same hooded eyes and the same tenacious expression, as if she had lived for centuries and was certain of living much longer. Yet just in that instant, just as his hand tightened on the camera and his eyes relaxed at seeing the picture the way he had planned it, something else swam into his mind. He thought of Miss Hattie coughing, in the center of that family reunion—not defiant then but very soft and mumbling, telling them all she was sorry. He frowned and raised his head.

"Well?" said Miss Hattie.

"Nothing," James said.

He bent down again, and sighted up the haughty old turtle-face before him and snapped the picture. For a minute he stayed in that position; then he straightened up. "I'm done," he said.

"I should hope so."

"I'll get one copy made, for Mrs. Hammond."

"I'm going in then. I'm tired."

"All right," he said. "Goodbye, Miss Hattie."

"Goodbye."

She nodded once, sharply, and turned to go, and James watched after her as long as she was in sight. Then he stared down at his camera. Just to his right Connie Hammond materialized—he caught a fold of lace out of the corner of his eye—but he didn't look at her.

"Well, now!" Mrs. Hammond said brightly. She was out of breath and looked anxious. She came around in front of him and went to stand where Miss Hattie had stood, with her eyes intent on the ground, as if by tracking down the print of Miss Hattie's Wedgies she could suddenly come to some understanding of her. "I'm sure it'll come out good," she called over her shoulder.

"Well."

"What's that?"

"Yes, I'm sure it will," James said. He folded up his tripod and gathered the rest of his equipment together. "I'm leaving now," he told her.

"Oh, are you?"

"I'll have the pictures ready in a day or two."

"That'll be fine," said Mrs. Hammond. But she was still staring at the ground and looking anxious; she didn't turn around to say goodbye.

James's pickup truck was parked on the road at the edge of the lawn. He circled around the children, being careful to stay clear of the ones playing statues. Their game was growing rougher now. Little Janice Hammond was frozen in the exact stance of a baseball pitcher, her right arm drawn back nearly out of joint, and even her face was frozen—she was grimacing wildly, showing an entire set of braces on her teeth. But she unfroze just as James passed her; she shook out her arms and smiled at him and he smiled back.

"I want to come out *pretty* in them pictures," she said. "You see what you can do about it."

"I'll see."

He placed the camera on the leather seat of the pickup and then went around to the driver's side and climbed in. It was like an oven inside. First he started up the motor and then he rolled down his window, and while he was doing that he caught sight of Maisie Hammond. She was standing high up on the lawn, waving hard to him and smiling. He waved back. This time when the heavy feeling hit his stomach he didn't shrug it off; he sat turning it over in his mind, letting the motor idle. As long as he sat there, Maisie went on waving. And when he had shifted into first and rolled on down to the bottom of the hill, he looked in the rear-view mirror and saw her still waving after him. He thought suddenly that she must be having two feelings at once—half one way and half another. Half angry at him, and half sorry because she had told him so. And now she had to keep on waving.

He looked down beside him at the camera, where Miss Hattie was so securely boxed now in her single stance. But the fields he drove through shimmered uncertainly in the sunlight; the road was misted with dust, and he was driving home now not knowing if he wanted to go there or not, not knowing for sure what he thought about anyone. All he could do was put the heavy feeling out of his mind, and let only the road and the fields alongside it occupy his thoughts.

4

THAT SUNDAY, JOAN BEGAN thinking about Simon's hair. She started out by saying, "Simon, tomorrow morning first thing I want to find you in that barber's chair," but Simon said, "Aw, Joan, I don't want to go downtown." Since that movie yesterday he had changed his mind about town; he hadn't even asked to eat in a restaurant today, and Joan could see his point. Going downtown meant people murmuring over him and patting his head, asking Joan in whispers, "How is he taking it? Is his mother coming out of it?" while Simon stood right next to them, his chin tilted defiantly and his eyes on their faces. Little boys who were usually his friends circled him widely, looking back over their shoulders in curious, half-scared glances. They had never seen someone that close to funerals before, not someone their own age. When Simon and Joan were coming out of the movie theater a member of Mrs. Pike's church had stopped smack in front of them and said to her friend,

"Oh, that poor little boy!" Her voice had rung out clearly and hung in the air above them, making other people stop and stare while Simon pulled on Joan's hand to rush her home. She could understand it if he had never went downtown again.

So instead of insisting, she said, "Well, all right. But we've got to cut your hair at home then. Today."

"It's not so long," he said.

"Curls down over your ears."

"Well, we've got nothing to cut it with."

"Scissors," Joan reminded him. "Your mother's sewing scissors. *Anything.*"

"Okay. Tomorrow, then," said Simon. "Bright and early."

"Tomorrow's a tobacco day; I won't be here. You know that."

"*Other* boys have hair *lots* longer."

"Orphans do," said Joan. "Will you fetch the scissors?"

He slid off the couch, grumbling a little, and went for his mother's sewing basket. It sat in one corner of the living room, gathering dust, odds and ends of other people's clothing poking out of it every which-way. (Mrs. Pike was a seamstress; she made clothes for most of the women in Larksville.) The materials on the top Simon threw to the floor, making a huge untidy pile beside the basket, and he rummaged along the bottom until he brought up a large pair of scissors. "These them?" he asked, and walked away from the basket with that heap of material still lying beside it. Joan let the mess stay there. She followed Simon into the kitchen, a few steps behind him, with her eyes on the back of his head. Where it had been pressed against the couch his hair was as matted as a bird's nest. It would take a sickle to cut all that off.

In the kitchen she found an apron and tied it around his neck, to keep the hair from tickling, and then she had him sit on the high wooden stool beside the kitchen table. He revolved on it slowly, making the seat of it squeak, while Joan looked him over and debated where to start. "I don't know where you *got* all that hair," she told him. "When was the last time you went to the barber's?"

"I don't know."

"It couldn't have been all that long ago."

"You sure you know how to cut hair?" Simon asked.

"Of course I do."

"Whose have you cut?"

"Well, my own," Joan said.

He stopped revolving and looked at her hairdo. "It's a little choppy at the ends," he told her.

"It's supposed to be."

"Will mine come out like that?"

"I surely hope not."

"If it does, what will we—"

"Now, Simon," Joan said, "I don't want to hear any more about it. Let's just get it over with."

He sighed then and gave in, but with his shoulders squinched up and his neck drawn into itself as if he thought she might slip and cut his head off. His hair grew in layers, lapping downwards like hay on a haystack. When Joan cut too much from one of the sun-yellowed upper layers it sprang straight up, choppy and jagged-edged, and she quickly pressed it down again and shot a look at Simon to see if he had noticed. He hadn't. He sat slumped on the stool, idly swinging one boot and gazing out the window. The only sound now was the steady snipping of scissors.

Out in the back yard Joan could see her uncle—just his head and his crumpled blue shirt. He was tilting back on an old kitchen chair in the sunshine, with one hand resting absently on Nellie's neck. That was the way he had been sitting all day. When Joan called him for his meals he came in docilely and ate everything set before him, and then he went out back again. Twice he had gone upstairs to see his wife, but that had taken only a minute; he must have given up trying to talk to her. Even Joan had given up. When she went to her aunt's bedroom, to where she was lying on her back with the covers pulled up around her, and asked her to come down for a bite to eat, her aunt only said, "No," and closed her eyes. Saying that one word seemed to take all the strength she could muster; Joan didn't dare argue with her. In the back of her mind she kept trying to think up little plots, planning ways to get her aunt interested in something, but she wasn't the kind of person who could do that. The most she could do was try and take care of the house for a while, and feed Mr. Pike and Simon. Even that was hard; she had never learned how to keep house.

The top part of Simon's hair was cut now. She squinted at it, not sure if this was how it was supposed to be or not. It seemed a little homemade-looking. But then she shrugged and began on the shaggy part along the back of his neck. She could always even it up later on.

Outside, Ansel called, "Is anybody home?" His voice was thin and wavered in the wind. Simon gave a sudden start and turned his head, so that Joan nearly gouged him in the neck. "Hold *still,* Simon," she said, and Ansel called again, "Is anybody home?"

"It's him," Simon said.

"Who do you mean? It's Ansel."

"I know. It's him."

"Just stop wiggling," said Joan. She raised her voice and called out, "We're out here, Ansel."

"Out where?"

"Out *here.*"

"Well, is someone going to come and let me in?"

"It's not locked," Joan said, and returned to her cutting. She didn't like Ansel and had never pretended to; he could open his own doors. When he came ambling out to the kitchen, walking in that shuffling way of his and stooping to get through the doorway, she didn't even turn around to look at him. "How are you," she said, making it a statement.

"Oh, not so bad, I guess."

"Turn a little to the left, Simon."

"Hey, Simon," Ansel said.

Simon frowned at his boots.

"*Hey,* boy."

"He's having his hair cut," said Joan.

"Ah, I see. That makes it impossible for him to speak."

"Will you have a seat?"

"I might," he said. He pulled out one of the chairs

from the table and sat down, facing Joan and Simon. He was looking better than usual today. The yellowish pallor of his face had faded and he sat nearly erect, with his arms folded across his chest. When he saw Simon frowning at him he smiled his dippy smile and said, "What's the matter with the barber, boy?"

"What?"

"Barber sick?"

But Simon only shrugged and didn't answer. Joan said, "I'm cutting his hair myself this time."

"I see that."

"I'm using the sewing scissors."

"I *see*."

That seemed to leave nothing more to be said. Joan hesitated a minute, with the scissors in mid air, and then she said, "Turn around, Simon."

"Are we done?" Simon asked.

"Almost. I want to think what to do about the front part of it."

"Where's Mr. and Mrs. Pike?" said Ansel.

"Uncle Roy's out back."

"Where's *Mrs.* Pike?"

Joan was frowning at Simon's hair, trying to figure out how to begin on that front shock. Any way she managed it, it was almost sure to end up looking like bangs. She snipped gingerly at one piece and held what she had cut off up to the light to examine it. Then she said, "Ansel, what're you here for?"

"Who, me?"

"Didn't James tell you not to bother her? Where *is* James?"

"He's taking pictures of the Hammonds."

"Didn't he tell you not to come around here?"

"Well, yes, he did," Ansel said. "He *suggested* that I not. But I was sitting reading on the couch and it occurred to me: I thought I might just wander over and see how you all are doing."

"We're doing fine," said Joan. She snipped off another piece of hair.

"Joan, you're ruining that boy."

"It'll turn out all right."

"Well. I was sitting reading a *Guideposts*," Ansel said, "and after that two outdoor-type magazines, and then I read them again. I would've read them a third time, if I hadn't come on over here. I read even the smallest inch-long ads for worm farms; I read the list of editors at the front and the entire information about the subscriptions. Then I thought I might come and see you."

"Simon, maybe you better get a mirror," Joan said. "I'm not sure what you're going to think of this."

"Aw, I don't care," said Simon. "Is it done?"

"You go look in a mirror and *see* if it is."

Simon stood up and little rags of hair fell around him, spilling off the apron around his neck. When he walked out of the room he trailed fuzz in a long path behind him.

"He won't thank you for this," Ansel said.

"I don't think it's so bad."

"Twice before, I started to come," Ansel said. "I got up and headed for the door and then I thought, 'No.' I cut my fingernails. I cleaned out my wallet. Then I thought I might as well come over. I thought—"

When he talked he had a way of leaning slightly forward and placing his fingertips together, as if words came hard to him and he had to consider. Yet in reality the words came flooding from him; it always made her feel swept away and drowned, with so many useless words spilling around her. Sometimes she could even get interested in what he said, but she never lost that drowned feeling. While he talked she stood silently by the stool, keeping her face blank and idly snipping at thin air with her scissors, but inside she was thinking, I wish you would *go*. The pale thinness of his face irritated her. She thought about all the long evenings of three long years, with James sitting next to her on the porch and never taking one step forward, never asking for more than tonight's kiss and tomorrow's date and never mentioning marriage or a family or any of those other things she was sitting there waiting to hear. And the reason for it all was Ansel, who hung limp and heavy in his brother's living room and expected to die any day, although actually he was stronger than any of them. He had that flood of words, after all, and that sad dippy smile, and that way of placing his fingers together as if asking people to be patient while he fumbled for what to say. "I thought I would come offer sympathy and then leave again," he was saying, and Joan snapped, "Well, you've offered it. Are you leaving?"

"Huh?" Ansel said. He looked up, bewildered. "Joan, I ain't even seen your Aunt *Lou* yet—"

Simon came in, with his hair plastered down by water. "It looks kind of like I expected it to," he said.

"You don't like it?"

"Well, yes. It'll grow out."

"I could trim it around the edges a little more," Joan said.

"No, that's all right. Thank you anyway."

"Or maybe tomorrow you could—"

"Hush!" Ansel said. He sat up straight, listening, and when the other two turned toward him he pointed at the ceiling. "Footsteps," he said.

It was the slow, clapping sound of Mrs. Pike's mules, crossing the upstairs hallway. "She's only going over to the bedroom," Joan said, but then the sound continued to the stairs, and Ansel said, "She's coming down." He stood up, preparing to meet her. Joan reached out and touched his arm. "Let her be," she said. "Why don't you go home?"

"I wanted to say hello."

"Do it some other time."

"No, I want—"

The footsteps descended slowly, like a child's—both feet meeting on the same step, then another hesitant step downwards. Joan left the kitchen, with a wave of her hand toward Ansel to show that he should stay there. He did, which surprised her a little. She crossed through the parlor alone and came to stand at the bottom of the stairs, looking up. Her aunt had just barely reached the halfway point. She was holding on to the railing and gazing steadily at Joan, her face blank without its makeup, her dark yellow hair straggly and uncurled, and her plump body wrapped in a chenille bathrobe. The grayness of her made her blend into the dark stairwell. She said, "Joan," and her voice came out blurred and gray also, without expression.

"What?" Joan said.

But her aunt didn't answer. She continued down the stairs laboriously, and when she reached the bottom she would have gone straight into the kitchen except that Joan took hold of her by one arm.

"Don't you want to sit in the parlor a while?" she asked. "I'll bring coffee."

"No."

"*Ansel's* out there in the kitchen."

"No."

Mrs. Pike went on walking, not pulling away from Joan but just walking off, so that Joan had to drop her arm or follow her. She dropped it. Her aunt said, "No," again, as if some new question had been raised, but Joan was trailing behind her now in silence, frowning at Mrs. Pike's back. Her back was soft and shapeless, and folded in upon itself at the waist where her sash was tightened. When she walked the hem of her robe fluttered out and Joan could see the dinginess where it had dragged across the floor.

Ansel was standing, ready to greet her. He said, "Mrs. Pike, I been waiting to see you," and Mrs. Pike said, "Ansel," and crossed to one of the kitchen chairs. Over by the window Simon stood with his back to her, his hands jammed awkwardly in his pockets and his chopped-at, straggly head wearing a stiff and listening look.

"I only came to tell you how I feel," Ansel said gently. "Then I'll leave."

"Where is Roy?" asked Mrs. Pike.

"Out back. You want I should get him?"

"No."

Mrs. Pike was sitting craned forward a little, with her hands on her stomach as if it hurt her. After a minute Ansel sat down opposite her, but Joan remained standing and Simon stayed by the window. Mrs. Pike didn't look at any of them. "I thought I would come downstairs a little," she said.

"That's the way," said Ansel. "You shouldn't sit alone."

"I wasn't sitting."

"What I actually came to say," Ansel said, "was how bad I feel about all this. That's all I wanted to tell you. I told James, I said, 'It's like the tragedy has struck at our own lives. I know just how she feels,' I said. I said—"

"No," said Mrs. Pike.

"Ma'am?"

But Mrs. Pike only looked away then, toward the screen door. Behind her, Simon picked up the cord of the paper window shade and began tying knots in it, small tight knots running up and down the length of the cord.

"What was you saying no for?" Ansel asked.

Mrs. Pike didn't answer.

"Was you saying I *don't* know how you feel? Mrs. Pike, I know how you feel better than you do yourself. I been through this before."

"Ansel," Joan said, "you've offered your sympathy now. I think you'd better leave."

"But I've got so much I want to *say* to her—"

"I came down to eat," said Mrs. Pike, "but I don't think I will."

Joan turned away from Ansel and looked down at

Mrs. Pike. She said, "Why, Aunt Lou, there's all kinds of things to eat in the icebox. Everyone's been bringing things."

"No," her aunt said.

"I know that when my mother died," said Ansel, "everyone kept trying to snap me out of it. They said that mourning has never brought the dead back. But it's only right to mourn; it's only natural. People have their faults but when they're dead you mourn them, and you expect to be mourned yourself someday."

"Janie Rose didn't have no faults," said Mrs. Pike.

"No, ma'am, of course she didn't. When my—"

"We don't know how it might have turned out. She was a little chubby but not, you know, really fat. She might have slimmed down some later on. I never *said* to her she was fat. I don't know what she *thought* I said but really I didn't. Never a word."

"When my mother died," said Ansel, "I thought of all the bad things I ever said about her. I got in a real swivet about it. She was a fine woman, but scared of everything. Wouldn't stand up against my father for us. When some sort of crisis was going on she had a way of sort of humming underneath her breath, slow and steady with no tune, and sewing away at someone's overalls without looking up. My father was—"

Joan came over and stood between Ansel and Mrs. Pike, bending down low so as to make her aunt look into her face. "I want you to eat something, now," she said. "There's a stew. Would you like that?"

"No."

"There's a whole icebox of things."

"No."

"My father was not what you'd call a man of *heart,*" said Ansel, placing his fingertips together. "Very strict. We always kept two goats around the place, to eat off the underbrush—"

"Isn't it funny," Mrs. Pike said, "that no one sent roses. Roses are a very normal flower, yet nobody sent them. Everything but, in fact."

"It's a little hot for good roses," Joan said.

"In the spring, when the goats had kids," said Ansel, "we would fatten them up for eating. Only by the time they were fat they'd be good pets, and we would beg for my father not to kill them. We would cry and make promises. But my mother sat humming (though she loved those goats the best of all and had names for every one of them) and my father always killed them. Only there was one thing that made up for that—"

"Ansel," Joan said, "Will you go home?"

"Wait a minute. When my mother brought a roasted kid in, or any part of it, holding it high on a wooden platter with potatoes around it, she always dropped it just in the doorway between the kitchen and the dining room. It never failed. The meat on the floor, and the potatoes rolling about like marbles and leaving little buttery paths behind them. 'Pick it up,' my father always said, but she would begin talking about germs and never let us eat it. I haven't *yet* tasted a piece of roasted goat. I think about that often now; it makes up for that humming, almost. I'm sorry I ever—"

Someone knocked on the front door. Joan said, "Ansel, will you go see who that is?"

"Why, Joan, it's *your* house."

"I don't care; just go."

"I'm not *well* enough to go bobbing up and down for people," said Ansel. But he rose anyway, moving slowly like an old man and holding his chest. "Who is it?" he called.

"Is that you, Ansel?"

It was James, with his voice sounding loud and steady even though he was still outside the house. Hearing him made Joan straighten up and feel suddenly more cheerful, and Simon turned around and let the window-shade cord slip out of his hand. "Ansel, what are you doing here?" James called.

"What're *you* doing here?"

"I'm looking for you. I been looking all over."

James had let himself in now, seeing that Ansel wasn't advancing to the door very quickly. He crossed the parlor in long strides, and appeared in the kitchen entrance with his hands on his hips.

"I'm taking you home for supper," he told Ansel. "I'm sorry about this, Mrs. Pike."

Mrs. Pike only gazed at him unblinkingly, without appearing to hear him. Joan said, "I wish you would, James."

"Come on, Ansel."

"Supper in the after*noon?*" asked Ansel.

"It's getting on towards sunset."

"Well, I don't feel so good, James. I'm not hungry."

"What's the matter with you?" James asked.

"My head is swimming."

"You been resting enough?"

"Well, yes. But after lunch this blackness started floating in, and then a little later this, um—"

Joan leaned back against the table, watching. She had never seen James actually *listen* to all this before; it seemed strange, and she couldn't figure out why he was doing it. The more James listened, the more Ansel's symptoms expanded and grew in detail; even his face looked paler. But James kept on nodding, saying "Hmm," every now and then. Finally he said, "I'll put you in bed. You can have your supper on a tray, if you want."

"Oh, I think I'll just stay here and—"

"It's time to go, Ansel."

Ansel sighed and let himself be led toward the doorway by one elbow. To Mrs. Pike he called, "I hope you're feeling better, ma'am. I'll be back tomorrow, maybe, or the next day—"

"Come on," James said.

They stopped trying to be graceful about it. James gave Ansel's arm a good tug and Joan followed close behind, almost on Ansel's heels, to hurry him out. After her came Simon, with his face looking small and curious under his ragged haircut. Mrs. Pike didn't go with them. She sat quietly in her chair, with her hands still pressed to her stomach, and it wasn't until the others were all the way into the parlor that she spoke.

"*Nobody* knows," she said distinctly.

Ansel wheeled around, fighting off Joan's and James's hands, and shouted, "*What's* that?"

Mrs. Pike didn't answer.

"Let's go," James said.

"I just want to tell you," Ansel shouted toward the kitchen, "I know better than you can *imagine,* Mrs. Pike. You're just sorry now you weren't nicer to her, but I know how it feels to *really* miss someone. I remember—"

Both James and Joan stopped then, looking first at Ansel and then back toward the kitchen. But all they heard was the creaking of a chair, as if Mrs. Pike had changed positions. And that seemed to show Ansel what they had been trying to tell him all along: that Mrs. Pike wasn't listening right now, and that nothing he could say would do her any good or any harm. So he shrugged and let himself be led the rest of the way out. When Joan stepped back a pace, indicating that he should go first and that she was staying in the house, he nodded goodbye to her gravely.

"One thing I'd like to make clear, Joan," he said. He was facing her squarely, acting very formal and dignified. "I *do* know," he told her.

"All right," Joan said absentmindedly.

"I *remember* how it feels. My memory's excellent."

"I believe you."

"Clutters my mind at night, it's so excellent."

James pulled him gently.

"When I want to sleep, it does. Clutters my mind."

"All right, Ansel," James said.

He led him on out to the porch. When he passed Joan she could smell the smoky, outdoors smell of James's hair, and he bent closer to her and said, "If you need anything, I want you to tell me."

"I will."

"And when you can get away, come over and see us."

"I will."

She stood in the doorway with her hand on Simon's shoulder and watched after them—Ansel tall and thin and leaning against James, who was solider and could bear his weight. She heard Ansel say, "Right through my temples it is, James. A sort of spindle of dizzy-feeling, right through my temples."

James said, "We'll lie you down. You feel tired?"

"Naw. I was thinking—"

"You sure now," James said.

"Huh?"

"I want you to tell me."

"Tell you what?" Ansel asked.

But James didn't answer that. And Joan, listening with a frown because it was so strange to her, felt suddenly lost and uncertain. She retreated into the parlor again, letting the screen door swing slowly shut behind her. But there was no one to listen to what was bothering her. Only Mrs. Pike, staring at the wall in the kitchen, and Simon beside her with his funny new haircut.

5

"Now, I CAN HAVE my ideas," said Missouri, "and you can have yours. Mind what you're doing there, Miss Joan. First off, I don't believe in sitting. I have never believed in sitting. Minute a person sits his mind gives way. Will you *watch* what you're *doing?*"

Joan sighed and handed her the next bunch of tobacco leaves. It was Monday afternoon, late in the day but hot, and even here under the shade of the pecan trees she could feel the sweat trickling down between her shoulder blades. Beside her stood three other women—two handing to Mrs. Hall, who was the fastest tobacco-tier in the county, and the other helping Joan do the handing to Missouri. Missouri was huge and black, and every move she made was a wide slow arc, but she could tie nearly as fast as Mrs. Hall. She stood at the end of her rod with her broad bare feet spraddle-toed in the dust, and first she yanked a handful of leaves from her daughter Lily and then from Joan, wrapping each handful to the rod with one sure circling of the twine so that the leaves hung points-down and swinging. If Joan or Lily was too slow with the next hanging she would click her tongue and stand there disgusted, holding the twine taut in her fingers, and when the leaves were ready she would take them with an extra hard yank and bind them so hard that the twine cut into the stems. Now it was Joan who was slow (they were down to the last of this table-load, and she was having trouble finding a full handing of leaves) and Missouri made her clicking sound and shifted her weight to the other foot.

"What it is," she called down the table to Mrs. Hall, "I bind *across* the stick. You bind on the same side, and I declare I don't see how. With Miss Joan on the left, I take her leaves and bind them on the right, and backwards from that with Lily. You follow my meaning?"

"Yes, and I think it's just as *inefficient*," Mrs. Hall said. She stopped her trying to brush a piece of wispy blond hair off her face. "That's three inches wasted motion every bunch you tie, Missouri."

"Ha. Fast as *I* move, who cares about three inches."

"It adds up. You see if it don't."

"Ha."

She yanked Joan's bunch from her and lashed it to the rod. That finished up the stick; it looked now like one long chain of hanging green leaves, with the rod itself hidden from sight by the thick stems that stuck up on either side. "You!" she said without looking, and Jimmy Terry raised himself from the side of the barn and set down his Coke bottle. By the time he had ambled over to Missouri she had lifted the stick from its notched stand

and stood making faces because of the weight of it, holding it very carefully so as not to crush the leaves. "Watch it, now," she said, and thrust it at him, and he started back to the drying-barn while she bent to take another rod and lay it in the notches. "I was saying something," she said. She tied the white twine around the end farthest from her and then snapped it off at a length of five feet or so, while Mrs. Hall stopped tying to watch her. (Mrs. Hall spent every day of every tobacco season trying to figure out how Missouri snapped off her twine ahead of time without measuring it.) "I was talking about sitting," Missouri said, grandly ignoring Mrs. Hall. "This table is *bare*, Lord; when they going to bring us more? Now, when you sit, your blood sort of sits along with you. It don't go rushing around your brain no more. Consequently, it takes that much more time to get rid of some sad idea in your mind. The process is slowed considerable. Whereas if you hurry your blood *up* some . . . There is a sizable amount of people could benefit from what I know. I could just go on and on about it. But do you get what I mean up to now?"

"Well, so far," Joan said.

"Good. Now, what started me on that—well, I do say. Took you long enough."

She was looking off toward the dirt driveway, where the men were just coming with the mule. Behind the mule was a huge wooden sled piled high with tobacco leaves, and it must have been heavy because the mule was objecting. He had stopped trying and began to amuse himself by blowing through his nose at the flies circling his head, and when Mr. Terry slapped his back he only switched his tail and gave an extra hard wheeze through his nose. Mr. Terry pulled out a bandanna and wiped his face.

"You stop that and bring him here," Missouri commanded. "We're out of leaves and getting paid for standing here with our ams folded."

"Well, I wouldn't want *that,*" Mr. Terry said, but he went on wiping his face with his back to the mule. He was an easygoing man; it was a wonder to the whole countryside how he ever got his tobacco in. Behind the sled was James Green, filling in for the day because Mr. Pike was at home with his wife, and he wasn't doing anything about the mule either. His face was dark from the sun and glistening, and his hair hung in a wet mop over his forehead. When he saw Joan he grinned and waved, but he didn't look as if he gave a hang whether that mule *ever* moved, so Missouri heaved a huge sigh and laid down her twine.

"I never," she said, and circled the long picnic table where the women were standing and headed for the mule. "Jefferson, you no-good, you," she told the mule, "you going to keep us waiting all day?"

"*That's* not Jefferson," Mr. Terry said. "That's my brother Kerr's mule, Man O'War. He's only a distant cousin to Jefferson."

"I don't care who he is." She reached up and grabbed the mule by one long ear, as if he were a little boy, and pulled in the direction of the table. The mule followed, sighing sadly. "In the end, it's the women that work," Missouri told him. "Stand still now, you hear?"

"I wish it *was* Jefferson," said Mr. Terry. "He was some good mule, old Jefferson."

"He sick?" Missouri asked.

"Nah. Dead."

"That's why this one is doddering around so, then. They know, them mules."

"Mr. Graves shot him down," Mr. Terry said. He and James were both at work now, lifting armloads of leaves from the sled and carrying them over to the table. "He says he has the right, because Jefferson kicked his boy."

"Nah, that ain't so. Only if Jefferson *killed* the boy, outright. Takes more than that to kill Sonny Graves. Sonny ain't dead, is he?"

"Oh, no."

"Well, you go on and sue then. Go on and do it."

"Well," Mr. Terry said. He took the mule and turned him around, and when he slapped him this time the mule headed back toward the fields with the empty sled skittering behind him. "We'll let Saul take care of him," Mr. Terry told James. To the women at the table he called, "That was the last load, there. Me and the men are going to cut out and have a beer up at the house."

"Don't you give Lem more than one," Missouri said. "You know how he gets."

"Well."

He headed toward the house, wiping his face again with the bandanna, and James turned and said, "You yell when you're ready to go, Joan."

"All right," Joan said.

When the men had left there was a different feeling in the air, blanker and stiller. The smell of sweat and mule and hot sun had drifted away, and for a minute the women just stood looking after them with their faces expressionless. Then Missouri said, "Well," and she and

Mrs. Hall took their places at their rods again and the others turned to the new heap of leaves on the table.

"That James stays out in the sun much more, he's going to change races," Missouri said to Joan.

"I guess he might," Joan said.

"He's a good man. Though a bit too quiet—don't let things show through."

"No."

Missouri waited, still without going back to her work. Finally she said, "Just where is he from?"

The others looked up. Joan said, "Oh . . . from around here, he says."

"Well, so are we all," said Missouri. "But what *town?*"

"He doesn't talk much about it."

"*That's* kind of peculiar," Mrs. Hall called. "You ever asked him?"

"He's not *wanted* or nothing, is he?" said Missouri.

"No."

"You never know. I'd been married two and a half years before I found out Lem had been married before. Mad? I tell you—"

"If I were you I'd ask him," Mrs. Hall said.

"Well, I did," said Joan. She was beginning to feel uncomfortable. "He *told* me where he was from but it was just an ordinary town, like Larksville—"

"Then why don't he say so?"

"Well, you know Ansel," Joan said.

"There's an odd one."

"He doesn't like for James to talk about it. He's afraid James'll send him back."

"Good thing if he did," said Mrs. Hall. "You ever been invited to meet their family?"

"Well, no."

"They had some kind of falling-out," Missouri's daughter Lily said. Everyone looked at her, and she said, "Well, that's what Maisie Hammond said."

"Maisie Hammond don't know beans," Missouri said. "Haven't you learned not to listen to gossip?"

"If I was you, Joan," said Mrs. Hall, "I'd just march right up and ask him. I'd say, 'James, will you take me to meet your family?' Just like that, I'd ask."

"No," Joan said.

They went on watching her, waiting for her to say more, but she didn't. She concentrated on grouping the leaves together by the stems, a small cluster at a time, so that they lay flat against each other, and then she held them out to Missouri and waited patiently until Missouri gave up and started tying again. Each time Missouri took the leaves from her there was a funny numb feeling in Joan's fingertips, from the leaves sliding across layers and layers of thick tobacco gum on her skin. Tobacco gum covered her hands and forearms, and it had worked in between the straps of her sandals so that there was black gum on the soles of her feet. Tonight when she walked barefoot through the house she would leave little black tracks behind her. She rubbed the tip of her nose against a clean spot on the back of her hand, and Missouri clicked her tongue at her to tell her to hurry. "I want to get *home*," she told Joan, and Joan swooped down on another bunch of leaves and handed them to her. In her sleep she would see tables full of tobacco leaves, stack upon stack of yellow-green leaves with their fine sticky coating of fuzz and their rough surfaces that reminded her of old grained leather on book covers. Whenever she told her aunt about that, about dreaming every night of mules and leaves and drying barns, her aunt thought she was complaining and said, "Nobody *asked* you to do it. I even told you, I said it right out, I didn't want you doing it. Secretaries don't work tobacco, honey." But then Joan only laughed and said she liked seeing leaves in her sleep. "There's lots worse I could dream of," she said, and Mrs. Pike had to agree.

Missouri had started talking again, now that she saw Joan wasn't going to answer any more questions. "Let's get back to sitting," she said. "What led me to speak of it was, your working and all so soon after that, uh, tragedy occurred. Now, honey, don't you mind Mrs. Pike. I know her, she feels like even James shouldn't of come. Feels like it shows disrespect. But look at it head-on and—"

"Well, not disrespect," Mrs. Hall called across. "Not that, exactly. But I see Lou's point. *I* wouldn't have come today, Joan. I don't mind telling you."

"What would I do at home?" Joan asked. "Sit?"

"Exactly what led me to my discussion," said Missouri. "What *sitting* does, is—"

"You could have stayed around and helped out," Mrs. Hall said. "Made tea and things. A person needs company at a time like this. And James there, why, he is very close to being Janie's cousin-in-law, or once removed, or whatever you call it—"

Once again they all looked at Joan, but she went on

grouping leaves and they sighed and turned back to the table.

"*Any*way," said Mrs. Hall, "with his own brother on the verge of—"

"Well, this is sort of pointless," Joan said. "You just think one way, and me another. I don't think she wants any more than her own husband there, and that's what she's got. And Simon too, if she wants him."

"Ain't *that* a funny thing," Lily said suddenly. "Up to last week, it was Janie *Rose* she never paid no attention to—"

"You hush," Missouri said. "This is Miss Joan's *relatives* we're talking about."

"Well, I know that. Now, won't it Simon she used to brag on all the time? Won't it Simon that was spoiled so rotten he—"

"Hush."

"My feet are killing me," said Mrs. Hall.

Her second hander, the pale one named Josephine, looked down at Mrs. Hall's feet and gave one of them a gentle kick with the toe of her sneaker. "With me it's sneakers or barefoot," she said. "What you wearing leather shoes for?"

"Because I'm older than you. I have to look decent." She snapped off her twine and turned to the barn. "Boy!" she called.

"Will you look?" said Missouri. "She's a stick and a half ahead of me, and you two are poking along. Hurry it up, Lily."

Lily handed her the next bunch and then stretched, raising her thin black arms an enormous length above her head. To show her disapproval Missouri jerked her string with a twanging sound, and one of Lily's leaves fell out of its bunch on the stick and landed in the dust. "Oh, Lord," Missouri said. She handed her string to Joan and bent to pick up the leaf, holding the small of her back with one hand. A pink slip strap slid down over her shoulder. "Four hours ago it was four o'clock," she said when she had retrieved the leaf. "Now it's four thirty. When'll it ever be five?"

"Won't help you if it is," called Mrs. Hall, "so long as you've still got leaves on your table."

"Well, I can't help it if they loaded the most leaves on me." She pulled her strap up again and took the end of the twine away from Joan. "I was saying something," she said. "I have that fidgety feeling, like I wasn't finished."

"Sitting," Joan reminded her.

"Sitting? Oh, sitting. My lord, how long I been *on* that? Well, anyway." She snapped her fingers at Lily, who was gazing open-mouthed at a pecan tree, and Lily jumped and handed her another bunch of leaves. "Originally," Missouri said, "I was getting around to a remedy for Mrs. Pike. Well, now I've gotten to it. Mrs. Pike is going to have to start working again."

"Working?" Lily said. "*I* didn't know Mrs. Pike worked."

"Will you *hush?*" Missouri switched the twine to her left hand and reached across to slap Lily's arm. "I don't know where you spend all your time, Lily," she said. She took up the twine in her right hand again and snatched Joan's leaves from her. "Well, it so happens she does work. She's a seamstress. Teen-iney stitches and a Singer for her machine work. Miss Joan can tell you. Most of it's altering things, but she makes things from scratch also. Reason you might not know," she told Lily, "is she does it at home. Works in. A lot of right important people go there. Mrs. Lawrence, the judge's wife, does—saw her drive up to the door once. Do you see what I'm getting at, Miss Joan?"

"Well, yes," said Joan. "You're saying this would snap her out of it. But being a seamstress is like working in a beauty shop—you have to carry on a conversation. And Aunt Lou just isn't capable right now."

"Of *course* not," said Mrs. Hall. "Why, she just don't have the heart to do that. Will you *look* at you people?"

"I got the answer," Mrs. Hall's first hander called. "I don't see why you are all worrying." She kept on handing as she spoke, thrusting precisely neat bunches at Mrs. Hall with lightning speed. "It's like when you've been sick," she said. "They have to walk you around by the elbow a while. Well, Mrs. Pike needs to be walked around too, only in the talking sense. Joan here only works every other day; she can spare the time. She can greet the customers and tell them the news and all, so's they won't even notice how quiet Mrs. Pike is. Then by and by Mrs. Pike'll start to get interested in what Joan is talking about. She'll begin uncurling and saying a few words herself. That's why she was such a favorite before, Mrs. Pike was; she could talk up a storm."

Missouri was watching her with her mouth open. "Charleen," she said, when Charleen had finished speaking, "you are just as silly as you look, Charleen. You must think Miss Joan is some kind of a walking newspaper. Do you? She don't say two words in a day, Joan don't. Customers would drop off like apples in the fall, and Mrs. Pike would have one more reason not to get a grip on things."

"Silly yourself," Charleen muttered, and bent closer over her pile of leaves.

"Mrs. Pike's no worse than my sister Mary was," said Mrs. Hall. "When Mary's oldest died she sat on the porch seven days and seven nights and it rained on her. I thought she'd *mold*, before we got her in again. Mrs. Pike is at least talking some."

"Not much," Josephine said. She was scraping tobacco gum off her hands with a nail file while Mrs. Hall tied a knot at the end of her stick. "I went up to her at the burying and, 'Mrs. Pike,' I said, 'I surely am sorry.' And you know what she said? She said, 'This is where Simon's bedroom was going to be.' I tell you, it scared me."

"Well, they were going to build a house there," Mrs. Hall said. She slammed another stick in the stand. "I say they should have put Janie Rose by the church, but that's a individual matter."

Missouri took off her straw hat and began fanning her face with it. "You can rest," she told Joan and Lily. "We're even now. Boy?"

"Yes'm."

"Well, come on and get it."

Joan and Lily leaned back against the table, half sitting on it, and Missouri tilted her head back so that she could fan her neck. "Sun's about gone," she said, "but still working. What was it I was thinking, now? Lily?"

"Well, I'm sure *I* don't know," Lily said.

"Hush. Wait, now—oh." She stopped fanning herself, clamped her hat on her head again, and bent for another rod. "Stop that standing around," she commanded. "Charleen, I take it back."

"What?"

"What I said. I take it back. You only half silly."

"Oh, why, *thank* you."

"Only half as silly as you look. Stand up straight, Lily, you're a mess. What's that all over your hands?"

"It's tobacco gum, what you think?"

"Oh." She snapped off her length of twine, with Mrs. Hall watching closely, and reached for Joan's leaves. "I'm a little vague, but I'm thinking," she said. Then she frowned into space for a while. Finally she said, "Growing old surely do damage a person."

"Well, is *that* what you've been getting ready to say?" Mrs. Hall asked irritably.

"*Oh* no," Missouri said. "It was something entirely different. I was working up to something."

"You were talking about Aunt Lou," Joan reminded her.

"Well, I know I was. If you all would just let me—"

"Personally," said Mrs. Hall, "I think this is a lot of fuss for nothing. You think it's something wrong if Mrs. Pike sticks to herself a few days. Well, something *is* wrong. Somebody died. And that's all I'm going to say."

"It's just as well," said Missouri. "You keep distracting my mind."

"Why, Missouri—"

"You *said,*" Missouri reminded her, "you said that was all you was going to—"

Mrs. Hall sighed and turned her back, muttering something but not attempting to argue any more, and Missouri nodded to herself several times. "There now," she said. "Now, what was I—?" But when Lucy clicked her tongue in exasperation, exactly like her mother, Missouri waved her free hand at her to tell her not to speak. "Now I remember," she said. "Growing old surely do— Well. Anyway. Now, of course we're not saying anything's wrong with Mrs. Pike. Sure she's sad. Going to go right on being that way, always a little sad to the end of her days. But that don't stop us from trying to make her feel better; that's just natural. We all got reasons. Maybe we want to stop remembering the dead ourselves. Or a host of other reasons."

She bent down and slapped a fly on her leg. "Oh, you," she said to the fly, and then reached out for Joan's leaves. Joan was holding the leaves too high and far away, and Missouri had to snap her fingers at her. "*Come* on," she said. Joan came to life and handed the leaves over.

"*Any*how," said Missouri. "Now I've lost my place again. Where was I?"

"Mrs. Pike," Joan said.

"Mrs. Pike? Oh, her. Well, no, I was passing on to someone else. What's-his-name. What's his name?"

"*Mr.* Pike?" Lily suggested.

"Just hush. Though he's in this too, of course. No, just hush—Simon. That boy of theirs. You know him, Joan?"

"He's my cousin," said Joan.

"Oh, yes. Yes. Simon. Going to go to pieces if things go on this way. Do you see now what I'm getting at?"

"Well, no."

"It's as plain as the nose on— Boy? Come on, now, quit that poking. I'm saying it's Simon should be in her beauty shop with her."

"In her—?"

"I mean in her sewing shop. Look what you done now, got me all confused. Well, that's who you want."

"You mean he should entertain the customers," Joan said.

"That was my point."

"Well—"

"He's the only one can help now. Not hot tea, not people circling round. Not even her own husband. Just her little boy."

"I don't see how," said Joan.

Missouri made an exasperated face. "*You* don't know," she told her. "You don't know how it would work out. Bravest thing about people, Miss Joan, is how they go on loving mortal beings after finding out there's such a thing as dying. Do I have to tell you that?"

She snapped her twine tight and held it there while she watched Joan scrape up the last of the leaves. "I despise finishing the day on half a stick," she said.

"Well, I'll be," said Charleen. She leaned back against the table, shaking her head and watching Mrs. Hall tie the end of her stick. "I never. Was *that* what you did all this talking to say?"

"It was," said Missouri.

At the other end of the table, Mrs. Hall suddenly looked up. "That's true," she said slowly, but when they turned toward her she only shook her head. "That's true," she said again, and lifted her tobacco rod gently from its notches and handed it to the waiting boy.

6

JAMES WAS HALFWAY THROUGH his second beer before he saw Joan coming toward him. He was sitting on Mr. Terry's porch, leaning back against the side of the house in a folding chair and lazily listening to the other men talking, and the beer can was making a cold wet ring on his knee. There were four other men there, all sitting just like he was in a line against the house. Maybe if Joan hadn't come he would have sat with them till supper, just to rest up from the long day's work and let the breeze dry his damp shirt. But then Mr. Terry said, "If you'll look out yonder—" and James raised his eyes toward the fields and saw Joan padding down the dirt driveway in bare feet with a sandal swinging from each hand. "Out yonder to the east is what I mean to cultivate year after next," Mr. Terry went on. He had been saying that for as long as James had known him. "I aim to extend the alfalfa a bit. No sense in letting good land grow wild, I say." James only nodded, not really listening. He squinted his eyes so as to see better—Joan was still far away—and watched how she picked her way so quickly and gently along the dusty wheel-tracks. Her head was bent, so that her hair fell forward and nearly hid her face. Way behind her were the other women, going in the opposite direction toward town, and once they turned back and waved at Joan but she didn't see them. The women bobbed on, farther and farther, until all that showed of them was their bright dresses between the tobacco rows and two huge black umbrellas shading Lily and Missouri from the sun.

"I also been thinking about the eight acres out back," said Mr. Terry. "They're Paul Hammond's, but he's not using them."

"No," James said.

"You listening?"

Joan had reached the edge of the Terrys' front yard. She crossed onto the grass, sliding her feet a little as if she liked the coolness of it, and Mr. Terry stopped talking and the others sat forward and took their hats off.

"Hey, Joan," said Mr. Terry.

"Hey." She stopped at the bottom of the steps and smiled up at them. "Lem," she said, "Missouri sent you a message. She said to come right on home."

Lem tipped back again in his chair, shaking his head. "Must be a mistake somewheres," he said. His eyes were faraway and dreamy, and the others laughed softly.

"Well, anyway," said Joan. "I came to see if you're ready to go yet, James. Or do you want to stay on a while."

"No, I'm ready."

He finished his beer in one gulp and stood up. Down at the end of the porch, Howell Blake looked up from cleaning his fingernails with a pocket knife and said, "You coming tomorrow?"

"Depends on Roy Pike, I guess. Looks like he'll be sitting with his wife a while."

"Well, just so's *one* of you makes it," said Mr. Terry. "You tell Roy I know how it is. *You* tell him, Joan."

"I will."

James went down the steps toward Joan, and she switched one sandal to the other hand so that he could take her free hand in his. Both of them were coated with tobacco gum. The gum had lost its stickiness by now but it still clung to their skin in heavy layers, so that it was like holding hands with rubber gloves on. He kept hold of her anyway, and turned partway back to nod at the others. "See you tomorrow, I guess," he said. "I or Roy, one."

"Okay. So long."

"So long."

They crossed the yard together and then they were on the dirt driveway again, heading toward the gravel road. When James looked down, he could see the dust rising in little puffs around Joan's toes every time she took a step. Her toes were gum-covered too, and the dust had stuck to them like a layer of sugar frosting.

"I have to have a bath," Joan said, as if she had been following his eyes.

"No. I like you this way."

"I'm serious. You have to have one too, and then we can sit outside and cool off."

"Okay," James said. He pulled her along faster, because he liked the idea of just the two of them sitting out on the porch a while. But Joan slowed him down again.

"I have to put on my sandals to walk fast," she said. "Do you want me to?"

"No, that's all right."

But she bent down anyway, and James stood waiting while she slid her feet into the sandals. She was wearing bermudas and a faded blue shirt with the tails out, and when a breeze started up it ballooned out the back of her shirt and made her look humpbacked. He put one hand on the hump. It vanished, pressed flat by the weight of his hand, and he could feel the ripple of her backbone through the thin cloth of her shirt. It seemed to him he knew Joan's clothes by heart. He could tell the seasons by them, and if she bought something new, he felt uneasy and resentful toward it until it had become worn-looking. When spring came he never really felt it until those old cotton shirts had come out again, though for days he might have known about the bits of green on the trees and the flowering Judas buds by the side of the road. He smiled down at Joan now and she straightened up and looked at him, not knowing anything about what was going on in his mind.

"What're you thinking?" she asked him.

"Nothing."

They turned onto the gravel road, holding hands again. A station wagon drove past, clanking and rattling as if it would fall apart before their eyes, and Joan waved at whoever was driving but James didn't look up.

He was concentrating on the gravel beneath his feet, and on steering Joan into the sandiest part of the road. Finally he said, "I've got an idea."

"What?"

"How about coming over and cooking supper tonight? We could sit out and eat it on the porch."

"You know I can't cook."

"Well, hot dogs is all right."

He dropped her hand and put his arm around her, so that he could feel her shoulder moving against his rib cage as they walked. They were going very slowly now; he had stopped caring if they never got anywhere at all. He would like to go on down this road indefinitely, with everything around him shining and wearing a clean, finished, end-of-the-day look. The sun picked things up slantwise, and the fields were very still in between the gusts of breeze. When they rounded the bend and their house appeared, long and shabby with its tin roof batting the sunshine into their eyes, it seemed surprising and out of place. Both of them slowed down still more to stare at it. Then Joan said, "Well, I'll race you home."

"Now?"

"Come on."

She started running, moving in bursts of uneven speed and letting her hands stay open instead of doubling them into fists the way most people did. Beside her, James ran at a slow easy pace because he didn't want to leave her behind. When he ran like this he was scarcely breathing hard, but Joan was out of breath and laughing. They reached the edge of the yard, and she stopped to tuck her shirttails in. "You weren't even trying," she told him. "That was no race."

But he reached out for a tall blue spiky flower and presented it to her gravely, as if she had won, and she accepted it.

"When you coming over?" he asked.

"In an hour or so. I have to take a bath and see that the others eat."

"Can you leave your aunt?"

"I'll see how she is," Joan said. She bent over suddenly and clapped her hands together, with the stem of the flower between them. "Hey, Nellie," she said. "That you?"

The bushes beside the lawn rustled and the dog poked just her head out, her nose pointed upwards. "Where you been?" Joan asked her. She made little coaxing motions with her hands. For a minute James watched, and then when it looked as if Nellie would be a long time making up her mind to come he turned toward the house.

"I'm going on in," he called.

"All right. Come on, Nellie."

James crossed the yard and climbed the steps at his end of the porch. In the seat of Ansel's chair was a rumpled magazine, which he picked up to take inside with him. "I'm home, Ansel," he said in the doorway. But Ansel didn't answer, and his couch was bare. "Hey, Ansel?"

On the coffee table was Ansel's entire collection of seashells, all laid out neatly with the hollow sides up.

This must have been one of his bored days, spent wandering aimlessly through the house with an occasional pause to glance over some possession of his before he grew tired of it and began wandering again. But he hadn't been flipping through James's photographs, the way he usually did on those days. And he wasn't in the kitchen, or up in his room. "Ansel?" James called once more, and his voice rang out into a waiting, ticking silence that worried him.

He went outdoors again. Joan was still in the yard, sitting on her heels and patting Nellie. When she saw James she said, "You're supposed to be in the tub by now," but James only shook his head.

"I can't find Ansel," he said.

Joan stood up then and came over to the porch. "He's probably just gone visiting," she told him. "Did you look for a note?"

"*Ansel* don't leave notes."

"Well, he'll be back."

"I don't know. I want you to check your aunt's for me; I don't like bothering her."

"All right." She turned and made a kissing sound at Nellie, who danced after her toward the porch. "It's time for your supper," Joan told her, and then led her through the Pikes' door by snapping her fingers high above Nellie's head. After they had disappeared into the house James stayed out on the porch, waiting to see if Joan had found his brother. If she had, she would need help coaxing him out. He had a sudden clear picture of Joan backing out the door again, snapping her fingers at Ansel to lead him forward the way she had led Nellie.

He smiled, and then relaxed and swung one foot up onto the porch railing.

But when Joan came out she came alone. "He's at the Potters'," she said, before James could ask. "Uncle Roy said he came calling, but Simon wouldn't let him in. He went on to the Potters."

"Well, maybe I'll just check," said James.

"Oh, he's all right, James. What's got into you lately?"

"I just want to make sure," he told her. "I wish you'd come with me. If I go alone I'll *never* get out, once they start to talking."

"Well, all right."

She came over to stand beside him, and he knocked on the Potters' door. There was no screen on it, because they didn't need one; they kept the inner door shut. Summer and winter their part of the porch had a closed, unbreathing look, and they had long ago paid James two dozen cinnamon buns for taking the baggy old screen door off its hinges and carting it out back. When James knocked there was first a faint movement of the paper shade—they had to make sure who it was—and then there was the sound of two bolts sliding back. The door cracked open; Miss Faye poked her round face out.

"Why, James," she said.

"Hello, Miss Faye."

"And Joan too. Both of you together. Joan, honey, don't you look fresh and outdoorsy today. I was saying to Miss Lucy just a—well, step on inside, step in."

"Actually," James said, "I just wanted to see if you had Ansel here."

"Ansel?" She had the door wide open now, and was

throwing back one arm to show that they were welcome. James kept trying to peer past her, hoping to see Ansel, but the way the Potters' house was arranged made it impossible. They had set up a labyrinth of tall black folding screens with needlework flowers on them, so that the house was divided into a dozen or more tiny rooms. No matter how James craned his neck around Miss Faye, all he saw was the screen behind her and more screens behind that. "Oh, Ansel," Miss Faye was saying. "James, I worry about that boy. I was saying just a while ago; I said—are you coming in? Don't stand outside; come on in."

"We've only got a minute," Joan said gently. "Is Ansel here?"

"Well, let's see." She stepped further back, leaving them the whole doorway to enter through, and after a minute the two of them came in. Who could tell what might be hidden in this maze of screens? The air was dark and stale, from being separated into so many cubicles in a tightly closed house. And there was a thick feeling to the walls that must have come from the heavy tapestries, because every place else in this house was shell-thin. When they were inside, Miss Faye shut the whole world behind them out; she said, "*Now,*" and slammed the door and slid the two locks into place. James frowned (it made him uneasy, being locked in this way) but Joan only looked amused.

"You were going to tell us if Ansel's here," she reminded Miss Faye.

"Yes. Yes, I was saying—Lucy? Lucy, are you coming to say hello?"

They heard Miss Lucy's footsteps, sounding very faint and taking a long time to weave in and out among the screens. First she came close and then went farther away again, and suddenly she popped out right behind Miss Faye. She wore a huge white apron with jokes about outdoor barbecues printed all over it.

"Lucy, look who's here," said Miss Faye.

"Well, isn't this nice?" Miss Lucy came towards them with both hands outstretched, making James wonder, just as he always did, what he was supposed to do when she reached him—hug her?—but Joan saved the day by stepping up and taking both Miss Lucy's hands in her own. "You're looking just as *healthy,*" Miss Lucy told her, and then gave a little giggle and shook her tight cap of curls. "We've had so much company today that I'm getting all—"

"Well, that's really what we came to talk about," said James.

"Aren't you going to sit down?"

"We wanted to ask—"

"You *have* to sit down." She began backing around the first screen, still holding Joan's hands. James glanced over at a puffy plush chair, with its layers and layers of antimacassars, and then shook his head.

"I'm sorry," he said, "but it looks like Ansel isn't here, and that's what we came about."

"*Oh* yes. Yes, he was here."

"When?" James asked.

"At three o'clock today, on the nose. No, more like three fifteen. I forget, Faye . . ."

"It was three twenty exactly," said Miss Faye. "It was

my turn to wear the brooch-watch today. I had looked down at it, while checking to see if my blouse was clean, just before I answered the door. And it was Ansel at the door. Will you sit down, please?"

"That was nearly two hours ago," James said.

"No, you're wrong, James."

"Well, it's way past five."

"Oh, it was nearly two hours ago that he *came,* all right. But it was more recently that he left, because he stayed to have a jam braid."

"Well—"

"Also a glass of milk. I said, 'Ansel, we've got to get some meat on your bones.' So did Miss Lucy. She said so too. Ansel said, 'Oh, Miss Faye, I just don't know.' He was feeling sad."

"What about?" asked James.

"He didn't say. Well, you know how he is. Some days the world is just too much for him. That's how he put it. 'Miss Faye,' he said, 'some days the world is just too much for me.' He told Lucy that too. 'Miss Lucy,' he said, 'some days the—' "

"Did he say where he was going?"

"Why, home, I reckon."

"I have to leave," James said.

"Oh, now. You only just—"

"I'm sorry, Miss Faye. Come on, Joan."

He reached the door before Miss Faye could, and he slid the bolts back himself, with Miss Faye's hands fluttering anxiously above his. Then he shot out on the porch, not even trying to be polite about it. Joan followed, but with her head turned toward the Potters, her voice drifting back to them as she tried to smooth everything over. "I'm sorry we have to leave this way," she said, "but I know you see how it is—" and the Potters made thin, sad little sounds to show that they did.

"Just please come back," Miss Faye told them, and James nodded tiredly and let the door swing shut. The two bolts slid back into place.

When they were outside again James just stood there, trying to think where to begin. Joan didn't seem worried at all. She said, "I got tobacco gum all over Miss Lucy's hands."

"That's too bad," James said absently.

"She was staring at her hands all funny-like; that's how I noticed. Little bits of black were sticking to them."

James turned around and looked at her. "Will you *listen?*" he told her. "I can't find Ansel."

"I'm sorry, James." She grew serious, and came over to stand beside him. "He'll come back," she said.

"I don't know."

"He always has before."

"Well, I just don't *know,*" James said. He knelt to tie his shoe and then stayed that way, looking down the porch to see who might be coming along the road. No one was in sight. "We don't know *what* might have happened," he said.

Joan squatted down beside him and said, "Well, he's come back every other time, James."

"You already said that."

"I just meant—"

"I *know* he comes back. I been through this a hundred

times. If I didn't even go looking for him, he'd come back. But I can't be a hundred per cent sure of that."

Down the road came a red hen, strutting importantly, sticking her neck far out as if she were heading someplace definite. As she walked she talked to herself, in little conversational clucks. James and Joan watched after her until she had disappeared.

"Somehow I can't get what Maisie said off my mind," James said finally. "How would I feel if just once he went too far? There'd be no one to blame but me, if that happened."

"Maisie who?" Joan asked.

"Maisie Hammond."

"Well, if you *did* go after him, you know how it'd be. You ever seen Ansel standing on a street corner waiting for you? He goes somewhere you'd never think to look, James. You go up and down town all night searching for him, waking every drinking man to ask him if he knows, and where does it get you? You always end up right here, waiting for him to decide to come back."

"I like to think I looked," James said.

"I know that." She stood up again, and the cotton smell of her shirt floated past him. "I can see it better than you can," she told him. "I don't like him. I can see easier than you how he will always come back."

"You can't see."

"Look," Joan said. "What's got into you? Things were getting better for a while. You weren't fussing over him, and he had almost stopped wandering off. Why have you started acting this way?"

He stared down at her feet, long and dirty in sandals

that had molded themselves to the curl of her toes. Her feet made him so angry that he almost didn't answer her. But then she looked down at him, with her face worried and unsure, and he said, "I don't know."

"Well, there's got to be some reason."

"Will you stop asking me that? *You* don't have a brother."

"Maybe not," Joan said, "but there is nothing I like or understand about you going to look for Ansel all the time. If he wanted he could have done a full day's work today, and been off at a dance right now."

"No, he couldn't."

"Yes, he could. He could be dancing and you and I could be going someplace. We could be doing something. We could be someone besides an old familiar couple that'll be courting when they're seventy and the town's fondest joke. Are you listening?"

"No," James said.

He got up off his knees and went down the porch steps. Bits of tobacco gum and dust from the floorboards clung to the knees of his pants, but he didn't brush them off. The sunset glowed red and dull across the roof of the pickup. "Don't bother fixing supper," he called.

"I wouldn't *think* of fixing supper."

He stopped and looked back at her. She was standing at the edge of the porch now, with her arms folded and her feet planted solidly apart. "I wish you'd wear some real *shoes* once," he said.

"What?"

"I'm sick of those sandals."

"Well, I'm sick of everything," Joan said.

Her voice was flat now, and only sad-sounding. It made him look back at her one more time, but by then she had turned away and was walking down the porch. "Joan?" he said. She went on walking, not answering. From behind, her folded arms gave her a thin, round-shouldered look, and she stepped in that gentle way she had, with her bare pointed heels rising and falling delicately across the long gray porch.

7

At night, when everyone was in bed, the house seemed to belong to one family instead of three. The separate sleeping-sounds mingled and penetrated through all the thin walls, and by now James could identify each sound exactly and where it came from. He knew Miss Faye's snore, as curlicued and lacy as she herself was, and the loud, honking sound that Mr. Pike made. He knew Miss Lucy's rat-a-tat on the walls, first on Mr. Pike's wall when the snoring grew too noisy and then on his own wall if he talked in his sleep. He thought it must be a thimble she tapped with. Because there was a big room's width between his end of the house and the Pikes' end, he wasn't sure of the softer sounds there—Simon's snoring, for instance, or Mrs. Pike's. And he had always wondered if Joan snored. But he had heard Janie Rose's nightmares often enough. They came through loud and clear, drifting up from the open window of her tacked-on bedroom downstairs. "*That's* not something you should be doing," she would say reasonably. And then, "Daddy, would you come *quick?*" and the floundering thuds across the floor as Mr. Pike began groping his way toward her voice in the dark. But if Simon talked in his sleep, he must have talked quietly. All James heard of him was in the morning, when they tried to wake him and he bellowed out, "Oh, *fine*, I'll be right there! I already got my socks on. Ain't this some day?"—yet all the while sound asleep, and just trying to fool people. Sometimes Mr. Pike shouted too. He would have too many beers on a Saturday night and throw all the pillows out the window. "Ninety-nine point two per cent of all the people in the southern *states* die of smothering," he would roar to the night, and then Miss Lucy would rap on the wall. Miss Lucy never slept at all; James was convinced of that. She spent her time policing the area. On nights when Ansel was restless, when he tossed around on his old wooden bed across the room from James (he wouldn't sleep in the other bedroom, for fear of waking alone and finding his feet numb), and when he kept calling, "James, how long has this night been going *on?*" Miss Lucy would tap very gently and ask if Ansel wanted her hot water bottle. "No, ma'am," James always said, and Miss Lucy would go back to her quiet, patient pacing. Sometimes James had a great urge to go see what she was wearing. He pictured her in a twenty-pound quilted robe with lead weights at the bottom, like the ones sewn into curtains, because it dragged so loudly across the floor at every step she took. But once he had had a horrible nightmare, right after eating two pizzas. He had shouted out, "My *God!*" and awakened shaking, with the terrible sound of his own shout still ringing in his ears. Then Miss Lucy had tapped and called, "Why, *it's* going to be all right," and the horror vanished. He had lain back down, feeling comforted and at home, and now it never annoyed him to hear Miss Lucy's bathrobe dragging.

In the Potters' bedroom the clock struck four, whirring and choking before each clang. James lay tensed, counting the strokes, although he already knew how many there would be. He had slept only in patches all night, and even in his dreams he was searching streets full of people for the thin stooped figure of his brother. In the last dream it had been a year ago—that time they had called from ten miles away to tell him Ansel had been run over, but neglected to add it was only a bicycle that had done it. After that he couldn't sleep at all. He thought of all the things that had happened to Ansel in the past, the really serious things, and all the things that might be happening to him tonight. When the clock had stopped whirring he found that he was frowning into the darkness so hard that the muscles of his forehead hurt. Then, as if that clock had been some sort of musical introduction, a faraway voice began singing outside:

> There's sunshine on the mountains,
> And spring has come again. . . .

James sat up and pulled back the curtain. Outside it was pitch black, with a handful of small stars scattered like sand across the blue-black sky. The trees beyond the field were only hulking dark shapes, and not one light glimmered from the town behind them.

My true love said she'd meet me,
But forgot to tell me when.

He climbed out of bed and untwisted the legs of his pajamas. At his bedroom wall there was one sharp tap, questioning (he had learned to read Miss Lucy's thimble language), and he called, "It's all right, Miss Lucy." She resumed her pacing again, with her robe trailing her footsteps like a murmuring companion. James shot out of his room, still buttoning his pajama top, and went downstairs in the dark. The voice was nearer now.

I was walking down the track, Lord,
With a letter in my hand,
A-reading how she'd left me
For that sunny Jordan land.

The front door was open but the screen was hooked shut. James pushed the hook up, jabbing his finger, and swung the screen door open. Then he walked across the porch barefoot, with the cold rough grain of the wooden floorboards stinging the soles of his feet. Around his ankles the cuffs of his pajamas fluttered and ballooned and nearly tripped him (they were Ansel's, and too long); he bent to roll them up. Then he descended the steps, scowling into the dark as he tried to see. He was halfway down the path before he stopped, more by sensing someone in front of him than by seeing him. Ahead of him was a long tall shape, swaying gently, smelling of bourbon. The voice was so close now that James could feel its breath.

> Oh, there's sunshine on the hills, Lord,
> And the grass is all of gold. . . .

His reedy roice was piercing, but the thinness of it made it seem still far away. James stepped closer. "Ansel," he said.

> My love has gone and left me,
> And I'll cry until I'm old.

"Ansel," James said again.

"I'm singing, please."

"Come on in."

He took Ansel by the arm. It was stone cold; he could feel the bone underneath. When he pulled Ansel toward the porch Ansel came, but lifelessly and with the shadow that was his face still averted. "People keep asking you in nowadays," he told the dark. "They got a thing about it."

"Careful," said James. "We're coming to the steps."

"The *Potters* downright *lock* you in. Slide little bits of machinery around. You mind if I finish my song?"

"I certainly do."

"I might just finish it anyway. Where you taking me, James?"

"*In,*" said James, and half lifted him up the first step. Ansel was as limp as a rag doll. His limpness made James realize suddenly how angry he was at Ansel, after all this worrying and waiting; instead of guiding him so carefully, he felt like giving him a good shove into the house and having done with it. "Get on in," he said, and took his hand away from Ansel's arm. Ansel gave him a deep lopsided bow and entered first.

"Certainly nice of you to ask me," he told James. "Certainly are a *hospitable* man."

"If you're hungry, Ansel—"

"I'm starved."

"Cook up some eggs," said James, and began making his way across the dark living room toward the stairs. Behind him Ansel said, "*Hey,* now—" but James paid no attention. The way he felt, he couldn't even make a cup of coffee for Ansel; he had been worrying for too long, and all he wanted now was sleep. Already he was unbuttoning the tops of his pajamas, preparing to go back to his bed.

"Don't you have food waiting?" Ansel asked.

"Nope."

"Don't you even *care* if I come back?"

"You know how to fry an egg."

"Well, I'll be," said Ansel, and sat down suddenly on something that creaked. "I take it back, James. What's so hospitable about you?"

The stairs were narrow, and James kept stubbing his toes against them. He touched the wall to guide himself, feeling the ripples and bubbles of the wallpaper as he slid his fingers along it. Behind him Ansel said, "You mad at me, James?" but James didn't answer. He could already hear the tapping sound that was coming from upstairs. Miss Lucy must be worried.

"I reckon you're wondering where I was at," Ansel said, and there was another creak when he stood up again. "You always *do* wonder." He banged into something, and then his footsteps wavered uncertainly toward the stairs. "You're taking all my places from me. Once I tell you, I can't go back no more. How long you guess it'll be before I've used up every place there is?" He was climbing the steps behind James now. His voice rang hollowly through the stairwell. For a minute James paused, listening to him coming, and then he continued on up and reached the top, with his hand still on the wall so that he could find his room. "It's all a question of time," Ansel said sadly. "Time and geography."

"If you're coming to sleep in *my* room," James told him, "you'd better shut up that talking."

"Well, I only want to explain."

"I'm sleepy, Ansel."

"I only want to explain."

James kept going, heading in the direction of Miss Lucy's tapping thimble. He could hear Ansel's hands sliding along behind his now on the wall, and then the sliding sound stopped and there was a click as Ansel snapped the hall light on. For a minute the light was blinding. James screwed his eyes up and said, "Oh, Lord—" and Ansel turned the light off again, quickly and guiltily. "I just thought," he said, "as long as we had electricity—"

"It's four a.m., Ansel."

"What're you, wearing my pajamas?"

"Go to hell, will you?"

"I never," said Ansel, but James was past listening. He was in the bedroom now, and on his way to bed he reached out and knocked on Miss Lucy's wall for her to stop that tapping. She did. He eased himself down between the sheets, which were cold already and messy-feeling. When he was lying flat he closed his eyes and wished away the figure of Ansel, standing like a long black stick and swaying in the bedroom doorway.

"I wisht I knew what was wrong with you," Ansel said. "You angry with me, James?"

"Yep."

"I only went out for a walk."

"You usually end up half dead after those walks. It's me that's got to nurse you back."

"Well, wait now," Ansel said. "I can explain. All you need to do is listen."

"How can I listen when I'm asleep?" asked James, and turned over on his side with his face to the window. He could hear Ansel's feet shuffling into the room, and he knew by the soft thumping noise that he had reached the other bed and was sitting on it.

"I tried and I tried," Ansel told him. "I went to the Pikes' first off, but Simon don't like me any more. I went to the Potters', and they locked me in and requested news of my hemoglobin. What could I do? At the tavern I said, 'Charlie,' I said, 'I got a problem.' But all Charlie did was sell me hard liquor under the counter; he didn't listen to no problem."

Ansel's shoes were dropped on the floor, first one and

then the other. There was a small whipping sound as he flung his tie around a bedpost. Even with his eyes shut James could picture his brother, how he would be leaning toward James with his shoulders hunched and his hands flung out as he talked, even though he knew he couldn't be seen. "Go to sleep, Ansel," he muttered, but Ansel only sighed and began unbuttoning his shirt with tiny popping sounds.

"This all has to do with Janie Rose," he told James. "Are you listening?"

"No."

"Just about everything has to do with Janie Rose these days. I don't know why. Looks like she just kind of tipped everything over with her passing on. Janie don't like gladioli, James."

James didn't answer. A button flew to the floor and then circled there for an endless length of time, and Ansel stamped one stocking foot over it and shook the whole house. James could feel the floorboards jar beneath his bed. There was a long silence; then Ansel bent, with a small puff of held-in breath, and scrapped his fingers across the floor in search of the button.

"Got it," he said finally. "All today, I was so sick and tired. I had looked at that picture of the Model A too long. I don't know why I do things like that. Then I thought, well, I'll just go up the hill and pay my respects to Janie Rose. I'll go slow, so as not to get overtired. And I did. I stopped a plenty on the way. But when I got close I saw her flowers, how they had got all wilted. I thought: I wisht I'd brought some flowers. I thought: I wisht I'd brought some bluets. You listening, James?"

James gritted his teeth and stayed quiet.

"There's four names for bluets I know of. Bluets, Quaker-ladies, pea-in-the-paths, and wet-the-beds. You can count on Janie Rose; she called them wet-the-beds. Well, she had problems herself in that line. But what I thought was: I wisht I'd brought some bluets. I *didn't* think: I wisht I'd brought some wet-the-beds."

"Oh, Lord," James said tiredly. He turned his pillow to the cool side and lay back down on it.

"Now, bluets are not good funeral flowers. Too teeny. But Janie Rose is not a funeral *person.* Usually it's only the good die young. Consequently I thought: I wisht I'd—"

James raised his head and shouted, "Ansel, will you *hush?*" and on his wall there was the sudden sound of frantic tapping. "I don't want to hear," he told Ansel more quietly, and then lay back down and forced his mind far away.

"I'll just get to the point," Ansel said. "I have to tell you this. James, there are *gladioli* on Janie's grave."

James heard a zipper slide down, and after a minute a pair of trousers was tossed shufflingly across the floor. Then Ansel's socks dropped one after the other beside his bed, in soft crumpled balls, and James heard them fall and winced because his ears seemed raw tonight.

"Janie Rose *despises* gladioli," said Ansel.

James said nothing.

"She hates and despises them. Believes they're witches' wands, all frilled up. She told me so."

James opened his eyes and rolled over. "Funerals are for parents," he said. "Ansel, Janie Rose is dead."

He waited, frowning. Out of the corner of his eye he could see the white blur that was Ansel in his underwear, standing before the bureau with his skinny arms folded across his chest. Finally Ansel said, "I know."

"She's dead."

"I know all about it. Nevertheless, she despises gladioli."

"The funeral is not really for her," James said, and rolled over again to face the wall. "It don't make any difference to her about those gladioli."

"*Oh* now," said Ansel. "*Oh* now." He crossed to his bed, heavily. "It's hard to bury people, Jamie. Harder than digging a hole in the ground."

"Will you go to bed?"

"They keep popping up again, in a manner of speaking."

James dug his head into his pillow.

"I remember Janie Rose's religious period," Ansel went on comfortably. "It was a right short one, wouldn't you know. But she took this tree out back, this scrubby one she was always drawing flattering pictures of. Dedicated it to God, I believe; hung it with tin cans and popcorn strings. Didn't last but a week; then she was on to something new. The birds ate the popcorn. But those tin cans are still rattling at the ends of the branches when a wind passes through, and Mr. Pike sits out back all day staring at them. Thought he had placed every last bit of her in a hole in the ground. Ha."

James reached behind him for the sheet and pulled it up over his head, making a hood of it. The rustling of the sheet drowned out everything else, and then when he was still again the sounds couldn't come through to him so clearly. The creaking of Ansel's bedsprings when he sat down was muffled and distant, and his voice was thin-sounding.

"I ought to studied botany," he was saying. "Don't you think? All I know about flowers, I ought to studied botany."

James lay still, and stared at the dark vines running up the wallpaper until his eyes ached.

"With Mama it was lilies," said Ansel. "Lord, she hated lilies. All she wanted, she said, was just a cross of—"

"We won't go into that," James told the wallpaper.

"We don't go into *nothing*. Getting so the only safe topic around here is the weather. Well, I was saying. Just a cross of white roses, she wanted. No lilies. And you know what they sent? You know what?"

He waited. The silence stretched on and on. James's arm, pressed beneath his body, began to go to sleep, but he didn't switch positions for fear of breaking the silence. He wiggled his fingers gently, without making a sound.

"Well, they sent lilies," Ansel said finally. "I thought you would have guessed. If you'd been there, I wouldn't have to be telling you all this. But I called you. I called you on the phone and said, 'James,' I said, 'will you kindly come to Mama's funeral?' I called you long distance and person-to-person, Caraway to Larksville. But you never answered me. Just hung up the telephone, neat and quiet. If I was the persistent type, I'd be asking still. I'd ask it today: 'James, will you kindly come to Mama's funeral?' Because you never have answered, never once, not once in all these years. I'll ask it now. James, will you kindly—"

"No, I won't," said James.

Across the room there was a little intake of breath, quick and sharp, and over behind the Potters' wall the measured pacing suddenly began again, with the weighted bathrobe sighing behind it. Ansel lay down on his bed.

"There's two kinds of sin," he said after a minute. His voice was directed toward the ceiling now, and sounded dreamy. "There's general sin and there's private sin. General sin there's commandments against, or laws, or rules. Private sin's a individual matter. It's hurting somebody, personally. You hear me? Listen close now; this is essential. What I chose was a general sin, that they'll be a long time forgiving. I did all that drinking, and ran around with that girl that everyone knew was no good. But what you chose was a private sin, that they'll *never* forgive. They got hurt personally by it—you forever running away, and telling them finally what you thought of them and leaving home altogether. Then not coming to the funeral. Think they'll forgive *that?* No, sir. Me they will cry over in church and finally forgive, someday. But not you. I'm a very wise man, every so often."

James didn't say anything. Ansel raised himself up on one elbow to look over at him, but he stayed within his hood of sheets. "James?" Ansel said.

"What."

"You don't care *what* I say, do you?"

"Yes," James said.

"Don't it bother you sometimes? Don't you ever think

about it? Here we are. You walked off from them without a backward wave of your hand, and I got thrown out like an old paper bag. Don't it—"

"Got *what?*" James asked.

"What?"

"You got *what?*"

"Got thrown out, I said, like an old—"

"You never got thrown out," said James.

"I did. Daddy said I was an alcoholic; he said I was—"

"He never said that."

"Well, almost he did. He said, 'Leave this house,' he said. 'You and your drinking and that girl in red pedal pushers, I never want to see you again.' That's what he told me."

James raised himself slightly from beneath the hood of the sheet. He peered across the dark room toward Ansel and said, "Don't you give me that, Ansel."

"What?"

"You *left*. You left, I left. Tell it that way."

"Well, what difference does it make? Who cares?"

"I care," said James. "Do *I* make excuses for leaving? Run out on him or don't run, but don't make it easy on yourself; don't tell me he *kicked* you out."

"Well," Ansel said after a minute, "I was drinking all that—"

"You don't even like the taste of it," said James.

"I do too."

James lay back down and pulled his sheet closer over him, and Ansel's voice rose louder. "It has a *won*derful taste," he said. And then, "Well, maybe he didn't exactly throw me out, but anyhow—"

Up on the tin roof, rain began. It started very gently, pattering in little sharp exclamation points that left spaces for Ansel's voice. "James?" Ansel said.

"Hmm."

"There's one thing I don't get, James. It was *you* they liked best. The others weren't nothing special, and I was so runny-nosed. I had a runny nose from the moment I was born, I think, and pinkish eyes. One time I heard Daddy say, 'Well, if there's ever a prize for sheer *sniveliness* given, he'll take it,' and Mama said, 'Hush, now. Maybe he'll grow out of it.' They didn't think I heard them, but I did."

"They didn't mean that," said James.

"You know they did. But *you* they liked; why did you leave? Why didn't you come to the funeral? I said, 'Daddy,' I said, 'you want I should ask James to Mama's funeral?' 'Which James is that?' he asks. 'James your *son*,' I tell him. And he says, 'Oh. Oh, why, anything you want to, Ansel.' This was when I was still home and they had hopes I would change my ways; they let me do some things I wanted. I called and said, 'James, will you kindly come to Mama's funeral?' Then he asked what happened. 'Ansel,' he said, 'did you invite that person you had mentioned previously?' And I said no, figuring it was better that way. Daddy said, 'He wouldn't have come. He was born that way,' he said, 'lacking our religion. There was no sense asking him.' "

The rain grew louder. Now it was one steady booming

against the sheets of tin, and all of Ansel that could be heard was his words; the quality of his voice was drowned out.

"I'm going back there sometime," he was saying. "They'll forget, and I'll go back. I crave a religious atmosphere." He lay back down and James nodded to himself, thinking maybe he would be sleepy now. "Churches here are somewhat lacking, I think," Ansel went on. "Quiet-like. At home it was better. Mrs. Crowley spoke in tongues. There was things that bound you there. A red glass on the windowsill in the choir loft, with something brown rising above it like the head on a beer. I think now it was wax, and the glass was a sort of candle. But before I thought it was a sort of brown fungus, some kind of mold just growing and growing. Do you remember, James?" He waited a minute. "*James?*" he said, and now his voice had an edge of desperation in it that rose even above the roaring of the rain.

"No, I don't," James said.

"Sometimes I think your mind is just a clean, clean slate, James."

"I keep it that way," said James.

"You do. I bet when I go back you won't even miss me. I'll go and bring presents. A natural-bristle hairbrush for each sister and a table game for Claude, and a French briar pipe for Daddy. Flowers for the grave and a set of them new, unbreakable dishes to go in the kitchen. A conch shell with the crucifixion inside to make up for that one you dropped, and a crane-necked reading lamp . . ."

The rain roared on, and James listened to that with all his mind. He thought it was the best sound he had heard all day. The heavy feeling was beginning to fade away, and the rain was lulling him to sleep.

". . . a new swing," Ansel was saying, "though none of us would use it now, I reckon. Before, it was a tire we swung on. It was all right and it went high enough, but there wasn't no comfortable way to sit in it. Inside it, your legs got pinched. Straddled above it, you'd be dizzy in no time what with all that spinning. 'Stop!' you'd say, and cling like a monkey on a palm tree while everybody laughed . . ."

8

ON TUESDAY MORNING, Mr. Pike was the second person awake. He arrived in the kitchen wearing his work clothes and carrying a nylon mesh cap, and when he sat down at the table he sat heavily, stamping his boots together in front of him and scraping the chair across the linoleum. "I'm picking tobacco today," he told Joan. Joan was at the stove, peering into the glass knob on top of the percolator to see what color the coffee was. When her uncle made his announcement she said nothing, because she was thinking of other things, but then she turned and saw him looking at her expectantly.

"I'm sorry?" she said.

"I'm going to pick tobacco," he repeated.

"Oh. All right."

But he still seemed to be waiting for something. He folded his big bony hands on the table and leaned toward her, watching, but Joan couldn't think what was expected of her. She picked the coffeepot off the stove and carried it over to the sink, in order to dump the grounds.

"We need the money," her uncle said.

Joan shook the grounds into the garbage pail, holding the coffee-basket by the tips of her fingers so as not to get burned.

"Well, *some*time I got to start work," he said.

"Of course you do, Uncle Roy."

"Things are getting worse and worse in this house. I thought they'd get better."

"Pretty soon they will."

"I wonder, now."

He watched as Joan set his cup of coffee before him. She handed him the sugar bowl but he just stared at it, as if he'd never seen one before.

"Sugar?" Joan prodded him.

He shook his head, and she set the bowl down at his elbow.

"It's no good sitting in a *room* all my life," he said.

"Drink your coffee," Joan told him. She poured a cup for herself and then sat down opposite him, hitching up the knees of her blue jeans. Her eyes were still foggy from sleep and things came through to her blurred, in shining patterns—the blocks of sunlight across the worn linoleum, the graduated circles of Mrs. Pike's saucepan set hanging on the wall, the dark slouched waiting figure of her uncle. When she stirred her coffee with a kitchen knife that was handy, the reflection of the sunshine on the blade flashed across the wall like a fish in a pool and her uncle shifted his eyes to that. He watched like a person hypnotized. She set the knife down and the reflection darted to a point high on the wall near the ceiling, and he stared upward at it.

"You going to want sandwiches?" she asked.

He didn't answer. She took a sip of her coffee, but it was tasteless and heavy and she set the cup down again. "Putting my foot down," her uncle mumbled. Joan drew lines on the tablecloth with her thumbnail. Outside a bird began singing, bringing back all the spots and patches of restless dreams she had had last night, in between long periods of lying awake and turning her pillow over and over to find a cool place. Ever since the rain stopped those birds had been singing. She rubbed her fingers across her eyelids and saw streaks of red and purple behind them.

"In regard to sandwiches," her uncle said suddenly, "I don't want them. I'll come home for lunch."

"All right."

"*Least* I can do."

"All right."

"What's the matter with *you?*" he asked, and reached finally for the sugar bowl. "You mad I'm picking tobacco?"

"No. I think it's the best thing you could do. Don't forget to tell James he won't need to work today."

"I thought you'd do that," said Mr. Pike."

"You can."

"You're not working today; you can spare a minute."

"No, I'd rather you do it."

"*Oh* now," Mr. Pike said suddenly. "You two have a fight?"

Joan took another sip of coffee. It still had no taste. A

hummingbird swooped down to the window and just hung there, suspended like a child's bird-on-a-string, its small eyes staring curiously in and its little heart beating so close and fast they could see the pulsing underneath the feathers. Mr. Pike gazed at it absently.

"I never *did* hold with long engagements," he said.

"What?"

"Longer the engagement, the more time for fights. Shouldn't allow it, Joan."

"I'm not engaged," Joan said shortly. "And anyway, it's none of *my* doing." Her uncle looked away from the hummingbird and frowned at her.

"I don't know about that," he said. "And I'll tell you. Some men need a little shove."

"I don't believe in shoving."

"Only way, sometimes. I ever tell you how I came to marry your aunt?"

"I'm not in the mood for that," said Joan.

"I was only going to mention."

"No, I don't want to hear," she said, and pictured suddenly her aunt, no longer young, lying so still upstairs. "*You* go tell James," she said.

"Aw, Joan."

"Someone has to."

"Aw, Joan, you know how it is. I'll go over and there will be Ansel, all talkative and cheerful. Cheerful in the morning—can you feature that?"

"Maybe he's still asleep," Joan said.

"Ansel? No. I heard him come in long after midnight just singing away, and I reckon he sang all night and is singing still. Where's Simon?"

"In bed."

"Been days since I seen that boy. Send *him* over."

"He won't go either."

"Look," said Mr. Pike. He stood up, jarring the table, and the hummingbird flew away without even preparing to go. "I can't see Ansel today," he said. "I don't know why but he gets under my skin nowadays. Will you *please* go?"

"Oh, all right," Joan said.

"All right, that's settled. Thank you very much."

He sat down again, and Joan went back to looking at the patterns in the kitchen. Everything she saw made her homesick, but not for any home she'd ever had. The sunlight on the linoleum reminded her of something long ago and lost; yet she had never lived in a house with a linoleum kitchen, never in all her memory. She kept staring at the design of it, the speckled white floor with bars of red and blocks of blue splashed across it, and the sun lighting up the dents and scrapes made by kitchen chairs. Finally she looked away and into her uncle's frowning, leather-brown face, but her uncle only said, "We need the money," so she looked away again. Her coffee had cooled, and the surface of it was greasy-looking. She drank it anyway.

When her uncle was through with his coffee he pushed the cup toward the center of the table and rose, clamping the mesh cap on the back of his head. "You can take care of things here, I guess," he said.

"Yes."

"I'll be running along, then."

He clomped off toward the front of the house, swinging his boots in that heavy way that Simon always tried to copy. His steps made the whole floor shake. She heard the screen door swing open with a twang of its spring and then slam shut again, rattling on its hinges. Then the clomping continued across the porch, and she waited for the extra-heavy sound of his boots descending the wooden steps to the yard but it didn't come. "Joan?" he called.

"What."

"*Joan!*"

She rose and went out front, wondering why men always had to shout from where they were instead of coming closer. Her uncle was standing on the edge of the porch with his back to the house and his cap off, scratching the back of his head. "What is it?" she asked him, and he turned toward her.

"Well, I already informed your aunt," he said, "but I'm not certain she heard."

"Informed her about what?"

"About my working. But I'm not certain she heard. Will you tell her again?"

"All right," said Joan.

"Say we need the money, tell her. Say I'm sorry."

"All right, Uncle Roy."

"I can't sit looking at *trees* all my life."

"No, I know," said Joan, and reached out to give his shoulder one gentle push so that he would turn and leave. He did, still frowning. Then halfway across the yard he slapped his cap back on his head and thrust his hands in his pockets and began walking more briskly, getting ready to go out into the world again. Joan watched after him till he was out of the yard, and then she went down toward the Greens' end of the porch.

Ansel was in his window, chewing sunflower seeds. He looked very happy. He spit the hulls out on the porch floor and then leaned over, his hands on the windowsill and his elbows jutting behind him like bird wings, and tried to blow the hulls all the way across the porch and into the yard. Joan wished he would fall out. She stood over him with her hands on her hips and waited until he had straightened up again, and then she said, "Ansel."

"Morning, Joan."

"Ansel, will you give James a message?"

"If I can remember it," said Ansel. "My health is poorly this morning. Seems to be growing worse and worse."

"Doesn't look to me you could *get* much worse," Joan said.

"At least you noticed. James just don't even care. He's in a ill mood today."

Joan gave up on him and stepped over to the door and knocked. For a minute Ansel stared out his window at her, puzzling this over; then he shrugged and withdrew. He came to the door and opened it with a flourish.

"Morning, Joan," he said.

"Where's James?"

"Ain't seen you in a long time. James? He's in the back yard, emptying out the garbage."

"Will you tell him he doesn't have to work today? Make up your mind, now. If you're planning to forget I'll just do it myself."

"Oh, I'll tell him," Ansel said. "Come in and set, why don't you. Old James'll be back any minute."

"No, thank you," said Joan.

"Well, suit yourself." He yawned. "Saw your uncle go off to work this morning," he said. "Seems kind of soon for him to be doing that, don't it?"

"No."

"Well, I just thought I'd point it out." He yawned again and fished another sunflower seed from the packet in his hand. The shirt he had on was James's, she saw. It was a dark red plaid and hung too loosely on him. She stared at it a minute and then, without a word, turned and went back up the porch. "Hey!" Ansel called after her, but Joan was inside her own parlor by now, letting the door slam shut behind her.

Upstairs, Simon was sound asleep, with his pajamaed legs sprawled and all his covers kicked loose from the foot of the bed. Joan went over and touched him gently, just on the outflung, curled-in palm of his hand. He stirred a little and then mumbled and turned away from her.

"Get up, Simon," she said.

"I *am* up. I am."

"Come on."

"I'm half dressed already. I got my—"

"Simon."

He opened his eyes. "Oh, light," he said, and Joan smiled and sat down on the bed beside him.

"I got something I want to talk over," she told him.

"Okay."

"You listening?"

"I just can't find any clean jeans," he said, and closed his eyes and was asleep again. Joan picked up his hand and shook it, but it hung loose and limp.

"Simon, this is about your mother," she said.

"I'm listening."

"I think your mother should start working today."

He turned over and squinted at her, through foggy brown eyes. "What at?" he asked.

"At her sewing. I want you to stay around and help with the conversation, all right? Missouri says I'm no walking newspaper."

"What?"

"Will you help me out?"

"Oh, why, sure," Simon said, and would have been asleep again if Joan hadn't pulled him to a sitting position. He stayed there, slumped between her hands, with his head drooping to one side. "I was in this boat," he said.

"Come on, Simon."

"Then we started sinking. They told me I was the one that had to swim for it. Do you believe that'll happen someday?"

"No," said Joan, and pulled hard on him till he was standing beside the bed.

"They say everything you dream will happen," Simon told her. "It's true. Last year I dreamed Mama would find out about me smoking and sure enough, that night at supper there was my half-pack of Winstons lying beside my plate and Mama staring at me. It came true."

He bent down to examine a stubbed toe and Joan stood up, preparing to go. "You come down when you're dressed," she said.

"I don't have any clean jeans to wear."

"That's just something you said in your sleep. You have lots of jeans."

"No, really I don't," Simon said. "No one's been doing the laundry."

Joan crossed to his bureau and pulled open his bottom drawer. It was bare except for a pair of bermudas. "Oh, Lord," she said. "I forgot all about the laundry."

"I told you you did."

"Well, wear bermudas till this afternoon, why don't you. By then I'll have you some jeans."

"Have my *knees* show?" Simon asked.

"What's wrong with that?"

"Boys don't *have* their knees out any more. You ought to know that."

"Well, la de da," said Joan, and rumpled the top of his hair. "Wear a pair of *dirty* jeans, then."

"They'd all call me sissy if my knees showed."

"All right. Hurry up, now."

She closed the door behind her and went downstairs. In the parlor she sat down on a faded plush footstool and reached for the telephone, which sat on a table beside her. She hooked the receiver over her shoulder and then opened the telephone book to the very back, where there was space for frequently used numbers. The page was filled to the bottom, and looked messy because of so many different handwritings. Mr. Pike had listed the names of bowling pals in a careful, downward-slanting script, and Simon had scrawled the names of all his classmates even though he never talked to them by telephone, and Janie Rose had printed names in huge capitals that took two lines, after asking several times how to spell each one—the four little Marsh girls, each listed separately, and the milkman who had once brought her a yellow plastic ring from a chicken's leg, which she had worn every day until she lost it. Mrs. Pike's handwriting was small and pretty, every letter slanting to the same degree, naming off her steady customers one by one with little memos to herself about colors and pattern numbers penciled in lightly beside them. Joan went down the list alphabetically. Mrs. Abbott, who never talked. Mrs. Chrisawn, who was in such a black mood most of the time. Davis, Forsyth, Hammond . . . She stopped there. Connie Hammond was always good to have around during a tragedy. She brought chicken broth whether people wanted it or not, and she knew little things like how to make a bed with someone in it and what to say when no one else could think of anything. As far as Joan was concerned, having a person talk incessantly would be more harm than help; but her aunt felt differently. Her aunt had actually sat up and answered, the last time Connie Hammond came. So Joan smoothed the phone book out on her knees and dialed the Hammonds' number.

Mrs. Hammond was talking to somebody else when she answered. She said, "If that's not the *worst* thing—" and then, into the phone, "Hello?"

"Mrs. Hammond, this is Joan Pike," said Joan.

"Why, Joan, honey, how *are* you?" Mrs. Hammond said, and then softened her shrill voice to ask, "How's your poor aunt?"

"Well, that's what I wanted to talk to you about," said Joan. She spoke at some distance from the receiver, in case Mrs. Hammond should grow shrill again.

"What's that you say?"

"I said, I wanted to *talk* to you about that. Aunt Lou is just miserable."

"Oh, my." There was a rustling sound as Mrs. Hammond cupped her hand over the receiver and turned away. "Lou Pike is just *miserable*," she told someone. Her hand uncupped the receiver again and she returned, breathless, to Joan. "Joan, honey, I told Mr. Hammond, just last night. I said, I haven't ever *seen* someone take on so. Well, of course she has good reason to but the things she *says*, Joan. It wasn't her fault; it was that no-account Ned Marsh who did it. How he manages to drive even a *tractor* recklessly is more than I can—"

"Um," Joan said, and Mrs. Hammond stopped speaking and snapped her mouth shut audibly, to show she had been interrupted. "Um, she hasn't even gotten up today. She's still in bed. And Uncle Roy's at the tobacco barns—"

"The where?"

"Tobacco barns. Working tobacco."

"Why, that man," said Mrs. Hammond.

"Well, he can't just sit staring at the *trees* all—"

"He could comfort his wife," Mrs. Hammond said.

"She won't listen. So I was thinking, as long as he's away today—"

"Men are like that," Mrs. Hammond said. "Work is all they think about."

"As long as he *is* at work," Joan said firmly, "I think maybe Aunt Lou should start working too."

"*Working?*"

"Working at sewing. Missouri said—"

"Mrs. *who?*"

"Mrs.—never mind. Wait a minute." Joan switched ears and leaned forward, as if Mrs. Hammond could see her now from where she stood. "Mrs. Hammond," she said, "I know how good you are at helping other people."

"Oh, why, I just—"

"I know you could help Aunt Lou right now, if anybody could. You could bring that dress she was working on, that—was it purple?"

"Lilac," said Mrs. Hammond. "Princess style."

"That's the one."

"Lou said it would add to my height a little, a princess style would."

"That's right," Joan said. "That's the one."

"Especially since it has up-and-down pinstripes."

"Yes. Well, I was thinking. If you could just bring it over and get her to work on it for you, just take her mind off all the—"

"You might be right," said Mrs. Hammond. "Why didn't I think of that? Why, the day before the funeral, when I came—*you* remember—I did feel she was doing wrong to sit so quiet. I said so. I have always believed that baking calms the nerves, so I said to her, 'Lou,' I said, 'why don't you make some rolls?' But she looked at me as if I'd lost my senses. After all, I'd just *brought* two dozen, and a cake besides. Yet I felt she ought to be doing something; that's what I was trying to tell her. You just might be right, Joan."

"Well, then," said Joan, "do you think you could come over sometime today?"

"I'll come over right this minute. I just wouldn't feel at rest until I had. You say your aunt's still in bed?"

"She was a minute ago," Joan said.

"Well, you try and get her up, and I'll be there as fast as I can find the dress. I'll be there, don't you worry."

"All right," Joan said. "It certainly is nice of you to come, Mrs. Hammond."

"Well. Goodbye, now."

"Goodbye."

Joan hung up and sat back to rub her ear, which felt squashed. Now that all that was settled, the next step was to get Simon downstairs. He would have to back her up in this.

Simon was standing in front of his mirror when Joan came in. He was wearing blue jeans but no shirt, and scratching his stomach absently. "Hey," Joan said, and he jumped and looked up at her. "Find yourself a shirt," she told him. "Connie Hammond's coming."

"Aw, gee, Joan. Mrs. *Hammond?*"

"She'll be here any minute. Come on, now. It's a special favor to your mother."

"I bet she'll never notice," Simon said, but he pulled a bureau drawer open. Joan closed the door and went on to her aunt's room.

Mrs. Pike was sitting up against two pillows, fat and

soft in a gray nylon nightgown. She had her hands folded across her stomach and was looking vaguely at the two points her feet made underneath the bedspread. "Good morning," Joan said, and Mrs. Pike raised her eyes silently and peered at her as if she were trying to pierce her way through mist. But she never answered. After a minute her eyes passed on to something else, dismissing Joan like the wrong answer to a question she had asked. Joan came to stand at the foot of the bed.

"Aunt Lou," she said, "would you like to get up?"

Her aunt shook her head.

"Mrs. Hammond's coming. Do you want her to find you in bed?"

"No," said Mrs. Pike, but she didn't do anything about it. She settled lower into the pillows, with her eyes worrying at the wallpaper now, and in so much dim clutter she appeared to be sinking, overcome by the objects around her. Under Joan's feet were cast-off clothes, everywhere, everything her aunt had been persuaded to put on in the last few days. She had stepped out of them and left them there, returning wearily to her gray nightgown. Mr. Pike, on the other hand, had made some effort at neatness. He had laid his clothes awkwardly on the back of the platform rocker, where they rose in a layered mountain that seemed huge and overwhelming in the half-dark. On the bureau were hairbrushes and bobby pins and old coffee cups with dark rings inside them. The sight of it all made Joan feel caved in and despairing, and she went over to raise the window shade but the light only picked up more clutter. "Aunt Lou," she said, "we just have to get organized here."

"What?"

"We have to start cleaning things up."

Her aunt nodded, without seeming to pay attention, but then she surprised Joan by moving over to the edge of the bed and standing up. She stood in that old woman's way she had just acquired—searching out the floor with anxious feet, rising slowly and heavily. For a minute she stood there, and then she shook her nightgown out around her and faltered toward the bureau. "I'm going to clean up," she told Joan.

"That's it."

But all Mrs. Pike did, once she reached the bureau, was to stare into the mirror. She put both hands on the bureau top and leaned forward, frowning into her own eyes. The alarm clock in front of her ticked loudly, and she reached out without looking to set it farther away. "Some people stop all the clocks when someone dies," she said.

"What're you going to wear, Aunt Lou?"

"If Connie Hammond's coming, why, she'll have to turn around and go off again."

"What *dress* are you going to wear?" Joan asked, and the sharpness of her voice made Mrs. Pike sigh and stand up straight again.

"Any one will do," she said. She pulled out a small plastic box from a half-open drawer and began putting bobby pins into it. One by one she scraped them off the top of the dresser, working like a blind woman with careful fingers while she kept her eyes on the mirror. Joan watched, not moving. Each bobby pin made a little clinking sound against the bottom of the plastic box, and each time the sound came Mrs. Pike winced into the mirror. "My *grand*mother stopped all the clocks," she said. "She would also announce the death to each fruit tree, so that they wouldn't shrivel up. But we don't have no fruit trees." Her fingers slid slowly across the bureau top, and when she found that all the bobby pins were picked up she closed the box and set it down again. Then she went back to bed. She tucked her feet down under the covers and drew the top sheet with great care over her chest.

"No, wait," Joan said.

"I did what I could, Joan."

Joan went over to the closet and pulled out the first thing she touched, a navy blue dress with white polka dots. "Is this all right?" she asked.

"No."

"This, then." And she lifted a brown dress from its hanger and laid it on the bed without waiting for an answer. "It's the prettiest one you've got," she said.

Outside, a car screeched to a halt and sent up a spray of gravel that Joan could hear from where she stood. She looked out and saw Mrs. Hammond's Pontiac swerving backwards into the yard with one sharp turn of the wheel, while Mrs. Hammond herself remained rigidly facing forward. The car came to rest right beside James's pickup, within an inch of running over Simon's bicycle. Then Mrs. Hammond shot out, clutching bits of cloth and tissue paper to her chest and leaving the car door open behind her. All she needed was an ambulance siren. Joan leaned out the window and called, "Mrs. Hammond?" and Mrs. Hammond looked up, with her fact startled and worried-looking.

"Just walk on in and come upstairs," Joan told her. "Aunt Lou's in bed still."

"Oh. All right."

She bent her head over her armload of cloth and started running again, and Joan could hear her quick sharp heels along the porch and then inside, across the parlor floor and up the stairs. "Oh, law," she was saying to no one. She sounded out of breath.

But Mrs. Pike didn't say a word to all this. She just lay back against the pillows and folded her arms across her stomach again, her face expressionless. When Mrs. Hammond burst into the room and said, "Why, *Lou!*" as if Mrs. Pike had somehow taken her by surprise, Mrs. Pike only nodded gently and watched the wallpaper. "Lou?" said Mrs. Hammond.

"She was just now getting up," Joan told her.

"Well, I'll help. That's what I came for." She set her load down on the dresser and peered into the mirror a second, pushing back a wisp of hair, and then she came over to sit on the edge of the bed. Every move she made was definite; now that she was here, the room seemed to lose its swampiness. Her face was carefully made up to cover the little lines around her mouth, and she was packed into a nice summery sheath that Mrs. Pike had made two years ago. The sight of so much neatness made Mrs. Pike sit up straighter and pull her stomach in, even though her face stayed blank.

"I was talking about stopping all the clocks," she told Mrs. Hammond.

"*Oh*, no."

"I've about decided to do it."

"Oh, no. I don't think that's necessary."

"But Mrs. Pike said, "Yes. I don't know why I didn't think of it before."

"It depends on the type," Mrs. Hammond said. "Ormolu, for instance, or mahogany—that you would stop. But those are the only kind. Isn't that so, Joan?"

Joan hadn't heard that before, but she said, "Well, yes," and Mrs. Hammond beamed at her and rocked gently on the bed.

"Only if it's *ornamental,*" she told Mrs. Pike.

"Oh. I didn't know that."

"You wouldn't stop a Baby *Ben* or anything."

"No."

"Do you want to get up?"

"Connie, I just can't," Mrs. Pike said. "I just don't have it in me. You're going to have to go off again."

"Oh, now." Mrs. Hammond shook her head and then began examining the room, as if anything Mrs. Pike said was to be expected and she was just planning to wait till it was over. "This place could use a bit of cleaning," she said. "Also, if I was you I'd add some patches of color to it. You know? I put an orange candlestick in Mr. Hammond's brown den and it just changed the whole atmosphere. He don't like it, but you'd be amazed at the difference it makes."

"I don't care about any of that," Mrs. Pike said distinctly.

"Now, Lou."

"I just want to sleep a while."

"After you make up my lilac dress, I'll let you sleep all you like," said Mrs. Hammond. "I need it for a party."

She stood up and went over to the bureau, where she pulled open the top left drawer as if she knew by instinct where Mrs. Pike kept her underwear. From a stack on the right she took a nylon slip and held it up to the mirror. "Oh, my, how pretty!" she said, and tossed it in the direction of the bed. Mrs. Pike caught it in her lap and stared at it.

From across the hall came the clattering sound of Simon's walk, closer and closer. He had his boots on now. When he reached his mother's door he walked on in without knocking and said, "I'm ready." Then he stood there at the foot of the bed, tilting back and forth in that awkward way he had and keeping his hands jammed tightly in his pockets.

"What're you ready for?" Mrs. Hammond asked interestedly.

"To be sociable at the sewing," Simon told her. "Would you like to know what was the cause of that fight Andy Point's mama and daddy had?"

"In a minute I would," said Mrs. Hammond. "Right now I'm trying to get your mother out of bed."

For the first time, Simon looked at his mother. He looked from under bunched eyebrows, sliding his eyes over slowly and carefully. But she wasn't watching. He kicked at one leg of the brass bed, so that a little jingling sound rose among the springs. Then he said, "Well, I'll be down getting me some breakfast," and sauntered out again. Mrs. Hammond looked after him and shook her head.

"Something is seriously wrong with that boy's hair," she told Mrs. Pike.

"No."

"How long you going to keep on like this, Lou?"

Mrs. Pike looked down at her hands and then shook her head, as if that were her secret. "Are you *sure* not to stop the clocks?" she asked, but Mrs. Hammond didn't answer. She had picked out the rest of Mrs. Pike's underwear, and she tossed it on the bed and then reached out to pull her gently to a sitting position. "That's it," she said. To Joan she said, "You go along and get that boy a decent breakfast. I'll have her down in a minute."

It didn't look to Joan as if they'd *ever* be down, but she was glad to leave the room. She shut the door behind her and descended the stairs quickly, taking two steps at a time, trailing her fingers along the railing. When she reached the kitchen Simon had already taken out the makings for a peanut butter and mayonnaise sandwich. He was running his thumbnail around the edge of the mayonnaise label, making little ripples in it. "Would you like some milk coffee?" she asked him, but he only shook his head. He stopped playing with the label and opened the jar, and Joan handed him a knife.

"From now on, I'm going on no more boats," he said. "I take *stock* in dreams."

"That's kind of silly," said Joan.

"I know when I been warned."

He slapped mayonnaise on top of peanut butter and clamped the two slices of bread together. Then he began to eat, starting with the crust and working his way around until all he had was a small crustless square with scalloped edges. When that point was reached he looked relieved, because he hated crusts. He took a bite out of what was left and began talking with his mouth full.

"Instead of staying here," he said, "I just might to on over to Billy's house. His daddy gave him a chemistry set." He looked up at Joan, but she didn't say anything. "I might do that instead of staying around here talking," he told her.

"Well, suit yourself," said Joan.

"*Mama'd* never notice."

"Sure, she would."

"I bet not."

Joan went over to the cupboard and took down a huge plate, a green glass one that looked like summer and river-water. She began laying out cookies and cakes on it, choosing from boxes that neighbors had brought, while Simon watched her and chewed earnestly through a mouthful of peanut butter. When Joan was finished she stepped back and looked at the cake plate with her eyes squinted a little.

"Aunt Lou does it better," she said.

"Oh, I don't know."

"She puts it in a design, sort of."

"One thing," said Simon, "she don't ever lay out that *much*. Not with just one customer, she don't."

"That's true."

"She uses that little clear sparkly plate."

"Well, it's too late now," Joan said. She picked up the plate and carried it out to the parlor, where she set it on a lampstand by the couch. Then she swung her aunt's sewing machine out into the middle of the room. It was the old kind, run by a treadle, set into a long scarred table. From one of the drawers underneath it she took her aunt's wicker spool box, and while she was doing that she heard the slow careful steps of Mrs. Pike beginning across the upstairs hall. "*That's* it," Mrs. Hammond was saying, "*that's* it." The kitchen door swung open and Simon came out, chewing on the last of his sandwich, to stand at the foot of the stairs and gaze upward. "Mama's coming down," he told Joan.

"I see she is."

"First time she's come before noon. How long have I got to stay here?"

"You don't have to stay at all."

"Well, maybe I will for a minute," said Simon. He swung away from the stairs and went to sit on the couch, and Mrs. Pike's feet began searching their way down the steps. "That's it," Mrs. Hammond kept saying. Joan pulled a chair up to the sewing machine and then stood waiting, with her face turned toward the sound of those heels.

When Mrs. Pike appeared she was dressed more neatly than she had been in days. Her brown dress was freshened up with a flowered handkerchief in the pocket, and her hair was combed by someone who knew how. The only thing wrong was that she had lost some weight, and her belt, which had had its eyelets torn into long slashes from being strained across her stomach, now hung loose and stringy a good two inches below the waist of the dress. Mrs. Hammond was following close behind her to pull the belt up from in the back, so that at least it looked right in front, but it kept slipping down again. "Doesn't she look *nice?*" Mrs. Hammond asked, and both Joan and Simon nodded.

In Mrs. Hammond's other hand was the bundle of cloth and tissue paper. She escorted Mrs. Pike to the chair Joan had ready and then she set the bundle down on the sewing table beside her, saying, "There you are," and stepping back to see what Mrs. Pike would do. Mrs. Pike didn't do anything. She looked at the lilac cloth as if she'd never seen it before. "Well, now," said Mrs. Hammond, and began opening out the bundle herself. "If you'll remember, you cut this out back in May, before all that business about Laura's wedding came up, and I haven't tried it on since. Joan honey, do you want to bring your aunt some coffee and a roll?"

"I'm not hungry," said Mrs. Pike.

But Joan escaped to the kitchen anyway, while Mrs. Hammond went on talking. "I've been on a tomato diet for three weeks," she was saying, "all in honor of this princess-style dress. So now, Lou, I want you to pin it on me again. Don't make it an inch too big, because I want to lose five *more* pounds, Lord willing—"

Joan took two cups and saucers down and set them on the tray. Then she poured out the coffee, taking her time because she was in no hurry to get back to the parlor. When the last possible thing had been seen to, she picked up the tray and carried it out.

"The older you get," Mrs. Hammond was saying, "the harder the fat clings." She had patches of lilac pinned on over her regular dress now, but she was more or less doing it herself. Mrs. Pike just kept smoothing down the already pinned-on patches, running her fingers along the cloth with vague fumbling motions. "There's only four pieces," Mrs. Hammond reminded her. "Plus the pocket.

Where's the pocket? You remember that's one reason we decided on this. You could whip it up in a morning, you said. Do you remember?"

In the silence that followed the question Joan set the coffee down by the cake plate and passed the two cups over. Her aunt's she put on the table, and Mrs. Hammond's she placed on the chair arm, but neither woman noticed. Mrs. Pike seemed fascinated by the little wheel on her sewing machine. Mrs. Hammond was waiting endlessly, with her hands across her breasts to keep the lilac cloth in place. She seemed to be planning to keep silent forever, if she had to, just so that one question of hers could be answered. But Mrs. Pike might not even have heard.

Then Simon said, "Um, why Andy Point's parents won't *speak* to each other—" and Mrs. Hammond looked up at him. "Why they sit in their parlor in chairs faced back to back," he said, "all dates back to Sunday a week. Least that's what Andy says. But I couldn't hardly believe it, it was such a little thing that set them fighting."

"It's nearly always little things," said Mrs. Hammond. Mrs. Pike nodded and took a packet of pins out of her spool box.

"They were on their way to church, see," Simon said. "Andy was along. They made him come. When suddenly they passed this sign saying, 'Craig Church two miles, visitors welcome.' Mrs. Point she said, 'Why, I never have seen *that* before.' Just being conversational. And *Mr.* Point says, 'Well, I don't know why not. It's been there a year or more,' he says. 'No it ain't,' Mrs. Point says. 'Yes, it has,' Mr. Point says . . ."

"Well, now, isn't that typical," said Mrs. Hammond. She turned slightly, but Mrs. Pike pulled her back again to pin two pieces of cloth together at the waist. Mrs. Pike's mouth was full of pins, and her eyes were frowning at everything her fingers did.

"So anyway," Simon said, "that was what began it. Andy says he never saw such a thing. He says they've even had to order another newspaper subscription, because they wouldn't share the one between them."

"If that isn't the limit," said Mrs. Hammond. "Ouch, Lou."

"Oh, I'm sorry," said Mrs. Pike. Everyone looked toward her, but she only went on pinning and didn't say any more, so Mrs. Hammond took up where she had left off.

"What doesn't make sense," she told Simon, "is Mary Point's *nature*. She's not the type to bear a grudge."

"Oh, it won't her fault," said Simon. "Andy says she had forgot about it. She just went on into church and never thought a thing about it. But then at dinner, Mr. Point wouldn't eat what she had cooked and made himself a sandwich right after. That's a sign he's mad. Mrs. Point said, 'Andy,' she said, 'I'll be. Is your daddy mad about something?' And Andy said, 'Well, I reckon he's mad you said that sign wasn't there.' So she said, 'Oh, I had forgot all about that,' but then it was too late. Now she's mad at him for being mad, and it don't look like it's ever going to end."

"You haven't lost a pound," Mrs. Pike said. She had finished pinning the pieces together now, and she was shaking her head at how tightly they fit.

"I have too," said Mrs. Hammond. "You allow a good inch for the dress I'm wearing underneath it, Lou." She acted as if it were perfectly natural that Mrs. Pike was speaking, but right on the tail of her words she shot Joan a meaningful glance. Joan nodded, although privately she didn't feel too sure of anything yet. But Simon kept on bravely, with his hands clutching the edge of the couch and his eyes on his mother, even though it was Mrs. Hammond he was speaking to.

"I asked him," he said. "I asked, 'Andy, how you think they're going to *end* it?' And Andy says, 'Same way it started, I reckon. By accident.' "

"Well, no," said Mrs. Pike, and once again everyone's attention was on her alone. She removed the pins from her mouth and laid them on the sewing table, and then she said, "It's not that easy. Why sure, one of them might speak by accident. Mary might. Then Sid might answer, being glad she'd spoken first, but by then Mary would have caught herself. She'd feel silly to speak first, and only snap his head off then. It's not that easy."

"No, you're right," said Mrs. Hammond, and Joan thought she would have agreed no matter what her aunt had said. "You have to think about the—"

The telephone rang. Mrs. Hammond stopped speaking, and Simon leaped over to pick up the receiver. "Hello?" he said. "What?" He was silent a minute. "No, I knew about it. I knew, I just forgot. Well, thank you anyway. Bye." He hung up.

"Who was that?" asked Mrs. Hammond.

"Just that station."

"What?"

"Just that radio station. They got this jackpot on. They call you up and if you don't say, 'Hello,' if you say instead, 'I am listening to WKKJ, the all-day swinging station—' "

"*I've* heard about that," Mrs. Hammond said.

"If he'd just called before, boy. It's not *me* who was prepared for them to—"

Mrs. Pike's spool box went clattering on the floor. All the colors of thread went every which-way, rolling out their tails behind them, and Mrs. Hammond said, "Why, Lou," but Mrs. Pike didn't answer. She had crumpled up against her sewing machine, leaning her forehead against the wheel of it and clenching both fists tightly against her stomach. "*Lou!*" Mrs. Hammond said sharply. She looked at Joan and Simon, and they stared back. "Did something happen?"

"I said something," Simon told her.

Mrs. Hammond kept watching him, but he didn't explain any further. Finally she turned back to Mrs. Pike and said, "Sit up, Lou," and pulled her by the shoulders, struggling against the dead weight of her. "What's the matter?" she asked. She looked into Mrs. Pike's face, at her dry wide eyes and the white mark that the sewing-machine wheel had made down the center of her forehead. "What's the matter?" she asked again. But Mrs. Pike only rocked back and forth, and Simon and Joan stared at the floor.

9

All Tuesday morning, Ansel had visitors. The first one was Joan. She mustn't have stayed long because she came and went while James was emptying the garbage, which only took a minute. When he returned Ansel said, "Joan's been here," and then dumped a cupped handful of sunflower hulls into an ashtray and sat down to read the paper.

"What'd she want?" James asked.

"Oh, nothing," said Ansel. He opened the paper out and stayed hidden behind it, with just one tuft of pale hair on the top of his head exposed to view. "You won't have to work tobacco today," he added as an afterthought.

"How's that?"

But Ansel didn't answer. Ever since he had awakened he had been angry; James could tell by his long silences, but he knew there was no point asking what was wrong. So he went on fixing breakfast, and while he was doing that he figured out that Joan must have come to say her uncle was working today. He flipped over a fried egg that was burning and called, "Ansel?"

"Hmmm."

"Is Roy Pike working today?"

But that was another question he never got to answer to. All he heard was the steady thumping of Ansel's foot (Ansel kept time to everything he read, as if it were a poem) and the crackling of newspaper pages. He didn't try asking again.

The second visitor was Maisie Hammond. She came while Ansel was eating breakfast off the Japanese tray, and when she walked in Ansel said, "Um. Maisie," and went on munching on his fried egg. (It was one of those days when James had brought a tray without being asked, simply because it was more comfortable to eat in the kitchen alone. Ansel had said, "*Well.* I see you've taken up cooking again," which hadn't even made sense.) Maisie was wearing a white summer dress with a full skirt, and she stood over his couch like Florence Nightingale and bent down to inspect Ansel's egg. "What's that?" she asked.

"Fried egg, of course."

"It looks kind of funny."

"It's James's," said Ansel.

"Ah." And she turned around, so that now she could see James where he sat eating in the kitchen. "Hey, James," she said.

"Hello, Maisie."

"Taken any pictures lately?"

"No."

That seemed to end the conversation; she turned back to Ansel. "You mind if I sit on your couch?" she asked.

"I'd prefer the armchair."

"Well."

She settled on the very edge of the armchair, spreading her skirt around her. When she bent her head toward Ansel, with the tow-white hair falling over her face, the morning sun seemed to pass right through her hair. She looked like glass. James studied her through the doorway as he munched on a piece of toast, but she didn't look his way again. "I came to ask you to a picnic," she told Ansel.

"Oh, no. Thank you anyway."

"Aunt Connie's giving it."

"Well, it's nice of you to ask," Ansel said.

"Don't you *want* to come?"

"Oh, I can't. James, I'm through with my tray."

"Put it on the table," said James.

"There's too much other stuff there."

James scraped his chair back and went to the living room, still chewing his piece of toast. By the time he reached the couch, Ansel was already preparing to lie down; he held the tray out in one hand, while he swung his feet up onto the couch.

"Ansel won't come to Aunt Connie's picnic," Maisie said.

"That's too bad," said James. He picked the tray up and went back to the kitchen.

"He just won't be reasoned with," Maisie called after him.

"Maybe he don't feel up to it."

"Will you hush?" Ansel asked. "*I'm* not giving any excuses; why should you?"

"Sorry."

James made another trip back for the salt and pepper, which were sitting on the arm of the sofa. As he bent to pick them up, Maisie said, "Will you talk to him?"

"Nothing I can say."

"Why doesn't he ever go places?"

"That's *my* secret," Ansel said. They looked at him. He was lying on his back, with his hands crossed over his chest as if he expected to be laid out any minute, and his eyes were staring upwards, wide and blank. But now that he had their attention, all he did was switch his eyes suddenly to the window overhead and say, "Well, now. Yonder goes a jet."

They both waited, still watching him.

"Little white tail behind it," he said finally.

"Are you in some pain?" Maisie asked.

"Well, yes."

She looked across at James. "Ansel's in pain," she told him. But James just sat down on a wooden chair, still holding the salt and pepper, and stretched his legs out comfortably in front of him. If Ansel began an answer by saying, "Well," there was no use believing him.

"What shall I do?" Maisie asked him.

"I don't know."

"Get him a hot water bottle?"

"Hot water bottle on my *feet* won't help," said Ansel.

"Oh. Is it your feet that hurt?"

"I think it is."

"I declare," said Maisie, and then looked at James again, but he didn't offer any suggestions. Finally she said, "Is that why you won't come to the picnic?"

"No."

"It's not till Sunday, you know. You'd be all better by then."

"I just don't want to come," Ansel said. "But thank you anyway."

Maisie couldn't seem to find anything to say to that. She sat there, twisting at the hem of her white skirt, and James began hitting the plastic salt and pepper shakers together until he had worked up to a good rhythm. He was considering starting some more complicated beat when Maisie said, "Will you *stop* that *noise?*"

James stopped. Outside a car suddenly drove up, making a great racket as it skidded to a stop on the gravel road. Maisie stood up and bent forward a little to peer out the window. "It's Aunt Connie," she said.

"Maybe she's come to invite me personally," said Ansel.

"No, she's going toward Mrs. Pike's."

"She won't stay *there* long. Mrs. Pike wants to be by herself."

"Aunt Connie's very cheering," Maisie said.

"Sometimes. *I'm* very cheering, but you know what happened when I—"

"It's Aunt Connie's biggest party of the summer I'm asking you to," Maisie told him. "That's all. The one where she hires the magician and all."

Ansel sighed and looked at the ceiling. After a minute

he said, "The actual place it hurts is right behind the anklebones. The pain is awful."

"The anklebones?"

"Last night I walked too much."

"Where'd you walk to?" Maisie asked.

James frowned at Ansel. He didn't want Maisie to hear about last night, not after that scolding she'd given him. But Ansel wasn't looking at James; he went on, placidly.

"I walked just about everywhere," he said. "I thought, 'I got to get out of here. This is no place for me.' I went everywhere I could think of."

"You shouldn't take such strenuous exercise," Maisie said.

"You have no idea how dizzy I was," Ansel told her. "How swimming in the head I was. I couldn't even pack my things. I had to have a little something first to steady my nerves."

"To—oh," Maisie said, and she shot a glance over at James and narrowed her eyes. "Ansel, you *know* what happens. If you get to drinking, you *see* how you feel."

"It was my mood," said Ansel. "I started walking."

James sat forward and said, "There's a pitcher of Kool-Aid in the icebox. Anybody want some?"

"No," Maisie said. "Where were *you* when all this was going on?"

"I was working," said James. He stood up, before she had a chance to say any more. "I've got to go see Dan at the paper. Take him those pictures."

"Well, goodbye," Maisie said, and turned back to

Ansel. James was relieved she had let him go that easily.

In the darkroom he got his pictures together—one fire, one family reunion, two ladies' meetings—for this week's paper. Then while he was hunting for a manila envelope he heard a knock on the door. He straightened up and listened (it might be Joan again) but it was only the Potter sisters, dropping in for their biweekly visit to see how Ansel was. He heard their little chirping voices, with Maisie's voice running flatly behind them. "We brought some Jewish grandmother cookies, the kind you like," Miss Lucy said, and Ansel said, "Why, that's real—" "I'll take them," Maisie said. Maisie was always butting in, James thought. He set down his pictures and came out to the living room, just to say hello, and saw that both the Potter sisters were still standing in the doorway while Maisie sat back in her easy chair with a bag of cookies in her lap. "Why don't you sit down?" he asked them, and then the chirping sounds began all over again, and the sisters came toward him with their hands outstretched. They had on those dressy white gloves of theirs with the ruffles around the wrists. Seeing that made him sad—they looked as if they were expecting so much out of the visit, when all they were going to do was sit on the threadbare plush chairs a minute and then go home again. He said, "It's good to see you, Miss Lucy. Miss Faye. Nice of you to bring the cookies."

"We *like* doing it," said Miss Lucy.

"Will you have a seat?"

Miss Faye took the chair he pointed out to her, but Miss Lucy chose to sit by Ansel on his couch. He didn't object. He was sitting upright now, and when she settled down next to him he only smiled at her. "I *heard* you tapping those walls last night," he said.

"Tapping the *what?*" asked Maisie.

Miss Lucy looked very severe suddenly and tucked her head further inside her high collar. She never mentioned her nightwalking during the daytime. "We came to see if you're well," her sister said, "and to remind you that tomorrow's Wednesday. Time for your shots."

"James already told me," Ansel said.

"Last time you forgot *anyway*. You went visiting."

"That's true, I did," said Ansel, and then he sat back and smiled around the room, looking so happy and pleased with himself that everyone else smiled back. The Potters made little ducking smiles down at their gloved hands, and Maisie smiled with narrow eyes straight into Ansel's face. James stood up; now that people were seated and comfortable he could go.

"I have to see Dan Thompson at the paper," he told the Potters. "Sorry to run off."

"Well, now, have a good time," said Miss Faye. "Will you remind him of that announcement about our niece's baby?"

"I sure will. See you later."

He went back to the darkroom. Here it was cool and distant-feeling; the voices in the living room were faded. He put the week's pictures in the envelope and then, to prolong his stay in the coolness, he set that down and began filing away the pictures that Ansel had been looking at a couple of days before—the Model A, Ansel on his couch, Joan in the dust storm. When he came to the picture of Joan he stopped and studied it; he thought it might be the best thing he had ever done. Her figure made a straight, black line through a circle of wavery blurs, and her head was bent forward in that way she had when she walked. He didn't know how many hundreds of times he had seen her like that. And facing that photograph head-on, having a tangible picture of the way he saw her in his mind, made him think about the quarrel again. All last night and all this morning, he had been trying not to.

It seemed to him, now that he stopped to consider, that if he wanted things to be smoothed over again it would have to be he who took the first step. Joan wouldn't. She would never change her mind about Ansel or even pretend to, in order to make things easier. He would have to go over and say, "Well, how*ever* we feel, I'm sorry that fight happened," or else she would just stay quietly in her own house, playing games with Simon and occupying herself with little private chores until she died. And all over nothing. He tucked her picture back into the file. Mr. Pike was always saying, "Someday, boy, that girl is going to walk off and leave you," and he didn't know how right he was. Last month Joan had packed her things and gone downtown to catch a bus for home, but then she had decided she might as well go to a movie first and by the time the movie was over she had changed her mind and come home again, dragging two big suitcases behind her and hobbling along on her dress-up shoes. She had told James about it, laughing at herself as she told it, but James hadn't laughed with her. If she were to go, what would he decide to do about it?

Out in the living room, he could hear Miss Lucy discussing her nephew, who was a missionary in Japan and a great curiosity there because of his red hair. "You ought to see him bow," she said. "They bow all the time, he tells me . . ." James half-listened, drumming his fingers on the steel file drawer.

If Joan were to go, he had only two choices. That was the way he saw it. He could let her be, and spend the next forty years remembering nothing but the way she used to walk across the fields with him from the tobacco barns and the peppermint smell of her breath when she kissed him good night. Or he could go after her and say, "Come back. And will you marry me?" In his *mind* he could say that, but not in real life. In real life he had Ansel, and would have him always because he couldn't walk out on that one, final member of his family that he hadn't yet deserted. And in real life, he could never make Joan and Ansel like each other.

"I'll take Africa any day," Miss Faye was saying. "Africans *know* they need a missionary, but these Easterners are eternally surprised." And Miss Lucy chirped something at the end, but James couldn't hear what she said.

He stood up and rubbed his knees where they ached from being bent so long. Then he picked up the pictures for the paper and left the darkroom. Instead of going out through the front he crossed to the back door, in order to make his escape as quickly as possible. Outside, his eyes searched out those daisies he had been meaning to pick, blowing in the wind and about to be too old. He tucked the pictures under his arm and went deeper into the field, heading toward the tallest ones. It always made him feel silly, picking flowers. He didn't mind doing it (Joan liked daisies far better than bought flowers, or any other kind of present), but he didn't like thinking that anyone might be watching. In case someone *was*, he picked very offhandedly—yanking the daisies up nearly by their roots, jumbling them together helter-skelter without looking at them. But while he was rounding the side of the house and heading toward the front yard he arranged them more carefully, and held them up to see if they were all right.

Mrs. Hammond's car was gone; that was one good thing. She must have left while he was in the darkroom. Now all he wanted was for Joan to be the one to answer the door. He knocked and waited, frowning tensely at the screen. For a long time nobody came. Then from somewhere else in the house, Joan called, "Was that a knock?" Her voice echoed; she must have been standing at the head of the stairs.

"It's me," James said.

"Simon, will you let James in?"

Simon came out of the kitchen, dragging his feet. Through the screen, all James saw of him was his silhouette—his spidery arms and legs, his shoulders hunched up as if he were scared of something. Before he reached the door he stopped and said, "You come by yourself?"

"Who would I be bringing?" asked James.

"Oh, no one." And he came the rest of the way to the door and pushed it open. "Joan's upstairs," he said, "putting Mama to bed. She'll be down."

"Your mother got up already?"

"Well, but now she's going back to bed. I said everything all wrong."

"I'll bet you didn't," said James, without being quite sure what he was talking about. He closed the door very softly behind him and went over to a chair. "Is Joan too busy to talk?"

But just then they heard Joan coming downstairs, walking on tiptoe and taking only one step at a time where usually she took two. Simon jerked his thumb toward the sound. "Here she is," he said. When Joan came into view she looked at James blankly a minute, as if she'd forgotten he was here, and then she smiled and said, "Oh. Hello."

"Hello," James said. He stood up and held out the flowers. "I brought you some daisies. I was walking through the field and happened to come across them."

"That was nice," she said, and then frowned at the daisies. James looked at them. They seemed old and draggled now, in a messy little cluster in his hand. "They're not all that special, I guess," he said, but Joan had come out of her thoughts. "I think they're fine," she said. "I'll get a vase."

"Oh, you don't have to get a *vase* for them—"

"Well, of course I do."

She went out into the kitchen, still seeming to walk on tiptoe. Now that James thought of it, there was an uneasy silence about this house. He couldn't tell if it was because of something to do with Mrs. Pike or because Joan was still mad at him, and he didn't know how to ask. He looked across at Simon, who was still standing and staring into space. "Did I come at a bad time?" James asked him.

"Huh?"

Joan came back, carrying a cut-glass vase full of water. He asked her, "Did I come at a bad time?"

"Oh, not really."

"Well, did I or didn't I?"

"It's all right," Joan told him. "Aunt Lou didn't feel well this morning, but she's upstairs now and everything's all right." She took the daisies from him. Her hands when they brushed his were cool and impersonal, and she didn't look at him. "We have to go gradually," she said. "I keep forgetting that. I don't seem to have a *light* touch with anything." Yet her fingers when she arranged the flowers were as light and gentle as butterflies, and the daisies stood up or bent gracefully over the minute she touched them. When she was done they had stopped looking draggled; James was glad now that he had brought them.

"You ought to work for a florist," he told her.

But she set the vase down on a table without even noticing how they looked. She hadn't glanced at them once, all the time she was arranging them. "Mrs. Hammond does," she said. "Have a light touch, I mean. But I'm not sure that's the kind I'm talking about right now."

"I don't know that I follow you," James said.

She shook her head and sat down, as if she had given up on him. "Never mind," she said.

"Mrs. *Hammond* has a light touch?"

"Never mind." She looked suddenly at Simon. "Simon, do you want lunch?" she asked him.

"I just had breakfast."

"Oh."

"*You* have a light touch," James said. "You have the lightest touch of anyone I know."

"Oh, James, *you* don't know."

"Well, I'm trying—" He stopped and glanced toward Simon. It seemed to him Simon looked cold. "Don't you want to sit down?" he asked.

"I'm okay."

"Come on."

Simon shrugged and sat down on the couch. Now that they were all seated here, facing each other and keeping their hands folded in their laps, it seemed more awkward than before. It seemed they should be having a *conversation* of some kind, something that made sense. Not these little jagged bits of words. He tried smiling at Joan but all she did was smile back, using only her mouth while her eyes stayed serious and maybe even angry; he didn't know. "Would you rather I come back another time?" he asked.

"It's all right."

"Well." He sat further forward and looked at his fingernails. "I guess your uncle's working today," he said.

"Didn't Ansel tell you so?"

"In a way he did."

"There's nothing *bad* about it," said Joan.

"Why, no, of course not."

"You have to *do* something. You can't sit around. It's not *fair* to sit around, reminding people all the time—"

She stopped, and James looked sideways at her while he kept his head bent over his fingernails. Her voice was so sharp-sounding it made him uneasy, and he didn't know what he was supposed to say to her. But then she said, "Well. So you don't have to work tobacco any more."

"No," James said.

"That's good."

He waited a minute, and then cleared his throat and said, "It'll be a good season, they say."

"Billy Brandon told me that," Simon said suddenly.

"Barns are nearly full already."

In his shirt pocket he found a plastic comb, with little pieces of lint sticking to it. By running his index finger across its teeth he made a sound like a tiny xylophone, flat and tinny. Joan and Simon both sat watching him. When he saw them watching he stopped and put the comb back in his pocket. "I guess I'll be going," he said helplessly. "I could come some other time."

"All right," said Joan.

"Do you want me to?"

"What?"

"Do you want me to come back?"

"Oh. Yes."

"Okay," he said, but he still wasn't sure. He stood up and went over to the door, with Joan and Simon following solemnly behind. Then he turned around and said, "I could take you to the movies, maybe, Thursday night. The two of you."

"We'll see," Joan said.

"Do you want to come or don't you?"

"I don't know yet if we can," she said.

"Well, I wouldn't ask so far in advance, but tomorrow night I can't go. I'm going to take Ansel playing cribbage. But Thursday—"

"We'll see," said Joan.

"I *know* I wasn't going to chauffeur him around no more, but lately he's been—Well. We don't have to go into that."

"I'm not going into anything," Joan said.

"Yes, you are."

"I wasn't saying a word."

"I could tell the way you were looking."

"I wasn't looking *any* way. I wasn't even *thinking* about it."

She sounded near tears. James stood there, trying to think of what to say next, but he figured anything he came up with would only make things worse. So he waited a minute, and then he said, "I think I'd better leave. Goodbye."

"Goodbye," Simon said.

He was down the porch steps and halfway across the yard when he heard their door close; Joan had never said goodbye. The only sounds now were from Ansel's window—the birdlike sounds of women laughing, all clustered around his brother, their laughter pealing out in clear happy trills that drifted through the window and hung like a curtain across the empty porch.

10

That afternoon, Joan had a telephone call from her mother. She was upstairs when it came, getting Mrs. Pike out of bed for the second time and finding it a little easier now than it had been in the morning. "What do you want to wear?" she asked, and her aunt actually answered, with only a slight pause beforehand. "The beige, I guess," she said. She waited while Joan lifted it off the hanger. "Can I wear the abalone pin with that?"

"Of course," Joan said. She would have agreed if her aunt had wanted to wear the kitchen curtains. She picked the pin out of the bureau drawer and laid it beside the dress, and then the phone rang. Both of them stopped to listen.

"Hey, Joan!" Simon called.

"I'm up here."

"Someone wants you on the telephone."

"Well, I'll be back," Joan told her aunt, and she went

down the stairs very fast, two steps at a time. She didn't know who she was expecting, but when she heard only the ice-cold, nasal voice of the operator she was disappointed.

"Miss Joan Pike?" the operator asked.

"Yes."

"Are you Miss Joan Pike?"

"Yes."

"Long distance calling."

"All right," Joan said.

There was a pause, and then her mother said, "Is that Joan?", formally, and waited for Joan to go through the whole business of identifying herself again.

"It's me," said Joan. "Hello, Mother."

"Hello," her mother said. "I called to see how Lou was. Your father said to ask."

"She's getting better," said Joan. She heard her mother turn and murmur to her father, probably relaying Joan's answer. In normal speech her mother had a very soft voice, held in as if there were somebody sick in the next room. But when she returned to the phone her tea-party voice came back, louder and more distinct, the voice of a plump woman who stood very straight and placed the points of her shoes outward when she walked.

"Your father feels bad we couldn't make it to the funeral," she was saying. "He says it's only a sniffle he has, but I don't like the sound of it. Is there anything we can do for Lou?"

"Not that I can think of. The flowers were very nice—Uncle Roy said to tell you."

"Well. We weren't quite sure. Some people have a dislike of gladioli."

"No, they were fine," said Joan.

"That's good. How's Simon?"

"He's all right, I guess."

"Tell him hello for us, now. Tell him—"

Her voice had grown almost as soft as it normally was. Joan could picture her, sitting on the edge of that rocker with the needlework seat, with Joan's father standing behind her and bending cautiously forward to hear what was going on. He was a little afraid of telephones himself; he treated them as though they might explode. She saw how her mother would be smoothing down that little crease between her eyebrows with her index finger, and then letting the crease come back the minute she dropped her hand. The thought of that made Joan miss her; she said suddenly, "I'm tired."

"What?"

"I'm just tired. I want to come home. I don't want to stay here any more."

"Why, Joan—" her mother said, and then let her voice trail off. Finally she said, "Don't you think you should be with Lou now?"

"I'm not helping," said Joan. "She just sits. Every place I look, Janie Rose is there, and I don't feel like staying here. Nothing is right."

"Doesn't Simon need you?"

"Well—" Joan said, and then stopped because her father must have asked to know what was going on. The two of them murmured together a while, her mother's voice sounding faintly impatient. Joan's father was growing deaf; he had to be told twice. When her mother finally returned to Joan she was sighing, and her voice was loud again.

"You know we'd love to have you," she said. "As soon as you can come. When were you planning on?"

"I don't know. A day or two, maybe. By bus."

"Or maybe James could drive you," said her mother. "We'd love to have him."

"He won't be coming."

"Your father's been asking about him."

"He won't be coming," Joan said firmly.

There was another pause, and then her mother said, "Is something wrong?"

"What would be wrong?"

"Well, I don't know. Shall we expect you when we see you, then?"

"All right. Don't go to any trouble."

"It'll be no trouble. Goodbye, now."

"Goodbye. And thank you for calling."

She hung up, but she stayed in the same position, her hand on the receiver. Out of the corner of her eye she caught sight of Simon. He was leaning against the frame of the kitchen door, eating another peanut butter and mayonnaise sandwich. "Hey," she said, but he only bit off a hunk of sandwich and chewed steadily, keeping his eyes on her face. "That was your Aunt Abby," she told him.

"I know."

"She called to see how everyone is."

He straightened up from the doorframe and came over to her, planting his feet very carefully and straight in front of him. When he had reached her he said, "I hear how you're going there," and waited, with the sandwich raised halfway to his mouth.

"We'll see," said Joan.

"You going by bus?"

"I might not go at all. I don't know yet."

"How long would you go for?"

"Look," said Joan. "I don't know that I'm going. I just think it might be good to get away. So don't tell anyone, all right?"

"Well, all right."

"Not even James."

"All *right*," said Simon. He was good at keeping secrets; it was an insult to suggest he might tell somebody. "If you do go—" he said.

"I might not."

"But if you do go, can I go with you?"

"Oh, Simon," Joan began, and stopped there because she didn't know what else to say. "Your parents need you here," she said finally.

"They won't notice."

"Your daddy will. So will your mother, pretty soon."

"No."

"Yes. See, she's coming downstairs now."

He turned and looked toward the stairs. Mrs. Pike was coming down of her own accord, taking each step uncertainly but not asking for help. She had pinned the abalone pin at the neck of her dress, and it was bunching up the material a little. When she reached the bottom of the stairs she looked from Joan to Simon and back again, as if she were expecting them to tell her what to do next. Joan went over to her.

"I could fix you a bite to eat," she said.

"I came to sew."

"To sew?"

"I came to sew Connie's dress together."

"Oh," Joan said. She looked around at the sewing machine, and was glad to see that the dress still lay there. (Mrs. Hammond had gone away all helter-skelter, talking to herself, leaving everything behind her.) "It's all here," Joan told her. "Is there anything else you need?"

"No. I just want to sew."

"Shall we sit here and keep you company?"

"I just want to sew."

"All right," said Joan, but she waited a minute anyway, and so did Simon. Mrs. Pike didn't look their way again. She went over to the chair at the sewing machine and lowered herself stiffly into it, and then she picked up the material and began sewing on it. She did it just that suddenly, without examining what she was about to do first or even looking at it—just jammed two pieces of cloth beneath the needle of the sewing machine and stepped hard on the treadle. Finally Joan turned away, because there was nothing more she could do. "Let's go to the kitchen," she told Simon. She steered him gently by one shoulder and he went, but he kept looking back over his shoulder at his mother. When they reached the kitchen he said, "See?" but she said, "Hush," without even asking what he meant. "Maybe we could go for a walk," she said.

"I found my ball."

"What ball?"

"That one I lost. I found it."

"Well, I'm glad to hear it," said Joan. "Is it all beat up?"

"It's fine. You want to play catch?"

"Not really."

"Aw, come on, Joan."

She frowned at him. "We should have taken you to a barber," she said finally.

"Just for fifteen minutes or so? I won't throw hard."

"Oh, all right," she said.

Simon went over to the door and picked up the baseball that lay beside it. It was grayer than before, and grass-stained, but lying out in the field for two weeks hadn't hurt it any. He began throwing it up in the air and catching it, while he led the way through the kitchen and out the back door.

"If we had a big mowed lawn, we could play roll-a-bat," Joan said.

"Roll-a-bat's a baby game."

They cut through the tall grass behind the house, parting the weeds ahead of them with swimming motions and advancing beyond the garbage cans and the rusted junk to a place where the grass was shorter. Janie Rose had set fire to this spot not a year ago, while trailing through here in her mother's treasured wedding dress and holding a lighted cigarette high in front of her with her little finger stuck out. James and Mr. Pike and Mr. Terry had had to fight the fire with their own shirts, their faces glistening with sweat and their voices hoarse from smoke, while Ansel leaned out the back window calling "Shame! Shame!" and Janie Rose sat perched in the tin can tree, crying and cleaning her glasses with the lace hem of the wedding dress. Now the weeds had grown up again, but they were shorter and sparser, with black scorched earth showing around them. Joan and Simon took up their positions, one at each end of the burned patch, and Simon scraped a standing-place for himself by kicking down the brittle weeds and scuffing at the charred surface of the soil. "Here goes," he said, and wound up his arm so hard that Joan raised both hands in front of her to ward it off before he had even let go of the ball. Simon stopped winding up and pounded the ball into the palm of his other hand.

"Hey, now," he said. "You going to play like a girl?"

"Not if you throw easy like you promised."

He squinted across at her a minute, and then nodded and raised his throwing arm again. This time the ball came without any windup, cutting in a straight clean arc through the blue of the sky. Joan caught it neatly, remembering not to close her eyes, and threw it back to him underhanded.

"Overhand," said Simon.

"Sorry."

Little prickles of sweat came out on her forehead. She tugged her blouse out of her bermudas, so as to make herself cooler, and almost missed the next ball when it whizzed low and straight toward her stomach.

"*Watch* it," Simon said.

"*You* watch it. That one burned my hands."

She threw it overhand this time, and it fell a little short, so that Simon had to run forward to catch it. While he was walking back to his place a screen door slammed behind them, and Joan automatically turned her head and listened to find out what end of the house it had come from. "Coming," said Simon, and just then Joan saw, in the corner of her eye, someone tall in James's plaid shirt, untangling his way through the field and toward Joan. She turned all the way. "*Watch—!*" Simon said, and something slammed into the side of her head and made everything green and smarting. She sat down, not because she had been knocked down but because she was so startled her knees were weak. Beside her, nestled in a clump of grass, was the baseball, looking whiter than she remembered. Her temple began throbbing and she lay all the way down on her back, with the scorched ground underneath her making little crisp brittle sounds. "*Joan!*" Simon was shouting, and whoever wore James's plaid shirt was thudding closer and closer. It was Ansel. She saw that and closed her eyes. In the same moment Simon arrived, with his breath coming fast and loud. He thumped down beside her and said, "*Joan,* oh, *shit,* Joan," which made her suddenly grin, even with her eyes closed and her head aching. She looked up at him and said, "Simon Pike—" and tried to sit up, but someone yanked her back by the shoulders. "*Where* did you—" she began, but then Ansel clapped his hand over her mouth. His hand smelled of Noxzema.

"You lie still," he said. "Don't you sit and don't you talk. I'll call a ambulance."

"An ambulance?" And this time she out and out

laughed, and sat up even with Ansel trying to press her back down again. "Ansel," she said, "I *really* don't need an ambulance. I just got surprised."

"I warned you," Simon said. "Oh, Lord, people *break* so easy." He settled back on his haunches, clutching his knees, and for a minute it looked as if he would cry.

"Oh, hey, now," Joan told him. She struggled all the way up, letting Ansel keep hold of one of her elbows, and then reached down to give Simon a hand up. When she stood her head hurt more; it was throbbing. She patted Simon's shoulder. "It was my doing," she said. "I turned to see who was coming."

Ansel kept hanging on to her elbow, too tightly. She tried to pull away but he only tightened his grasp and bent closer over her, looking long and pale and worried with his light eyes blinking anxiously in the strong sunlight. "You're coming inside," he told her. "I'll call a doctor."

"I don't *need* a doctor, Ansel."

"Terrible things can happen."

"Oh, for heaven's sake," she said. "I'm not *about* to die on you."

"You never know. You never can—"

She pulled away from him, this time so hard that he had to let her go, and reached out for Simon's hand instead, in case she got dizzier. Simon accepted her hand like a grave responsibility and led her, soberly and silently, toward the house. Ansel followed, panting from all this unexpected exercise.

"We'll go to my house," he said, "where I have iced tea."

"No, thank you."

"I *want* you to go to my house. I feel responsible. And anyway, I'm lonely. James has gone off to Dan Thompson's."

"Oh, all right," Joan said. It was true that she didn't want to go back to that parlor again. They veered toward the Greens' end of the house, with Ansel parting weeds ahead of them and kicking aside bits of rusted car parts so that Joan could have a clear passage. When they reached the back door he held it open for them and ushered them in with a bow, though neither Simon or Joan paid any attention to him.

"Head on to the front room," he said. "I'll tell you what, Joan: you can lie on my couch."

"Oh, well, Ansel, I don't need—"

"It's not often I let someone do that."

"All right," she said, and went on toward the couch, feeling too aching to argue. The house smelled like James—a mixture of darkroom chemicals and shaving soap and sunshine—and there was a little of that medicine smell of Ansel's there too. She lay back on the couch and closed her eyes.

Ansel brought iced tea, with the ice cubes tinkling in the glasses and a sprig of fresh mint floating on top. It surprised her, because Ansel was used to being waited on himself. She had thought he wouldn't even know where the glasses were. He set the tray down on the coffee table and handed a glass to both Simon and Joan. Then he picked up his own glass and carried it over to the easy chair, where he sat down a little uncertainly, as if he had never sat there before. Maybe he hadn't.

"Cheers," he said, and held his glass up high. "In reference to this doctor business, Joan—"

"I feel *fine*."

"But maybe you should see one anyway," said Simon. "You just don't know *what* might have happened."

"Nothing happened. Will you hush?"

She took a sip of iced tea and closed her eyes. It felt good to be cool again. The room was dim and quiet, and the couch was comfortable, and the heat of outdoors had made her feel relaxed and sleepy.

"What else is good," Ansel was telling Simon, "is to drink iced tea with peppermint candy in it. You ever tried that?" His voice was far away and faint, because Joan was half-asleep. She heard him shift his position in the creaky old chair. "You ever tried it?" he asked again.

"No," said Simon. He was still being cautious with Ansel, although Joan couldn't figure out why.

"You ought to have your mother make it for you," Ansel told him.

"She won't care."

"Sure she will. Sure she will."

"We drink mainly Cokes," said Simon.

"This is better."

There was a long silence. Joan reached over to set her glass on the floor, and then she lay down again and put the back of her hand across her eyes to shut the light out.

"James is at Dan Thompson's," Ansel said.

"You told me that," said Simon.

"He just walked out and left me here, alone."

"I don't care."

"If I drop dead today, he'll forget what name to put on the headstone."

"I don't care."

"Ah, well," Ansel sighed, and there was the sound of his stretching in the chair. "There is a collection, in this world," he said, "of people who could die and be mourned approximately a week. If they're lucky. Then that's the end of it. You think I'm one?"

"I don't know," said Simon. "I'm not listening."

"Oh."

There was another pause, and someone's ice tinkled. Ansel's, probably. Ansel said, "I'm going to go away from here."

"Everyone is," said Simon.

"What?"

"Grown-ups can go and not even let on they're going. I wish I could."

"You can come with me," Ansel said.

"Where's that?"

"This town of mine. This place I come from."

"Is it north?" Simon asked.

"North of what?"

"*North* north. Is it?"

"It's south," said Ansel.

"Oh. I want to go north."

"It's all the same. Who you kidding? This town has got a cop that acts like a night watchman. He goes through the town on foggy nights crying out the hours, singing 'Sunshine on the Mountain' and all other sunny songs, middle of the night. Ain't *that* a thing to wake in the night to, boy."

"Yeah," said Simon.

"To wake up after a nightmare to."

"Yeah."

The throbbing in Joan's head kept time to Ansel's words. She wanted to leave now, and stop listening to that thin voice of his going on and on, but the throbbing made a weight on her head that kept her down. She listened dreamily, without interrupting.

"Lately I've been thinking about home," Ansel said. "It was the funeral that did it, somehow."

"You didn't go to the funeral."

"It did it *anyway*. The only problem is, it's hard to know what way to think about it. No telling how it's changed, and I get no letters from there. James does, from our sisters. He writes them once a month, letters all full of facts, but when he gets an answer he pretends he doesn't. I don't know why. I mean he goes on writing but never mentions what their letters to *him* have said, never comments on them. Why do you think he does that?"

"I don't know," Simon said. "This cop, does he sing every night?"

"*Just* about. And there's a feed store that gives away free hats. Big straw hats, with red plumes curling down like Sir Walter Raleigh's. Walk down Sedad Street and it's just an acre of people wearing hats, red plumes bobbing up and down. Merchants wearing hats, farmers wearing hats, everyone but little old ladies wearing hats. Old ladies don't like them hats. You go down to Harper's

River and find little boys and colored men fishing in leaky boats, wearing red-plumed hats. Why, you can tell when you're coming home again. You look out the bus window into those country fields and find farmers plowing, wearing hats with red plumes, and the mules wearing them too but with holes cut in them for the ears to stick out. That's how you know you're nearing home."

"How about me?" asked Simon.

"How *about* you."

"If I was to ask, would they give me one too?"

"Why, surely."

"I'll ask, then."

"You do that."

More ice tinkled. Joan's hand had stuck to her damp forehead and she took it away, making a tearing sound, and sighed and turned over on her side.

"What exactly is the name of this town?" Simon asked.

"Caraway, N.C."

"Is there buses to it?"

"Six a day."

"Is there people my age?"

"Is there?" Ansel asked, and he laughed suddenly, a chuckle deep in his throat so that he sounded a little like James. "*Is* there, boy. Well, lots. I ought to know. Another thing. This is something I've never seen in any other town, now: the boys wear one gold ring in their ear."

"*Earrings?*"

"Oh, no. No, this is like pirates wear. Pierce their ears and put one gold hoop through. Everyone did it."

"Did you?"

"My family didn't want me to. Well, I wasn't actually in that particular group, anyway. But James was. He had a hoop, but he took it off finally. Only got one because the family told him not to. Eventually *every*one takes them off, when they've grown up and settled down. You'll hear someone say, 'So-and-so's engaged now. He's got a steady job, and there's no more gold in his ear.' But I never had gold in my ear to begin with."

"Does it hurt?" Simon asked.

"Does what hurt?"

"When they pierce your ears."

"Oh, no. At least, I don't think so. Not for long."

"If I went there, would I wear a earring?"

"Sure you would."

"How long is it by bus?"

Joan felt herself drifting off. The house seemed to be spinning around her, making streaky yellow shimmers of sunshine through her eyelids, but when she found that she wasn't even hearing the others' voices now she pulled herself sharply awake. She opened her eyes and found that she was looking at one of Ansel's shoes, tapping lazily on the floor. "Have I been asleep?" she asked. Simon and Ansel looked over at her. "What time is it?"

"Not yet three," said Ansel. "How's your head?"

"It's fine."

"You sure?"

"Yes. Sorry to disappoint you." She sat up and tucked her blouse in. "Simon, we got to get going," she said.

"Aw, I was just hearing something interesting."

"It can wait."

She let him go through the front door first, and then she turned to Ansel and smiled at him. "Thank you for the use of the couch," she said.

"Nothing to it." He poked his head out the door, past Joan, and looked at Simon. "You be making your plans, now," he said.

"All right."

"Plans for what?" Joan asked.

"Nothing," said Simon.

Joan yawned, and followed him down the porch toward home.

11

"THERE'S NOT MUCH DIFFERENCE between one person and the next," Ansel said. "I've found that to be true. Would you agree with me?" He raised himself up from a prone position on the couch to look at James, who was sitting nearby with the paper. "Would you?" he asked.

"Well, more or less," said James, and turned to the sports section.

"Course you do. You have to. Is that the Larksville paper?"

"Larksville paper's not out till tomorrow."

"Oh. I thought today was Wednesday."

"It is," said James. "The paper comes on Thursday."

"Oh."

Ansel lay down again and stared thoughtfully upwards, lacing his fingers across his chest. He had been flat on his back all morning, complaining of dizzy spells, and James had been sitting here keeping him company. It was easier that way. Otherwise Ansel would continually think up reasons to call him into the room and things to ask him for. "James," he would call, "what was the name of that old woman who gave sermons on the street corner?" Or, "Whatever happened to that seersucker suit I used to have?" And in the long run James would have to spend just as much time in this room as if he'd been sitting there all along. He yawned now and turned another page of his newspaper, and Ansel switched his eyes back over to him.

"It's a fact, James," he said. "People don't vary a heck of a lot, one from the other."

"You told me that," said James.

"Well, yes, I did. Because it's true. If you will hark your mind back to that Edwards boy, that bucktoothed one that joined the Army—what was his name?"

"I don't know."

"Oh, sure you know. Sure you know. What was his name?"

"Ansel," said James, "I just don't make a point of *remembering* all these things."

"Well, I wouldn't brag about it. Clarence, that was it. Or Clayton; I don't know which. Now, Clarence, he went almost around the world with that Army outfit of his. Almost everywhere. And you know what he said when he got back? He said that every single country he'd been in, one thing always held true: when mothers and children climb into a car to go visiting, the first act a mother undertakes is spitting on a hanky and scrubbing her children's faces with it. Always. Canada, France, Germany—always. If that doesn't prove my point, what does?"

James ran his eyes down the baseball scores. He

frowned over them, absentmindedly making a little *tch* sound under his breath when he came upon a score he didn't like. After a while he became aware of the silence, and he looked up to see Ansel watching him with his eyes wide and hurt. "You weren't even listening," Ansel said, and James sighed and folded his paper up.

"I was listening and reading both," he said.

"No. What's it take to make a man listen?"

"Well, I'm sorry. You can tell it to me over again, if you want."

"No."

Ansel turned slightly, so that his cheek was resting on the sofa cushion, and closed his eyes. "I've noticed more and more," he said, "that no one listens when I talk. I don't know why. Usually I think about a thing before I say it, making sure it's worthwhile. I plan it in my mind, like. When I am dead, what will they remember but the things I talked about? Not the way I looked, or moved; I didn't look like much and I hardly moved at all. But only the things I talked about, and what is that to remember when you never even listened?"

"I listen," said James.

"No. Sometimes in one of those quiet periods after I've said something, when no one's saying anything back because they didn't hear me, I look at myself and think, well, my goodness. Am I *here?* Do I even *exist?*"

"Oh, for heaven's sake," said James. He opened the paper again.

"When I am dead, I wonder what people will miss me. You? Simon? Mrs. Pike will wish she'd brought more hot soup. Joan won't notice I'm gone. Will you miss me?"

James read on. He learned all about a boy named Ralph Combs, who was planning to be Raleigh's contribution to the major leagues. He read Blondie and Dick Tracy and Part 22 of the serialized adventure story, and then he noticed the silence again and he lowered his paper to look at Ansel. Ansel was asleep, with one arm flung over his head and his fingers curling in around the sofa arm. His eyelids were translucent and faintly shining, and over his forehead his hair hung rumpled, making him look the way he had when he was twelve. Seeing him that way made James feel sad. He rose and came over to the couch, standing at Ansel's head and looking down at his long pale face tipped back against the cushions. If he hadn't known better, he would have tapped him on the shoulder and said, "*Now* I'll listen." But then Ansel would wake up and be twenty-six years old again, nervously testing himself for new symptoms, beginning some long monologue that he had begun before, changed forever from that scared small brother who could sit a whole evening without saying a word or raising his eyes from the floor. That twelve-year-old would vanish without a trace, leaving not even an echo of himself in the way Ansel smiled or said a certain word. James moved away from the couch and went over to the window.

Because of the way he felt, the view from the window took on a sad, deserted look. Everything was bowed low under the breeze, straightening up for a second only to bow again. Simon's bicycle lay on its side with a drooping buttercup tangled in its spokes. At the edge of the yard the Potters' insurance man was just climbing out of his Volkswagen. (He came every week, because the Potters had to be constantly reassured that their policy really was all right.) He looked tired and sad. While he was crossing the yard he mopped his face and straightened the plastic carnation in his buttonhole, and then on the first porch step he snapped his head erect and put a bright look on his face. After that James lost sight of him. But he could hear the knocking, and the sound of the Potters' door cautiously opening and the bolts being slid back after the insurance man was taken inside. They slid easily in their little oiled tracks. The quickness of them made James smile, and he could picture Miss Lucy's eager fingers fumbling rapidly at the locks, shutting little Mr. Harding in and the loneliness out for as long as she and Miss Faye could manage. He stopped smiling and moved away from the window.

Back in the kitchen it was even worse. There was one daisy on the counter, a stray one from the field in back, and it was dead and collapsed against Ansel's untouched lunch tray. ("I'm not eating today," Ansel had said. "Do you care?" "Suit yourself," said James.) Out the back window was the half-mowed field, looking bald and straggly. Simon Pike was leaning against an incinerator staring at it all, and while James watched, Simon straightened slowly and began wandering in small thoughtful circles around the incinerator. With the toes of his leather boots he kicked at things occasionally, and he had his shoulders hunched up again so that he looked small and worried. James stuck his head out the window.

"Hey, Simon," he said. "why don't you come in?"

Simon raised his head and looked at him. "What for?" he asked.

"Well, you look kind of lonely out there."

"Aw, no."

"Well, anyway," said James, "I want to take a picture of you."

That made Simon think twice. He stood still for a moment to consider it, with his chin stuck out and his eyes gazing away from James and across the field. Then he said, "What kind of picture?"

"The kind you like. A portrait."

"Well, then, I reckon I might. I'll come in and think about it."

"*That's* the way," said James.

He let Simon come in his own good time, stopping to kick at a bootscraper and wasting several minutes examining some blistered paint on the door. When Simon was troubled about something, this was the way he acted. He circled all around the kitchen without once looking at James or speaking to him, and he picked up several things from counters and turned them over and over in his hands before setting them down again. Then he jammed his hands into his back pockets and went to the window. "Mama's hemming a dress," he said.

"That's good."

"She talks a little, too, but not about any concern of mine."

"Well, you got to give her time," said James. "First thing people talk abut is weather and things."

"I know," Simon said. "Daddy is at the fields, and Joan too. It's her tobacco day. Everybody's busy."

"So're you," said James. "You're having your picture taken."

"Yeah, well."

But when James headed toward the darkroom, Simon followed him. "Where are we going to take it?" he asked.

"Outdoors, if you like."

"I'd rather the living room."

"All right," James said. He opened the door of the darkroom and led the way to where his cameras stood. "You got to be quiet, though, because that's where Ansel's sleeping."

"*Now?*"

"It's one of his dizzy days."

"Oh, cripes," said Simon, and he started walking in circles again. He put the heel of one boot exactly in front of the toe of the other, and keeping his balance that way made him fling both arms out and tilt sideways slightly. "It's a bad day for *every*one," he said. "I declare." He seemed to be walking on an imaginary hoop, suspended high above the ground.

James had seen the kind of portraits that Simon and Janie Rose liked best—the ones taken against a dead white screen, with the faces retouched afterwards. He favored a homier picture, himself. He left the screen behind and brought only a couple of lamps, not the glaring ones, and his favorite old box camera. "We'll put you in the easy chair," he told Simon. He had given the camera to Simon to carry, and Simon was squinting through the view-finder as he walked. "Do you want to be doing anything special?"

"Yes," Simon said. "I want to be smoking a cigar."

"Be serious, now."

"I *am* serious. You asked me what I wanted to be doing. Well, all my life I've been waiting to get my picture took with a cigar. I been counting on it."

"Oh, what the hell," said James. He set his lamps down and went over to the living-room mantelpiece. From the old wooden cigar box that had belonged to his grandfather he took a cigar, the fat black kind that he smoked on special evenings when no one was around to complain. "Here you go," he said. "But don't you light it, now. Just get your picture took with it."

"Well, thank you," said Simon. He crossed to the easy chair, giving Ansel a sideways glance as he passed, but Ansel only stirred and didn't wake up. "He don't know what he's missing," Simon whispered. "Me with a cigar, boy."

"It'll all be recorded for posterity," said James.

While James was setting up the lights, Simon practiced with the cigar. He opened it and slid the paper ring off, and then he sat with his elbow resting on the chair arm and his face in a furious frown every time he took a suck from the unlit cigar. "I'm getting the hang of it," he said, and looked around for an ashtray to practice tapping ashes into. "When do you reckon they'll let me smoke these for real?"

"Never, probably," said James. "Always someone around that objects to the smell."

"Ah, I wouldn't care. I'm going to start as soon as I'm out on my own, boy. Soon as I turn sixteen or so."

James smiled and tilted a lamp closer to Simon. He had been listening to Simon for some years now, and he had a mental list of what he was planning to do at age sixteen. Smoke cigars, take tap-dance lessons, buy his own Woolworth's, and grow sideburns. Janie Rose hadn't even been going to wait *that* long. She asked her mother weekly, "Do you think it's time I should be thinking of getting married?" And then she would smile hopefully, showing two front teeth so new that they still had scalloped edges, and everyone would laugh at her. James could see their point, though—Jamie's and Simon's. He couldn't remember that being a child was so much fun. So he nodded at Simon and said, "When you turn sixteen, I'll *buy* you a box," and Simon smiled and settled back in the chair.

"Might not wait till then even," he said. "You never can tell."

"Well, I would," said James. "Tobacco stunts your growth."

"No, I mean to go out on my own. I might go earlier." He stuck out his tongue and flicked an imaginary piece of tobacco off the tip of it. "I been thinking where I could go."

"It's kind of early for that," James said.

"I don't know. You know Caraway, N.C.?"

James stopped fiddling with his camera and looked up. "What about it?" he asked.

"I just thought you could tell me about it. If that's where you are from."

"Nothing to tell," said James.

"Well, there's hats with feathers on them, and them gold earrings the boys all wear. Do you think I might like that town?"

In the view-finder his face was small and pointed, with a worried line between his eyes. He was leaning toward James with the cigar poised forgotten between his thumb and forefinger, and in the second of stillness that followed his question James snapped the picture. "That'll be a good one," he said.

"Will I like Caraway?"

"I don't see how. Do you ever see *me* going to Caraway?"

"Well, the boys wear gold earrings,"' Simon said again, and he sighed and rubbed the top of his head and James snapped that picture too.

"Sure, the *boys*," he told Simon. "They're the worst in the state, Caraway boys. Got tight little Church of God parents. All they want to do when they grow up is come somewhere like Larksville. What you want to do in Caraway?"

"I could board with your family," Simon said.

James looked up from his camera with his mouth open and then threw back his head and laughed. "*Hoo!*" he said, and Ansel stirred in his sleep at the noise. "I'd like to see that," he went on more quietly. "Would you turn sideways in your chair now, please?"

Simon turned, but he kept his eyes on James. "*Ansel* says—" he began.

"*Ansel* don't know."

"Ain't he *from* there?"

"He don't know."

"Well, anyway," said Simon, "I could go and look it over."

"Your mother would love that. Now, quit watching out of the corner of your eye, Simon. Look at the fireplace."

"Do you think she'd miss me?" Simon asked.

James clicked the picture and stood up, squinting at him sideways to see which way to turn him next.

"I think my mother'd say, '*Who* you say's gone? Oh, *Simon!*' she'd say. 'Him. My goodness. Did you remember to bring the eggs?' " He sat forward again then and frowned at James, twining the cigar over and under the fingers of his left hand. "You see how it'd be," he said.

"You know that ain't so," said James.

He stepped a little to one side and got Simon focused in the camera again, all the while waiting for the argument to continue. But it didn't. In the square of the viewfinder Simon suddenly sighed and slumped down like a little old man, staring abstractedly at the wet end of his cigar. "Ah, hell," he said. "It don't matter."

That made James look up, but he didn't say anything. Instead he snapped the picture and frowned over at the lamps, measuring how much light there was. "Outdoors would've been better," he said finally.

"I also hear," said Simon, "that they sing all night in the dark. And them plumed hats, why, even the mules wear them. With holes cut for ears."

"Look over toward your left," James said.

"There's six buses going there a day, Ansel told me."

James folded his arms across the top of the camera and watched Simon a minute, thinking. Simon stared straight back at him. In the light from the lamps his eyes seemed black, and it was hard to see beyond the flat surface of them. His chin was tilted outward a little, and his lashes with their sunbleached tips gleaming were like curtains over his expression. Who knew what was in his mind? James uncrossed his arms then and said, "Put your cigar away, now. This last one's for your mother."

"Aw, my mother won't even—"

"She wants a picture she can show to the relatives. What would they think, you with a big fat cigar in your hand?"

"She won't—" Simon began again.

But James said, "You're growing so much, this summer. She wants to get you in a picture before you're too big to *fit* in one."

"She tell you that?" asked Simon.

"Why, sure."

"She ask you out and out for a picture of me?"

"Sure she did," James said. "She said, 'James, if you got time, I wish you'd snap a picture of Simon. We don't have a picture that looks like him no more.' I said I'd try."

"Well, then," said Simon after a minute. He rose and crossed over to the mantelpiece, where he laid down the cigar. When he returned to his chair he settled himself very carefully, tugging his jeans down tight into his boots, running both hands hard through his hair to smooth it back. He looked more posed now; the relaxed expression that he had worn in the other pictures was gone. With both hands placed symmetrically on the arms of the chair, his back very straight and his face drawn tight in the beginnings of a smile, he stared unblinkingly into the lens of the camera. James waited a minute, and then he pressed the button and straightened up. "Thank you," he said formally.

"Oh, that's all right."

"I'll have them for you this afternoon, maybe. Or tomorrow, early. Perle Simpson is coming by for a passport photo and I want to take that before I start developing."

"Okay," said Simon. He stood up, frowningly tucking in his shirt, and then suddenly he looked over at James and gave him a wide, slow smile, so big that the two dents he was always trying to hide showed up in the center of his cheeks. "Well, I'll be seeing you," he said, and sauntered on out, slamming the screen door behind him. When James went to the window to look after him he saw him in the front yard, picking up the bicycle he hadn't ridden for days and twirling the pedal into a position where he could step on it. The buttercup still hung in the spokes, its little yellow head dangling drunkenly from the front wheel and its withered leaves fluttering out like banners when Simon rode slowly off. He rode in the direction of the Terrys' farm; he would be going to see the tobacco pickers, the way he used to do.

When Simon was out of sight, and when James had turned and seen that Ansel was sleeping still, he himself went out the screen door and down the long front porch. The Pikes' window shades were up now. He peered in through the dark screen door and saw Mrs. Pike at her sewing machine, not running it at the minute but sewing by hand on something that was in her lap. "Mrs. Pike," he called gently. She lowered the sewing and looked up at him, her mouth screwed up and lopsided because of the pins in one corner of it. "Mrs. Pike, can I come in a minute?"

"Joan's handing tobacco," she said. Speaking around the pins made her seem like a different woman, like that waitress at the Royal Crown who always had a cigarette in her mouth when she talked. "Did you want to see Joan?"

"Well, no, I just wanted to tell you—" said James. He pulled open the screen door and stepped just inside it, even though he hadn't been asked. "I took a picture of Simon," he said.

"Oh."

"Sitting in an easy chair."

"Well, that's real nice," said Mrs. Pike, and bowed her head to nip a thread off the dress she was sewing.

"Well, I took it for *you*, Mrs. Pike."

"That's real nice of you," she said again. She held the dress up at arm's length and frowned at it. James shifted his weight to his other foot.

"What I actually told him," he said, "was that you *asked* for it. Asked me to take it for you."

She lowered the dress to her lap again and looked over at him, and James thought that surely she would say *some*thing now. But when she did speak, all she said was, "It must be right hard, taking pictures of children" —politely, as if he were a stranger she was trying to make conversation with.

James waited a minute, but she didn't say more. She had lowered her head to her sewing again, fumbling at it with quick, blunt fingers and absentmindedly working the pins from one side of her mouth to the other. So he said, "Well, ma'am, not really," and then turned and quietly let himself out the door again. All the way down to his end of the porch he kept thinking of going back and trying once more, but he knew already it wasn't any use. So he entered his own part of the house and then just stood there a minute, thinking it over, watching Ansel as he slept.

12

THE THINGS Joan Pike owned in this world could be packed in two suitcases, with room to spare. She was putting them there now, one by one, folding the skirts in two and laying them gently on the bottom of the big leather suitcase her father's parents had given him to take to a debating contest fifty years ago. Her own suitcase, newer and shinier, stood waiting on the floor already filled and locked. She had saved out her big straw pocketbook, which was hard to pack and could hold all the things she might need on the bus. It stood on the floor, with one corner of a Greyhound ticket envelope sticking out of it. The ticket she had bought this morning, after spending all of Wednesday night lying in bed rolling up the hem of her top sheet while she thought what to do. She had ridden into town for it on Simon's bicycle, and come back with it hidden inside her white shirt. Nobody knew she was going.

When her closet was empty she cleaned it out carefully, picking up every stray bobby pin and button from the floor and bunching the hangers neatly at one end of the rod with the hooks all pointing the same way. Mainly she wanted to save her aunt the trouble, but also she wanted to go away feeling that she had left a clean sweep behind her—not a thread, not a scrap of hers remaining that she could want to return for. She would like to have it seem as if she had never been here, if that was possible. So she closed the closet door firmly and turned the key in its lock. Then she began on the rest of the room.

She rolled her silver-backed dresser set in sweaters, so that none of the pieces would get scratched. Seeing the set, which her parents had given her on her eighteenth birthday, made her remember that she should be bringing back presents for them, and she frowned into the mirror when she thought about it. Always before, after two weeks at Scout camp even, she had brought back gifts for each of them and formally presented them, and her parents had done the same. But this time she hadn't thought far enough in advance; she would have to come home empty-handed. The idea bothered her, as if this were some basic point of guest etiquette that she, always a guest, had somehow forgotten. She shook her head, and laid the wrapped silver pieces carefully on top of her skirts.

Out in the back yard Simon was running an imaginary machine gun, shouting "ta-ta-ta-ta-tat" in a high voice that cracked and aiming at unknowing wrens who sat in the bushes behind the house. She could see him from her window—his foreshortened, blue denim body, the swirl of hair radiating out from a tiny white point on the back of his head. With luck, he wouldn't see her go. He would stay there in the back yard, and his mother would stay in bed for her afternoon nap, and she could sneak out of the house and across the fields without anyone's seeing her. It might even be supper before they noticed. Mr. Pike would fuss a little, feeling responsible for his brother's child. Mrs. Pike was still too sad to care, but Simon would care. He would ask why she had left without telling them, and how would they answer him? How would *she* even answer him? "Because I don't want to think I'm really going," she would say. It was the first time she had thought that out, in words. She stopped folding a slip and looked down at where Simon sat, with his legs bent under him and the toes of his boots pointing out, sighting along a long straight stick and pulling the trigger. As soon as she got home, she decided, she would telephone to make it all right with him.

Then after supper James would come. "Joan ready?" he'd say. "She's gone," they'd tell him. Then what would he do? She couldn't imagine that, no matter how hard she tried. Maybe he would say, "Well, I'm sorry to hear that," and remain where he was, his face dark and stubborn. Or maybe he would say, "I'll go bring her back." But that was something she didn't expect would ever happen now. A week ago, she might have expected it. She'd thought anything could happen, anyone would change. But now all she felt sure of was that ten years from now, and twenty, James would still be enduring, on and on, in that stuffy little parlor with Ansel in it; and she couldn't endure a minute longer.

She turned away from the window and went back to

her suitcase. Everything was in it now. The bureau was left as blank as the bureau in a hotel room; its drawers were empty and smelled of wood again. On the back of the door hung her towel and washcloth, the only things left of her. She plucked them off the rack and carried them out to the laundry hamper in the hall, and then she was finished. No one would ever know she had lived here. When she had locked the second suitcase, and stepped into the high heels that she had taken off so as not to make a noise, she stood in the doorway a minute making sure of the blankness in the room. Then she picked up the two suitcases and the pocketbook and went downstairs.

Carrying it all was harder than she remembered. She kept having to switch the pocketbook strap from one arm to the other, and although the suitcases weren't heavy they were big and bulky and banged against her legs when she walked. Before she was even off the front porch she was breathing hard. Then in the yard, the spikes of her high heels kept sinking into the earth and making things more difficult. If she'd had any sense, she thought, she would have called Mr. Carleton and his taxi service. Except then everybody and his brother would have known she was leaving. She waited until she had crossed the road and was into the field and then she took her first breather, chafing the red palms of her hands and looking anxiously back at the house. No one had seen her yet.

All the evening walks through this field with James or the children had taught her the shortest way to town— the straight line through burrs and bushes, leading apparently to nowhere but more field, emerging suddenly upon Emmett Smith's back yard and from there to Main Street. She walked carefully, to avoid getting runs in her stockings, and kept her eyes strained ahead for the first sight of the Smith house. Around her ears the breeze made a hot, lulling sound, drying the dampness on her forehead to a cold thin sheet. Then another sound rose, like wailing, and she turned and saw Simon running to catch up, his brown hands fluttering to part the weeds in front of his chest and his face desperate. "*Jo*-oan!" he was calling. He made two syllables out of it. Joan set down the suitcases and waited, with her hands crossed over her pocketbook. "Joan, *wait!*" he said, and floundered on. "Oh, Simon," she said, but she kept waiting.

When he came up even with her he was out of breath, and covered with burrs. For a while he just stood there panting, but then his breath came more slowly and he straightened up. "Can I come?" he asked.

"Oh, Simon—"

"I came in to see what you was doing. I couldn't *find* you; I thought—" He stopped, and switched his eyes from her face to the field behind her. "I wouldn't be a bit of trouble," he said softly. She leaned forward, trying to catch his words, and he said it louder: "I wouldn't be a *bit* of—"

"Well, I know that."

"Old James came over with that picture he took yesterday," he said. "You were gone off on my bicycle. He brought it in a special brown envelope like he does to customers. I said, 'Mama, here is that picture you was asking for.' She says, 'What?' I pulled it out to show her.

She said, 'Oh,' and then went back to her sewing and didn't look any more. I put it back on James's doorstep."

"Well, now, don't you worry—" said Joan, but she had to stop there, because she wasn't sure what he was talking about. She stood frowning at him, with the wind whipping the hair around her face and her hands clenched white on the pocketbook.

"I won't be a *bit* of trouble," he said again.

She said, "No," and stooped nearer to him. "I can't take you," she said. "I have to go off, Simon. And you have to stay with your family. When they are back to normal, though, you can come and visit."

Simon just stood there, very straight. She didn't know what to do, because he had his head drawn back in that way he had and if she'd hugged him he would have hated her. So she waited a minute, and then she said, "Well, goodbye." He didn't answer. "Goodbye," she said again. She kept on facing him, though, because she couldn't turn first and just leave him there. Then when she was beginning to think they would stand that way forever he swung around and left, and she watched him go. He stumbled through the field in a zigzagging line, not parting the grass ahead of him but pressing on with his hands at his sides. "Simon?" she called once. But Simon never answered.

When she turned away herself, and bent to pick up her bags again, she was thinking that out of all the bad things she had ever done this might be the one sin. It made her feel suddenly heavy and old; the weight of her sadness dragged behind her through the fields like another suitcase, and she couldn't look up or let herself think about anything but walking, putting one foot ahead of the other.

The Smith house loomed up suddenly, just beyond a little rise in the ground. Inside a wire fence the hens scratched irritably at the dirt, and from the house came the sound of someone's singing. Joan set her suitcases down and looked back, thinking to see some sign of what she had left, but there was only the gentle slope of wild grass stretching as far as she could see. Behind that was James, dark and slow and calm, rocking easily in his chair and never knowing. And that long front porch where she and Simon used to shell peas on summer evenings, while Janie Rose sang "The Murder of James A. Garfield" through the open window. She picked up her suitcases and walked on, with that sudden light, lost feeling that came from walking in a straight line away from people she loved.

The clock in the drugstore where the buses stopped said there were ten minutes to go. Tommy Jones behind the soda fountain checked her bags and handed her the tags, and she said, "Thank you," and smiled at him dazedly without thinking about him.

"Coke while you wait?" he asked.

"No, thank you."

"On the house."

"Oh, no."

Her voice sounded thin and sad. She felt like a stick, very straight and alone, standing upright with nothing to lean against. Surely people should have noticed it, but they didn't; Tommy smiled at her as if this were any normal day, and the two other people in the store went on leafing through their magazines. Dan Thompson's wife came in, wearing one of Dan's baggy printing aprons the way she usually did and carrying a fresh stack of this week's newspapers. The insides of her forearms were smeared with ink from them. When she saw Joan she smiled and came over toward her. "Hi," she said. "You want a paper?"

"I guess so," said Joan. She fished in her purse for the money and handed it over, and Carol gave her a paper off the top of the stack.

"Nothing but the most startling news," she said. "We took it all from the Rockland paper this week. Usually we get it from Clancyville."

"Well, that's all right," Joan said. "I haven't read the Rockland paper either."

"Good. You know what I think sometimes?" She heaved the papers onto a soda fountain stool and began rubbing the muscles of her arm. "Sometimes I think, what if *every* paper gets its news from the other papers? What if this is twenty-year-old news we're reading, just circulating around and around among newspapers?"

"I don't suppose it'd make much difference," Joan said absently.

"Well, maybe not." She picked up the papers again. "You bring James over for supper some night, you hear? We haven't had the two of you together in a long time."

"All right," said Joan. She didn't see much point in telling Carol she was leaving, not if Carol hadn't noticed for herself. And she hadn't. She went off jauntily, with a wave of her hand, and threw the papers on the floor in front of the magazine rack and left the store. Yet there was Joan, all dressed up in her high-heeled shoes. She looked around at the other customers again, but they went on reading their magazines.

When the bus drew up, she was the only person to board it. The driver didn't smile or even look at her; already she was outside the little circle of Larksville, and only another stranger to the people on this bus. She sat in a seat by herself, toward the rear, and smoothed her skirt down and then looked at the other passengers. None of them looked back except a sailor, who stopped chewing his gum and winked, and she quickly looked away again and sat up straighter. The bus started with a jerk and wheezed up to full speed along Main Street, making a sad, going-away noise. Through the green-tinted windows Larksville looked like an old dull photograph, and that made her sad too, but once they had passed the town limits she began to feel better. Some of that light feeling came back. It crossed her mind, as she was pulling on her gloves, that all she was going to was another bedroom, to years spent reading alone in a little house kept by old people, remembering to greet her mother's friends on the street, smiling indulgently at other people's children. But then she shook that thought away, and folded her gloved hands in her lap and began looking out the window again.

It was almost an hour before the bus made its next stop, in a town called Howrell that Joan had always hated. Gangling men stood lined along the street, spitting tobacco juice and commenting on the passengers whose faces appeared in the bus windows. Underneath

Joan was the slamming and banging of bags being shoved into the luggage compartment, and then the driver helped a little old lady up the steps and into the bus. She wore a hat made entirely of flowers. From the way she advanced, clutching her pocketbook in both hands, examining the face of each passenger and sniffing a little as she passed them, Joan knew she would sit beside her. Old ladies always did. She stopped next to Joan and said, "This seat taken?" and then slid in, not waiting for an answer. While she was getting settled she huffed and puffed, making little comments under her breath; she would be the talkative kind. "I thought this bus would *never* come," she said. "I thought it had laid down and died on the way." Joan smiled, and turned her face full to the window.

When the bus had started up again, and was rolling through the last of Howrell, Joan checked her watch. It would be nearly suppertime now. If she were in Larksville she would be sitting at the kitchen table cutting up a salad. She pictured herself there, her bare feet curled around the rungs of the chair. In her mind she seemed to be sitting an inch or so above the seat, not resting on anything but air. She ran through other pictures of herself—sitting in her parents' parlor, sitting on the porch with James, even sitting now beside this old lady on a bus rolling west. In all the pictures, she was resting on nothing. She turned her mind back to the firmest seat she knew—James's lap, in the evenings when Ansel had already gone to bed. But even there, there was a good two inches of air beneath her and she seemed to be balanced there precariously, her arms tight around James. She turned away from the window quickly and said to the old lady, "It'll be getting dark soon."

"It certainly will," said the lady. "My daughter will be getting supper on now. The married one. I left them a cold hen, barbecued the way I like to do it."

Joan went back to looking out the window. She stared steadily at the clay banks that rose high and red along the side of the road, and the tall thin tobacco barns from which little strings of brightly dressed women were scattering home for supper. Who would take her place tomorrow at the tobacco table? She stopped watching the barns. All around her in the bus, people were settled firmly in their seats, with their hands relaxed on the arm rests and their heads tipped against the white starched bibs on the backs of the seats. They talked to one another in murmuring voices that mingled with the sound of the motor. A little boy was playing a tonette.

"I'm going to my *other* daughter," the old lady told her. "The one that never married. She has a kidney ailment."

"I'm sorry to hear that," said Joan.

"She's in terrible pain, and there's no one to take care of her."

Out of the corner of her eye Joan saw the Larksville paper she had bought, folded neatly and tucked down between her seat and the wall of the bus. She picked it up quickly and unfolded it, and the old lady turned away again.

There would be nothing interesting in the paper, but she read it anyway. She began with the first page and read through the whole paper methodically, not even skipping the ladies' meeting announcements or the advertisements. There had been one birth in Larksville this week, she saw, and two deaths. The first death was Jones, Laramie D., whom she had never heard of, but she read all about him anyway—the circumstances of his death, the highlights of his life, the list of relatives who had survived him. The second death was Pike, Janie Rose. The name hit into her stomach, as if she hadn't known of the death until this instant. She started to pass over it, but then she went back to it and read it through:

> Pike, Janie Rose. At County Hospital, in her sixth year, of internal injuries caused by an accident. Beloved daughter of Mr. and Mrs. Roy J. Pike, sister of Simon Lockwood Pike. Funeral was held from Collins Memorial Home, July 16, interment in family cemetery.

She read it twice, but it seemed unreal still, something vague and far off. Nothing that bad could happen. When she had finished with it a second time she folded the paper very carefully in half, so that the obituaries were out of sight, and then went on to the rest of the paper. She read very closely now, even moving her lips, so as to shut out all thought of anything she had read before. "Teller-Hokes Wedding Held in First Baptist Church," she read, and although neither name meant anything to her she was careful to find out exactly what the bride wore and who her guests were. Next came the memorial notices, ringed in black like the obituaries. She had never looked at the memorial notices before. She read about someone named Auntie Peg Myers, who had passed away on July 16, 1937, and was dearly remembered by her two nieces. Then she read about Nathan Martin, who had been taken from his wife in 1941. For him there was a quotation. "Too dearly beloved ever to be forgotten," it said. Further down, for other people, there were little poems, but Joan stopped reading. She had a sudden picture of all the years of this century, stretching far back in a chain of newsprint that grew yellower and yellower as the years grew older. 1937 was almost orange, older than she herself was; 1941 was growing brittle at the edges. How would this year look? The print on January was already blurred. And then she pictured how it would be when today was yellowed too, years from now, and the Pikes themselves were buried and Simon an old man. Then on the third week in every July he would print his notice: "In memory of Janie Rose, who passed away just fifty years ago July 13th. Fondly remembered by her brother Simon." He would be remembering her as someone very small with spectacles, who had lived in the tacked-on bedroom in back of the house. But he himself would be a grandfather then, and nobody Janie would recognize. How would Simon look in fifty years? Joan tried to think, but all she saw was Simon as he was today—hunching his shoulders up, tucking his head down in that uncertain way he had.

She looked quickly out the window and saw the town of Graham rolling up, and the bus station with its line of coin machines. "Is this where you get off?" the woman asked her.

"No."

"Oh. You just sat up so sudden—"

"No," said Joan, "but I think I might buy a Coke."

She stood and wormed her way out past the woman's knees, and as soon as she was out the woman slid quickly over to the window. Joan didn't care. She went down the aisle without looking at anyone, and then descended the bus steps. A team of some kind was waiting to board, a group of boys in white satin windbreakers with numbers on them, and when Joan stepped down among them they remained stolidly in her path, ignoring her. "Excuse me," she said, "excuse me, please," and then when no one noticed she shouted, "*Excuse* me!" For a minute they stopped talking and stared at her; then they moved aside to let her through. She walked very quickly, holding her head up. Out here she felt thinner and more alone than before, with the team of boys all watching her down the long path to the Coke machine. And when she reached the machine she found she didn't even want a Coke. But she put her dime in anyway, and just as she was reaching for the bottle someone said, "Ma'am?"

It was a young man in sunglasses, standing beside her and looking straight at her. She felt scared suddenly, even with all those people around (had he been able to *see* how alone she felt?) and she decided not to answer. Instead she uncapped the Coke bottle and then turned to go.

"Ma'am?" he said again.

She couldn't just leave him there, still asking. "What is it?" she said.

"Can you show me where the restroom is?"

"Why, it's right inside, I guess. Over there."

"Where?"

"Over there."

"I don't see."

"Over *there.*"

"I don't see. I'm blind."

"Oh," said Joan, and then she just felt silly, and even sadder than before. "Wait a minute," she told him. She turned around and saw two bus drivers walking toward her, looking kind and cheerful. When they came even with her she tapped the older driver on the arm and said, "Um, excuse me."

"Yes."

"Can you show this man the restroom? He doesn't see."

"Why, surely," said the driver. He smiled at her and then took the blind man by the elbow. "You come with me," he said.

"Thank you, sir. Thank you, ma'am."

"You're welcome," Joan said.

The other driver stayed behind, next to Joan. He said, "Can you imagine traveling blind?" and stared after the two men, frowning a little.

"No, I can't" Joan said. She automatically followed the driver's eyes. Now that she looked, she couldn't think why the blind man had frightened her at first. He wore his clothes obediently, as if someone else had put them on him—the neat dark suit with the handkerchief in the pocket, the shoes tied lovingly in double knots. He reminded her of something. For a minute she couldn't think what, and then she remembered and smiled. That slow, trusting way he let himself be guided forward, with his hands folded gently in front of him, was like Simon during the first year she'd lived there, when he was six and still had to be awakened at night and taken to the bathroom so he wouldn't wet his bed. He had gone just that obediently, but with his eyes closed and the shadows of some dream still flickering across his face. (You couldn't stop walking with him for a minute, not in a doorway or going around the bend in the hall, or he would think he had reached the bathroom and proceed to go right then and there.) He had held his elbows in close to his body that way, too, against the coolness of the night. Joan stopped smiling and looked down at her feet.

"You all right?" the driver asked.

"I want to go back."

"Ma'am?"

"I want to go back where I came from. Can I take my bags off my bus and wait for the next one going back?"

"Why, surely," the driver said. "You on that bus over there?"

"Yes. I know this is—"

"Women got a *right* to change their minds," the driver called. He was already heading toward her bus, and Joan followed him with her untouched Coke bottle still in her hands.

"I always do this," she said. "But this time it's—"

"You got the right," said the driver.

"This time it's different. I can't help it, this time; I'm not just—"

But the driver didn't hear her. He was walking up ahead of her and laughing over his shoulder, thinking it was all a joke. She stopped trying to tell him it wasn't.

13

SOMETHING WAS WRONG at home. James knew it instantly, the moment he stepped out of the pickup carrying his two bags of groceries. There on the porch stood the Potter sisters and Ansel and Mrs. Pike, all huddling together, and Mr. Pike was a little distance away from them. He was facing toward the road, frowning down at an Indian elephant bell that he held in his hand. When he heard the pickup door slam he looked up and said, "James." The light from the setting sun turned his face strange and orange.

"What's wrong?" said James.

"We can't find Simon."

"Well, where is he?" he asked, and then to cover up the stupidity of that question he said quickly, "He was here at lunchtime."

"We thought you might have him with you," Mr. Pike said.

"No."

They all kept looking at him. Even Ansel. James hoisted his groceries up higher and then said again, "No. No, I've been running errands all afternoon. All by myself."

"Well, then," Mr. Pike said. He sighed and turned back to the others, who still waited. Finally he said, "He's not with James."

"Maybe he's with Joan," James offered.

"No. Joan must have gone off somewhere, but after she left Simon was still around. Lou says so."

James looked over at Mrs. Pike. She was dry-eyed and watchful; her arms were folded firmly across her chest.

"When was the last time you noticed him?" he asked her.

"I don't know."

"Ma'am?"

"I don't *know*," she said, with her voice slightly raised.

"Oh."

"We called the boys he plays with," Mr. Pike said. "And we called the movie-house."

"Did you ask about buses?"

"No. Why?"

"I'd do that," said James. He climbed the steps at his end of the porch and set the groceries on Ansel's chair, and then he straightened up and rubbed the muscles of his arms. "Call the drugstore," he said. "Ask them if he's—"

"Well, I *went* to the drugstore, to see if he'd gone there for a soda. Mary Bennett was on; only been there a half hour or so, but she hadn't seen him."

"Might have gone earlier," said James. "Did you look at the bus schedule?"

"*No* I didn't. What would I want to do that for?"

"Just in case," James said. "Who was there before Mary Bennett?"

"Tommy was, but I can't find him. If it weren't for Lou I'd just sit and *wait* for Simon, but Lou thinks he left with a purpose. Thinks she might have sent him away somehow."

James looked over at Mrs. Pike again. For a minute she stared back at him; then she said, "You believe he's on some bus."

"I didn't say that," said James.

"You think it."

"Now, Lou," Mr. Pike told her.

"I can tell."

"Well, it wouldn't hurt to ask," said James. "I'd track that Tommy down, if I was you."

"*Oh*, now," Mr. Pike said, and accidentally clanged the elephant bell. Everyone jumped. "Sorry," he said. For the first time, Ansel lost his blank tense look; he winced, and leaned back limply against the front of the house. Mr. Pike said, "Sorry, Ansel. But where would he take a bus *to*?"

"There's lots of places," said James.

"Not as many as you'd think," Ansel said. "World's shrinking."

"Hush," James told him. He jingled his keys thoughtfully. "Roy, can I use your telephone?"

"What for?"

"Let him," Mrs. Pike said. The Potter sisters stepped

closer to her on either side and patted her shoulders, as if she had suddenly had an outburst of some kind. "You know where it is," she told James.

"Yes, ma'am."

He walked toward the Pikes' end of the porch, with everyone's eyes following him. At the door he stopped and said, "Did he have any money?"

"He gets an allowance," said Mr. Pike. "I don't know if he saved it."

"Did he get some this week?"

He was asking this of Mrs. Pike, but she just shook her head. "I don't know," she said. Finally James turned back again and went on inside.

It was Tommy Jones's mother who answered the telephone. Her voice was breathless, as if she had had to come running from some other part of the house. "Hello?" she said.

"Mrs. Jones, this is James Green. Is Tommy there?"

"No, he's not."

"Do you know where he is?"

"No. Is this about Simon still?"

"Yes, ma'am."

"They haven't found him?"

"No. Do you think Tommy'll be getting back soon?"

"I really don't," she said. "He's off someplace with his girl. Shall I have him call?"

"No, thank you. Sorry to bother you."

"It's no bother."

He hung up and stood thinking a while, and then he went out to the front porch again. In just the short time that the telephone call had taken the color of the evening had shifted, turning from sunset into twilight. The others were standing where he had left them, still looking in his direction as if their eyes had never moved from the spot where he had disappeared. "Tommy's not there," he said.

"Well, *I* could have told you that," Mr. Pike said irritably. He swung his arms down, making the bell clang again, and started toward the front yard. "I'm going to round up a couple others," he called back. "We'll look in all the places where he goes, and ring bells or fire guns if we find him. Want to come, James?"

"I'm not sure that's the way," James said.

"Only thing I can think of. Mind if I use your truck?"

"Well, wait," said James. He came down the steps and crossed over to Mr. Pike. "No, I'd like to take the truck and follow up an idea of my own. I think I—"

"When *I* was a little boy . . ." Ansel announced, and everyone turned around to look at him. He had recovered from that last clang and was standing erect now, placing the tips of his fingers together. "When I was a little boy, I had to tell my mother *every*where I went. It was a rule. And I could never go out of hearing range of this old Army bugle, that my father would stand in the doorway and blow at suppertime—"

"If you could come along," Mr. Pike told James, "and bring a noisemaker of some kind, why, we could start by—"

"I was thinking of Caraway," James said.

"Caraway?"

"I was thinking that was where he might've gone."

"Oh, *Caraway*," Mr. Pike said impatiently. "*I* been

there. No, more likely he went off on some hike or other, and forgot to let us know."

"Well, I'd like to try Caraway anyhow," said James.

"But James, that's a waste of—"

"Let him," said Mrs. Pike, and once again the Potter sisters closed in on her and patted her shoulders. "Hush, hush," they whispered. James pulled out his billfold and checked his money; there was plenty for gas. He turned to Mr. Pike.

"I'm sorry," he said. "I just feel I know where he's at."

"Well, that's all right," said Mr. Pike. "Sure wish I could have the loan of your pickup, though."

"I'll make the trip as fast as I can."

"Well, sure." Mr. Pike sighed, and then he set off wearily across the yard. He carried the elephant bell upside down, with his fingers poked through the inward-curling teeth of it to hold the clapper silent. When he reached the gravel road he turned back and said, "Ansel? You feel up to coming along?"

"Not really," said Ansel. "I just feel miserable about all this."

Mr. Pike nodded several times and then continued down the road in the direction of the Terrys. "Poor man," said Miss Lucy, and then she and Miss Faye began patting Mrs. Pike harder than before.

James said, "Ansel, take in the groceries. And fix yourself something for supper, in case I'm late getting back."

"Well, all right," Ansel said.

"I don't expect you want to come with me."

"No."

James descended the porch steps. In the distance he could see Mr. Pike, far and small already, marching on steadily with his shoulders set. It seemed so clear to James that Simon was in Caraway—where else would he be?—that he felt sorry to see Mr. Pike going to all this trouble. He wanted to call him back, but he knew there was no use. So he just turned around and said, "Ansel—" and bumped squarely into Mrs. Pike, who was standing right behind him. "Oh, excuse me," he said. "I didn't hear you coming." She remained silent, with her arms still folded and her head bowed meekly. "Well," he said. "Ansel, I'm going to call you at the Pikes' number when I get there. To tell you what happens, in case Mrs. Pike is going to be over at the Potters'."

"All right," said Ansel. "Does that mean I can stay at the Pikes' until you call?"

"I don't care, for heaven's sake."

He continued on toward the pickup, and Mrs. Pike kept following after him. When he opened the door on the driver's side she opened the other door, and it was only then that he realized she meant to come along. They stood staring at each other for a minute across the expanse of seat; then Mrs. Pike lowered her eyes and climbed in, and he did the same. He could see that the others on the porch were just as surprised as he was—they came closer together, and turned to look at each other—but Mrs. Pike didn't offer to explain herself. She sat quietly, with her eyes straight ahead and her hands clasped in her lap. Even when he craned his neck around to look out the rear window as he was backing out, she stared ahead. The stoniness of her face gave her a calm, sure look, as sure as James felt inside; she must know where Simon was by instinct.

When they were on the main highway James turned his lights on. Already the opaque white look of early twilight was growing bluer and more transparent, and other cars as they came towards him clicked their own lights on. But he could see around him clearly still: the landmarks of the journey to town slipping by, and then a brief glimpse of Main Street itself before he passed it. It felt funny to keep going straight, instead of turning there. A strange sinking feeling began in his stomach, and he looked into the rear-view mirror and watched the town lights fading away from him. "Don't worry," he said suddenly to Mrs. Pike, but Mrs. Pike wasn't looking worried at all; she only nodded, calmly.

"I'm just waiting," she told him.

"Oh."

"I'll take what I get. Whatever I deserve."

"Yes, ma'am," James said.

He swerved around a little boy riding a bicycle. Where was Simon at this minute? Maybe swaggering down a street alone, trying to look as if he knew where he was going. Searching for some sign—a boy with a ring in his ear or a woman in a red-plumed hat, someone who would expect him the way he had expected them. James frowned. The clomping of Simon's leather boots seemed louder than the sound of the motor; the fuzz down the back of Simon's neck seemed clearer than the road ahead of him.

"It's been a pretty day," he said.

"Yes."

"Where's Joan?"

"I don't know," said Mrs. Pike. She looked out at the road a while, and then she said, "I sewed a dress today."

"Oh, did you?"

"Yes."

"Well, now," James said. He cleared his throat. "I always thought a dress would take *days* to make."

"Anything that happens," said Mrs. Pike, "it's only my fault. My fault."

"Well, now," James said again.

The truck was traveling too fast, he thought. Already the countryside looked like Caraway countryside; not Larksville. In his mind he had added mile upon mile to this trip, stretching the road out long and thin till Caraway might have been in Asia. Yet before they had been on the road half an hour they reached Stevens's Esso Station—the halfway mark—and he braked sharply and turned in. "Need gas," he told Mrs. Pike. She nodded. The meter said the tank was half full, but stopping this way would slow things down a little.

Mr. Stevens himself washed the windshield and filled the tank, with only a brief smile to James because he didn't recognize him. "Three dollars, ten," he said. "Nice evening." He held his hand out flat, palm up, outside James's window, and James counted out the exact change very slowly. When he had paid he said, "This the road to Caraway?" to stretch the stop out even longer.

"Sure is," the man said.

"How much further?"

"Be there in half an hour."

"Thank you," James said. He started the motor and looked over at Mrs. Pike, but she didn't seem surprised at the questions he had asked. She just looked down at her hands and waited for him to drive on.

Almost no one else was on the road now. He drove at a steady pace, and in silence, looking at the country around him whenever they were on a straight stretch of road. At first it was just the occasional, very noticeable things that he recognized—that humped bridge that looked like something off a willowware plate, the funny barbecue house off in the middle of nowhere with pigs chasing each other rapidly in neon lights across the front porch. But after another ten or fifteen minutes, he began to recognize everything. The objects that flashed by were all worn and familiar-looking, as if perhaps without knowing it he had been dreaming of them nightly. Even the new things—the brick ranch houses rising baldly out of fresh red clay, the drive-ins and Dairy Queens—seemed familiar, and he glanced at them mildly and without surprise. When he reached the town limits it was just beginning to grow really dark, and his headlights glared briefly against the slick white surface of a newly painted sign. "Caraway. Bird Sanctuary," it read. The last time he had been here it had said only "Caraway." And he had looked at it and thought, I'll never see that sign again, not for *any* reason. He hadn't known the Pikes then, nor Joan, nor the Potters; he hadn't foreseen the existence of Simon.

He slowed down as soon as they reached the actual town, and Mrs. Pike straightened up and began looking out the window more intently, perhaps already searching for Simon. James kept his eyes straight ahead until they got to Main Street. Then he pointed to an all-night grill and said, "This is where the buses stop."

"Oh," said Mrs. Pike.

"Do you want to go ask if they've seen him?"

"I guess so," she said, but she was looking at him, obviously expecting that he would be the one to ask. He sighed and swung the truck into a diagonal parking place.

"I'll be right out," he told her.

"All right."

Once on the street, out from behind the shield of the pickup, he felt clumsy and conspicuous. Girls in bare-backed dresses waited with their dates in front of the movie theater next door, and when he stepped on to the sidewalk they pivoted on their high heels and glanced over at him. He stared back, but there was no one he recognized. And the waitress in the grill was a new one—a fat blond he didn't know. He came up and laid both hands palms down on the counter and said, "Were you here when the last bus from Larksville came?"

"Yes," she said. Her voice was tired, and she seemed hardly able to raise her eyes and look at him.

"Did you see a little boy get off?"

"I wasn't watching," she said.

She began swabbing off the counter with a pink sponge, and James walked out again without thanking her. On the street he looked up and down, hooking his thumbs in his belt and staring over the heads of passersby, but there was no sign of Simon. For the first time he felt uncertain about him, and frightened. He returned to the truck.

"She wasn't watching," he told Mrs. Pike.

"She wasn't," she agreed, and went on looking calmly out the window.

James knew where he was heading, but he was hoping he didn't have to go there. So he drove down Main Street very slowly, looking right and left, peering into the windows of restaurants and soda shops and scanning the faces of people out for evening walks. Several times he saw people he knew. Seen through the truck window, walking in half-dark, six years older and unexpected in new clothes that James had never known, they looked worn and sad to him. He would look after them a minute with a feeling of bewilderment, almost forgetting Simon until Mrs. Pike touched him on the arm. Then he would drive on.

Mrs. Pike didn't ask what he was doing when he turned off Main Street. She seemed to think that this was part of a tour around Caraway that anyone might follow, and she gazed in tourist-like respect at a three-foot high statue of Major John Caraway. ("This is Major Caraway," James's father always explained to them. "He fought in the Big War." Meaning the Civil War, though there'd been others since. "He certainly was a *small* man," said their mother. Their father never answered that.) Even when they turned down Hampden Street, where there were no statues and only private houses, Mrs. Pike said nothing. She kept on searching the sides of the road, poking her nose toward the window so that the skin between her chin and the base of her throat made one slanted line. James drove more and more slowly. He turned left on Winton Lane and then drew to a stop, letting the truck roll into the grass at the side of the road. They were in front of an old gray house with a great many gables, its yard sprinkled with the feather-white skeletons of dandelions. No one was on the porch. For a while James sat silent, tapping the steering wheel with one finger. Then he looked over at Mrs. Pike. She was still searching out the window, almost as if she thought they were still moving. "I'll be back," he told her.

"All right."

He opened the truck door and climbed out stiffly, careful not to make too much noise. But no dog barked. In his mind, he saw now, he had pictured the dog's barking first. He had imagined that everyone would come to the door to investigate, long before he had reached the front steps; he had seen the long rectangle of yellow light from the doorway and the silhouettes of many people, watching as he walked awkwardly through the dandelions. Yet he came to the door in utter silence, with no one noticing. He opened the screen, which creaked, and knocked several times on the weatherbeaten wooden door and waited. For a while no one came. Then there were footsteps, and he stepped back a pace. He fixed his eyes on a point just a little above his own eye level, where he would see that hard white face as soon as the door opened.

But when the door did open, he had to look lower than that. He had to look down to the level of his shoulders, much lower than he had remembered, into the old man's small lined face and his eyes in their pockets of bone. His hair was all white now, gleamingly clean. He wore suspenders, snapped over a frayed white collarless shirt which was only folded shut, without buttons. And his trousers bagged at the knees.

"The dog didn't bark," said James.

"She died," his father said, and stepped back a step to let him into the house.

14

THE FIRST THING Simon said was, "If I'd known *you* were coming, I'd of hitched a ride with you." He was sitting in old Mr. Green's platform rocker, with his elbows resting lightly on the arms of it and his fingers laced in front of him. "Did you just leave home and not tell anyone?" he asked.

"I told *every*one," said James, and looked straight across at the others. They stood in a line behind Simon, the three of them—his father, Claude, and Clara, the one brother and sister still at home. They were standing very still, all three of them in almost exactly the same position, with their eyes on James. When James looked at them Simon turned around and looked too, and just in that one turn of his head, with his chin pointed upwards and the shock of hair falling back off his forehead, he seemed to be *claiming* them somehow, marking them as his own. James's father looked down at him soberly, and Clara smiled, but by then Simon had turned to James again and couldn't see her. "I came on a bus," he said.

"I guessed you had."

"I found them in a telephone book."

Clara said, "James, will you sit down?"

"Oh, I guess not," said James. "Did you call the police?"

"I don't hold with police," his father said.

"I forgot."

"We figured you'd come after him. We didn't call no one."

"I see," James said. He folded his arms and stared down at one shoe. "His mother was wondering where he was."

"Well, now she'll know," said his father. "*Your* mother used to wonder."

"Sir?"

"What did she say?" Simon asked. "Did she see I was gone? What did she say about it?"

Instead of answering, James turned around and looked out the open door. There was Mrs. Pike, picking her way through the dandelions and toward that rectangle of light across the porch. She had come unasked, having waited long enough in the pickup, and because she didn't know whose house this was or what she was doing here her face had a puckered, uncertain look. She stumbled a little on the porch and then came forward, her eyes squinting against the light. "James—" she began, and then saw Simon and stopped. "Is that Simon?" she asked. Her fingers began plucking at her skirt, and she stayed poised there on the porch.

Simon stood up and looked at James, but he didn't say anything.

"Simon, is that you?" his mother asked.

"Yes."

"Where did you go?" She called this into the room from her place on the porch; she didn't seem able to step inside. "Why did you leave?"

"Oh, well," Simon said uncertainly. He looked over at James's family, as if they might tell him what was going on here, but they were all staring at Mrs. Pike. "I just came to see these people," he said.

"Oh," said his mother. She looked down at her skirt. The longer she stood there the more distant she seemed to become, so that now James couldn't imagine her *ever* walking in of her own accord. He said, "Mrs. Pike, will you come in?" and then Clara, who had been gazing open-mouthed, came to life and said, "Oh. Yes, *please* come in."

Mrs. Pike took a few steps, just enough to get her safely into the room, without moving her eyes from Simon. "What happened to your hair?" she asked him.

"What hair?"

"I wish you'd have a seat," Clara said.

"Simon, were you not going to come back?"

"Well, I don't know," said Simon. "I just came away, I guess."

"Oh," Mrs. Pike said. She wet her lips and said, "Will you come back *now?*"—not looking at Simon any more but at James, as if he were the one she was asking.

"What for?" Simon asked.

"Why—just to be back."

Whatever Simon was thinking, he didn't show it. He began walking in those small circles of his, with his eyes on his boots. And James suddenly thought, what if he *won't* come back? The same idea must have hit Mrs. Pike. She said, "Don't you *want* to come?"

"Well," Simon said.

"You can't stay *here*."

"How did you happen to come by?" he asked.

"James thought of it."

"I mean, what for? Did you just go off driving?"

Mrs. Pike frowned at him, not understanding. "*James* thought of it," she said. "He thought you'd be in Caraway."

"You mean you came specially?"

"Well, *yes*," said Mrs. Pike. "What did you think?"

"*Oh*," Simon said, and the sudden clear look that came across his face made James feel light inside and relieved. It was that simple, he thought; Simon didn't know they had come just for him. "You mean you're here on *account* of my going off," he said.

"Of course we are. Will you let us take you home?"

"Sure, I guess so."

Everyone seemed to loosen up then. James's father said, "*Well*, now," and Mrs. Pike crossed over to Simon and hugged him tightly. He stood straight while she hugged him, looking very stiff and grown up, but there was a little shy, pleased smile pulling at the corners of his mouth. "I came on a bus," he said.

"Wasn't anyone *with* you?"

"No."

"I'm glad I didn't know about it, then. I'm glad I—oh, goodness. Miss, um—"

"Green," James said. "Clara Green, and Claude, and my father. This is Mrs. Pike."

"Your *family?*" said Mrs. Pike. She looked at them more closely. "Well, of *all* things," she said. "I never thought I'd—well. Miss Green, do you have a telephone?"

"In the dining room," said Clara. "I'll show you."

"I want to reach my husband somehow. I hope someone's at the house."

She followed after Clara, with one arm still around Simon, and James watched after them because he didn't know where else to look. Simon walked very straight, holding up the weight of his mother's arm but keeping himself tall and separate from her, and Mrs. Pike moved almost briskly. "They'll be half insane," James heard her say. "Oh, good. Thank you." They were out of sight now. Clara reappeared in the doorway, and James turned away and put his hands in his pockets.

He was standing squarely in front of the fireplace, a small one with a marble mantelpiece. Everything in the room was exactly the way it had been before—the linoleum rug with the roses painted on it, the bead curtains, the turquoise walls made up of tongue-and-groove slats. On the mantelpiece was a Seth Thomas clock that his mother had brought when she came, and a picture of Jesus knocking at the door and a glass plate that looked like lace. At first, not knowing what else to do with himself, James absentmindedly stooped nearer to the fireplace and held out his hands to be warmed. It was only after a minute that he remembered it was summer and the fire unlit. So he had to straighten up again, his hands in his back pockets and his face toward the others. They were all looking at him. Clara had sat down on the footstool, thinner and sharper and with the look of an old maid beginning to set in around her mouth. And Claude was on the couch, twisting a leather lanyard in his hands. He was grown now. The last time James had seen him, Claude was in his early teens and had turned red from the neck up every time he was directly addressed. There had been more of them then. His mother, small and dark, scared of everything, humming hymns under her breath in a tinny monotone as she sewed. His sister Madge, whose one romance they had broken up and who was now in China doing missionary work. And Ansel.

If he had ever imagined coming back here—and it seemed to him now he had, without knowing it—he had not imagined standing like this, wordless. He had thought that of all the mixed-up, many-sided things in the world, his dislike of his father was one complete and pure emotion and that that alone could send words enough swarming to his mouth. Yet his father stood before him like a small, battered bird, the buttonless shirt folded gently over his thin chest and the worn leather slippers searching out the floorboards hesitantly when he walked. He was making his way to the rocker. All the time that Simon had sat there, the old man must have been watching shyly and eagerly, waiting for his chance to reclaim it. (It had always been his property alone, forbidden to the children. On Bible Class nights, when both parents were gone, James would sit in that chair and rock fiercely, and the other children stood around him with wide scared eyes.) Now James's father sat down almost gratefully, feeling behind him first to make sure it was there and then slowly lowering himself into it. When he rocked, the chair complained; it had grown old and sullen with time.

"Yes, the dog died," he said. He surveyed his three children out of eyes the same startling blue as Ansel's, and he smiled a little. "She died."

"I'm sorry to hear that," said James.

"It happens."

"She had cancer," Claude said.

"Can dogs get cancer?"

"Get everything people get," said his father, rocking steadily. "The vet told us so, at the time."

"I never heard that."

There was a silence. Clara sat forward suddenly, throwing her arms around her knees in that swooping way she had and craning her neck up, and everyone looked at her as if they expected her to say something but she didn't. She just smiled at them, with her lips tightly closed.

"You've got your hair a different way," James told her. Clara went on smiling at him and nodded.

"Yes, I do," she said.

"Every thought of every curl is another stroke for the devil," said her father. "Have you ever thought of that? But *Clara* here don't care; she *likes* short hair."

"Yes, I do," Clara said again. The tone of her voice was indifferent, and she included her father in her smile. No one seemed to be as James remembered.

Out in the dining room, Mrs. Pike said, "Yes? Miss Lucy, I'm glad you're there. I was hoping you would hear the phone and—"

"You're back," James's father said.

The others looked at him.

"You're back in this house."

"Yes," James said. "Just for—" He stopped.

"Just for a while," his father said. "Just for the boy."

"Yes."

"Ah, well."

Mrs. Pike was talking loudly, apparently trying to break in on something Miss Lucy was saying. "Yes, I know," she said. "I know—Miss Lucy, will you try and find Roy? First go and shout for him. Yes, I'm feeling fine, thank you. Then if he's too far away I'll leave a message. But I'd like to have Simon tell him—"

"The phone is a precarious instrument," said James's father.

"Hush, now," Clara told him. "There's not a machine in this world you don't say that about."

"A *wavery* thing," said the old man, overriding her. "On a thin line between what's real and what isn't. Is that person *really* sitting next to you, the way he sounds? When I called you at your neighbors, three Christmases ago—"

"Sir?" said James.

"When Clara called three Christmases ago, and Ansel wouldn't talk to her but stayed in the other room, I happened to be passing near enough to hear what was going on at the other end. Heard Ansel shouting how he wouldn't come. And it seemed to me his voice was trembly-like, unsteady. Is his sickness worse?"

"No," James said. "He's just a little weak sometimes."

"It's the forces from inside that weaken."

"He's all right," James told him.

Simon was on the telephone now. He was talking to Miss Lucy. "Yes, ma'am," he said. "Then I got on the bus. I figured out the schedule in the drugstore." James's father rocked sharply forward and slapped both slippers on the floor.

"That boy is too *young* to travel alone," he said.

"He ran away," said James.

"I realize that. He came to our door and asked to be a lodger. Did you tell him this family ran a boarding house?"

"No."

"He seemed to think you had."

He rocked on in silence for a minute; the only sound was Simon's voice. The Clara looked up and, finding her father's eyes on her, gathered her skirts beneath her and spoke. "He likes mayonnaise," she said.

"Who does?" asked James.

"The little boy. He wanted a mayonnaise sandwich."

"Oh." He frowned at her a minute, and then looked over at his father. "What were you going to do with him?" he asked.

"The boy? I figured someone'd come after him."

"What if they hadn't?"

"You *did*," said his father. "Someone *did*. I don't hold with police."

"You could have called the parents."

"I don't speak on telephones."

"His sister just died," said James. "His mother had enough to worry about."

"Most do."

"*More* than enough. Clara could have called."

"I never turn a stranger from my door," his father said. He let his head fall back against the rocker. "Can *you* say that? Did *you* never let a man down?" He looked at James from under white, papery eyelids, waiting for an answer. No one said anything. It seemed to James that his father had raised a banner in the room—the same one as in old days, long and dark and heavy. His lowered eyes were asking "What can you do about it? Can you take my flag down?" and smiling faintly. Yet the lines around those eyes were deep and tired; his children sat limp, not bothering to answer. "Ah me," said the old man, and rolled his head to the other side and then back again and closed his eyes.

"This has nothing to do with me," James said. "It was his *mother* you made worry; it wasn't me."

"Stop it," Clara told him.

"Clara, are *you* against telephones?"

"You could have telephoned here," his father said suddenly. He opened his eyes and looked over at James.

"I was hoping he hadn't got this far," said James.

"I see. Have you got a telephone yet? I didn't think to ask."

"No."

"And money. Have you made a lot of money in your life?"

"No. But I get along."

"Get along, do you." He nodded to himself, several times. "Changed your ways?"

"No."

"No," his father agreed, and relaxed against the back of the rocker again.

Mrs. Pike and Simon came out of the dining room, Mrs. Pike's hand still on Simon's shoulder. She said, "We called collect. I'm sure you're relieved to hear that," and then laughed a little and looked down at Simon. "They're going to relay the message to Simon's daddy," she said.

"Well, I'm glad you got through to them," said Clara. "Will you have a seat?"

"Oh, we couldn't. I'm sorry, I know I haven't said two words to you. Mr. Green, it's nice to see you." She advanced, smiling, heading straight for James's father and holding out one plump hand. He had to rise from his rocker and take it. She said, "You're smaller-boned than James or Ansel. But you've got Ansel's fair skin." The way she spoke of him made him seem like a child being compared to his parents, but he smiled graciously back.

"James gets his skin from his mother," he told her.

"I guessed that."

"He's back in this house now."

Clara said, "Mrs. Pike, I wish you'd sit down and have some lemonade."

"No, we really can't. I have to get Simon home—and I do thank you for taking care of him." She said that directly to Clara, and Clara smiled at her with her narrow, gaunt smile. "He don't *usually* run away, I don't want you thinking—"

"He's too young to be on his own," said Mr. Green.

"He's *not* on his own."

"James used to run away." He sat down in his rocker

and looked up at her, staring out from under white arched eyebrows. Mrs. Pike waited, and then when she saw that he wasn't going to continue she turned to the others.

"I thank my Lord we found him," she said. "I feel it's some kind of sign; I've been let off with a warning." She squeezed Simon tight against her, and he smiled at the middle button of her dress and then broke away.

James stood up, preparing to leave, and Mrs. Pike said, "James, I thought we could go back by bus. You probably want to stay on a bit, now you're here."

"No, I'll drive you back," said James. He crossed over to his father and said, "I guess I'll be going."

"We still have your old bed," said his father, but he seemed to know beforehand that James would say no. He rose again from the rocker, very slowly, and shook James's hand while he looked at the floor. It was a small, clean hand, that offered no resistance when James pressed it. To Mrs. Pike, James's father said, "It began when he was four. He ran everywhere."

"What?" asked Mrs. Pike.

"James."

"Oh," she said. "Well, I'm glad to've met you, Mr. Green—" and she shook his hand once more, holding her wrist slightly curved and offering just the tips of her fingers. "I can't thank you enough for all you've done; any time you're in Larksville you just stop in on us."

"We locked doors and tied knots," said Mr. Green, "but he was like Houdini."

Mrs. Pike shook hands with Claude and Clara and made Simon do the same, and James followed behind

them. He shook Claude's hand but Clara he kissed, feeling that she would prefer that. Her cheek was bonier than he had expected, and the skin dry. She would probably never get married, he thought. None of them would.

When they went out the door his father followed them, and stood on the porch in his slippers. "Well, goodbye, James," he said. "You'll be back someday, I expect." But his smile when he looked up at James was timid and uncertain, and James smiled back.

"Tell Madge hello for me," he said.

"All right."

They climbed into the pickup at the edge of the yard —Mrs. Pike at the window, and Simon in the middle next to James. Simon said, "Hey, James, can I steer?" but James was starting the engine up and didn't answer. He looked in the rear-view mirror and saw his father still standing on the porch, his arms hugging his chest, his knees bagging, his small white head strained toward the truck. As long as James took getting started, his father remained there, and when he drove away Mr. Green lifted one arm for a goodbye and stayed that way until the truck was out of sight. James drove staring straight ahead for a while, holding that picture of his father in his mind.

When they had turned into the center of Caraway again, Mrs. Pike said, "It's a nice town, isn't it?"

"Some ways," James said.

"Yes." And she settled back, one hand patting the back of Simon's neck. Simon was restless and fidgety after all his adventures. He sat on the edge of the seat, kicking one foot nervously and gritting his jaw in that way he had when he'd had too much excitement. The passing streetlights gleamed briefly on his face and then left it dark again, and his eyes were strained wide against the night.

"Sit back in your seat," James told him.

"I am."

"No, you're **not**. You'll go through the windshield."

"Yes, Simon," said his mother, and pulled him back. Simon leaned against her side, still kicking that one foot.

"James," he said, "will we ever go back visiting there?"

"I don't know."

"I better tell Ansel."

"Tell him what?"

"I bet New York is better any day."

"Well, maybe so," James said.

"Those earrings were just teeny gold wires, you know? And there *weren't* no feather hats."

"Well, that was just one summer they had those," James said. "Some kind of free sample."

"Why didn't he tell me that?"

"I don't know."

"Why did he say it was all year every year?"

"Go to sleep," said James. "I don't know."

15

JOAN ARRIVED at the Pikes' house in Mr. Carleton's taxi, rattling over the gravel road in pitch dark with the taxi's one headlight making a swerving yellow shaft in front of them. Her suitcases were on the back seat, where they bounced around at every bump in the road, and she sat up front with Mr. Carleton but she didn't talk to him. Twice he tried to begin a conversation. He started off the first time with, "Well, now. Well, now. I didn't know you were even *gone*, Miss Joan." And when she didn't answer that, except for a single motion of her head that might have been a nod, he rode on in silence for a while and then tried again. "Wher*ever* you were," he said, "I sure hope the weather was good." But Joan's face was turned away from him, and she went on looking out the window without even changing expression.

When they turned into the Pikes' yard Joan sat up and opened her straw handbag. She didn't look toward the house. Mr. Carleton said, "Some kind of party?" and then she heard the noises that were floating from Ansel's window. Music, and voices, and someone laughing. The light from that window flooded the yard, fading out the pale yellow of the taxi's headlight. The rest of the house was dark. "I don't know," she said, and reached forward to hand him his money. "Don't worry about my bags; I'll take them in."

"They look pretty heavy for you."

"I can take them."

He climbed out his side of the taxi to drag the bags from the back seat. Somehow the bag that had been her father's had had a strap broken; the strap dangled, looking ridiculous and defeated. When Mr. Carleton handed the bag to her she swayed for a minute, surprised by the weight of it, and then she said, "Okay. I've got it."

"You sure now."

"Sure. Thank you, Mr. Carleton."

"Oh, it's nothing," he said. "Good night." He climbed back into the taxi, slamming the door behind him, and backed out into the road. Joan started for the porch.

The suitcases were hard to get up the steps. She swung them onto the porch one at a time, and then she climbed the steps herself and picked them up again. This all felt so familiar; how many times had she lugged these suitcases into this house? She thought of the first time, coming here in a dust storm, met on the steps by Janie Rose who wore nothing but her underpants and carried one half of a brown rubber sheet that they hadn't been able to get away from her in those days. Now there was no one at all to meet her. When she opened the front door the house was so empty it seemed to echo. She turned on a lamp, and it threw long, black, lonely shadows across the parlor walls.

The first thing she did was put her suitcases back in her bedroom. Whether they had noticed she was gone or not, she didn't want them to come back and find those suitcases. Then she closed her bedroom door and went directly to Simon's room. He wasn't there. The room was black and the door was open, and everything had a strange blank look.

Downstairs, she poured herself a glass of milk from the refrigerator and then wandered through the rooms drinking the milk and switching on every light she came across. Soon all in the house were on, but it didn't seem to change things. When the motor in the refrigerator started up she jumped a little, half frightened for a second. Then she set down the glass of milk and walked very slowly and deliberately out of the house, with that feeling of loneliness prickling the back of her neck as she walked.

The way the music was pouring out, she couldn't identify the voices from Ansel's window. All she heard was words and phrases, and occasional laughter. She stopped at the Potters' window and peered in, but not a single light glimmered there, not even from the very back of the house. They couldn't be far, then. If they planned to be gone for any length of time they turned all the lamps on and set up a cardboard silhouette of a man reading that was guaranteed to fool burglars. And they couldn't be in bed; it was no later than ten o'clock. She turned away from the window and looked out at the yard, hoping they might come walking up, but they didn't. The only thing left to do was to go on to Ansel's.

No one answered when she knocked. It was too noisy for them to hear her. She opened the screen and knocked once more on the inner door, hard, and then she heard Ansel say, "Wait! Did someone knock?"

"I didn't hear anyone," said Miss Lucy.

Joan knocked again, and Ansel said, "See!" She felt the doorknob twist beneath her hands; then Ansel was standing there, swaying slightly and smiling at her, leaning his cheek against the edge of the door. "Came back, did you," he said.

"What?"

"*I* saw you go.

"I don't—"

"But I didn't tell," he said, and then swung the door all the way open and threw back one arm to welcome her. "Look what *we* got!" he called to the others. "*Who* we got. See?"

Joan stepped inside and looked around her. The room was full; it looked as if someone had tipped the house endwise so that everyone had slid down to James's parlor. Now they sat in one smiling, rumpled cluster—the Potter sisters, the Pikes, Ansel, and James. When Ansel shouted at them they all turned toward Joan and waved, with their faces calm and friendly. The only one who seemed surprised was Simon. He stood up and said, "*Joan!*" but she frowned at him. "Hush," she said. The voices rose again, returning to whatever they'd been talking about before. Simon shouted, "What?"

"I said, '*Hush*'!" called Joan.

"Oh, *I* didn't tell. It was like I promised you, I didn't—"

The rest of his words were drowned out, but Joan understood his meaning. Nobody had told. Maybe they thought she'd just been to a movie, or off visiting. Maybe they knew that wherever she'd gone, she'd be back. And now they sat here, cheerful and in a party mood—but what was the party about? Just by looking, she couldn't tell. Miss Lucy and Miss Faye were making a silhouette of James—Miss Lucy holding a lamp up so that James winced in the light of it, and Miss Faye tracing the shadow of his wincing profile on a sheet of paper held against the wall. But that was something they always did; some instinct seemed to push them into making silhouettes at parties, and now everyone in the house had at least one silhouette of everyone else. Nor could she tell anything from Mr. Pike, who seemed to be a little tiddly from some wine he was drinking out of a measuring cup. He sat smiling placidly at something beyond Joan's range of vision, tapping one finger against the cup in time to a jazz version of "Stardust" that the radio was sawing out. And the person who confused her *most* was Mrs. Pike, sitting in a chair in the corner with her hands folded but her eyes alert to everything that was going on. "Fourteen!" she called out; she seemed to be counting the swallows Simon took from his own glass of wine. But her voice was lost among all the other voices, and Joan had to read her lips. She turned to Ansel, to see if he could explain all this. He had lain back on his couch now, like an emperor at a Roman festival, and when he saw her look his way he smiled and waved.

"Have a seat!" he shouted. He pointed vaguely to several chairs that were already occupied. "We're celebrating."

"Oh," Joan said. "Celebrating."

"Simon ran away."

"*What?*"

Simon smiled at her and nodded. "I went to Caraway on a bus," he said.

"Oh, Simon."

"I saw those gold earrings."

"But how did—"

"James and Mama came and got me. They made a special trip," he said. "We're drinking Miss Faye's cooking wine."

Joan felt behind her for a footstool and sat down on it. "Are you all *right?*" she asked.

"Sure I am."

"Oh, I wish I hadn't gone off and—"

"No, really, I'm all right," said Simon. "Look, they're letting me have wine. They put ice cubes in it to make it watery but I drink it fast before the ice can melt."

"That's nice," Joan said vaguely. She kept looking around at the others. Ansel leaned toward Joan with his own jelly glass of wine and said, "*Drink* up," and thrust it at her, and then lay down again. "Ansel had to find his own supper tonight," Simon told her. "He had one slice of garlic bologna, all dried out. James is going to cook him a steak tomorrow to make up for it."

Joan took a long swallow of cooking wine and looked over at James. He was swiveling his eyes toward the silhouette while he kept his profile straight ahead, so that he seemed cross-eyed. When he felt Joan looking at him he smiled and called something to her that she couldn't hear, and then Miss Faye said, "When you talk your nose moves up and down," and erased the line she had drawn for his nose and left a smudge there. Mr. Pike laughed. He clanged when he laughed; it puzzled Joan for a minute, and then she examined him more closely and found in his lap the elephant bell from Mrs. Pike's mantlepiece. "Why has he got that bell?" she asked Simon.

Simon shrugged, and Ansel answered for him. "He used it while hunting for Simon," he called. "Weird thing, ain't it? Such a funny shape it has. Everything Indians do is backwards, seems to me—"

"Fifteen!" Mrs. Pike said.

"*India* Indians, of course," said Ansel. "Not American. Hey, James."

Miss Faye's pencil had just hit the bottom of James's neck. She finished off with that same little bump at the base of it that sculptors put on marble busts, and then James stretched and turned toward Ansel.

"What," he said.

"Funny feeling in my feet, James."

James sighed and rose to go over to the couch. "Well, thank you, Miss Faye," he called over his shoulder.

"No trouble at all. Joan, dear, it's your turn."

"How about Simon?" asked Joan.

"They did me first," Simon told her. "I'm the guest of honor."

"Oh." She stood up and went over to the Potters, still carrying her glass of wine. "My hair's not combed," she told them.

"That's all right, we'll just smooth over that part on the paper. Will you have a seat?"

They sat her down firmly, both of them pressing on her shoulders. The lamp glared at her so brightly that it made a circular world that she sat in alone, facing Miss Lucy's steadily breathing bosom while Miss Faye, strange without gloves, skimmed the pencil around a suddenly too-big shadow of Joan. Outside the circle was the noise, and the beating music and the dark, faceless figures of the others. Their conversation seemed to be blurring together now.

"I had a cousin once who did *group* silhouettes," said Miss Faye. "I don't know how. It's a talent I never had—he could make everyone be doing something so like themselves, even in a silhouette of twenty people you could name each person present."

"That was Howard," Miss Lucy said.

"Howard Potter Laskin. I remember him well. If he was only here tonight, why, we could put him right to work. I wish I knew how he did it."

"Where is he now?" Miss Lucy asked.

"I don't know."

Joan looked at her shadow, staring almost sideways the way James had done. "There is a whole *gallery* of silhouettes in this house," she said suddenly.

"Quiet, dear, you've moved."

"Didn't I have this blouse on the last time? There was that same sticking-up frill around my neck."

"Yes," said Miss Faye. She sighed and her pencil moved briefly outside the shadow of the frill. "Simon had the same shirt, too," she said.

"How do you remember?"

"The collar's worn out. Little threads poking up."

Joan looked over at Simon; he nodded and held up the corner of his collar. "This is the shirt I ran away in," he called.

"Didn't you get dressed up to go?"

"You didn't do the laundry yet."

"Oh," said Joan, and she turned back to fit her head into the silhouette. Miss Faye started on the back of her hair, skimming past the shadows of stray wisps the way she had promised.

"The mornings after parties," she said, "Miss Lucy and I cut these out and mount them. Don't we, Lucy?" We talk over the parties as we cut."

"I think we should take a picture," said Simon.

"A what?"

"A picture. A photograph. With a camera." He took a swallow of wine.

"Sixteen," said his mother, still counting.

"I *know*. James could take it when you're done with Joan there. Me in my shirt that I ran away in. Everybody else standing around."

"Cameras are all very well," Miss Faye said. "But who can't press a button? If Howard Potter Laskin was here—"

"Howard did *every*thing well," said Miss Lucy.

"I could take you and Miss Lucy drawing silhouettes," James called. He looked up from rubbing Ansel's feet. "Could Howard Potter Laskin do that?"

"Well, now—" Miss Faye said. She lowered her pencil and frowned into space a minute. "A silhouette of a silhouette? I don't know. But Howard could—"

"I'll get my camera, then," said James. He left Ansel's couch and crossed toward the darkroom, stepping carefully through the other people. But the minute he was gone, Miss Faye finished Joan's silhouette with two quick strokes, ending in a point on top of her head that wasn't really there.

"You weren't *supposed* to finish," Joan said. "How will he have you doing a silhouette if there's no more left to do?"

"Oh, now," said Miss Lucy. "People don't *get* photographed making silhouettes. We'll just sit down, I think —maybe on Ansel's couch, if he doesn't object."

They began gathering up their pencils and paper. All over the room, people were getting ready for that camera. Simon had buttoned the top button of his shirt, so that he looked as if he would choke, and Ansel was sitting ramrod-straight with his numb feet on the coffee table in front of him. By the time James returned the whole room seemed tense and silent. Even the radio had been turned off. James said, "I don't hardly recognize you all," and everyone laughed a little and then got quiet again. "You're going to have to bunch up, now," he said.

They moved closer in, heading toward Ansel who for once allowed someone else to sit on the couch. "Simon can sit on the floor," said James. "That would help. Miss Faye, can you move your silhouettes in?"

"Oh, I don't think—" said Miss Faye, but James cut her off as if he already knew what she would say.

"Sure you can," he said. "*Every*one gets photographed making silhouettes these days." And though Miss Faye smiled, to show she didn't believe him, she brought one of her silhouettes over and set it on the back of the couch against the wall. "That's better," he said. He was carrying his little box camera, and he held it in front of his stomach now and squinted into the viewfinder. "Almost," he said. "Joan, where are you? All I get is your foot."

Joan moved over, squeezing in against Simon on the floor. "Ouch," said Simon. "James, are you going to get in the picture?"

"Not while I'm taking it I'm not," said James.

"You should," Miss Lucy said. "You're the one that went and got him."

"No. I hate being photographed."

"Then what's the use?" Simon said. He looked around at the others. "*James* made that special trip—"

"I'll take it," said Joan. She stood up. "You show me how to aim it, James."

"How to—"

"No, Joan should be in it too," Simon said.

But Mr. Pike came to life suddenly and reached down to touch Simon's shoulder. "Can't have everything, boy," he said. "Come on and get in the picture, James. *Joan* didn't go nowhere; she don't mind."

"No, I don't," Joan told James. "Give it here."

"Well, all right."

He put it in her hands and then showed her the button. "This is what you press," he told her. "It's not all that hard."

He went over to sit on the arm of the sofa, next to Ansel, and now even James looked self-conscious. When Joan peered at them through the view-finder she saw all of their faces made clear and tiny, with their smiles stretched tight and each person's hand clamped white around a glass of wine. Ansel's feet were bigger than anyone. He still had them propped up, and when Joan raised her head to glare at them he ducked a glance at her and said, "They hurt."

"They're in the way," Joan told him.

"They hurt."

"If you'd get the right size *shoes*—" said James.

Mr. Pike bent forward to stare at Ansel's feet; his elephant bell clanged again and Ansel said suddenly, breaking in on what James was saying, "I had a *cousin* engaged to a India Indian. I ever mention that?"

"No," said Joan. "Your feet, please, Ansel." She lowered her head and stared into the finder again, but Ansel showed no sign of moving his feet.

"I'd nearly forgotten about it," he said. "This particular Indian used to sing a lot. All the time long songs, India Indian songs, without no tune. He'd finish and we'd clap and say, 'Well, wasn't that—' when oops, there he'd go, on to the next line. Got so we were *afraid* to clap. On and on he'd go, on and on."

"Are you *sure* we shouldn't just sit in a chair?" asked Miss Lucy.

"Wednesday came and went," James said. "When will you remember your shots?"

In the finder of the camera Joan could see them moving, each person making his own set of motions. But the glass of the finder seemed to hold them there, like figures in a snowflurry paperweight who would still be in their set positions when the snow settled down again. She thought whole years could pass, they could be born and die, they could leave and return, they could marry or live out their separate lives alone, and nothing in this finder would change. They were going to stay this way, she and all the rest of them, not because of anyone else but because it was what they had chosen, what they would keep a strong tight hold of. James bent over Ansel; Mrs. Pike touched the top of Simon's head, and Mr. Pike sat smiling awkwardly into space. "It starts near the arches," said Ansel, "right about here . . ."

"Be still," said Joan.

She kept her head down and stared at the camera, smiling as if it were she herself being photographed. The others smiled back, each person motionless, each clutching separately his glass of wine.

A SLIPPING-DOWN LIFE

1

Evie Decker was not musical. You could tell that just from the way she looked—short and wide, heavy-footed. She listened to marches without beating time, forgot the tune to "The Star-Spangled Banner," and moved soddenly around the high school gym in a bumbling two-step. At noon, while Evie munched a sandwich, boys from the band played Dixieland in a corner of the cafeteria. Sharp brass notes pierced the air above the tables; they darted past like red and yellow arrows. Evie ate on, a plump drab girl in a brown sweater that was running to balls at the elbows.

So when she invited Violet Hayes (her only friend) to a rock show at the Stardust Movie Theater, Violet couldn't understand it. "What would you go to a thing like that for?" she said. "Are you serious? I don't believe you even know what a rock show is."

"Well, I do listen to the radio," Evie said.

And she did. She listened all the time. With no company but her father and the cleaning girl (and both of them busy doing other things, not really company at all) she had whole hours of silence to fill. She turned her radio on in the early morning and let it run while she stumbled into her clothes and unsnarled her hair. In the afternoons, advertisements for liver pills and fertilizers wove themselves in among her homework assignments. She fell asleep to a program called "Sweetheart Time," on which a disc jockey named Herbert read off a list of names in twos to dedicate each song. "For Buddy and Jane, for Sally and Carl, for George and Sandra, he loves her very much. . . ." Herbert was an old man with a splintery voice, the only disc jockey the station had. He read the dedications haltingly, as if they puzzled him. "For Paula from Sam, he hopes she'll forgive last night . . ." and there would be the rustle of a paper lowered and a pause for him to stare at it. At the end of a song he said, "That was the Rowing —the Rolling Stones." His faltering made him sound sad and bewildered, but no more bewildered than Evie.

She listened carefully. She lay on her back in the dark, wearing a great long seersucker nightgown, and frowned at the chinks of light that shone through the radio's seams. Sometimes the names were familiar to her—couples she had watched floating hand in hand down school corridors in matching shirts, or girls called Zelda-Nell or Shallamoor, so that they couldn't hope to pass unnoticed. When she knew the names she paid close attention to the songs that followed, ferreting out the words with a kind of possessiveness but ignoring the tunes. Pop songs and hard rock and soul music tumbled out of the cracked brown portable, but the only difference she heard between them was that the words of the pop songs were easier to understand.

One evening in February there was a guest on the program. He came right after the "News of the Hour." "I have here a Mr. Bertram Casey," said Herbert. "Better known as, known as Drumstrings." He coughed and shuffled some papers. "It's an honor to have you with us, Mr. Drumstrings."

No one answered.

Evie was sitting on the bed, twisting her hair into scratchy little pincurls. When the silence grew noticeable she took a bobby pin from her mouth and looked at the radio. All she heard was static. Finally Herbert said, "Well. This is the beginning of a new feature on 'Sweetheart Time': interviews. May I ask if you are a native North Carolinian, Mr. Drumstrings?"

Someone said, "Not for long I won't be."

His voice was cool and motionless, like a stone plunked into a pool. Herbert coughed again.

"*Whereabouts* in North Carolina?" he asked.

"Farinia."

"Farinia, yes. Off of Highway—"

"But I'm leaving there," said Drumstrings Casey.

"All right. Where is it you're going?"

"A city, some city. It ain't quite clear yet. I aim to cut records and play night clubs, and if I once wiggle out of here I'm never coming back again, not even for Christmas. If my family gets to missing me they can come to where I'm at, I'll buy them a house with white telephones and a swimming pool."

"That's very nice," said Herbert. "Have you done much recording yet?"

"No."

"What are the names of your, um, records?"

"There ain't none."

"Oh. Well, your style, then. Would you care to describe it for us?"

"Style?"

"Your style."

"Style, *ain't* no *style*."

"Well, what, what do you *do*, exactly?"

This pause was even longer than the first one. Second after second ticked away in dead air. "If you don't know what I do," said Drumstrings finally, "then how come you got me on your program?"

Herbert mumbled something.

"What's that?"

"Because they told me to, I said. Heavens, boy, just answer the questions. Let's get this over with."

"Oh," Drumstrings said. "All right."

"Only thing they gave me was a little scrap of paper with your name on it."

"Well, don't blame me. I just show up where I'm asked for."

"All right, all right. Where was I?"

"You want to know what I do. I sing and play guitar. Rock."

"You have one of those groups," Herbert said.

"I sing alone. All I got is a drummer, but I don't know about him."

"How's that?"

"He kind of trods the beat."

"Oh, yes," said Herbert.

There was a series of tiny explosions; someone was tapping his fingers.

"You could ask me where I get my material," Drumstrings said.

"Where do you get your material?"

"I make it up."

"That's very interesting."

"Some is other people's, but most is my own. I make it up in my room. I lie on my bed arguing with the strings, like, and sooner or later *something* comes out. Then my fingers get to hammering, reason they call me Drumstrings. How many people do you know could carry a set of drums singlehanded with one little old electric guitar? Lots will say you can't do it. *I* can. I don't go along with all them others. Well: how my songs start. Words come out. Things I hear. 'Oh, Lord, why can't you ever come home on time like decent people do. . . .' " He was singing now, and his fingers kept a beat upon a hard surface. The suddenness of it surprised Herbert into clearing his throat, but Evie listened without changing expression, chewing absently on the rubber tip of a bobby pin. "Nothing more to it," said Drumstrings. "Just putting hard rhythm to what floats around in parlors, just hauling in words by their tails. Nothing more."

"Is that right," said Herbert.

Drumstrings Casey was silent again.

"Do you think we—well, I guess we covered near about everything now. Folks, say good-bye to—"

"Goodbye," the cool voice said.

"And give him a nice hand."

But there was no one to give him a hand, of course—only the Beatles, starting up brokenly in the middle of a line, hurried-sounding, without any list of names to lead them in.

"Do you know a singer named Drumstrings Casey?" Evie asked the boy behind her in algebra class. He was a bongo player. Sometimes she heard him whistling soundlessly at the back of her neck, tapping out the beat on his desk and moving his shoulders in rhythm. But, "Never heard of him," he said.

"He's a rock-and-roll singer."

"Rock-and-roll is *out* now."

"Oh, I see," said Evie.

She walked most places alone. She carried her books clutched to her chest, rounding her shoulders. Her face, which was pudgy and formless, poked itself too far forward. And like most heavy people, she had long ago stopped expecting anything of her clothes. Her coat was old-fashioned, wide-shouldered, falling in voluminous uneven folds around her calves. The white collar she wore to brighten her complexion had a way of twisting sideways and riding up her neck, exposing a strip of skin above the collar of her coat. When classmates met up with her they passed in a hurry, barely noticing her. Evie never spoke to them. She bent to pull up a swallowed sock, or tied the knotted laces of her oxfords. Then she walked on.

On her way home from school one day, she saw a poster in a laundromat window. "Rock the Nite Away!" it said. "Pulqua's first all-local rock show!" Below that was a column of names that she had never heard of: the Huddlers, Spoony and James, Daphne Liggett. And at the bottom, Drumstrings Casey. "Bertram 'Drumstrings' Casey." The name had a worn, vulnerable look, like something she was too familiar with. She pulled a scrap of paper from a frayed zipper notebook and wrote down the time and place of the show. Then she folded the paper and placed it inside her history book.

"Are you serious?" Violet said on the phone. "I don't believe you even know what a rock show is."

"Well, I do listen to the radio."

"What's that got to do with it? You're sitting in your bedroom, listening to the radio. But do you know what kind of trash goes to a live rock show?"

"I don't care," Evie said. She was shut up in her closet to avoid being heard by Clotelia, the cleaning girl. Her voice was muffled by clothes and boots and suitcases, and what was meant to sound lighthearted came out secretive and urgent. "It's at the movie house. What could happen there? I think we should go, Violet."

"Well, listen," said Violet. "My uncle went to one of

those shows in Raleigh, back before he was married. He said they danced the dirty bop all up and down the aisles. He said he was so embarrassed he just sat transfixed to his seat, never saw anything like it."

"What's the dirty bop?" Evie asked.

"*I* don't know."

"Well, it's bound to be out of style by now. They wouldn't still be doing it."

"No, but they'll have thought of something else," Violet said.

"That's all right. I want to hear just one special singer. Then we can go."

"Really? What's his name?"

"Oh, it's nobody famous."

"What's his *name?*"

"Bertram Drumstrings Casey."

"Drumstrings?"

"Do you know him?" Evie asked.

"No. How do *you* know him?"

"I don't. I just heard him on the radio."

"What kind of stuff does he do?"

"I only heard him talking."

"Well, for heaven's sake," said Violet. But she seemed to be thinking it over, because after a minute she said, "Did you ask your father about it?"

"No," Evie said. Her father was a high school math teacher, a vague, gentle man who assumed that Evie would manage just fine wherever she was. In her talks with Violet, though, he kept turning out to be the kind of father who put his foot down. "I don't think I'll bother him with it," she said.

"Oh-oh."

"Will you come?"

"Oh, well, sure," said Violet. "Now that I know the reason why."

When she had hung up, Evie waited a second and then gave her closet door a sudden shove. But Clotelia was nowhere around. Downstairs a soap-opera star said, "This is going to be very hard for me to tell you, Bertha—"

"Oh, Bertha, watch *out!*" Clotelia shouted.

Evie got to her feet and smoothed her wrinkled skirt down.

Violet met her in the lobby, wearing a purple spring coat. She was an enormously fat girl with teased black hair and a beautiful face, and she always wore brilliant colors as if she hadn't read any advice to the overweight. Beside her, Evie seemed almost thin, but lifeless—gray-skinned and dull-haired. She had on her school coat and oxfords. "Are you going to dance in *those?*" Violet said.

"Who would I dance with?"

They were shoved by slick-haired boys in leather jackets, girls in tight sweaters and false eyelashes the size of small whiskbrooms. Almost nobody from school was there. "We are cut off from civilization here, I hope you realize that," said Violet. "I swear, will you look at that girl's *earrings?*" Her voice was rich and lazy. Every time she spoke, boys turned to see who she was and then slid their eyes away again.

Inside the theater they had to work their way through more boys who roamed the aisles in packs. Above the "No Smoking" signs, blue smoke was already beginning to haze the ceiling. Couples with their arms around each other leaned against walls and exit doors and the pipe railing down front—anywhere but in the chairs. "Are we supposed to stand during this?" Evie asked, and Violet said, "No, not me." She flung herself into one of the wooden seats, bought second-hand from a larger town nearby. A boy who was sidling down their row said, "*Move*, sweetie."

"Move yourself," Violet said.

Oh, nothing bothered Violet. She smiled a beautiful bland smile at the empty stage, and the boy struggled past her large pale knees and then past Evie's, muttering all the time. "You'd think they would serve popcorn," Violet said calmly. She smoothed her skirt down and went on gazing at the stage.

But the popcorn stand was closed tonight. The theater had turned into something else, like a gym transformed for a senior prom or an American Legion hall into a banquet room. There was a cavernous chill from the tongue-and-groove walls, in spite of the heavy velvet window curtains. The ceiling seemed higher and dingier, and when Evie looked up she saw light-fixtures poised dizzyingly far above her, their bowls darkened by pools of insects that she had never noticed before. Down front the movie screen had been rolled up. The wooden stage with its electric amplifiers looked like a roomful of refrigerators. A man in shirt sleeves was unraveling microphone cords. "Testing," he said. "Anybody out there?" The volume was high, but it melted away among the voices in the audience.

When the first group began, only a few people had found seats. Four boys in pink satin shirts came out carrying instruments and stood in a semicircle, and one of them spent some time getting his French cuffs adjusted. Then they began playing. Their music was too loud to be heard. It blended with the voices out front, the volume reaching a saturation point so that it was impossible to separate the notes or distinguish the words. "This is *hurting*," said Violet, but she had to shout directly into Evie's ear. Nobody else seemed to mind. They shuffled about in groups, not quite dancing, or draped themselves on the arms and backs of the seats and snapped their fingers and wagged their heads as they continued their conversations. When the music stopped, they cheered. After three more numbers they clapped raggedly and the musicians gathered their instruments and left. Nobody watched them go.

"Who was that?" Violet asked. But they had no program to tell them. A few minutes later three boys and a girl came on, and the girl sang a song and did a tiny intricate dance step. The words of the song were slippery and whining: "*Oh, ya, ya, my honey knows how. . . .*" Evie felt a sort of seeping discomfort, but the rest of the audience listened cheerfully and clapped and whistled afterward.

Following the fourth group, there was an intermission. A phonograph somewhere played a Montovani record. A few of the boys went out to the Coke machines in the lobby, and others took flat curved bottles from their hip pockets. Only Evie and Violet stayed in their seats. They had kept their coats on, as if they were only dropping in on their way to somewhere else. "Where is Drumstrings Casey?" Violet asked. "Was he one of them?"

"No. I don't think so."

"How will we know him?"

"He will only have a drummer. Look, maybe we should go. Do you want to?"

"What for?"

"I feel like I've made a mistake. Shall we go?"

"Oh, why? I'm enjoying myself," Violet said. "At least let's stay till Drumstrings comes."

Drumstrings Casey was preceded by a blond boy who set out drums in a circle around a stool. The largest drum had a blurry black "Casey" stamped on it with a grocery store stencil. "Now," Evie said. She sat up straighter, clutching her coat across her chest. A dark boy had followed the blond one out. He had long black hair, too shiny, cut square across his neck and falling in a slanted line over his forehead. His clothes were black denim, a short zippered jacket and tight jeans ending in high leather boots. Instead of walking, he glided. His spangled guitar dragged a tail of cord which the drummer took charge of while Casey slid coolly on, almost keeping time with Mantovani's violins. "Cut it," someone shouted. Mantovani stopped playing in the middle of a note. There was a second of pure silence while the blond boy seated himself at the drums. Then he picked up the sticks.

He set up a rapid, choppy rhythm that made the dark boy's foot tap, and after that one second of silence, Drumstrings Casey's guitar-playing seemed to break the air into splinters around Evie's ears.

If there were words to his song, Evie couldn't make them out. She heard a clanging of guitar strings, a patter of drums which sometimes subdued the guitar into a mere jingle at the end of a beat, and a strong reedy voice that softened consonants and spun out vowels. "Nnhnn," he said occasionally, close to the microphone. Then the singing stopped, but the music went on. Drumstrings turned his narrow, unseeing face toward the audience.

"*Why do you walk on my nerves this way?*" he asked suddenly.

Evie turned and looked around her.

"*Have I got to tell you again? Have I got to say it?*

"*We met him on the mountain. He was picking blueberries.*

"*She was emptying trashcans.*

"*Don't leave now!*"

The guitar grew louder, and the drums along with it. The song started up no different than before, with the same blurred words. Not many people clapped when it was over.

"Well, thank you for coming," Evie told Violet as they were starting home.

"Was it like you expected?"

"Oh, more or less."

They crossed a silent, neon-lit street. Watery reflections of themselves slid along an optician's darkened window.

"What I meant," said Violet, "was Drumstrings Casey—was *he* like you expected?"

"Not exactly," Evie said.

"You sorry you went?"

"Well, no."

She paused at the corner, in front of the town library. Their paths were supposed to split here, but instead of turning down Hawthorne Street, Evie stood still with her hands in her pockets and her oxfords set wide apart. "That speaking out he did," she said.

"That *was* peculiar," said Violet. "I never heard anyone do that before."

"Me neither."

"Well, in slow songs, of course. Those sappy kind of songs, some girls reading out a love letter between two verses."

"This is different. Drumstrings Casey wasn't sappy."

"No."

"What," said Evie. "You liked it?"

"Well, yes, I did."

"Me too." Evie started moving one foot in a slow arc in front of her, watching it closely. "It made me want to answer. You know those girls who scream on the Ed Sullivan show? Well, now I know why they do it."

"Of course, he is kind of trashy," said Violet.

"Sure, I know that."

"That greasy hair."

"Those tight pants."

"Walking that slinky way he has."

"Would you like to come to my house for a Coke?" Evie asked.

"Oh, I might as well."

They both turned down Hawthorne Street, ambling in fits and starts toward the yellow light above Evie's porch.

2

After the show the days seemed longer and duller. Evie walked to school at a slow, aimless pace, stopping often to stare into store windows. She had changed to spring clothes by now. Her skirts were full, with waistbands that kept folding in upon themselves, her sleeveless blouses came untucked and her sandal straps slipped off her heels—all problems needing constant attention. She walked along continually tugging at hems and rebuttoning buttons, as if she were nervous. Yet her face, seen close to, was blank and listless. She complained to Violet that she had nothing to look forward to. "Summer is coming," she said, "and there I'll be on the porch. Getting fatter. Reading romances. My father will be home all day just picking at the lawn. Don't you wish there was something to do?"

"You could be a camp counselor," Violet said.

Evie only sighed and yanked at a slip strap.

In the changing-room, on gym days, half-dressed girls sat on long wooden benches and named their favorite singers. Their lockers were lined with full-color pictures of the

Beatles and the Monkees, their notebooks were decorated with the titles of the top forty, and they traded stacks of pulpy gray magazines filled with new lyrics and autographed photos. Their favorites lived in Detroit or Nashville or London, and switched like baseball players from one group to another, from group-singing to solo, and from an outdated style to a new one. Evie couldn't keep up with them. While the others talked she dressed behind a slatted partition, shielding the front of her 40-D bra as she reached for a blouse, concentrating glumly on what she overheard.

"Fill in your name, they say. Mail it off. If you win you get a date with the singer of your choice, dinner and dancing and a photograph to remember it by. It tells you right here, see?"

"Yes, but what if I win?"

"Lucky you."

"I mean, wouldn't you *die?*"

"Not me."

"I would. I wouldn't say a word all evening. How could you talk to a singing star?"

"That's why you have to watch who you pick. You can't just choose for looks, you got to get someone with personality."

"Paul McCartney has personality."

"His name isn't on here."

One day a tenant farmer's daughter named Fay-Jean Lindsay said, "Those people in the magazines are all right, I reckon. Those Rolling Stones and all. But me, I'll take Joseph Ballew."

"Never heard of him," someone said.

"He's from Pulqua. Right around Pulqua."

"How come we never heard of him?"

"*I* don't know. You ought to have. He sings real nice."

"Where's he at now?"

"Pulqua."

"Well, for heaven's sake," they said, and then they changed the subject.

But later, when Evie was fully dressed, she came out from behind her partition to talk to Fay-Jean. Fay-Jean was kneeling on the end of a bench, drawing her comb through a ribbon of pale, shining hair. "I heard you liked Joseph Ballew," Evie said.

Fay-Jean tucked away the comb and brought out a mirror, which she looked into for some time. There was nothing else to do with it. She had one of those tiny, perfect faces, not yet sharpened enough to show the tenant farmer in her. "Who?" she said finally.

"Joseph Ballew."

"He's all right."

"Was he at that rock show a few weeks back?"

Fay-Jean looked up. "Why, yes, he was," she said. "I didn't see *you* there."

"I was near the back."

"Did you like him?"

"Well, really I—which one was he?"

"Oh, you couldn't have overlooked him. He sang 'Honeypot.' Now you remember."

"Well," said Evie. "I was wondering. Do you know Drumstrings Casey?"

"Him? Wait a minute."

Fay-Jean started rummaging through her notebook. She came up with red-slashed quizzes, a *Silver Screen* magazine, and finally a sheet of ruled paper which she handed to Evie. It was a pencil drawing of a narrow-faced boy with high cheekbones, one eye smaller than the other. His features were vague, hairy lines, and his mouth had been erased several times and redrawn heavily. "Who's this?" Evie asked.

"It's Drumstrings Casey, who do you think."

"Do you know him?"

"No. Do you think it's a good likeness?"

"Oh, well, sure," said Evie. "But how were you—did you ask him to sit for it?"

"No, I did it at the Unicorn. That's where he plays, same as Joseph Ballew. Joseph Ballew is my real favorite, but I think this one is kind of cute too. You ever been to the Unicorn?"

"I don't even know what it is," Evie said.

"It's a roadhouse. Just south of Pulqua a ways. You can come with me sometime, I got a car I can borrow."

"Tomorrow?"

"What?"

"Are you going there tomorrow?"

"Tomorrow's Friday. Casey only plays on Saturdays."

"Will you be going there this Saturday?"

"Sure, I guess so."

"I'll come with you then," Evie said. "Could I bring a friend?"

"Sure. And keep the picture, if you like."

"Well, thank you. I don't have anything to trade for it."

"To—?"

"Trade. Trade for the picture."

"Why would you want to trade for it?"

"I don't know," Evie said.

She pasted the picture in the middle of her mirror. Drumstrings Casey's penciled head took the place of her own every time she combed her hair. "When we go to the Unicorn," Violet said, "bring a camera. Hanging out with the likes of Fay-Jean Lindsay is bad enough; I fail to see how you can live with her art work."

"I don't mind," Evie said.

The Unicorn was out in the country, a gray windowless rectangle on a lonesome highway with darkness closing in all around it. Cars and motorcycles and pickup trucks sat any old way in a sand parking lot. In front, beside a baggy screen door, stood a policeman with his arms folded. It was not a place that people dressed up for, but Evie and Violet didn't know that. They came wearing full, shiny dresses and high-heeled pumps. Fay-Jean had on a skirt and blouse decorated with poodles on loops of real chain, and she twirled her car keys lightheartedly around her index finger as she passed the policeman.

It seemed to be noise that bellied the screen out—pieces of shouts and guitars and drums and an angry singer. Noise hit Evie in the face, on a breath of beer and musty-smelling wood. Someone wanted pretzels, not potato chips. Someone wanted to know where Catherine had gone. The singer's voice roughened and he sang out:

You ask me to be somebody I'm not,
How can you say you're my honeypot?

"Hear that?" Fay-Jean said.

Evie thought if she heard any more the noise would turn visible.

She followed Fay-Jean through darkness, past rows of long tables and seated couples. Once she nearly tripped over someone's outstretched leg. When they came to a table that had room for them, she found that a hand holding a lighted cigarette rested on the back of her chair. "Excuse me!" she shouted. Her voice disappeared as soon as it left her mouth. Finally Fay-Jean reached over and lifted the hand away, and Evie pulled her chair out.

"*What did you do with that ring I bought?*" the singer asked. He stood under a dim red bulb, moving constantly in a small circle as he sang. "*You ain't* acting *like no honeypot.*" Besides his guitar there were three other instruments and possibly a piano, although Evie couldn't be sure. All she saw was someone soundlessly pressing the keys. Behind them, on the same platform, a few people danced. The smell of beer gave the air a cold feeling. The rough walls and tables, built of the grayed wood used in picnic pavilions, made the building seem flimsy and temporary.

A fat man in a butcher's apron was handing out beer. When he started toward them Fay-Jean shouted, "How old are you?"

"Seventeen," said Evie.

"How old is Violet?"

"I'm eighteen," Violet said. "I caught scarlet fever in the fourth grade and was held—"

"What?"

"Eighteen, I said."

"You're okay. *You—*" and she pointed to Evie, "go *way* over. Say you're twenty. Then they won't ask for proof."

But the fat man did not even question her. He wanted to see Fay-Jean's driver's license, which she showed him. Then he looked over at Evie, slumped against the table with her arms folded under the billowing bosom of her dress. "What's for you?" he said.

"What?"

"Budweiser," Fay-Jean told him.

"Same for you, ma'am?"

Violet nodded.

Joseph Ballew left the platform. The dancers remained, pivoting on their heels and gazing around the room, until someone started a record of Frank Sinatra singing "Young at Heart." Then they gave up and wandered back to their seats.

"That Joseph Ballew is my ideal," Fay-Jean said. "You can *have* your big names, I don't care. He is only nineteen but looks twenty-five, at least, those two cool lines running down alongside his mouth."

"Have you ever gone up and talked to him?" Evie asked.

"Oh, sure, all the time. Once I called him on the phone and he let on he was busy, but I could tell he was right tickled to be called."

"What would you *say* if you went up?" Evie asked.

"Why, anything that comes to your head. You'll see. Aren't you going to go talk to Casey?"

"Oh, I couldn't," Evie said.

Her beer was brought to her in a chipped glass mug. She took small sips of it and looked sideways at the other customers.

"Once," said Fay-Jean, "a girl fell out, right about where I am sitting. She was listening to the music and then next thing you know had fell out. Laying out on the floor with her eyes shut. I would have been right embarrassed, if I was her."

"Who was it over?" Violet asked. "Drumstrings Casey or Joseph Ballew?"

"What? Oh, I don't know. It turned out to be a fit of some kind, nothing either of them bothered taking credit for. I will say this, though, she got a right smart of attention for it. They had to lay her out clear across a table. When she come to, Casey said, 'This here is for that pretty little girl yonder on the table,' and he played her a song. It was all wasted, though. Seems she didn't even know she had fell out; she just slid down to her seat and looked around her for some time, smiling kind of baffled-like."

"Is that right?" Evie said. She studied the foam on her beer a minute. Then she said, "Well, talking about attention. Would it cause a fuss if I were to snap his picture? I brought my Kodak."

"Oh, I thought I had give you that portrait," Fay-Jean said.

"You did," Violet told her. "I remember it, clearly."

"Well, I can't see how taking a picture would do any harm. Joseph Ballew once had a lady here snapping photos all evening long, writing him up for a motel newspaper."

Drumstrings Casey slid onto the platform as silently and as easily as some dark fish, the spangles on his guitar flashing dapples of red light. Nobody hushed or looked in his direction. He might have been anyone. Yet his face, which was a smooth olive color, gave off a glow across the cheekbones and down the bridge of his nose, and surely the audience must have noticed the separate, motionless circle of air he moved in. He hooked a chair with the toe of his boot and slid it to the center of the platform. With one foot resting on it he stared out over Evie's head, and the blond boy ambled forth from behind an amplifier to seat himself at the drums. "Where is the drum with 'Casey' on it?" Evie asked Violet.

"How should I know?"

"He should be using his own drums."

"Maybe these are better."

"I wish he'd use his own. These could be just anyone's."

"Maybe it's too hard to set them up each time. What difference does it make?"

"Well, still," Evie said.

They played a song called "My Girl Left Home." All Evie understood were the first four words. Halfway through, the music slowed and Drumstrings frowned.

"*Hold on,*" he said.

The audience stopped talking.

"*She left, you say?*"

He hit one note several times over.

"Where were you? Did you see her go?
"The meter man's coming.
"Buy the tickets. Wait in the lobby.
"Have you noticed all the prices going up?"

"My girl left home!" the drummer called. As if that had reminded him, Casey hit all the strings at once and continued with his song. Here and there conversation picked up again, but a few girls stayed quiet and kept their eyes on the guitar strings.

Fay-Jean danced with a boy chewing bubble gum. At the end of the first song she rested her hand on his shoulder and talked about something, steadily. Then a new piece began and another boy took the first one's place. She talked to him too, looking out toward the audience as if what she said took no thought. Her feet wove a curved, slithering pattern on the bare floorboards. The music seemed familiar. It was probably the song Drumstrings Casey had played at the rock show; but then when he slowed his guitar and spoke out, where was the man picking berries and the woman emptying trashcans? This time, he told about someone throwing soda-bottle caps at the moon. And then a bicycle.

"Basket on the front. Shiny in the dark.
"If I tell you again, will you listen this time?
"Never mind."

The song went on. Evie fumbled in her handbag for her camera, and then without allowing herself to think ahead she stood up and aimed it at the platform. Casey looked out beyond her. "Casey!" she called. He turned, still playing, not seeing. When the flashbulb went off he blinked and his eyes snagged on her. "Oho, she lied," he sang, and studied her white, shaky face. Then she sat down. He looked out beyond her again. Her hands were so tight upon the camera that the circulation seemed to have stopped.

"Evie, I declare," Violet said.

Evie said nothing.

He sang someone else's song next, one she had heard before on "Sweetheart Time." When his guitar slowed, the drummer beat louder, prodding him to hurry, and Drumstrings didn't speak out after all. At the end he bent his head slightly. It must have been a bow; everyone clapped.

After that he walked off the platform and past Evie's table. An envelope of cold air traveled with him, as if he had just come in from a winter night. Evie heard his denim jacket brush Violet's chair, and when she felt that it was safe she turned to look after him. But he had not passed by, after all. He stood behind her with his chin tilted up, his eyes on her beneath half-shut lids.

"You from some newspaper?" he asked.

"No," said Evie.

"Oh," he said, and then he walked on out.

" 'Oh,' he said. Was it 'oh'? Or 'Well.' I should have had an answer planned."

"It's not something you would have expected, after all," Violet said. She was spending the night with Evie, up in her flowered bedroom where the radio still spun music out. They were the only ones awake in the house. They had come home late, packed three abreast in the front seat of Fay-Jean's father's Studebaker, while a bushel basket full of tools rattled around in the back. Now Violet sat yawning and blinking as she unpinned her hair, but Evie was wide awake. She wandered around the room fully dressed, snapping pictures. "I want to use up the film," she said.

"Wait till tomorrow, why don't you."

"I want to drop it off at the drugstore tomorrow. Is Lowry's open on Sunday? Do you think that his picture will turn out halfway decent?"

"Oh, I imagine so." Violet yawned again and reached for her comb.

"Once I was standing up, I couldn't think what to call him," Evie said. "Bertram or Drumstrings." She photographed her bulletin board, hung with programs and newspaper clippings and a hall pass handwritten by a man teacher whom she had liked the year before. Then she said, "It's those quotes that confuse me. 'Drumstrings' in quotation marks. Which does that mean I should call him by?"

"Like Nat 'King' Cole."

"Oh, that's right. I'd forgotten. What did they call him?"

"Nat."

"Then I should have said 'Bertram.' But I could never do that. I'd feel silly saying 'Bertram.' " She snapped her own picture in the full-length mirror. "I was so scared, I was shaking," she said.

"I know. I saw."

"My hands were shaking. You mean it showed?"

"Well, I was right next to you."

"It wasn't something I had thought up first, you know. It was spur-of-the-moment. 'Why not?' I thought, and did it. Just stood up and did it." She turned toward Violet, who had lain down on the other side of the bed. "*Impulse*. That's what it was."

"Right," Violet said with her eyes closed.

"If I'd thought before, I would have fallen on my face. Or dropped the camera. Or lost my voice. Impulse was the clue. Are you listening?"

There was no answer. Evie fitted another flashbulb into her camera and snapped Violet's sleeping face.

3

Fay-Jean Lindsay was always dancing, and sometimes going off to huddle in dark cars with boys who only showed up once. She wasn't the kind to chauffeur two girls around indefinitely. So Evie and Violet started borrowing their fathers' cars, taking turns at it, and coming to the Unicorn by themselves every Saturday night. They still sat at Fay-Jean's table, although generally her chair was empty and her purse left spilled open beside her beer mug. They wore skirts and blouses now, and waved when they passed the policeman at the door. Evie's skirts were dark, to slim her down. Her blouses were white cotton that turned gray and limp halfway through the evening. Violet's skirts were rose and purple and chartreuse. She seemed to have taken the place over for her own—striding between chairs like a huge, stately queen, serene in the face of whistles and catcalls, ordering draft beer by the pitcher and pouring it expertly down the side of her mug so that there would be no foam. She reminded Evie of the lady chaperones she had learned about in Spanish class, except that Violet did no chaperoning: Fay-Jean returned from long absences with unknown partners, tilting against their shoulders like a solemn rag doll, and Drumstrings Casey slid his hips in easy circles under Violet's calm gaze. She said she liked this kind of life. "I should be a barmaid," she said. When a boy at the next table said, "Hey, fat mama," she threw back her head and laughed.

Only Evie seemed uncomfortable there. It was she who planned ahead for the evenings, rinsed her hair in malt vinegar and mourned a broken fingernail and begged Violet not to disgrace her by wearing her wiglet. Yet in the Unicorn she sat slumped behind her beer, chewing her thumb and scowling. She turned often to study the faces of other customers, especially when Drumstrings Casey was playing. Who was that blond who hushed everyone as soon as Casey came on the platform? Wouldn't you know that Evie could never have anything for herself without a lot of other people butting in and certain to win in the end? As if her coming here were a mysterious sort of publicity, the audience grew larger every Saturday and the clapping louder. "There, you see. I know what's what," she told Violet. "Now *everybody's* catching on to him." But she didn't look happy about it. She watched with a thoughtful, measuring look on her face when he ruffled a strange girl's hair on the way up to the platform.

"*You know I'm late,*" he said. "*Will you let me be?*

"*I've listened all night.*

"*I've pondered all day.*

"*Faces don't stick with me half as much as names.*"

The drummer slammed down on his drums. The music

grew louder. Oh, it was that talking out of his that made the difference. He never should have begun it. While he spoke Evie held very still, but afterwards, with her eyes wandering over the room, she said, "What would make him do like that?"

"I kind of like it," said Violet, starting her second mug of beer.

"Is he saying something? Is there something underneath it? Is he speaking in code?"

Other girls thought nothing of going straight up to him. They crowded around as soon as a set was done. "Now, how did you ever . . ." "Where did you get . . ." Casey slouched easily with his guitar at his side and looked straight through them. He seemed to think they were part of the program. Meanwhile Evie sat by Fay-Jean's empty chair and drew faces in a ring of beer.

"If I were to get his attention," she told Violet, "it would have to be without thinking of it first. Something that just happened. Can you see me going up with those others? I would be planning it ahead, smoothing down my skirt, tucking in my blouse, saying something memorized that would come out backwards, in a reading tone of voice."

"Oh, he wouldn't notice," Violet said.

"That's exactly what I meant."

One Saturday a redhead who was dancing on the platform stood stock still while Casey did his speaking out. It was only one line.

"If I called your name wrong, would you still say yes?"

When the music crashed down again, the redhead said, "You *bet* I would!" Then she left her partner and pulled

Casey around by one shoulder to finish the dance. He danced as he played, laughing. It was the first time Evie had seen him laugh. The sudden breaking up of that smooth olive face made him look unfinished and angular, like someone's comical little brother.

"*There's* how to get his attention," Violet said. "Just give him a yank." But when she turned, she saw that Evie was several tables away by now, pushing toward the ladies' room. The boy at Violet's right said, "Hey, little marshmallow, you're all alone." Violet smiled and poured more beer.

Or was it Joseph Ballew they all came for? He swaggered onto the platform with his head down and one fist raised, like a prize fighter. Everybody clapped. Fay-Jean appeared in a man's leather jacket and said, "Will you look at how his hair curls up? Oh, I wish *mine* would do that way."

"*Nobody got a right to leave me like you left me,*" Joseph sang. All of his songs were angry. His voice was furry and dark, roughening on vowels, and he stood very close to the microphone. When he started his second song Fay-Jean said, "Will you listen? Evie Decker can have *six* of Drumstrings Casey. Where'd she go, anyhow?"

"Excused herself," said Violet.

Someone screamed.

Joseph Ballew looked pleased, and twanged two sharp notes on his guitar. Then he lowered it to sing another line. He never did both at once. Behind him a murmuring arose, and the other players began looking around, but Joseph sang on with his eyes closed.

"Who screamed?" Violet asked.

Fay-Jean moved away, her jacket swinging from her shoulders. As soon as she was gone Violet turned back to her beer, but then there was another scream. This time the voice was Fay-Jean's.

"My Lord in heaven, Evie Decker!" she said.

Violet stood up. Joseph Ballew stopped playing. The commotion was in a rear corner, by the door to the ladies' room, but even when Violet had angled her way over there the crowd was too tightly packed for her to see anything.

"Will you let me through?" she said. "What is it? Will you let me through?"

Someone bumped into her from behind. "Police," he said. "Clear the way. *Clear* the way." The crowd divided. Violet passed through, widening the path for the policeman. When she reached the door of the ladies' room she stopped suddenly and rocked backward against the policeman's chest.

"Evie?" she said.

Evie was smiling. Two people supported her, the redhead and a skinny blond girl. They held her in a professional, movie-like way, each with one hand beneath Evie's elbow and one at the small of her back. Evie's face was ridged with vertical strands of blood. There were crimson zigzags across her forehead, dampening her hair. "Evie, what *happened?*" said Violet.

"It's his name," Evie said.

The policeman stepped forward, carrying a small pad of paper and a retractable ball-point pen. He clicked the pen. "Name?" he asked.

"Drumstrings Casey," Evie said.

4

She had cut the letters with a pair of nail scissors. They ran all the way across her forehead, large and ragged and Greek-looking because straight lines were easier to cut: ϒƎƧAƆ. In the emergency room, after they had swabbed the blood away, there was a silence lasting several seconds. "*Backwards?*" someone said finally. It looked as if she were staring out at the letters from within, from the wrong side of her forehead. Or maybe she had cut them while facing a mirror. Whatever the reason, Evie wasn't telling. She sat in a white enameled chair beside an instrument case, her shoulders slumped, the lower part of her face round and blank and pale beneath the red slashes. Her pudgy feet in their vinyl sandals were twined around the chair rungs. Beside her stood the policeman who had brought her in, still curious although he had already taken down the necessary information; and opposite her, right alongside the doctor and nurse, was Violet. Oh, it would take more than this to shock Violet. She had ridden with Evie in the back of the squad car, patting her hand absently. "Evie Decker, I declare," she said, "I wish you would tell me—Goodness, will you listen? Sirens. They're for you." Evie only blinked and watched as the headlights scraped the edges of a tobacco field. When they drove up to the hospital door she said, "I left my pocketbook in the ladies' room."

"Oh, don't worry. I'll call about it."

"And then what about your car? And I never paid for my last beer."

"Don't worry."

The others treated her as if she were unconscious, resting their hands on her shoulder while they leaned forward to discuss her. "Is she all *right?*" the nurse said once, and patted Evie's cheeks sharply, almost slapping her. "Do you think she's all right?"

The doctor shrugged and filled a hypodermic needle. "Who knows?" he said. "Damn fool teen-agers. Find her a room, will you? I'm keeping her the night till I see her state of mind." The nurse left, and so did the policeman, still staring backwards over his shoulder as he closed the door. "Should we have tipped him?" Violet asked.

"No," said the doctor. "You might as well call her family. Does she have a family?"

"Only her father."

"He'll have to be told about this."

So Violet left too, rippling the fingers of one hand at Evie. "Just be a minute," she said. "Take care."

Evie was the only patient in the emergency room. The doctor worked in silence, snapping threads just above her eyes with gloved, dead-feeling hands while water dripped somewhere behind him. "Casey your boyfriend?" he asked finally.

"No."

"Who, then?"

"Just a singer."

"Rock-and-roll, I suppose."

"That's right."

"Mmhmm." He snapped another thread. "This is nothing dangerous, you understand. First-degree cuts. But they're ragged. They'll leave scars. You'll need a good plastic surgeon to get rid of them for you."

Evie stared at a crease in his white coat.

"You all right?" he asked her.

"Yes, fine."

"Well, I can't think why."

Violet returned, swinging her purse by its long strap so that it jingled against her shins at every step. "Your father's on his way," she said. "I said you had to have a little cut stitched up. Was that what you wanted? I couldn't see just out and out *telling* him." She settled on a stool beside the doctor and arranged her skirt around her. "Would you rather I had?"

Evie shook her head.

"Hold still," said the doctor.

He worked for what might have been hours, snapping threads endlessly and sometimes letting out a long whistling sigh between his teeth. Beside him, Violet twirled on her stool and hummed. A clock over the exit jerked each minute by with a deep, pointed click. When finally the doctor laid a strip of gauze over the stitches, Evie saw that it was nearly midnight. "This sets some kind of record," he said. "Aren't there any singers called Al? Or Ed?"

"His first name was Drumstrings," Violet told him.

"Well, then, I suppose she did the best she could." He peeled his gloves off. "You can go home tomorrow, if you're in a normal state. Though what *that* would be—Help her to the nurses' station, would you, miss? Ask for Miss Connolly. I'll talk to her father before I send him in."

"Thank you," Evie said.

"You'd be better off in the Peace Corps," said the doctor.

Evie's room held two white beds, both empty, and a maple dresser with a mirror over it. There was only a night-light on. When she looked in the mirror she saw a wide dark shadow with a band of startling white across the forehead. She touched the band with one finger. "Oh, look, you get a johnny-coat," Violet said. "Only two ties down the whole back of it, and one of them broken. Shall I bring you fresh clothes to wear home tomorrow? Your father'll never think of it."

"No, he probably won't," Evie said.

She pulled off her clothes, which felt creased and heavy from being worn too long. As she dropped each piece to the floor, Violet fumbled for it in the dark and laid it on a chair. Their movements were slow and soundless—Evie's because she felt awkward, Violet's for no known reason because Violet never felt awkward. When Evie had put the gown on, she climbed into the bed farthest from the window. She sat up against the metal headboard, her hands folded across her stomach.

"They'll bring you breakfast in bed, I suppose," Violet said.

"Does Drumstrings Casey know about this?"

"Well, I'm not sure."

"There was a lot of commotion over it. Wouldn't you think he'd have heard?"

"He wasn't singing then. Joseph Ballew was. *I* don't know."

"Didn't you look?"

"Honestly, Evie, I don't *know*. I was with you. I and the policeman. We were busy taking you out."

"I believe this might be the best thing I've ever done," said Evie. "Something out of character. Definite. Not covered by insurance. I'm just sure it will all work out well."

Violet bent to line up the vinyl sandals beneath the bed. "Why don't you tell me what you want to wear tomorrow," she said. "I'll stop by your house and pick it up."

"Oh, anything. Skirt and blouse. While I was walking through that crowd with the policeman, I kept thinking of my name: Evie Decker, *me*. Taking something into my own hands for once. I thought, if I had started acting like this a long time ago my whole *life* might've been different."

"Well, *that's* for sure," said Violet. "Anyway. Skirt and blouse. Do you want me to stay till your father comes?"

"No, I guess not. Your family will be wondering where you are."

"All right. See you in the morning."

Violet's shoes made a soft, plodding sound out of the room and down the hall. When the sound had faded Evie pulled the sheets over her and lay on her back, staring at the ceiling. Headlights swung across it in slow white wedges. Some sort of blower beneath her window made a steady rushing noise that turned other noises unreal and distant. Her forehead was a tight, thin sheet. There was only a surface pain, but the tightness gave her the feeling that her skin might split into shallow cracks at any moment. She bridged her forehead with one hand, clamping it inward with her thumb and middle finger to ease the stretch.

"Evie?" her father said.

She lowered her hand and winced toward the lighted door. Her father was a tall black angular silhouette, bent at the waist. He entered with his head leading, just as he entered his classroom while students whispered and passed notes and ignored him. "I brought you some clothes," he said.

"Oh. You did?"

"Don't you need them?"

"Well, Violet was going to bring some."

He reached over to the bureau and turned on a lamp, so that her eyes contracted into a sudden ache. "Is that, does that bandage have to be so big?" he asked her.

"It has to cover my whole forehead."

"All of it?"

She shaded her eyes to look at him. "I thought the doctor had told you," she said.

"He did, yes."

"Do you want to see?"

"Oh, no, that's all right."

"I don't mind." She sat up and undid the gauze, which was fastened by adhesive at both ends, and laid it in her lap. "It's only a flesh wound," she said.

"Yes, he said that. He—" Her father looked for only one second before he dropped his eyes again. "I don't understand," he said.

"It's a singer."

"Yes, I know. Casey. I know."

"You know him?"

"I mean, I know that's what the name is. I never heard of Casey before."

"Oh."

"I never even heard of him."

"Well," said Evie.

Her father bent over the bag at his feet, a shopping bag with string handles. "Clothes," he said. He brought out a blouse, a flowered skirt, and underpants but no bra. Finally he came to a pink frilled bedjacket sent her by an aunt two years ago but never used. He laid it in her lap. Evie picked it up and turned it over, smoothing the frills. "A bedjacket," she said.

"I thought you might need it."

In Evie's stubby hands, the frills seemed fussy and out of place. A bedjacket must have been what he brought her mother when Evie was born—something he had been told was expected of him, along with flowers and a bottle of cologne. Evie's mother had been the last woman in Pulqua County to die of childbed fever. Her father never mentioned her (and never said, "You are what I traded your mother for, and it was a bad bargain at that," which was what Evie continually expected to hear). But the bedjacket, with its satin buttons, seemed to be giving him away without his realizing it, speaking up out of all those years of silence. "Well, thank you very much," Evie said.

He went over to the window, jamming his hands into his pockets. Everything about him was long and bony; nothing but his awkwardness had been passed on to Evie. His hair and lashes were pale, his eyes set in deep shadowed sockets, his skin sprinkled with large freckles so faint that they seemed to be seeping through a white over-layer. "Plastic surgeons take money, of course—" he was saying.

"I don't want one."

He barely heard her. His mind had snagged on a new thought. "Evie, had you been drinking?" he asked. "Was that it?"

"Half a beer."

"But then, why would you do it?"

Evie spread her fingers in front of her and studied them like a deck of cards while she chose her words. "Now, I'm not trying to be rude," she said finally, "but it *was* my face. It is. It's my business how it looks."

"You'd feel awfully silly with 'Casey' across your forehead all your life."

"I'd feel sillier having it erased the day after I did it," said Evie.

"Well, that's the worst of it. You *can't* erase it the next day, you have to wait until it heals. Could you maybe cut bangs, meanwhile?"

"No," said Evie.

Her father rubbed the pouches under his eyes, smoothing and re-pleating them. "Evie, honey," he said. "There are *plenty* of nice boys in the world. Just give yourself time. You're a sweet-looking girl, after all, and when you lose a, when you're older, boys are going to fall all over themselves for you, take my word. You're only sixteen now."

"Seventeen," said Evie.

"Seventeen. So why should you ruin your life for some singer in a roadhouse? Listen. The doctor's giving you a tranquilizer. You have a good night's sleep, and tomorrow I'll come get you and we'll talk it over. Things will look different in the morning. You'll see."

Evie said nothing. She rolled the strip of gauze into a small cylinder.

"Well, good night, Evie."

He clicked off the lamp. Then at the door he stopped and turned. "Another thing," he said. "Tell that Casey boy not to bother coming around again. I won't allow you to see any more of him."

Evie looked up, with two small pleased folds beginning at the outer corners of her eyes. But by then he had jammed his hands back in his pockets and walked away.

They gave her some sort of pill but she spent a bad night anyway, tossing beneath a light, frowning sleep. Strange beds bothered her. Splinters of dreams came and went, leaving only echoes of themselves to remember in the morning. And when she awoke, all her muscles ached. She sat up and looked out toward the corridor, where specks of sunlight floated slowly above the polished red floor. "Nurse!" she tried. No one answered.

Somewhere in her waking, the thought of her forehead floated by like yesterday's surprise, some new possession which would have to be confirmed again today. She slid off the high bed and padded over to the bureau mirror, keeping her nightgown hitched shut behind her.

Her forehead was an angry doll's, crisscrossed with black stitches. The word "Casey," reflected right side around, formed itself only after several seconds, during which she stood stunned and motionless with her mouth barely open. Later, maybe, it would be immediately legible. But today the threads turned her forehead first into a jagged design, a grayish-white crazy-quilt covering the space between her hairline and her straight brown eyebrows, which were flaked with dried blood. All her other features seemed to have drained away. Her lips were pale, and her eyes had lightened. Her nose looked flatter. For years she had cherished the few surprises hidden away in her shapelessness: a narrow nose, slender wrists, and perfect oval fingernails. Now, still looking into the mirror, she held up both wrists and turned the blue-veined, glistening insides of them toward the glass. Then she backed away, very slowly. But when she was as far as she could get, pressed against the wall behind her, the letters still stood out ragged and black. "Casey." A voice inside her read the name out, coolly: "Casey."

Something on wheels was coming down the hallway. Evie climbed back into bed and sat there, with her wrists still upturned in her lap, while her heart began thudding at an uneven rate. There was no way she could steady it. She breathed deeply, gazed at a blank wall, straightened her back. Her heart kept racing and then pausing, collecting itself to race again.

A nurse wheeled in a cart laid with pills in paper cups and a jarful of thermometers. "*Here* we are," she said. She looked over at Evie, with a thermometer in mid-air, and opened her mouth but said nothing. Her face had the same pale, startled look that Evie's had had in the mirror. But when she spoke again all she said was, "Have a nice night?" She slid the thermometer into Evie's mouth and reached for a wrist. Evie was too intent on her heartbeat to answer. She went on staring at the wall, keeping her lips conscientiously tight around the thermometer. In a minute, now, the nurse would know from her pulse that something was wrong. She would drop the wrist and run to fetch doctors, oxygen tents, digitalis—taking the responsibility from Evie, letting her rest finally while someone else steadied her heartbeat. But when the minute was up, the nurse had still said nothing. Evie stopped looking at the wall. She found the nurse's eyes just brushing her, very briefly, and then settling on the thermometer which she plucked out and shook down with no more than a glance at it. "Breakfast'll be along," she said. She set the thermometer on a paper napkin and wheeled the cart out.

If she lay still, Evie kept hearing the blood thudding unevenly through her ears. She drowned the sound by struggling out of bed, trailing one sheet halfway across the floor and limping on the foot that was tangled in the sheet's folds. Her hospital gown bellied out like a sail when she bent to free herself. Her hair fell forward in dark, rigid strings, matted with blood. After she had kicked the door shut she dressed in a flurry of deliberate noises: clicking snaps, shuffling sandals, slamming drawers as she looked through the bureau for a stray comb. All she found were a box of Wipettes and a booklet called "Our Daily Bread." She shut the final drawer and then raised her head, listening. Her heartbeat was regular again. Or if not regular, at least unnoticeable. In the mirror a steady pulse quivered one point of her collar, and a black-pointed design was plastered above it like a label.

After breakfast, a nurse's aide appeared in the doorway and folded her hands across her pinafore. "Photographer's coming," she said. "You're going to be famous."

Evie sat on the foot of her bed, snapping her watchband over and over and waiting for someone to remember she was there. "Famous?" she said. "What? Photographer?"

"They heard what you did," said the nurse's aide. She spun out of the room. Just before she disappeared she remembered to say, "That singer guy, too. He's coming."

"What singer?"

"Yezac."

Evie got off the bed. It was better to be standing. No, sitting. But there was no place to sit except the bed, whose sheets were still strung out across the room. She stood in the middle of the floor with her hands clasped behind her, straight-armed, shifting from one foot to another. She felt like a package at a post office, stamped and addressed, and the heel-taps of the addressee were clicking closer and closer down the hall. She could hear him clearly now. She heard how the swing in his walk created silences between his steps: click, space, click, while whoever was with him luff-luffed steadily along in soft-soled shoes. The photographer, a small bald man hung with several strapped objects, arrived in the doorway first. "Paul Ogle, Pulqua *Times,*" he said. Then he crossed the room to the far corner, holding a light meter to Evie's chin on the way. And there, finally, came Drumstrings Casey. He wore his black denim and his high leather boots. He had on sunglasses made of a silvery black that mirrored Evie perfectly and turned his own face, what you could see of it, into something as hard and as opaque as the glasses themselves. "Shades off, Casey," the photographer said. "I want a reaction."

Drumstrings Casey leaned against the doorframe, crossed one boot, and removed his sunglasses. His face lost its smoothness. He had, after all, the narrow brown eyes that Evie expected, so straight-edged that each seemed formed from a pair of parallel lines. The slant of hair was not greased down today; he ruffled it through his fingers, stroking his forehead with the same motion. "It's the newspaper lady," he said.

"No," said Evie. She meant no, she was not from the newspaper at all and had told him so before; but Casey, misunderstanding, said, "Well, you sure do look like her."

"More reaction, Casey," the photographer said. Casey stretched his mouth into a wide straight line. "Will you turn this way, miss?" Evie turned, focusing her eyes upon a drawer-pull for as long as she felt Casey watching. The photographer clicked the shutter. "Now, Casey, put your arm around her. Smile. Don't you know how to smile?" But Casey only stared fixedly at the bottom half of Evie's face. Every now and then his eyes darted up to her forehead and then down again, as if they had run away with him for a second. Across Evie's shoulders his arm was limp and motionless, the hand falling open off the edge of her sleeve. He had the pleasantly bitter smell of marigolds. Even this close, he seemed filmed by cold air.

The camera clicked again. For the first time, Evie remembered that the purse she had left at the Unicorn contained her snapshot of Drumstrings Casey. "Oh—" she said, but when the two men turned, she went back to staring at the drawer-pull. The snapshot had come out dappled by tiny pools of light, glinting for no apparent reason on the edges of his dark clothes and on his face, which was tilted slightly up, the veiled eyes turned in her direction.

"Now, it's Evie, that right? Evie Decker," said the photographer. He was writing on a scrap of paper with bitten-looking edges. "Age?"

"Seventeen."

"Seventeen. Really? Occupation?"

"I go to school."

"I thought you were older," the photographer said. "Now. Could you tell me what end you had in mind?"

"End?"

"What your goal was in doing this."

"Oh," said Evie.

"Your reason, then. Could you tell me your reason?"

Drumstrings Casey shifted his weight, his fingers hooked in his back pockets.

"Let's put it this way," the photographer said. "We'll say you're just a music fan. You dig rock, especially Casey's rock. That sound about right?"

"Oh, well, I guess so."

"We'll put it in quotes, then. Now, would you mind telling what you did it with?"

"I don't remember," said Evie, suddenly tired.

"Was it all of a sudden? Had you planned it?"

"It's hard to say."

"Well, I suppose that's enough," the photographer said. "It's only going to be a caption."

Drumstrings Casey straightened up. "A caption, what's that?" he asked.

"The writing under a photo. *You* know."

"Couldn't you give it more?"

"It's not *me* that says, boy, it's the boss."

"Well, God almighty," Casey said.

"What now?"

"Wasn't it you that was waking me at seven this morning? Shouting about publicity? I don't see what *that* was all about. Little old grainy newspaper picture, heap of gray dots nobody'll recognize."

"Don't talk to me, talk to your drummer," said the photographer. "He's the one called *me*. Well, thanks, folks." And out he walked, leaving the two of them alone in the middle of the room.

"Well," said Casey. He slipped his dark glasses back on and jammed his shirt down tighter into his pants. Then he turned toward Evie. Behind the glasses it was hard to tell where he was looking. "What'd you go and cut it backwards for?" he asked her.

"It just worked out that way," said Evie.

"Worked out that way, how do you mean."

"I don't know, that's just the way it happened. Can't you read it?"

"Sure, I can read it."

"Now I can see that it's uneven," Evie said. "I know that's going to bother me. Every time I look in a mirror I'll think, why did I let the Y droop? Why did I shake on the C?"

"Why did you make it 'Casey'?" Casey said.

She stared, mistaking his meaning. She thought he had asked the only question she minded answering.

"Why not my first name?" he asked. "There're thousands of Caseys around."

"What, *Drumstrings?* I don't have that big of a forehead."

"Drum," he said. "Nobody says the whole thing, for Lord's sake."

"They call you Drum?" asked Evie.

"That's right."

"Well, I certainly wish I'd of known."

"Yeah, I suppose it's too late now," he said.

He was teetering on his heels, his hands in his back pockets again, plainly thinking of going. Evie pressed her palms together and said, "You are going to be famous someday."

He raised his sunglasses to stare at her. His eyes were bleached-looking in the sudden light. "It's funny," he said finally. "I would never have took you for a rock fan at all." Evie held still under his gaze, until he dropped the glasses and turned toward the door. "Certainly was a peculiar feeling," he said to nobody special. "Feels like meeting up with your own face somewhere." He was halfway out the door now, but still with no good-byes, no summing up, no rounding off of the conversation before he left. "Almost like something you would dream in bed at night," he said, but by then he was out of sight. His voice was sliding away and his boots were ambling down the hall. Evie remained where she was for several minutes, staring out the open doorway. She was used to definite endings. When Drum Casey left he trailed bits of conversation like wisps from a cotton ball, clouding the air behind him. His voice remained in the hall, disembodied. His heel-taps clicked for a long time without seeming to get farther away. The doctor when he came found Evie alone in the middle of her room, surveying the insides of her wrists, and he shook his head and signed her discharge papers in silence.

5

Messes rose up wherever she sat; that was the kind of mood she was in. For days after she came home from the hospital, she stayed in a draggled bathrobe, as if she were truly an invalid, while clutter collected magically in an oval around her chair. Flakes of lint speckled the rug. Candy papers overflowed the ash trays. The slipcover sagged on the chair cushion and grew creased and dingy. Yet from morning to night Evie hardly moved, just sat on the back of her neck with her arms limp at her sides and an open magazine in her lap. Clotelia, passing through the living room, jabbed a broom under Evie's legs. "Excuse, please. Move," she said. Evie frowned at the broom and picked a chocolate out of the box at her elbow.

People called to ask about her. Not classmates, but friends of her father's. "*You* talk to them," Evie told Clotelia. She heard conversations from outdoors, at twilight, while her father was sprinkling the lawn. "Evening, Sam. Is Evie, I hear she had a little accident. Or rather—" "Go on now," someone said, "they tell me that girl of yours has slashed her wrists with a movie star's initials. Is that true?" "Forehead," said her father. "A singer. His full last name." When he came in, his face would be pouched and sagging. Grownups wearing that expression usually said, when asked, "No, not angry. Just disappointed." Only Evie never asked and her father never said it, not out loud.

She covered her forehead with gauze from the medicine cabinet and taped it at both ends, the way the doctor had. Her hair, which she still had not washed, remained stiff with blood in front and limp and damp-looking behind. She wore a bathrobe faded from sky blue to gray, grayer along the edges, and her slippers were gray too, a matted pile that had started out white. Even without the mysterious clutter around her, any corner she inhabited would still have seemed untidy. "You are a sight," Clotelia said. "You constituting a mess all by your lone self." Evie only stared at her and turned a page of her magazine.

Her teachers sent her assignments home with her father. At first her father seemed relieved that she was staying out of school. In the mornings as he left he said, "That's the girl. You just take it easy a while, I'll see you tonight." But it was clear that he expected things to fall into some sort of progression—the blood to be washed from her hair, the gauze removed, bangs cut. Evie took no steps at all. Toward the end of the week she kept an appointment to have her stitches out, but then she came home and got back into her bathrobe. "Let's see you," her father said that evening. Evie tilted her face up, exposing a naked forehead with "Casey" running across it in dried red dots. "Ah, yes," said her father. He looked away again.

She rose every morning just as he left for work, and drank a glass of orange juice in her easy chair. Then she opened a magazine. Her father bought her magazines at a newsstand, carefully choosing those which had nothing to do with rock music, or teen-agers, or even love. If she was not in a reading mood she held one of his selections open on her lap while she stared into space, but when she got bored she dove under the skirt of the chair for what Clotelia read: *Jet*, *Ebony*, and *Revealing Romances*. She chewed a fingernail and raced through vague, hopeful confession stories and smeared advertisements for hair straighteners and bust creams. By then Clotelia would be making passes at the living room with a dirty dustcloth. "What you read that trash for?" she asked Evie. "You know it only snarl your mind."

"I want to see where you get your outlook on life," Evie said.

Clotelia emptied one wastebasket into another, piece by piece.

Clotelia's skin was the color of pale cocoa, but since she had started dating Brewster Miggs she called herself black and wore her hair in a bush. "Brewster don't want me doing day-work no more, either," she told Evie. "Say I got to quit. I tell him I will." Yet she continued to show up every morning, at nine or nine-thirty or ten, wearing ski pants and an African cape. When she chose to do any cleaning she kept up a running conversation with the dirt. "Come out of there, you. I see you. How come you to bug me this way? That's all this house is, filth. Filth."

"You should know," said Evie. She felt continually disappointed by Clotelia. Four years, and Clotelia was still an indifferent stranger kicking dust puffs with the toe of a cream suede high-heeled boot. Other people would have turned into members of the family by now. Clotelia carried her purse with her from room to room all day long, and massaged pink lotion into her hands while staring out the kitchen window. When she poked a mop beneath a radiator, Evie felt that the whole house was suffering from some sort of disdain. It was such a leaden, damp-smelling house. The flowered furniture and lacy figurines had sat so long in their places that they seemed to have jelled there, hardening around the edges. Clotelia passed among them scornfully, with earrings as big as slave bands flashing knives of light across the walls.

At noon, when the soap operas came on, Clotelia always settled before the television with her feet outstretched and a beer between her knees. "Clotelia, where is lunch?" Evie asked.

"I'm watching the stories now."

"Well, I see you are."

"Something happen to your feet?"

"I just did get home from the hospital," Evie said.

"What, was it your feet give you trouble? *No* sir. Your head." She tapped her temple and went back to watching "Love of Life." Evie wouldn't have eaten lunch anyway. She ate chocolates, or the last of the pack of Nabs in Clotelia's purse. Meanwhile the soap operas toiled on, one after the other. People quarreled and sobbed and flung out of rooms to organ music, and Evie kept saying, "Oh, for—" but watching, anyway, caught up in what was going on. Clotelia talked about the characters as if they were relatives.

"I don't know what *she* doing. That boy don't care two flicks for her. You ever seen her mother? Talk about nosy. At Christmastime she trail that girl all the way to New York, that's where she went for the holidays, and eagle-eyed? Oh, she give me the creeps. I despise a woman to be that way."

"She's got no sense of privacy," said Evie, crumpling the Nabs wrapper.

"Oh, don't tell *me*. You remember when her boy got engaged?"

"I didn't see it."

"Well, it was to a sweet girl but I wasn't easy about her. Something she was hiding. Naturally his mother saw it right off. She don't miss a trick. Stop wagging your foot, will you? Like to driving me crazy."

"It's all I've got to do," said Evie, but she stilled her foot.

"Every time I get out of here Brewster say, 'Honey, why you so *evil* today? I never seen you so evil.' I say, 'It's that Evie. She driving me crazy,' I say."

"I don't do one thing to you," Evie said.

"Oh, no? Look at you, wherever you sit you just causing a shambles. I already cleaned that space today. Will you look at it?"

Evie looked. Crumpled cellophane lay beside her chair, and cheese cracker crumbs littered her lap and the rug. "What do you expect?" she said. "I just came out of the hospital."

"Hospital is right. And you be right back in, if you don't rise off that fat butt of yours. You hear what happen if you sit too long?"

"What."

"You bust your skin seams. You pop right open, you leak out the cracks."

Clotelia never would act the way she was supposed to.

After school Violet would stop by. She carried her books and all the odds and ends she had accumulated during the day—someone's broken looseleaf binder, blank newsprint from the journal office, a tissue flower found in a wastebasket. She saved things. She saved bits of gossip she had heard third-hand, so far removed from the outer circle she and Evie inhabited that sometimes even the names were missing. "You know that real tall cheerleader? The one that does the split after the fight song? She had to get married. Lola Nesbitt has fought with that boy she dates. I saw him send a note into her class and hang around outside waiting for her to read it, but she never did."

Pulled from one set of plots into another, Evie frowned at the television set and tried to collect her thoughts. "Is he the one that debates?" she said.

"I think so. Miss Ogden is back from her honeymoon. She's Mrs. Bishop now. Has a florentined wedding-ring set with diamond chips. It looks kind of tacky; everybody says so."

"What do they say about me?" Evie asked.

"Oh, well, I don't know."

"They don't say anything?"

"Well, bits and pieces. *You* know."

On the television screen a tense married couple sat gingerly circling each other's feelings, casting significant looks after a simple sentence, causing the music to swell ominously over no more than a phrase and a pair of lowered eyes. Violet watched them and tapped a fingernail against her front teeth.

"My father thinks I'm going to a plastic surgeon," Evie said.

"Well, aren't you?"

"Ha," said Clotelia. "You think she got that much sense?"

"I don't know yet," Evie said, "but I doubt if I am."

"You could cut bangs."

"That would be worse. Showing up at school wearing bangs all of a sudden, everyone knowing why."

"Then go to the surgeon."

"Watch, now," Clotelia said. "This man here is some operator. Listen to his sweet-talk. Yesterday he was after that blond, the one before the commercial. Fickle?"

"I'm not sorry the letters are *there,*" Evie said. "I'm glad. I'm talking about something else."

"What, then?"

"Well, I don't really know."

"School will be out in just a few more weeks anyhow," said Violet.

"I keep forgetting."

"That's because you don't get outdoors. It's hot now."

"Is it?" Evie twisted in her seat, tearing a shank of hair through her fingers. "I just hate summer," she said.

"Every year you tell me that."

"I mean it. What have I got to look forward to? You know what I thought, Violet: This summer might be different. Now it looks like it won't be."

"Why would it be different?"

Evie didn't answer, but Clotelia did. "Ha. Thought that

Casey boy would come riding up and spirit her away, once he heard what she done."

"You hush," said Evie.

"I don't see him beating down no doors. Do you?"

"Ignore her," Evie told Violet.

Violet sighed and wrapped her hands around each other. "You could take your finals at home," she said. "Your father could arrange it."

"You think I'm scared to go back."

"Well, Evie, here you *sit*. What are you staying around home for?"

"Look. Can't you tell me what they're all saying? I won't care. I promise I won't. Just tell me what you've heard."

"I already did," said Violet. "Just bits and pieces, that's all. Someone will come up and say, 'Is it true what I heard about that friend of yours?' 'What'd you hear?' I say, and they say, 'Oh, *you* know.' "

"But you must have to answer sometime," Evie said. "What do you tell them?"

"I tell them yes, I believe there *was* something like that."

"Do they act surprised?"

"What would they act surprised for? If they asked, they must have already known."

"Well, shocked then. Do they laugh? What do they *say?*"

"Oh, they just think a while. Like when—but no, not exactly—"

"Like when."

"Like when the cheerleader had to get married, I was going to say."

"They think I did something evil, then."

"No, I didn't mean that. Good Lord. Like when someone has crossed over where the rest of them haven't been. Getting pregnant, or dying, or that boy in the band who shot himself. Remember that? You think, 'Why, I saw him in the hallway, often. And sat behind him in algebra. But I never *knew*, and now he has gone and done it.' That's what they sound like."

"Ah," said Evie.

At suppertime, Evie and her father sat opposite each other at the tiny kitchen table. Clotelia would have set out the food and left by then, slamming the front door behind her and clicking away down the sidewalk. She rarely said goodbye. The silence she left behind seemed an angry one, as if she had said, "*Now*, you've done it. See? I'm leaving. I've had all I can take." The two of them looked guilty and awkward as they sat poking their baked beans. "*Well*, now," her father would say finally. "Tell me what you've done with yourself today. Talked to anyone? Been out much?" But all Evie ever answered was, "I didn't see anyone. I didn't go anywhere."

"Violet come over?"

"Yes."

"How was she?"

"Oh, fine."

His impatience was controlled, showing up only in the way he fidgeted with a fork or drank water in deep, hasty gulps. He did no reading at the table nowadays. He concentrated solely on Evie, as if he had made some sort of resolution. When Evie tried to keep on reading herself, she felt his eyes on her and his premeditated smile, burdening her mind until she had to give up and shove the magazine aside. "All right," she would tell him.

"What?"

"Was there something you wanted to say?"

"Why, no. Not that I can think of."

They finished the meal without speaking, every clink of fork against plate sounding as loud and as artificial as a sound effect. Food she didn't enjoy, Evie thought, was not fattening. She waded through her mound of baked beans and frankfurters, lukewarm rings of canned pineapple and instant mashed potates, and everything sank heavily to her stomach and left her feeling uncomfortable but virtuous. When her father brought sherbet glasses full of Jello from the refrigerator, she ate every last mouthful and set her spoon down neatly beside her knife. Then they were free. They could go off to opposite ends of the house and do whatever kept them busy.

She no longer listened to the radio. She lay on her bed filing her fingernails or leafing through more magazines, and sometimes she fell into daydreams that involved one-sided, whispered conversations. "Aren't you Drum Casey? I thought you were. I heard you sing once, years ago. Yes, I'm Evie Decker. I was fat back then, I didn't think you would recognize me." She would toss her hair back, exposing a smooth white forehead. But not surgically smooth. She pictured the effects of plastic surgery as being just that, plastic, a white poreless rectangle like a blank label surrounded on four sides by a thin border of scar tissue. In her daydream, the smoothness was natural and the ragged letters spelling "Casey" would have been only a joke, something she had written in red ink as a prank or, better yet, just something Casey had made up. "Letters, you say? I never cut letters. Where did you get *that* idea? Do you think I go around cutting strange names in my face?"

But she always ended up feeling hopeless and betrayed. Rising to fetch a Kleenex or an emery board, she would catch sight of her reflection whispering in the bureau mirror and she would clamp her lips shut and lie down again. Then by nine o'clock she would have started trying to sleep. All her muscles lay coiled from a day of sitting. She turned from one side to another, tightening her sheet over and over in order to erase the untidy feeling that followed her even to bed.

On Tuesday morning, ten days after she had returned from the hospital, her father said, "Evie, honey, I'd like to talk to you."

"Hmm?" said Evie. She was already in her easy chair, a bag of marshmallows beside her.

"I was wondering about school. Don't you feel like going back now?"

"Oh. Well, no, I don't," Evie said. She looked up at her father, who stood rocking gently above her. The morning sunlight bleached the tips of his lashes. "I'm not really up to it yet," she told him.

"Up to it? What do you mean?"

"Well, I believe I have a low-grade virus. I would go back otherwise, but I think I should stay out till I'm well. My head aches."

"But if that's all—"

"And my stomach's upset. My joints are stiff."

"Evie, honey, the school has made quite a few allowances for you. With finals so near—"

"Well, maybe tomorrow," Evie said.

"Do you mean that?"

"Sure."

But when he went he paused at the door for a moment, jingling his keys, and the silence behind him left Evie with a suspended feeling.

She sat very still for a long time, staring into space with her hands in her lap. A clock struck. A lawnmower started up. Clotelia banged the front door and went straight to the kitchen to make coffee, showing Evie nothing but the back of a swirling cape. "Clotelia!" Evie called.

Clotelia didn't answer.

"*Clotelia!*"

But there was only the rattling of cutlery.

Evie waited a minute longer, and then she heaved herself out of her chair and went over to the hall telephone. Dust outlined the directory beside it. She thumbed through the pages until she came to the listings for Farinia: a page and a half of names, mostly Frazells. There were three people named Casey. The first was Asquith, which didn't sound likely. Then there was a B.L., and after that an Obed E. If his father's name were B. for Bertram, wouldn't Drum have to be called Bertram junior? She dialed the number anyway. A woman answered, out of breath. "Hello," said Evie. "May I speak to Drum?"

"Who?"

"Drumstrings."

There was a silence.

"Bertram?" Evie said.

"Who?"

"Well, I must have the wrong number."

"I reckon you must."

The woman hung up. Evie pressed the dial tone and then called Obed E., where another woman answered. "Yes, hello."

"I'd like to speak to Drum, please," Evie said.

"To—Oh." The receiver at the other end clattered against something, and the woman called, "Bertram? Phone." Evie stood hunched over the hall table, clutching folds of bathrobe to her stomach.

"Hello," Drum Casey said.

"This is Evie Decker."

"Huh?"

"I carved your name on my forehead."

"*Oh*, yes," said Drum. He seemed to be eating something; he chewed and swallowed.

"I was wondering if I could see you for a minute."

"Oh," Drum said. "Well. . . ."

"It'll only take a second. There's something I wanted to discuss with you."

"What's that?"

"I'll have to tell you when I see you. Will you come over?"

"I'm in Farinia," said Drum.

"I know you are. Don't you have a car?"

"Look. What do you think, my wire is tapped? Just tell me on the phone, why don't you."

"It would be to your advantage," Evie said. Her speech

seemed to be turning formal. To make up for it she said, "No skin off *my* neck."

"Well, wait a minute," said Drum. She heard him farther off, calling "Mom?" It stunned her to think of Drum Casey as someone's son, part of a family, possessing even an age which she had never thought to wonder about. When he came back he said, "Okay. Where you at?"

"I'm at home."

"Where's *that?*"

"Fourteen-twenty Hawthorne."

"Now, you sure you can't say this over the phone."

"I'm positive," said Evie.

When she hung up she found Clotelia right behind her, holding a cup of coffee and shaking her head. "*Oh,* Evie," she said. "What call you got to act so ignorant?"

Evie turned and went upstairs without answering.

Nothing was fit to wear. She didn't have a single dress she could stand, and she went through her closet flailing at skirts and jingling hangers. Finally she settled on a red taffeta party dress. Its hem was far too long for this year or even last year, but at least it was red. She slipped it over her head and tugged until the buttons met the buttonholes. Then she put on her vinyl sandals. In the bathroom, she bent over the sink to wash her hair with a bar of Ivory. It was lucky she had not cut bangs. Her hair lay plastered to her skull in dark wet lines from an almost central part, and coiled into snaky circles at her jaws. Freckles that were usually invisible stood out clearly on her pale skin, more dots of red echoing the dots above. She smiled in the mirror, exposing large square teeth. She frowned and turned away.

While she waited on the front porch, clutching her books to her chest, disapproval hung like a fog up and down her street. A lady in a gardening hat clipped her hedge, throwing Evie sharp, sidelong looks with every snick of her shears. Blank-faced houses watched her sternly. Behind her, in her own house, Clotelia slammed doors and shoved furniture and muttered to herself, although Evie couldn't hear what it was she said. Once she came to stand behind the screen with a crane-necked watering pitcher in her hand. "I've a good mind to call your daddy," she told Evie.

"What would you tell him?"

"You know he don't want you seeing that trash."

"I'm not doing anything wrong," said Evie. She straightened, throwing a sudden smile at the gardening lady. Her father had banned Drum Casey as if Drum were storming the front hedge, bearing flowers and a ladder, begging to be let in. She could almost pretend that her father knew something she didn't. But when finally Drum drove up, in a battered black Dodge with upside-down license plates, all he did was lean out his window and give her a long, unsmiling stare. Evie hugged her books tighter and started toward him.

"You going somewhere?" he asked.

"I have to get to school. I thought you could drive me there while we were talking."

"Funny time to go to school."

"I know. I'm late."

She opened the car door and climbed in beside him. The car had a hot, syrupy smell in the morning sunlight. Instead of the black denim that he sang in, Drum Casey wore blue jeans and a T shirt with sleeves rolled up past his biceps.

The soft colors gave him a gentler, faded look. He was leaning on the steering wheel, the shock of hair falling forward over his face. He slid his eyes past her forehead without ever quite looking at it. "I ain't got much time," he said.

Evie only smiled. "I thought you might have a motorcycle," she told him.

"Me, a bike?"

"A motorcycle."

"Naw, they're too dangerous."

"Oh, I see," said Evie. She watched Drum set the car into motion, steering easily with his forearms resting on the wheel. He wore a wristwatch with a silver expansion band, which gave her a smaller version of the shock she had felt when she heard him call his mother. Did he wind his watch every morning, check its accuracy, try to be places on time like ordinary people? "How old are you?" she asked him.

"Nineteen."

"I'm seventeen."

Drum said nothing.

"If you're nineteen," said Evie, "do you go to school?"

"No."

"What, then."

"I don't do much of nothing."

"Oh."

The car turned onto Main Street. They passed a clutter of small shops and cafés, the bowling alley and the Christian Science Reading Room. Evie pressed tight against the window, but there was nobody to see her.

"What was it you wanted to tell me?" Drum asked.

"Well, I had an idea this morning."

"Is this where I turn?"

"No, one block farther."

"Only been here once before, but I'm good at directions."

"We got written up in the paper. Did you see it?" Evie asked.

"Yeah, I saw it. Just a picture, though."

"Well, it's better than nothing."

"Sure."

"Somebody sent me a copy in the mail." She rummaged through her notebook until she had found it: a plastic-sealed photograph of her in her hospital room, rising from a wave of strung-out sheets, and Drum scowling beside her. Taped to the plastic was a printed message. "Congratulations on your recent achievement. And when it's the *tops* in achievement you want, just think of Sonny Martin, Pulqua County's Biggest Real Estate Agent." "This rightly belongs to you," Evie said. "Here. Keep it." Drum took his eyes from the road a minute to glance at it, and then he nodded and put it into his back pocket.

"Thanks," he said.

"It's good publicity."

"Sure, I reckon."

"How do you usually get publicity?" she asked him.

Drum gave a sudden short laugh, as if it had been startled out of him. "Well, not *that* way," he said.

"Do you put in ads?"

"I got a manager."

"Oh. I thought only fighters had managers."

"Well, no," said Drum. "Well, them too, of course." He had drawn up before the school by now but sat frowning, tapping one finger on the wheel, as if he were no longer sure that a manager was what he had. "Of course, he's only my drummer," he said finally.

"Does he put in ads?"

"Sometimes. Or talks around, mostly. Goes to see people."

"Wouldn't he like it if you got more publicity?"

"What you getting at?"

"I was thinking if I started coming to all your shows, where people could see me. Wearing my hair off my face. Wouldn't it cause talk? They'd say, 'You see what she did for him. There must be something to him, then.' Wouldn't they?"

"Oh, I reckon," said Drum. "Until you got healed up."

"Healed up? What are you talking about? *I'm* not going to get healed up."

He didn't react the way she had expected. He stopped tapping his fingers and slumped back in his seat, staring at the windshield. After a minute he said, "*What?*"

"I thought you knew."

"Are you going to have, um—"

"Scars," said Evie.

A line of girls in gym shorts crossed the playing field, followed by Drum's darkened eyes. "Jesus," he said.

"Well, it's done now. Wouldn't you like to have me sitting there while you played? People would say, 'We better go hear Drum Casey, there's this girl who cut—' "

"Are you out of your head?"

"Why? What's so crazy about that?"

"For you, maybe nothing," said Drum. "But I ain't going to sing under those conditions."

"What conditions?"

"How do you think I would feel?"

"Well, I don't see—"

"Go on, now," said Drum. "Get out. I'm real sorry about what happened, but I got my own life to live."

"Nobody said you didn't."

"Will you *go?*"

"You can live your own life all you want," said Evie, but she could feel her words fading away from her. Drum had reached across her to open the car door. His arm was covered with fine brown hairs, dotted with the faintest sheen of sweat, and for one motionless second she stared down and mourned it, just that isolated arm which she had only now started to know. Then she said, "All right. If that's the way you feel." She stumbled out onto the sidewalk, clutching at slipping books and smoothing the back of her rumpled skirt. Her face felt heavy, as if some weight at her jawline were pulling all her features downward.

Yet when she started up the front steps of the school, two girls in gym shorts were staring past her at the disappearing Dodge. They looked at her, then at the Dodge again. Evie smiled at them and went inside. If two people saw, the whole school would know by noon. They would pass it from desk to desk and down the lunchline: "That girl who slashed the singer's name in her face, well, now she's hanging out with him. He drove her to school. Sat a long time in the car with her. What were they doing in the car?"

She smiled at a boy she didn't know and set her books down in front of her locker. If the boy stared at her forehead, she didn't notice. The letters stood out clear and proud, framed by damp hair, finer than any plastic rectangle a surgeon could have pasted there.

6

Drum Casey's drummer's name was David Elliott. Some people had tried calling him "Guitar" for a joke, just rounding things off, but David was the kind who slid out from under nicknames. He was not light-minded enough. He played the drums intently, watching his hands, sitting very straight instead of hunkering over the way other drummers did. This made him seem childlike, although he was a good six feet tall. He had white-blond hair that fell in an even line, hiding his eyebrows. His face was fine-boned and his eyes transparent, the color of old blue Mason jars. Yet girls never took to him. They liked his looks but not his seriousness. He spoke too definitely; there was a constant, edgy impatience in the way he moved, and he planned ahead too much. "We're good. We're going good," he told girls. "I want to hit a night club next. We're getting up there. We're ready to move." Drum, beside him, was slow and cool and dark. He made plans too; but while David talked about up, Drum talked about out. "When we get out of this place, I want me a custom car. Going to go so far I'll lose the way home, forget the name of the town, mislay the map. Also new singing clothes; I want me something shiny." Girls understood what he meant. They fluttered after him when he drifted off, and David stayed behind to think up more publicity.

David solicited clubs and roadhouses and church organizations. During the day he sold insurance policies door to door, but he never forgot to work the conversation around to music. "Spring is here. Are you going to have a dance? Do you know of any dances? You'll need a band, records aren't the same. What about Mrs. Howard, the one in the house on the hill? She gives a dance every May. Won't she need a band? Ask her. It's cheaper to hire the two of us; those big groups can get out of hand." He believed in gimmicks, little eye-catching traps for people to fall into while they were making up their minds. Bright red cards with gilt lettering on them—"Drumstrings with guitar, David with the sticks, 839-3036"—were thumbtacked to every bulletin board. David's Jeep was painted with psychedelic swirls and a purple telephone number. In December, he had sent Christmas cards picturing an orchestra of angels to every leading businessman in Pulqua, Farinia, and Tar City. He instructed Drum to carry his guitar slung over his shoulder at all times, but Drum didn't. ("In the *pharmacy?*" Drum said. "At the liquor store? You're putting me on.") And when Evie Decker slashed "Casey" across her forehead, it was David who called the newspaper photographer. "This is why you need a manager," he told Drum. "Would you have thought of it by yourself? You haven't got the eye for it."

"You're right, I ain't," said Drum. "I got to hand it to you."

Drum got along well with David, better than other people did. He liked riding on the tail of all that energy, letting someone else do the organizing, listening to the rapid, precise flow of talk which he thought came from David's having spent half a semester at Campbell College. But it was only words that should be so precise, not drums. David's drums never skipped a beat, and yet somehow the spirit was missing. Other drummers went into frenzies; David remained tight, expressionless, speeding faster and faster without so much as bending forward. "You drag," said Drum. "Oh, I feel it."

"I don't drag. I'm there all the way."

"Well, but you're holding me back somehow. Tying me in. *I* don't know."

"Get another drummer, if you feel like that."

But he never did. Together they went over each new piece, juggling lines and bickering and giving little wheezes of disgust at each other. When it came to music, Drum always won. He had the feel for it. "What's this talking out in the middle of a piece?" David once asked. "Where does that get you? Most of what you say is not even connected."

"I ain't going to argue about that," said Drum. "I just do it. If you have to ask why, you shouldn't be here."

"Oh, all right. I don't care."

He had the sense not to go against Drum on things like that. He believed that Drum was a real musician, someone who deserved to climb straight to the top. When an audience talked instead of listening, David muttered curses at them all the while he played. When Drum hit one of his low moods, David followed him around rescuing scraps of songs from wastebaskets. "What call have you got to slump around like this? What you throw away those other cats would give their teeth to write. You're nearly there. You've almost made it."

"You reckon so? I don't know. Maybe you're right," Drum would say finally.

David paid a visit to Evie Decker on a Saturday afternoon during finals. She was on her front porch studying. She lay in a wooden swing with her head on a flattened, flowered cushion, one foot trailing to the floor to keep her rocking. When she heard the Jeep, she turned and blinked. Swirls of color chased around its body and across the canvas top, where they blurred and softened. And there came Drum Casey's drummer out of the little tacked-on door, smoothing down his bangs with his fingers. "The Missouri Compromise," Evie went on out loud, "was supposed to maintain a . . ." but her eyes were on David. She watched him cross her yard and climb her steps, rifle-straight and full of purpose. Because of the edgeless shimmer of his hair in the sunlight, he seemed only another daydream, nothing to get nervous about. "Afternoon," he said.

"Afternoon," said Evie. She sat up, laying a finger in her history book to mark the place.

"You Evie Decker?"

But he would have known, having seen her forehead by now. She didn't answer.

"I'm David Elliott. I play with Drum Casey."

"I know, I recognized you," said Evie. She waited for him to go on, but he seemed to be getting his bearings. He gazed around at the dim white house, at the lawn twinkling beneath a sprinkler, and finally at Evie herself, who wore a billowing muu-muu and no shoes. Then he said, "Mind if I talk with you a moment?"

"All right."

He sat on the top porch step, with his forearms resting on his knees. Now that he was in the shade he had lost his shimmer. He was made of solid flesh, damp from the heat. Evie began swinging back and forth very rapidly.

"I'm also his manager," said David.

"Yes, I know."

"I do his publicity, line up parties and things. I think we got a good sound going." He flashed her a look. "*Drum* has."

Evie stopped swinging.

"Drum has really got it," he told her. Why was he watching her feet? She curled her toes under. "Don't you think so?" he asked.

"Well, yes," said Evie. "You know I do." She brushed a loose piece of hair off her forehead. David peered at the scars and then lowered his eyes—something that usually made her angry. "What was it that you wanted to talk about?" she asked him.

"Oh. Well, you spoke to Drum the other day about a plan you had. Plan for publicity."

"Tuesday," said Evie.

"Was that right, you had a plan?"

"I thought if I went to his shows, and sat up front. *You* know. People would say, 'This boy has got to be good, look at what she did because of him.' Only your friend said—"

"It's not a bad idea," said David.

"Your friend said no."

"Ah, *he* don't know. That's why he has me."

"He said he couldn't sing under those conditions."

"'What does he know?"

"He knows if he can sing or not," Evie said.

"Look. Do you want to try it? Just once, just tonight. If people take notice, you can stay. If not, you go. All right?"

"What, try just sitting there?"

"That's right. Tonight. I'll give you a lift, pick you up at eight. Three dollars and beer. Only don't drink a lot, you hear? It wouldn't look good."

"I never have but one beer anyway."

"Though on second thought, nothing wrong if you *did* drink a lot. It wouldn't hurt anything."

"I never have but one," Evie said.

"Oh, well."

He stood up and Evie stood with him, clutching her book. "Wait," she said.

"What is it?"

"Well, I don't know. I haven't thought it out yet, really—"

He paused, not arguing, just waiting. "About your friend," she said. "Drum, I mean. Well, I hate to go against him this way. Riding right over what he said to me. What will he do? Did he say anything about you coming here?"

"He didn't know about it," David said.

"Oh," said Evie.

"He leaves this kind of thing to me," David told her.

He looked up suddenly, straight into her eyes. "You can't ever listen to *him*. Then where would he be? Playing in a room to himself, wasting all that music alone. I hate to see things wasted."

It seemed more settled then. Evie nodded and let him go.

At eight o'clock that night Evie came down the front steps in a skirt and blouse, her vinyl sandals, and a blue plastic headband that kept her hair off her face. The Jeep was already parked outside. In the back seat, behind David, Drum Casey sprawled out with both feet up and his guitar in the crook of his arm. It hadn't occurred to Evie that he might be there. She froze on the sidewalk, gripping her purse. Then David said, "Nope. It's not what I was thinking of."

"What?" she said.

"You need something black. Dressy."

"No one dresses up at the Unicorn."

"*You* do. You want to stand out. We'll wait."

"What? You want me to change *now*? I can't do that, my father will start wondering. He thinks I'm at a friend's."

"We'll wait around the block then."

"Oh, for Christ's sake," said Drum. David shooed him away with one hand.

"You leave this to me," he said. "I've got it all clear in my mind. We'll be over there, Evie."

Evie ran back to her room. She changed in a rush, mislaying things that had been right at her fingertips and tearing stockings, jamming zippers, tripping over cast-off clothing. If she took one minute too long, she felt, the Jeep would vanish. It would drift off like a tiny, weightless boat, piloted by careless people with short memories. She put on a scoop-necked black blouse and a black skirt. Then she picked up a pair of pumps and ran down the stairs in stocking feet. "Back in a while, Daddy," she called. Her father didn't answer. He might not even have heard.

The Jeep waited around the corner. Drum was plucking one guitar string over and over. He didn't stop when she climbed into the front seat, but David looked her over carefully and said, "That's right. Much better."

"Is this what I should wear all the time?"

"All the *time?*" said Drum. "How often you figure on doing this?"

Evie looked at David, who was backing the car up. He didn't answer. Finally she turned toward the back seat, and without actually meeting Drum's eyes she said, "If it works out, I'm coming every week."

"Ah, David," Drum said. "You've went too far this time."

"Will you leave it to me?" said David.

"You've went too far, man."

They drove the rest of the way without speaking. David frowned at the road, making some sort of calculations, shaking his head from time to time and then brightening as if an idea had struck. In the back, Drum kept plucking at the guitar string. Whenever the Jeep slowed, Evie could hear the single note repeating itself tinnily in the twilight.

They pulled in beside a motorcycle in the Unicorn's parking lot. Not many other cars had arrived yet. After he had shut the motor off, David said, "Now, listen. You'll sit at a table for one, right up front. I've brought you a candle. It'll stand out. While the other guy's on, Joseph Ballew, read a newspaper."

"By candle?"

"Oh, shoot now," Drum said. "Joseph Ballew is a friend of mine. She can't do that."

"Oh, all right. Stare down at your beer, then. What I want is a difference, you follow me? A difference that people will notice when Drum comes on. Sit up. Look close. I was thinking of some other things, but there hasn't been time to work them out. Sending him flowers, for instance."

"I would send them back," said Drum.

"I figured you would."

"Another thing," said Drum. "I want you both to listen good, now. I am not for any part of this plan. I don't approve, I never will approve. It makes me sick. And on top of that it won't work, because while I am playing, my entire audience will be whispering and pointing at a fat girl with a name on her forehead. I just thought you should know that."

Evie said, "Oh, well, I don't want to—"

"Got you," David told Drum. "Then I had thought of having her scream, maybe, but I guess not. She's not the type for it."

He looked at Evie for a minute longer, and then shook his head and climbed out of the Jeep. Evie had to trail behind them all the way across the parking lot.

The policeman at the door recognized her. He nodded at her and then rested his hands awkwardly on his gunbelt and stared into the distance. The proprietor recognized her too. When she walked in, he stepped out from behind the bar, smoothing his apron and looking worried. "You're the girl that, uh. Look, I hope you're not planning to pull something like that again. I had an awful time. Cops were down my neck all night, thinking there had been a cutting."

"There had been," David said.

"Not *that* kind."

"Well, never mind. She's here to watch Drum sing, that's all. Have you got a table for one?"

"You know I ain't. People like sitting in groups."

"Give me a bar stool then, we'll use that."

He dragged the stool up next to the dance platform, and set a chair beside it. It was the right height for a table but much too small, which David said was all for the better. "Ruin everything if someone came and sat with you," he said. From a brown paper bag he took a tablecloth and a net-covered vase with a candle in it, the kind used in restaurants. Meanwhile Evie stood by awkwardly with her hands across her purse. Drum had disappeared somewhere. From a door behind the dance platform she heard laughter and the twanging of guitars.

"Sit down," said David.

She sat.

"No, not like that. Straighter. And don't put your purse on the table. I want you half-turned from the audience, not quite sideways, so that they can get a glimpse of—"

"I know how," Evie said. "Leave it to me. I can figure it out for myself."

And she did. She sat erect, her hands folded in her lap, an untouched beer in front of her. The candle glimmered more brightly on her face as the room grew darker. People filing in called out greetings to the proprietor, joked with their dates and scraped paths for themselves between the chairs, but when they saw the candle their voices seemed to skip a beat. They glanced at the candle and then at Evie. Evie stared straight ahead at nothing at all.

Drum Casey was the first to play that night. When he came onto the platform Evie looked up; nothing more. David signaled to her silently all through the first piece: "Do something. Move around. Could you stand? Take a drink." Evie ignored him. "*My girl has done and boarded a Carolina Trailways,*" Drum sang, "*She's scared to death of planes and she can't stand railways,*" and Evie stared at his face without blinking. Out of all the chattering couples dancing or at least beating time, Evie was the only one motionless. She showed them the white mound of her back disappearing into a scoop of black cotton, the curve of one cheek turned rigidly away. Her dowdy clothes gave her a matronly look; her scars, what could be seen of them, seemed in the candlelight to be mainly vertical, a new kind of age-line or tear track which made her appear experienced and incapable of being surprised. "See that girl?" someone whispered. "I believe it's the one in the newspaper. No, wait till she turns. Remember when I showed you her picture?" They were careful not to point. Girls indicated her by no more than a glance. "That's her. No, don't look now." In the back of the room, a boy half stood to peer at her before Fay-Jean Lindsay pulled him sharply down.

"*Will you see me to the door?*" Casey asked.

"*Don't come no further.*

"*Don't mind the lights.*

"When you going to leave off that hammering?
"When they going to let me be?"

Evie looked down at the table. David had stopped signaling to her by now. His eyes skimmed the roomful of people, who stared from Evie to Drum as if following a dotted line. Then he nodded to himself and turned all his attention to the song.

7

She was hired for life, David said, meaning for as long as she could cause any kind of stir, make a ripple cross a room and bounce off the wall to cross back. But how long would that be? She had felt, the first night, a buzz and a whispering at the back of her neck. On the following Saturday it was quieter. "Maybe I shouldn't be riding with you," she told David, although she would have fought against giving the rides up. "Won't it look funny? You and Drum bringing me here just to sit admiring you?"

"*They* don't care," said David. "It's like watching a magician. They would like to believe his cards really come from thin air."

David had other plans in mind. Now that Evie's had worked he had grown jittery, impatient to improve on it. He was nervous about the sheer understatement of a single dumpy girl sitting there with a beer. Shouldn't she drink too much? Cry? Send notes? But Evie said no. She walked a narrow line; it was all right to take money for lifting a scarred face toward a rock player every Saturday night but only if what she did was real, without a single piece of play-acting. Her sitting still was real, and so was pinning her eyes on Drum. So were her scars, which turned white in time, raised and shiny, gleaming clean even if the rest of her face became smudged in the heat. "How about a new costume?" David asked. "Blacker and shinier. With a rhinestone necklace." "*No*," said Evie. It was as clear a no as Drum's when he refused to stop his speaking out. David never brought the subject up again.

She offered to come to the Unicorn free. It wasn't as if she needed the money. David said, "Fine," but Drum, when he heard about it, said, "What is she trying to do to me? She gets paid. Then she can burn it, for all I care. But she gets paid, anyhow."

"Sometimes I feel like I am dealing with porcupines," David said.

School had ended. Evie spent the last few weeks of it feeling blurred and out of focus, with classmates looking carefully to the right and left of her and speaking to the middle button on her blouse. Even Fay-Jean Lindsay seemed to have trouble finding things to say to her. On the final day, they autographed annuals out on the school lawn. They had overlooked Evie other years—reaching across her to pass their annuals to someone else, sending her home with only a few scattered signatures in her own. But this year, everyone wanted her autograph. They shoved their books at her silently, with lowered eyes. "Best wishes, Evie Decker," she wrote. She felt awkward about trying the clever rhymes that other people used. Then, after signing for the twentieth or thirtieth time, she began marking the forehead of her photograph with YƎƧAƆ and nothing more. When the bell rang, she cleared out her locker and left the building without a backward glance.

"What do you do with yourself these days?" her father asked.

"Nothing much."

"Are you bored? Have you got a lot of time on your hands?"

"Oh, no."

Time hung in huge, blank sheets, split by Saturday nights. She spent her days bickering with Clotelia or carrying on listless, circular conversations with Violet. In the evenings she sat at her window slapping mosquitoes, gazing into darkness so heavy and still that it seemed something was about to happen, but nothing ever did. She awoke in the mornings feeling faded, with clammy bedclothes twisted around her legs.

On Saturday nights she took hours to dress. Her hair would be limp from constant re-arranging, her black skirt and blouse shiny at the seams from too much ironing. She held up and threw down endless pieces of costume jewelry. She brushed her black suede pumps until little rubbed spots appeared. "Oh," her father would say, meeting her on the stairs. "Are you going out?"

"Just to Violet's."

"Have a nice time."

Why hadn't anyone told him where she went? He continued up the stairs, pulling keys and loose change and postage stamps from his pockets and stepping over the turned-up place in the carpet without even seeming to notice it.

She waited on the corner for the Jeep. Her arms were folded across her chest, as if, in this heat, she were cold. Sometimes her teeth chattered. What held her mind was not the time spent in the Unicorn but the rides there and back, the two half-hour periods in the Jeep. She thought of them as a gift. Someone might have said, "Do you want Drum Casey? Here is a half hour. Here is another. See what you can do." For while she was at the Unicorn, she never exchanged a word with Drum. He was either performing or off in the back room. Bearing that in mind, she talked non-stop all the way over and all the way back. She went against her own nature, even. She shoved down all her reserve and from her place in the front seat she drilled him with words.

"Can you read music? Do you believe in drugs? What was it got you started playing?"

"Course I read music, what do you think I am," said Drum, following a passing car with his eyes. "Marijuana gives me headaches. I won a talent show, that's how I started."

Oh, questions were the only way to grab his attention. She had tried, at first, declarative sentences: laying her life before him neatly and in chronological order, setting out minute facts about herself as if it were important he should know. Drum seemed not to hear. But she had only to say, "Is *all* your family musical?" for him to wade up from his silence and start framing an answer. "None of them's musical, they just admire it a whole lot. My mama said she would give every cent she had into seeing me be a singer."

"Doesn't she come to hear you play?"

"At the rock show she did. All my family did."

"Did I see them? What do they look like?"

"Nothing extra. Just a parcel of brothers and her and him."

"Him? Oh, your father. What does your father do?"

"What have you got up there," Drum said, "a questionnaire?" David, taking him literally for a second, glanced sideways into Evie's lap. But then Drum said, "He works in a filling station. I help him out some."

"I bet he's proud of you. Isn't he?"

"Oh, well."

"He would have to be," said Evie. "Anybody that plays like you, his family must just *die* of pride."

His eyes would flick over to her, as sudden and as startling as the appearance of someone in a vacant window. If she spoke about his music he would listen all day, but what would he answer?

"Oh, well. I don't know."

She entered the Unicorn alone and went to her table, keeping her head erect, holding her stomach in. Eyes lit on her back. Whispers flitted across tables. "Oh, it's you," the proprietor said. "Budweiser?"

"Yes, please, Zack. Have you got a match for my candle?"

She thought of herself as a bait-and-switch ad. People came out of curiosity, bored by the long summer days. They figured they might as well go stare at the girl who had ruined her face. But after two minutes of that, there was nothing left to do but concentrate on the singer who had caused it all. Even Drum had to see that. People who returned came for the music alone; Evie was only a fixed character to be pointed out knowingly to new customers. "*Will you be waiting?*" Drum called. "Where *will you be waiting?*" Customers who were used to his speaking out began answering. "Yeah, man! Here!" A reviewer commented on him in the *Avalice and Farinia Weekly*. "Rock music of his own making, leaning toward a country sound, original at first although he tends to get repetitious." Evie was not mentioned, any more than the color of his clothes or the brand of his guitar.

Evie always had to hang around for awhile before the ride back. The wait was nerve-wracking. It sometimes stretched on till after one o'clock in the morning, while at home her father might be telephoning Violet at any moment. She watched the customers gather their belongings and leave. The proprietor washed his glass mugs. The dance platform was dark and empty, and all she heard of Drum was fits of music in the back room. "David," she would say, catching his sleeve as he hurried by, "are we going now? What's taking so long?"

"Be just a moment," David always said. But he would be carrying in a new pitcher of beer and a fistful of mugs. Eventually Evie gave up. She tucked her purse under her arm and left, sidling between vacant chairs and crossing the dim-lit, hollow-sounding floor to the door. Outside, the darkness would be cool and transparent. She took several deep breaths before she curled up in the back seat of the Jeep.

The slick surface of Drum's guitar would jog her awake. "Move over," he would say. "Here we are."

"What time is it?"

"I don't know."

Until she looked at her watch she always had a lost, sinking feeling. Her sleep had been troubled and filled with muddled dreams; it might have lasted for minutes or for hours. Had her father called the police yet? She pressed forward in her seat, as if that would help them get home faster. Every pickup truck dawdling in front of them made her angry. Then she remembered Drum. On the rides home he sat beside her, with only the guitar between them. "Did you think it went well?" she asked him.

"Mmm."

"They liked the Carolina Trailways song."

No answer. David took over for him. "I thought so too. Why always that one? The walking song is a hell of a lot harder to do."

He was kind-hearted, David was. Or maybe he just wanted to keep Evie's good will. During Drum's silences he picked up the tail of the conversation and moved smoothly on with it, rescuing her. For a while they would shoot sentences back and forth—"Oh, well, the walking song takes getting used to." "Not if they had *ears* it wouldn't"—but there was always the consciousness of Drum's silence, which they played to like actors on a stage. Questions, that was the only way. Questions.

"What is your favorite song, Drum? Drum?"

"Oh, I don't know."

"Don't you have a favorite?"

"Not for all time I don't. The one about the blue jeans, maybe."

"Why don't you have regular titles?"

"Never had no need for them."

"You will when you make a record," Evie said.

His eyes flicked over to her again; she felt them in the dark. She moved his guitar slightly so as to speak straight at him. "Someone is going to make a record of you that will sell a million copies," she told him. "What will they put on that little center label? You've got to think up some titles."

"She's right," David said.

"What's so hard about that?" said Drum. "I'll name them what I call them—'The Walking Song,' 'The Blue Jeans Song,' nothing to it. Wait till they ask me, first."

"You think they won't ask you?"

"They haven't yet, have they? I been sitting in that dump for seven months now. Haven't got nowhere."

"You will," Evie said.

"How? When? You seen any talent scouts around?"

After a show he was always like that. She had seen girls clustering around him three deep at the end of a set, paying him compliments and brushing bits of nothing off his shoulder while Evie frowned fiercely into her beer and thought, "Now he'll find out; they'll show him he's too good for Pulqua and the Unicorn and me"—although she had always counted on his becoming famous. But when the girls left he would only seem more uncertain. His proud cold envelope of air temporarily left him. "You sound better than *anyone* I hear on the radio," Evie would tell him, and he would stun her by turning on her suddenly and saying, "You think so? Is that what you think? Ah, but what do *you* know?"

"I know if it sounds good."

"*I* don't know that. How do you know?"

Those were the only times they met face to face. They were the only times Evie lost the feeling that she was tugging at Drum's sleeve while he stood with his back to her, gazing outwards toward something she couldn't see.

Early in July, the Unicorn began hiring Drum for Fridays as well. People were asking for him, the proprietor said. Joseph Ballew was no longer enough. But Fridays Drum worked late in the A & P, bagging groceries. "The only solution," said David, sitting in the Jeep with one of his lists on the steering wheel, "is for me to pick you up first, Evie. Then we'll get Drum at the very last minute. Even then it'll be close. Does that suit you?"

"Of course," Evie said.

"Or you could keep coming just on Saturdays, if you wanted."

"Why? Do you think I'm not working out any more?"

"No, Lord, you're working out fine. But if your father starts worrying, you being gone two evenings and all—"

"No, I'll come," Evie said. Although it did seem that her father might begin to wonder. She frowned down at her skirt, gathering it in folds between her knees, while David made more lists on more scraps of paper.

The next Friday they drove to Farinia to pick up Drum. Evie had been through Farinia often, but without really noticing. She stared out her window now at the town's one paved street, with its double row of unpainted stores covered in rusty soft-drink signs. On a corner next to a shoe repair shop, a service station sat under a tent of flapping pennants, its lights already shining. David drove in and honked his horn.

"You haven't run over the bell thing yet," Evie told him.

"Bell thing? Oh. No, I don't want gas, this is where Drum lives."

"*Here?*"

Then she saw that the service station was an unpainted Victorian house, its bottom story tiled with shiny white squares. Above, lace curtains wavered in narrow windows. "What the hell," David said. "I'll run up and get him."

"Can I come too?"

"If you want."

She followed him across the service area and up a flight of rickety outside steps. The door had a card thumbtacked to it saying "ObeD E. CAseY" in pencil. David knocked. "Who is it?" a woman called.

"It's me, David. I've come for Bertram, tell him."

The door opened. After the rickety steps and the penciled card, Drum's mother was a relief—a plump, cheerful woman in a bibbed apron, smile lines working outward from Drum's brown eyes. "Evening, David," she said. Then she saw Evie, and she raised her fingers to her lips. "Oh, my Lord," she said. "Why, you must be—my Lord. Come in, honey. I hate to say it but I've forgotten what they called you."

"This is Evie Decker, Mrs. Casey," David said.

The name on Evie's face, of course, was Mrs. Casey's own—something Evie hadn't thought of before. But Mrs. Casey didn't seem to mind. She only looked worried; she shepherded Evie to a chair and hovered over her while Evie sat down. "Here, honey, put a cushion at your back. It's much more comfortable. My!" she said, staring openly at Evie's forehead. "I never thought it would be so, so *large!*"

David, still beside the door, shifted his weight uneasily. "Where is Bertram?" he asked. "We're running late."

"Oh, he's just now changing. I'll hurry him along."

She disappeared, looking backward one last time, and David sank down in a flowered armchair. The room was dim but clean, with a line of vinyl plants on the window sill and stiff plastic antimacassars on every piece of furniture. Over the mantel was a picture of a cross with a radiant gilt sunset just behind it. The glass-faced bookcase contained three books and dozens of photographs in white paper folders, which Evie rose to look at more closely. Tow-headed boys scowled out at her, three or four to a picture. One was Drum, his hair turning darker and longer as he grew. In the most recent picture he was posed all alone with his guitar held vertically on one knee. "Would you believe that he was ever blond?" Mrs. Casey said behind her. "Then one day it seemed it all turned black, surprised the life out of me. The others, now, they're turning too. Bertram's daddy says his did the same."

"It's a good picture of him," Evie said.

"Would you like it?"

"Oh, no, I—"

"Go on, take it, we have more. It's the least I can do. Honey, I feel I *owe* you something. 'Bertram,' I said (I never call him Drum), 'that little girl has put your name in the paper and started you on your way. Now don't you forget that,' I said, and sure enough, here they are having him work Fridays too and I just know you had a part in it. Oh, how can you sit up at your little table that way? I heard all about it. 'She is doing you just a magnificent service, Bertram,' I said—"

"I'm sure they'd have started him on Fridays anyway," Evie told her. "He's the best singer I know of."

"Now aren't you sweet? Well, I can't say it myself, of course, being his mother, but deep down I know he has a wonderful career in front of him. He is what I am pinning my hopes on. 'You remember,' I tell him, 'that wherever you go, you are carrying my hopes around with you.' And it's on acount of me that he's not just a filling-station attendant like his daddy. 'Boy's lazy,' his daddy says. 'Nineteen years old,' he says, 'and spinning out his days plucking music, only pumping gas when it suits him.' I tell him I won't stand for that kind of talk. 'You just remember,' I tell him, 'that Bertram is going to be famous one day. He's carrying all my hopes,' I say. There's a spark in Bertram, you know? He gets it from my side. My father played the banjo. Not just being musical but a sort of, *I* don't know—"

Evie nodded, over and over. Agreement welled up inside her like tears, but even saying yes meant breaking into Mrs. Casey's web of words. "There was always something special about him," said Mrs. Casey. "Right from when he was born. I felt it. Would you like to see the album?"

"We got to go, Mom," Drum said. He was standing in the living room doorway, buckling his belt. "Don't wait up for me."

"Oh, why do you rush off like this? Bertram, honey, I

want you to bring Evie back again, you hear? We just get along like a house afire. I hope you will never be so famous you forget the people who did you a good turn."

"A good turn, what's she been telling you? I'm paying her, ain't I?"

"Not to do all that cutting you didn't. Can't *any* money pay for that. Evie, honey, what do the doctors say?"

"I don't know," said Evie.

"Well, you might just inquire. When Bertram leaves this area I expect they could fix you up just like new."

"Mom, for Lord's sake," Drum said.

"Well, she don't want it all her life, now does she?"

"We better be going," David said. He stood up and ran his fingers through his hair. "Nice seeing you, Mrs. Casey."

"Well, hurry back." And at the door, as she handed Evie the picture in its paper folder, she said, "Don't be a stranger, Evie, we'll welcome you just as often as you want to come. Next visit I'll let you see Bertram in the photo album, you hear?"

"Thank you," said Evie. She was surprised to feel David's hand suddenly clasp her elbow as she started down the steps.

She went back often. Drum usually had to be called for on Fridays, and it was Evie who ran up to knock on the door while David waited in the Jeep. "I don't see how you stand that woman," he said.

"Why? I think she's sweet."

"How can you listen to all that talk? And going on about your forehead and all, how can you put up with that?"

"Oh, I don't mind," said Evie.

She thought that David might even like her now, in an absent-minded way. They had had so many long rides together, with the filling of the silence resting on the two of them—Drum being absent or as good as absent, twanging that one guitar string. Once when they were alone David said, "I've been thinking about your forehead. I mean, they're only white now, the letters. Have you ever thought of wearing bangs?"

"Then no one in the Unicorn would see them," Evie said.

"Well, no."

"Don't you want me to come to the Unicorn any more?"

"No, I was thinking about the rest of the time. People must stare at you a lot. Your friends and them."

"I don't have any friends," said Evie.

"Oh."

"Only Violet, and she doesn't stare. And besides, by now I don't notice. I don't even see the letters in the mirror, half the time. Sometimes I wonder: Does *anybody* see them? Or have I just gotten adjusted? Do they come as a shock to strangers still?"

"They do stand out some," David said.

"A lot?"

"Well, I don't know—"

"You can tell me, I don't care. Are they bad?"

"Well, not with bangs they wouldn't be."

"I see," said Evie.

But she still didn't get around to cutting bangs.

. . .

At the end of July a heat wave struck. Crops shriveled, lawn sprinklers ran all day and all night, Clotelia carried a black umbrella to fend off the sun and Violet stopped wearing underwear. "Seems like this summer will just go on forever," people said. But Evie thought of the heat wave as the peak of the season, a dividing point after which summer would slide rapidly downhill toward fall. And how could she go back to school? She had never planned past August. She had cleaned out her locker with the feeling that she was leaving for good, and the thought of going back to the rigid life of winter smothered her.

Lately her rapid-fire questions to Drum had slackened off, grown easygoing. "I suppose you'll be playing at a party tomorrow," she would say, too hot and lazy even to add a question mark. All Drum had to answer was, "Mmm" and lapse into silence again. But the thought of summer's ending came to her one Friday night at the Unicorn. Drum was speaking out: "*Was it you I heard crying?*" "Yes!" someone shouted. But Evie hadn't been listening. She didn't even know what song he was on. Then she was riding home in the Jeep, picking absently at a seam in his guitar. Drum jerked it away from her. His face was turned to the window, only the smooth line of one cheek showing. What had happened to all her spring plans? Things were no different from the very first night.

She changed her tempo. She concentrated on Drum alone, running a race with time, which she pictured as a hot, dark wind. "Why do you speak out in songs? Oh, you're going to say you don't know, but you could tell me what started it. Was it by accident? Did you just want to give a friend a message or something?"

"I forget," Drum said.

"Think. When was the first time you did it?"

"Oh, well, the picnic song, I reckon. That's right. It was too short. I tossed in extra lines, speaking out, like, just the pictures in my mind. Then a girl told me it was a good gimmick."

"What girl? Do I know her?"

"That's none of your business."

"Nothing you speak out is connected," Evie said. "How can so many pictures come to your mind at once?"

"I don't know."

She noticed that people in the Unicorn had stopped staring at her. No one whispered about her; no one stood up to get a better look. They craned their necks around her in order to see the musicians. Sooner or later David would notice too. She dreaded his firing her. As if she could change anything by beating him to the draw, she came right out with the news herself one evening when they were alone. "People are not whispering when I walk in nowadays," she told him.

"I saw."

"Does that mean I should stop coming?"

"Well, let me see what Drum says."

She knew what Drum would say.

The next Friday night when David picked her up, she told him the entire plot of a movie without giving him time for a single word. When the plot was finished she analyzed it, and when that was finished she told him Clotelia's life story. By then they had picked up Drum and arrived at the Unicorn. Neither Drum nor David had had a chance to say she was fired. It will be afterwards, she thought, when we are riding home. All during the show she sat memorizing the cold smell of beer, the texture of her netted candle-vase and the sight of Drum Casey tossing his hair above her as he sang. After that night it would all be lost, a summer wasted.

But on the ride home they had other things to talk about. "You hear the news?" Drum asked her. Evie only stared. Drum never began conversations.

"We're going to a night club in Tar City. A man came looking for me, all the way to the Unicorn, hired me for a two-week run. I thought it would *never* happen."

"This is the beginning, now," David said. "Didn't I tell you? A genuine night club where they serve set-ups. From here on out we'll be heading straight up."

"But what about the Unicorn?" Evie asked.

"Oh, we'll take two weeks off. It's all set."

"And may not be back," said Drum. "I tell you, after this I'm going to buy me some new singing clothes. Spangly."

"Well, congratulations," said Evie, but no one heard her. They were discussing lights and money and transportation.

When they reached Farinia, Drum said, "Let's wake Mom and tell her the news. Tell her we want a celebration." He might have been speaking only to David; Evie wasn't sure. The two of them bounded across the darkened service area while Evie followed at a distance, hanging back a little and looking around her and stopping to search in her pocketbook for nothing at all.

Mrs. Casey wore a pink chenille bathrobe, and her hair was set in spindly metal curlers all over her head. When she opened the door her hand flew to the curlers. "Bertram, my land, I thought you was alone," she said.

"Now, Mom, did you wait up again?" Drum circled her with one arm, nearly pulling her off her feet. "Listen, Mom. We want us a celebration. A man came and hired us to play two weeks at the Parisian."

"Is that right? Well, now," she said. When she was pleased her cheeks grew round and shiny, and little tucks appeared at the corners of her mouth. "I was just mixing up hot chocolate. Will you all have some?"

"Nah. Beer."

She talked even while she was out in the kitchen, freezing the three of them into silence. They sat in a row on the couch and looked toward the doorway. "I just know this is the break you been waiting for," she called. "Once you're in the city your name gets around more. Oh, I've half a mind to wake your daddy. Won't *he* be surprised. 'Now,' I'll say, 'tell me again who's wasting time when he should be pumping gas?' The Parisian is a right famous place, you know. A lot of important people go there. Remember your cousin Emma, Drum? That's where she had the rehearsal supper, before her wedding. I was there. Well, little did I *dream,* of course, at the time. Is Evie going too?"

Evie stared at the doorway until it blurred.

"What for?" Drum asked.

"Why, to sit at her little table."

"Nah," said Drum.

"Oh, go on, Evie."

David cleared his throat. "As a matter of fact, Evie's been thinking of quitting," he said. "Weren't you, Evie?"

"That's right."

"She feels the point has been made, by now. No sense going on with it."

"Well, no, I suppose not," said Mrs. Casey.

She appeared in the doorway with three cans of beer on a pizza tin. "She might want to come with your daddy and me and just *watch,* though," she said.

"She don't," said Drum.

"Will you let her speak for herself?"

Everybody looked at Evie. Evie stared down at her laced fingers and said, "I don't know. If it was up to *me,* I mean —I might want to come just once and hear him play."

"There now. You see?" Mrs. Casey told Drum.

Drum slammed his beer down on the coffee table. "Will you get her off my *back?*" he said.

"Bertram!"

"Now, I mean this. I have had it. How do you think it feels to look at that face night after night when I'm playing? Do you think I like it? Following me with those eyes, watching every move. It wasn't *my* fault she cut those fool letters. Am I going to have to go on paying for it forever?"

"Bertram. No one's asking you to pay for it. She just wants to come hear your music, that's all."

"Don't make me laugh," said Drum.

"Oh, you're turning hard, son. Are you going to be one of those stars that forgets the little people?"

"Well, wait now," said David. He stood up. "Seems to me we're getting worked up over nothing. If Drum don't want Evie in the audience she won't come. Right, Evie?"

"Right," said Evie. The word opened a door, letting through a flashing beam of anger that took her by surprise. "I won't come now or *ever*. Ever again. Not if that's the way he feels."

"Praise the Lord," said Drum.

"And another thing, Drum Casey. If I had known what a cold and self-centered person you are those letters wouldn't be there, I can promise you that. And your music is boring, it tends to get repetitious, and I hope everybody at the Parisian notices that the very first night and sends you home again. I hope you cry every mile of the way."

"Why, Evie," Mrs. Casey said.

"Not only that, but you can't even play the guitar. You just hammer out noise like any fool at a Coke party, and I hope they notice that too."

"That's a lie," said Drum. "You're talking crazy."

"Oh, am I?" She stood, but her knees felt shaky and she sat down again. "I may not be musical but I know *that* much. Joseph Ballew can play better any day."

"He can not. Joseph don't know one end of the guitar from the other."

"That's more than you know."

"You're out of your head. I play a great guitar. Don't I, David?"

"Why, surely you do," Mrs. Casey said.

"All you've got going," said Evie, "is the speaking out and me. Well, the speaking out does not make sense and I'm going to cut my hair in bangs. *Then* see how far you go."

"I was working at the Unicorn before I ever heard your name. I didn't notice anyone asking how come no girl had cut 'Casey' in her forehead. Did you, David?"

"It was a waste," Evie said.

"Will you stop that talk?"

"It was all for nothing."

"I play a great guitar," Drum said.

On the way home, Evie cried into the hem of her skirt. David kept quiet. When they had reached her house he said, "That ties it, I guess."

"I'm sorry," Evie said.

"No harm done."

From what she could see in the dark, he seemed to be smiling. She smiled back and smoothed her skirt down. "Well, it looks like I won't be seeing you again," she said.

"No, I guess not. Been quite an experience knowing you, though."

"Well. Good-bye."

Before she shut the car door behind her she made certain she hadn't forgotten anything. She wanted to leave no traces, not even a scrap of paper fluttering on the floor to make them remember her and laugh.

. . .

Her father was downstairs reading, wearing his faded plaid bathrobe. "I was just about to call Violet," he said. "Aren't you a little late?"

"We ran into some friends."

"Oh. There's cocoa in the kitchen."

"I don't want any."

She started toward her room, but halfway up the stairs she thought she heard his voice. "Did you say something?" she called.

"I said, are those the only clothes you've got? Remind me in the morning to give you some shopping money."

"I don't want any," Evie said.

8

She cut herself a set of bangs, long enough to cover her eyebrows. Her eyes without eyebrows looked worried and surprised. And because her hair was puffy at the sides, she sometimes had the feeling she was living under a mushroom button. "*There's* my girl," her father said. "I'm going to find you a plastic surgeon, too. Would you go? I always knew you would come out of this, if I just let you be." Then he went off to paint the back porch, whistling a tune she couldn't recognize.

She threw away her black skirt and blouse, her snapshot of Drum at the Unicorn, Fay-Jean's pencil drawing and the posed photograph his mother had given her. That was all that was left of him. She walked downtown under Clotelia's huge umbrella and laid in a stack of school supplies for the coming year. On the way home she bought a Tar City newspaper. "Like everything else," she read, "night-life seems to be suffering from the heat wave. The Manhattan Club has no entertainment at all this week, and the Parisian's Drumstrings Casey is strictly amateur." She refolded the newspaper and pushed it through the swinging door of a trashcan.

Afternoons, she visited Violet. All summer she had stayed home and let Violet come to her, and now she felt as if she had returned from some long hard trip that no one else knew about. The off-hand clutter of Violet's room and her smiling fat family had a clear and distant look. New china horses had joined the parade across Violet's bureau. On the closet door was a life-size poster of a movie star she had never even heard of. "What have you been doing all summer?" she asked Violet.

"What do you mean? You've seen me every day, haven't you?"

"Well, yes." She sat forward on the bed, cupping her chin in her hand. "Seems like I had *two* summers," she said. "Two different ones. Sometimes I think, was that *me*, riding large as life between two boys to a roadhouse? Why, I never was on a date, even, except with that peculiar Buddy Howland whose voice never changed. I can't believe I did it all."

"Oh, remembering things is always that way," Violet said.

"Not for me. Nothing to *bother* remembering, before. And I would rather not remember this. Why was I such a fool? You should have stopped me."

"The best thing now is just to drop the subject from your mind," Violet said.

"You're right. I will. Let's talk about something else. Did you know my father is taking over Miss Cone's class? He said that she—"

"You told me that."

"I did?"

"Last month."

"Oh. I forgot." She rose sharply from the bed, causing Violet to grab for her bottle of nail polish. "You see what I mean. I don't remember telling you a thing about it. Oh, how am I going to get over all this? I wish I had spent the summer swimming or being a camp counselor. Or just snug in my house reading books, even. I wish someone would give me back all the time I've known Drum Casey, and I would change everything I did."

"You were going to drop the subject," Violet said.

But she couldn't. She spent her mornings skating a slick surface, keeping busy, but afternoons she sprawled across Violet's unmade bed and said the same things again and again, and Violet listened with a sort of cheerful tolerance that made it seem safe to say them.

On Monday morning, over a week since her fight with Drum, Evie settled down to cleaning out her desk. It helped to do things with bustle in them. Just as she started on the second drawer she heard Clotelia call, "Evie? You wanted down here."

"Coming," said Evie. She came out and looked down the stair well to the front hall. Clotelia stood waiting there with her arms folded and her feet apart. "You got a guest," she said.

"Who is it?"

"Come on down, I told you."

"Oh, all right."

"Your father be home any minute, now."

"Well, what about it?"

But Clotelia only jerked a thumb toward the living room.

Downstairs, Drum Casey was sitting on the couch with

his boots on the coffee table. His head lolled to one side, as if he were asleep. Evie stopped short in the doorway and stared at him. She felt separated from him by a wall of glass, protected by the thick new bangs on her forehead and the days she had spent removing him from her mind in bits and crumbs. His eyes were closed; she could look at his face without feeling he might blind her by looking back. His mouth was relaxed, almost open. He needed a shave. His hands, with their nails cut short for the guitar strings, lay loosely curled on his legs. When she saw his hands she made a small movement, only enough to smooth her bangs down, but Drum rolled his head toward her and looked from beneath lowered lids. "Hey," he said.

"Hello," said Evie.

He sat up and moved his feet off the coffee table. The silence grew to the point where it would be hard to break. "I didn't know it was you," Evie said finally. "Clotelia didn't say. Do you want a lemonade? You're hot, I bet—"

Behind her, Clotelia said, "Your father be home any minute, Evie."

"Oh. Yes, my father's coming," Evie said.

But that didn't seem to mean anything to Drum. He sat forward and rubbed his eyes with the heels of his hands. "I ain't slept since Saturday," he said.

"What happened?"

"I got fired."

"*What?*"

"Fired, I said."

"Oh, well, they don't know," said Evie, thinking of the

reviews. "It's the weather. In this heat they can't tell good music from bad."

"Music, hell. That was just an excuse. I was getting on good with the manager's daughter and he didn't like it, that's all. Said I hadn't worked out well. 'Goddam man that *hires* these people—' he said. I said, 'Nobody does that to *me*.' End of it all was a fight."

"A fight? With fists?"

"What else. Fists and the police station and the works. He was just peeved over his daughter is all."

Evie blinked, cutting off the daughter forever with a single movement. "That's illegal," she said. "You can hold him to his contract."

"*Contract*, what do you think I am? A movie star?"

"Well, he can't just fire you."

"Guess again." Drum took a comb from his shirt pocket. "Now they got my name on the books, down at the police station. Just what I needed. You ever seen those movies where the mother tells the cops, 'He's a good boy'? That's what *my* mother did. 'He's a good boy,' she says. 'Oh, I just don't understand it,' she says. Then she paid the damages and yanked me outdoors and said she might've known this would happen. Said I had disgraced them all, what would my daddy say, if she had had any sense she would have put me to work like everyone told her to. Now, I ask you. Won't my own *family* even stand by me? When I got home my daddy wouldn't let me in the house. 'I am just too pissed off to look at you right now,' he says. 'Sleep down in the car. I'll talk with you in the morning.' 'Well, if *that's* the way you feel,'

I said, and walked right off. I don't care if I never see the place again."

"Where is David?" Evie asked.

"David. Home, I reckon. *He* didn't get in no fight, not him. I would've gone and spent the night at his house but you know his mother, she hates my guts."

"What for?"

"No reason *I* know of. I never did a thing to her."

Out in the hallway, Clotelia gave a sudden sharp sigh. "Go fix some lemonade," Evie told her.

"Evie, your father going to hit the roof if he find him here."

"Never mind, fix some lemonade."

Clotelia pivoted on one heel and left. Drum seemed not to have noticed her. He combed his hair, ran one hand across it, and put the comb back in his pocket. "I spent the night on someone's porch," he said, "but didn't sleep none. Now my eyelids feel scratchy. I don't know what my daddy has against me, but he never will listen to reason, not for one second. Never asks my side of nothing. Oh, well, him I'm used to. But Mom? 'Bertram, you have just killed my soul,' she told me. 'I ain't got no more faith in you.' Mom! What would you say to that? I went by home this morning after I saw his service truck pull out and, 'Mom,' I said, 'could I just have some biscuits and a little side meat for my breakfast?' She said, 'Yes, here, I done saved you some, but you better not come by no more, Bertram, until you set it right. Meaning make up the money and apologize and get you a steady job.' Well, I never thought I would live to hear *her* talk that way. 'Now, you *know* it wunt my fault,' I told her.

'That man is just real possessive over his daughter and for no good reason either, since she is right wild and always has been. But he just won't see it,' I said, 'and up and fired me on some manufactured cause.' Mom says, 'Oh, Bertram, where are you going to end up? Sometimes I feel you won't even amount to a hill of beans,' she says, and then she pushed a little brown bag of food on me. Well, it was like I had just heard something crack, the final floorboard I was resting on. I won't be going back now."

He stood and began walking around the edges of the room. Every now and then he took a hand from his back pocket to pick up a figurine or a photograph. "Who's this?" he asked.

"My mother."

"She dead? Who's this?"

"My uncle."

"You got a real nice place here. You reckon your father might let me sleep on the couch?"

"Well, no, I doubt it."

"How about your porch?"

"Not there either, I'm sure of it."

"He'd never know."

"He might," said Evie. "If a neighbor saw you, or he went out on the porch some night."

"I'd be real careful."

"But I was just getting all *straight*," said Evie. "How can you ask me a thing like that?"

All Drum did was pick up a china goose girl and lay it against his cheek, as if it cooled him.

"Oh, go ahead, then," said Evie. "I don't care."

. . .

So he slept on the porch, on the heavy, flattened cushions in the wooden swing. Not just one night, but all week. Evie would lie awake until midnight or so, when she heard through her open window the rusty sound of boots on the floorboards and then the creaking of the swing as he settled himself. The creaking died away immediately, with nothing following. He seemed not even to turn in his sleep. He would be one of those people who lay down without a fuss and lost consciousness until morning, frustrating whoever was with them, the way Violet did when she spent the night. It was Evie who stayed awake. She listened to crickets and breaths of music and other people's parties, and she thought of a hundred different things that could happen if her father came upon Drum. Would he shout? Call the police? Or only apologize for disturbing Drum's sleep and tiptoe back to bed? She expected to have nightmares about it, but when she finally slept her dreams were of struggling in water as thick as gelatin, running from a fire on boneless legs, climbing a ladder which swooped backwards under her weight but never quite fell over. When she awoke in the mornings, Drum was always gone.

After the first night she came out on the porch in her bathrobe and stared at the swing, whose cushions were not even dented. She was still there when Clotelia came. "He gone?" Clotelia asked. No one had told her Drum was staying there, but she seemed to know anyway. Evie nodded.

"Well, go on get dressed. Nothing attractive about sitting out here in your bathrobe."

At ten o'clock, her father went off for an errand. As soon as his car was out of sight Drum opened the front screen door a few inches and slid into the hallway. "I wonder if I could have breakfast?" he said. Evie was at the foot of the stairs, sorting out the mail. It was the first time all morning that Drum had not been in the center of her mind, and she raised her head and stared at him a minute. Then Clotelia called, "Come on out, it's on the table." She had set a place, even —a dinner plate heaped with ham and biscuits, which Evie and her father never ate. When Drum walked in, Clotelia looked up from the sink to say, "It's waiting on you, over there. I know *you.*" Then she emptied the dishwater and walked out, peeling off pink rubber gloves. Drum shrugged and sat down.

"She is a mite uppity," he said.

"Did you sleep all right?"

"Sure. It's a little short, but better than the ground. You got any syrup?"

Evie handed it to him and then sat down. "Have you been to see David yet?" she asked.

"Not yet."

"How about your friends?"

"How about them?"

"Well, you do have some."

"Sure."

"Are they worried about you?"

He frowned at her over a biscuit. "What you getting at?" he asked.

"I'm not getting at anything."

"You want me to clear out?"

"No, of course not."

"What you asking about friends for, then?"

"I just wanted to know—" said Evie. She drew rays out from a coffee ring, with Drum watching. "I was wondering why it was me you came to," she said finally.

"Oh. I don't know."

"There must have been lots of other people."

"Sure."

She gave up. She waited until he had finished eating, and then she brought him an ash tray. Drum tipped back in his chair to smoke a cigarette. At his elbow was the back door, unlocked and waiting in case her father should appear. There was no telling when he might walk in. She sat braced to move suddenly, her mind tracking down and identifying every sound from the street, so that when finally Drum decided to answer her question she didn't take it in. "You and me really had some fight that night," he said. Evie said, "Mmhmm." She was listening to a jingling motor noise that could have been her father's Volkswagen. When it passed she said, "What?"

"You and me really had some fight, I said."

"Oh, well."

Drum blew out a funnel of smoke and watched it dissolve. Then he said, "I thought about it later. That fight is where I went wrong, I thought."

"Oh, well, it's over now," Evie said.

"It came to me the night I got fired. I said, 'Oh, damn, I missed all the signs, will you look at that?' "

"What?"

"Are you listening to me?"

"I just don't see what you're saying," Evie said. "It's all right about the fight, really. I'm the one that should apologize."

"I ain't apologizing, I meant every word. You weigh on my head. But you bring luck, too. Or take it away, like when you hoped I would mess up at the Parisian."

"Well, wait—" Evie said.

"If I'd of took you to the Parisian like you asked, they wouldn't have fired me."

"That's just silly," Evie said.

"Nothing silly about it. Except I wish if you bring me luck you wouldn't have to weigh on my head. Don't you ever *smile* none?"

"Of course I do."

"Not to notice. Just sitting there paper-faced with your forehead showing. Now you've cut bangs."

"I thought it was time to."

"Does that mean you were serious?"

"Serious about *what?*" Evie said. "I don't understand what we're talking about."

"The fight. When you said I couldn't play the guitar."

"Oh, that."

"I can play one hell of a lot better than Joseph Ballew, I'll tell you that. And sing too. If you don't agree, you got no ears."

"Well, I was just angry," Evie said. "I never really meant it."

"Did you know I took lessons? Up at Farnham's Music

Company, where I got my guitar. Then I won a talent show before I had even finished my lessons. Fifteen dollars and a medal."

"You know I never meant it," Evie said. "It was just one of those things you say when you're angry. I could listen all day when you play."

"Well, then," said Drum. It seemed to be what he had come for. He stubbed his cigarette out and then just sat there, tipping his chair against the wall, until they heard Evie's father climbing the porch steps. "See you around," Drum said. He was up from his chair and out of the house before Evie could answer. He must have taken note of that door right from the beginning.

When he was gone, she felt she had made a mistake. He had come to make sure she still liked his singing; if she had had any sense, she would have kept him wondering. She plodded from room to room pulling sharply on one strand of hair, muttering under her breath when she was sure she was alone. "Was I serious? I don't know. I've forgotten what you sound like by now." Clotelia passed her several times, and threw her a look but said nothing. Her father asked if she were bored. "No, why?" Evie said.

"I thought you looked restless."

"Oh, no."

"Well, school will start soon. Summer always drags about this time."

He looked so cheerful nowadays. He had made her an appointment with a plastic surgeon for September, and at supper he had grown talkative and sometimes made small jokes. What she should have said was, "No. I don't like you anymore, I don't like your music, I don't want you sleeping on my porch." Then life would be simple again. No more hanging around waiting and wondering, no more secrets hidden from her whistling, unsuspecting father.

Drum set up a pattern. He came whenever her father was gone, as if he kept close watch on the house, and he seldom spoke. Conversation was up to Evie. If she was silent he seemed irritable, tapped his fingers or swung his foot, left before he had to. If she talked he seemed not to listen, but he kept very still. He rested the back of his head against the wall and watched the ceiling while she searched for any words at all to fill the space. "You mustn't mind Clotelia. Does she get on your nerves? Once I went home with her when my father was out of town and I met her boyfriend, not the one she has now but another one, who sat around drinking beer all the time and matching pennies, living off her money. She thinks all men do that way. That's the only reason she acts so snippy. His name was, wait a minute. Not Spencer, no—"

She had never been given so much time before. No one interrupted her, no one shifted impatiently. She could choose her words as slowly as luxury items in a department store. "Not Stewart, not Stengle. It will come to me in a moment. Spindle. I knew it was something peculiar. Have you ever heard of anyone named Spindle? He had a black knitted skull cap on in the middle of summer. His shoes were the big high kind with metal toe-caps."

Drum stubbed his cigarette out and passed a hand over his eyes. "Are you tired?" Evie asked him.

"No."

But his face was pinched and tight, and his tan was turning yellow. Sometimes, lost in what she was saying, she forgot that anything was wrong. Then she would look up accidentally and notice how he sat, limp and heavy-limbed, not bothering to protect himself from the net of words she had wound around him. She would break off and say, "Do you want something? Iced tea?"

"No."

"Are you not sleeping nights?"

"I'm sleeping fine. Go on talking."

"How can I talk if I never get an answer? You talk to *me*. What's been happening? Have you been back to see your mother?"

"No."

"Are you going?"

"No."

"She can't still be angry with you."

"I don't care if she's angry or not, I'm not going."

"What, not *ever?*"

"I've had it," said Drum. "All this time telling how famous I'm going to be, and then she goes to pieces at one little setback. I'm nineteen years old. I got a right to get fired once, don't I? Oh, it looks like I will never get anywhere in this life. Never do a thing but bag groceries on Friday nights. A lot *she* cares."

"If you're not going back," said Evie, "where *are* you going?" She was careful about her tone of voice. Even a sudden movement, she felt, might frighten him away. But Drum only shook his head. He didn't seem to care what she said.

He spent five days moving between her house and David's, where he was allowed to visit but was not asked for meals. He shaved in the restroom of an Esso station, borrowed a change of clothes from David, and kept his guitar in David's tool shed. At Evie's house he saw only Evie and Clotelia. Once Violet came, pink-cheeked with curiosity after what Evie had told her on the phone, but Drum left immediately. "I believe he doesn't like me," Violet said.

"No, that's not it. It's some mood he's in," Evie told her. When Violet was there, she could draw back from things and see how strange they were: Evie Decker making excuses for a rock guitarist, protecting a fugitive sitting boldly in her kitchen chair. She said good-bye to Violet as soon as she could and went out back to signal toward the tall grass behind the house.

On Friday afternoon Drum's mother called. "This is Mrs. Ora Casey," she said stiffly. "Is that you, Evie?"

"Yes, ma'am," said Evie.

"I am trying to get ahold of Bertram. He's wandered off somewhere. Has he been by your house?"

"No, ma'am."

"If you see him, will you say I'm looking for him?"

"All right."

There was a pause.

"I've called David too," Mrs. Casey said. "*He's* not seen him. Now, where would a boy go off to like that?"

"Well, I'll certainly tell him you were looking for him."

"Evie, I'll be honest with you. I been looking for him all week now. Since Sunday. We had a little falling-out. Oh, it was all over nothing—a misunderstanding at the Parisian—but you know how sensitive he is. I told him he had let me down—well, I had my reasons. We may not be college-educated in our family but we are *law*-abiding, we don't give no one cause to complain about us. I did speak sharp to him, but only because I was disappointed, nothing permanent. What call did he have to take it to heart so?"

"Well, if I see him—" Evie said.

"Yes, yes. All right. Good-bye."

Evie hung up and went back to the living room, where Drum and Clotelia were watching soap operas. Drum had grown bolder now. When the television was on he sat watching it as if he were an invited guest, talking back to all the actors. "This here doctor," Clotelia was telling him, "think he's the center of the universe. Selfish? Watch." Drum nodded, probably not listening, concentrating on the screen so hard his eyes had turned to slits. He and Clotelia shared the couch. Clotelia had grown used to him, although she still said he was trash. "Now, here is what I want to know," she told him. "When that doctor mince in such a stuck-up way, is it *his* way? Or do he just act like that for the play? Which? Pull your gut in, Evie. Who was that on the phone?"

"No one," said Evie.

"If I don't get on her tail," Clotelia told Drum, "she would go around looking like a old bedsheet. What am I going to do? I tell my boyfriend, 'Brewster,' I say, 'you ain't going to believe it, but I know a white girl seventeen years old need a full-time nursemaid. Maid ain't enough,' I say. 'She need a nursemaid.' "

Drum rolled his head back on the couch and watched Clotelia. During commercials he would listen to anyone. It didn't have to be Evie.

" 'Why won't you quit then?' he say. I tell him I will. Nothing more disgraceful, he say, than me spending my lifetime picking up over Evie Decker."

"I wish you *would* quit," Evie said.

"Oh, I will, miss, I will." She made a face and twisted her watch around sharply. "Week to week I say I will. Only if I could find me something else to do. Factory job. Do you know how long I wasted on her? Four years. Now I got to say it was all for nothing and quit. My land."

"Go to some city, why don't you," Drum said.

"Sure. Be glad to."

"I would too, if I had the money."

Evie stood above him, folding her hands on the back of the couch and looking down at the top of his head. There was no part in his hair, just a dense sheet of black separating into thick strings. Sometimes, watching him sprawled in her house, she felt an unpleasant sense of surprise hit her. There were things about him that kept startling her each time she noticed them: the bony, scraped look of his wrists, the nicotine stain on his middle finger, the straggling hairs that edged his sideburns. He was sunk into the couch cushions as if he were permanent. If her father walked in right now, what would Drum do? Raise his hand no more than an inch, probably, say "Hey" and let the hand drop again.

"Drum Casey, what do you want out of me?" she asked him.

"Huh?"

"What do you want, I said. Why are you hanging around here?"

"Evie, well, I never," Clotelia said.

Drum had turned to face her, with his mouth slightly open. "Well, if *that's* the way you feel," he said.

"I didn't say one word about the way I feel. I asked you a question."

"Some question."

"Well, have you ever been known to answer one? Have you ever had a real conversation, one that goes back and forth like it's supposed to? I asked you something. I want to know. What do you want out of me?"

"Watch now," Clotelia said loudly. "The lady in black going to cry; she's cried every show. How do you reckon she makes tears spurt that way?"

"It's fake, it's only water," said Drum. He stood up. "Talk like this just gets me down. If you don't like me sleeping on your porch, come out and say so. None of this roundaboutness."

"*Porch?* Who said porch? I asked you—"

"I got ears, I can hear."

"I wonder more about that every day," Evie said.

But Drum was already leaving, stuffing his cigarettes into his shirt pocket as he crossed the hallway. "So long," he said.

"Well, wait a minute—"

She saw his back as he loped down the front steps. Anyone could have seen him. Her father could have run into him on the sidewalk. When he reached the street he paused for a minute and then turned to the right, where he was half hidden by the hedge that bordered the yard. "I don't see you running after him," Clotelia told the television.

"I didn't know if I wanted to," Evie said.

10

She lay awake most of the night, listening for the creak of the swing. It never came. In the morning when she got up she seemed to have returned to the way she was a week ago, brisk and cheerful, willingly sitting on a board while her father sawed it and then humming while she washed the dishes, since it was Clotelia's day off. But toward noon she grew restless. She followed her father aimlessly while he built shelves in the kitchen. Once she pointed to his work pants and said, "Are you going to wear *those* all day?"

"What's wrong with them?"

"Well, if you're going out, I mean. Aren't you going downtown?"

"No, I hadn't planned on it."

"Tomorrow's Sunday, you know."

"Was there something you needed?"

"Oh, no," Evie said.

She went out into the back yard and sat on the steps, looking toward the field of grass where Drum used to wait.

Nothing moved. She sat there for hours, for an entire afternoon, without so much as a book in her lap. Her eyes began to sting from staring at one place so steadily.

After supper she went outside again, this time to the front porch. Neighbors' televisions blared up and down the street. From the window behind her she heard her father's shortwave radio flicking rapidly across continents. "Evie, come here, I've got Moscow," he called once. And then, a little later, "There is too much Spanish in this world." Evie picked up a cushion and set it in her lap. It smelled musty, like the inside of an old summer cottage. If every evening lasted this long, how much time would it take to get her whole life lived? Centuries. She pictured herself growing older and fatter in this airless dark house, turning into a spinster with a pouched face and a zipper of lines across her upper lip, caring for her father until he died and she had no one left but cats or parakeets.

Her father went to bed with a book. Lights blinked off up and down the street, and chairs were scraped off porches through bright yellow doors that finally closed and darkened. Then someone came up the sidewalk, all alone. She watched him swing over the hedge and cut across the lawn to the front porch steps. "Oh, you know better than anyone, don't you," he said.

"Know what?"

"How come you're sitting out here? You're waiting for me to slink back, nowhere else to go."

He climbed the steps and sank down on the swing, at the opposite end from her. "Everybody asked about you," he said.

"Who do you mean?"

"At the Unicorn."

"I thought you weren't going there this week," Evie said.

"No call not to, is there? Sure we did. Last night and tonight, same as ever. People said, 'Where is that girl who cut herself up, has she found her someone else by now?' I was thinking of saying you had killed yourself. 'Finished what she started,' I would say. *That* would have gone big."

"You don't know what you're talking about," Evie said, "Do you think I would kill myself over the likes of you?"

"Then I went back home with David and slept in the tool shed. His mother came out in the morning with a broom. Old witch, should have been riding it. 'What are *you* doing here?' she asks. I swear if she wasn't about to sweep me right out."

"Well, I don't blame her," Evie said. "You just hang on and *hang* on, Drum Casey. When are you going to leave me alone? As soon as I get used to you being gone, you turn up again. Will you ever just get out and stay out?"

"Oh, now, don't make me go," said Drum. "It's late. I'm tired."

"Well, so am I."

She drew in her breath, waiting for him to say something else that she could fire back at him, but he seemed to have given up. He sat slumped against the arm of the swing. All she saw was a black shadow with his T shirt making a triangle of white above his jacket. Finally he said, "You know Joseph Ballew? He says, 'Where is that plump girl with "Casey" on her forehead? Lost her interest? You're slipping, man,' he says."

Evie didn't answer.

"Have you ever thought of losing some weight?"

It took a moment for his words to sink in. Then she said, "Well, my God in heaven."

"Have you?"

"Why do you feel free to act so rude? I eat less than *you* do."

"I was just asking. You know, in Tar City they got this slenderizing place. Steam baths and exercise machines. You ever been to one?"

"No, I have not."

"Well. This girl was telling about it. Seems they can really slim people down. And make-up, and hair styles— You know, I saw in this magazine once where they decide the shape of your face and then fix your hair to fit it. They had before-and-after pictures; it looked real good."

"I wish you would go," Evie said.

"What, *now?*"

"Nobody *makes* you sit here. If you can't stand my looks, find someone else's porch to sleep on."

"Well, wait now," Drum said. "You got it all wrong. I'm trying to help out."

"I didn't ask for any help."

"I just want you to look your best. There's no reason you should get mad about it."

"What business is it of yours if I look my best?"

"Well, I was thinking we might could get married," Drum said.

Evie held still for a minute, not breathing. Then she began to laugh.

"Did I say something funny?" Drum asked.

"Yes," she said. But the laugh, which should have flowed on, suddenly rusted and broke. "I believe you're out of your head," she said.

"Why? Don't you want to?"

"No, I don't," said Evie.

"I don't know what you got to lose. You must like me some or you wouldn't have, you know, cut the letters. You wouldn't hang around me all the time. And here I am with no home. And my career's at a standstill, we could get our pictures in the papers. Human interest. Plus I do like you. I wouldn't be asking if I didn't."

"What do you like about me?" Evie said.

"Jesus."

"Well, go on. Name something."

"*I* don't know. I like the way you listen to people. Is that enough?"

"No," said Evie.

"Look. I like you. I want to get married. I feel like things are just petering out all around me and I want to get married to someone I like and have me a house and *change*. Make a change. Isn't that enough? Don't you want to change your life around some?"

Evie held the cushion closer to her and breathed in its musty smell. Then she lifted a hand and ran one finger across her forehead, tracing the narrow ridges of the scars, which always felt pleasantly crinkled. In the opposite house, the last of the lights went out. People slept fitfully in hot, rumpled beds hollowed to fit their shapes, in houses they had grown up and grown old in. Beside her, Drum shifted in the swing. He was waiting for her answer, which would be yes, but only after she had taken her time over it. Things moved too fast. She had wanted a courtship, with double dates and dances and matching shirts, but all she got was three minutes of staring at sleeping houses before she said, "Oh, well. Why not?" and Drum slid over to kiss her with cool blank lips.

11

She awoke from a dream in which she slipped through slimy clay, trying to escape a reckless woman driver in an army car. It was nearly ten o'clock in the morning. The second hand of her alarm clock spun off circle after circle while she lay watching, unable to move her eyes or gather her thoughts together. A steeple bell rang. The Sunday paper slapped against the screen. Her father passed her door on his way to church, and she wondered if he would find Drum asleep in the swing. But even that was not enough to unfasten her eyes from the clock.

Long after her father's car had driven off, she heard the front door slam. Drum's boots crossed the downstairs hall. "You there?" he called.

Evie didn't answer.

"Evie?"

"All right, I'm coming," Evie said.

Lying still so long without breakfast had made her dizzy. Black and blue buttons swarmed toward her when she climbed out of bed. As soon as her eyes had cleared she stepped into last night's clothes and then went to the mirror to unravel her pincurls. How would she curl her hair if she were married? Clotelia's magazines said no man liked to see his wife in curlers. The word "wife" hit her strangely, stilling her fingers for a moment. It was more definite than "married," which had merely floated shapelessly in her mind since the night before. She saw herself in a housecoat, mixing orange juice; saying no to a vacuum-cleaner salesman; wondering if it were time to start supper. None of the situations seemed likely. What Drum had come for, she thought, was to tell her he had changed his mind. She would never be a wife, after all. She felt so certain of it that she descended the stairs blank-faced, shut against everything, and when she saw him lounging in the living room doorway she failed to smile.

But all Drum said was, "Could you fix some breakfast?"

"All right," she said.

She fried eggs and bacon while he leaned on the stove and watched. The shut feeling was still with her, causing a brisk competence which she had never had before. Eggs plopped neatly into the frying pan, and she laid down strips of bacon in exactly parallel lines. Then Drum said, "No biscuits?"

"You'll have to do without," she told him. "I don't know how to make them."

"Can't you get Clotelia to show you? Breakfast is not breakfast without no biscuits."

"Clotelia isn't here today."

"I mean later. For the future. I'm used to having biscuits every morning."

"Oh. Later," Evie said. She let out a long breath and laid the spatula on the stove top. "Well, sure, I guess so."

"That's the girl," Drum said.

She left him to eat his breakfast alone while she fried more eggs for herself. She had turned hungry suddenly. While the eggs popped and sputtered in the frying pan, Drum finished everything on his plate, sopping it up with slice after slice of white bread. "I've got the Jeep tomorrow," he said with his mouth full.

"You do?"

"David's lending it to me. I asked him this morning. We can drive to South Carolina and be back in time for supper."

"South *Carolina?*"

Drum looked up from his plate. "What's the matter?" he said. "Did you forget all about it? Last night you said you would run off with me. I was counting on it."

"But South Carolina. I can't go there."

"Why not?"

"Well, Dillon, you mean. Where everybody goes when they have to get married, all the trash goes. You expect me to run off to *Dillon?*"

"Well, sure," said Drum.

"No, we have to go somewhere else."

"But there ain't nowhere else. Dillon's the only place you don't have to wait for three days."

"I'm sorry, I just can't help it," said Evie. Which was exactly what she meant; she had had no idea that she was going to object to Dillon. Words popped forth ready-made, strung from her mouth like comic-strip balloons. "I would rather wait for the license, even. Anything. Do you think I want to go around the rest of my life with a South Carolina marriage certificate? Oh, you just have no *respect*, Drum Casey."

"Well, my Lord," said Drum.

"Besides, we'd have to lie about my age anyway. Even in Dillon. We might as well do it in Tar City, or Raleigh."

"We'd have to lie *more* in Tar City," said Drum. "I would be underage too, if we went there."

"I don't care."

"They'd ask for proof. Then where would we be?"

"I don't care."

She waited to see what she would say next, but nothing more came. And there sat Drum, tapping a cigarette against his thumbnail over and over until the tobacco had settled a good eighth of an inch, but still he didn't light it. He would be framing a way to say, "All right, then. Stay home. Die an old maid." He was joined to her by a piece of elastic which she had stretched too far. With Drum, even an inch was too far. "I know what you must be thinking," she told him. "I'm sorry, I really meant that. But can't you go along with me this once? I'll never ask you again."

"Oh, well. Shoot," said Drum. Then he finally struck a match, but her father's car was just driving up. He had to leave by the back door, hunching his shoulders and cupping the match flame as he went.

"Evie," her father said, "why do I smell smoke?"

"Well, I've taken up cigarettes," Evie said.

"I thought so. Just so you are straightforward about it, then. I know young people have to try these things."

"All right," Evie said.

"I was young myself once," said her father.

It was Violet who helped most with the arrangements. ("*Eloping?*" she had said. "Evie. Aren't you excited? Oh, and here I thought this Drum business was all in your head.") She investigated marriage laws, arranged for the blood tests, chauffeured them to the doctor in her mother's convertible. "As far as the license goes," she said, "lie. Don't bother pulling out phony documents and such, lie through your teeth. You'd be amazed how much you can get away with." She drove Evie to Tar City to apply for the license, and Evie lied and no one questioned her. All the way home Violet sang "O Promise Me," causing people to slow down and stare as they passed. Planning things seemed to turn Violet larger and more brightly colored. She took up over half of the car seat, and every time she thought of how they had fooled the clerk she laughed her lazy rich laugh. Meanwhile Evie sat in the corner with her hands between her knees. She pictured Tar City policemen swooping down on them to hand a summons through the window for perjury, or the clerk having second thoughts and alerting all ministers and J.P.'s, or her father coming out front to point at Violet's car and say, "That's Tar *City* dust on those wheels. What have you been up to in Tar City?" But the ride home was smooth and quick, and when she went in Clotelia didn't even look up from the television.

They had to wait three days after they applied for the license. During that whole time it rained, breaking the heat wave and pulling the town from its stupor. Evie kept finding Drum on the back doorstep, under the eaves, huddled into David's windbreaker to keep warm. She pulled him in whenever her father wasn't around, but once they were sitting side by side they had almost nothing to say to each other. Drum discussed houses. He had heard of a cheap one for rent, twenty-four dollars a month. When he had finished with that, Evie went over and over the details of applying for the license, as if that were the one solid link that would hold them together till Thursday. "The clerk said, 'Date of birth?' I had it all worked out beforehand, but still I thought I would slip. Where I did slip was your name. 'Drum Casey,' I said. 'No, Bertram.' I must have sounded half-witted, not knowing the name of my, of the boy."

"I reckon so," said Drum.

They were quiet for a minute. He was beside her on the couch, one arm draped across her shoulders and his hand dangling free.

"They wanted to know your mother's maiden name," said Evie. "Did I tell you that? I made one up. What was your mother's maiden name?"

"I don't know. Parker."

"I forget what I told them. Maybe Parker, after all. Wouldn't that be funny? I had to think even for *my* mother's maiden name, which shows you how flustered I was. Eve Abbott: my own first two names. It should have been on the tip of my tongue."

When Clotelia was far enough away Drum would pull Evie closer, choosing the first pause in her speech. Evie had been waiting to be kissed for years. She had rehearsed it in her mind, first with someone faceless and then with Drum, who looked as if he would know all about it; but now she didn't think it was what it had been built up to be. They stayed pressed together between kisses, looking out over each other's shoulders like drivers meeting on opposite lanes of a highway. Drum smelled like tobacco and marigolds and the flattened porch cushions, which had turned mustier than ever now that the rain was here.

On Thursday, she got up early and put on a white eyelet dress that she had saved from junior-high graduation. The seams had grayed and it was a little tight, but she had set her heart on white. She filled her purse with absolute necessities, in case her father told her never to darken his door again: make-up, two diaries, all the letters received since fifth grade, a photograph of her parents taken before she was born, and a billfold containing twenty-eight dollars. Then she tiptoed out of the house. Her father was still dressing. Just as she reached the stairs she heard him slam a drawer and say, "Oh, drat." It surprised her that she could do something so momentous without his sensing it.

She set out for a corner halfway between her house and Violet's, where Drum and David were going to pick them up. ("If Violet's coming, then so is David," Drum said. "I ain't going to be outnumbered"—as if this were some sort of contest, girls against boys.) The rain had stopped, but the streets still glistened and the lawns were a dark, shiny green. She edged puddles not yet dried by the sun and hopped across flowing gutters, feeling like a star in an old movie with her high heels clacking so importantly and her full skirt swirling around her calves. On the corner where they were to meet, Violet was already waiting. She wore a pink nylon cocktail dress. "I believe this is the most exciting day of my life," she called out. Evie hushed her. She was certain someone would notice them and guess what was happening.

They waited five minutes. Evie stared very hard in a direction away from where the Jeep would be coming. When she heard it pull up behind her, she began smiling widely and couldn't stop. "Hop in," David said. Evie climbed into the back, where Violet was already settling herself. She looked steadily eastward so that the smile would be taken for a squint against the sunlight. Up front Drum sat lounging in the corner of her eye, one of his feet resting on the dashboard. He wore a white shirt with his jeans and his hair was slicked down too neatly. David was dressed the same as always—a sign of protest, it turned out. He was against the wedding. In all these days of planning Evie had never thought to ask how David felt, and it took her a minute to understand when he said, "All right, here we go. But it's against my better judgment, I just want you to know."

"You already said that," Drum told him.

"He did?" Evie said. She sat forward and looked at the back of David's neck. "Said what? He thinks we shouldn't be getting married?"

"Damn right I do," said David. "There is something too half-baked about this deal. And besides. Here I am. His manager. Aren't I supposed to know what's good for him? Career-wise, marriage is suicide. Look at the Beatles."

"*I* still like the Beatles," Violet said.

"But you don't swoon away when you hear them, now, do you?"

"I never did," Violet said.

That ended the conversation. For the rest of the ride everyone sat in his own corner, staring out at the scenery. Evie's smile had faded. She watched tobacco barns zip by, each standing out bare and lonely along the flat highway. Men in filling stations turned their blank faces slowly to follow the Jeep out of sight. Barefoot children strung across the pavement drew in while they passed and then fanned out again.

When they reached the outskirts of the city, the buildings tightened together. They pressed Evie's heart out of rhythm; she kept clearing her throat and swallowing. All around them people were busy with humdrum things, waiting for buses or driving the groceries home, bearing loads of children and picnic baskets and diaper bags to some sunny playground. They sped by in small circles of cheerfulness, with Evie watching enviously until they were too tiny to see.

When they were nearly downtown, they stopped for a red light. A very short fat man with a child's face stepped up to wipe their windshield, using a greasy cloth. He smeared the dirt around and stepped back to wait for a tip, but David only scowled at him. And still the light didn't change. They were going to wait there forever, eye to eye with a watchful little man. "Oh, I tell you," David said. "Everything has gone wrong today, everything. I can't wait to see what'll happen to me next."

"Name one thing that has gone wrong," Violet said.

"Other than that man," she added, for by then the light had changed and they were pulling away.

"Isn't it enough that we are heading for Drum's wedding? I'm driving my own hearse wagon, I don't know why I do it. Inside of a month he'll be a full-time pump attendant and I'll be out of a job. And *you*," he said, nodding to Evie in the rear-view mirror, "don't look at me like that. It's your own good I'm thinking of, partly."

Evie didn't argue with him. None of it seemed real anyway. Time was speeding up and slowing down in fits, like her pulse. The argument between David and Violet moved as rapidly as a silent film, jumping so suddenly into anger that Evie felt she must have missed a whole section of it. "Where is your *tact?*" Violet was asking. "We are here to get my girl friend married, it's the happiest day of her life, and you sit talking about hearse wagons. Well, stop right here. Let us out. We'll *walk* to the wedding."

"Tact, nothing," said David. "It's a free country, ain't it? I got a right to voice an opinion just like anybody else."

"Voice it by yourself, then. We three are walking."

"Go ahead," David said. "But let me tell you one thing, fat girl. I didn't like you the moment I set eyes on you. Organize, organize, I know you like a book. Why don't you get something of your *own* to organize?" He stopped the car with a jolt and reached across Drum to open the door. "Get out, all that wants to. You won't hurt my feelings a bit."

"Fine," Violet said. "Pick us up at the nearest J.P., in an hour."

"Minister," Evie told her. "And anyway—"

"Minister, then. I don't care. You just go have yourself a beer, David Elliott."

"What?" said Drum. He had been watching pedestrians all this time, not appearing to listen, but now he turned halfway in his seat and raised his dark glasses. "*Minister*, what's that for? What's wrong with a J.P.?"

"Well, nothing," said Evie. "Only I was always hoping, well, I was counting on a minister. Also a church."

Violet nodded.

"What next," David said.

"Things are getting out of hand here," said Drum. "I had never looked for all *this*."

"Well, now's the time to back out," David told him.

Violet said, "Will you just *hush?* Evie, climb out. We're walking."

"No, wait," Evie said.

"Do you want him to ruin your wedding?"

"It'll be ruined for sure if you walk," said Drum. "Because *I* ain't coming."

"*Wait,*" Evie said.

Time slowed to its regular pace. Everyone hushed and stared at her.

"Nobody walks," she told them. "I plan to have a normal, ordinary wedding, with witnesses who aren't called in off the street. No fighting. No disapproving. We are going to do this one thing the way it ought to be done, and afterwards we will have a bottle of wine to celebrate. Now, is that too much to ask?"

"Well—" said Violet.

"All right. Shut the door," Drum said. "Looks like we got to find us a minister."

"Methodist," Evie said.

The minister had a face she forgot an hour later. He perched, childlike, on the edge of his seat when they drove him to his church, and he stayed that way forever in Evie's mind. All she remembered of the wedding itself was the smell of musty swing cushions when Drum stood beside her at the altar. For souvenirs she had a wire-thin ring and a marriage certificate in old English lettering, two engraved doves cuddling at its head and David and Violet's ball-point signatures on the witness lines.

12

For twenty-four dollars a month they rented a tarpaper shack on the outskirts of Pulqua. A series of tenant farmers had once lived there. Tobacco fields stretched away from it on all sides, and the gravel road in front was traveled by barefoot children and mule wagons. Evie thought it was a wonderful place to start out in. The tenant farmers had been too poor to leave even a strip of carpeting or a one-eared sugar bowl; the house was blank, waiting for Evie to make her mark. Nothing she could do would hurt it.

She plastered the papery walls with posters advertising the Unicorn. She spent eighteen dollars at the dimestore, entering the amount carefully in a budget book, and lugged home tea towels and cutlery and a set of dishes the bluish color of skim milk. Their furniture came from Evie's father's house. They had moved it in a U-Haul-It the afternoon of the wedding, because they couldn't afford a night in a motel.

First her father said, "Married?" Then he sat down on the porch steps and said, "Married. I don't believe it." He was slumped and hollow-faced, exposed before Drum and

David and Violet, whom Evie had brought, without thinking, up the front walk with her. They stood in a semicircle around him and frowned at the ground. "Have you ever met Drum?" Evie asked finally.

"No, I don't believe I have," her father said. He rose and held his hand out, not quite looking into Drum's eyes. He could have threatened annulment, but he didn't. He didn't seem to have the energy to think it up.

"And this is David Elliott," Evie told him. "Violet you know."

But her father wasn't paying attention.

"Are you the rock singer?" he asked Drum.

"Yes, sir."

"Casey."

"Yes, sir."

"Well, I don't understand. I was going to take her to a plastic surgeon; none of this was necessary."

"Sir?"

"Oh, it's all beyond me," Evie's father said.

"Mr. Decker," said Drum, "Evie and I will need furniture. Do you reckon we could borrow what you have extra?"

"Well," said her father. He turned and went into the house. Would he lock the door behind him, say he never wanted to set eyes upon them again? But when he was inside he said, "Take what you want, then. Evie will show you."

"Thank you, sir," Drum said.

His mother was different. She clutched at Drum's shoulders and said, "You *what?* You fool. What would make you go and do a thing like that?" And Evie stood in the doorway, wondering where to put her hands. She hadn't wanted to come in the first place. "You said you were never going back," she had told Drum. "Why now? Why drag me with you?"

"Because I want to show her I'm settled and done with her," Drum said.

He stood motionless in his mother's grip, although she was trying to shake him. "It was you always telling me I didn't appreciate her," he said.

"Well, I didn't mean *marry* her."

"It's done now. Do we have to get in a swivet over it?"

"In a swivet, you say. My life is broke in pieces and you tell me not to get in a swivet. You, Evie Decker. Don't you look at me so smug. I'll get every lawyer in town after you. I'll annul it, I'll have your marriage license tore up by the highest judge there is. Oh, where is your father when I need him the most?"

She grabbed the hand of one of Drum's little tow-headed brothers, who shifted his feet and grinned.

Drum said, "Mom, can I have the record player from my room?"

Who would have thought that Drum Casey would be so homey? He wanted cushions for all the chairs and curtains for the windows, a checkered skirt for the stilt-legged kitchen sink and a frilly bibbed apron for Evie. During the first three days they were married he spent his time installing can openers, toothbrush holders, and towel rods. He directed their settling in as if he had had in mind, for years, a blueprint for a home of his own complete to the last detail. "That easy chair goes in the bedroom, for when I'm making up songs. No more lying around on a bed to play my guitar. The other chair goes in the corner of the living room. We want our furniture in corners. We want to sit snug in corners when we're home of an evening. Do you know how to make biscuits yet?"

Evie paid a call on Clotelia, choosing nighttime so that she could go to Clotelia's own house instead of her father's. "Well, look who's here," said Clotelia, kicking open the screen door. "The girl with the peabrain, I declare."

"I came to see how to make baking-powder biscuits," Evie said.

"Ain't you got no cookbook?"

"You know a cookbook wouldn't do it right. Drum has a special recipe in mind."

"Sure. Him and his kind use bacon drippings," said Clotelia. "Nothing special to *that*. Oh, come on in."

She led Evie through the darkened living room, where an old woman with powder-puff hair sat nodding on a vinyl couch. In the kitchen, she sat Evie on a step-stool decaled with panda bears. She whipped up a mound of crumbling dough, mixing it with quick, angry fingers and cutting it out with a drinking glass before Evie even realized it was finished. Meanwhile Evie stared around her to see how other people's kitchens were kept. "What is that china thing on your stove?" she asked.

"Spoon-rest."

"Oh, I see."

"Cost me fifteen cents at a rummage sale."

"Well, that's the trouble. Fifteen cents here, a quarter there—you don't know how they add up. *I* didn't know."

"Should have thought of that before you got married," Clotelia said.

"Why are you talking like this? I thought you had started liking Drum."

"I tell you why: go look at your father. You've broke his heart."

"You never cared before how he felt."

"Nor don't now," said Clotelia, "but it kills me to see somebody's heart broke. When you going to visit him?"

"Well, maybe in a day or two."

"All right. You got your recipe; important thing is mix it with your fingers. Now go before Brewster comes. You know he don't like to see you here."

She fanned Evie out the door with floury hands. Drum was waiting for her in David's Jeep, with a crowd of little boys closing in like moths to touch the headlights and run their fingers over the canvas top. "Shoo now," Drum told them. "You get the recipe?"

"I think so," Evie said.

He drove her home carefully, as if the recipe were something precious and she the shell that held it.

On Wednesday school began. She went, even though Drum couldn't see the point. "*I* never finished, and I ain't sorry, either," he said.

"But it's silly to quit my senior year."

"All right, suit yourself."

There was Mr. Harrison to argue with too. He was the

principal, a close friend of her father's, but even so he had to tell her about the rule against married students. "We make exceptions, sure," he said. "Especially when their grades are as good as yours. But not if you, not if there's a little one on the way, so to speak."

"No, of course not," Evie said.

"And then too, it would depend on your discretion. We have a lot of impressionable young girls here. Knowing you as I do, I'm sure you wouldn't *talk* about, well, but still—"

"Of course not," Evie said again.

Even if she did talk, what would she say? She had overheard more in the girls' gym than she had yet found out with Drum in the papery bedroom. Their love-making was sudden and awkward, complicated by pitch dark and a twisted nightgown and the welter of sheets and blankets that Evie kept covering herself with. Besides, there weren't many people she could talk *to*. She arrived every morning at the last minute, having caught a Trailways bus out on the highway and ridden it in to the drugstore terminal. In class, people stared at her and were too polite. She didn't mind. She had known that getting married would set her apart. And there was always Violet, who ate at her table in the cafeteria and walked her to the drugstore after school. Violet was full of talk. Witnessing a wedding seemed to have the same effect as being godmother at a christening: she was proprietary, enthusiastic. "Evie! Do you *cook*, just like that, every night without a single lesson? Does he like what you feed him? Have you had your first quarrel? Oh, I can't wait till I'm married. Nights when I pass lighted houses I think,

'All those people, so cozy with someone they belong to, and here I am alone.' I think you're the luckiest girl in the senior class."

Coziness, that must be what the world was all about. It was what Violet wanted, and David, who sank onto their borrowed couch and kicked off his shoes and said, "Oh, man, a place all your own. I might get married myself someday." And most of all it was what Drum wanted, when he rolled over in bed to watch her dress and said, "Ah, *don't* go to school. Stay home and make me pancakes. I'll do more for you than any schoolhouse will."

"But we're getting ready for a test."

"So what? It's cold outside. Stay in the house where it's warm."

And often she did, more and more as fall set in and the fields were frosted over every morning. Drum worked very little now—just odd jobs at the A & P, and then the two evenings at the Unicorn. If she stayed home their days were unscheduled and almost motionless, with great blocks of time spent on manufactured tasks. Afternoons, Drum practiced his guitar or made up songs. He tested new lyrics in a mumble, almost inaudible—"*My girl's wearing patent leather shoes*—" No. "*My girl wears*—" The guitar strings barely tinkled. At first Evie stayed in the other room, thinking she might get on his nerves, but eventually he would crash down on all the strings at once and say, "Where are you? What are you doing out *there*, come in and keep me company." Then she sat on the edge of the bed, watching how the slant of his black hair fell over the guitar just as it had the first night she saw him.

She worried that he would get tired of her. She spent weeks feeling she had to walk on tiptoe and check everything for stupidity before she said it, since she had never imagined that Drum would settle quickly into being married. He would be hard to live with, she had thought. She had seen his moody silences and the way he shrugged off what people said to him. But he turned out to be the easiest person she knew. All he wanted was a wife. He ate what she fed him, kept her company when she washed the dishes, slept with one arm thrown across her chest, and rose in the morning asking for her baking-powder biscuits. Gradually she stopped tiptoeing. She talked about anything that came to mind—a casserole in *The Ladies' Home Journal* or a new way to stop runs in stockings—and he kept cheerfully silent and mended chairs. These were the things she was *supposed* to talk about. Wearing her bibbed apron, tying a scarf over her pincurls, she began to feel as sure and as comfortable as any of the feather-light girls floating down high-school corridors.

"*All I saw was a cat, slinking on a fence,*" Drum called out at the Unicorn.

"*Will he be there tonight?*"

"Yeah!" his audience said.

"*Will* I *be there tonight?*"

He wore black. He was cool and glittering. Evie sat smiling below him in a baggy brown skirt and a sweater that rode up around her waist.

"*My girl is at a hymn-sing.*

"*What happened to double ferris wheels?*"

"Yeah!" they said again.

She still couldn't understand what that speaking out was about.

She had to darn socks now instead of throwing them away, and she clipped recipes for meatless meals and carried her lunch to school in a brown paper bag. They never paid the rent on time. "There is nothing for it," said Drum, "but to get me a part-time job. I wish now I hadn't fallen out with my daddy. Pumping gas was not too enjoyable but the pay was sure good, and where else would they let me work such loose hours?"

"Make peace with him, then," Evie said.

"I don't much feel like it."

"Well, I didn't say apologize. Just get on speaking terms. We'll have them to dinner with my father, settle all this family business at one sitting."

"Nah, it'd never work out," Drum said.

"We could give it a try, though."

She set the dinner for the second Sunday in November. That Friday in school she invited her father, choosing one of those moments when they met in the hall and stood awkwardly searching for something to say. Then she telephoned Drum's mother from the drugstore. "Thank you, but we'll not trouble you by coming," Mrs. Casey said, and hung up. Evie dialed again. The receiver was lifted on the first ring. "Mrs. Casey, we were *expecting* you," Evie said. That was the only argument she could think of, but it seemed to be enough. "Oh, well then," Mrs. Casey said, "I reckon we can fit it in. I don't believe in letting people down."

Evie fixed a casserole a full day ahead: tuna fish and canned peas. Early Sunday morning she washed all the ash trays and filmed them with floor wax, the way *Good Housekeeping* had told her to. She refused to let Drum use them after that; he had to carry around a Mason jar lid. "This is getting on my nerves," he said. "Can't you just *relax?*"

But she couldn't. She worried that her father might be dismayed by the house, or that Mrs. Casey would start a fight. All these weeks she had been half expecting an annulment to come through (a scroll of parchment, she pictured it, stamped with the state seal and "*Esse quam videri*," arriving in a mailing tube to prove that she was nobody's wife after all) and now she wondered if Mrs. Casey planned to bring it in person. "Here. A little housewarming gift." She remembered exactly the flowing tone of Mrs. Casey's voice, soft but pushing steadily forward, and the rhythm it set up with the other voices trying to survive beside it. What if an argument started somehow between Mrs. Casey and Evie's father? Her father would be beaten to the ground. She straightened the table settings nervously, stood back to squint at them, and then straightened them again.

Her father arrived first. When she opened the door to him he stood folded into his thin overcoat with his hands in his pockets. He entered stooping, as if he were coming to inspect a child's playhouse. "Well," he said. "So this is where you live." Then he smiled and kissed her, looking at the floor.

"Do you like it?" Evie asked him.

"It's a little cold, isn't it?"

"No, it's very comfortable."

"What do you use for heat?"

"We have a very good oil stove. There, see? Over there."

"Oh, yes," said her father. But he still didn't look.

Then Drum's parents came, and Drum appeared from the bedroom buttoning his shirt cuffs. He stood still while his mother kissed him on one cheek. Mrs. Casey wore a feathered hat and a rayon dress with a draped bosom; Mr. Casey was in a blue suit and white spectator shoes. He was sharp-boned and whiskery, with very round bright eyes. Nothing like Drum. Evie had never seen him before, but instead of introducing them Mrs. Casey just tipped her head toward him and he nodded gravely. "We like to got lost," Mrs. Casey said. "Well. I was *wondering* what kind of house you all had. My, it surely is—I understand you teach, Mr. Decker." The neckline of her dress pouched outward, framing a V of skin reddened by the constant pinching motion of her fingers. Gardenia perfume powdered the air around her. She carried no documents.

At dinner they all outdid each other in compliments and small courtesies. They circulated serving dishes, spoon side outward; they leapt to pass the butter to whoever asked for it and they filled silences with hopeful questions. Like salesmen, they over-used each other's names. "Mr. Decker, have you lived in Farinia all your life?" "Evie tells me you run a service station, Mr. Casey." "Do you bowl, Mr. Decker?" Meanwhile Evie watched anxiously as her food disappeared into people's mouths, and Drum ate in silence with his face calm and distant.

The only tension was over the contest to be best-behaved. Evie's father won. He said, "Evie, Drum, I'm giving you a late wedding present. Well, nothing very fancy, but I'm buying myself a new car. Would you like the VW?"

"Boy. Sure would," said Drum. "We got the devil's own time getting anywhere."

"That's what I thought. I know that Evie isn't, doesn't keep a perfect attendance record these days. Not that it's any of my business, but I figured a car might help."

"Thank you, Daddy," Evie said. The afternoon was too perilous to bother arguing about her attendance record. Her father sat with his fingers together, the tip of his nose whitening as it always did under strain. Mrs. Casey was pleating the V of skin again.

"Lord knows we don't have extra cars to hand out," she said, "or anything like that; we're only simple folk. But your daddy here was thinking you might want your old job back, Bertram. Plenty would give their right arms for that job."

"Well, I could use it, I reckon," Drum said. "Sure."

The three parents sat side by side, keeping their backs very straight, as if the couch were something breakable.

At three o'clock they left. Mrs. Casey said, "Well, I surely did—Obed, where is my purse? Now, don't be a stranger, Bertram. You come by whenever you like—even if you just get lonesome, or hungry for a snack. Thank you for the sweet lunch, Evie."

"Joyed it," said Mr. Casey.

Evie's father carefully buttoned all the buttons of his coat. He kissed Evie on the cheek and shook Drum's hand. "My car will be coming next Wednesday," he said. "Thursday I'll give you the keys to the VW. Won't you come by and see me sometime?"

"Oh, of course," said Evie. "It's just that these last few weeks have been so busy. Getting settled and all."

"You could come for supper some night. Will you do that?"

"Of course," Evie said.

She stood beside Drum in the doorway, shivering slightly, watching the two cars grow smaller. "Now," Drum said. "It's over and done with."

She nodded.

"And hot dog, we got us a car. Ain't that something? I always did like stick-shifts."

"I believe that's all you can think about," Evie said.

"Huh?"

"Well, you could at least have said thank you. Or talked to him more. Oh, I know that car, it smells woolly like his school suit and I will think about that every time I get in it. Couldn't you just tell him you appreciated it?"

"Nothing wrong with a woolly smell," said Drum.

"No," Evie said, giving up. So when he suddenly tightened his arms around her, pulling her close, it came as a surprise.

"Don't fret, I'm here," he said.

Beneath his shirt she felt his rib cage, thin and warm, and she heard the steady beating of his heart.

13

Then one Saturday at the Unicorn, Drum got into an argument. Not a fist fight, this time; just a shouting quarrel. It was almost midnight. Evie was splitting a burnt-out match into tiny slivers of paper while she waited for the evening to end, and the crowd had thinned enough so that she heard clearly when Drum's voice rose in the back room. "The hell you say. What you trying to pull, Zack?" She looked up, first toward the back room and then at the people sharing her table—three couples, talking softly over empty beer mugs, separated from other couples by a jungle of vacant chairs. None of them paid any attention. "Ah, don't give me *that*," Drum said. Evie rose and pushed through the chairs and behind the band platform. When she reached the back room she squinted in through layers of smoke. There was Drum, facing the proprietor and holding his guitar by the neck. David stood beside him. ". . . to be sensible about this, Drum," he was saying. Nearest Evie were Joseph Ballew and Joseph's bass player. "I don't see *Joseph* getting treated so light," Drum said.

"Joseph's our lead player," the proprietor told him. "You know that."

"Have you got some method to tell who draws in what people? No. All you got is—"

"Look, Drum, you'll still play on Saturdays. But Fridays, face it, there ain't all that big a crowd nowadays. You want me to lose money?"

"What's going on?" Evie asked.

They looked at her and then turned away again, not answering. Finally David said, "Zack was just saying how—"

"I been cut back to one night a week," said Drum. "There was a full house tonight and it's almost Christmas and now Zack here decides he's losing money."

"Now, Drum, if I could see my way clear you *know* I'd—" Zack said. He looked fatter than ever and very sad, with sweat running down the sides of his face like tears. "Spring, of course, we could see about having you for both nights again. It all goes by *seasons,* don't you see."

"He's right," said Joseph.

"*You* can talk," Drum told him. "How would you feel to get cut back without no warning?"

"Sure, I know how—"

"Ah, forget it," Drum said. "Where's my coat?"

"It's right behind you," Evie said.

But Drum went on stamping through the room, shoving chairs aside and looking under instrument cases. When finally he found the coat he said, "Another thing. You can forget Saturdays too, from now on. I ain't coming back here. You'll have to get along without me."

"Now, Drum, wait," said David.

"Do you want a ride or don't you?"

He pushed his way out of the room, right past Evie, and David looked at the others for a minute and then shrugged and followed him. Evie had to run to catch up with them.

Outside, the air was crackling with a sharp dry cold that made her ears tighten. She stumbled after Drum and David, struggling into her coat on the way. Their car was haloed with frost. While Drum unlocked the door Evie shifted from one foot to the other to keep warm, but Drum didn't look cold at all. He pulled the key out of the handle and then just stood there a minute, staring out over the icy roofs of other cars. "Hop in," David told Evie. "Let me sit up front. I'll talk to him."

Evie perched on the edge of the narrow back seat. One knee rested against Drum's guitar, which had kept some of the warmth from the Unicorn. While Drum was backing out no one spoke, but then on the highway Drum said, "Damn fat fool."

"He's just having to look out for his business," David said.

"What, over Christmas? School's letting out, the place'll be jammed. And how about Joseph, now? How does he get to stay?"

"Zack told you. Joseph is the—"

"All right, all right. The lead player. Who don't even have a sense of rhythm. I tell you, we're well out of that place. Got to find us something *lively* now."

"Well, where, Drum? Do you think you can pick up a new job just by snapping your fingers? I can't even find us private parties nowadays, and here it is Christmas time and I have sent ads all over town."

"Something will turn up."

"Nothing will turn up. Tomorrow I'm calling Zack. I'll tell him we'll be there next Saturday same as usual. You were just a mite put out, I'll tell him. He'll understand."

"No, he won't, because I ain't showing. Me and Evie are going to the movies."

"Suit yourself, then," David said. And he was quiet for the rest of the ride, although he whistled under his breath.

When they dropped David off at his house, Drum jerked his chin toward the front seat. "Come up here and sit," he said.

"What for?"

"Come talk to me."

She looked at his face in the rear view mirror. It was pale and shadowed. And after she had settled herself beside him he said, "I made a fool out of myself, didn't I?"

"Oh, no."

"Seems like I am just going through one of those low periods. Last Christmas we played at three different parties; this Christmas they forgot all about us."

"Maybe you need more publicity," Evie said.

"I don't see how I can *get* anymore. Oh, pretty soon he will fire me for Saturdays too, I can feel it coming. I will have to play at those free things he has on Sunday afternoons, everybody drinking coffee. That's how low I'll come to."

"You just need a good night's sleep," Evie told him. "Things will look different in the morning."

"Oh, sure, I know."

When they got home, he pulled off his shirt and jeans and then climbed into bed with a jelly glass half full of bourbon. He watched Evie while she moved around the room straightening up. She folded his clothes and laid them in a chair, she changed into her seersucker nightgown and then stood before a mirror to curl her hair. From one of her drawers she took a plastic barrette and pinned her bangs back. They would have to be trained that way. She planned to leave her forehead bare again, showing Drum and all the rest of the world what his music was worth to her.

"This business about Saturdays," Drum told her. "I ain't going to change my mind; I meant it. I don't want to play there at all any more. Why should I go where I'm not appreciated? I would like to find me something new, switch over. Now, are you going to side with David and start beating me down about this?"

"You know I wouldn't," Evie said.

"Well, I was just wondering."

He set the empty jelly glass on the window sill, and by the time Evie had put the lights out he was asleep.

But Evie stayed awake, long after she had come to bed. She lay on her back, stiff and still, watching how the cold moonlight frosted the rim of the jelly glass. That had been the last of the bourbon. It was a reckless purchase one weekend when they had extra money, and for two months the bottle had sat in the kitchen cupboard growing sticky and fingerprinted, brought down rarely and measured out carefully. Now how long would it be before they bought more? Their money came in dribbles—five dollars here, fifteen there, sometimes a little from her father who said, "This is for a sweater," or for books, or a new hairdo, making it too explicit for Evie to object, although she never spent it on what he suggested. What they had they kept in billfolds; it wasn't enough for a bank. And it was paid out in dribbles, too, so that the dimestore budget book with its headings—"Mortgage," "Insurance," "Transportation"—seemed unrelated to their lives. They spent it on cigarettes or records, or on a can of artichoke hearts which Drum said he wanted to try just once before he died. When they were poorest they ate stale saltines and spaghetti in dented tins, reduced for quick sale. They turned out coat pockets and dug between sofa cushions. And in the end, more money always dribbled in again.

But now their only income would be from the A & P and the filling station. It wasn't much. If she didn't want Drum pumping gas all day she would have to find a job, and she even knew where: at the public library. Her father had told her about a position there, intending it for Drum. (Money was something her father worried about. Money and balanced diets.) But how would Drum ever endure a library? He would sit behind a circulation desk in spurred boots and a black denim jacket, sinking lower every time he jabbed a rubber stamp against an ink pad. It would have to be Evie who did it, afternoons when school was out. She even thought she might like it. She pictured herself in a blue smock, calm and competent, going through a set of crisp motions with catalogue drawers. When she finally slept the dreamed she walked up to the Unicorn's band platform with a stack of historical romances, and one by one she laid them in Drum's lap. "Thank you," said Drum, strumming his guitar. "It's what I always wanted."

But in the morning Drum turned out to be against the idea. He heard it with his eyes on something far above the bed, his face smooth and blank and patient. Then at her first pause he said, "No."

"But don't you see?" Evie asked. "It works out so well. You would never be pressed into doing some job you hated; you would know you had me to fall back on."

"I don't like it," said Drum.

"Well, Drum, I never. Are you one of those people that doesn't like working wives?"

"No. Well, no, of course not. But it wouldn't look good. People will say I must have got cut back at the Unicorn."

"You have," Evie wanted to say, but she didn't. She had read in *Family Circle* about how wives needed tact at times like this.

On Monday afternoon, she passed the library twice very slowly and then made up her mind and walked in. All she wanted to do was satisfy her curiosity. She smelled the familiar library smells, paste and buckram and polished wood, and she saw how the cheerful yellow curtains framed narrow rectangles of winter light. Behind the desk sat Miss Simmons, red-haired and spectacled, sliding pencils into an orange-juice can some child had painted for her. "Why, Evie," Miss Simmons said. "How nice to see you."

"I only came by for a minute," Evie said. She shifted the heap of books she held against her chest.

"Was there something I could help you with?"

"Oh, no. Well, I was curious, is all; my father said you had a job open."

"That's right, Naomi's job. She got married. I hated to lose her. Are you interested?"

"Well, I don't know. There's my, Drum, he doesn't—but it sounded like something I'd like."

"It's after school hours, you know. No problem there."

"Yes, I know, but—"

"Dollar and a half an hour."

"Would it take up any evenings?"

"Evenings, no, we're not open evenings. Three to six every afternoon; you'd be home in time for supper. Won't you think about it? I'd love to have someone I knew."

Miss Simmons had a wide, lopsided smile that changed the shape of her face, making her look young and hopeful. When she smiled Evie said, "Oh well, all right. I think I'd like to," without even planning it. Drum was in some far unlighted corner of her mind. She wouldn't think about him until later. She followed Miss Simmons into the workroom behind the desk, still carrying her books, listening carefully while the job was explained to her. "Could you start today?" Miss Simmons asked. "There are all these cards piled up. Oh, I hope you like it. Some people get the fidgets in libraries. It's the importance of details that bothers them."

But to Evie, importance of details seemed peaceful and lulling. She settled herself on a high stool in the workroom, with an electric heater warming her cold stockinged feet and a mug of cocoa at her elbow. For three solid hours she alphabetized Library of Congress Cards and stacked them in neat little piles. Abbott, Anson, Arden—the cards snapped crisply under her fingers, and when she had finished with the A's she evened up the corners, slipped a rubber band around them, and moved smoothly into the B's. "Are you getting tired?" Miss Simmons called. "Do you want to take a break? I know this must seem tedious." But Evie didn't get tired all afternoon. At six o'clock, when Miss Simmons moved around the reading room closing blinds and straightening magazines, Evie was sorry to have to go.

Drum was lying on the couch at home with an old copy of *Billboard*. "What took you so long?" he asked.

"I stopped by the library."

"Oh," Drum said.

"Do you—shall I open up some chili?"

"Sure, I reckon."

He never asked what she had been doing at the library.

She went to work every day that week. Although Miss Simmons kept up a steady patter of tea-party talk Evie stayed silent, soaking up the words and the warmth from the heater as she filled out overdue-reminders. Sometimes she wandered through the reading room with a trolley of books to shelve, and the memorized classification numbers hummed peacefully through her head while she searched for shelf-space. Or she sat behind the circulation desk, swiveling in a wheeled metal chair and stamping first books and then cards—thump-tap, thump-tap—until she was lulled into a trance. People rarely spoke to her. If Violet came by and said, "Hi, Evie. Evie?", Evie looked up with a blank smile for several seconds before she realized who it was.

"Oh, aren't you just bored out of your *mind?*" Violet asked. "I don't see how you stand it here."

"It's all right," Evie said.

She kept preparing explanations for Drum—how Miss Simmons was desperate, how the job was only temporary—but she didn't have to use them. Drum asked no questions at all. On Friday he said, "It's my late night at the A & P. Can you come early so I can have the car?"

"I have to stay at the library till six," Evie told him.

"Well, I'll come pick you up and take you home, then. That all right?"

"I guess so."

At six o'clock she looked up from the desk to find him leaning in the doorway, looking sleepy. "I'm ready any time you are," he told her. She had never thought it would be so easy. She wondered if he were just waiting till they were alone to say, "Hey. What's this? I thought I said I didn't want you working." But even after they had left the building, he kept quiet. She had him drop her by the bank to cash her paycheck, and when she returned to the car she handed him the money. "Good, I'm out of cigarettes," he said. She was relieved, but she had a let-down feeling too.

Meanwhile nothing seemed to have been settled with the Unicorn. Friday night David stopped by the house and said, "I wanted Drum, but maybe you could tell me. What am I supposed to do about this Unicorn business? I been letting it ride; I never thought he'd go this far. Now tomorrow is Saturday and we still don't know if Drum will change his mind and play there."

"He hasn't mentioned it," Evie said.

"Shall I just go on and say we'll show? I thought of it. But then Drum could always make a liar of me, and that's bad for business." He sat down on the edge of the couch. He was still wearing the suit he sold insurance in, grey wool with a pinstripe. It made him look unusually straight-edged and sure of himself. "*You're* around him all week," he said. "And you know he likes the Unicorn. Even I am sure of that much. So what should I do? You must have *some* idea."

"David, I don't. Really."

"But if you don't take the decision out of his hands he might just say no from pride. You know how he is."

"Well," Evie said.

"Shall I do it?"

"He *is* proud."

"So shouldn't I go and tell Zack he's coming?"

"Well, I don't know. I guess you could."

"Good enough," David said. "It'll work out. You'll see."

And it did. On Saturday night she talked Drum into his singing clothes, polished his boots and set them beside the door, followed him around holding his guitar out level, like a tray, until he grew nervous about its safety and yanked it away from her. "Why are you doing this to me?" he asked.

"I'm not doing anything to you, I'm saving you from making a mistake. You'll be sorry later if you throw this job away."

"Don't you care how I feel about it?"

"Of course I do, that's why I'm telling you to go."

"Well, I won't," said Drum. He sat down sharply and lay his guitar on the couch. Already he was almost late. Evie kept sliding her eyes toward her watch, on which time seemed to pass with a hurried, grating motion that she could feel against her skin. "Drum," she said, "I stuck my neck out for you, I and David both. I got him to patch things up with Zack. Now what will Zack say when you don't show up?"

"Well, you had no business doing that," said Drum.

"What else could I do? You always *used* to like the Unicorn."

"I got a right to change my mind, ain't I?"

"Not when there's nothing to change *to.*"

Drum was quiet. She thought that she had lost, and already her mind was rearranging itself to accept the defeat when Drum said, "All right. All right."

"You're going?"

"I don't see I have much choice."

At the Unicorn he played heavily, for once overcoming the drums behind him. He did his speaking out without ceasing to twang the guitar strings, so that his voice fought out from beneath the notes like a swimmer beneath the peaks of waves.

"How did it gray?
"When were they pink?
"They've made him a major.
"How long did it take?"

His audience kept silent.

School stopped over the Christmas holidays, but Evie hardly noticed. She went less and less often now. When she did go the sharp rhythm of electric bells and the herding from class to class seemed misted and foreign. Her teachers spoke in loud, evenly paced voices, emphasizing the names of authors and the dates of wars; students scribbled frantically in loose-leaf notebooks, taking down every word, but what Evie wrote trailed off in mid-sentence. She often stared into space for long periods of time without a thought in her head. When she collected herself, whole minutes might have passed. There was not even an echo of what the teacher had said, and her classmates, still bent over their notebooks, seemed to have ridden away from her on their scurrying ball-point pens. "Please excuse Evie D. Casey," Drum wrote in his notes to the principal. "She was not feeling well and couldn't come to school 'Wednesday,' 'Thursday,' and 'Friday.' Sincerely Bertram O. Casey." Mr. Harrison put on his clear-rimmed glasses and puzzled out the penciled words, bunchy and downward-sloping. The notes were an embarrassment to him. To have her husband write them seemed a mockery, yet her father could not logically be asked to do it instead.

For Christmas, Evie gave her father a pair of gloves and Drum a sweater. Drum gave her a bottle of perfume—"My Sin," which pleased her. She put up a little tree and they had Christmas dinner at the Caseys. Then the next day she went back to work in the library. Miss Simmons had offered her a week's vacation, but Evie felt they couldn't give up the money.

Evenings, when she came home, the house would be filled with the clutter of Drum's day—overflowing ash trays, empty record jackets, stray dishes in the sink. "Were you practicing?" she asked him, but he rarely had been. "I don't know, I just can't get started right," he said. "Seems like I am messing around all the time. My fingers forget what they was doing." He talked more now. His voice tugged constantly on the hem of Evie's mind, so that she almost forgot how it had been in the old days when he never talked at all. "What is the point in me sitting here strumming? I'll never get anywhere. I ain't but nineteen years old and already leading a slipping-down life, and hard rock is fading so pretty soon nobody won't want it."

"That's not true," Evie said.

"Well, it *feels* like it is. Feels like I have hit my peak and passed it. I was just a fool to ever hope to be famous."

"Will you *stop* that?" Evie said.

She wanted to get pregnant. She had latched on to the idea out of the blue, flying in the face of all logical objections: her job, their lack of money, the countless times that Drum had whispered, in the dark, "Is it safe?" The thought of a baby sent a shaft of yellow light through her mind, like a door opening. Yet getting pregnant was turning out to be easier said than done. Drum in this new mood of his often drifted into sleep while listening to the radio, a weighted, formless figure face-down on the living room couch. "Drum," she would say, "aren't you coming to bed?" Then he would stagger up and into the bedroom, where he fell asleep again with all his clothes on. She tugged at his boots, working against the dead heaviness of his legs. She put on her nightgown, and in her mirror the bathroom light lit up her silhouette almost as wide as the billowing gown, a blurred stocky figure broadening at the hips and not narrowing below them. She thought of crash diets, exercycles, charm school. Whcn shc lay down, Drum would be snoring. She stayed awake for hours with all her muscles tensed, as if she were afraid to trust her weight to the darkness she rested on.

14

In February a revivalist named Brother Hope came to preach at the Pulqua Tabernacle of God. His anxious face appeared in every store window, above interchangeable numerals showing the number of souls he had saved. His sermon titles were posted on a signboard on the Tabernacle lawn: "One-Way Street," "Do You Have a Moment?" and "For Heaven's Sake." Above the signboard were strings of pennants, triangular like the ones in Mr. Casey's filling station.

"Someone is shouting your name in the Tabernacle of God," a bass player told Evie. Evie felt a sort of inner jolt, a bunching together of the chest muscles. Then the bass player said, "You ought to go hear, they say it's right comical."

"Have *you* been?" Evie asked.

"Naw. I don't go places like that."

None of the Unicorn's musicians did; yet still they sieved the news from unnamed sources and passed it on. False gods were multiplying on every corner of the earth, Brother Hope said, even in this green and pleasant town of Pulqua: drugs, liquor, and the mind-snatching rhythms of rock-and-roll. Right here in Pulqua some poor girl had ruined her face during an orgy over a roadhouse rock singer, it was in all the newspapers, and if that was not idolatry then what was? Evie Decker was her name, if no one believed him; the Unicorn was where the singer sang.

"At least it's publicity," Evie said.

"Publicity won't do us no good in the Tabernacle of God," David told her.

"Well, I don't know why not."

"Do you think that congregation is likely to show up at the Unicorn?"

But he was wrong. They did show up. Not the entire congregation but at least the younger members, probably slipping out on their straight-backed country parents. They came that Saturday in small clusters, pale and watchful, as if Brother Hope had been their trained guide on the paths to sin. The tables were lined with dressed-up boys and dowdy young girls who seemed hit in the face by every beat of the music. Drum slid his pelvis easily beneath the spangled guitar. Evie's scars shone like snail tracks. Brother Hope's congregation leaned forward to watch and then back to whisper, taking in the sights in small gulps. "Well, this is the place all right," Evie heard one boy say. "There's the girl. This is the music." When she rose to meet Drum in back, she walked slowly and proudly, as if she were carrying something important.

That Saturday she was happy. She felt that things were going well again. But by Monday everything had changed.

Zack Caraway drove out in person to say that Drum was no longer needed, even for Saturdays. He stood in the middle of the room looking around him unhappily, twisting his hat in his hands. "I was going to say it two nights ago," he said, "but they was a rush toward the end and I put it off. Now, all I've had this winter is bad luck and I know you will argue, Drum, but what can I do? My money has *went*. If you want to come on Sundays to the free-for-all, I would be right happy to have you, but that's the most I . . ."

Drum never said a word. She had expected another fight, but he just sat on the couch with his face toward the window, his long brown eyes reflecting the winter light, not even protesting as Zack cut the last inch from him. After Zack had left he drank two beers and listened to a record. Then David came by, and they played a game of darts. Drum seemed insulated; if Evie mentioned Zack, he looked away from her and all she saw was the smooth olive line of his cheek.

"Zack is slipping," David told her. "If he had eyes he could see that what that Tabernacle crowd is after is you and Drum."

"Well, tell him that."

"*I* can't tell him."

"Somebody should. Brother Hope is giving the Unicorn free publicity and nobody even takes advantage of it."

Publicity was everything. She felt that more and more. She thought of publicity as the small, neat click that set into motion machines that had previously been disengaged. Drum's music, beating like a pulse, had started leaving her ears with a cotton-wool feeling, and his speaking out was harder to understand with every show; but if there were crowds of screaming fans, then everything would click into working order. "If we could only *spread* Brother Hope," she said. "Get his sermons where they mattered more—not just to little old scared country people."

"No way of doing *that*," David said.

"Why not? We could go to the Tabernacle and make a big fuss, get a newspaper write-up."

"Naw," David said.

But she wore him down. Over a two-day period she filled his mind with pictures—Brother Hope looking startled, a reporter asking what all the trouble was about, a news item on Drum Casey's protest at a church attack. David moved forward inch by inch, balking sometimes so that she wished she could just give up. There was too much expected of her, she thought. All this arguing, urging, encouraging. Alone, she heard the driving rhythm of her own voice echoing wordlessly through her mind. But there was Drum. She watched him when he wasn't looking, and felt hollow with worry when she saw him slumped on the couch endlessly circling the rim of a beer can with his index finger. "Oh, why not, let's go and give Brother Hope a try," David said one evening. Drum didn't even look up.

And when David came by Thursday night and said, "You ready?" Drum said, "Ready for what?"

"The Tabernacle of God, of course," David said.

"You wouldn't catch me dead in the Tabernacle of God."

"Well, what the hell, Drum, where you been all this time? We been discussing the Tabernacle three days now and you never said a word against it."

"Oh, never mind," said Evie. "We'll go alone. It's only for a couple of hours."

"Then what about me?" Drum asked.

"You said you didn't want to come."

"Well, what am I supposed to do, just sit here till you get back? Looks like everyone is *leaving* me all the time."

"Lord," said David.

So they all went. They rode in David's Jeep. Wind whistled in under the canvas flaps, and Evie shivered inside her thin school coat and huddled closer to Drum's side. Her hair was pulled straight off her forehead, held by a flaking gold barrette. When she looked into the rear-view mirror her scars glinted back at her, right side to, but dim as an old photograph. Her features were wavery and uncertain. "Now that we're really going I feel like a fool," she said. "I don't even have a plan in mind."

David said, "Well, I did call that photographer from the newspaper. Publicity's no good without a photograph."

"If I hear that word publicity again," Drum said, "I'm going to puke."

"Now, Drum."

The Tabernacle was on Main Street, an old white clapboard house between a pizzeria and a shoe repair shop. A sign across the porch said, "Pulqua Tabernacle of God. Everybody 'Welcome.' Come on in Folks," with the sermon title tacked beneath it: "What Next?" Nailed to a pillar was another of Brother Hope's posters, with his eyes unfocused and frightened, as if he could see straight to hell. Spinsters in high-heeled galoshes and old men in suit jackets and overalls filed past the poster toward a brightly lit door. Evie followed, holding tightly to Drum's hand so that nothing would separate them. She had pictured something bigger and more anonymous, like a lecture hall; not this oversized front parlor lined with folding chairs and hung with dusty curtains. An old lady with lace laid across her shoulders like antimacassars pressed Evie's hand in both of her own. "Good evening, children, you won't regret this," she said. When she saw Evie's forehead she smiled harder and gazed far away, blinking several times, as if she had received an insult she wanted to overlook. Evie clutched Drum's and David's elbows and led them toward the chairs in the back of the room.

"I wish we hadn't come," she said.

"Told you so," said Drum.

"Well, I forgot how creepy these places are. I don't like the smell."

David was the only one who stayed cheerful. "Smells all right to *me*," he said, and he took a deep breath of the air—dry wood, hand-me-down hymnals, and dust. "Yonder is the photographer," he told Evie.

"What's he doing way up front?"

"He has to be far enough away to photograph us."

"Us?" Evie said.

"Who else?"

"Well, yes, of course," Evie said, but she wished she had thought this thing through before she came.

Brother Hope appeared on a small raised platform up front. He was red and knotty-faced, like a man swelling with anger but choking it down. His hair was plastered sleekly across his skull; and he wore a long black robe with a striped woolen scarf hanging from his shoulders. "All rise," he said. His voice was thin and stifled.

Everybody rose. Forty chairs creaked and snapped.

"I was glad when they said unto me, let us go into the house of the Lord. 'In the Garden.' "

"In the Garden" sounded strange without a piano. The women sang in high, sliding voices, as if they were complaining, and the men made muttering sounds beneath the tune. Evie, who disliked hymns, stayed silent. When all the verses had been sung they sat down again, and Brother Hope gripped both sides of the pulpit.

"We are gathered here," he said, "as lone survivors on a sinking ship. Only you and I know that ship is sinking. Only you and I seek to find the rotting planks. Art thou weary? Art thou languid? Then thou art smarter than thy neighbor, for thou hast seen the water rising beneath the planks. Last month, my friends, I was in Norville. A man buying a popular magazine was told that the price had gone up, and I heard him ask, 'What next?' 'What next?' he said. Well, that started me thinking, my friends. What next for *us*, in the life beyond, I thought, if things continue like they're going now? Today there are women wearing the garb of men, men in stupors from the fumes of alcohol and the taste of foreign mushrooms, dancers dancing obscenities in public and everywhere, on every corner of the earth, sacrifices made to false gods and earthly idols. What next? What next?"

His voice stitched in and out of Evie's thoughts, rising above them sometimes as a new topic jolted into view and then submerging while she decided whether to go to school tomorrow, planned a menu, wondered what Drum was thinking with his mouth so straight and set. At her left, David shifted his weight but kept his eyes pinned on Brother Hope. The congregation commented on the sermon during each pause. "It's true. It's true." "Amen." "Ain't that so?" Like poor listeners in an ordinary conversation, they seemed likely to jump up at any moment and interrupt to tell experiences of their own. Only none of them did. Instead, Evie began to worry that it would be she herself who interrupted. Pauses between paragraphs grew longer and quieter, swelling until they might burst forth with her own voice saying something terrible. Ordinary ministers picked a single, narrow theme for each sermon; Brother Hope tried to cover the world in an hour. Faced with the leap from one topic to another, from the evils of pre-teen dating to the inevitability of death and from there to the unnaturalness of working mothers, he kept taking a breath and hesitating, as if he worried about the abyss he had to span; and every time it happened Evie drew in her breath too. She was not certain what would burst forth. She gripped the chair in front of her, and the man who sat in it turned to show her the expectant, circular eyes of a baby.

"Our children are no longer safe," said Brother Hope. "Golden nets are cast to reel them into evil and we say, 'It's only music. *We* had music,' we say, but we had the waltz and 'Mairzy Doats.' My friends, I say unto you, go into your parlors some night and watch your children dancing. Is that innocence? I can cite chapter and verse. A young man driving home from a jukebox joint crashed into a Good Humor truck and died; marijuana in his glove compartment. His name was Willie Hammond, if you care to check on that. A young girl living within your own town limits slashed her forehead with the name of a rock-and-roll singer; ruined her life for nothing. If you don't believe me, her name was Eve Decker; the singer sang at the—"

"Wait," Evie said. "That's *me*."

She stood up, still gripping the chair in front of her, and looked around at all the upturned faces. Hearing her name in public, even when she had expected it, gave her a ripped-open feeling. She couldn't think why David was smiling at her and nodding. "You take that back," she told Brother Hope.

"We are all friends here," said Brother Hope.

"Well, *I'm* not. You're speaking libel. Slander. I did not ruin my life, it was not for nothing. How can you say such a thing?"

Brother Hope was fiddling with the ends of his scarf and staring at her forehead. "Please, now, please," he said. "Any burden you have—"

"I don't have *any* burdens!" Evie shouted. "I didn't ruin my life, I married him!"

A flashbulb snapped in her face, an explosion of light that faded to a squirmy green circle. It took her a moment to remember about the photographer. She watched the circle drift over to Brother Hope's face, and then she let go of the chair.

"Well," she said finally. "The place he was talking about is the Unicorn, out on the south highway. The singer is Drum Casey, who is my husband and just got fired for—"

"Sit down," Drum said.

"—for the last day of the week he was working. Just got his working time cut day by day, raising his hopes and then lowering them again, and if anybody *really* cared about Christian love they would call up the Unicorn and say, 'Where is Drum Casey? Why isn't he there? We want—' "

Drum rose. "I don't have to allow this," he said.

"Why, Drum."

"Shut up," Drum told her. "Sit down."

"Please, my friends. Please," said Brother Hope, and he looked over either shoulder although there was nothing but a blank wall behind him.

"Drum, I am only trying—"

"She's doing great, Drum," David said.

"You shut up too," said Drum. "I have had enough publicity tonight to put me six feet under. And *you*—" he said, turning suddenly on Brother Hope, who opened his mouth and took a breath, "you and your sacrifices to false gods, that's a bunch of bull. It'd been a hell of a lot more sacrifice if she'd been prettier to begin with. Get going, Evie. We're through here."

He took hold of her arm just above the elbow. He pushed her out ahead of him and Evie went, boneless and watery, knocked sick by what he had said. David had her by the other hand. "Now, then," he kept whispering. "Now, wait. . . ."

They rode home in a swelling, suspended silence, as if this

were just another pause in Brother Hope's sermon. David kept clearing his throat. Evie expected to cry but could not. Drum sat beside her with his face set straight ahead, his hands on his knees. Once he drew in his breath as if he meant to speak, but he said nothing.

15

That week's newspaper carried a photograph of Evie hunched forward behind a seated man, as if she were pushing him in a wheelchair. Her face looked surprised. "Evangelist Ends Sojourn in Pulqua," the caption read. "Brother Evan Hope left Pulqua yesterday after two weeks at the Tabernacle of God. He described his stay as 'heartwarmingly successful.' Above, a local teen-ager protests his attack on rock music." Evie threw the newspaper aside, not bothering to show Drum. But the next day David drove all the way out to their house to tell them that Drum had been re-hired at the Unicorn. "You can thank Evie for this," he said. "Word of mouth spread what she did all over town. People kept calling Zack and asking where Drum Casey was."

"What do you know," said Drum. He didn't look up from the magazine he was leafing through. "Anything I hate, it's indecision. I wish Zack would just fire me for good and get it over with."

"When are you going to be satisfied? You got your Saturday nights back, didn't you?"

"Sure. I guess so." Then Drum turned another page of his magazine.

What he had said to Evie at the Tabernacle was buried now, not erased but buried beneath the new grave courtesy he showed toward her. He had never apologized. For several days he treated her very gently, helping her with the dishes and listening with extreme, watchful stillness whenever she spoke to him. It was the most he could do, Evie figured. She shoved down the Tabernacle memory every time it floated up in her mind; yet evenings, when they sat doing separate things in the lamplight, she sometimes wanted to leap up and ask, "What you said, did you mean it? You must have or you would never have thought it. But did you mean it for all time, or just for that moment? Are you sorry you married me? *Why* did you marry me?" None of the questions were ones Drum would answer. She kept quiet, and only watched him from across the room until he looked up and raised his eyebrows. Then the questions began to occur to her less frequently. Whole days passed without her remembering, and gradually she and Drum drifted back to the way they had been before.

Drum returned to his Saturdays at the Unicorn without a word, played his songs and came home as soon as his last set was over. He never went without Evie. She felt that her hold on her school work was slipping, and sometimes she suggested that he go alone while she studied, but Drum said, "Nah, you can study some other time. You're so smart, one night won't hurt you." Yet while he played he stared over her head, never directly at her.

"We went two-ing on the one.

"We went circling on the square.

"We went adding on the divide."

Evie listened without changing expression, clutching her coat around her for warmth.

She thought she might be pregnant. She pictured her stomach as a thin, swelling shell, like a balloon, and since something so fragile had to be guarded with a half-drawn breath, she put off going to the doctor and she said nothing to Drum. It was too early yet, she told herself; and then, as she reached the end of the second month, it was too late. How could she explain keeping it a secret so long? What held her back was this thin-skinned feeling. The baby, she thought, was a boy, still and grave and level-eyed like Drum, and the picture of those eyes in such a small face made it seem necessary to protect him in fierce silence every second of the day. She made a circle of herself, folding more and more inward. She carried herself like a bowl of water. At moments when she opened her mouth to say, "Drum? Guess what," the sense of something spilling or breaking always changed her mind.

In department stores she picked up free magazines for expectant mothers and studied every word. Babies, it seemed, nested in vast jungles of equipment, wheeled and decaled and safety-railed and vinyl-covered. She had never been exposed to babies before, and she was not sure how much of the equipment was essential. Would it take a Jolly Jumper to keep him happy? Was it true that babies needed to ride their mothers' backs in canvas carriers in order to feel secure? And if so, how would she ever buy it all? She put her name in a drawing for an English pram, and she clipped a newspaper coupon for a free week of germ-proofed diaper service. Like a mother cat, she wandered through the house counting up bureau drawers and staring for long periods of time into corner cupboards. She hung over the toilet bowl in the mornings, sick and dizzy, and worried about finding the money for a tip-proof high chair with a snap-on tray and safety straps.

Meanwhile Drum sat in the bedroom chair with his feet slung over one of its arms, and for hours on end he played his guitar. He sang very softly, reaching for notes deep on the scale. Even Evie could tell the songs weren't rock. "St. James Infirmary" he sang, and "Trouble in Mind," and something called "Nobody Knows You When You're Down and Out." The words slid about more, the beat was not as clear, and the tunes were sadder. Evie said, "Did you make these things up?"

"Shoot, no," said Drum.

"They're not rock, are they?"

"Shoot, no."

It had been weeks since he had written any rock music. At the Unicorn he did the same pieces he always did, but at home he played nothing but these new ones. Evie began to recognize them. She could pick out the patterns, the verses that recurred with only slight variations from song to song. The parts that she liked she sang alone in the kitchen, with the tunes all wrong:

One morning you'll wake to an empty bed,
You'll bury your eyes and bow your head.

But she never told Drum she liked them. If he started playing those things in the Unicorn it would be the end of him. How could people dance to "Nobody Knows You"?

"You never write any songs these days," she said.

"I'm getting weary of them."

"What will you do, then?"

"Ah, I don't know. Seems like I am always pushing to lift something I don't have the muscles for. Every song I wrote, I thought, 'This is it. This is something singular,' I thought, but later I see how it is no different from anyone else's except maybe worse. Little old crabbed, stunted lines. Nothing new. Same old beat. Now, why would I want to write more of them?"

His lashes cut across his eyes, straight and even; his pupils seemed pricked by tiny points of gold. Evie touched the hand that lay nearest her on the couch. "Everything will work out," she said. "This is just a low period. What you need is publicity."

"Publicity. Huh."

"Let me think about it a while."

"Forget it, I tell you."

"Well, it's for your own good, Drum."

"Not for *my* own good, no ma'am," Drum said. "I hate it."

"How will you get ahead, then, if nobody knows your name?"

"That's *my* business."

"It's mine too. It was me you were complaining to."

"I wasn't complaining, I was talking," said Drum. "And you weren't listening. You were thinking about publicity, which makes me tired. And I am tired too of getting nagged at all the time and having to face that nagging forehead of yours. I don't know why you don't wear bangs anymore."

"I don't wear bangs because I don't back down on things I have done," said Evie. "And I have never said a nagging word to you in my life."

"All right, all right."

"Have I?"

"No, forget it. I was just talking. Evie," he said, "where has my luck gone? When am I going to rise above all this? Am I going to grow old just *waiting?*"

But Evie couldn't answer that. All she could do was sit quiet, leaning gently toward him as if that would do what words could not, watching him run his fingers through the slant of his hair.

That Sunday David came over for lunch. While Drum was in the kitchen opening beers, Evie said, "Listen, David. What would you think of Drum getting kidnapped?"

"Huh?"

"For publicity."

"Evie. You couldn't even fool a traffic cop with a stunt like that."

"I know we couldn't," Evie said. She looked toward the kitchen, checking on Drum, and then she came to sit beside David on the couch. "But listen to what I have in mind. It wouldn't be a *serious* kidnapping, nothing to call in the FBI for. He would be spirited away by fans, that's all, just for a couple of hours. What would be the harm? And still the newspapers would pick it up."

"Sure," said David. "Nothing wrong with that at all, except it's too much work. It's not worth it."

"It is to me. *I* will do the work. I'll get Violet and maybe Fay-Jean Lindsay, she'll do it if she thinks it's tied up with the Unicorn. And Fay-Jean might have a friend. I'll arrange the whole thing. All right?"

"You can't arrange Drum," David said.

"Drum?"

"He will never go along with this, you know that."

"I'm not going to tell him about it."

"Oh, well, wait now."

"It's for him, David. I know he doesn't like things like this, but *I* don't like seeing him just curl up around the edges, either. What else can I do? Besides, I have to think about the baby."

"What baby?"

"I believe I might be having one," said Evie, and she felt something lurch inside her just the way she had expected it to.

"Oh," David said. "You are?"

"Don't tell Drum."

"Well, shouldn't—"

"Evie," Drum called, "what have you done with the beer-can opener?"

"Coming," Evie said. "Listen, David. If I did the work, would you go along with it?"

"Oh, Evie, I don't—"

But at the end of the afternoon, when Drum and Evie were seeing him to the door, David said, "Evie, you know I would always try to help you in any way you wanted."

"Well, thank you," Evie said.

"What was *that* about?" Drum asked when they had shut the door.

"I don't know," Evie said.

In the library she looked up Fay-Jean's number and then reached for the telephone. Even before she had dialed, her throat prepared itself for the tone she wanted. She slipped into it like a needle into a groove: the sure and reasonable voice needed to lay plans before people whom she did not expect to agree with her.

On Tuesday evening at seven, Drum said, "Why are we waiting so long to eat? I'm starved."

"In a minute," Evie said. She stood at the living room window, pressing her face against the glass so that she could see past her own reflection.

"You ain't even started cooking."

"In a minute, I said."

A pair of headlights swung up the road, recognizable even at this distance. The headlights were round and close-set, like the eyes of some small worried lady. They floated gently up and down, bouncing on the uneven road. "Who's that coming?" Drum asked.

"I don't know."

"Who's it *look* like?"

"I don't know."

Drum sighed and moved up next to her. She could smell the marigold smell of his skin. "That's David's Jeep, as any fool can see," he said.

"Is it?"

The Jeep parked in the dirt yard, but the lights stayed on. A minute later there was a knock at the door, and when Drum said, "Come in," the three girls entered first—Violet, Fay-Jean, and Fay-Jean's sister Doris, all dressed up. David came behind. "Well, hey," Drum said. He nodded to Violet and Fay-Jean, and then looked toward Doris and waited to be introduced. No one bothered. The three of them kept walking until they had surrounded him. Then Fay-Jean brought out a shimmering length of nylon cord and reached for one of his hands. For a minute it looked as if it would be as easy as that—just tie him up while he stood waiting. But as her fingers were circling his wrist, Drum said, "What in—" and jerked away. "What the hell's going on?" he said.

"They're kidnapping you," Evie told him.

"They're—"

"Kidnapping. It's only for publicity."

"Are you out of your head?"

"Now wait," David said. "It's not such a bad idea, Drum. We're taking you to my shed. Evie will tell the police a bunch of crazy fans got you, and then you'll be returned. No more than an outing."

"You have went too far this time," Drum said, but it wasn't clear whether he was speaking to David or to Evie. He backed away, holding both arms ready at his sides, while the three girls advanced. "I would help you," David told them, "but it wouldn't look right." Fay-Jean made another pass with the nylon cord and Drum lashed out, clipping the side of her face with his forearm and sending her crashing into the wall. "Ouch," she said. "Get him, Doris!"

But it was Violet who got him. All she did was fling herself against him like a pillow, knocking him flat on his back. She set her one hundred and eighty pounds squarely on his chest. Even though he was still hitting out at them, Fay-Jean and Doris between them managed to tie his wrists together. Then they all sat there, breathing hard, and Drum lay scowling on the floor. "This is laughable," he said.

"Well, sure," said Violet. "So laugh. Enjoy yourself. We're only going for a little ride."

"*Oh*, no."

He heaved until they couldn't sit on him any longer. He tripped Violet with one kick of his foot and rammed an elbow into Doris's stomach. "Now, you better stop that," Doris said. Her voice was on the edge of tears. "Didn't anybody ever tell you not to go hitting girls?"

"Here," Violet said, and tied his feet together with enough space between them so he could walk. Then they raised him up, keeping tight hold of his elbows.

"Evie," Drum said.

Evie pressed both hands together and shook her head.

"Now, Evie, I know this was your idea. It couldn't be nobody's else's. You tell these girls to let me go, right this second. I don't adapt well to being kidnapped."

"It's only for a while," Evie said.

"I mean it, Evie."

"I packed you a supper. It's in the Jeep. A brown paper bag."

"David?"

David hesitated.

"The worst part's over anyway," Evie told him.

"She's right, Drum. No point untying you now. If I'd of known you'd take it so hard I would have said no, but what have you got to lose? You'll be back by bedtime."

Drum seemed to have nothing more to say. When David had opened the door, the girls led him out with no trouble at all.

After the Jeep had driven off, Evie sat on the couch for a while with her hands pressed together. She had not expected a kidnapping to be so difficult. The room was a shambles—furniture kicked over, cushions and papers scattered across the floor. When she finally crossed to the closet for her coat she nearly tripped over the rug, which lay in a twisted heap. She closed the door behind her before she had even put her coat on and ran toward the Volkswagen.

More headlights floated down the road, wide apart and rectangular. While she stood waiting beside the VW the other car drew to a stop, and a man said, "Evie?"

"Sir?"

"It's me. Mr. Harrison."

"Oh, Mr. Harrison." Evie said. As if this evening had been none of her doing, she felt shaky and relieved at the sight of him. "Drum's been kidnapped," she said. "Not for real, but a bunch of fans got him. What'll I do? I'm getting worried." And she was. Her throat muscles knotted, and that uneven heartbeat was beginning in her ears again.

"Drum can wait," Mr. Harrison said. "Your father's sick. I want you to come with me."

"Drum's been *kidnapped.*"

"Evie, we haven't got time for that. Your father's in the hospital."

"Will you *listen?*" Evie said. She had drawn closer to the car now. Her hands clutched the window frame; she felt them trembling. "Drive me to where Drum is. No, never mind, I'll drive myself. Do I have the keys? Tell my father I'll be there soon. It doesn't matter about the police, just tell my—"

"Your father," said Mr. Harrison, "has had a heart attack and is dying. I didn't want to say it but I see I had to. Climb in. I'll take you to the hospital."

He opened the door on the passenger side, flooding the car with a dingy yellow light. Evie circled the car and climbed in slowly.

"Hospital," she said. Her voice was as clear and sudden as if it were an order, but she was merely echoing him without any idea at all of what to do next.

16

In the hospital lobby, on a sectional vinyl couch, sat Mrs. Harrison and Mrs. Willoughby, the old lady who lived next door to Evie's father. They stood up when Evie entered —a bad sign. Evie and Mr. Harrison clicked toward them across polished tiles, between potted palms and standing ash trays. As they came up to the two women, Mrs. Harrison tugged her skirt down and straightened her belt and smoothed the gray pom-pom of hair on her forehead. "Evie, dear—" she said. Her tone made everything clear, there was no need to say more, but Evie was in the grip of a stony stubbornness and she refused to understand. "How is he?" she asked.

"He passed, dear," Mrs. Willoughby said. Mrs. Willoughby was as small and as dumpy as a cupcake, raising her creased hands to her bosom and furrowing her powdery face into sympathy lines. Everyone else was small too. The scene was miniaturized and crystal-clear, like something seen through very strong prescription glasses. Lights were sharp pinpoints. Sounds were tinny.

"Would you like to see him?" Mrs. Harrison asked.

"No, thank you," said Evie.

"It happened not long after you left, Bill. I wished you had known, so as to prepare Evie. I thought of coming out after you."

"Well," said Mr. Harrison. "This is very very sad news. Very sad. Sam Decker was as fine a man as I've known. How long have we known him, Martha?"

"Oh, years. Since back before—Evie, we will expect you to come stay the night. You don't want to go all the way out to your place again, do you?"

"I think I'll go to my father's," Evie said.

"Oh, no, dear. Not alone."

"I'd rather."

"Well, anything you say. If it were *me*, though—"

They drove there in Mr. Harrison's car. Mrs. Willoughby sat in back, and Evie was urged to wedge herself in the front seat between the Harrisons. Touches kept grating against her—Mr. Harrison's elbow as he shifted gears, Mrs. Harrison's sharp-edged purse, her cold gloved fingers patting Evie's wrist. Every now and then Mrs. Harrison clicked her tongue and shook her head. "Such a patient man, he was," she said. "Oh, and all those troubles. First his wife passing —well."

"He was just leaning across the fence, like," Mrs. Willoughby said. "He said, 'Mrs. Willoughby, all my potted plants are dying. I don't understand it.' 'It's that maid of yours,' I told him. 'Not that I have any proof, but in my heart I feel she neglects them. Yellowy leaves never pinched off, a sort of unwatered look to the soil. I could be wrong,' I said. Or meant to say, but then he took in a breath and opened his mouth and slumped over. I couldn't get straight what had happened. I said, 'Mr. Decker? Why, Mr. Decker!' The fence held him up. He seemed to be resting."

"Now, now," said Mrs. Harrison.

" 'All my potted plants are dying,' he told me. Oh, little did he know!"

"Now, now."

They stopped in front of Evie's father's house, where all the lights still blazed. At first they planned to come in and keep her company, but Evie wouldn't allow it. "I'd rather be alone," she said.

"Oh, no, dear, not at a time like this. I know it *seems* you'd rather. But we'll be quiet as mice. I'll just make tea and not say a word—"

"No. I mean it."

"Well, maybe Mrs. Willoughby, then."

"Oh, I'd *love* to!" Mrs. Willoughby said.

"No. Thank you."

"Whatever you say, of course," said Mrs. Harrison. "I would think, myself—but that's not important. Just try and get some rest, and we'll be by to talk about the arrangements in the morning."

"Arrangements?" Evie said. She thought of song arrangements, then furniture, then flowers in vases. Meanwhile Mrs. Harrison and Mrs. Willoughby looked at each other in silence, as if there were no possible synonym they could think of to offer her. "Oh. Arrangements," Evie said finally.

"Will you call us if you need anything?"

"Yes. And thank you for all you've done."

"He was a mighty fine man," Mr. Harrison said suddenly. He coughed and looked down at the steering wheel.

Evie and Mrs. Willoughby climbed out of the car and watched it drive off. Against the lighted house Mrs. Willoughby was only a silhouette, topped by a scribble of hair. Charms jingled when she moved. "There is the fence," she said. "He was leaning over it, like. I was standing in that patch of earth, wishing it was spring and time to plant petunias. He came up slow. Leaned his elbows on that fence and said . . ."

She padded away, maybe still talking. Evie waited until she was lost in the darkness before she climbed her own porch steps.

The house had not yet heard of the death. Clocks ticked, the refrigerator whirred, a desk lamp lit an ash tray with a pipe resting on it and the short-wave radio was speaking Spanish. Evie clicked the radio off and then moved through the house, still in her coat. She didn't touch anything. She looked at the dishes in the kitchen sink, then at the bed upstairs which Clotelia had left unmade. She leaned forward to study an oval photograph above the bureau: a woman in a high-necked dress, perfect creamy fingers curled over the back of a chair, a tail of hair tied low on her neck with a wide black bow. An ancestor, maybe; no one could tell her any more. Under her father's bed two socks lay like curled mice, startling her.

Her old room held a bulletin board, a pennant-covered

wastebasket, and the upstairs telephone. Everything else had been borne away by Drum in the U-Haul-It truck. Evie sat down on the floor and pulled the telephone by its tail until it rested between her feet. Then she dialed Clotelia's number.

"Clotelia?" she said.

"Who's this."

"It's Evie."

"Oh. Hey."

"I'm calling with bad news, Clotelia. My father died."

There was a silence. Then Clotelia said, "Oh, my Lord have mercy."

"It was a heart attack."

"Well, Lord have mercy. That poor man. Was he all alone when he passed?"

"He was talking to Mrs. Willoughby."

"Her. I could think of better to die with."

"Well, I was wondering. Could you come stay the night with me? I'll be here till tomorrow."

"Sure thing," said Clotelia. "I be right over. Well, Lord. Did you ever?"

"I'll see you then," Evie said.

She hung up and dialed again. "David?" she said.

"This is his brother. David ain't here."

"Well, this is Evie Decker. Could I speak to Drum Casey? He's out in your shed."

"Shed? What shed is that?"

"Your toolshed."

"Is this a joke or something?"

"He's out in your toolshed."

"What would he be doing out there?"

"Oh, Lord, I don't know," Evie said. "Just messing around. Give him a message then, I don't care."

"Well, I will if I ever run into him."

"Say my father died. Say I'm sorry but I can't bother sending the police after him right now and I'll see him in the morning."

"*What?*"

"Just tell him to come on home, will you?"

"Oh, well, if I—"

She hung up and started wandering through the rooms again. Now the house was quieting down. Beneath the surface noise of clocks and motors there was a deep, growing silence that layered in from the walls, making her feel clumsy and out of place. Her shoes clacked against the floor boards. Her full coat snatched at ash trays and figurines as she passed them. In the living room her mother smiled hopefully from a filigree frame, her hair tightly crimped and her lipstick too dark, remembered now by no living person. Her father's textbook lay in an armchair on top of a sheaf of graded quizzes. And everywhere she looked there were props to pass time with: completed crossword puzzles, a face made out of used matches, a *Reader's Digest* vocabulary test neatly filled out in pencil.

Clotelia arrived wearing a long striped robe, like one of the three wise men. Her head was wrapped in a silk turban. Darts of gold dangled from her ears. "My Lord, I can't take it in," she said. "The news don't stick in my head. Well, been one of those days, I might have known. Where is your bangs, may I ask?"

"I'm pinning them back now," Evie said.

"You look like trash. Go comb them down. If you want I fix you some cocoa and then you tell me how it come about."

"There's nothing to tell. I wasn't there," Evie said.

But Clotelia only waved a hand and swept on into the kitchen—swept literally, gathering with the hem of her robe all the dust balls she had left behind that day. "Now then," she said as she took down the cocoa box. "Did he pass peaceful? What was his last words?"

"I wasn't there, I said. He wondered why his potted plants were dying."

"Oh, that poor man. Blamed me, I bet."

"He didn't say."

"You don't look good, Evie. How far along are you?"

"What?"

"How far? Two months? Three?"

"Three, almost."

"Oh, my, and never told your daddy. What is it makes you act like that?" She lit the flame under a saucepan of milk. "Well, they is a silver-backed mirror in the guest room he always said he would will to me. He tell you that?"

"No, but you can have it anyway. I don't care," Evie said.

"He give you the house, I reckon. Well, I will say this: He always was a gentleman. Never cause me trouble, like others I could name. Now I got to find me another job."

"You could get yourself a factory job," Evie said.

"Oh, you be roping me in to take care of that baby of yours, I expect."

"Are you crazy? You might sacrifice him up at a Black Panther rally."

"Listen to that. A death night and you talk as mean-mouthed as you ever did. Here, drink your cocoa."

She passed Evie a flowered mug and then leaned back against the sink, folding her arms in her long flowing sleeves. Her hands, striped a soft glowing yellow at the outsides of her palms, gripped her elbows. "And now I hear you quit school," she said.

"Who said that? I never quit."

"Been weeks since you been, I hear."

"Well," said Evie. She ran her finger around the rim of her mug. It was true; she couldn't remember the last time she had attended a class. "Anyway, I'm starting back next week," she said.

"You separated, too, ain't you," said Clotelia.

"Separated?"

"From that husband of yours."

"*No*, I'm not separated."

"Where's he at, then?"

"Oh, at home, I guess."

"Why ain't he here, in your time of trouble? Or why ain't you there?"

"It's complicated," Evie said.

"Oh, I just bet it is. No point in a husband if you ain't going to lean on him during stress, now, is there?"

"Clotelia, for heaven's sake," Evie said. "Will you stop just *harping* at me? Will you leave me *be?*"

"Well. Sorry," said Clotelia. She unfolded her arms and gazed down at her fingernails, shell-pink with half-moons left unpainted. "If I'd of thought, I'd of brought my mother," she said.

Evie put her head in her hands.

"My mother is a consoler at the Baptist Church. She go to all the funerals and console the mourners till they is cheered up."

"How would she go about that?" Evie asked in a muffled voice.

"Oh, just hug them and pat their shoulders, offer them Kleenex. How else would she do?"

Then Clotelia, who was not like her mother at all, turned her back and rinsed out the cocoa pan, and Evie cupped her hands around her mug for warmth.

17

It's been weeks since I've been out in the country," said Mrs. Harrison. "Wouldn't you think winter would be *over* by now? Look at that sky. Look at those trees, not a sign of green. If you like, I can turn on the heater, Evie."

"I am a little cold," Evie said.

Mrs. Harrison reached for a lever somewhere beneath the dashboard. She drove with a look of suspense on her face, as if she constantly wondered how she was doing. Her back was very straight; six inches separated her from the back of the car seat.

Mr. Harrison couldn't come, of course. It was a school day. Evie understood that but Mrs. Harrison seemed afraid she hadn't. She said, "Oh, if only Bill could have made it. He wanted to, you know that. And naturally he will be coming to the funeral. He feels just terrible about all this. Your father was the first teacher we met when Bill came here to be principal. 'I'm Sam Decker,' he said—Oh, I remember it just as *clear!* Had on that baggy suit of his. There was some confusion in his mind about whether or not I meant to shake hands. And now look. But if Bill was to turn his back for a second, even, that school would just shatter into pieces. 'Bill,' I said, 'Evie will understand. You are coming to the funeral, aren't you?' and he said, 'Martha, you know I am.' I felt sure you wouldn't be insulted."

"No, of course not," Evie said. "He did more than enough last night."

"Oh, that was nothing," said Mrs. Harrison.

"Well, I did appreciate it."

They seemed to have reached the end of a dance set, both of them curtsying and murmuring a pattern of words. But Evie had trouble remembering what to say. Her voice wandered, searching for the proper tone. Had she shown the right amount of gratitude? Was anything else expected of her? A row of grownups lined the back of her mind, shaking their heads at the clumsiness of Evie Decker.

"You'll have to tell me where to turn, dear. I've never been out this far before."

"Oh. Right up there at the tobacco barn," Evie said.

"Don't you have trouble with undesirable neighbors around here?"

"I don't know any of them."

Mrs. Harrison swung to the right, onto deep clay ruts hardened by frost. It sounded as if the bottom of the car were dropping out. Her gloved hands were tight on the wheel, strained shiny across the knuckles, and she looked anxiously around her while the car seemed to bound of its own accord through the dry fields. Around a curve there were two thin children, ropy-haired, lost in clothes too big for them, holding a dead rabbit by the heels and offering it forth. "My stars," said Mrs. Harrison. She sailed on past them while a narrow line suddenly pinched her eyebrows together.

"One thing I told Bill," she said. "I told him, 'Thank heaven she's married, Bill,' We hadn't thought it at the time, of course, but *now* look. You won't be all alone in the world. You have yourself a hand-picked guardian. Are you certain this is the road?"

"Yes. Our house is just over there."

"Where?"

"*There*," said Evie, and she nodded at the tarpaper shack. Yet for a minute, she hadn't been sure herself. It looked different. The sky today was a stark gray-white, arching over treeless billows of parched land and dwarfing the house and the single bush that grew by the door. Blank squares of gray were reflected off the windowpanes. A dribble of smoke rose from the rusted chimney pipe. Mrs. Harrison drove into the dirt yard and parked between a wheel-less bicycle and a claw-footed bathtub, but before she had turned the motor off Evie said, "Oh, don't come in. Really. I'll be all right."

"Well, are you sure?" Mrs. Harrison asked.

"I'm positive. Thank you very much."

"Well. We'll see you at the funeral, then. Or before, if you think of anything you need. You let us know."

She waited while Evie collected her coat around her and fumbled for the door handle. Then she raised one gloved hand and shot off into the road, still stiff-backed. A spurt of dust hovered behind her.

. . .

Evie climbed the two wooden steps, avoiding the corner that was rotting off its nails. When she opened the door she was met by a damp smell, as if the wintry sky had seeped in through the cracks around the windows. It took her a minute to understand why things were in such a jumble; the kidnapping had slipped her mind. A chair lay on its side, poking splintery legs into her path. The shaggy rug, worn down to bare fabric in spots, was twisted beneath it. At the other end of the room there was a half-finished game of idiot's delight on a footstool, a heap of paper airplanes made by Drum on an idle day, five empty beer cans and an ash tray full of cigarette butts and chewing-gum wrappers and the metal tabs from the beer cans. A grape-juice stain on the wall had seeped through the white poster paint she had covered it with. The room might have been left weeks ago, hardening beneath its stale film of dust.

"Drum?" she called.

She heard something from the bedroom, not quite a sound.

"Is that you, Drum?"

By the time she reached the bedroom door, Drum was already sitting up. One side of his face was creased from the pillow. Beyond him was Fay-Jean Lindsay, wearing an orange lace slip which seemed to have drained all the color from the rest of her. Her face and her pointy shoulders were dead white; her tow hair streamed down her back as pale as ice. "*Oh*-oh," she said, and reached for the black dress crumpled at the end of the bed. Drum only looked stunned.

He and Evie stared at each other without expression, neither one seeming to breathe.

"What are *you* doing here?" he asked her finally.

"This is where I live."

"Well, where you been? You think you can just stay away all night and then pop back in again?"

"I've been home. My father died."

"Oh. Oh, Lord." He looked for help to Fay-Jean, but Fay-Jean sat among the blankets groping her way upward through her black dress. Nothing showed but two limp arms raised toward the ceiling. When her face had poked through she said, "Well, excuse me for being here but you were away, after all. Will you zip me up?"

"Certainly," Evie said. Now, too late, she hit upon the polite tone of voice she had needed for the grownups. She zipped the dress while Fay-Jean held her hair off her neck; she waited patiently while Fay-Jean trailed long toes beneath the bed feeling for her spike-heeled shoes. Meanwhile Drum had risen and was shaking out his dungarees. He wore yellowed underpants and an undershirt with a hole in the chest, its neckband frayed. He hopped one-footed into the dungarees, clenching his muscles against the cold. "Look," he kept saying. "Wait. Listen." But nothing more. Evie handed Fay-Jean her coat and saw her to the door. "How do I get out of here?" Fay-Jean asked.

"Walk to the highway and catch a bus."

"Walk? In these shoes? Couldn't you just drive me?"

"I don't have the time," Evie said, and shut the door.

She went to the kitchen and began making coffee, still in her coat. The coat gave her a brisk, competent feeling.

While she was waiting for butter to melt in the frying pan Drum came out, dressed in his dungarees and a khaki shirt, and stood behind her. "Well, I don't know what to say," he said.

Evie tilted the frying pan, evening the butter.

"And then about your father. Well. He was a right nice guy."

She rapped an egg and broke it, neatly.

"I don't know what got into me," Drum said. "It was that kidnapping. How could you do me that way? And then it looked like you had decided not to come back again. Either that or forgot all about it. We waited and waited, those three girls just tapping around the toolshed. Violet trying to start up campfire songs. Evie, say something. What are you thinking?"

"I am thinking that we have to get organized," Evie said. "Have you ever *looked* at this place? It's a mess. And I'm freezing to death, it's much too cold."

"Well, is *that* what you want to talk about? *Housekeeping?*"

"Not housekeeping, just things in general. You've got to pull yourself together, Drum. I keep meaning to tell you this: I'm expecting a baby. It's coming in six months or so."

She scrambled the eggs around rapidly, not looking at him. Drum said nothing. Finally she let out her breath and said, "Did you hear me?"

"I heard."

"Well, you don't act like it."

"It just took me by surprise, like," Drum said. "Why didn't you mention this before?"

"I was waiting for the right time."

"Is *this* the right time?"

Then she did look at him, but she couldn't tell what he was thinking. He leaned against the wall with his boots crossed, his eyes fixed on the swirling eggs, so that all she could see were the straight dark lines of his lashes. "Right time or not," she said after a minute, "we are going to have to make some arrangements. Now, my father has left me his house. We can move in this afternoon—just pack up and leave this place. Start a new life. Give some shape to things."

"You mean *live* there? Live in his house?"

"It's our house now."

"It's *your* house."

"Well, what's the difference?"

"I like it where we are," Drum said.

"We can't stay here, Drum."

"I don't know why not."

"We just can't."

"Well, *I* can't go *there*," said Drum.

"What do you mean?"

"What I said. I can't do it."

He sat down at the kitchen table, bracing himself with his hands as if he had a headache. Evie stared at him, but he wouldn't say any more. He folded his arms on the table and waited. She poured his coffee, dished out his eggs, and found him a fork. Then she said, "All right. I'll go there alone."

"You mean leave me?"

"If I have to."

"You don't have to," said Drum. "Evie, I don't know why you are talking this way. Is it Fay-Jean? Fay-*Jean* don't mean nothing, I swear it. Oh, how am I going to convince you?"

"Fay-Jean. Don't make me laugh," said Evie. "All I'm asking is for you to pick yourself up and move to a decent house with me. If you don't do it, then it's *you* leaving *me*. I did give you the choice."

"That's no choice," Drum said. "Evie, I would do almost anything for you but not this. Not get organized and follow after you this way. You used to like it here. Can't you just stay and wait till my luck is changed?"

He laid one hand on her arm. His wrist was marked with a chafed red line. Evie felt something pulled out of her that he had drawn, like a hard deep string, but she squared her corners as if she were a stack of library cards.

"I have the baby now," she said.

"I don't see how that changes anything."

"No, I know you don't. That's why I'm leaving."

"Can't we talk about this?"

But he had to say that to her back. She was already leaving the room. She went to the bedroom and pulled out a suitcase, which she opened on the bed. Then she began folding the blouses that hung in her closet. Hundreds of times, in movies and on television, she had watched this scene being rehearsed for her. Wives had laid blouses neatly in overnight bags and had given them a brisk little pat, then crossed on clicking heels to collect an armload of dresses still on their hangers. There was no way she could make a mistake. Her motions were prescribed for her, right down to the tucking of rolled stockings into empty corners and the thoughtful look she gave the empty closet.

Drum came to be her audience, leaning awkwardly in the

doorway with his hands in his pockets. "You are moving in too much of a rush," he told her.

"What?" said Evie, and she stared down at her hands, overflowing with scarves and headbands.

"People don't just take off like this. They think things through. They talk a lot. Like: How will you support that baby, all alone?"

"I'll get along."

"Yes, well," Drum said. "*That's* for sure." He picked up a barrette from the floor and studied it, turning it over and over in his hands. Then he said, "How will you explain to strangers, having 'Casey' wrote across your face?"

"I'll tell them it's my name," Evie said. Then she paused, in the middle of rolling up a belt. "It *is* my name."

Drum frowned at the barrette. "Now that you have done all that cutting," he said, "and endured through bleeding and police cars and stitches, are you going to say it was just for purposes of *identification?*"

He tossed the barrette into the open suitcase. Evie dragged an airline bag from under the bed, and filled it with underwear and stray bottles from the medicine cabinet. In the bathroom, holding a tube of toothpaste and watching her smudged face in the mirror, she said, "*I* didn't do it."

"What?"

"*I* didn't cut my forehead. Someone else did."

"You don't make sense," Drum told her.

"Well, you were there. You remember how it was. The singing was good and there were fans shouting back at you and lots of people dancing. When I went into the restroom an argument started up. I forget just how. Me and a redhead and some friend of hers. She got mad. She told her friend to hold me down and she slashed your name on my face. 'I hope you're satisfied,' she said. *That* was how it happened."

"Life is getting too cluttered," Drum said.

"Didn't I tell you so?"

She zipped the airline bag. There were other things of hers all over the house, books and records and pieces of clothing, but all she wanted now was to finish up. In movies the packing did not go on so interminably. She picked up the suitcase, but Drum moved forward to take it away from her. "Evie, don't go," he said.

That was said in movies too. Then the whole scene would end with his changing his mind, saying he would come with her anywhere, but what did Drum know about things like that? "Come with me, then," she said, and all Drum said was, "No. I can't."

He had never once done what she had expected of him.

He carried the suitcase, she carried the airline bag. They crossed the cold dirt yard to the car. "Keys," said Drum, and when she handed them to him he opened the trunk and slid the bags in. He was going to let her go, then. She climbed into the driver's seat and waited for him to slam the trunk lid down. "Maybe—" he said, when he had come around to her side of the car.

She rolled the window down. "What?"

"I said, maybe later you will change your mind. Do you reckon?"

"I never back down on things," Evie said.

He reached in with the keys. He didn't even say good-bye;

just laid the keys in the palm of her hand, leaving her with a trace of his cool, slick surface and a smell of marigolds and a brief tearing sensation that lasted long after she had rolled out of the yard toward town.

On Saturday night at the Unicorn, Joseph Ballew and Drumstrings Casey played rock music on a wooden dance platform, the same as always. Joseph Ballew sang two new songs and Drumstrings Casey sang old ones, stopping his strumming occasionally to speak out between verses.

"*Where is the circular stairs?*" he asked.

And then, "*But the letters was cut backwards.*

"*Would you explain?*"

His audience just nodded, accepting what he said. The only person who could have answered him was not present.

A NOTE ABOUT THE AUTHOR

ANNE TYLER was born in Minneapolis, Minnesota, in 1941 and grew up in Raleigh, North Carolina. She graduated at nineteen from Duke University and went on to do graduate work in Russian studies at Columbia University. Her first novel, *If Morning Ever Comes,* was published in 1964, and her stories have appeared in such magazines as *The New Yorker, The Saturday Evening Post, Redbook, McCall's,* and *Harper's.* Her eleventh novel, *Breathing Lessons,* received the Pulitzer Prize in 1989. She is a member of the American Academy and Institute of Arts and Letters. She and her husband, Taghi Modarressi, live in Baltimore, Maryland, with their two daughters.

A NOTE ON THE TYPE

The text of these novels is set in Electra, a Linotype face designed by W. A. Dwiggins. This face cannot be classified as either modern or old. It is not based on any historical model, nor does it echo any particular period or style. It avoids the extreme contrasts between thick and thin elements that mark most modern faces and attempts to give a feeling of fluidity, power, and speed.